THE KING OF YS
Volume I

THE KING OF YS
Volume I

ROMA MATER
GALLICENAE

Poul and Karen Anderson

NELSON DOUBLEDAY, INC.
Garden City, New York

Published by arrangement with
Baen Publishing Enterprises
260 Fifth Avenue
New York, New York 10001

Printed in the United States of America

**This tale is all for
Astrid and Greg
with our love.**

ROMA OCCIDENTALIS

.... Antonine Wall
-- Hadrian's Wall
-x- Boundary of Empire
-x- East/West Boundary
Corvorum Insulae—Channel Islands
Eburacum—York
Dubris—Dover
Gesoriacum—Boulogne
Condate Redonum—Rennes
Lutetia Parisiorum—Paris
Caesarodunum Turonum—Tours
Augusta Treverorum—Trier
Lugdunum—Lyon
Vienna—Vienne
Vindobona—Vienna
Mediolanum—Milan
Burdigala—Bordeaux
Narbo Martius—Narbonne
Massilia—Marseilles
Caesaraugusta—Saragossa
Tarraco—Tarragona
Chersonesus—near Sevastopol
Sequana—Seine
Liger—Loire
Garumna—Garonne
Rhenus—Rhine
Albis—Elbe
Rhodanus—Rhone
Iberus—Ebro

Luguvalium—Carlisle
Isurium—Aldborough
Eburacum—York
Mona (1)—Man
Mona (2)—Anglesey
Deva—Chester
Viroconium—Wroxeter
Lindum—Lincoln
Glevum—Gloucester
Isca Silurum—Caerleon
Segontium—Carnarvon
Abonae—Sea Mills
Aquae Sulis—Bath
Borcovicum—Housesteads

Isca Dumnoniorum—Exeter
Vectis—Wight
Venta Icenorum—Caister St. Edmunds
Venta Belgarum—Winchester
Anderida—Pevensey
Rutupiae—Richborough
Dubris—Dover
Durnovaria—Dorchester
Camulodunum—Colchester
Calleva Atrebatum—Silchester
Corstopitum—Corbridge
Sabrina—Severn
Tamesis—Thames

BRITANNIA

ÉRIU AND ALBA

CALEDONI

PICTI

Airgíalla

DÁMNONII

Dál Riata (2)

NOVANTAE

SELGOVAE

OTADINI

Luguvalium
Borcovicum
Corstopitum · Hadrian's Wall

BRIGANTES

Isurium
Brigantum

ALBA (BRITANNIA)

Mona (1)

Mona (2)

Deva

ORDOVICES

Segontium

Dál Riata (1)

QÓIGET N ULAT

Emain Macha

MIDE
Mag Slecht
Tailtiu
Bend Etair
Temair
Cnóc Tarui

Dún Ailinni

QÓIGET LAGIN

Casel

Siuir

CONDACHT

ÉRIU (HIVERNIA)

MUMU

Emain Macha—near Armagh
Mag Slecht—in Co. Cavan
Temair—Tara
Cnóc Tarui—Clontarf
Casel—Cashel
Dál Riata (1)—Antrim
Dún Ailinni—near Kildare
Tailtiu—Teltown
Bend's River—Boyne
Ruirthech—Liffey
Siuir—Suir
Qóiget n Ulad—Ulster
Condacht—Connaght
Mide—Meath
Mumu—Munster
Qóiget Lagin—Leinster

Dál Riata (2)—Argyll
Mona (1)—Man
Mona (2)—Anglesey
Luguvalium—Carlisle
Borcovicum—Housesteads
Corstopitum—Corbridge
Segontium—Carnarvon
Deva—Chester
Isurium Brigantum—Aldborough

PROMONTORIUM GOBÆUM

(Garomagus)

To Vorgium and
Condate Redonum

To Aquilo

(Audiarna)

OCEANUS AQUITANICUS

Redonian Way

Aquilonian Way

Nymphaeum
Power? of the King
Amphitheatre

Old Roman station

Old Gallic fort

POINT VANIS

Seat's Landing
and Ghost Quay

CAPE RACH

Pharos

Menhirs

House of the
Goddess

Lÿr Aliar

Sena

Promontorium Gobaeum–Cap Sizun
Point Vanis–Pointe du Van
Cape Rach–Pointe du Raz
Sena–Sein
(Garomagus)–Douarnenez
Condate Redonum–Rennes
(Audiarna)–Audierne
Aquilo–Locmaria

THE CITY OF YS

B.-B. Bastions for missile throwers
Site of Ys–Baie des Trépassés
Point Vanis–Pointe du Van
Cape Rach–Pointe du Raz

Point Vanis

Radonian Way

North Spira Way

Processional Way

Path and Canal to Nymphaeum

King's Head

Sacred Wood

Amphitheater

The Gull

High Gate

The Roman

Water Tower
Star House
Library
Basilica
Belisama Temple and Elven Garden
Warriors'
Dragon House
WAY
FORUM
Theater
Palace Grounds

Northbridge Gate

Epona Square

Corn Market
Ishtar Shrine
Lir Shrine
Taranis Temple
Mars Temple
Baths
TARANIS
Aurochs Gate
Phares Way

Arch it
LIR
Shippers' Market
Menhir Place
Melqart Shrine
Sweet Fair

The Gull
The Sisters

HARBOR

Gate
B
B
B
B
B
B
B
Shippews

The Brothers
The Raven

Cape Rach

Contents

ROMA MATER

I

1

At noon upon that Birthday of Mithras, the sun blazed low in an ice-clear heaven. As Gratillonius looked south, he saw its brilliance splinter into rainbow shards amidst his eyelashes. Hills afar, ditch and earthworks nearby, terraced fields below, lay whitened and still. Smoke rose from Borcovicium fort and the settlement huddled against its ramparts, but so straight that it scarcely marred the purity. When he turned his gaze north, there was nothing of man save the shadow of the Wall, huge and blue, down a cliff whose own shadow filled the hollow underneath. Heights beyond were dark with forest in winter sleep. Light flashed star-like off icicles. A few crows aflight set their blackness against his breath, their distant cawing against his heartbeat, and that was all that stirred.

For a moment he felt wholly alone. The summer's warfare was not only past, it was unreal, a dream he had had or a story told him in his child-hood, fading out of memory—but what, then, was real?

A glance right and left brought him back. Foursquare, the murky bulk of a tower blocked off most westward view; but eastward, vision ran along the walkway past the two intermediate observation turrets to the next milecastle, and the next, until the Wall swung under the horizon: fifteen feet from base to battlements, seventy-seven miles from sea to sea across Britannia. Metal made small fierce gleams where men stood watch down that length. Cloaks and drooping standards splashed their colors athwart its gray. Below them, some two hundred Roman paces from him, the legionary base rose in a gridiron of streets and lanes which seemed doubly severe next to the paths twisting between houses in the vicus. Everything he saw belonged here.

And so did he. His body rested easy under helmet, mail, greaves. Be-neath them, his tunic hung lower than the skirt of studded leather straps;

a scarf protected his neck from chafing by armor; woolen half-breeches, stockings inside the hobnailed sandals, fended off the season; all was familiar. Sword at hip, stick cut from the mainstem of a grapevine, were as much limbs of his as were arms and legs. Because the day was holy, he had not yet taken food, nor would he until the Mystery at eventide, and hunger somehow spurred awareness of his own strength. The chill in the air made it feel liquid, it bathed him within and without. And now trumpets sounded, echoes rang, high noon had come.

To most in the army, that signalled no more than a change of guard. It called Gratillonius to prayer. He faced the sun again, removed his helmet and set it on the parapet. A scarlet horsehair crest, attached for the round of inspection which he was on, scratched his wrist and scritted. He raised his arms and began the office—soft-voiced, because such was seemly and it would be his heart that the God heard—"Hail, Mithras Unconquered, Saviour, Warrior, Lord, born unto us anew and forever—"

"Centurion."

At first he barely noticed, and did not imagine it meant him. "—hear us, You Who did slay the Bull that Its blood might make fruitful the world, You Who stand before the Lion and the Serpent—"

"Centurion!" yelled in his ear.

Rage flared. Had the contumely of the Christians swollen to this?

An instant before snatching his vinestaff and giving the intruder a slash across the mouth, Gratillonius checked himself. It behooved an officer both of the Halidom and of Rome to curb a temper he knew was too quick, not profane his devotions with violence. He shot a glare which made the fellow step back alarmed, and continued.

The words were soon finished. It was as well, he thought, when anger seethed in him. He turned to confront the stranger, and beheld insignia of the Sixth Victrix. His mind sprang. Although that legion was based at Eboracum, closer than either of the other two in the island, it had not joined them against Picti and Scoti raging down from the north, but stayed behind. Supposedly that was to stand off any Saxon raiders. However, some few of its men had accompanied Maximus as bodyguards, couriers, confidants.

No matter yet. Gratillonius picked up the stick that marked his rank, tucked it under an elbow, and rapped forth: "Attention! Have you no better manners than to interrupt a man at his worship, soldier? You disgrace your eagle."

The other stiffened, gulped, abruptly recovered and answered, "I beg the centurion's pardon. No bishop ever told me this is a time for services. I had my orders, and only supposed the centurion was deep in thought."

Insolent knave indeed, Gratillonius knew. He sagged a little, inwardly. Of course he was dealing with a Christian. Most legionaries were, these days, or pretended to be. This very year the rescript had arrived that banned the old faiths, along with tales of how the authorities were despoiling Mithraic temples first. Men at war on the uttermost frontier paid scant heed, and Maximus knew better than to enforce such a decree . . . until today, when the immediate danger was past?

Within Gratillonius, his father drawled anew, "Son, you're too rash, you always court trouble. No sense in that. She'll come on her own, never fear. Better just court girls." A curious tenderness followed. Gratillonius must even quell a smile as he said:

"I should take your name and remand you to your unit for punishment drill, if not a flogging. But since you admit ignorance, I'll be merciful. What do you want?"

An awakened caution replied. "Mine is . . . the honor of addressing Gaius Valerius Gratillonius, centurion of the Second . . . is it not? I asked the squad where you were."

"Which is here. Speak on."

The messenger donned importance. "The Duke of the Britains sent me. You are relieved of your regular duty and will report to him at once in the praetorium."

"The Duke? What, not at Vindolanda?" Gratillonius was surprised. The old fort and settlement, close by but somewhat behind the Wall, was where the grand commander had generally stayed when in this area.

"He is making a progress of inspection and . . . other business, it seems. He summoned you by name."

What could that mean? A mission? The blood thrilled in Gratillonius.

2

The close-packed buildings of the strongpoint shaded streets and turned the lanes between into tunnels of cold and gloom. Nonetheless several men were passing time off watch with a dice game on the verandah of their barrack. But they were Tungri, auxiliaries such as formed the permanent garrisons of the Wall; regulars only arrived in emergencies like this year's. Well wrapped in furs, the barbarians doubtless found the dry air a blessed change from their native marshlands. Their speech went croaking and hawking through a quiet otherwise broken by little more than footfalls, although those rang loud enough on frozen earth.

Entering on the west, Gratillonius must pass the headquarters block standing sheer around three sides of its courtyard. He halted to salute the basilica, for it held the legionary shrine and standards: not his legion, true, but equally Rome's. The sentries saluted him in their turn. The smartness of it pleased, now when the Tungri had reminded him of the slovenly ways he found when his vexillation first came here. Maximus had done marvels in restoring discipline. To be sure, Gratillonius thought, the long campaign helped; poor soldiers were apt to become dead ones.

Memory ranged across the months that were past: the march up country through springtime rains to a stone wonder he had never seen before; settling in, getting to know the hills and heaths, exploring what often sleazy pleasures the civilian villages had to offer; shamefaced purification before he sought the Mithraeum, but then, for no good reason that he could see to this day, his elevation in grade—well, they said he had fought valiantly, but that hardly sufficed, and most likely it was that pious Parnesius had recommended him to the Father, and after all, the congregation had grown so pitifully small—

The warring itself was somehow less vivid. It had been an endlessness of expeditions from this base to seek whatever band of painted Picti or gaudy Scoti had been reported, of weather wet or hot, of troubles with supply trains and troubles among the men such as a centurion must handle, of having them shovel trenches and ramparts for encampments they would demolish the next dawn, of finally—most times—coming upon the enemy and going to work, of the dead afterward and the wounded, the wounded. . . . You did what you and the surgeons could for your own, and tried to keep your men from being needlessly cruel when they cut the throats of tall dark highlanders and fair-skinned warriors from over the water. There was no safe way of bringing prisoners to a slave market, and you could not risk that any would recover from his injuries. You had seen too many homesteads plundered and burnt, slain men, ravished women who wept for children carried off because the Scoti did do a brisk trade in slaves; and this was not only north of the Wall, among tribes friendly to Rome, but south of it, in territories thinly peopled but still subject to Caesar. The foe came around every defense in their leather coracles. So as leaves withered and fell, Gratillonius killed his last opponent (hail rattled on helmets; its pallor across the ground made blood spurt doubly red) and Britannia lay at peace. But thus it had been again and again in the past, and surely would in the future.

He curbed his mind, squared his shoulders, and strode onward. Forebodings were foolishness. The truth was that Maximus had prevailed, had reaped so widely among the wild men that they would not soon come back, and had something to tell an infantryman who was chafing at the sameness of garrison life. What better omen than getting that word on the holiest day of the year?

The praetorium was almost as large as the principia. When Gratillonius identified himself, the guard called a man to guide him. Inside, the warmth of a hypocaust radiated from tiled floors; frescos on the walls glowed with flowers, fruits, beasts, Homeric Gods and heroes; more servants than soldiers passed by. But such was usual, Gratillonius knew. His own commandant's house in the base at Isca Silurum made this one on the far frontier look impoverished. Maximus had the reputation of living austerely wherever he was.

Another legionary of the Sixth stood at a certain door. Upon learning who had appeared, he opened it and waited at attention until bidden to speak. "Gaius Valerius Gratillonius, centurion of the seventh cohort, Second Legion Augusta," he then announced, and gestured the newcomer in. The door closed. Gratillonius saluted.

Light, straggling bleak through a glazed window, got help from lamps. It showed lavishness neglected. Two men sat at a table whereon were beakers, bescribbled notebooks of thin-scraped wood, a map drawn on parchment, an inkwell and quill, a waxed tablet and stylus. One man, big, young, freckle-faced, was clearly a native. He had donned Roman garb for this occasion, but a mustache flared, his ruddy hair was bound in a knot, a golden torque gleamed around his neck. His companion, whom Gratillonius knew by sight, was the Duke of the Britains.

Magnus Clemens Maximus hailed from the uplands of Hispania Tarraconensis. It showed in his height and leanness, hatchet features, olive skin, hair stiff and black and slightly grizzled. It also softened his Latin as he said, "At ease, centurion. Take off your cloak and helmet." The steel of him was in his voice, though, and his eyes were always probing.

To the tribesman he added: "This is the officer whom I have in mind to lead your escort." To Gratillonius: "You have the honor of meeting Cunedag, a prince among the Votadini and Rome's loyal ally. Your assignment will be to accompany him and his following to the Ordovices, on your way back with your century." Smiling: "Look well, you two. I trust you both like what you see."

Gratillonius sped through memory. Dwelling north of the Wall, the Votadini had formerly been subjects and, after the tide of empire ebbed southward, had stayed on reasonably good terms. Indeed, their leading families claimed Roman descent and often bestowed Roman names. He had not met Cunedag before, but had heard of him as a useful warlord throughout the year's campaigning.

The chieftain's gaze searched over the centurion. It found a man of twenty-five, medium tall for a Briton—which made him overtop most Italians—and robustly built. The visage of Gratillonius was broad and square, clean-shaven, with craggy nose and wide-set gray eyes. His complexion was fair, his close-cropped hair auburn. He moved like a cat. When he spoke, the tone was deep and rather harsh.

"You have won a high name," said Cunedag in his own language. "I think we shall travel well together."

"Thank you, lord. I will do my best," replied Gratillonius. He used the tongue of the Dumnonii, which was not too alien for the Northerner to understand and chuckle at.

"Good," said Maximus, sensing the accord. "Prince, we have talked a long while and you must be weary. The centurion and I have matters to discuss which can scarcely interest you. Why do you not seek your guest-room, or wherever else you like, and rest until we meet at the evening meal?"

Cunedag, an intelligent barbarian, took the hint and uttered a stately goodbye. A gong summoned an attendant to lead him out and a second man to bring Gratillonius a goblet of wine and water. The officer took the vacated stool at his commander's word and peered across the clutter on the table. His pulse drummed anew.

Maximus stroked fingers across his prow of a chin. "Well, soldier," he said, "you must be wondering how I even knew who you are, let alone found a rather special task for you."

"The Duke surely has many ears," Gratillonius ventured.

Maximus shrugged. "Fewer than he could use. In this case, you've become a friend of Parnesius, and it happens that I am acquainted with his father and have kept my eye on the son. Parnesius praised you to me: less your valor, which any dolt could show, but skill and coolness overriding a temperament hot by nature, a talent for improvising, a gift of leadership." He sighed. "That is a gift, you know, a mystery. God's hand touches a man, and that man turns into one whom others will follow though it be past the gates of hell. Would I had more like that to follow *me!*"

A chill tingle passed through Gratillonius. The provinces of the Empire bred men who claimed the purple by right of the sword, and Britannia was among them. Here the legions had first hailed great Constantinus, almost a hundred years ago. More recently there had been Magnentius, rising in Gallia but born in Britannia and supported by Britons; his failure and its terrible aftermath need not discourage later dreams. As warfare ended and winter closed in, legionaries had time to think, wonder, mutter

. . . fifteen years was a long time to keep as able a leader as Maximus off on the frontiers . . . he declared that he held the Sixth in reserve at Eboracum against Saxon attack, and maybe this was true, but it was likewise true that the Sixth had come to be his adoring own . . . the real rulers of the West were not the co-Emperors but a barbarian, a woman, and a churchman . . . the hour might be overpast for putting a man of proven metal on the throne. . . .

Maximus's voice levelled. "I've kept your detachment, together with that from the Twentieth and all the sundry oddments, on the Wall to make sure our pacification was nailed down. The Picti wouldn't worry me by themselves. Their little quarrelsome packs will never do more alone than snap up some loot, take a drubbing, and scatter back to lick their wounds. But lately the Scoti have been leagued with them, and—the Scoti are a different breed of wolf." He scowled. "Somebody in Hivernia has been behind the last onslaught, somebody powerful and shrewd. I would not have put it past him to deliver a surprise blow just when we thought we were safely finished."

Maximus tossed off a laugh and a swallow from his cup. "Well, he didn't. Now he couldn't possibly before spring, and one may doubt he'll care to try again that soon. So the vexillations can return to their legions: a cold trek, but not one that I think they'll mind. On your way, Gratillonius, I want you to guard Cunedag on his. At Deva you and your century will part company not only with the Valeria Victrix troops, but with your fellows of the Augusta. Proceed with Cunedag into Ordovicia, stop where he wants, and do whatever is necessary to establish him."

"Would the Duke explain why?" Gratillonius requested.

"It won't likely be a severe task," Maximus said. "I have had negotiators there, and on the whole, the clans will welcome him. See here. Stationed where you are, you must know how law and order have been breaking down in those parts, leaving people well-nigh helpless before the Scoti, not to mention home-grown brigands. I can't have that sort of thing at my back when—" He broke off. "Cunedag possesses a fairly sound grasp of both military and political principles. He'll take charge. Your century shouldn't have a great deal to do, nor need to linger long, before it can return to Isca Silurum."

"I understand, sir," Gratillonius said. "In part."

"Never fear, you'll know more before you leave. Half a dozen men, both Roman and tribal, are set to instruct you. Meanwhile," and Maximus smiled, "you can get to know Cunedag better this evening at supper."

Gratillonius stiffened. He must summon up as much of himself as he had ever needed in combat in order to say: "I regret that I cannot accept the Duke's invitation."

Maximus raised his brows. "What?"

"Sir, this day is sacred. I may only take part in the feast of the God."

"Oh." Maximus was silent for a space. When he spoke, it was like the winter outside. "I had forgotten. You are pagan."

It prickled in Gratillonius's armpits. "Sir, I do not worship Jupiter, if that's what you mean."

"But Mithras. Which is forbidden. For your soul's good, understand. You'll burn forever after you die, unless you take the Faith."

Gratillonius bridled. "The Duke has not yet seen fit to close our temples."

Maximus sighed. "As you will, as you will. For now, at least. After all, Parnesius is obstinate too. But he serves Rome well, like you and, I dare hope, me. Come, let us drink to the well-being of our Mother."

The wine was excellent, unlike what was issued the troops. Yet its sweetness dimmed on Gratillonius's tongue as Maximus frowned, lowered his beaker, stared into the shadows that filled a corner, and murmured: "Little enough well-being is hers any longer. You've never seen Rome, the City, have you? I have. Our Mother is fallen on evil days. There are more ghosts than living folk in her streets, and the Emperor reigns from Mediolanum, Augusta Treverorum, or . . . anywhere except poor, plundered Rome. The Emperor of the West, that is. No, today the joint Emperors of the West, the first a plaything of his Frankish general, the second of his mother, and the West divided between them. And even the Augustus of the East feels Constantinople tremble beneath him. It is but four or five years since the Goths rode down the Romans at Adrianople. Have you heard about that, centurion? The Emperor Valens himself died on the field. His successor Theodosius must needs buy the alliance of those barbarians, Arian heretics, those that are not still outright heathen —" He straightened. His voice clanged forth: "By the Great Name of God, Rome shall not suffer this! Mother, your hour of deliverance draws near."

Then immediately he was again the self-contained man whose patience had forged victory. He raised his cup, sipped, regarded Gratillonius over the rim, and smiled afresh before he said, "Be not alarmed, centurion. I've no wish to scare off the few trustworthy men left me. Rather, I've work in mind for you, more challenging and more glorious than the mere delivery of a leader and his warriors to some ragged hillfolk. Indeed, that assignment is essentially a final test of you. If you carry it off as well as I expect—"

Leaning forward: "I've made inquiries about you, of course, since Parnesius's mention of you drew my attention your way. Now I wish to talk freely with you, explore what sort of *person* you are."

"A very ordinary soldier, sir," Gratillonius replied uneasily.

Maximus laughed, straightened on his stool, crossed shank over knee. Such putting aside of dignity, by the Duke himself, caught at Gratillonius's heart. Eagerness rekindled in him. "Oh, no, you don't, lad!" Maximus crowed. "You'll never make that claim stick, not after this summer. And I hear you did well in the South, earlier."

"That was nothing unusual, really, sir. Sometimes Scoti or Saxons came visiting, and we went out to meet them. Otherwise it was plain patrol and camp duty."

"Um-m, I've heard of a fire in town, and a young legionary who risked his life to rescue the children from a burning house. I've also heard how that same fellow gets along well with natives, whether they be his familiar Silures and Belgae or the half-tame dwellers in these parts."

"Well, I'm of Britannic blood myself, sir."

"Unusual— No, you are a regular, of course, not an auxiliary. Almost a namesake of the Emperor Gratianus."

The centurion felt his muscles grow tense. Likening his family to that Scythian-loving sluggard! "Pure chance, sir," he stated. "My folk are Belgae, living near Aquae Sulis since before Claudius. Naturally, we've long been civilized, and a forebear of mine gave the name a Latin form, but we've kept our ties to the land."

Maximus seemed a trifle amused. "Have you no ancestors who were not Belgae? That would be strange."

"Of course there were some, sir. Soldiers stationed in Britannia, Italians, a Dacian, a Nervian. And a couple of Gauls, though they were female, brides brought home."

Maximus nodded, once more grave. "Sound stock throughout. You are of the curial class, I understand."

Gratillonius grimaced. Maximus hastened to bespeak happier matters: "Your grandfather had a distinguished military career, did he not? And your father went into trade out of Abonae, and prospered. That took real seamanship—those tides in the estuary—and fighting skill, too, when pirates infest the waters."

The Duke must have queried Parnesius closely indeed, to dig out things casually related over a span of months. The voice quickened: "His main business was with Armorica, true? And he took you along on his voyages."

"Well, between the ages of twelve and sixteen, when I joined the army, I used to go with him, sir," Gratillonius replied.

"Tell me about it."

"Oh, we'd coast along Britannia, taking on cargo here and there, then cross over to a Gallic port—maybe as far east as Gesoriacum—and work our way west, stopping off to trade. Sometimes we'd leave the ship and travel inland to markets in places like Condate Redonum or Vorgium—" Gratillonius shook himself. Those joyful years were far behind him and his father both.

Maximus's tone sharpened. "Did you ever visit Ys?"

"What?" Gratillonius was startled. "Why . . . why, no. Does anybody any longer?"

"We shall see. You appear to have an ear for language. Did you acquire fluency in any Gallic tongues? I'm interested especially in whatever they use on the western end of Armorica."

"I got along, sir. That was quite a while ago, and I haven't returned since." Gratillonius began to realize what Maximus was driving at. The hair stirred on his neck and arms. "But I ought to regain it pretty quickly. Those dialects aren't too different from the southern Britannic, and I had a Dumnonic nurse when I was small." Awkwardly: "She stayed on in the house for my younger siblings, and we used to talk in her speech, she and I, till I enlisted—and afterward, when I was home on leave. I do hope old Docca is still alive."

The wistfulness flickered out, for Maximus was saying low, while he stared before him as if his vision could pierce the wall and fly away over Europe: "Excellent. The Lord is gracious to me, a sinner. It may actually be Providence that you are an infidel; for there could be things yonder that are not for a Christian man to deal with."

A fire leaped up in the breast of Gratillonius.

3

Once the temple had not been as far as it now was from a vicus of several hundred veterans, artisans, merchants, innkeepers, harlots, wives, children, hangers-on, a settlement akin to the rest that clustered south of the Wall, from sea to sea, within a mile or a few each other. But nearly two hundred years had passed since Caledonic invaders laid the Borcovicium region waste while Rome writhed at war with itself. After Severus restored things, rebuilding was done farther uphill, next to the military base. Perhaps in awe, the reavers had spared the Mithraeum. Thus it stood alone on a knoll near the ditch, only brush surrounding its temenos. Northward, darkness rose like a tide toward the battlemented horizon the Wall made; southward, the ground rolled off in ridges which the setting sun reddened. Frost creaked underfoot, voices mumbled through smoke signals of breath, silence everywhere else deepened with cold.

Arriving early for the service, Gratillonius found Parnesius among those who waited outside. His friend was wrapped in a cloak but had not drawn the hood over his black hair. It curled back from his forehead to show the tiny brand of initiation which Gratillonius also bore, both now faint; hot iron had made larger and deeper marks on their bodies when they first entered the army. Beneath the religious sign, Parnesius's eyebrows formed a single bar over his jutting nose. "Hail," he said, more cheerfully than might be suitable at this hour. "How went it with the Old Man today?"

They clasped forearms in the Roman manner. "Lad, you're all aquiver," Parnesius exclaimed.

"How I wish I could tell you," Gratillonius replied. "It's—oh, wonderful—but he made me vow secrecy for the time being. When I can talk, when actual operations are in train, then I'll be far from here."

"Well, I'm glad to see you're glad. Although— Come." Parnesius plucked at the other's mantle. "Step aside for a bit, shall we?"

More men were climbing the trail hither. While they numbered under a score, they were of many sorts, not only soldiers but workmen, serfs, slaves. Rank on earth counted for nothing before Ahura-Mazda.

As it did not before the Lord of the Christians . . . but they welcomed women to their services, passed fleetingly through Gratillonius. His father, his brother, himself followed Mithras; but his mother had been Christian and so, by amicable agreement, were his sisters raised. Could that alone be the reason why Christ was triumphing?

He thrust the thought away and followed Parnesius off as he had followed this comrade in arms, and the still more experienced Pertinax, on days when they could "take the heather"—fare off with a native guide to hunt, fish, be at ease in clean and lonesome country. "What have you to say?" he asked. "Time's short." Because the service was conducted on sufferance, military members had better be in their quarters by curfew.

Parnesius looked off and beat fist in palm. "I'm not sure," he answered roughly. "Except . . . I couldn't help getting hints when he quizzed me about you. And . . . Pertinax and I have had an offer . . . but we'll stay on the Wall, we two. You're going south, aren't you? Not just back to Isca, but on to Gallia."

Gratillonius swallowed. "I'm not supposed to say."

"Nevertheless—" Parnesius swung about and seized him by the shoulders. His gaze probed and pleaded. "He wouldn't have told you outright, but you must have a fair idea of what he intends. You must be aware you're to guard his back while— Well, what do you think about it? The next war will mean a great deal more than this last one, you know. Don't you?"

"I am . . . a soldier," Gratillonius answered most carefully. "I follow my orders. But . . . an Emperor who is a soldier too might be what we all need."

"Good!" cried Parnesius, and pummeled him lightly on the back. "And here in the North, Pertinax and I'll hold fast. Ho, I see him coming. Hail, Pertinax!"

But then the Father appeared, and men ranked themselves for the ceremony.

The Mithraeum was plain and low. It could not hold even as many as the remnant who were gathered. However, it was not meant to. The junior initiates, Ravens, Occults, Soldiers, did not attend the holiest of the rites. They joined their seniors in hymning the sun as it departed.

Flame glimmered across a green southwestern heaven, and went out. More and more stars gleamed forth, and lights along the blackness of Wall and fortress. Elsewhere the world sheened phantom gray. The song ended. The three underling ranks formed their squad and saluted while Lions, Persians, the Runner of the Sun, and the Father whom he attended went inside.

There was no space for a pronaos. There was, though, a vestibule, where Gratillonius and his fellows changed into their sacred garb. For him it was robe, mask, and Phrygian cap, because in the past year the elders had promoted him to Persian. Solemnly, they entered the sanctuary.

Lamplight amidst restless shadows picked out the altars that jutted into the narrow nave. At the end of the chamber, reliefs depicted Mithras slaying the Bull and His cosmic birth with the signs of the zodiac around. The stone was pierced so that illumination behind created the halo about his head. Flanking were the graven Dadophori, the brother figures, one with torch held high, one with torch down and guttering out. It was very quiet. After the chill outside, air felt merely cool. The sweet smoke of pine cones breathed through it.

The celebrants crossed the floor of oak planks and birch logs to their benches along the walls. The Father took his place before the Tauroctony.

He was an aged man, as was the Heliodromos who served him. Their deaths would surely spell the end of worship here.

Gratillonius raised up his heart. However men blundered, Mithras remained true to His world; and meanwhile he, Gratillonius, had his own victory ahead of him.

II

Imbolc marked the season of making ready for the year's work, the lambing that would soon begin, spring sowing later, fishing whenever Manandan and the merfolk would allow. People took stock of what supplies remained in household and farmyard. On the coasts they gathered seaweed to cut up and strew on their fields, as well as shellfish when the tide of Brigit stood at its lowest. Yet the day itself and the vigil of the day were hallowed. Along the shores of Condacht and Mumu, live periwinkles or limpets were buried around each house for luck on strand and water. Many tuaths elsewhere did no work that called for the turning of a wheel, such as carting; it might bewilder the sun on his homeward course. Families wove new talismans of straw and twigs and hung them about dwellings for protection against lightning and fire. They celebrated the eve with the best feast their stores could provide, putting some outside for the Goddess, Who would be traveling that night, and grain for Her white cow. They reckoned, however, that Brigit was also pleased if the food went to the needy, or to those parties of youths and maidens that carried Her emblems from home to home across the land—as long as the gift was given in Her name.

Anxiously they watched for weather signs. Rain was welcome, to soften the ground and hasten growth of new grass; but storms were ominous, and if the hedgehog did not appear, that meant he was keeping his burrow in expectation of more winter followed by a hard summer. This year, what happened was so shifty across Ériu that no one knew what to await. Wisewomen said it portended strange doings and great changes; druids generally stayed silent.

On Temir was the most splendid of all festivals, for it was the King's, and Niall maqq Echach bade fair to become the mightiest since Corbmac maqq Arti, or even to outreach that lord. Not only his household and following were on hand, learned men, ollam craftsmen, warriors, their women and children; not only free tenants of both his and theirs, and families of these, from end to end of Mide; not only kings of the tuaths over whom he held sway, and their own attendants and underlings. From Condacht, whence the forebears of Niall had sprung, came many to greet their kinsman. From Mumu, where he had friends, came not a few. From the Lagini came some, more in hopes of mildening him toward themselves than in love. From the Ulati, alone among the Fifths, came not a man, unless it be a few outcasts begging. But then, in Emain Macha they held a revel too, which they said was as royal and sacral as this.

Throughout the day of the vigil Niall had been taken up with welcoming his guests as they arrived, in such ways as became their standings and his. Now at eventide he would open the festivities.

Bathed and freshly clad, in stately wise he walked from the King's House to the point where the southward-running of the Five Roads to Temir came up on the hilltop. There his chariot awaited him. Its matched gray horses snorted and pawed; Cathual the driver must keep tight reins. Niall mounted easily. When the wheels groaned into motion, he stood steady amidst the rocking and jouncing. His spear swayed like a ship's mast. Sunlight streamed level to make its head shine as if newly bloodied.

From here Niall saw widely over his domains. Down along the road clustered the booths and tents of lower-ranking folk for whom the buildings had no space. Many were striped in colors, and pennons fluttered above some. On the next summit loomed the hill fort sacred to Medb. Heights round about were still bright, but hollows were filling with shadow. Though leafless, forest hid Boand's River to the north; yet the air, damp and turning chill, bore a sense of Her presence among the spirits that thronged nigh. Westward land dropped steeply to the plain, its pastures winter-dulled, save that mists had arisen to beswirl them with molten gold. The sun cast the same hue on clouds above that horizon, with heaven violet beyond them. Ahead of Niall bulked the Great Rath, its lime-whitened earthwork and the palisade on top likewise aglow.

People crowded the paths to watch him and his guards go by. Men's tunics and cloaks, their breeches or kilts, the gowns of women were vivid in red, yellow, blue, green, orange, black, white; gold, silver, amber, crystal, gems glistened around brows, throats, arms, waists; spears, axes, drawn swords flashed high in reverence; on shields, round or oval, the painted marks of their owners twined or snarled or ramped. Children, dogs, pigs ran about among the grown and joined their clamor to the shout that billowed for the King.

Well did he seem worthy of hailing. His chariot of state bore bronze masks on the sides; the spokes of its two wheels were gilded; at either rail hung the withered head of a Roman, taken by him in the past summer's warfare. Cathual the charioteer was a youngling short but lithe and

comely, clad in tunic of scarlet; headband, belt, and wristlets were set
with silver. From the shoulders of Niall swung a cloak of the finest wool,
striped in the full seven colors permitted a king; his undershirt was of
Roman silk, his tunic saffron with red and blue embroideries; rather than
breeches he wore a kilt, dark russet to show off the whiteness and shapeliness of his legs, with shoes of kid on his feet. His ornaments outweighed
and outshone all others.

Finest to see was himself. At some thirty years of age, after uncounted
battles against men and beasts, Niall maqq Echach remained without any
flaw that might cost him his lordship. Taller than most he reared, wide in
shoulders and slender in hips, skin fair even where weather had touched it
and not unduly shaggy, wildcat muscles flowing beneath. Golden were his
long hair and mustaches, his close-trimmed beard. His brow was broad,
his nose straight, his chin narrow; eyes gleamed fire-blue.

Behind the chariot paced his hounds and his hostages, the men's attire
revealing his generosity. They wore light golden chains, that everyone
might know them for what they were, but strode proudly enough; their
position was honorable, and most times they went unhampered. Behind
them, and also in front of the chariot, walked his warriors. Closest to him
were the four bodyguards and the gigantic champion, bearing helmets
and dress shields of polished bronze; but the rest were hardly less brilliant, in tunics like their master's, axes glimmering and spearheads nodding on high.

Folk cheered themselves hoarse to see the power of King Niall. Few
were so close as to make out the grimness upon his lips, the bitterness in
his face.

The procession turned where a gate stood open in the Great Rath and a
bridge had been laid down across the ditch. It went over the lawn within,
past the lesser enclosure of the Royal Guesthouse and the embanked
mound whereon rose the King's quarters. A ways farther on, it halted.
There the Mound of the Kings lifted itself athwart the outer palisade.

Niall did not dismount and climb its grassy slopes. That was only done
when a new King was taken. Then he would stand on the sacred slab at
the top, make his three turns dessiul and widdershins, receive the White
Wand, invoke the Gods. On this holy eve, Cathual guided the chariot past
the Phallus below, five lichenous feet of standing stone. A fighting man
stationed at that menhir swung a bullroarer to proclaim that this was
truly the King who came by.

The procession went on, out a northern gate, past other stones to which
Niall dipped his spear, past the Rath of the Warriors, between the small
mounds Dall and Dercha, on to the Feasting Hall. Niall's Queen, his

sons, his counselors, their chief servants stood waiting. Cathual drew rein and the overlord sprang down. He gave his weapon to the charioteer and first greeting to the druid and the poets, as was seemly. Thereafter he received the salutations of the others according to their status.

"Now we've a time to wait," he said. "Is it a good sign that we are free of rain the while?"

"It is that," answered the druid, Nemain maqq Aedo, gravely, "but other signs have been such that you will be wise to sacrifice more than is wont tomorrow."

Niall scowled. "I did so last year, at both Imbolc and Beltene, and meager gain did we have of it."

Some people looked aghast at this defiance of the Powers. Nemain simply raised his hand. He was gaunt, snowy-bearded, his eyes dimmed by years and by peering into mysteries. Unlike everyone else, he wore a plain white robe and blue cloak; but his staff was carved with potent ogamm signs. "Speak not rashly, dear heart," he said. "If you failed to overrun the foe—then, sure it nonetheless is that you brought home alive yourself and most of the men, with not so little plunder. Would it not have been easier, now, for the Mórrigu to let you lie raven-food under the Roman Wall? The signs I have read, in stars and staves and secret pools, are signs of mighty deeds, of a world in travail with a new birth. Give freely, and receive back honor."

Flame flickered up through Niall's sullen mood. "Warfare already again this summer?"

"That is as may be. Thus far the red wind only whispers, and I know not from what quarter it is blowing."

Niall's glance flew about, south toward the Lagini, north toward the Ulati, east toward Alba across the water, which the Romans called Britannia. There it lingered.

Breccan, his eldest son, advanced. "Father, dear," he cried, "you'll be taking me along, will you not?"

Niall turned and regarded him. The sun had just set, but light remained in heaven to make the boy shine forth against a world going dun. Breccan was tall for his fourteen years but not filled out; his limbs thrust spidery from the garments that covered his slip of a body. The hair tumbled flax-white past huge blue eyes and a face whose beauty was redeemed from girlishness by the down on its upper lip. Yet he moved with a certain coltish grace; few could match him in a race afoot or on horseback; he was fierce in the games that his kind played and in practice with weapons.

"You are a stripling," Niall said, though he smiled more kindly than he had done since his return. "Be patient. You'll be winning fame aplenty in due course."

Breccan swallowed, stood his ground, and said stoutly, "Seven years it's been since I took valor. You told me then that I should have to wait no longer than that." He appealed to the Queen. "Mother, did he not indeed?"

She, who was in truth his stepmother but had always gotten along with him, smiled in her turn. "Niall, darling," she said, "I remember you promised he should—fare widely, those were your words—after seven years. And did not yourself do the same?"

Niall's countenance darkened. She made a mistake when she reminded him of his own stepmother and how Mongfind schemed his destruction for the sake of her sons by his father.

Laidchenn maqq Barchedo spoke softly: "It is to the glory of the King when someone recalls his exploits. This is also true of deeds done together by brothers among whom there was faith."

For a heartbeat Niall's mouth tightened. But he could not gainsay an ollam poet, who moreover was a guest and the former pupil of his foster-father. Nor did the man from Mumu intend anything but good. He merely called to mind that the sons of Mongfind had themselves never conspired against Niall but had become his trusty followers; and that he had no right to suspect his wife of urging Breccan into early battle, to get him out of the way of her sons.

The King eased. "We shall see," he told the boy. "Do you begin by learning how to wait. You will do enough of that in war." Suddenly he grinned. "And likewise you will know chills, rains, mud, growling belly, weary feet, grumbling men, and baggage trains gone astray. Not to talk of dripping noses, runny guts, and never a woman for your bed!"

Gladness went through listeners like a wave. For the first time since coming back to Ériu, himself seemed cheerful. Well, this was the eve of Brigit, and She a healing Goddess.

Meanwhile guests had come crowding about. Men gave their weapons into the care of attendants, for it was gess to go armed into this house. The very eating-knives must be solely in the hands of the servers who would carve the joints. Their shields the men turned over to the steward. Aided by household staff, he bore them inside. There the royal senchaide directed where they should hang, in order of dignity, so that each owner would go straight to his place without scrambles or quarrels. It took a knowledge of lineages and histories through long generations. Dusk had deepened before all was ready and a horn blew invitation.

Magnificent was the Feasting Hall on Temir. The earthwork that sheltered it was not round but seven hundred fifty feet in length, ninety feet in width; and the building left scant room between. Although it had stood for more than two years, and would be torn down this year before a new one was raised for the next Harvest Fair, it did not much show wear. Peeled upright poles making the walls were still bright, ties and chinking still solid; winds had not disturbed the intricately woven patterns of the thatch.

Within, the double rows of pillars upholding that high roof would be reused, as great as they were and as thickly carved with magical figures. Lamps hanging from the rafters and a fire in a pit at the middle gave light to see by, reflecting off gold and burnished bronze. Down the length of the nave, servers stood ready to carve the meat that kitchen help were bringing in from the cookhouse. Guests took benches along the aisles, before which were trestle tables bearing cups of mead. Foremost, at the center of the east side, was Niall's place, flanked by the men of greatest honor. Fifty guards stood in attendance, also disarmed but their shields and helmets asheen in unrestful shadows.

The Queen and other women sat opposite. Unlike most homes, at Temir it was not usual for them to join the men at feast. Instead, they dined in the Royal Guesthouse. This, though, was time sacred to a female God and to the fruitfulness of the coming season. Besides, some of them flaunted scars from battles, and had brought back several of the skulls which stared emptily from the walls. Medb Herself could take pride in celebrants like these.

The surf-roar and clatter of people finding their seats died away. Looks went to the King's companions. Before anyone touched food here, always a poet spoke.

Laidchenn stood up, rang the chimes on the baton that declared what he was, lifted from its carrying case a harp he had already tuned, and cradled it in his left arm. There had been no question but that he would take the word, among those poets who were present. Not only was he a visitor from afar, he was from the school of Torna Éces. A barrel-chested man with bushy red hair and beard, richly but a little carelessly clad, he did not seem one who could call forth such icy-sweet notes as he did. Power pulsed in his deep voice when he looked straight into the eyes of Niall and chanted:

"Lúg, bright God, of war the Lord,
Long-Arm, hear my harp!
Hark to tales that I will tell,
Talking unto all.

"Heaven sees how Temir's holy
Hilltop now bears Niall,
Never conquered, as its King,
Keeping warlike watch.

"See him seated in his splendor.
So it was not once.
Well that men should know how much
Might wrung wealth from woe."

A happy sigh went over the benches. Listeners knew they were about to hear a grand story.

And Laidchenn told it; and those who had heard it often, growing year by year, found newness, while others found wonder.

Niall, sang the poet, Niall, descendant of Corbmac maqq Arti, son of Eochaid maqq Muredach who was called Magimedon—Niall was born of dark curly-haired Carenn, a princess whom his father had carried away from Alba. In those days his grandfather still ruled. Eochaid had a wife named Mongfind, daughter of a tuathal king in Mumu, who was a witch and a ruthless woman. She bore him four sons, Brión, Féchra, Alill, and Fergus. Because Niall showed early promise, Mongfind plotted to do away with him, lest he succeed to lordship instead of Brión or a brother of Brión. She had him carried off, a small boy, while his father was gone warring. When Eochaid returned, Mongfind persuaded him that the loss was due to Carenn's carelessness, and Eochaid let Mongfind make a menial slave of his erstwhile leman.

But Torna, great poet in Mumu, knew by his arts what had happened, and foresaw what was in Niall. He rescued the child and fostered him. When the early signs of manhood were upon Niall, Torna sent him back to reclaim his own. Eochaid, now King, joyously received this son he had thought lost, and Carenn was released from her bondage.

Once Eochaid wished to test the five youths. A blacksmith's shop caught fire, and he commanded them to save what they could. Brión fetched out the chariots, Alill a shield and sword, Féchra the forge trough, Fergus merely some firewood; but Niall rescued anvil, block, sledges, and bellows, the heart of the smith's trade.

On another time when they were hunting and had grown sorely thirsty, they came upon a well deep in the forest. However, its guardian was a hideous old hag, who would give a drink to none unless he lie with her. No son of Mongfind could make himself do that; at most, Brión achieved a hasty kiss. But Niall led her aside and laid her down. Then rags and shriveled skin fell from her, she came forth radiant in youth and beauty, for this was the Goddess Who bestows sovereignty. Afterward Niall made his half-brothers pledge fealty to him before he would let them drink. They abided honestly by that, and Brión presently fathered a line of chieftains.

But meanwhile Mongfind lived and schemed. Through her magics— and, no doubt, kinsmen in Mumu of whom Eochaid had need—she kept him from putting her from him. Upon his death, she succeeded in having her brother Craumthan maqq Fidaci chosen as his successor.

He, though, proved to be no clay for her molding, but instead a man who laid a firm grip on the land and warred both in Ériu and across the waters. After years, despairing of aught else, Mongfind sought to poison him. He required that she drink first of the cup she proffered; and so they both died. Spells were still cast on certain nights to keep quiet the ghost of Mongfind the witch.

Throughout this time, Niall had been at the forefront of battles. In council his words were shrewd, later wise. It was upon a tenant's daughter, Ethniu, that he begot his eldest child, Breccan; but she was lovely and high-hearted, and everybody mourned when she died in giving birth. Niall soon married well—behold how his sons by the Queen are already shooting up! Thus after the death of Craumthan four years ago, it was no surprise when the Mide men chose him to be their King.

And he has wrought deeds that will live in memory as long as valor is cherished. Besides much else closer to home, he has harried the coasts overseas, bringing back huge booty. When the Cruthini of Alba, whom the Romans call the Picti of Caledonia, threatened the settlement of Dál Riata, Niall made alliance with its mother kingdom for its rescue; then, having cast the Cruthini back, he made alliance with them in turn. In Ériu, too, he called warriors to him from far beyond the bounds of Mide. No vaster hosting has been seen since the Cattle Raid of Cóalnge, than when the men of tribes conjoined roared down to the Wall of Rome.

And this time it was not Cú Culanni who stood alone in defense, it was Cú Culanni reborn at the van of attack. Many a Roman soldier sprawls headless in the heather, many a Britannic estate lies plundered and burnt, many a slave has gone to market and today herds sheep or grinds grain for a worthy master; and if the Wall of Rome still stands, why, the more glory to reap when we return!

"Never shall the hero Niall
Kneel to any other.

Witness, all You Gods, my words,
Aware I tell the truth."

The last notes shivered away. Cheers thundered from benches to
ridgepole. The King took from his arm a heavy coil of gold. Standing up,
he put it in the hands of Laidchenn. "Have this of me in token of thanks,"
he said amidst the din, "and let me ask of you that you abide with me a
long while—forever, if I may have my wish."

Flushed, breathing hard, eyes asparkle, Niall sat back down. The druid
Nemain stroked his beard and murmured, "Your fame grows by leaps,
darling."

Niall tossed his head. "What a poet says is true. He may find fresh
words for the clothing of truth—but—you would not be denying that I
wedded the Goddess of the land, would you?"

"I would not," replied Nemain, "nor speak against anything I have
heard tonight; for indeed truth is a lady who has many different garments
to wear. I would simply lay caution upon you. Not qualm, only caution,
for sadly would we miss our lord should he fall, and worst if it was
needlessly."

Niall did not hear. Again his head was aflame with dreams. Long
though the nights still were, he did not look for much sleep in this one, if
any; for among the gessa laid on a King of Mide was that sunrise must
never find him in bed on Temir. It did not matter. He *was* the King.

As host, he should make a speech of welcome. Rising, he lifted his
goblet—Roman glass, loot from Alba. Out of full lungs, he shouted: "It's
glad I am to see so great and fair a company here, and glad Herself must
be, and every God. If I name not the kings and nobles among us and their
honors, it is because dawn would break well before I was done. Let us
instead make merry, let us no more grieve over our losses or brood on our
wrongs, let us look ahead to a year of revenge and victory!"

III

His father's house felt strangely empty to Gratillonius.

Or not so strangely, he thought. When he arrived the evening before, joy was too tumultuous for him to pay close heed to his surroundings. Notified in advance, Marcus had had a feast prepared for his soldier son. The food was local, fish and meat and dried garden truck, but seasoned with such things as pepper and cloves, scarce these days, while the wines were from Burdigala and Narbonensis, not a mediocre Britannic vineyard. If the tableware was of poor quality and the attendant an untrained yokel, talk between the two men made up amply for that. When it turned to Gaius's older brother it grew evasive—Lucius was "studying in Aquae Sulis; you know what a bookish sort he's always been, not like you, you rascal"—but then the news quickly came that his youngest sister Camilla had married an able farmer, Antonia and Faustina continued happy in their own homes, and another grandchild was on the way. And his old nurse Docca had earlier hugged him in arms crippled by rheumatism, and he learned that three or four more of those who had been dear to him in his boyhood were still above ground.

Soon after supper weariness overwhelmed him and he went to bed. It had not been any route march to get here, only a few miles from Isca to the Sabrina, a ferry ride across the broad rivermouth, and a little way inland beyond that. He had, though, been at work since dawn preparing, as he had been for days previously. It won him an early enough start that he could justify spending two nights at home before he began his journey in earnest.

Thus he awoke ahead of sun and household. When he got up, the air nipped and the floor was cold. He recalled that the place had been chilly yesterday too, nothing but a couple of charcoal braziers for heat; he had avoided asking why. Fumbling his way through murk, he drew aside a curtain that, as spring approached, had supplanted shutters. On the leaded window, bits of leather were glued over three empty panes. The glass must have been broken in some accident or juvenile mischief. Why had his father, who always took pride in keeping things shipshape, not had it replaced?

Sufficient moonlight seeped through for Gratillonius to use flint, steel, and tinder. When he had ignited a tallow candle, he dropped the curtain back to conserve warmth and took care of his necessities. Clad in tunic and sandals, candlestick in hand, he padded forth in search of all he remembered.

The house reached shadowy around him. It had grown, piece by piece, for almost two hundred years as the family prospered; but his grandfather had been the last to make any additions. Doors were closed on this upper story, though only he and Marcus occupied bedrooms. (Once the hall was a clamor of footfalls and laughter.) Well, no sense in leaving chambers open when servants were too few to keep them dusted.

Gratillonius went downstairs. The atrium was still elegant, peacock mosaic on the floor and Theseus overcoming the Minotaur on a wall. Colors glimmered where the candlelight picked them out of darkness. However, most of the heirloom furniture was gone. Replacements were conscientiously built, but by carpenters, not artists.

An ebony table was among the few ancestral pieces remaining. Upon it lay several books. They were copied on scrolls, not bound into modern codices, because they too had been in the family for generations. Gratillonius's left hand partly unrolled one. A smile passed faint over his lips. He recognized *The Aeneid*. That he had enjoyed reading, along with other hero stories, as he did hearing the songs and sagas of the Britons from those backwoods folk who knew them yet—and did emphatically not enjoy Fronto and other bores he was supposed to study so he could become a proper Roman. Learning Greek turned out to be impossible for a boy who could be rambling the woods, riding, swimming, boating, fishing, playing ball or war with his friends, alone in the workshop making something—later, hanging around neighbor Ewein's daughter Una— Finally his tutor gave up.

Lucius was different, of course. Their mother had been proud of him.

Sadness tugged at Gratillonius. He left the atrium, went down a corridor to the west wing, and opened a door he knew well. Behind it was a room Julia had used for sewing and such-like lady's work. And for prayer. Her husband let her have a fish and Chi Rho painted on a wall. Before them each day, until a fever took her off, she humbly called on her Christ.

Gratillonius's free hand stroked the air where her head would have been were she sitting there. "I loved you, mother," he whispered. "If only I'd known how to show it."

Maybe she had understood anyway. Or maybe she now did in whatever afterworld had received her.

Gratillonius shook himself, scowled, and went out. He wanted to inspect the kitchen and larder. That wasn't supposed to be any concern of his. But every soldier developed a highly practical interest in grub. Though supper had been fine, what were ordinary meals like, in this house where they couldn't pay to fuel the furnace? Gratillonius meant to make sure that his father was eating adequately, if perhaps frugally.

He should have looked into that on earlier visits. Even before he enlisted he was aware of a pinch that strengthened year by year. But his awareness was only peripheral, as stoic as his father was and as lost as he himself was in his dreams of Una, the lightfoot and golden-haired—until she perforce married elsewhere, and he flung himself into the army— She no longer haunted him, much. He should have become more thoughtful of his own kindred.

Yet regardless of Isca's nearness, his appearances here had been infrequent, the last one three years back. And they had been short. He'd spent most of his furlough time ranging the Silurian hills, forests, remote settlements where men were friendly and girls friendlier; or else he'd be off to the baths and frivolities of Aquae Sulis, or as far afield as smoky Londinium. The recollection hurt him, on what might well be his last sight of home and these people, hurt him both with guilt and with a sense of having squandered a treasure.

When he had finished his tour, the sky showed wan through glass. The cook and the housekeeper yawned their way forth, too sleepy to greet him. He could forgive that in the former, who had been here longer than he could recall, but the latter was a young slattern. Gratillonius considered giving her a tongue-lashing for insolence. He decided against it. She would merely be the surlier after he was gone. Besides, maybe she was the best Marcus could find. The older man had bespoken a dearth of good help. Not only was the countryside population dwindling as small farms were swallowed up by plantations or abandoned altogether by owners whom taxes and weak markets had ruined. Those folk who stayed were generally bound by law to the soil, and serfs seldom raised their children to much pride of workmanship.

As he re-entered the atrium, Gratillonius met his father coming from upstairs, and was especially filial in his salutation. "Good morning," replied Marcus. "I hope you slept well. Your old bed is one thing I've managed to keep."

Touched, Gaius gave him a close regard. The dawnlight showed a face and form resembling his own; but Marcus's hair was gray, his counte-

nance furrowed, the once powerful body gaunt and stoop-shouldered.
"Thank you, sir," Gaius said. "Could we talk today . . . privately?"

"Of course. You'll want a walk around the place anyway. First, though,
our duties, and next our breakfast."

They went forth together onto the verandah, sought its eastern end,
lifted arms and voices to Mithras as the sun rose. It stirred Gaius more
than rites in a temple commonly did. He paid his respects to the God and
tried to live by the Law, because that was upright, soldierly, everything
this man at his side—and this man's stern father, once—had tried to
make him become. But he was not fervent about it. Here, somehow, a
feeling of sanctity took him, as if borne on those rays bestorming heaven.
Tears stung his eyes. He told himself they must be due the wind.

Everydayness came back. The men spoke little while they had their
bread and cheese. Afterward they dressed against the weather and left the
house. "Let's begin at the stable," Marcus suggested. "There's a colt
you'll appreciate."

Gaius looked about him more closely than yesterday. The house stood
firm beneath its red-tiled roofs, and likewise did the farm buildings to
either side, around a cobbled courtyard. But he saw where whitewash had
flaked from walls, the cowpen and its barn gaped almost empty, a single
youngster went to feed pigs and chickens where formerly the grounds had
roared with life.

The wind shrilled and plucked at his cloak. He drew the garment tight
against those icy fingers. Northward he saw the land roll in long curves to
the woods where boys went—sometimes in defiance of orders from parents who feared Scoti might pounce from the river and seize them for
slaves—and where Gwynmael the gamekeeper had taught him how to
read a spoor and set a snare. Closer in, the acres were cleared, but most
had gone back to grass and brush, still winter-sere, although quickened by
the faintest breath of new green. Through an apple orchard he discerned a
cultivated field, dark save where wind-ruffled rain puddles blinked in the
sunshine. Rooks and starlings darted above, blacker yet. A hawk high
overhead disdained to stoop on them. Its wings shimmered golden.

A thought struck Gaius. "I haven't seen your steward, Artorius," he
said. "Has he died?"

"No—"

"Good. He used to tell me wonderful stories about his days as a legionary. That was what started me thinking I'd want to enlist, myself." Gaius
forced a laugh. "After I did, I discovered what a liar he'd been, but no
matter, he's a grand old rogue."

"Too old. Nearly blind. I retired him. He's moved in with a son of his."

"Um, who do you have now?"

Marcus shrugged. "Nobody. Can't find a competent man and couldn't afford him if I did. I'm my own steward. The villa's no longer so big or busy that I can't handle it."

They neared the stable. A hound sprang forth, baying, until a word from Marcus brought it to heel. A white-haired man shuffled out behind the creature. He stopped short, blinked, squinted, and quickened his pace. "Why, bless my butt if that's not the young master!" he cried in Belgic dialect. "We'd heard you were coming, but I thank the Gods just the same. Welcome, lad, welcome!"

Gaius took a hand gnarled into a set of claws, regarded a visage withered and well-nigh toothless, and remembered how Gwynmael had drifted like a shadow down forest paths till his bow twanged and the arrow found its mark. He hadn't been nearly this aged three years ago. Well, Gaius thought with pain, you grow old, suddenly you can't run fast enough, and Time the Hunter overtakes you in a pair of leaps. "Are you working here?" he asked in the vernacular.

"So 'tis, so 'tis. I'm no use any more for chasing off poachers or bringing back venison. But your dad's a kindly sort and lets me pretend to earn my keep being his head groom. That's easy, because except for a boy I'm the only groom, heh, heh. Not that I could've carried on in my real job after our woods got sold off." In his shock at hearing that, Gaius hardly noticed when Gwynmael fondled the hound's ears and said, "Splendid dog, eh? Remember Brindle, what coursed the stags so well? Here's a pup from the last litter she bore. Too bad we can't let this 'un do what his blood meant him for." Taking the centurion's elbow: "But come inside, young sir, come in and look at what we got in a stall. Juno foaled him last summer, and if he don't live up to his promise, why, he's the biggest braggart in horsedom."

The stable was dim and warm, smelling sweetly of hay and animal, pungently of manure. Gaius stopped to stroke the two beasts he knew, mare and gelding—their noses were silk-soft, and Juno whickered for pleasure—before he went on to the stallion colt. That was indeed a superb creature, like a cross between flesh and wind. "Epona Herself'ud be glad to ride him when he's full-grown," Gwynmael said. He had never made any bones about his devotion to the ancient Gods of the Belgae.

"What sire?" Gaius asked.

"Commius's prize stud," Marcus told him.

"Really? Commius the senator? He must have charged you a pretty solidus."

"He did, but I should profit eventually. You see, I think I can fence in most of what land we have left, take out the scrub, sow pasturage, and breed horses. Blooded horses, for riding. Skilled help may not be too hard to come by in that business: veteran cavalrymen from the eastern provinces, especially, or their sons."

"But who could pay the price you'd have to set?"

"The army. I may have swallowed the anchor, but I still get word from overseas, as far as Constantinople. Given the new Asiatic saddles, horsemen are the soldiers of the future. Cataphracts could roll the barbarians back—though we won't get them in Britannia during my lifetime. However, I expect we'll begin to see more and more cavalry in Gallia, and here I'll be, prepared to export." Marcus's smile turned grim. "Also, rich men everywhere will want fast mounts in case of raiders or uprisings."

His mood gentled. He touched Gaius's arm. "I'll need this fellow for breeding," he murmured, "but I'll set aside the best of his get for you."

The son gulped. "Thank you," he said unsteadily. "I'm not sure whether—oh, we have to talk about all this."

They went out and set off toward the Roman road. Little used, the wagon track alongside which they walked was not very muddy. Rounding the orchard, Gaius saw two men, no more, at work in the grainfield. They were plowing with ards drawn by cows. Gaius halted. "Where's the proper gear?" he wondered.

"Sold, like much else," Marcus replied.

Keen as its coulter there rose before Gaius the memory of a wheeled moldboard plow and the mighty oxen that pulled it. Rage rose acid in his throat. "But this is wrong, wrong!"

"Oh, the villa hasn't enough land under cultivation to need better equipment."

"You've sold . . . still more? Besides the woods?"

"Had to. They slapped an extra assessment on me for waterworks, after Tasciovanus went bankrupt, Laurentinus suicided, and Guennellius disappeared—ran off to Londinium and is hiding in its proletary, some say."

"Who bought your land?"

"Commius. Who else?"

Fury lifted higher. Commius the gross, Commius the crooked, Commius the unmerciful squeezer of tenants, servants, slaves, Commius who bought his way to senatorial rank—everybody knew that was a question of bribing the right people—and thus escaped the burdens of the curials, Commius who thereupon had the gall to boast how public-spirited he was because he maintained a theater, whose pornographic shows must swell business at the whorehouse everybody knew he owned—

"Calm down," Marcus advised. "His sort, they come and go. Rome's had them since first the Republic began to rot, if not earlier; but Rome endures, and that is what matters." When he grinned, his leathery face looked, briefly, wolfish. "In fact, last year, at a series of council meetings, I had the pleasure of frustrating him. He wanted to close our Mithraeum as the Emperor had decreed. I got my friends behind me and we agreed that if that was done, we'd see to it that his precious theater was shut down too. Those plays pretend to show myths of the ancestors, you know, and we'd claim this made them not 'educational displays' but pagan ceremonies. An Imperial inquiry would have turned up more about his affairs than he could well stand—investments in commerce and industry such as are forbidden a senator, for instance. He stopped calling for any religious prohibitions. It was marvelous, seeing him flush red and hearing him gobble. The God does send His faithful a bit of fun once in a while."

But the God's faithful die or fall away, year after year, and ever fewer take their places, Gaius thought.

The somberness dampened his wrath. "At least you've lowered your tax by selling off," he ventured, "and with this horse-breeding scheme you may win back to something better . . . for Lucius and the grandchildren he'll give you."

Marcus's mouth drew tight. They trudged on in silence, except for the wind. Finally the father said, tonelessly, looking at the far hills: "No. I didn't tell you earlier because it would have spoiled our evening. But Lucius has turned Christian. He's studying under the bishop in Aquae Sulis, with the aim of becoming a churchman too. He talks about celibacy."

Gaius' feet jarred to rest. Emptiness grew from his heart until it engulfed him. "Not that," he whispered.

Marcus stopped likewise and squeezed his shoulder. "Well, well, don't take it overly hard. I've learned to live with it. We've stayed on speaking terms, he and I. It *was* his mother's religion, and is that of his sisters and their husbands and . . . Maximus, who cast back the wild men. . . . I can't blame him greatly. If he'd waited till I died, he'd have been trapped in the curial class himself. Taking Christian holy orders now is his way out of it."

Out! thought Gaius. The army was another way, and he had chosen it, although that would not have been allowed if he were the older boy. Since Diocletianus, a son and heir must follow in his father's occupation. The law was frequently evaded, but the curials—the landowners, merchants, producers, the moderately well-off—were usually too noticeable. Once it had been an honor to belong to their class. They were the councillors and magistrates; they did not endow the grandiose spectacles that Caesars and senators and ambitious newly rich did, but they underwrote the useful public works. That had been long ago. The burdens remained; the means were gone.

"I hoped to be free of it myself, you know," Marcus was saying. "That's why I went into sea traffic. High profits for men who didn't mind the risk. Your grandfather approved—and he was a man of duty if ever there was one—and got me started. But at last . . . well, you know. It had taken all my father's influence, and a stiff bribe, to get permission for me to become a navicularius when I wasn't the son of one. Then your uncle, my older brother, died, and the guild was only too happy to 'regularize' my status. That laid this estate on me. It's devoured everything I had."

"I do know. But I've never quite understood how."

"I didn't explain because I didn't want to whine at you, who were young and had neither gift nor wish for this kind of thing. I did have my good, quiet Lucius, who was supposed to inherit anyway. It's the taxes and assessments. You'd think, as debased as most money is, coin wouldn't be hard to find. But that's not so, we're more and more going over to barter, and meanwhile the Imperium wants its cash. The taxes in kind, they get higher all the time too, as the number of farmers shrinks. In my seafaring days I was a sharp bargainer, you may recall; but I don't have Commius's talent for grinding wealth out of the poor underneath me."

Abruptly Marcus lifted his head, glanced at Gaius through crow's-footed eyes, and laughed. He might almost have been standing at the prow of his ship as a gale blew up. "At ease, boy, at ease!" he said. "You're safe. The law will scarcely haul a battle-proven officer back to the farm, especially when you're known to none less than Duke Maximus. He'll probably get you senatorial rank. As for this place, why, if my plan pays off, I should have a chance of joining forces with my sons-in-law after they inherit. Between us, we might yet put together a villa that will last."

"But if you fail to?" Gaius breathed.

"I won't consider that till it's upon me, which the God forbid. At worst, I'll never do what too many broken curials have, slunk off under changed names and become underlings, even serfs. No, your old man will die a Gratillonius."

"I would help you if I could. I hope you know that, father. But . . . I'm bound afar, and what will happen to me I cannot foresee."

"Let's go on," said Marcus. A while of walking passed until he remarked, "You've told me nothing but that you're off to Gallia on a special mission for the Duke. Crossing the Channel before equinox— Did he give you the funds you'll need to persuade a skipper to take you?"

Gaius smiled. "Better than that. A writ letting me commandeer a naval transport. And I mean to cross by the shortest way, from Dubris to Gesoriacum, where one can scarcely get lost in anything less than an oatmeal fog. Cutting out that hazard makes the added overland travel worthwhile."

"Then your march will take you through Londinium," said Marcus, also trying to lighten the mood. "Give the fleshpots a workout for me."

Gaius shook his head. "We won't stop after today, except for sleep. We've this breadth of Britannia to cross, and then it's more than four hundred miles over Gallia, and . . . the task is urgent."

Marcus squinted into the wind. Some distance off, Gaius's legionaries had pitched their tents in a vacated field. That was all they had done, being too few for the labor of constructing a standard camp, but they had done it properly. The leather was drawn so taut over poles and guys that the air got no purchase on it but must be content with flapping a banner.

Metal gleamed on statue-like sentries. Men detailed to camp chores were in plain tunic and trousers, but neat. The rest were outside in full battle dress, drilling. When they hurled their javelins, it called to mind a flight of bright birds. Tethered pack horses stood placidly, used to the sight, but the centurion's mount and remount, more spirited, stirred as if impatient for action.

"Four tents," Marcus counted. "Thirty-two men, eh? Not much."

"I chose them carefully, the best I have who aren't bound to wives. Most are Britons; we'll understand each other's thinking. I didn't order them to follow me but offered them the privilege of volunteering. They're eager. Over-eager, maybe, but I think the march will shake them down into a crack unit."

"Still, I can hear in your voice you'd have preferred a larger force."

"Maximus sent direct word to my commandant that I was to have no more than this. He . . . can't spare many."

"So I've been suspecting. . . . But he obviously doesn't expect you'll meet serious opposition."

"No. Yonder fellows will be my bodyguards and, um, the presence of Rome. That should suffice."

"Where?"

"Father, I'm not supposed to tell—"

"Four hundred-odd miles of Gallia. Not south, because that's where the main action will be. Also, your experience has been with Armorica, as Maximus must know. Westbound, you'll fetch up at Gesocribate, or else fairly close. But Gesocribate already has an ample Roman presence. And I don't think the Duke of the Armorican Tract would welcome troops dispatched by the Duke of the Britains—certainly not before he knows which way the cat is going to jump. Therefore he's doubtless not been informed, nor is he meant to get the news until too late for him to do anything about it." Marcus nodded. "M-hm. Your task is to secure a critical area and thus help assure that Armorica will stay safe—for Maximus."

Gaius's bark of laughter flushed a hare from a briar patch. It lolloped off as if a fox were at its tail. "Father, you're too shrewd!"

"I told you I get word from outside." Marcus bleakened. "For some time, now, I've caught the smell of war on the wind, stronger and stronger. Civil war. Maximus will get the Britannic legions to hail him Augustus. The Sixth may be doing it in Eboracum at this very hour. He'll cross to Gallia and try for the throne."

"Wait, wait! He didn't say that to me. He said only that affairs of state are approaching a crisis and Rome will need a loyal man in Armorica."

"Loyal to him. You're not stupid. You know what he meant."

"He is . . . a valiant leader, father. And intelligent and just. Rome perishes for want of right governance."

"Those sound like words you got from him," Marcus said, low in his throat. "Oh, we could do worse. Provided the struggle doesn't wreak the kind of harm the last such did, or give the Northfolk their chance to invade."

Gaius recalled Parnesius. "The Wall will abide, I swear."

"Scoti sail past it. Saxon galleys sweep in from the eastern sea."

"Against them—Rome will have new help."

Once more they halted. Marcus's gaze probed like a sapper's spade. "That's your task," he said finally.

Gaius swallowed hard and nodded.

"I believe I know where. I'd liefest hear it from your lips, son. Mithras be witness that I'll keep the secret."

Gaius thrust the name forth. "Ys."

Marcus drew a sign before him, the Cross of Light that marked the shield of his warrior God. "That's an uncanny place," he said.

Gaius mustered courage. "It's been left alone so long that all sorts of wild stories about it have sprung up. What do we know for certain? What do *you* know, father?"

Wind roared and whistled. Clouds were appearing over the horizon. Their shadows raced across winter-gray hills and the few springtime-wet croplands. A solitary willow nearby lashed its withes around. At their removes, the manor house and the soldiers' camp looked very small. The hawk wheeled scornful overhead.

Lines deepened in Marcus's brow and beside his mouth. "I was never there myself," he said. "I did speak with Britannic and Gallic captains who'd called. But they were just three or four, and none had done it more than once. The Ysans don't seem to want any trade with the outside that they don't carry on for themselves. No more involvement of any kind with Rome that they can avoid. Not that they act hostile. My talkmates said the city is still more wonderful than they'd heard, Ys of the hundred towers. But even in the joyhouses there was always . . . an otherness."

"It's a foederate of ours," Gaius reminded.

"After a fashion. And only in name for—what? These past two hundred years? When did the last Roman prefect leave?"

"I'm not sure." Gratillonius straightened. "But I will be the next."

"Keeping Ys neutral, at least, and a counterweight to people elsewhere in Armorica who might otherwise side with Gratianus and Valentinianus against Maximus."

Gaius responded louder:

"And, I hope, taking a more active part than hitherto in measures against pirates. Ysan commerce has shrunk with Rome's. From what little I recall or could find out these past months, Ys trades mainly with its Osismiic neighbors, overland; but once it was the queen of the Northern seas. I should think it'd welcome guidance in rebuilding security and commerce. Father, I don't see how any living city can be the kind of witch-nest those rumors tell of. Give me a few years, and I'll prove as much to the world."

Marcus Valerius Gratillonius smiled, more in pride than in pleasure. "Good for you, son. Sink or sail, you're a Roman!"

And how many such are left? he did not ask. Men who have hardly a drop of blood in them from Mother Rome, and who will never see her whom they serve. Can she hold their faith, today when new Gods beckon?

IV

1

It was good to be on salt water again. Gratillonius braced himself at the taffrail of the transport, near a swan's-head figure that decorated the after section, and looked happily about. Forward of him was the deckhouse, on top of which two men strained to hold their steering oars against seas running heavy. It hid from Gratillonius the main deck, with lifeboat, cargo hatch, crewmen, and his soldiers. The mast rose over it. Square mainsail and triangular topsail bellied against swift gray clouds and malachite waves. Gratillonius could also glimpse the spar that jutted out over the prow and the artemon sail it bore.

No other craft was in sight. Their whiteness dulled by spindrift, the cliffs of Britannia were sinking under the horizon, though he could still make out the pharos that loomed over Dubris. Ahead, hillscape was shouldering out of Gallia, likewise vague and distance-dimmed.

The ship rolled and bounded like a live creature. Waters rushed, boomed, clashed. The wind skirled and flung briny spatters across his lips. Timbers and rigging creaked. Gratillonius's muscles rejoiced in the interplay that kept him erect. Tomorrow he'd be on the road again, and that was good too, because he'd fare through country new to him until he reached magical Ys. But Mithras be thanked that first he got this brief voyage.

He laughed aloud at himself. Had the Gods really carved out a strait at the Creation in order that Gaius Valerius Gratillonius could have a day's worth of feeling like the boy he once was?

The captain strode around the deckhouse. His blue uniform was hidden beneath a cloak he hugged to him in the cold. Approaching, he said through the noise: "Come forward with me, Centurion. A fight's brewing between your men and mine."

"What? How?"

"Several of yours are miserably seasick, and when one of them puked on the deck, the sailors didn't want to clean it up. Then they started mocking those landlubbers."

Gratillonius bridled. "What kind of discipline do you have in the fleet?"

The captain sighed. "They resent being forced out this early in the year, in this tricky weather. I do myself, frankly, but I realize you have your orders, whatever they are. Now do come along. It'll work better if we both take charge."

Gratillonius agreed and accompanied the other. On the broad expanse around the mast, men stood at confrontation. They were not all there were in their units. Some deckhands would have been flogged if they left their duty stations—though they too gibed and made obscene gestures. Half the legionaries huddled shivering, turned helpless by nausea. The rest had reflexively formed a double rank; their weapons were stowed but their fists were cocked. The sailors bunched loosely, about an equal number. They were not professional fighters. The garrison commander had ruled that the danger of Saxons was so slight at this season that he wouldn't subject any of his too few soldiers to the real hazard of the crossing. However, each crewman bore a knife, and fingers had strayed to hilts.

Quintus Junius Eppillus stood before his troops, growling at a sailor who appeared to be a leader. Eppillus was a stocky, paunchy man in his forties, big-nosed, bald on top, a Dobunnian with considerable Italian in his bloodlines, Gratillonius' appointed deputy. His Latin came hoarse: "Watch your tongue, duckfoot. The bunch o' you watch your tongues. You're close to insulting not just us, but the Augusta."

The sailor, a tall redhead, leered and answered with a thick Regnensic accent: "I wouldn't do that. I only wonder why your legion allows fat swine like you in it. Well, maybe they've gotten tired of sheep, and pleasure themselves now with swine."

"Take that back before I remove some o' those rotten teeth from your turnip hatch."

"Very well, I'll take it back. You're not swine. It's just your fathers that were. Your mothers were whores."

Cynan, who was young and of the still half-wild Demetae, yelled a battle cry. He broke from the army rank and threw himself on the sailor. They went down together, to struggle for possession of the knife and each other's throats.

"Stop!" Gratillonius roared. "Eppillus, break that up! Nobody else move!"

The legionaries who were standing froze. The captain grabbed a belaying pin and bloodied a head or two among his tars. They retreated in confusion, babbling excuses and pleas for mercy. Eppillus gave the combatants a couple of efficient kicks. They separated and crawled to their feet, gasping, spitting, and shuddering.

"Attention!" Gratillonius barked. He lifted his vinestaff of authority, which seldom left him. "Captain, I want that man of yours whipped."

"Five lashes," the skipper agreed. "The rest of you bless whatever saints you know about. Hop to it!" The redhead was immediately seized. He didn't resist, doubtless realizing he was lucky to escape with nothing worse. The captain turned to Gratillonius. "We'll make the same example of your fellow, eh?"

The centurion shook his head. "No. He must be in shape to march. But we can't have this kind of conduct, true. Keep still, Cynan." The vinestaff cut a crimson line over the youth's cheek. "Go to the horses and stay there till we land. The rest of you who were involved, except the deputy, hold out your right arms." He gave each wrist a blow that raised a welt but would not be disabling. Eppillus possibly deserved punishment too, but not enough to make it worthwhile compromising his dignity.

Fingers plucked at Gratillonius's ankle. He glanced down and saw that his follower Budic had crawled to him. The youngster's ash-pale hair fluttered around eyes hollowed by misery. He lifted a hand. "Here, sir," he mumbled.

"What?" asked Gratillonius.

"Strike me, sir."

"Why, you didn't do anything." Gratillonius smiled. "You were too upchucking sick."

The blue gaze adored him. "But . . . I might have . . . when that . . . that sailor said what he did . . . about our legion. And surely I failed my centurion, me, useless when he needed his men. Please, sir. Make it right."

Gratillonius quelled an impulse to rumple those locks, as if this were one of his small nephews. "It is already right, soldier. Just remember and learn." He paused. "Oh, and be sure you shave before we march tomorrow. I want this outfit smart."

Adminius snickered at his comrade's discomfiture. "Spruce," he said, "not peach-fuzzy. I'll guide yer 'and if it's been so long you've forgotten 'ow." He was from Londinium, given to teasing country boys like the Coritanian Budic.

Stripped and triced to the stays, the deckhand choked off screams as the lead-weighted cords of the whip reddened his back. Cynan slunk down the hatch. Gratillonius gave the captain a discreet grin and muttered, "Fresh air's the best medicine against seasickness. He'll be where it's warm and stale."

"You're sharper than you look to be," the captain said. "Uh, best we absent ourselves for a while, you and I."

"Right. Let them regain control on their own. It takes hold firmer, that way."

The commanders sought the captain's room within the cabin. There he lifted a flagon from its rack and offered wine, thin sour stuff that didn't call for watering. "Military honor isn't high in the fleet," he admitted, "and it drops year by year. I can't blame the men too much. Time was, you may know, when Rome had a navy in these parts. Now there's just some tubs like this one, that the Saxon galleys can sail or row rings around. They land anywhere they will, the heathen do, and when next we pass by, all we find is ashes and corpses. That wears the spirit away, I can tell you. How do the inland legionaries feel?"

"Not so badly," Gratillonius replied. "We did win our war last year, and afterward my particular detachment had fun getting a new chief installed among the Ordovices. No one objected to him, so we'd nothing more to do than hike around in the hills showing the eagle and proclaiming the news officially. People were delighted to see new faces, and laid themselves out to be hospitable."

"The girls especially, I hope?"

Gratillonius laughed. "Well— Anyhow, we came back to Isca Silurum and settled into winter quarters. It's our home, you know; has been for hundreds of years. The older men generally have wives and children in town, and the younger men are apt to acquire their own after the usual pleasures of courtship. On furlough, you can reach Aquae Sulis in a day, baths, foodshops, joyhouses, theaters, games, social life, even learned men for those who care to listen. It's no Londinium, but still, in season you'd think half the world was jostling through its streets." He drank. "No, a man could do worse than join the army. Not that we don't keep the troops in line. They gripe. But they'd be appalled if we let their . . . strength fall away from them."

The captain gave him a narrow stare and said low, "From time to time the legions raise up an Emperor. That must be a heady feeling."

Gratillonius veered from the subject. The communities where he had sometimes overnighted, on his march through Britannia, were abuzz with rumors about Maximus, like beehives which were being toppled. He didn't want to give any hint of confirmation, most particularly not to this man who would often be crossing the Channel. If the governors of Gallia got sufficient advance warning to mobilize, the fighting could become disastrous.

"I trust we'll make port before dark," he said. "I wouldn't care to spend the night hove to."

"The wind's not from too bad a quarter, though stiffer than I like. You talk as if you've been a mariner yourself."

"Oh, more of a supercargo, on my father's ship when I was a boy. We called two or three times at Gesoriacum. But that was years ago."

"And a kid would scarcely see much. Can you stay over? The circus is small, but gets a canvas roof in bad weather, so it may be open tomorrow. Pretty good spectacles, not like those wretched bear-baitings which are the best we see in Dubris. In Gesoriacum they know how to stage an animal fight, and once I saw actual gladiators."

Gratillonius grimaced. "No, thanks. Torture and killing, for the amusement of a lot of rabble who'd loose their bowels if they saw teeth or a sword coming at *them*—I don't even permit my men to draw blood when they must touch up the horses."

"I hope you're not so soft-hearted in combat," said the captain, miffed.

"No insult intended. Anyhow, I can't stay. We've got to be off in the morning."

"Really pressing business, eh? Well," said the captain as his irritation passed, "I know a whorehouse in town that keeps late hours."

Gratillonius smiled. "Again, no, thanks. It's the hostel and an early bed for me." He grew serious. "Also frankly—and, again, no offense—I'm trying to stay clean. Aside from prayers, it's the only chance this trip gives me to honor the God."

"Why, you could've stopped off at any church or shrine along the way."

Gratillonius sighed. "The Mithraeum in Londinium was closed—closed forever. Does Gesoriacum have one any more?"

The captain sat straight, or as straight as the heeling ship would allow. His eyes bulged. "What? You're joking!"

"Certainly not. I serve Mithras. Doubtless you serve Christ. What matter, as long as we both serve Rome?"

The captain made a V of two fingers and jabbed them in Gratillonius's direction. "Out!" he shrilled. "Go! It's unlucky enough having a pagan aboard, without sitting here and drinking with him. If you weren't an officer on a mission, I swear I'd have you thrown overboard. Don't think I won't report you when I get back. Now go! Out of my sight!"

The centurion did not argue, but rose and went forth onto the deck, into the wind.

2

Dusk was falling as the ship glided between jetties and docked at the naval wharf. The soldiers collected their gear and tramped down the gangplank under the stares of the crew. Gratillonius had them wait in formation while the horses were unloaded, a process which called forth words that sizzled. In the meantime he queried the harbormaster, who had come from his office to watch this unseasonal landing, about accommodations for the squadron. To his relief, he learned that most of the garrison were away on joint maneuvers with those of two other towns. Their barracks would thus have plenty of available beds.

Marching his men there, he found the prefect of the cohort that had stayed on guard and presented his written orders. They declared that he was on a mission of state, as directed by the Duke of the Britains, with rights to food, lodging, and whatever else his band required along the way. The prefect refrained from asking questions. These days there were many curious comings and goings. His only inquiry was: "Do you require a room for yourself?"

Gratillonius shook his head. "I think I'll put up at a hostel, and return about sunrise to take your guests off your hands."

The prefect chuckled wryly. "You may as well be comfortable."

Gratillonius made somewhat of a nuisance of himself, seeing to it that his men would have decent quarters and, though it was well past the regular hour, an adequate meal. Not until they were seated in the mess—complaining about food meant for auxiliaries from some forsaken far corner of the Empire—did he leave. It was quite dark then, but the prefect assigned him a guide with a lantern. The wind had chased most clouds away before lying down to rest, letting stars and a partial moon add their light. Air was cold, breath smoked and footfalls rattled, but a breath of spring softened it and leaf buds were pale upon trees.

The inn for official travelers was a two-story building, its tile roof rime-whitened. A stable and a shed flanked the courtyard in front. It stood outside the city, on a highway leading south. Beyond that pavement reached cropland, out of which remnants of two houses poked ghostly.

Like many other Gallic cities, Gesoriacum had shrunk during the past several generations, cramping itself within its defenses. Walls, towers, battlements gloomed under Draco and the Milky Way.

Passing by the stable, Gratillonius heard a noise that brought him to a halt. "What on earth?" He listened closer. Someone behind the door was weeping—no, more than a single one. The sounds were thin. His skin crawled. He did not think he had ever before heard such hopelessness.

The door was merely latched. He opened it. Murk yawned at him. The sobbing broke off in wails of terror. "Come along," he ordered his escort. "Be careful about any hay or straw, of course."

"Don't hurt us!" cried a child's voice. "Please don't hurt us! We'll be good, honest we will!"

He followed the words without difficulty. This was Belgica, whence the forebears of his own tribe had come to Britannia, and language hadn't changed much on either side. Fair-skinned and flaxen-haired, the children might have been playmates of his boyhood.

They numbered five, three boys and two girls, their ages seeming about nine or ten. They were dirty and unkempt, but not too poorly clad; two of them sported brightly colored wool scarves that their mothers must have given them at the farewell. Some horses in the building kept it warm. But it had been altogether dark here, and the children were penned in a stall. Slats nailed around and over it confined them, and made it impossible for them to stand upright.

Lanternlight glistened off tears on cheeks and, elsewhere, caused shadows to dance monstrous. Gratillonius hunkered down. "Don't be afraid," he said, as gently as the tightness in his throat allowed. "I won't hurt you. I'm your friend. What can I do for you?"

A girl's skinny arms reached out between the bars. He took her hands in his. "Oh, please," she stammered, "will you take us home?"

He couldn't help it, his voice harshened. "I'm sorry. I'm very sorry. I can't—now—but I will see if there is anything I can do, sweetheart. Be brave, all of you."

"You're not Jesus?" came from a boy. "I heard Jesus is the God in the city. I heard He is kind."

"I am not He," Gratillonius said, "but I promise Jesus will always watch over you." He kissed the hands he held, rose, and turned his back. "Goodnight. Try to sleep. Goodnight." The wails broke out anew as he left the stable and shut the door.

"New-taken slaves, sir," the escort observed.

"That's plain to see," Gratillonius snapped. He strode quickly to the hostel and thundered its knocker.

Candleglow spilled around the ruddy man who responded. "What do you want?" he asked. Gratillonius was in civil garb. "It's past supper-time."

"I'll have supper regardless," Gratillonius snapped. "For your information, I'm a legionary officer traveling on Imperial business. Furthermore, I'll have an explanation of those kids caged outside."

"Oh." The manager thought for a moment, then jerked his thumb over his shoulder. "He's in there, he can tell you better than me. Come in, sir." He didn't require credentials, doubtless reckoning that the soldier who had accompanied the stranger was sufficient.

Gratillonius bade that man farewell—be courteous to subordinates who deserve it, more even than to superiors—and followed the hostelkeeper into a long room feebly lit by candles. Their burning tallow filled it with stench, like an announcement of the poverty into which the Empire had fallen. Four guests sat benched around one of several tables. "Hail," called a portly fellow. "Welcome." Judging by his robe and the rings that sparkled on his fingers, he was the leader of his companions, who wore ordinary Gallic tunics and breeches. They were having a nightcap.

Gratillonius ignored the greeting. The manager asked him to register—name, rank, avowal that he was on an errand of the state—before taking a pair of candles and guiding him on upstairs. "We don't get many so soon in the year," he remarked. "You say you're of the Second Augusta? Isn't that off in Britannia? Well, well, these be uneasy times, and me, I know to keep my mouth shut. Here you are, sir. I'll go after my wife. Can't make anything fancy, I'm afraid, but we do keep a kettle of her good lentil soup on the hob. We'll get you something pretty quick, sir."

He left Gratillonius a light and departed. The centurion glanced around the room. Little was in it but a water jug, basin, chamber pot, and a pair of narrow beds. At this slack season, he'd be alone. He unpacked the small bag he had carried, stripped, scrubbed as well as he was able, dressed anew, and said his prayers—well after sunset, but better than not at all.

When he returned downstairs, the portly man called to him again: "Hoy, there, don't be so aloof. Come have a drink with us."

Briefly, Gratillonius hesitated. But . . . he had sought here not for the sake of comfort, as the prefect supposed, but in the hopes of picking up more gossip, a better feeling for how things were, than he could likely get in barracks. Parts of the Continent were devastated or in upheaval, while he had scant exact information. "Thanks," he said, and took a place beside the inviter. A youth, son or underling of the keeper, scuttled forth with a cup, and he helped himself from the pitchers on the table.

"My name's Sextus Titius Lugotorix," the portly man said. "My attendants—" He introduced them. They were a ruffianly-looking lot.

"Gaius Valerius Gratillonius, centurion, on a special assignment."

Lugotorix raised his brows. Seen close up, his face carried a gash of a mouth and eyes that were like two hailstones. He smelled of cheap perfume. His affability was undiminished. "My, my, you're the silent one, aren't you, friend?"

"Orders. What are you doing here?"

"I'm a publican."

"I thought so."

"We were delayed—some bumpkins got obstreperous and we had to teach them a lesson—and didn't reach Gesoriacum till the gates had closed for the night. I suppose you walked around the city wall, from the military post? It wasn't worthwhile persuading the guard to let us in, when this hostel is so close by." Lugotorix winked and nudged Gratillonius. "And free."

"I didn't know your business entitled you to government accommodations."

"The governor has authorized me. Specifically authorized me." Lugotorix rolled a pious glance ceilingward. "After all, the state must have its internal revenue."

"Those youngsters in the stable—you're dragging them to the slave market?"

A man laughed. "Not exactly dragging," he said. "Give the little buggers a taste of the whip, and they run along so fast their leashes nearly choke 'em."

Lugotorix peered at Gratillonius. "Did you take a look? Well, don't get mawkish, my friend." He drained his goblet and refilled it. A certain slurriness suggested he was a bit drunk. "They weren't abused, were they? Properly fed, I swear, and you saw for yourself they have a warm sleeping place and clean straw. Why damage the merchandise? Not that it'll fetch much. Hardly worth the trouble of collecting and selling. But I'm a patriot like you, Centurion. I feel it's my duty to the state to crack down on tax delinquents. I'm very patient, too, especially considering that this is my livelihood and I have mouths of my own to feed. I give those families plenty of time to find the money. Or if they can't, I'll take payment in kind, cattle or grain or whatever, marked down no more than necessary to compensate me for the added inconvenience. But they snivel that they'd starve. What can I do then but confiscate a brat? It helps keep the rest honest. If you let somebody evade his taxes, soon you must let everybody, and the government will have no more internal revenue."

"What will become of the children?" Gratillonius asked slowly.

Lugotorix shrugged. "Who knows? I pray they'll land in nice Christian homes and learn the Faith that will save their souls. See what a good work is mine in the sight of God! But I do have to take the best offer I get, you realize, or else how could I meet my own obligations to the state? And whelps like that don't command any large price. They have to be housed and fed for years, you know, before they're grown to field hands or maid-servants or whatever."

A man leered. "Got a whorehouse in town where some of the customers like 'em young," he said.

"I don't approve, I don't approve!" Lugotorix maintained. "But I must take the best price I can get. Besides, those rustic brats are seldom pretty enough. We may have one this time, but believe me, she's a rarity."

Her hands had lain in Gratillonius's.

He gulped his wine more fiercely than it deserved. The Empire still did fairly well by its officers, most places. In return, his immediate duty was to sound out these people. They must travel rather widely and hear news from farther yet.

"Well, never mind," he achieved saying. "Look, I'm bound west to Armorica. I can't tell you more. Now I have, um, been out of touch. If you can give me some idea of what to watch for along the way, I'll be grateful. So will . . . Rome."

Flattered, Lugotorix rubbed his chin and pondered before he replied: "We don't hear much from those parts. Courier service across them has gotten precarious, at least for private messages. Official dispatches have nearly absolute priority, and I understand they aren't too sure of getting through any more. I actually know better what's been happening in Mas-silia than in Baiocassium, say. . . . You shouldn't have trouble here in Belgica. It suffered little from the Magnentian War, and the Germanian province eastward has stayed quiet too—good Germans, those, not Hun-like Franks. You should find Belgica easy; and, if I do say so myself, it's concerned citizens like me who keep it that way. But beyond, as you enter Lugdunensis—my information is that the more west you go, the worse conditions get. I trust you're not alone?"

"No, I have soldiers with me."

"Good. Just the same, watch out. I don't *think* the Bacaudae would attack a military unit, but you never know, these days. The word I have is that they're growing ever more brazen."

Gratillonius searched his memory. He had encountered the word be-fore, but only the word, and that was back when troubles were a not quite real thing that happened to somebody else. "Bacaudae?" he asked. "Bandits?"

"Worse than bandits," Lugotorix said indignantly. "Rebels. Men, if you can call them men, who've fled their obligations, gone into the woods, and don't just live by robbery and extortion—no, they have some kind of organization, they call themselves 'Bacaudae'—'the Valiant'—and they war against the very state. Wolves! Vermin! Crucifixion would be too good for them, if we still did it."

"It was not too good for your Saviour, was it?" Gratillonius murmured.

Luckily, perhaps, that was the moment when the boy carried forth his meal. He ordered it put on a different table, and made clear that he wanted to eat by himself and go to bed immediately afterward. Lugotorix quacked a few questions—what was the matter?—but, getting no response other than a glower, soon quit.

There was no more to learn from him, Gratillonius thought, and so there was no need to spend more time at his board. Nothing could be done for the children except to beseech that Mithras—or Christ, or whatever Gods had stood over their cradles—would at last receive their weary spirits. The faith of Gratillonius was pledged to the man who could save Rome. Later that man would set about restoring her true law, making her again the Mother of all.

3

The military highway dropped well south before meeting one that bore west, but pavement offered faster going than most secondary ways in this rainy month. Gratillonius set no fixed daily goals. He took his men as far as they could make it under the given conditions without becoming exhausted. That usually meant about thirty miles, since they were spared the labor of constructing a wall and ditch at the end. It took a gauging eye to know when he should call a halt, for he was on horseback. He would have preferred to share the footwork, but dignity required he ride, as it required a private tent. The men expected it and didn't mind.

They made a brave sight on the march. Gratillonius ranked them four abreast so they wouldn't be slowed by any civil traffic they met. To spare hoofs without the trouble of sandalling them, he rode on the graveled side-strips when those were provided, while three men at the rear led the pack horses. On the highway, Eppillus named a different man each day for the honor of striding in the van, holding the standard on high and with the bearskin over his armor. Everybody wore full battle gear; in sunny weather, light flashed off helmets, mail, javelin heads, the oiled leather of shield facings. Gratillonius displayed silvery coat and greaves, together with crest athwart his helmet and cloak flowing away from his throat, both as vivid a red as the eagle banner. Hobnails crashed down in drumlike unison, but the lines were not rigid, they had that subtle wheatfield ripple that bespeaks men whose trade is war.

At first they traveled through country such as Gratillonius had heard described. It was smooth terrain, grazed by livestock or worked by gangs of cultivators. Aside from woodlots, trees were few. Hamlets generally amounted to a pair of long houses, half-timbered and thatched, divided into apartments for the dwellers and, in winter, their beasts. Carts trundled along the roads, driven by men in smocks and wooden shoes. Other passersby rode mules, or walked carrying baskets or tools. What few women appeared were afoot but seemed unafraid. When they saw the squadron, people gaped, then often waved their hats and cheered. Every fifty or sixty miles the highway passed through a small town. This country lay at peace.

Yet Gratillonius noticed how hastily those towns had been walled of late, with anything that came to hand, even tombstones and broken-up monuments. And they had shrunk. Deserted buildings on the outskirts, stripped of everything valuable, were crumbling into grass-grown hillocks. The inhabitants looked poor and discouraged, save those who sat in taverns getting drunk. On market days the forums remained half empty. As for the hinterlands, the farmers ate better, but most of them were serfs. Or worse; Gratillonius remembered the publican. Whenever he passed a villa—a fundus, they called such an estate in Gallia—or a latifundium, a plantation which had devoured many a farm, he thought a malediction.

He would have liked commandeering fresh rations from those places as the need arose, but that was too chancy. Instead, he levied on military warehouses. Sometimes he had trouble getting what he wanted, because the garrisons were composed of alien auxiliaries with their own ideas about diet. His requirement was for what would keep in this wet climate, while being nutritious and easy to prepare: parched grain, biscuit, butter, cheese, dry sausage, preserved meat, beans, peas, lentils, pickled cabbage, dried apples, raisins, wine. That last was apt to be poor, and the water that would dilute it to be muddy, but beer was too bulky for what you got out of it. Not that he allowed drunkenness. However, it was wise to let the men have a treat at day's end while supper cooked or in their tents if rain forced a cold meal.

The first night out was mild. They pitched camp in a pasture and grinned and winked at some towheaded youngsters, driving cattle home, who stopped to stare timidly. Gratillonius ordered a kettle of warm water brought him when it was ready, sought his shelter, removed his armor, and sighed in relief. Give him a scrub and change of linen, and he'd be ready for a drink himself. He insisted the troops keep clean too, but if he bathed out in the open among them, it would be bad for discipline.

Budic carried the water in, set it down by Gratillonius's bedroll, and straightened. He could stand upright in an officer's tent, though his blond hair brushed the leather. He saluted. "Sir," he said in a rush, "may I ask a great favor?"

Gratillonius laughed. "You may. You won't necessarily get it."

"If . . . the centurion would allow me an extra ration of bread and cheese . . . and if, when the chance comes, we could lay in some kippered fish—"

"Whatever for?"

It was getting dim in here, despite the flag being folded back. Did the boy blush? He certainly gulped. "Sir, this is Lent."

"Lent. Ah. The long Christian fast. Are you sure? I've gathered the Christians can't agree among themselves how to calculate the date of their Easter."

"I didn't—didn't think, I forgot about it, in all the excitement of departure, and then on the march I lost track of time. But that terrible happening on the ship, it shocked me into recalling—this, and all my sins, like lust when I see a pretty girl or anger when some of the men bait me— Equinox has just passed, with the moon new. Lent is already far along. Please, sir, let me set myself a penance, and also do right in the Faith." Budic swallowed again. "The centurion is not a Christian, but he is a pious man."

Gratillonius considered. He wanted everybody fit, not weakened by a growling belly; and special privilege might well cause discord. Yet this was a deprivation, not a luxury. He doubted others would want it, he having picked men he knew weren't holy-holy sorts—men who, Christian or Mithraist, would not feel uneasy about there being no observance on the Sundays that both religions made their sabbaths. Budic he hadn't known so well, the lad being newly enlisted, an orphaned rustic; but Budic had fought like a wildcat beyond the Wall, been a good if perhaps overly earnest trailmate on the way home, and would have been crushed if his leader had passed him over for this expedition. Young, strong in spite of his gangly build, he should get along, no matter his curious practice. Maybe he was so fervent because Christians were scarce where he came from, and other children had jeered at him. Maybe he enlisted partly in hopes of finding friends.

"You may, if it's that important to you," Gratillonius decided. "Just don't act sanctimonious if nobody else follows your example. Go tell the cook."

"Oh, sir!" Adoration blazed forth. "Thank you, sir!"

Presently Gratillonius emerged to find the squadron at ease except for sentries and kitchen detail. The campfire crackled, raising savory fumes out of a pot suspended above. A low sun gilded the earth. Grass was dry enough to sit on, but several men, with goblets in hand, stood clustered before Budic and teased him.

"You mean you didn't think to get a special dispensation?" asked Adminius. "Why, the bishop was 'anding 'em out like 'otcakes at a love feast. Dibs on yer porkchops."

Cynan sneered, which made the mark of his punishment writhe on that cheek. It marred his dark handsomeness, and must still hurt, but should heal soon. Probably he wasn't quite over his resentment. Those Demetae were inclined to be broody sorts. "I suppose somebody among us may as well get in good with Jesus," he said, "though I hear this countryside is still blessedly free of Him." He heard Mass when that seemed expedient, but made no bones about reckoning the faith one for women and soft city dwellers. Himself, he sought the temple of Nodens when he could.

"Can't stop and dicker with any cleric we might come across." Adminius's thin features split in a gap-toothed grin. "Tell you wot, though, Budic. If we do meet one, I'll 'elp you grab 'im up and sling 'im over a 'orse, and 'e can oblige you as we travel."

The youth reddened. He doubled his fists. Eppillus's burly form pushed close. He had sensed trouble brewing. "That will do," the deputy rumbled. "Leave off the jibes. Every man's got a right to his religion."

The tormentors drifted away, a little abashed, to mingle with their comrades. "Thank you," Budic said unevenly. "I, uh, may I ask what your belief is? I've never seen you at . . . our services."

Eppillus shrugged. "I follow Mithras, same as the centurion and two others amongst us. But I admit that for luck I look more to a thunderstone I carry." It was a piece of flint in the form of a spearhead, found near a dolmen many years ago. He chuckled deep in his hairy breast. "Could be that's why I've never made better than second grade in the Mystery. But I'm too old to change my ways, when there's no wife to badger me out of 'em."

"I thought . . . you would be married."

"I was. She died. Two kids, both grown and flown the nest. I've got my bit of a farm still, back near Isca, and when my hitch is up—couple years to go—I'll find me a nice plump widow." Eppillus grew aware of Gratillonius, who had stood quietly listening. "Oh, hail, sir. Budic, don't stand there like a snow man in a thaw. Go get the centurion his wine."

Gratillonius smiled. On the whole, this episode seemed to bode well.

4

The land began to rise after they crossed into Gallia Lugdunensis. Roads must curve, climb, swing back down again, around and over hills that were often steep. Nevertheless, the legionaries continued day by day to eat the miles.

Or the leagues, which were what waystones now measured. Unlike Britannia, Gallia had reverted from Rome's thousand paces to the larger Celtic measure. Gratillonius didn't know just when or why that had happened. But he did know that the Gallic provinces, together with the Rhenus valley, had been the richest, most populous and productive territories in the Empire. What they wanted, they could likely get—including a new Emperor?

Certainly this land clung unhindered to its own old ways. Cynan had been right; Christianity was a religion for towns. Frequently Gratillonius spied a cella, a Celtic temple. Even smaller than a Mithraeum, it consisted of a single square room surrounded by a porch. Public rites took place in the temenos outside; the chamber could barely hold one or two persons who had some special need of their Gods.

Now and then the legionaries passed a hill fort, earthworks raised on a height before ever Caesar arrived. Most were deserted, their outlines time-blurred, but Gratillonius observed that some had lately been refurbished, refuges against the failure of everything Roman.

Spring rolled northward apace. Trees leafed, hawthorn hedges bloomed white, wildflowers bejeweled meadows gone intensely green, larks jubilated aloft. Where fields lay under cultivation, the first fine shoots thrust out of furrows and orchards were riotous with blossom. Views became splendid from the ridges, down over dappled valleys where rivers gleamed and clanged in spate. Rain turned into scattered showers, after which rainbows bridged the clouds. Most days were clear, warm, full of sweetness. They grew swiftly longer too, which made for better time on the road, although Gratillonius liked the gentle nights and would sometimes stroll from camp to be alone with the stars.

Speech changed across the country, shifting from dialect to dialect until you could say that Caletes and Osismii spoke distinct languages. However, he could always make himself understood, whether or not anybody knew Latin—which many farmers, who never went more than a few miles from their birthplaces, did not. Barely enough commerce still trickled along that he could obtain information about conditions ahead. Thus advised, he twice took shortcuts over local roads that were adequate. The gravel on them was washing away and not being replaced, but in dry weather they still served.

That neglect was a sign of much else. The farther west the men came, the more desolation they saw. At first it was not unlike parts of Britannia, vacant huts, acres gone back to weeds, squalid serf shacks well away from the mansions of the honestiores, towns listless and half empty. The larger towns had garrisons, which saw to such things as the maintenance of bridges, but these were auxiliaries from as far away as Egypt, foreign alike to Roman and Celt, generally sloppy. Or, worse, the troops were laeti, Germanic or Alanic barbarians who had forced their way into the province and carved out settlements for themselves: men surly, shaggy, fierce, and filthy, on guard more for the sake of their own kin than for the Empire to which they gave nominal allegiance.

Thirty years had passed since Magnentius failed in his try for the throne. The ruin left by the war was not yet repaired, nor did it seem likely ever to be. Why? wondered Gratillonius. Nature was no less generous here than erstwhile: rich soil, timber, minerals, navigable rivers, fructifying sunshine and rain. The Gauls were an able race, to whom Rome had brought peace, civilization, an opening on the rest of the world. Her armies and navies easily kept prosperity unplundered by outsiders. In return she asked for little other than loyalty, obedience to laws that were more tribal than Roman, a modest tribute so the engineers and soldiers could be paid. Gauls grew wealthy, not only from agriculture and mining but from manufacture. Art and learning waxed brilliant in their cities. Gallia became the heartland of the Empire. Why could she not now recover? What had gone wrong?

Gratillonius didn't ask his questions aloud. The men were already oppressed by what they saw. In camp they didn't sing or crack jokes, they sat wistfully talking about their homes. The centurion heartened them somewhat with a speech on the marvels awaiting them at Ys, but he was hampered by the fact that he didn't know just what those were.

The more they marched, the grimmer it was. The road ran near the coast. Saxon raiders had been coming yearly out of the sea, in ever greater fleets whose crews would go ravaging far inland. The Duke of the Armorican Tract could do little to check them. His forces were depleted, and the shore forts had never been as tightly interlinked as those of Britannia. If a detachment was not simply too small to fight a barbarian swarm, it was seldom fast enough to catch them before they had wrought their havoc and were off elsewhere. They took care to demolish message towers, so that Roman signals of fire by night and smoke by day were no longer visible at any very useful distance; it looked to Gratillonius as if the army had given up attempts at rebuilding.

Otherwise the Saxons were as insensate as wildfire. They slaughtered men, ravished women, made quarry of children. Having clumsily sacked, they burnt. Were a place too poor to rob, they kindled it anyway, for sheer love of destruction. Gratillonius came upon ash heaps that had been houses, buildings of brick and stone rooflessly agape, towns where a few who fled had returned to squat in the ruins and tell their tales of horror, defensive walls broken and never repaired, orchards chopped down, fields charred, harbors empty of their fishing boats. He glimpsed livestock skeletons, strewn human bones which nobody had come back to bury, wandering beggars who had once had homes, three or four women who had gone mad and went about unkempt, ragged, and gibbering. Wild dogs were more dangerous than wolves. One rainy day at the remnant of a manor house, he saw a peacock dying of chill and starvation, its tail dragged down in the mud, and wondered why the sight moved him so.

Scoti out of Hivernia had been arriving too. They were fewer in number than the Saxons, not as wantonly cruel, and their leather coracles could hold less loot than German galleys. They did their share of damage, though, especially by carrying off able-bodied young captives for slaves.

Not every stronghold had fallen, not every farm stood abandoned. A measure of civilized life went on, however wanly. The land itself was beautiful, wide beaches, long hills and dales whose grass rippled and trees soughed in the wind off the sea. Birds filled heaven, gulls, gannets, cormorants, ducks, geese, swans, cranes, herons, a hundred smaller sorts and the eagle high above them. Fish flashed in every stream, bats and swifts darted about at dusk while frogs croaked in chorus, lizards basked on sunny rocks. Squirrels streaked like meteors, hares bounded off, deer browsed in the distance. At least wildlife was coming back.

At Ingena Gratillonius planned to turn south of west, inland, toward Vorgium. There he would collect fresh supplies and have the men put their equipment in top form before the last leg of their journey. The military commander, a grizzled Italian, counselled him against it.

"Yonder's only a husk, scarcely a village, after what the Saxons did to it—Osismiis, that was once the finest city in Armorica, after Ys," he said. Gratillonius felt a slight shock at hearing how the Roman name had fallen out of use, even for this man. "A few Mauretanians stationed there yet, but they don't keep proper stores, they rely on outside supply mostly. No, I'd say you should head south from here to Condate Redonum. It's about your last chance to restock, if you're bound west. I suppose you've business among the Veneti?"

"Farther north," Gratillonius evaded.

"Well, then, first proceed to Fanum Martis. Don't bother exchanging courtesies with the garrison, they're a lot of scruffy Egyptians. It's a detour, but you'll make better speed, because you'll have trunk roads to there and then down to Redonum. Thence it's secondaries, but graveled and well kept up, because the Osismii and sometimes the Ysans use it for their wagons. A good deal is through wildwood, but you should have no trouble; I scarcely think Bacaudae will jump Roman regulars. At the coast you'll come to Garomagus—m-m, the ruins of Garomagus—and from there another good secondary road will take you down to the maritime station near Ys. That's ruined too, been ruined for a long time. However, I hear the Ysans maintain the roads through their hinterland, and they should certainly allow you passage, if that's the way you're going."

A thrill passed through Gratillonius. "I've heard tell about Ys," he said carelessly. "Things hard to believe. What's it like in truth?"

The commander frowned. "Who knows, any more? A city-state on the west coast. I've never been there, but people say its towers are the eighth wonder of the world."

"Surely you know more, sir."

The commander scratched his head. "Well, let me think. I've heard it began as a Carthaginian colony, back before the Celts arrived. The colonists interbred first with the Old Folk, those who're said to have raised the great stones, and afterward with the Osismii. They grew prosperous on trade. Julius Caesar made a foederate of Ys, but relations were never close and the last Imperial resident departed, oh, one or two hundred years ago, I guess. Ys no longer even pays tribute. Lately the Duke asked it to cooperate in the defense of Armorica. I hear the answer he got—in polite words, no doubt—was that by patrolling its own waters Ys was doing the best possible service to Rome. He hasn't the manpower to enforce anything on the city; it's well protected by its wall and there'd be no way to close its sea lanes. Besides, maybe the Ysans are right. I don't know. I told you I've not been there myself."

"Few seem to. Odd. I should think curiosity alone—"

The commander pressed lips together. "I should too, now you say it. But that isn't the case. I never wondered much about Ys either, even when I was young and lively. You see practically no mention of it in any records. I've read Caesar and Tacitus and Plinius and—and many more— and nowhere have I found a word about Ys, not in the *Gallic War* itself, though native tradition insists Caesar paid a visit in person." He sighed. "Christ and all angels help us, there's something damnably strange about Ys. They have a grisly kind of royal sacrifice, and nine witch-queens who go out on a desert island and work black magic, and—Well, I don't want to talk about it. I've troubles aplenty as is."

Gratillonius did not pursue matters.

At sunrise he led his men onward. After two days they came to Fanum Martis, where the tower dedicated to the war God loomed huge and empty above houses, many of which were also deserted.

There they swung south. In that direction they found ample traces of former habitation. Armorica had once been thriving and well populated, except for the heavily forested interior; but little remained. Land rolled gently, taken over by grass, brambles, young trees. Often the travelers spied megalithic monuments. Gauls said Gods, or elves, or wizards, or the Old Folk had raised those gaunt menhirs, solitary or in cromlech circles, those massive dolmens and passage chambers. Once the party made camp by one of the latter. Gratillonius took a torch inside and came upon relics of a family who had sheltered there—a well-off family, whose glassware gleamed while furniture decayed and silver corroded on the earth. He wondered what had happened to them. Thieves had not dared enter this haunted place afterward. Gratillonius left the things where they were, out of respect for the dead, and did not mention them.

None of his followers had volunteered to accompany him, though he knew they would have done so if asked. Gratillonius was not himself afraid. He didn't think Ahriman would deign to employ mere spooks, and in any event they must flee from the light of Ahura-Mazda which Mithras bore. He could not understand why otherwise rational people had all those vague superstitions about Ys.

Next morning the soldiers rose at first light as usual, paid their various devotions, got a meager breakfast, struck camp, and marched. They reached Condate Redonum before noon.

This riparian city too had withdrawn behind fortress walls; but those were unbreached, the houses within unplundered, if dirty and dilapidated. More life flowed over the cobbles, between buildings and across the forum, than Gratillonius had seen for some time. After passing through areas where folk tended to be dark-haired, here he found them again generally fair, as well as robust and rather tall.

Most were local Redones, but quite a few were Osismii come from the west to market. Gratillonius observed the latter with special interest; their country bordered on Ys. The men ran to sweeping mustaches and hair in long braids. Their clothing was of good stuff and frequently fur-trimmed. They carried themselves boldly. Gratillonius recalled that the honestiores had never taken root among them, nor had there ever been many curials to grind between the millstones.

In contrast, the garrison appalled him. It was mainly of Frankish laeti. They were big men, armored in conical helmets and leather reinforced with iron rings. Sword and francisca, the dreaded throwing-ax, were their principal weapons; shields were small and round, garishly painted. They swaggered about pushing others out of the way, daring anybody to defy them.

Gratillonius sought the military prefect at headquarters. That Iberian could only say, "I'm sorry. I'll see to it that you get what you need, of course, but in this confusion it may take a little time, and meanwhile I urge you to camp well away from town. Our people have gotten used to the Franks, if not exactly liking them, but your men could too easily get into a fight. You see, it happens they're holding one of their festivals tonight."

"Hm-m. Drunk and rowdy."

"To say the least. They're heathen, did you know? They'll swill themselves into madness and believe they're inspired by Mercurius—Wotan, they call Him, chief of their Gods." The officer grimaced. "It won't be as bad as the quarter days. Then they go out in the country and make human sacrifices. True, that does take them out of town. Redonum won't be safe tonight. But what can we do?"

Gratillonius thought furiously that he knew very well what *he* could do. Still, he must not lose men in the chastising of Franks . . . who were allies against barbarians from outside. . . . His mission lay before him, in glorious Ys.

Next day his troop marched westward.

V

At midnight the Nine left the House of the Goddess and set forth. They bore no lanterns, for the moon was nearly full and the sky clear. Their weather spell had seen to that. But there was a wind, whistling and cold from the east, over the island and away across Ocean. This too was the will of the Nine, for it was such a wind as rode with the souls of many among the dead. The Gallicenae would need every unseen power they could raise to strengthen them in that which they were about to do.

Sena was small, flat, treeless. Moonlight lay hoar on harsh grass, darkling on rocks, ashimmer on tide pools and the kelp strewn around them. It frosted the manes of waves as they rolled and tumbled, it made white fountains where they crashed on outlying reefs and rocks, it glimmered off the coats of seals that swam along as if following the procession. It drowned most stars; those that were left seemed to flicker in the wind.

The women walked slowly, silent save when a cloak flapped or a pebble gritted underfoot. The wind spoke for them. Forsquilis led. She stared before her, blind and deaf in trance. Vindilis and Bodilis guided her by either arm. They were those who could hold themselves steadiest when next to such a vessel of strangeness. The other six followed in file. Quinipilis was in front, as befitted the oldest, the presiding one. Fennalis came after, and then her daughter Lanarvilis, then Innilis, then Maldunilis. Last was Dahilis, who crowded a little as if the bulk ahead could somehow shield her from the terrors that prowled about. A covered firepot she carried glowed out of airholes like red spider eyes.

It seemed long, but was not, until the Queens reached the Stones. Those two pillars, rough-hewn and raised by the Old Folk, stood close together near the middle of the island. The beak of the Bird, the more pointed head of the Beast—vague resemblances—were some two man-heights aloft. Vindilis and Bodilis helped Forsquilis in between them. They engulfed her in shadow; hardly any of her was now to be seen other than the manifold linen windings of her headdress, phantom-wan. She laid her palms against the rock and stood motionless except for quickened breath.

The rest ranged themselves in a circle, Quinipilis facing the seeress. The aged woman lifted her arms and countenance on high. "Ishtar-Isis-Belisama, have mercy on us," she called in a voice still strong. "Taranis, embolden us. Lir, harden us. All Gods else, we invoke You in the name of the Three, and cry unto You for the deliverance of Ys."

Her prayer used the ancestral speech because of its sacredness and potency, but thereafter she returned to the vernacular: "Forsquilis, Forsquilis, how go you, what find you?"

The priestess between the Stones answered like a sleepwalker: "I go as an owl. The treetops beneath my wings are a net wherein the moon touches buds and new leaves with argent. It is lonely being a spirit out of the flesh. The stars are more far away than ever we knew; the cold of those vastnesses comes seeping down over the world, through and through me.

"I see a glade. Dew sparkles on grass around a camp where a fire burns low. Metal gleams on its guardians. I glide downward. The forest is haunted tonight. Do I glimpse the antlers of Cernunnos as He walks amidst His trees?

"They are soldiers, yon men, earthlings only, naught in them of fate. Am I misled? Did the Gods not hear us or heed us? Oh, surely these men are bound hither and surely that is a sign unto us. Yet—Bewildered, I flutter to and fro in the air."

Suddenly her voice came alive: "A man steps forth from darkness. Was it him that I espied under the boughs? Sleepless, he has walked down a game trail to sit by a spring and love the sky. Sleepless—he knows not why—but I know him! Now when he is drawn this near, his destiny has reached out of the future and touched him.

"He feels it. He looks upward and sees my wings beneath the moon, the moon that turns his eyes to quicksilver. The dread of the mystery in him comes upon me. I fly from his terrible gaze. It is he, it is he, it is he!"

Forsquilis shrieked and fell. Quinipilis stood aside while Bodilis and Vindilis pulled her out into the open and stretched her carefully on the ground. The rest clustered about. Between dark cloaks and blanched headwraps, most visages were paler than was due the light.

Bodilis knelt to examine the unmoving woman. "She seems in a swoon," she said.

Quinipilis nodded. "That is to be awaited," she replied. "Our Sister has traveled along weird ways. Cover her well, let her in peace, and she should arouse soon."

"Meanwhile, what shall we do?" asked Lanarvilis.

"Naught," quavered Maldunilis, her wonted placidity torn apart. "Naught save abide . . . abide that moment."

"Surely *something* else," was Innilis's timid thought. "Prayer?"

Fennalis stroked her hand, responding, "Nay, I think not. We have held rites since sunset. It were not well to risk the Gods growing weary of us."

Bodilis said slowly: "Hold, Sisters. Belike those same Gods have given us this pause. We can think on what our wisest course may be."

Wrath flared in Vindilis. "What mean you?" she cried. "We held council and made decision at equinox. We cast our spells and tonight we know they've wrought well. What else remains but to curse Colconor?"

"That . . . that is such a dreadful thing," Dahilis dared say. "Mayhap we shouldn't—"

Vindilis turned on the girl as if to attack. "You dare?" she yelled. "Has he won your heart, little traitress?"

"Please, darling, please," Innilis begged. She tugged at the sleeve of the older woman, whose anger thereupon abated somewhat.

Dahilis helped by blurting, "I meant no cowardice, in truth I did not. It was but that Bodilis said—oh—"

"Bodilis said," declared that one, "we should take heed this last time ere we do what cannot be undone. Magic is ever a two-edged sword, ofttimes wounding the wielder. I loathe Colconor as deeply as do any of you, my Sisters. But we have called his death to him. May not that be enough? Need we hazard more?"

"We must!" Lanarvilis exclaimed. "If we stand by idle at this pass, well shall we deserve it that our whole enterprise comes to grief." She crooked her fingers aloft like talons. "Also, I want my share in the death."

Vindilis hissed agreement.

"Calm, Sisters, calm, I pray of you," urged Fennalis. "I've no wish myself for black sorcery. Yet if 'tis needful, 'tis needful."

"I believe it is," Quinipilis told them. "Forsquilis is most profound in the lore, aye, but over the years that have been mine I've had to do certain deeds, and watch others done. You, Bodilis, are wise, but it is the wisdom of your books and philosophers. Bethink you. Thus far we have at best brought a man who *may* prevail, and thereafter prove a better King than Colconor."

"He could never prove worse," whispered gentle Innilis.

"This man may choose not to fight," Quinipilis went on. "If he leads soldiers, he is on duty he would be reluctant to set aside. If he does fight, he may lose. I doubt me Colconor's strength has much dwindled since he won the crown."

Bodilis nodded thoughtfully. "True. If then the soldiers slay him who killed their comrade, why, we would be rid of the monster, but how shall we have a new King? The sacred battle may never be of more than one against one. Ys beholds too much desecration already. I believe that is why the powers of the Gallicenae are fading and failing."

"Oh, nay," Innilis shuddered and crept close to Vindilis, who laid an arm about her waist.

"Fear not, my sweet," Vindilis assured her. "We will cast our spell in righteousness, that the hero shall indeed take lordship and redeem us."

Dahilis clasped her hands together. "The hero!" Her eyes shone.

Forsquilis groaned, stirred, looked up with merely human sight. Her colleagues aided her to sit, chafed her wrists, murmured comfort. Finally she could rise.

"Feel you that we should go on as we've planned?" Quinipilis asked. "And if you do, have you the strength?"

The witch straightened. Teeth gleamed between lips drawn thin. "Yea and yea!" she answered. "Wait no more. Our might sinks with the moon."

The Nine had, earlier, brought wood and laid it on a blackened site near the Stones. Dahilis had had the honor of carrying the fire: for the Sisterhood had agreed, upon Quinipilis's proposing, that Dahilis, youngest and fairest of them, should be the bride of the new King's first night. She prayed to Belisama while she emptied glowing charcoal onto kindling. The wind made flames leap quickly.

From under the cloak Forsquilis took a silver vessel whence she dusted salt across every palm. The Queens licked it up in the name of Lir. Quinipilis called on Taranis while she drew forth a knife, nicked her thumb, and flung drops of blood onto the fire. They spat when they struck the coals. Each by each, the Sisters passed before her and made the same sacrifice.

They joined hands around the blaze. It roared, streaming and sparkling on the wind. Red and yellow unease below, icy white above, were all the light there was; everywhere else reached blindness. Sang the Nine:

"Winter wolf and sheering shark,
Whip and tautened traces,
Shame by day and fear by dark,
Hobnails down on faces,
Worms at feast in living hearts,
Dulled and rusted honor—

From his spirit, let these parts
Rise to curse Colconor!

"May he fall as falls a tree
When its roots are rotten
And a wind whirls off the sea,
Angry, Lir-begotten.
Lord Taranis, in Your sky
Hear the tempest clamor.
Long those poisoned boughs reached high.
Smite them with Your hammer!

"Belisama, may our spell
Make You come and take him
Down to doom, and there in hell
Evermore forsake him.
Hitherward his bane we draw
In this vengeful springtime.
Stranger, heed the holy Law
All throughout your King time."

Aboard their boat at the dock, looking beyond the House, the fishermen who had brought the Nine hither saw the fire. They did not know what it portended, they had only obeyed when called upon, but they shivered, muttered charms, clutched lucky pieces and made forfending signs; and they were Ferriers of the Dead.

VI

1

West of Vorgium the hills became long and steep. Forest thinned out until there were only isolated stands of trees, and none wherever heath prevailed over pastureland. The soldiers were rarely out of sight of one or more megaliths, brooding gray amidst emptiness. Winds blew shrill and cold, drove clouds across heaven and their shadows across earth, often cast rainshowers. Yet here too it was the season of rebirth. Grass rippled like green flame, mustard and gorse flaunted gold, flowers were everywhere—tiny daisies, blue borage, violets, hyacinths, cuckoopint, speedwell, primrose, strewn through filigree of wild carrot and prickle of blackberry. Only willows had thus far come to full leaf, but oak and chestnut were beginning, while plum blossoms whitened their own boughs. Bumblebees droned, amber aflight. Blackbirds, starlings, sparrows, doves, gulls filled the sky with wings and calls.

Farmsteads were apt to be far apart, tucked into sheltering dells: a thatch-roofed wattle-and-daub house for people and animals together, perhaps a shed, a pigpen, a vegetable garden, an apple tree or so. Mainly folk in these parts lived by grazing sheep and, to a lesser degree, cattle. They were all Osismii, and Gratillonius would not have been able to speak with them had he not picked up some of their language as a boy. It used many words unique to itself, words he thought must trace back to the Old Folk. Invading Celts, centuries ago, had made themselves the leading families of the tribe and mingled their blood with that of the natives, but more thinly, this far out on the peninsula, than elsewhere in Gallia.

Some words, he thought with an eerie thrill, must stem from another source, from Ys. They resembled none he had heard before, but stirred vague memories in him of names he had met when studying the history of the Punic Wars.

Although folk were friendly, much excited to see legionaries, he didn't stop for talk except one evening when he chanced to camp near a dwelling. There he learned that the neighborhood had suffered little from raiders, being too poor to draw them, but the western shore was an utter wreck apart from Gesocribate and Ys. The former was tucked well into a narrow bay and Roman-defended. The latter fronted on Ocean, but— The farmer signed himself to his Gods in awe of the power protecting that city. He would be glad to come under its guardianship. Unfortunately, Ys claimed only a few eastward miles of hinterland.

Disturbance crept about within Gratillonius. What forces indeed did such a minikin state command, that it endured while Rome crumbled?

He found himself thinking about that again when his squadron reached the coast and spent a night at Garomagus. He and his father had called there several times, in years as lost as the lives they had found. Small but bustling, the town once embodied those industries, that prosperity, which ringed its great bight: ceramics, metalwork, salt, and garum, the fish sauce Armoricans exported to the farthest ends of the Empire. Now, as sunset smoldered away, Gratillonius stood fingering a shard of a jar, among the burnt-out shells of buildings surrounding a forum where only he and the whimpering wind had motion.

He saw no bones lying about. Survivors who crept back to town after the final sack must have buried their kindred before abandoning their homes. Stains still darkened a fountain gone dry, where the heathen had held a sacrifice, and rubbish littered pavement. A book sprawled mildewing outside a church, its cover stripped of jewels, its vellum capriciously slashed. Gratillonius bent over to peer at the rain-blurred pages and recognized Greek letters and ink drawings. A Gospel. Christian or not, the dead book saddened him. He carried it into the church and laid it on the altar.

Later the moon rose, a day past the full. Unable at first to sleep, he wandered from camp. Following the stream beside which the town had nestled, he came to the mouth and turned onto a beach. Wavelets on the bay glimmered and lulled, sand scritted underfoot. The air was not very cold. He made out stars, old friends, the Bears, the Dragon, the Lion that heralds the northward-swinging sun. Tonight they seemed remote and alien. Did they really rule over the fates of men? Most people believed so. If they were right, then the star of Ys—Venus?—was still ascendant; and the Mars of Rome was sinking?

Without having pondered the matter, which could have led him to question seriously a tenet of his religion, Gratillonius had always doubted astrology. At most, he supposed, whatever planet a man was born under might influence him; but so would the heritage of blood and circumstance that he had from his parents. Manhood required him to make his own fate.

But if the blind circle of the spheres was not what kept Ys alive: what did? He should have learned far more than he knew before embarking on this mission. The knowledge had, though, not been there for him, in any chronicles he could find or any spoken accounts he could elicit. Ys kept itself wrapped in enigma—how?

For no good reason, he remembered another evening a few days back, and a great owl he had glimpsed above a glade. Why should that make him shiver? He turned from shore and sought his tent.

2

Out of what had been Garomagus, a road ran almost due west along the coast, twenty miles or a bit less to the Gobaean Promontory. It was merely graveled, like most secondary Roman routes, but well maintained. The troops started early and marched with redoubled briskness. This night they would be in the fabulous city.

They had covered half the distance when they came to a pair of stones flanking the track. Ten feet tall, those granite pillars were not prehistoric; weather had softened their squared edges, but the characters chiseled into them were still legible. Gratillonius dismounted to read. On the southern column, a gracefully curving alphabet was unknown to him. On the northern he found Latin, surely the same message. His finger traced what his lips murmured: *"In the names of Venus, Jupiter, Neptunus, here I mark the frontier of land that has been of Ys since time immemorial, along this Redonian Way. Hold me and my sister sacred, for we bear the Oath, forever binding. Raised DCLXXXVIII AVC obedient to orders of the SPQR, year XIII since the Sign came upon Brennilis, who with C. Julius Caesar did make the Oath."*

"Old," Gratillonius whispered. "Four and a third centuries. But the wording—I've seen things like this elsewhere, from nearly that far back— the wording here is—" a chill went up his spine—"unusual."

Eppillus looked around. "Boundary marker, eh?" he grunted. "Where are the sentries?"

Grass waved in a salty breeze, down to a cliff's edge on the north, with water agleam beyond it under a clear sky, and southward up to the spine of the peninsula. Afar in that direction, the men could just spy a flock of sheep near some wind-gnarled trees, but no other sign of habitation. Out where sunlight winked on whitecaps, sails showed boldly colored across the arc of vision. They were too remote for Gratillonius to be certain, but he supposed they belonged to fishing boats. Ys took little from its modicum of thin-soiled hinterland; its communion was with the sea.

"I don't imagine the city feels any need of pickets," he answered slowly. "Relations with the Osismii, and with Rome, have been peaceful. Trade must go unhindered, and across a long stretch, too. 'Redonian Way.' That seems to mean the Ysans think of this as their road to the Redones in eastern Armorica—nowadays to Condate Redonum—though those tribesmen seldom get to these parts."

"But what about pirates?" the deputy argued. "Pirates could land and walk on in."

"They don't. Something keeps them away. I don't know what."

"The old Roman Gods?" Cynan asked from his place as today's standard bearer. "Do They still have power . . . in this place?"

"Those are not Roman, those Gods the stones bespeak," Gratillonius said. "They're only Latin names. Romans used to suppose any Gods they met were the same as their own, but it was never true. You, my friend, must know better, must know Sulis is not really Minerva or—See, the inscription puts Venus first. A mother Goddess? Maybe. If we could read it, the second stone would tell us something very different from the first, about the Gods of Ys."

"The demons!" Budic exclaimed. He raised his arms. "Christ Jesus," he beseeched, "watch over us, drive off the powers of darkness."

"Fall in," Gratillonius snapped. "Forward march."

Mithras, Lord of Light, ride with us, Your soldiers, he thought as he sprang back onto his horse. He could not make it feel like a prayer. Had he wandered so far, into such foreignness, that the God of his fathers no longer heard him?

Angry at his weakness, he tried to thrust the question away. What was there to fear? Most likely less than anyplace else in the Empire, here where robbers dared not come. However lonesome, the landscape was gauntly beautiful. Ys of the marvels awaited him, and would scarcely deny him obedience. His demands would be modest in any case, simply that Ys remain at peace, and help keep the rest of western Armorica at peace while Maximus campaigned. The leaders of the city would not fail to see how they too would benefit by an Emperor strong and able.

And afterward—why, that grateful Emperor ought at the very least to bestow senatorial rank on a man who had served him well. Perhaps he would lift the man's entire kin out of the curial class. And the officer would go on to mighty deeds, power, wealth, undying fame.

With an abrupt shock, Gratillonius realized that he did not know what his ambitions were. Hitherto he had been content to live day by day. When he thought about the future, he hoped for eventual promotion to senior centurion, followed by retirement in a home he would acquire somewhere among his Belgic tribesfolk. There he would have a woodworking shop for pleasure, horses, dogs, a cat to sleep on a sunny windowsill. Of course, he would already have married and begotten sons. . . . Never before had he imagined the world open to him. Did he truly want it?

A bulk ahead drew his attention. "Keep on," he ordered, and turned his horse off the road onto a point of land. What he found was the remains of a fortress on the brink of a precipice. Ditched and triple-walled, it was from before the Romans, and long unused. Grass billowed across ridges and mounds that had been earthworks. Yards below, waves foamed and growled; overhead, a gull cruised mewing.

The sight was like an omen of mortality. Gratillonius drew the sign of Mithras, wheeled his mount, and hastened back to the van of his party.

The end of the headland wasn't far now. He knew this road went to a maritime station the Romans had built, back when they maintained a constant presence; later the Ysans manned it for them. From there, he supposed, the way would turn south till it went down to the bay where the city was. Impatience leaped in him. He wanted to gallop straight across. But that wouldn't be dignified. Besides, grass and brush might well conceal footing dangerous to a horse. His heels prodded the animal into a trot while he reined in his spirit.

At the bend in the route he diverged for a look down a side path. Under granite of the promontory, above rage of water among rocks and reefs, he saw the ruins of the station. Holes knocked in walls—whether by enemy rams or by storm-driven surf—gaped full of darkness. Rain had washed away the soot of the fire that consumed roof and dock; he glimpsed only a few charred timbers from either, tumbled and bleached like driftwood.

"This happened years, maybe decades ago," he muttered. "Ys is supposed to be safe. But already then—"

Eppillus trod forward to stand by his leader and see. "Maybe their Gods are dying too," he said. Yet the rusty voice and the barrel-shaped figure somehow called Gratillonius back to hopefulness. Here was reality, prosaically Roman. Whatever ghosts haunted this country were no more solid than those cloud shadows which the sea wind sent scudding over it.

"We'll see," the centurion answered. "Onward!"

Southbound he passed a hillock which he suspected covered more wreckage. He scarely noticed, for towertops were coming into view ahead. When he reached the descent, there was Ys.

From this height the road swept to a deep dale, walled on both sides by the land. Thus protected, the northern slopes were fit for more than rough pasture. Orchards and woodlots stood around the red tile and white walls of wealthy homes, the thatch and clay of clustered cottages. Brown plots amidst the greenness showed where gardens would soon be bearing. The southern side of the hollow was less occupied, because it climbed steeply to form another headland. Between those two nesses was the bight which Ys filled. Eastward the valley ran lengthly, well populated, toward distance-blue hills.

Soldier's training made Gratillonius first survey the terrain. A branch way plunged directly down to a short bridge between this promontory and the wall around Ys. Another road led from the eastern city gate, inland. An arm of it swung north, and then east under the heights, to a grove of oaks, after which it became a mere trail.

On the near side of the shaw, Gratillonius spied three large wooden buildings around a courtyard giving on that road. Beyond the trees, in a low swale, was an amphitheater, modest in size but clearly Roman save for—something subtle, some difference he could not identify from this far off. There the highway went south, and then east again out of sight. Elsewhere ran several dirt roads, and a graveled one out onto the southern cape, which held a pharos at the tip. From the far hills, down the middle of the valley, cutting through the grove, gleamed a narrow canal.

His gaze sought Ys. Strange, he thought as he caught his breath—part and parcel of the strangeness everywhere around—that he and his father had traded as close as Garomagus, yet not until now had he glimpsed Ys of the hundred towers.

Thus they bespoke it around Armorica. If the count was not really that high, if this was in fact a rather small city, what matter? Ys soared out of the sea.

Its wall formed a rectangle about a mile long, to which were added semicircular ends of a diameter slightly less. The shore arc snugged close between the two forelands, and there the rampart loomed fifteen feet. Westward its elevation above water would depend on the tides, which Gratillonius knew to be large. He could only wonder how deep those foundations lay. Red-brown, the material must have been quarried from the cliffs. A band of color below the parapet, a frieze, relieved the murkiness. Twin turrets lifted battlements over each of the three landward entrances. Along the western arc, if he gauged rightly, a fourth pair stood about a hundred and ten degrees apart, to guard the harbor and its marvelous gate.

He could not discern that basin from here, because too many buildings were in the way—towers indeed, high, narrow, reaching for the sky out of the crowd of lesser structures. Mosaics and patternings formed brilliant fantasies up their sides. Glass, gold, even tiled and patinaed copper caught the early afternoon sunlight and flung it back in a dazzle. A slight haziness, borne in from Ocean, made the sight a dream. He could scarcely believe that human beings dwelt yonder, not elves or Gods.

But the first of the Caesars had walked those streets, the first Augustus had ordered those outer defenses erected. Gratillonius had come to reclaim a heritage.

The knowledge thrilled in him. "Silence!" he cried at the amazed swearing of his men. "Dress ranks. We'll enter in Roman style."

The Ysans had paved this section of the way, since gravel would have washed downward. Hoofs rang on stone. Gratillonius tightened knees against the hairy warmth of the horse. Weight pulled hard on him, hauling him on toward the sea.

Faintly through the wind he heard a trumpet call, and another and another. Watchmen had glimpsed his soldiers. The land portals stood open and he supposed townsfolk would soon be swarming forth—past the smithies and carpenter shops and other worksteads that stood just outside along the eastbound road—unless an official delegation forced itself in front of the crowd.

But the first human motion he spied was at the oak grove. Several people came from the house. For an instant they paused in the courtyard to stare. Then a man took the lead, loping out while the rest scurried after. Clearly they meant to intercept the newcomers.

Gratillonius thought fast. Amidst what scanty information he had been able to gather, much of it doubtless false, was a story that the King of Ys spent the three days and nights around full moon in a sacred wood, and that at all times he must hold himself prepared to fight any challenger for his crown. Last night had ended the period in this month; but he might have lingered for some reason. If not, those might be priests of importance . . . and priestesses? Gratillonius identified women among them. Probably he would do best to meet them as they wished, allay whatever fears they had, ask that they accompany him into town.

A rutted track offered a shortcut between this road and the one that led to the grove. He gestured to his men and turned off, angling downward.

3

The parties met nearer the shaw than the city. They halted a few feet apart. For a space there was stillness, save for the wind.

The man in front was a Gaul, Gratillonius judged. He was huge, would stand a head above the centurion when they were both on the ground, with a breadth of shoulder and thickness of chest that made him look squat. His paunch simply added to the sense of bear strength. His face was broad, ruddy, veins broken in the flattish nose, a scar zigzagging across the brow ridges that shelved small ice-blue eyes. Hair knotted into a queue, beard abristle to the shaggy breast, were brown, and had not been washed for a long while. His loose-fitting shirt and close-fitting breeches were equally soiled. At his hip he kept a knife, and slung across his back was a sword more than a yard in length. A fine golden chain hung around his neck, but what it bore lay hidden beneath the shirt.

"Romans," he rumbled in Osismian. "What the pox brings you mucking around here?"

The centurion replied carefully, as best he was able in the same language: "Greeting. I hight Gaius Valerius Gratillonius, come in peace and good will as the new prefect of Rome in Ys. Fain would I meet with your leaders."

Meanwhile he surveyed those behind. Half a dozen were men of varying ages, in neat and clean versions of the same garb, unarmed, their own hair braided but beards closely trimmed. In form they resembled Osismii, except for tending to be more slender and dark, but the visages of four were startlingly alike, long, narrow, curve-nosed, high-cheeked. Brothers? No, the gap between a gray head and a downy chin was too great.

Nearest the Gaul stood one who differed. He was ponderous of body and countenance. Black beard and receding hair were flecked with white, though he did not seem old. He wore a crimson robe patterned with gold thread, a miter of the same stuff, a talisman hanging on his bosom that was in the form of a wheel, cast in precious metal and set with jewels. Rings sparkled on both hands. In his right he bore a staff as high as himself, topped by a silver representation of a boar's head.

The women numbered three. They were in ankle-length gowns with loose sleeves to the wrists, of rich material and subtle hues, ornately belted at the waist. Above hung cloaks whose cowls bedecked their heads.

Gratillonius guessed their disheveled appearance was due to haste, after his sudden advent, rather than to carelessness.

The Gaul's voice yanked him from his inspection: "What? You'd strut in out of nowhere and fart your orders at *me*—you who can talk no better than a frog? Go back before I step on the lot of you."

"I think you are drunk," Gratillonius said truthfully.

"Not too full of wine to piss you out, Roman!" the other bawled.

Gratillonius forced coolness upon himself. "Who here is civilized?" he asked in Latin.

The man in the red robe stepped forward. "Sir, we request you to kindly overlook the mood of the King," he responded in the same tongue, accented but fairly fluent. "His vigil ended at dawn today, but these his Queens sent word for us to wait. I formally attended him to and from the Wood, you see. Only in this past hour was I bidden to come."

Gratillonius laughed. "He was sleeping it off, eh?"

The man shrugged and smiled. "After so much time alone with three of his wives—" He grew serious. "Let us indeed go meet with the rest of the Gallicenae and leading Suffetes. This is an extraordinary event. My name is Soren Cartagi, Speaker for Taranis."

The Gaul turned on him, grabbed him by his garment and shook him. "You'd undercut me, plotting in Roman, would you?" he grated. A fist drew back. "Well, I've not forgotten all of it. I know when a scheme's afoot against me. And I know you think Colconor is stupid, but you've a nasty surprise coming to you, potgut!"

The male attendants showed horror. A woman hurried forth. "Are you possessed, Colconor?" she demanded. "Soren's person when he speaks for the God is sacred. Let him go ere Taranis blasts you to a cinder!"

The language she used was neither Latin nor Osismian. Melodious, it seemed essentially Celtic, but full of words and constructions Gratillonius had never encountered before. It must be the language of Ys. By listening hard and straining his wits, he got the drift if not the full meaning.

The Gaul released the Speaker, who stumbled back, and rounded on the woman. She stood defiant—tall, lean, her hatchet features haggard but her eyes like great, lustrous pools of darkness. The cowl, fallen down in her hasty movement, revealed a mane of black hair, loosely gathered under a fillet, through the middle of which ran a white streak. Gratillonius sensed implacable hatred as she went on: "Five years have we endured you, Colconor, and weary years they were. If now you'd fain bring your doom on yourself, oh, be very welcome."

Rage reddened him the more. "Ah, so that's your game, Vindilis, my pet?" His own Ysan was easier for Gratillonius to follow, being heavily

Osismianized. " 'Twas sweet enough you were this threenight agone, and today. But inwardly—Ah, I should have known. You were ever more man than woman, Vindilis, and hex more than either."

"My, my lord, you rave," stammered Soren. "Be calm, I pray you, for your own sake and everyone's."

"Calm—after what *you* said to me when yon invaders came in sight?" Colconor's shout was aimed past him, at a younger woman: tall, well-formed in a rangy fashion, her face recalling Minerva in its cold regularity and gray eyes. "You adder, you sorceress, you—you Forsquilis, trafficker with devils—" Then she returned him a look that sent a shudder through the centurion.

"Colconor, dear, please, please," begged the third woman. She was big and plump, with brown eyes and pug nose. Her manner was mild, even timid. Was she less formidable than her companions? "Be good."

The Gaul gave her a leer that was half a snarl. "As you were good, Maldunilis? 'Twas your tricks more than aught else that kept me belated in the Precinct. But meseems you too were conspiring my betrayal—"

He swung on Gratillonius. "Go, Roman!" he roared. "I am the King! By the iron rod of Taranis, I'll not take Roman orders! Go or stay; but if you stay, 'twill be on the dungheap where I'll toss your carcass!"

Gratillonius fought for self-control. Despite Colconor's behavior, he was dimly surprised at his instant, lightning-sharp hatred for the man. "I have prior orders," he answered, as steadily as he could. To Soren, in Latin: "Sir, can't you stay this madman so we can talk in quiet?"

Colconor understood. "Madman, be I?" he shrieked. "Why, *you* were shit out of your harlot mother's arse, where your donkey father begot you ere they gelded him. Back to your swinesty of a Rome!"

It flared in Gratillonius. His vinestaff was tucked at his saddlebow. He snatched it forth, leaned down, and gave Colconor a cut across the lips. Blood jumped from the wound.

Colconor leaped back and grabbed at his sword. The Ysan men flung themselves around him. Gratillonius heard Soren's resonant voice: "Nay, not here. It must be in the Wood, the Wood." He sounded almost happy. The women stood aside. Maldunilis seemed shocked, though not really astonished. Forsquilis breathed what might be an incantation. Vindilis put hands on hips, threw back her head, and laughed aloud.

Eppillus stepped to his centurion's shin, glanced up, and said anxiously, "Looks like a brawl, sir. We can handle it. Give the word, and we'll make sausage meat of that bastard."

Gratillonius shook his head. A presentiment was eldritch upon him.

"No," he replied softly. "I think this is something I must do myself, or else lose the respect we'll need in Ys."

Colconor stopped struggling, left the group of men, and spat on the horse. "Well, will you challenge me?" he said. "I'll enjoy letting out your white blood."

"You'd fight me next!" yelled Adminius. He too had been quick in picking up something of the Gallic languages.

Colconor grinned. "Aye, aye. The lot of you. One at a time, though. Your chieftain first. And afterward I've a right to rest between bouts." He stared at the woman. "I'll spend those whiles with you three bitches, and you'll not like it, what I'll make you do." Turning, he swaggered back toward the grove.

Soren approached. "We are deeply sorry about this," he said in Latin. "Far better that you be received as befits the envoy of Rome." A smile of sorts passed through his beard. "Well, later you shall be. I think Taranis wearies at last of this incarnation of His, and—the King of the Wood has powers, if he chooses to exercise them, beyond those of even a Roman prefect."

"I am to fight Colconor, then?" Gratillonius asked slowly.

Soren nodded. "In the Wood. To the death. On foot, though you may choose your weapons. There is an arsenal at the Lodge."

"I'm well supplied already." Gratillonius felt no fear. He had a task before him which he would carry out, or die; he did not expect to die.

He glanced back at the troubled faces of his men, briefly explained what was happening, and finished: "Keep discipline, boys. But don't worry. We'll still sleep in Ys tonight. Forward march!"

By now people were spilling out of the city. Three of Soren's attendants stood in line across the road to keep them from coming farther. This combat would be a rite, not a spectacle. The other three ran ahead, passing by Colconor, to make things ready. Evidently all of them were household staff in yonder place. Since their attitude was not servile, that must be an honored position.

The Speaker walked at Gratillonius's left, the women at his right. Nobody talked.

It was but a few minutes to the site. A slate-flagged courtyard stood open along the road, flanked by three buildings. They were clearly ancient, long and low, of squared timbers and with shingle roofs. The two on the sides were painted black, one a stable, the other a storehouse. The third, at the end, was larger, and blood-red. It had a porch with intricately carven pillars.

In the middle of the court grew a giant oak. From the lowest of its newly leafing branches hung a brazen circular shield and a sledge-hammer. Though the shield was much too big and heavy for combat, dents surrounded the boss, which showed a wildly bearded and maned human face. Behind the house, more oaks made a grove about seven hundred feet across and equally deep.

"Behold the Sacred Precinct," Soren intoned. "Dismount, stranger, and ring your challenge." After a moment he added quietly, "We need not lose time waiting for the marines and hounds. Neither of you will flee, nor let his opponent escape."

Gratillonius comprehended. He sprang to earth, took hold of the hammer, smote the shield with his full strength. It rang, a bass note which sent echoes flying. Mute now, Eppillus gave him his military shield and took his cloak and crest before marshalling the soldiers in a meadow across the road.

Vindilis laid a hand on Gratillonius's arm. Never had he met so intense a gaze, out of such pallor, as from her. In a voice that shook, she whispered, "Avenge us, man. Set us free. Oh, rich shall be your reward."

It came to him, like a chill from the wind that soughed among the oaks, that his coming had been awaited. Yet how could she have known?

The storehouse door crashed open and Colconor strode forth. He had outfitted himself well for a barbarian—conical nose-guarded helmet, scale coat reaching to his knees, calf-length leather boots reinforced with studs. His left hand gripped a small round shield. The longsword shone dully in his right.

"Well, well, you're here 'spite of being a Roman," he gibed. "Let's have done fast. I've business with yon traitor wives of mine."

"My lord, your demeanor is unseemly," Soren protested. "It cannot please the God."

Colconor spat. "I've given Taranis deaths enough whilst I was King. Think you He'd want a lackey of Rome instead?"

"Kneel." Soren pointed to a spot below the tree. Gratillonius and Colconor obeyed, side by side. An attendant brought water in a bowl, another a sprig of mistletoe. Soren used the herb to sign the contestants as he chanted a prayer in a language Gratillonius did not recognize at all.

Thereafter: "Go forth," said the Speaker for Taranis in Ysan, "and may the will of the God be done."

Colconor led the way between the red house and the stable, in among the trees. Gratillonius followed, never looking back. Light rays struck between branches still largely bare. Shadows welled up in the farther depths of the grove. Last year's leaves rustled underfoot, smelling of damp. Moss and fungi grew on fallen boles. A squirrel darted ruddy, like a comet foretelling war. Gratillonius heard a pig grunt—wild, sacred to whatever mystery dwelt in this place?

Near the middle of the shaw was a grassy space, narrow but clear. Colconor stopped and faced about. "Here I'll kill you," he said in a voice gone flat.

Gratillonius raised his oblong Roman shield. Javelins would be hampered under these conditions, and he bore just the shortsword in his fist, the dagger at his hip. Fleetingly, he wished he had had a chance to swap his parade mail for workaday armor. He smiled bleakly at himself. This was good equipment despite the damageable ornamentation. It was with such gear that Rome's legionaries had conquered much of the world. However, they did it in disciplined units, each a single many-legged machine. With two men alone, the barbarian outfit was as useful, maybe better.

Mithras, he thought, I stand as a soldier, obeying my orders. Into Your hands I give my spirit.

Then at once he became entirely seized by the business before him.

The fighters circled, seeking an opening. It was always an odd feeling to Gratillonius when he looked into the eyes of an enemy. A perverse comradeship—

Colconor lunged. His sword whirred down. Gratillonius moved his shield slightly to intercept. The blow thudded loud, radiated back through handle and arm, pulled the strap hard across his shoulder, but the metal rim of the plywood stopped it. He stabbed. Colconor was skilled too. The point smote into the soft pine of the Gallic shield and stuck for an instant. Colconor twisted it while he slashed at that wrist of Gratillonius. So confined, the long blade was awkward. The centurion had time to block it with his own shield. He freed his weapon and tried for a knee. Colconor recoiled. Blood wet a ripped trouser leg, but from a minor cut.

Colconor bayed. He kept his distance, sword leaping, crashing, seeking. Gratillonius must stay on the defensive, unable to counterattack with his smaller blade. His shield did not catch every blow. Two rang on his helmet, one hit mail, one slid along a greave. They hurt.

Coldly, Gratillonius peered beyond his foeman, found what he sought, began maneuvering. A frenzied Colconor dogged his step-by-step retreat. Gratillonius got his back against a great trunk. Colconor yelled and hewed, right, left, up, down, metal a-clang among the rising shadows. He bounced about like a wolf slashing at a bull.

Gratillonius spread his feet right-angled and tensed his knees. Abruptly he released the left. He pivoted, and Colconor nearly ran past him. Gratillonius jabbed. Colconor drew back . . . and now it was he who stood pinned against the tree.

Gratillonius gave him no time to work his way out of the trap, but moved in. The longsword dinned on his helmet. A shallow slash opened on his forearm. Then he was close. He feinted at the legs. Colconor lowered his shield to cover. Gratillonius drove the boss of his own straight into his enemy's belly. Scales or no, wind whooped out of Colconor. Gratillonius brought the top edge of the shield aloft, catching Colconor beneath the chin. Bone crunched. Red ran forth. Colconor wailed.

Gratillonius saw a rare opportunity. He drove his sword upward and home. It entered at the cheek and went on. He felt bone give, and next the soft mass of the brain. That was a chancy stroke, but therefore unexpected. Blood gushed from Colconor's mouth and nose. His face became a Gorgon's. He crumpled and flopped. Gratillonius withdrew his sword and reinserted it beside the larynx, to complete the task.

For a while the centurion poised over the corpse. Breath went in and out of him, cool and cooling. He felt sweat chilly on his skin and smelled it, an arrogant odor. His mood was calm, though. He had done what he must—good riddance to bad rubbish—and inspection showed his wounds to be trifling.

He'd not wipe his steel on Colconor's greasy, death-fouled clothes. Squatting, he used earth and old leaves. Meanwhile he considered what might happen. King of the Wood? That doubtless entailed duties, he didn't know what, but seemed to bestow a certain amount of power as well. Thus a prefect who was also the monarch should be able to carry out his mission very handily.

Regarding the slain man, he realized that Ys would expect him, too, to fight future challengers, until at last one of them bested him. He shrugged. Surely he could cope while he finished his work here. Later he surely could leave. At worse, he and his men might have to cut their way out, or send for reinforcements; but he would regret that if it happened. The Ysans were probably decent people, on the whole. He'd try to do well by them.

Today he'd be busy with whatever ceremonies they held. He said a belated noontide prayer, added a word of thanks, and stooped to close the eyes below him and straighten out the body. Colconor had been brave enough to deserve that much.

As he performed the office, Gratillonius noticed anew the chain around the fallen man's neck. Wondering at something so delicate on someone so uncouth, he gave it a tug and drew forth from under padding and mail the object it held—an iron key, longer in the shank and more intricate in the prongs than he had ordinarily seen.

A talisman? Gratillonius felt the unknown touch him, cold as the wind. With reverence he laid the key back on the breast. Rising, he sought the red house.

VII

1

When he strode into sight, his men drew blade and gave him three honest cheers. Soren led the Ysan males in genuflection. The women remained standing. Maldunilis's soft features offered shyness, uncertainty, but from Vindilis and Forsquilis blazed an exultation terrifying in its savagery.

At once events swept Gratillonius along. Soren conducted him into the house. He saw that the columns of its portico represented a man, bearded and majestic, who bore a hammer like that which hung at the Challenge Oak, and attributes such as eagles, wild boars, and stylized thunderbolts. The name Taranis he recalled from former visits to Gallia, as well as the same image. So the Ysans had made Taranis their chief God? Gratillonius suspected matters were not that simple.

Within, the right half of the house was a feasting hall, high-raftered and gloomy, where fire licked out of trenches in a clay floor and smoke stung eyes before escaping from a hole overhead. Pillars upholding the roof formed two rows of idols, some clearly Celtic, others impossible for him to identify. Wainscot panels behind the built-in benches along the walls seemed to depict heroic tales. Banners hung from the crossbeams, sooted and frayed with age. Magnificence so rude must have stayed in use because ancientness made it holy. "Is this the temple of the God?"

Soren shook his head. "No, Taranis has a splendid marble fane in the city, and many lesser shrines. This is the House of the King, also known as the Red Lodge. Once he was required to live here always, with each Queen spending a night in turn. But for centuries, now, it has only been during full moon, and he summons those wives or other persons whom he will." He paused before adding, grimly matter-of-fact: "Of course, wherever he may be, he must come back when a challenger strikes the Shield. The resident staff dispatches a messenger."

Again a prickling went through Gratillonius's skin. Colconor could have left at dawn today for the comforts and pleasures of town. In that event, the Romans would have entered Ys directly, and might well have settled matters with the city magistrates before even meeting the King, who would most likely have decided to accept what he could not easily or safely change. Instead, though, three of his—wives?—had kept him carousing, and at the same time piqued him, as subtly and cruelly as a bullfighter, until he stormed forth when he saw the newcomers and, in besotted fury, forced the quarrel that ended in his death.

And just how had he done so? Gratillonius knew himself for a short-tempered man, and the insults he suffered were unforgiveable. Yet he was a legionary officer on duty. For the sake of Rome, he should have armored his pride in dignity and merely returned contempt—not plunged headlong into action of whose consequences he had no idea. What demon had entered him?

A burning log cracked. Flames and sparks leaped high. Shadows moved monstrous in dimly lit corners, and it was as if a rustling went through the blackened banners overhead.

Gratillonius ran tongue over lips. "You must understand, Priest Soren—"

"No, my lord, I am simply the Speaker." The interruption was bluff but not discourteous. "I serve Taranis by leading certain rites and by helping govern the worldly affairs of His temple. Otherwise I am a Councillor of the Suffetes and the director of a Great House—an industry. You, sir, are the ordained one, high priest and, in a sense, Incarnation."

"You must understand," Gratillonius persisted, "that I am a Roman citizen in the service of the state. I am also a votary of the God Mithras. Never ask me to compromise my conscience about either of these things."

He could not be sure, in the dusk, whether Soren showed a flicker of unease. The man did reply steadily: "I do not believe we need fear that. If I am not mistaken, Mithraists may and do honor other Gods. For the most part, a King does as he will. Apart from meeting his challenges— and I would not expect any to you for a long while, my lord—apart from that, a King's reign is very much what he himself makes it. Ys is old. Through the hundreds of years it has seen many different kinds of men on its throne, Romans among them. But come, please."

The second half of the Lodge was divided into smaller rooms. These had been modernized, with glass windows, tile floors, frescoed plaster, hypocaust heating. Furniture was comfortable. It included a remarkable number of chairs, with arms and backs. Gratillonius remarked on that and was told that such seats were common in Ys, and not confined to the rich, either.

There was no space for a full-panoply bath, but a large sunken basin had been filled for him. Servants helped him out of his armor and under-garments. He sank gratefully into hot, scented water. His encounter had strained him more than he realized, and Mithras knew what would come next. He needed a rest.

Emerging, he had his injuries poulticed; just the cut on his arm received a precautionary bandage. Thereafter he enjoyed a skilled massage, was anointed, was guided to a chamber where new raiment lay. Resembling Soren's but more sumptuously worked, the robe fitted him well, as did the soft shoes. He supposed the house kept several wardrobes in different sizes. His pectoral was a gold sunburst, hung from a massive chain and set with pearls and rubies. However, instead of a staff he would bear a full-sized sledgehammer, whose oaken haft and rounded iron head were dark with antiquity. True to his religious vows, he declined the laurel wreath offered him.

More men bustled around than before, making preparations. Soren had gone to oversee matters in the city, and no Ysan present had much if any Latin. His halting Osismian won Gratillonius a little information from the chief steward, about what was happening and what to expect.

Trumpeters and criers went through the streets. *"Allelu, allelu!"* resounded between walls and up into heaven. There followed words in the ancestral language of Ys, which had been Punic. Few other than sacerdotes and scholars knew it today, but it was sanctified. The message then repeated in the vernacular. *"The King is dead, long live the King! In the names of Belisama, Taranis, Lir, come ye, come ye unto the coronation of your lord!"*

The steward's account continued from the immediate past to the present and immediate future.

From the temples of the Three, Their images rolled forth on wagons never used for aught else, drawn by paired white horses for Belisama, black for Lir, red for Taranis. Folk garlanded themselves and heaped the wains with what greenery and blossoms they could find. Led by drums, horns, harps, they went singing and dancing out the gates and to the amphitheater. The clear weather, which gave no cause to unroll the canvas roof, seemed to them a good omen. Some must stay behind, though, making ready for a night's wild revelry.

The royal feast would be more sedate. Huntsmen tracked down a boar, out of the half-wild swine that ranged the Wood. At risk of life, they captured it in nets and hung it above the body of Colconor. There they cut its throat and bled it, down onto the fallen King. Stewed in a sacred cauldron, its flesh would be the center of a meal here at the Red Lodge.

Taken aback, Gratillonius asked what would become of the human remnant. Ys, he heard, was like Rome in forbidding burials within city bounds; and the cemetery out on Cape Rach, under the pharos, had long since grown to cover as much land as could be allowed. Dead Ysans were taken to sea on a funeral barge and, weighted, sent down to Lir. But a former King lay in state in the temple of Taranis until he was burned, which was too costly for anyone else. A warship took his ashes out near the island Sena. There they were strewn, given to Belisama (Ishtar, Isis, Ashtoreth, Aphrodite, Venus, Nerthus . . .), the Star of the Sea.

As for his conqueror, following the victory feast, he spent his first night in the house. Thereafter he was free to move to his city palace. If he chose, he could visit his Queens in their separate homes, or call them to him—

"Queens!" burst from Gratillonius. "Hercules! Who are they? How many?"

"The Nine, my lord, the Gallicenae, high priestesses of Belisama. But, um, the King is not compelled—save when 'tis Her will—Forgive me, great sir, a layman should not talk of these matters. They touch the very life of Ys. The Speaker will soon rejoin you and explain what my lord needs to know."

Dazedly, Gratillonius received a herald, all in green and silver and with a peacock plume on his head, who announced that the processional was beginning. They must want their new King consecrated immediately, he thought. Well, they believed that somehow he embodied a God, or at least the force of that God, upon earth.

Outside, it was late afternoon, and the air boisterous. Soren waited with several fellow dignitaries of his temple. Nearby stood the legionaries. He had made arrangements for them to march along and have seats, later to be quartered in town: unusual, but then, every King was unique. How many had fought, won, reigned, fought, perished, how many ghosts were in this wind off the sea of Ys? Long hills, stark headlands, glimpsed towers and gleam of waters beyond, seemed remote to Gratillonius, not altogether real; he walked through a dream.

Where Processional Way, which led to the Wood, met Aquilonian Way, which ran out of the city's eastern gate, the Gods received their King. The idols of Taranis and Belisama were handsome work in marble, twice life size, done by Greek sculptors whom the Romans brought in as a gesture of alliance in earlier times, He the stern man, She a woman beautiful and chastely clad. The emblem of Lir was immensely older, a rough

granite slab engraved with Celtic spirals. Later Gratillonius would learn
that that God was never given human shape. Sometimes folk described
Him as having three legs and single eye, in the middle of His head, but
they knew that was only a way of bespeaking something strange and
terrible.

A jubilant crowd followed the wagons. Gratillonius had a feeling their
joy was not pretended. Colconor appeared to have made himself hated—
mostly among the first families of Ys, whom he daily encountered, but
their anger would have trickled down to many commoners. And yet there
had been no thought of overthrow, assassination, anything but enduring
that which the Gods had chosen to inflict.

Unless—Again bewilderment laid hand on Gratillonius.

As the servant in the house had said they would, the throng moved
eastward, down onto low ground, and neared the amphitheater. It was
Roman-built, a gracefully elliptical bowl of tiered benches within an outer
wall of marble whose sheerness was relieved by columned doorways and
sculptured friezes. Nevertheless Gratillonius confirmed the impression he
had gotten on the promontory, that it was alien. The proportions were
not . . . quite . . . classic. The portals were pointed. The fluting and
capitals of the pillars hinted at kelp swaying upward from the sea bottom.
The friezes mingled seals, whales, Northern fish with fabulous monsters
unlike centaurs or gryphons, and with curious Gallic symbols. How much
mark had Rome ever really made on Ys?

The people swarmed in right and left while the sacred cortege entered
by a centrally southern archway, through a vaulted passage and out onto
the arena. This was not sanded, to take up blood, but paved. A spina told
Gratillonius that chariot races were held. That low wall ran down the
middle of the arena, leaving space clear at either end; there rose posts for
the hoisting of scorekeeping markers. In the middle, however, this spina
broadened into a cornice, a balustraded stone platform. Stairways led up
to it, as they did to the boxes in the stands reserved for magnates. That
meant, Gratillonius realized, this place did not see beast combats—nor
human, he felt sure.

When benches had filled with brightly clad spectators, the Gods made
a circuit of the arena before stopping under the cornice on the south side.
Gratillonius noticed that Belisama was in the middle. Soren told him to
bow to Them as he, accompanied by the Speaker, went up onto the platform. Acolytes followed, bearing ewers, censers, evergreen boughs. Behind them, a rawboned graybeard carried a bronze casket. It was a position of honor; his robes were blue and silver, and Soren had introduced
him as Hannon Baltisi, Lir Captain.

Standing aloft, these celebrants waited until a hush had fallen. The
lowering sun still spilled brilliance down into the bowl, though shadows
lengthened and chilled. A trumpet rang, high and icy sweet. From the
middle northern archway came a band of girls and young women, gor-
geously cloaked above white gowns, bearing tall candles in silver holders.
"The vestals, virgin daughters and granddaughters of the Queens, those
who do not have vigil today," Soren murmured to Gratillonius. They
moved wavelike to ring the spina while they sang:

"Holy Ishtar Belisama,
Lady of the starry sky,
Come behold Your sacred drama
Taught to men by You on high.
You the Wise One are our teacher.
Spear-renowned of ancient days,
Hear the words of Your beseecher.
Mother, come receive our praise.

"Great Taranis, heaven-shaker,
Lord of sky and inky cloud,
You the rain- and thunder-maker,
Wrap not this Your day in shroud.
Shed Your light on Your procession.
Bless us with Your golden rays.
Giver of all good possession,
Father, come receive our praise.

"Lir of Ocean, dawn-begotten,
Lifter of the salty tide,
Be Your servants not forgotten
When in hollow hulls they ride.
Lord of waves and rocks, bereaving,
Draw us into safer ways,
And, our fears of wreck relieving,
Steersman, come receive our praise.

"Threefold rulers of the city,
Star and Storm and Ocean Deep,
For our praise return us pity
While we wake and while we sleep.
Grant we keep our worship faithful,

Sung aloud in sacred lays.
Turn on us no faces wrathful.
Holy Three, receive our praise."

And now arrived the Nine. Those whom Gratillonius had met this day
were become as strange to him as were the rest, in gowns of blue silk
bordered with figures akin to the friezes, white linen wrapped high over
their heads and pinned by orichalcum crescents, faces stiff in solemnity.
Pace by pace they approached the stairs and ascended one by one. A tall
old woman led them . . . they seemed to be going in order of age . . .
Soren spoke the name as each paused before Gratillonius, bent her head
above folded hands, then entered a rank forming on his left hand and
stood like soldiers, war captains of the Goddess, nothing further of humil-
ity about them. . . . Quinipilis, Fennalis, Lanarvilis, Bodilis, Vindilis,
Innilis, Maldunilis, Forsquilis—

Dahilis.

Dahilis rammed through Gratillonius. He would not confuse that
name. O Gods, she was so much like Una the neighbor girl whom he
loved when he was fifteen and ever since had sought to find again, for Una
must needs marry wealth in Aquae Sulis if she would help her father stave
off ruin. . . . Dahilis reached to the base of Gratillonius's throat. She was
slender though full-bosomed, her hue very fair save for the tiniest dusting
of freckles over a short, slightly flared nose; her mouth was soft and a
little wide, dimples at the corners; her face was heart-shaped, high cheekbones delicately carven, chin small but firm; her dress brought out the
changeable blue-green-hazel of big eyes under blond brows; her movements kept an endearing trace of coltishness, as young as she was. . . .
When she looked at him, her look was not like that of any of the others,
proud or rapt or victorious or wary. A blush crept up from her bosom,
her lips parted and he heard her catch her breath before she moved on.

Invocations sounded forth, first in Punic, next in Ysan. Gratillonius
could not make himself pay close heed. Reality struck him in the stomach
when the Lir Captain opened his casket and held it out to the Speaker,
who lifted forth a key on a fine golden chain. Gratillonius knew that key.
"Kneel," Soren commanded, "and receive the Power of the Gate that is
the King's."

Gratillonius obeyed. When the loop went over his head and the thing
hung from his neck it felt heavy, and as if so cold as to freeze his heart
through the pectoral and robe. That passed over. He forgot it in the next
moment, for out of the casket Soren had brought a crown.

"Receive the sigil of your lordship and the blessing," the Speaker said.

"No, I cannot," Gratillonius whispered.

Soren almost dropped the circlet of golden spikes. "What?"

"I told you I follow Mithras," Gratillonius replied in hasty Latin. "When they raised me to Soldier of the Mystery, I was thrice offered a crown and must thrice refuse it, vowing never to wear any, for the God alone is Lord."

"You shall—" Soren broke off. Glances clashed. He made a wry mouth. "Best not risk a disturbance. The Key is what truly matters. Hannon, keep silence. Gratillonius, may I briefly hold the crown above your head? Answer, quick!"

I must not let them order a Roman about, passed through the centurion. "Do that and nothing else. Or I'll fling it from me. My legionaries sit yonder, still armed."

Soren flushed. "Very well. But remember Colconor."

Gratillonius heard a buzz go around the seats at the change in the ceremony, but it died away and everything further was soon completed. Afterward the maidens led the Queens out; Suffetes came down from their boxes to meet the new King in the arena; the amphitheater emptied; last, the Gods of Ys went home to Their temples, to abide the future.

2

After sunset the wind loudened and bleakened, driving rainclouds before it low above the land. The first few spatters were flying when the magnates bade their host goodnight and departed with their lantern bearers for the city, a mile hence. Gratillonius left the door and paced the length of the hall.

It had been a polite gathering, but cautious and formal, when neither side knew what to make of the other. He was no desperate adventurer or runaway slave, he was an agent of the Empire, come to serve its purposes; and though he promised those would enhance the welfare of Ys, he could not blame its leading men if they took that incident of the crown as a bad sign. He had to win their trust. Before he could do so he must understand them in some measure, and what his position among them really was. Well, he thought, tomorrow I'll begin, I'll take my earliest few steps into the labyrinth.

He grew aware that the household staff had assembled before the wall that divided the two portions of the lodge. Flickers of firelight and lamplight showed them expectant. What, more procedures? He stopped and waited.

The chief steward touched his brow, salutation to a superior. "Is my lord ready for bed?" he asked.

"Oh, I . . . I'm not sleepy, but suppose I may as well—"

"Presently comes the bride of my lord's first night."

"Uh?" No, he would not reveal perplexity. Had he, with his limited knowledge even of Osismian, misunderstood something? Well, let that happen which the Gods willed. Certain it was that he had slept solitary for months. He felt sudden heat in his loins. Of course, if they went by precedence of age—maybe he could blow out the lights and use his imagination. "Aye," he said, as calmly as might be, "let us do what may beseem this occasion."

Servants guided him to a well-outfitted chamber, helped him disrobe, brought in a flagon of wine, cups, cakes and cheeses and sweetmeats, several lamps, incense which they set burning, and left. Abed, unable to lie down, Gratillonius sat with arms folded across nightshirted knees. Warmth from the floor, fragrance from the sandalwood and myrrh, enfolded him. Noise of wind and rain sounded remote beyond the shutters. Much louder was his heartbeat.

Nine wives—He wondered wildly what his duty was toward them. He had married them in a heathen rite and because he had no choice if he was to carry out his mission. When he was done here and could go home, need he legally divorce them? He should ask a Mithraic Father. Yet meanwhile they were human, they could feel pain, and, O Gods, there would likely be children—

Faintly there reached him a hymeneal hymn. It could only be that. His pulse quickened still more. Who had arrived? Wrinkled Quinipilis, bitter Vindilis, handsome Forsquilis, what could happen with any of them? Somehow they had *known* he was on his way hither.

The door opened. "May all Gods bless this holy union," said the steward. Dahilis entered. The steward closed the door behind her.

Dahilis.

She stood as if frightened. One small hand fumbled at the brooch of a rain-wet cloak. She swallowed before she could speak. "My lord King, is . . . is Dahilis, his Queen . . . is Dahilis welcome?" Her voice was a little thin, but the timbre caused him to remember meadowlarks.

He surged from the bed and went to take both her hands in his. "Welcome, oh, indeed welcome," he said hoarsely.

The cloak came off. He took it and tossed it aside. She had changed to a simple gown of gray wool whose belt hugged it against her slimness. Her hair was piled high, held up by a comb. He saw that it was thick and wavy, sun-golden with just a tinge of copper. He clasped her shoulders, looked down, and said in his lame Osismian, which he tried to give an Ysan lilt: "How wonderful that you, you, should seek me this night."

She lowered her gaze. "They, the Sisters, they decided it when—when we called you, my lord, called you to deliver us."

He did not want to think about that, not now. "I will strive to show kindness . . . unto all—Fear me never, Dahilis. If ever I blunder into wrongdoing, tell me, only tell me."

"My lord—" She received his embrace, she responded, the kiss lasted long, she was not skilled but she was quick to learn, and eager.

"Well, uh, well," he laughed breathlessly, "come, let us sit down, refresh ourselves, get acquainted."

Her glance was astounded. "Col—" she began, and checked herself. Colconor, he thought, Colconor would never have troubled to put her at ease. (Supposing that he, Gratillonius, could do it in this first encounter.) "Already you are being kind," she whispered.

They took chairs opposite each other at the table. He felt in a remote fashion what a curious arrangement that was. But naturally, she was used to it. He poured wine. When he was about to add water, she made a shy negative gesture, so he refrained too. Her cup trembled as she lifted it. The drink was dry and full-bodied, warming both flesh and spirit. He thought he would readily learn to like taking his wine like this.

"Do you speak Latin?" he inquired in that language.

"I can try," she gave him back with difficulty. "We study it in vestal school. But I've seldom had any practice since."

He smiled. "Between the two, we'll get along." And thus they did. Sometimes it required much repetition or search for a word, but that became part of a game they played, helping them feel more comfortable with each other; and he found himself actually beginning to acquire Ysan.

"I know well-nigh nothing, Dahilis," he said. "You understand, don't you, I did not intend to take the Kingship. I stumbled into it." Her look sharpened, and he hurried on before she could respond. "I do not even know what questions to ask. So let us talk freely, dear. Will you tell me about yourself?"

She dropped long lashes. "Naught is there to say. I am too young."

"Tell me anyhow."

She lifted her eyes. A bit of mischief danced forth. "If you will do likewise, good my husband!"

He laughed. "Agreed. Not that we can say much in an hour or, or two. How old are you, Dahilis?"

"Seventeen winters. My father was King Hoel, my mother Tambilis. Queen Bodilis was her daughter too, my older half-sister, by King Wulfgar. But mother died in my fifteenth year and . . . and the Sign came to me."

And Colconor, then reigning, took her.

"There is, is scarce anything else, my lord," Dahilis said, "but I think I shall be glad you are King. Pray won't you speak of your own life?"

When ever was a man loth to parade his exploits before a lovely girl? thought Gratillonius. Nevertheless he kept the tale laconic. Her eyes widened and widened. To her, Rome must be as glamorous as Ys was to him. And he traveled on affairs of Rome. . . .

When her clothing fell to the floor, he saw that above the cleft of her breasts was a tiny red crescent, its horns to the left, like a birthmark. She noticed his attention drawn to it from other sights, touched it, and said diffidently: "This? 'Tis the Sign. Ever when a Gallicena dies, it appears on one of the vestals. That consecrates her a priestess. I know not why Belisama chose me out of all the rest—but oh, this night I thank Her that She did."

And afterward she snuggled close to him and murmured drowsily, "Yea, I do thank Her, truly I do thank Her, that She made me a Queen of yours. Never erenow have I known what glory She may bestow."

His lips brushed along the summery odor of her hair. "And I thank Her too," he said.

VIII

1

"It were well that we talked together, unheard, you and I," said Quinipilis. "Would it please you to walk the wall? Then I could also show you somewhat of this your newly-won city."

Gratillonius looked more closely than hitherto at the eldest of the Gallicenae. With five-and-sixty winters behind her, she still bore herself tall. A once opulent figure had become stout, her hands were gnarled by the aging that had made her gait rocking and painful, her visage was furrowed and most teeth gone; but underneath abundant white hair, gathered in a Psyche knot, gray eyes gleamed wholly alive, while good bones and arched nose held a ghost of her youthful comeliness. She was simply clad and leaned on a staff whose ferrule was plain iron. Her house was unostentatious, requiring just a pair of domestics, for she used only a part of it. Yet he felt he had never encountered anyone else more truly like a queen.

And her note borne to him at his palace, written by herself in excellent Latin, had less requested his presence than summoned him. He believed he could not well decline. His few days in Ys had overwhelmed him more than they had taught him. He badly needed advice. Still, not knowing what she wanted, he had come in some uneasiness.

"Is that what my lady intended?" he asked.

Quinipilis brayed a laugh. "Oh, ho! Did you fear me dragging you from lovely Dahilis to soothe my lust? Me, barren, crippled, my face like forty leagues of bad road?" She patted his arm. Her palm was warm and dry. "Nay, I gave up that three reigns agone. King Hoel and I were good friends, no more. As I hope you and I shall be, Gratillonius."

"As you were not with Colconor," he ventured.

Her mood darkened. "Never. Oh, he had me, again and again, for well he knew how I abhorred it from him. However, that was less bad than what he made the rest of the Sisterhood suffer. He had the animal cunning to sense it would be dangerous to goad me overmuch. And indeed, at the last—" She shook her head. "No matter. 'Tis behind us, thanks be unto you. We should take counsel for the morrow, foremost concerning that Sisterhood."

"I will be grateful, my lady."

"Then let us begone. A mummy like me does best to use the morning, for she is weary by afternoon."

"Could we not spare you, stay here and talk Latin?" asked Gratillonius in that language. "I'm told all educated Ysans know it, more or less, but don't suppose your slaves do."

"Servants, boy. Temesa and her husband are free, and well rewarded," Quinipilis replied sharply in her mother tongue. He was already able to follow it fairly well, though his speech stumbled. "We have no slavery or serfdom in Ys. Too much have we seen of what they have done to Rome."

"I've heard of Ysans capturing and selling folk."

"Aye, abroad, among the barbarians. Ys lives mainly by her ships. Most are fishing craft and merchantmen. A few are raiders. But do stop spilling my scanty time and come along. I'd fain point out this and that, and see how you respond. 'Twill tell me things about you. And I want to make you practice Ysan." She grinned. "Besides what you've been cooing at Dahilis."

Gratillonius felt himself redden. He helped her on with her cloak and resumed his own. Otherwise he wore the shirt, decorated jacket, breeches, and low shoes that were everyday male garb in the city. They were of fine material but of colors more subdued and cut more simple than was usual among the well-to-do here. As King he could have carried a sword, but was content with the knife at belt which was all that unauthorized persons were allowed to have on the streets. He did not care to be conspicuous this day. Best might be if he went unrecognized—though that was unlikely, when his companion was one whom everybody must know.

They left the house. Like its neighbors, it was of rectangular outline. Dry-laid sandstone blocks and red tile roof glowed mellow beneath rays of a sun that was as yet not far above the eastern towers. It gave directly on the street, and the flower garden behind it was minute, for even this wealthy district was crowded. Most homes nearby were larger, rising two or three stories, smoothly stuccoed, figured with inlays or frescos. What those showed might be scenes but were often ideals: spirals, Greek keys, geometric arrangements. The effect was brilliant in the clear, cool air, as if jewels had tumbled out of a great coffer.

Not being a commercial thoroughfare, the street was narrow, nonetheless paved and clean. Ys required the hauling away of rubbish. Upon inquiry Gratillonius had learned that the sewers did not drain into the sea, which would have angered Lir, but into tanks of fuller's earth in chambers excavated below the city. From time to time these were emptied and the muck carted inland, where farmers were glad to have it for their fields.

Most people he saw as he walked were menials, in vivid liveries, on errands to and from markets and the like. The rich who dwelt hereabouts were already off to their businesses, while their wives were indoors managing the households. He met an occasional artisan carrying tools for some task, and flocks of children too small to attend any of the various schools, and sometimes an elderly person or a leisured youth. Where leaded windows stood open, he glimpsed a few pets—a songbird, a cat, a ferret. Ys lacked room for larger creatures, except draught animals admitted only onto major routes.

To him, folk generally looked happy. Well, he thought, why should they not? The city-state is at peace, safe, less prosperous than formerly but in no dire want, seemingly well governed. True, for years it lay in the shadow of Colconor, but the harm he could do was limited, and now I have plucked him out of the world.

"Yours seems a nation the Gods have favored," he said.

"They've sent us our share of grief," Quinipilis answered, a bit harshly.

"Whence came Ys? I've heard tell it stems from Carthage of old, but little else. 'Tis a puzzle to me how Ys could flourish this long a while and remain obscure abroad."

"Bodilis can best recount the history. She's the scholar among us. Seek her out." Quinipilis paused before she added: "Seek them all out, and soon. Aye, liefest would you lie with Dahilis only; that's graven upon you. And we are seldom jealous of each other, and . . . the yoke of Colconor united us. However, we brook not scorn. If naught else, that would through us dishonor the Goddess."

"I, I will do my best, my lady. But I've so much to learn, so much to do—"

She smiled at him. "Verily, if you be the man of duty I suppose." A chuckle. "Feel no pity for yourself. They may not be equally well-favored, but nine wives with incomes of their own should fulfill the daydreams of the friskiest young fellow. Well, eight, though I trust you'll reckon me a helpmate. That had better suffice, you know."

He sensed an underlying meaning. "Nay, I do not know."

She turned grave, almost motherly. "You are the King; the Father is in you. We are the Queens; the Mother is in us. Never will your manhood fail with any of these your wives. But never will you have your way with any woman else."

He stopped short. "What?"

"That is the law of Belisama, Who is present at every act of procreation." Her voice went steely. "Colconor tried, and could not, and that is one thing which made a monster of him, though he did find tricks whereby his whores in Old Town might give him pleasures of a low sort." Again the tone softened. "I think you will be too proud for that."

"It . . . it is not a wish for—Nay. A man is more than . . . a penis. But, but I have heard that only daughters—"

Compassion spoke. "Aye. We bear no sons. Ever. This too is the law of Belisama; for we are Hers." Quinipilis squeezed Gratillonius's hand. "Surely it is honorable to father Queens."

Stunned, he accompanied her in silence when she walked on. "You shall, my dear, you shall," she said presently. "Those of us who are of childbearing age will open their wombs for their liberator as they would not for Colconor, no matter how that maddened him. The Goddess gave unto Her first priestess in Ys the secret of an herb which bars conception—"

Mithras lives, he thought. Mithras will not leave me bound forever by a heathen spell. When my task here is done, He will free me, and I will go home and beget me sons to bear the name.

He squared his shoulders and rallied his spirit. If nothing else, he had Dahilis, he had Dahilis.

Cheer mounted as he passed through more and more of the city, its variousness and plenitude.

The street climbed gently in this eastern end of town, unlike the steep downwardness of its western half. Near the end he could look over roofs to Elven Gardens: arbors, topiaries, early-blooming flowers. Adjoining, the temple of Belisama was like a miniature Athenian Parthenon—he had seen a drawing in a book—although its marble was not painted but left pure. That was somewhat northward; southward lifted the dome of his palace.

The street gave on Lir Way, the principal east-west avenue, and suddenly he was in a millrace of traffic, walkers, riders, porters, oxcarts, mulecarts, donkeycarts, a clattering, a chattering, creaking, calling, whistling, singing, laughing, swearing, dickering, hoping—city folk, farmers and herders out of the hinterland, fishermen, merchant sailors, traders, now and then a party of Osismii or Veneti trying not to be yokels, one party of Redones trying to be Romans, bound for the marketplaces or on other business. . . . Few actual transactions went on in this vicinity. It was full of blocky apartment buildings, with statues at intervals to lend stateliness, heroes, animals, chimeras, each with a hint of something neither Greek nor Roman.

Lir Way debouched on the pomoerium, the space kept clear under the city wall for defensive purposes. Beyond that paved ring, and High Gate standing open, Aquilonian Way ran out broad past the amphitheater, bent southward to climb the heights, turned east again and sought the distant hills. Immediately in front of the pomoerium, two large edifices flanked the avenue, Warriors' House on the left as a barrack for marines, Dragon House on the right as quarters and conference rooms for their officers. Gratillonius gave Quinipilis his arm when they crossed to the wall and went up the staircase on the north side of the gate.

The tower there was generally called the Gaul. Its bulk, battlemented and severe, reminded Gratillonius of the milecastle at Borcovicium and its kind. This, though, was not mortared in their fashion, but of closely fitted, dry-laid granite blocks, their edges rounded off by the weathers of many a lifetime. And so was the entire wall around Ys. He wondered why.

Sentinels recognized Quinipilis, realized who Gratillonius could be, and slanted their pikes, crashing the butts downward, in salute. She waved back cheerily. They wore studded skirts like his men, but helmets were peaked, shoulderpieces and greaves flared, cuirasses loricated and engraved with spirals, shields oval, swordblades of laurel leaf shape, cloth never red but blue or gray, insignia abstract—a foreignness Gratillonius found faintly disturbing, as he did not that of Scoti or Picti or Saxons, because this was more subtle.

Quinipilis led a southward course, over the arch above the gate, past that twin tower called the Roman, on around the half-circle of this end. "I've heard your state has had no army since Caesar made it his protectorate," Gratillonius remarked.

"Nor do we, nor did we ever," Quinipilis snorted. "Why should our men squander their best years in drill, or we pay a pack of flea-bitten mercenaries? Nay, what you see is a cadre of professionals, marines, who double as peacekeepers at home. Besides them, every sailor has training for combat afloat or ashore."

"Suffices that, in times like these?"

"Aye. Not for an empire, but then, we've no wish to rule over outlanders. Have you Romans not had enough woes with your Gauls and Jews of yore, your Goths and Vandals today?" He was surprised that she knew of such rebellions, and a touch disconcerted. His task was to keep the Ysans loyal to Rome—to Maximus—and to that end, much history was preferably ignored. "True, our ships afar may at times meet peril, but no oftener than yours. And as for our defenses, what need we fear when the Gallicenae command the weather?"

Once more he halted in startlement. "My lady, can that be? I mean, well, surely you have the love of your Gods, but the Gods do not always answer human prayers."

Likewise stopping on the walkway, Quinipilis laughed; it made him recall hearing wolves. "You misheard me, boy. I said we *command* the weather. Oh, we abuse our power not, lest the Three take it from us. We call upon it only in the worst need. But no few reaver fleets were wrecked among the skerries, until the barbarians learned to leave us be. Landward, you can see, is merely a narrow arc of wall to hold, should attack come from that side; and our sea lanes will stay open for supply. Not that we've had many threats on land either. Caesar himself, flush from his crushing of the Veneti, knew better than to dare an outright conquest of Ys."

Gratillonius stood for a spell, silent in the breeze that blew tangy off Ocean. A merlon lay sun-warmed under his hand. When he had on a previous circuit leaned over and glanced down through the crenel beside, he had seen the frieze that ran around the wall. A mosaic of colored stones, it showed sacrificial processions, mythical battles, visions out of the deeps that glittered quicksilver to worldedge.

His glance shot to and fro. Bleak and windswept, the headlands enclosed Ys, Point Vanis reaching away on the north, Cape Rach on the south extending more than two miles westward. At the far end of the latter, beyond its clustered necropolis, he saw the pharos tower. Rocks stood rugged out of the waves, reefs lurked just below, surf burst white and green.

The promontories were of the same dark-red granite as the wall. However, he had learned that Ys stood between them on a downward-sloping shelf of sandstone. Its softness was easily quarried—those caves underneath had yielded much building material as they were enlarged—but it was just as easily gnawed by great tides and murderous currents. Indeed Ys had need to stay friends with Lir.

Well, had it not done so? Did wonder not nestle within its rampart? From this elevation, the city was speckled with silver, sunlight off rainwater in multitudinous rooftop catchbasins. He had been told that these drained into bottomless tanks below ground, set in fine sand within clay cisterns. Water passed through the filtering material to central wells, whence people drew it. In this wet climate there was never a lack. Nonetheless, beyond the Gaul and Warriors' House another water storage place rose high, a tower into which the canal discharged through a culvert. There ox-driven Archimedean screws raised the fluid, whereafter pipes delivered it to the homes of the rich and to public troughs, fountains, baths. He had heard that the canal ran from a spring in the hills, sacred to Belisama, its shrine tended by virgin daughters and granddaughters of the Gallicenae.

He recalled his wandering mind to its surroundings. Turrets at the wall did not match the height of numerous buildings in the middle and lower town. Those soared from levels of stone to upper stories of wood, flamboyantly ornamented, taller than the Emperors had ever permitted in Rome. If the climb was wearisome to a lodging on a tenth or fifteenth floor—one dwelt in Ys! Gulls winged white between those pinnacles; tops sheened many-hued, tile, patinaed copper, painted gilt.

A faint drummming came up to Gratillonius, the blended noise of wheels, feet, hoofs, machines, pulsebeat of the living city.

"Shall we go on?" Quinipilis suggested.

Where the arc straightened out to run almost due west, Cape Rach thrust a mass inward that had been too large to chisel away. The architects had taken advantage of this; they need not build a causeway as they must on the northern side. Flanked by those towers called the Brothers, Aurochs Gate opened on Taranis Way, which ran northward to intersect Lir Way at the Forum and thence onward to Northbridge Gate and its defending Sisters. Down on the left, the plaza of Goose Fair bustled with countryfolk bringing their products to market. Savoriness drifted in smoke from foodstalls, merchants cried their wares from booths.

"You've a livelier commerce than aught I've seen elsewhere, even in Londinium," Gratillonius observed.

Quinipilis shrugged. " 'Twas better aforetime, when the Roman peace kept traders safe and Roman money was honest. But still we cope."

"Roman money? You strike not your own?"

"Nay, what sense in that? Formerly Roman currency was taken everywhere. Now, if we made coins for ourselves, they must either be good, and vanish into hoards like your solidi, or else be as worthless as your nummi. Gold, silver, and bronze circulate within the city but seldom leave it. For most dealings we're back to barter."

Quinipilis drew breath. "Yet we have wherewithal for bargaining," she said. "Our soil is poor, but its sheep yield a wool long, fine, well-nigh as precious as Asiatic silk. We must import most raw materials, but from them we fashion ships and boats, metalwork and jewelry, cloth, pottery, glassware, of a quality that makes them much desired. Our waters are the source of salt, preserved fish, garum, whale oil, tusks, and such-like exports.

"Though scarcely a foreign ship calls here any more, ours still fare widely, if quietly. When our merchantmen do not sail off trading for themselves, they carry freight for others, from Britannia to Hispania. Our adventurous young men travel out among the barbarians to get amber and furs or to be slavers, pirates, mercenaries—never against Rome, dear —and those who live return at last carrying wealth. Aye, Ys endures."

Gratillonius's glance flew northward. "On Point Vanis I've seen the wreckage of a station that was Ysan as well as Roman," he said roughly. "It was meant to serve ships when your sea gate must be shut. What happened to it?"

The old woman's staff thudded harder on the stone as she walked. " 'Twas nigh three score years agone, in the reign of my father Redorix, when I was a girl. Suddenly, there a score of Saxon warcraft were. The Gallicenae had not foreknown. The crews landed, harried widely about, destroyed the maritime post as you saw. Redorix died in battle against them. Our men cast them back at the wall, and they made off. The Gallicenae sought Sena and raised a gale they hoped would avenge us, but they never knew if it did or no."

She sighed. "Prefect of Rome, I will not lie to you. Ys was always less than omnipotent; and now, ever more are our ancient powers flickering and fading. Once any high priestess could heal any sickness by laying on of hands; today, seldom. Once her soul could range afar through space and time; today, few of us can have a vision, and for those who do, it may as well be false as true, with Forsquilis alone granted some measure of assurance. Once—ah, but you too have seen your God in retreat, have you not?"

She clutched his wrist. "We wanted you for more than a liberator, Gratillonius. We hoped for a redeemer. May you be he, and not a destroyer we brought upon ourselves."

His throat felt tight. "I will do my best," he said, "but remember I am pledged to Rome."

They walked on in silence to the western arc of wall and along it to the Raven Tower. There a sentry forbade promenading civilians to go farther. Behind him, on the stone curve that ran onward until the sea portal interrupted it, Gratillonius saw bastions upon which stood rain shelters of leather and light timbers. Beneath them, he knew, were ballistae and catapults. He could have demanded access, but he had already been there and Quinipilis was starting down a stairway to the pomoerium. He came after. Let her be the guide throughout.

While the top of the wall was everywhere level, ground dropped sharply beneath the western half of Ys, which was thus overshadowed. Buildings on his right crowded time-worn, mostly bare of decoration; here was Old Town, where industry and poverty intermingled. On his left, the shipyard extended to the harbor. Quinipilis went along its fence until she reached a street which ran beside it in the direction of the water, called the Ropewalk because it doubled as that. This she took. It was not in use today. Looking into the shipyard, Gratillonius spied a single small vessel under construction, albeit there were facilities for several large ones. As the Queen had said, Ys too felt the hard times that afflicted the Empire.

Where a launching ramp went down to the basin, the waterfront began. Its curve paralleled that of the city wall to seaward, a grand sweep two thousand feet in length, set back five hundred feet. Hard against its stone wharf, warehouses, belonging to the great traders reared proud. But their inlaid façades were faded, and for the most part they seemed almost empty of men and goods. A number of hulls rested between the floating piers that reached out from the dock like fingers. None at this end were big, mainly fishermen in for unloading or overhaul. Their crews were off on leave, and only a few workers moved among them.

Nevertheless the harbor was a noble sight. Water sparkled as if dusted with crystal, lapped, gurgled. Gulls rode it like white boats or skimmed above in a snowstorm of wings. Some young boys were joyfully swimming, oblivious to the coldness of the water; it was a skill that sailor folk desired. Behind lifted the sheer cliff of the wall, ruddy-dark but its upper battlements brave with flags and the cloaks of watchmen.

Halfway along the waterfront, Quinipilis stopped. Here was a break in the line of buildings, for here began Lir Way. It started off through a triumphal arch, raised by the Roman engineers who built the wall but not to commemorate any victory in war. This was the sign of the saving of Ys, of the Pact between the city and its Gods. Beyond, the square of Skippers' Market was astir as dealers took seat in their booths.

The priestess, though, gazed outward, to where the western entry stood open. "That is the masterwork of all," she said low.

"Aye," Gratillonius agreed in awe.

Fifty feet wide, the gap in the wall faced upon illimitable reaches, Ocean itself. The doors on either side were beginning to close as the tide flowed higher—enormous oaken doors, iron-bound and sheathed in copper weathered green, silent and easy on their hinges despite the mass. Hemp and leather sealed their edges. On the bottom, when they shut, they would press against a sill carved out of the rock shelf that upbore Ys.

As yet, ample space remained between them for an incoming merchant-man. Few Romans would willingly put to sea this early in the year, but Ysan mariners were more bold. The craft was leaner and handier than most in the Empire. Gilt trim, horse-headed stempost, red- and blue-striped sails were like a defiance of any dangers. Those sails were being furled, since the wind was not straight from the west and the wall had therefore laid calm on the basin. Towboats darted from their piers on spidery oars. Already their coxswains were shouting bids for the job of bringing the ship in. A customs officer and his amanuensis came out a door and took expectant stance. Oh, there was still life in Ys!

"You have been on the gate?" Quinipilis asked.

"Yestereven," Gratillonius replied. The memory thrilled in him afresh.

2

That was the final rite confirming him as King. Lir Captain and a delegation of sailors, deckhands as well as officers, called on him at the palace when the tide was nearly full. They took him out on the wall to the northern edge of the portal. There he looked downward, at the sea, and they showed and told him how the gate worked.

It was as simple as a heartbeat, and as vital. High on either side, aslant, jutted a great stone block. The feline heads into which these two were sculptured had blurred in the centuries, but their strength abided. Through each, a chain passed over a sheave within. One end of the chain was fast to its adjacent door. From the other end depended a giant bronze ball, cased in padded leather, hollow so that it floated.

"Without this, half the city would lie drowned at high tide," Hannon declared gravely. "Given a spring tide and a hard storm behind it, neither would the eastern side escape. Look. The doors are shaped so that they continue the curve of the wall. This helps them resist the force of the waves. They angle inward from bottom to top. This makes them *want* to close.

"As the water rises, likewise do the floats, giving ever more slack on the chains and thus letting the doors draw ever more near together. When they do shut, water level in the basin is still some three feet below the wharf. The tide outside goes on flowing, of course, until it may crest close under the battlements; but our city rests safe behind its gate.

"You see the floats are sheathed. This is to keep them from damaging themselves and the wall when storms fling them about. From time to time that protection must be renewed, as must the caulking along the edges and bottoms of the doors. This is done at the lowest low tides, on the calmest days. At that, 'tis difficult, dangerous work. The divers who do it are both well paid and honored. For they keep us alive.

"Now when the sea ebbs, the floats drop, pulling out their chains by their weight, hence drawing the doors open again."

"A marvel!" Gratillonius exclaimed. "Indeed the eighth wonder." And even then it perplexed him that this was all but unknown beyond Ys.

"The Romans wrought well," said Hannon, "but only by the leave of Lir; and He set conditions upon that."

"Um-m-m . . . when the doors do stand wide . . . could not an enemy fleet enter? Or what if there is violent weather?"

Hannon beckoned. "Come." He led the way down a stone staircase. Meanwhile, with a huge hissing sound, the gate closed. Gratillonius heard surf rumble outside; he saw the basin tranquil beneath him.

The stairs ended at a ledge halfway down the wall. There stood a capstan, from which a cable ran through another cat's head to the inner top of this door. Hannon pointed to corresponding structures on the opposite side. "At need," he said, "we use these to pull the portal shut against the weight of the floats. And we've a further security—which is in your hands, O King. Follow me."

He was rather brusque with his lord, Gratillonius thought. But that was understandable. He spoke for his God and his guild. Besides, like everyone before him in his present office, he was a retired skipper who had dared seas from here to Africa, here to Thule.

The doors, like the wall which they matched, had such a large radius of curvature that the inner surface they presented to the harbor was not far from being flat. A narrow, railed walkway reached across either, each terminating in a platform at the juncture. There Hannon and his party took Gratillonius.

On the southern door, a mighty beam—it must have been hewn from an entire oak tree—stood upright, pivoted above a lead counterweight. A cable ran from its upper end to a block high above, and back down to an equally solid cleat. Hannon stepped to the southern platform, released the cable, lowered the beam. The counterweighting was so well done that he could swing the mass up or down by himself. The beam crossed over both doors and settled into a massive iron U bolted to the northern one.

"This holds the portal tight against aught that may seek to come through," Hannon said. "We've less dread of pirates than of storms. Even in good weather, you've seen, the doors swing slightly to and fro as the floats bob on the waves. In a gale, those floats are mightily stirred. Descending into the troughs, they'd fain drag the doors wide apart. Did that happen, especially at high tide, the sea would pour in and wreak catastrophe on Ys. But the bar keeps the gate fast."

Stapled to the northern door beside the U was a chain on which hung a heavy padlock. Solemnly, Hannon passed it through holes in the beam and the iron, tightened it, and put the hasp of the lock through two links. "Lord," he said, "bring forth the Key."

The Key Colconor bore—and Kings before him and before him, back to the time when Ys and Rome and the sea made their treaty— Wordless, Gratillonius drew it from off his bosom and its chain of gold over his head. Hannon had him close and reopen the lock, release the bar and haul it back upright and secure it.

"That is our final safeguard," said the old man. "In times of threat, from war or weather, we shut the gate, lower the beam, and by the lock make sure that no evil chance can somehow fling it loose from its holder and free the doors to the waves. Always, save if he must needs leave Ys, the King bears the Key upon his person. It is his sacred duty to make fast the gate like this when danger nears, and unlock it when the threat is past. Thus went the word of Lir, Taranis, and Belisama."

Half numbed, Gratillonius donned the emblem again. "But what if I were elsewhere, leading your men off to battle, perhaps?" he mumbled.

"Then the Key awaits your return in the Temple of Lir, and I or another high person uses it. As for its loss, the Gallicenae keep the only duplicate; where, is known but to them." Hannon gave him an austere smile. "You understand this is all ceremonial, a repeated sealing of the Pact, rather than absolutely necessary. If we must, we can change the lock. Fear not. Our Gods do not forsake us."

3

Standing beside Quinipilis, Gratillonius recalled those words. Unthinkingly, he murmured them. She gave him a keen look. "But someday we may forsake the Gods," she said.

"For which others, do you think?" he asked very quitely.

Her laugh was bitter. "I've no fear of Christ. Nay, I feel sorry for the minister the Romans have forced on us. Poor little lonely man."

"I must tell you that I serve Mithras." In haste: "He does not forbid me to honor your Gods, if my acts keep within His law and I hold him in my heart to be supreme."

"Hm. That may bring you trouble, lad." Quinipilis brooded. "But I'll not fret about your Bullslayer either. Nay, what plagues me is a fear that we of Ys may become Gods unto ourselves."

She began walking again, he beside her. The northern half of the dock was given over to large ships, civil or naval—a number lay empty, idle— and to office buildings ornate behind colonnades. At the end of the basin, woman and man turned left, back toward pomoerium and wall. Below an ascending staircase stood the temple of Lir. Older than the Roman work, small but thick-built, it was pillared with rough-hewn gray stones akin to the menhirs found throughout Armorica.

The two climbed up past the Gull Tower and continued the circuit of the city bulwark. Quinipilis breathed hard and leaned heavily on her staff. Gratillonius offered his arm. She smiled and let him help her. "You should not exhaust yourself for my sake," he said.

She smiled. "Be not sorry. At home I can rest as long as I wish. Ere many years have fled, I'll be resting snug forever. Let me now enjoy my good-looking young escort."

"You have seen much, my lady," he said with care. "Methinks you've thought much too, and won wisdom thereby. Will you share it with me?"

"Ha! Scarce would I call myself wise, a hard-drinking hag like me. Anyhow, wisdom lies in nobody's gift. We must each forge it for ourselves, alone as best we can."

"But you have known the life of Ys for over half a century. Will you not tell me of it? I do want to be good for your people, but I am wretchedly ignorant."

She regarded him for a time. "The omens were unclear when we called you hither," she said slowly. "But I dare think it likely that we did well." Her mood lightened. She cackled a laugh. "Aye, why should the garrulous crone not gossip as we walk?"

While she narrated, the wall grew straight again beneath their feet and brought them to the higher and newer part of the city, where its powerful families dwelt. At Northbridge Gate the landside length began. They went above the portal. Between those turrets called the Sisters, it gave on a short bridge across waters wild among rocks, to the northern cape. There ran Northbridge Way, along which he had come. . . . The pair continued east and then south.

They passed Star House, a Grecian-like building set in a garden near the wall, next to the Water Tower where astronomical observations took place. Those were essential. Although the secular calendar of Ys had become Julian, the religious calendar remained lunar. The holiest festivals were set by the moon and the planet Venus, which were Belisama's; the clans of the Suffetes each took name from one of the thirteen lunar months.

"The learned foregather, here," Quinipilis remarked. "Philosophers, scholars, poets, artists, mystics—'tis a setting better for their discourse than a tavern. You'll often find Bodilis amidst them. Belike you'd enjoy it too. You carry yourself soldierly, lad, but I suspect you use that pate for more than a helmet rack." In Ys the idea was current that consciousness resided in the head.

Mainly, in slow sentences broken by pauses when she must wheeze for air, she spoke of her men. The talk went on past the Water Tower, down the staircase at the Gaul, back through the streets to her house. There Gratillonius bade her farewell. His mind awhirl but his heart warm with the feeling that he had made a friend, he sought home to the royal palace and Dahilis.

4

Now these were the Kings whom Quinipilis knew.

Redorix. He was a landholder near Vorgium until a barbarian raid left him widowed and ruined. Unable to mend his fortunes under the laws of Diocletianus, he went to try his luck at Ys, and overcame him who kept the Wood. The reign of Redorix lasted nine years and was fondly remembered, for he was personable and conscientious. On one of his Queens he begot a girl who received the name Gladwy—the name her mother had borne as a maiden, which was the custom for first-borns of a high priestess. A great horseman, Redorix sought to organize a cavalry troop among the Ysans, but this was not very successful and disbanded after his death. That happened when Saxon rovers appeared. There had been no forewarning, either through agents abroad or visions sent the Gallicenae. Folk wondered if this meant the Gods were failing, or if They were angry because too many Ysans had abandoned strict ancestral ways in favor of pleasure and luxury. The Saxons laid waste the maritime station and neighboring homesteads. Redorix led his raiders against them and perished in the charge. They assailed the city but could not take it. Archers, slingers, catapults, and boiling kettles wrought havoc on them from the wall. At length they gave up and departed before navy ships out on patrol at sea should return. The Gallicenae raised a storm to hound them, but never knew if it had destroyed the galleys or not. Already Roman commerce was slumping so badly that no effort occurred to rebuild the station.

Calloch. Whenever a King died otherwise than in combat at the Wood, Ys must find a successor as soon as might be. The King was expected to lead his men in war, where his death was not the evil portent that demise from sickness or accident would be. He must always be a foreigner, lest grudges fester and feuds flame in Ys. In Condate Redonum a delegation bought an Osmisian slave, a gladiator. Calloch was happy about this; he would live better, and probably longer, than as a fighter in the arena. For six years he defended himself ably. Else he was not outstanding and had the sense to stay in the background, letting the Suffetes govern unhindered by him. He begot a number of children, of whom two, by Ochtalis, would become the high priestesses Fennalis and Morvanalis.

Wulfgar. This was a Saxon adventurer, outlawed among his folk for a manslaying that, he claimed, was righteous. Most Ysans believed him, for despite his heritage Wulfgar proved another good King, forcefully taking leadership but considerate of the magnates and mild to the lowly. His greatest service was the enlargement of the navy, which had dwindled under the Roman peace. An enormous strength kept him nineteen years alive. In his reign an aged Queen died, and the Sign appeared above the breasts of young Gladwy. For her religous name she chose Quinipilis. She and Wulfgar much enjoyed each other, and of their three daughters, one would become Karilis. He also begot Quistilis-to-be by Donalis, Lanarvilis-to-be by Fennalis, and Tambilis-to-be by Vallilis, as well as numerous girls to whom the Sign never came. These also served as vestals for the required term. Free on their eighteenth birthdays, some married, some renewed their vows and became minor priestesses, some went into curious byways of life: for a strangeness always lay over the Sisterhood. Meanwhile Wulfgar cut down challengers until word got about and none came for a long time. Then at last a second Queen died, and the Sign marked a daughter of his own. She took the name Tambilis. Horrified, he would have refused, but when they were alone in the bridal chamber, the power of the Goddess descended. Unable to help himself, he made Tambilis his, and she became the mother of Bodilis. It was afterward thought that Wulfgar lost the will to live, as easily as he fell to the man who next arrived.

Gaetulius. This was a Mauretanian auxiliary stationed at Vorgium, who deserted when he saw no future worth having in a military career. While the Gallicenae missed Wulfgar, they did not hold his death against his killer. Such was the will of the Gods; and the slaying of the old King, the crowning of the new enacted the rebirth of the year and of all beloved dead. Gaetulius, though, proved to be a gaunt, ascetic man with a certain streak of cruelty and a temper apt to flare in violence—perhaps because he found himself hemmed in whenever he tried to accomplish something noteworthy and could never make his way through or around the opposition. On Quistilis he fathered Maldunilis-to-be, on Donalis he fathered Innilis-to-be, besides unchosen girls by different Queens. Quinipilis could never bring herself to like him. She discovered she was with child so soon after Wulfgar's death that she was not sure but what it was his. Features and nature revealed it to be of Gaetulius, and the infant grew to womanhood and became Vindilis. The reign of Gaetulius lasted for eleven years.

Lugaid. This was a Scotian from Mumu. He said he was of royal blood, driven out by a feud, but nobody ever learned much about him, for he was a brooding, solitary man. Against the Law of Belisama, Quinipilis regarded him as Wulfgar's avenger. Else he meant little to her. He was not a bad King, and when the mood struck him he sang and played the harp most wonderfully, but otherwise he attracted small love; and it was whispered that, alone, he carried out eldritch rites. By Karilis he fathered Forsquilis-to-be. The mother died in childbed and the girl was fostered by grandmother Quinipilis. The reign of Lugaid was for only four years.

Hoel. When a boy in the tribe of the Namnetes, this person had been sold into slavery for taxes. He ran away and drifted venturesomely about for a long while before coming to Ys and, almost on impulse, taking the Kingship. Handsome and cheerful, he quickly won hearts. He was intelligent, too, but content to stay first among equals, suggesting and persuading rather than invoking the full powers that were his in law. A great sportsman, reveler, and lover, he was likewise strong in battle. (While its wall and its high priestesses protected the city of Ys, its commerce more and more required warlike help.) Hoel took charge of convoys at need. He also led punitive expeditions which taught Scoti and Saxons a lesson they did not forget until after his death. Indeed, under him Ys prospered as it had not done for generations. Trade picked up southward, especially, with his native Namnetes and on down the gulf as far as Hispania. The wealth and the Southern influences that this brought were not an unmixed blessing—said the old and the moody: for they loosened morals and undermined patriotism. Yet Hoel was deeply mourned when he fell, not least by his wives and their plentiful daughters.

Colconor. This was an Osismian farm hand who fled (after having ravished the wife of another, or so the rumor went) and joined the Bacaudae. There he flourished brutally for several years before he decided to become King of Ys; surely, with his strength, he could hold that position until none dared go up against him. Soon he was hated, less for having struck down good King Hoel than for his coarse and overbearing ways. He was just shrewd enough to avoid provocation immediately unbearable. There did come to be an unusual number of challengers, as had happened in the past when Ys fell under a wicked man, but for five years he prevailed over all. None of the Gallicenae bore him a child, though he had them often and savagely—except for Maldunilis, and hers did not come to term, an ill omen. In his reign Tambilis died and the sign came upon youthful Estar, offspring of Tambilis and Hoel. Estar took the name Dahilis. Colconor had special delight in using her. But whatever he did, he found her spirit too sunny to break, as he found that of her fellow Queens too hard or, in the case of Maldunilis, too loose and lazy. This deepened his rage, as it did his loneliness. In Old Town he had his cronies and toadies, among them harlots who could amuse him despite his impotence outside the circle of the high priestesses. On these people he squandered much of the royal treasury. Perhaps it was not perfect justice that blame fell upon him for the decline in trade and the renewed rise of piracy and banditry since Hoel's time. These things were happening everywhere else, and in general the affairs of Ys went on independently of him. But rightly was Colconor blamed for causing the death of Tambilis, through abuse and heartbreak. Whispers of knife or poison went through Ys. This, though, would have been sacrilege, which might well cause the Gods to end the Pact and Lir to send His waves through a shattered gate. Slowly the Nine groped their way to an answer. If Suffetes could in secrecy persuade men to come strike the Shield, then it would be lawful for Queens to cast a spell drawing hither one whose chances were better and causing him to do battle. The omens they took were ambiguous but did not forbid. And so they gathered on Sena, the holy of holies, and there they cursed Colconor.

Gratillonius.

5

About sunset, clouds blew out of the west across heaven. It was already dark when Soren Cartagi raised a bronze knocker and brought it back down on the door of Lanarvilis.

The homes of the Gallicenae were not together, nor were they far apart, in the neighborhood of Elven Gardens and the temple of Belisama. Outwardly plain, they were inwardly Roman, from the time when they were built. Yet that time lay almost four hundred years in the past. Each of the nine dwellings had descended from Queen to successor Queen, each of whom had left her traces that never quite went away. Here the knocker, worn smooth by lifetimes of hands, was in the form of a serpent that bit its own tail. . . .

The door opened. The steward saw who stood at the threshold and brought hand to brow. While Soren was in civil garb, few ever failed to recognize that broad hook-nosed visage and heavy frame. "Our lady awaits you, my lord," the steward reported, and stepped aside. Soren entered. His two lantern-bearers followed. The steward guided the party through the atrium and rooms beyond to a certain inner door, which he swung wide. When Soren had passed through, he closed it and led the escort off. Nobody would venture to question what went on in private between the Speaker for Taranis and a high priestess of Belisama.

Windowpanes in this chamber were full of darkness, but lamps gave ample soft light. It fell on blue carpeting, crimson drapes, fine furniture inlaid with walrus ivory and upholstered in leather. Flagon and cups on a table were cut crystal; a plate for cheeses and spiced mussels was millefi-ori glass. Lanarvilis took what pleasures she wanted, so they be permissible. What she wanted the most was not.

She rose from a settee and went to meet Soren: a tall blond woman, small-bosomed and thick-haunched, her nose too wide and her blue eyes too small, but not ill-looking when she took trouble about her appearance. Today she had had her tiring maid do her hair up in an intricacy of knots and braids, topped by a jeweled comb. Ointments and powders gave fresh coloring to a face whose bearer neared her fortieth year. Gold shimmered under her throat, above a gown cut low; those folds of rich brown fabric were kind to a woman who had fivefold been a mother. She took both his hands in hers. "Welcome and blessing," she said.

"Elissa!" he blurted, half dazed. "You're beautiful tonight. What witch-craft made you a maiden again?"

Her smile mingled enjoyment and sadness. "I was Elissa once," she murmured; "but that was long ago. I am Lanarvilis now. Elissa is my daughter by Lugaid, finished with her vestalhood, soon to wed and make me a grandmother."

"For an instant I forgot," he said harshly. "Only an instant. It shall not happen more."

"Oh, Soren, dear, forgive me," she begged, contrite. " 'Twas myself I felt I should remind. I did wish to receive you well—in celebration—but mayhap 'twas a mistake." She released her hold on him. "Come, be seated, take refreshment."

They placed themselves on the settee, separated a foot or two. She poured. The wine gurgled and glowed. It was a choice Aquitanian, whose fragrance met them before they tasted.

He looked from her, across the room to a mural of Diana the Huntress. "I've been stewing ever since I got your reply to my message," he said. "Why could you not see me earlier?"

"I'm sorry." This regret was calm, with an undertone of resolve. "Three Sisters were needed for a certain emprise, and Vindilis asked that I be among them. What is your desire?"

"I decided 'twould be wise to talk beforehand about this Council the King summons. You and I have worked well together over the years."

"We have that." She regarded him. "But what is in your mind?"

"Let us prepare ourselves against surprises."

"Why, there should be none. For us, at any rate. This Gra—Gra-lo—Gra-til-lonius has met the leaders of Ys severally, well-nigh since he won the crown—since he took the Key. We've all accepted his purpose. The assembly should but ratify our agreement."

Soren scowled. "He's been less than candid. *Why* has Rome sent a prefect, after letting generations go by? Gratillonius speaks vaguely of troubles anticipated and the desirability of keeping Armorica out of them. Methinks he knows more than that, and does in truth plan a surprise later."

Now when Lanarvilis smiled it was not womanly but an aspect remote from humanness, the look of Knowledge. "Aye," she said evenly. " 'Tis that which concerned Forsquilis, Vindilis, and myself this day."

He started. "Forsquilis! Did she learn—?"

Lanarvilis nodded. "We believe so. Politically, I deem it very plausible."

He set his glass down most carefully, lest he smash it. "Will you tell me?"

She did.

At the end, he drooped his lids, stroked his beard, sipped his wine, and said in measured tones: "I'd guessed, of course, though I could not be positive. I daresay Gratillonius withholds the news in hopes of first making his grip the firmer. Think you, like me, that 'twill be a shrewd stroke, telling him in Council that we know already? Thus taken aback, he may be the easier to deal with. For sure 'tis, we've no figurehead King here."

"He does not wish us ill."

"Nay, but he has his own aims—or Rome's, whatever Emperor's those may come to be. They may not prove the best for Ys." Soren barked a laugh. "If naught else, let us ride the current to our advantage. We may perchance wring substantial concessions out of the Imperium."

Woman again, Lanarvilis laughed too and touched his hand. "Ever were you the calculating one, Soren."

"I seek the welfare of my city, my House, my sons, and myself," he replied. "What else is there to strive for?"

Her gaze darkened. Unspoken was the truth that they would have wedded, had not the Sign come upon her a single month before the end of her vestalhood.

"Oppose this King when you feel you must," she said. "But lay no plots to confound him. I tell you, he is not evil. Else would the Gods have allowed our summoning of him?"

He stared at her through a silence before he breathed, "Then you did indeed, you Nine."

"Certes." Her tone stayed level. "Did you never suspect?"

"Oh, aye, aye," he stammered. "And yet . . . was deed like that done any time before in Ys?"

"Nay, and best 'tis that it not be noised abroad. Mere rumor will die away. The new King knows—Quinipilis told him, on purpose—albeit she doubts he can yet believe it. You do."

"I must." Soren passed hand over eyes. "That morning—" he whispered. "What did you do to entrap Colconor? He was strong, and you meant to weaken him as much as might be, but—" He beat fist in palm. "A-a-ah, I've heard of his wallowings in the Fishtail brothels—"

The calm went out of Lanarvilis. Tears trickled, blurring the malachite so carefully painted around her eyes. "Soren, dear, *I* was not there. I knew, I helped plan it, aye, but . . . but never could I do such a thing to you."

Bitterness lashed: "Why not? What difference? We're not the boy and girl who babbled endearments under a midsummer moon. Your satisfactions have been plain to see on you. I daresay you await more of them from Gratillonius."

She drew herself straight and retorted, "You've taken your own pleasures, Soren Cartagi, and well I know 'tis not been with your wife alone. Should I embalm my spirit? Lugaid was no bad man, and Hoel was grand." Anger collapsed. She struggled not to weep. "But oh, how often with them would I pretend to myself 'twas you. And I tried with Colconor, but as nasty as he was . . . 'twould have been wrong to have even the memory of you present . . . whenever he took me, I would go away anyplace else."

"Oh, Elissa," he croaked. They reached.

She drew back before they had quite met. "Nay. Nay. We are what we've become. 'Twould be desecration."

He slumped. "True." After a while he stirred. "Best I depart."

She had rallied. "Not yet, Soren. We *are* what we are, Speaker for Taranis and high priestess of Belisama, in Ys. I said we should not conspire against the new King. But let us think how best we may cope with him."

IX

1

Unwontedly solemn, Dahilis asked, "Beloved, have you an hour to spare for me this morning?"

Gratillonius clasped her to him. How wonderfully slender and lithe she was. His free hand cupped a breast, roved down across the curves of hip and belly, rested briefly on golden fleece, returned to chuck her under the chin. "What, immediately again?" he laughed. "I'll need that hour to recover my strength, as spendthrift of it as you've made me."

"I mean talk, the two of us alone." He heard what a need was hers, and read it in the lapis lazuli of her gaze. "Oh, I understand you are engaged, you've been around among people like a whirlwind since first you arrived, but if you have any time free— It concerns us both, and the whole city."

He kissed her. "Of course, of course," he did his best to say in Ysan. "It was never my wish to leave you behind. If you too would discuss affairs of state, why, every magnate and officer should be as delightful."

At his movement, an object stirred between his shoulderblades—the Key that he must always wear but had put at his back, out of the way. Somehow, shifting it onto his chest again felt like closing a door. He pushed the thought off, banned it from Dahilis and himself.

They left the bed to which they had impulsively returned after breaking their fast, and sought the bath. Dahilis became playful once more, giggling as she soaped him and her and rinsed them clean, diving about in the warm water like a seal. They toweled each other as well but did not call anyone to help them dress. He would summon his barber later, he decided. He slipped on a robe, cloak, and sandals. She took an equally simple white gown belted at the waist, slippers on her feet, a fillet on her head. The yellow tresses she had merely combed and let hang free. Many young women of the best families often used plebeian styles these days, rather than the traditional elaborate coiffures. Ready to leave, she seemed to him a maiden, almost a child.

Hand in hand they wandered down a hallway on which opened the doors of luxurious chambers, across the mosaic of charioteers which floored the atrium, past servants who touched the brow, and out into the morning. Uniquely in Ys, the palace had a walled garden around it, not large but so intricate in its hedges, bowers, topiaries, flowerbeds, paths that one could walk long about and never feel cramped. The building and the outbuildings behind it were likewise of modest dimensions, but ample for their uses and pleasing to behold. The northern and southern sides of the palace formed ideal rectangles, their plaster flaunting vigorous images of wild beasts in a forest. Sculptures of a boar and a bear flanked a staircase leading to the portico and the main door, whose bronze bore reliefs of human figures. The upper story was set back above a roof of green copper, and itself carried a dome, on top of which the gilt figure of an eagle spread wings.

It was a glorious day, springtime in bloom, each breath like a draught of cool wine. Dew still glittered on leaves and moss, newly born blossoms, crushed shell that scrunched softly underfoot. Birds were everywhere, redbreast, warbler, finch, linnet, wren, singing in a chaos of joy. High overhead, white as the cloudlets they passed, winged a flight of storks, homeward bound.

Dahilis walked mute, her trouble again upon her, until she and Gratillonius reached the wall. Vines growing over its sandstone did not hinder the warmth of sun that it had begun to give back. He spread his cloak over the dampness on a stone bench and they sat down. He laid a hand across the fist she had made in her lap. "Tell me," he said.

She stared before her, unseeing, and spoke with difficulty: "My lord, my darling, I can no longer abide here. Grant me that . . . that I may go to my own house."

"What?" he exclaimed, dismayed. "I thought you happy."

"Oh, I was. Gladsome beyond measure. But—it is not right . . . that I have the King all to myself. Five days it has been. Six nights."

He clenched his teeth before saying, "Well, true, I suppose we should—"

"We must! You are the King. And they, they are my Sisters in the Mystery. They too are of Belisama. Oh, do not anger Her! I would fear for you yet more than I already do."

"I will certainly give them proper respect," he forced out.

She turned her face to him. He saw tears on her lashes. "Do more than that," she begged. "Cherish them. For my sake at first, if naught else will

serve. Later for their own. They are my Sisters. They bore with my child-
hood flightiness, they were gentle and patient when I grew too restless to
study what I ought, the older were like my mother unto me and the
younger like loving elder sisters in the flesh. When my father Hoel fell,
they upbore me in my grief. When my mother died, they did more, for the
Sign was upon me that same night, and— And they consoled me, gave me
back my heart, after Colconor, until they had schooled me in how to
endure him. And at last it was they, they, they who had the bravery and
the skill to bring you. I was their acolyte. Yet me only have you honored— It is not right!"

She fell into his arms and sobbed on his breast. He stroked her, crooned
wordlessly, at length murmured, "Aye. Indeed. It shall be as you wish.
And you speak truly, I've been unwise in this. I can but plead that I've
been too taxed with my business among men to think, otherwise, of aught
than you, Dahilis."

She gulped her way to self-mastery and sat straight. He kissed the salt
off her cheeks and lips. His mouth slipped on down to the angle between
jaw and ear; he kissed the softness of her skin there, too, and drank odors
of her warmth and her hair. "Th-thank you," she whispered. "You are
ever kind."

"Nay, now, what else could I be, toward you? And I've agreed you are
right. Can you explain to . . . the rest . . . that no insult was intended?"

She nodded. "I'll go about today doing that, since tomorrow comes my
Vigil."

"What's this?" he inquired.

"You did not know?" she replied, amazed. "Why, I took it for given
that my learned lord— Well, then, Sena is the sacred isle. Always must at
least one of the Gallicenae be there. Save at a few certain times, Council
meetings or the Crowning and Wedding, when all of us are needed here.
Oh, and in war, for safety's sake, though I scarcely believe even the
fiercest pirate would dare—We go out for a day and a night by turns, on a
special ferry. The crew are navy men whose officers decide they've earned
this honor for a month."

He forebore to ask what the high priestesses did yonder. That might be
knowledge forbidden him. Instead, he regarded her in some slight
bemusement before saying, "You've depths I did not suspect, my sweet."

The bright head shook. "Nay, nay. I'm a shallow little person, really."

"You're unjust to yourself."

"I am truthful. The deaths of four aged Queens did not touch me, I was only sorry and missed them for a time. Not until my father was slain did I understand what sorrow is."

"He surely adored you."

A smile quivered. "He spoiled me, he did. You are much like Hoel as I remember him, Gra—Gratillonius." Her Latin weak, she occasionally had trouble keeping the syllables of his name in place. He found it easiest to chop along in Ysan when with her, telling himself he needed the practice.

"Even afterward," she continued, "when I'd stopped mourning him aloud, I'd no real thoughtfulness in me. I expected to serve out my vestal term, and then after I turned eighteen belike marry a pleasant young man, the sort who was in my daydreams." Her smile writhed away. "But mother died, and the Sign came, and—" She stared beyond him. Her fists doubled anew.

"That must have been horror," he said.

Bit by bit, she eased. "At first. But my Sisters took me in charge, Bodilis foremost. She's my true sister, you know—half-sister—also daughter of Tambilis, though her father was Wulfgar. But the rest comforted me too, and taught me. Colconor was seldom there for long. When he was finished he'd dismiss me, or fall asleep and snore if it was night. Then I could go home next morning. And when he used me—however hurtfully or, or shamefully—I could leave him. I sent my spirit back through time, or forward, to when things had been better or when someday they would be good once more. Forsquilis taught me how. And most days he let me alone, I could live my own life."

"Tell me," he said, trying to help her back to gladness, "how did you pick the name Dahilis? I know your mother called you Estar. How do any of you Gallicenae choose your names when . . . you have been chosen?"

"They come from places, They bring the blessing of whatever spirit is tutelary. My name means 'of Dahei.' Dahei is a spring in the eastern hills where the nymph Ahes indwells. I picked that because it is cool and bubbly, hidden among trees. When I was a girl and my mother or Bodilis took me along on a trip to those parts—'tis beautiful countryside—while she meditated I would seek the spring and give Ahes a garland and ask her for happy dreams at night."

She sighed, but no longer in misery. "Could we go together sometime, Gratillonius? I'd like to show you."

"Of course, when I can find leisure. There's too much on hand now. Hm. You need not feel overly hurried about passing my message on. Your Vigil on Sena shall be postponed. I should have told you, but you make me forgetful of everything outside. And it was preoccupying, making those arrangements—when I was ignorant of all the ins and outs—for a full Council. It meets tomorrow." He grinned. "That requires your presence."

"As a matter of form," she said humbly. "I can offer nothing."

"Your presence, I repeat. We'll need the loveliness."

"Oh, my own only!" They embraced. "I did not know," she breathed in his ear. "I thought, yea, the new King will carry a better day for us on his shoulders, he cannot help but do that. I did not look for joy such as you've given. Last night after you were asleep, I prayed to Belisama Mother, I prayed you be spared for many, many years—and whatever happens, I might die before you. Was that terribly selfish of me? I'll come back in the sea and wait for you. Always will I wait for you."

"Now, now, I have many a battle in me yet," he boasted. She strained against him. Arousal stirred. "M-m, I've a meeting with some Suffetes at noon, but that's hours hence. Shall we?"

She crowed in glee. "And you thought you'd need more time!"

"With any woman but you I would." Briefly, he wondered. Quinipilis had bespoken the power of the Goddess. . . .

As she skipped along beside his more dignified pace, she said laughing, "Could we wait long enough for you to be shaved? Later you might grow a beard. 'Tis the style in Ys."

He rubbed his chin. "I might. These past days my whiskers have been sprouting at a furious rate."

"Well, but do put the razor to them this time. When I call on my Sisters and explain, best would be that I not flaunt marks on my face. Not but what they won't know from my gait, dear stallion!"

2

The Forum of Ys had never been a marketplace. It merely received that familiar name from the Roman engineers who reconstructed it as they did much else while the wall against the sea was going up. At the middle of the city, where Lir Way and Taranis Way crossed, it was a plaza surrounded by public buildings. These were likewise on the Roman model, marble-sheathed, colonnaded, stately, albeit of no great size. The temple of Taranis, the baths, the theater, and the library were still in use. The basilica was also, less often, despite having seen no Imperial official permanently in residence for the past two hundred years. The temple of Mars had echoed empty almost as long, until Emperor Constantinus I required Ys to take in a Christian minister. Then it became a church.

Budic went looking around the square. Mosaics of dolphins and sea horses ringed a triple-basined fountain at the center. No water splashed; on festival nights, pump-driven oil did, set alight to leap and cascade in fire. At noon today, not many folk were about. They stared curiously at the young soldier. He was out of uniform, but height, pale-blond hair, tunic falling down to bare knees—a garment his Coritanic mother had sewn for him—identified him as a foreigner. Though sunlight descended mild, his calves felt the breeze as a cold caress. His sandals slapped the pavement too loudly.

Because the former temple faced south, the Christians had cut a new entrance in its western side. Mounting the stairs to the portico, he found that door open and passed through. Before him was a stretch of bare floor, the vestibule, ended by a wall—which its peeling plaster revealed to be wooden—that subdivided the great chamber where the pagan rites had taken place. A door in it was also open, giving Budic a glimpse of the sanctuary. It was nearly as devoid of furnishings. The altar block stood in the middle beneath a canopy replacing the cupola of a proper church; the cross upon it was neither gilt nor of especially fine workmanship. At the far end were a table and a couple of seats.

An aged man was languidly sweeping in there, hunched over his besom. Budic halted at the divider. "I b-beg your pardon, sir," he ventured.

The other stopped, blinked, and shuffled forward. "What would ye?" he asked. His Latin had a heavy Redonic accent. "Be ye a believer?"

"I am, sir, though only a catechumen."

"Well, ye're young yet. Can I help ye, brother in Christ? I be Prudentius the deacon."

Budic declared his name and origin. Too bashful to seek higher, he asked, "C-could I see a priest?"

"Priest?" The old man blinked. "Haven't got any priest. What for? How big d'ye think our congregation be? I only get the name of deacon because I'm baptized and have time to help out with the chores. All the rest of the believers are busy making their livings."

"Oh. Then the bishop? If I may?"

"Haven't got a bishop either, not here in this nest of heathens. Eucherius is the chorepiscopus. I'll go ask if he can see ye just now. Wait." The man went off. Budic shifted from foot to foot, gnawed his thumbnail, stared into the sacred room he must not enter before he himself had received baptism. That wouldn't likely be for years and years—

The oldster reappeared. "Come," he said, and led the way through a door in the original transverse, marble wall on the left. Having followed a corridor past an unused space, they reached another door. The deacon signalled the soldier to go in.

Beyond was poverty huddled in what had been opulence. The chamber where the pastor made his home, once the temple treasury, was too big for him. However, decent if modest furniture occupied a part, and a threadbare carpet warded off some of the chill. Windows were glazed. At the north end, where a smokehole had been knocked through the ceiling, was a kitchen, crude but sufficient for cooking. Soot from it had obliterated ancient decorations above and had grayed murals. Several books rested on a table, together with writing materials: pens, inkwell, thin slabs of wood, a piece of vellum off which earlier notations were scraped.

Budic halted and made awkward salute. Two people sat on tall stools at the table. That must be why the deacon had questioned whether the chorepiscopus would receive a new visitor. One person was a short, frail-looking man, gray, Italianate of features, stoop-shouldered in a robe much darned and patched. He blinked nearsightedly and smiled uncertainly. "Welcome," he said in Latin.

"Father—" Budic's voice entangled itself.

"I stand in for the bishop, your proper father in Christ. But let me call you 'son' if you wish. My name is Eucherius. Where are you from?"

"I am . . . I am a legionary . . . of those who follow Gratillonius, he who is your King. My name is Budic."

The pastor winced and signed himself, as many Christians had taken to doing. The woman across from him turned and asked in a husky, excited tone: "A man of Gratillonius? Do you have a message from him?" Her Latin was excellent.

"No, honorable lady," faltered Budic, unsure how to address her. "I came on my own account. Father, having leave today, I inquired my way here. We were long on the march. We got no time for anything but hasty private prayers. I've much on my soul, to confess and repent."

"Why, of course I'll hear you." Eucherius smiled. "You come like the flowers of the very Paschal season. But you have no more need to hurry. Join us. I imagine you too, Lady Bodilis, would like to know this young man better. Eh?"

"I would that," said the woman.

"Budic," said Eucherius, "pay respect—not religious, but civil—to Queen Bodilis of Ys."

Queen! A woman of the infamous Nine? Yet . . . a woman of the centurion's? Dazedly, Budic saluted her.

She was a handsome woman, at least: tall, well-formed, singularly graceful in her movements. Dark-brown, wavy hair lay braided around features blunt-nosed, wide in the cheekbones, full in the mouth. Her eyes were large and blue under arching brows. The gown she wore was of rich material, soft green in color, sleeves worked with gold thread, its leather belt chased in undulant patterns. A silver pendant in the form of an owl hung on her bosom.

"You can take a goblet from yonder shelf." Eucherius pointed. "Come share this mead that my lady was so generous as to bring for the warming of these creaky bones. Don't be surprised. She and I have been friends since first I came here, and that was ten years ago, was it not, Bodilis?"

A fit of coughing seized him. She frowned in concern, reached over to clasp his hand. Budic fetched a wooden vessel for himself and diffidently took a third stool, one of the ordinary low sort from which he would have to look up at the others. Bodilis gestured at the flagon. Well, a queen—whether or not she was a heathen priestess—wouldn't pour for a common soldier, would she? Budic mustered courage and filled his cup.

Bodilis smiled at him. This close, he saw fine lines crinkle at the corners of eyes and lips. "We share no faith, the pastor and I," she explained, "but we share love of books, art, the wonders of earth and sea and heaven."

"Queen Bodilis has been more than a companion in my isolation," Eucherius wheezed when he was able. "She saw to it that I got proper furnishings and enough to eat. The pagan Kings had done nothing about that, and—and there are no more than a score of Christians in Ys. Otherwise this church serves what transient Gauls and sailors are believers. My predecessors dwelt in wretchedness. I trust that speeded their salvation, but—but— Hers is a noble soul, my son. Pray that she someday see the light, or that God will reveal it to her after she dies."

Sardonicism tinged Bodilis's smile. "Beware," she said. "Do you not skirt heresy?"

"The Lord forgive me. I must remember—" Eucherius gave Budic his full attention. "When I can, I travel to Audiarna—Roman-held town, the closest, on the west bank of a river that otherwise marks the frontier— You'd not know the geography, would you? . . . There I make my own confessions, and obtain the consecrated bread and wine. But I cannot travel often. My health—"

He straightened as best he could, with an apologetic look. "Now it's you who must forgive, my son," he finished. "I didn't mean to appear unmanly and chattery, before a soldier at that. It's only, oh, to see a *Roman* again— Are there Christians among your fellows?"

Budic nodded. Eucherius beamed.

"Drink, lad, and let us talk," Bodilis counselled. "We've each a bundle of news to exchange, I'm sure."

Budic sipped. The mead was dry, delicately flavored with blackberry. "I'm just a rustic from eastern Britannia," he demurred. "This journey has been my first. Well, my vexillation was on the Wall last year, but that was fighting, and garrison duty in between. Nobody told us anything."

"The Wall last year! Where Magnus Maximus rolled back a barbarian midnight." Her tone sank. "Although— What do you know about him? What sort of man is he?"

"I *am* only a roadpounder—a common legionary, honorable lady," Budic faltered. "I know nothing about great matters. It is enough to follow my centurion."

"But you heard talk," she said fiercely. "You are not deaf."

"Well, camp and barracks are always full of rumors." Budic attempted evasion. "The lady is very well informed about Rome."

Bodilis laughed. "I try. Like a snail reaching horns out of the shell into which it has drawn itself. Word does come in. I'm here today to share with Eucherius a letter lately arrived from Ausonius. He too hears talk."

"Let us get acquainted," the chorepiscopus urged.

His story soon emerged, as glad as he was of fresh company. He was a Neapolitan who, after attaining the priesthood, had been sent to the school of rhetoric which Ausonius then maintained in Burdigala, for he showed promise. Exposure to ancient philosophers and to the attitudes of his teacher bred in him a doubt that man since Adam is innately depraved —especially new-born children. When he expressed such ideas on his return home, he was quickly charged with heresy, and had no influential clergyman to argue on his behalf. Though he recanted, his bishop afterward trusted him with no more than the work of a lowly copyist.

Then it chanced that that bishop received a letter from his colleague and correspondent in Gesocribate. Among other things, the writer lamented that the ministry at Ys had fallen vacant some time ago and there seemed to be no man both competent and willing to take it over. Thus the Church had lost even this tenuous contact with the city—the comings and goings of its traders were altogether unmonitored—and there was no guessing what the powers of darkness wrought around the Gobaean Promontory.

The Italian bishop wrote back proposing Eucherius, and this was agreed to. The feelings among Eucherius's superiors was that in the midst of such obstinate pagans any errors into which he might again stray would make small difference, while he ought to administer the sacraments sufficiently well to whatever few Christians came by. Also, serving in yonder post would be an additional penance, good for his own soul.

Hence he was elevated to chorepiscopus—"country bishop," as slang put it—with authority to govern a church, teach, lead services, give Communion and last rites, but not to baptize or consecrate the Bread and Wine.

Reaching the city, he learned the language, but remained lonesome, not so much scorned as ignored, until Bodilis's desire for knowledge brought him and her together. She tried to get him membership in the Symposium, the gathering of thinkers at Star House, but the vote failed. For his part, he put her in touch with Ausonius, and those two exchanged letters even though the poet had since joined the Imperial court and attained to a consulship.

Eucherius's own correspondence was perfunctory, confined to his ecclesiastical masters. Beguiling his empty hours was the labor of a treatise on the history and customs of Ys. These had come to fascinate him as greatly as they appalled him; and—who knew?—one day the information might help a stronger man guide this poor benighted people back from the abyss.

Tears stung Budic's eyes. "Father," he blurted, "you are a soldier too, a legionary of Christ!"

Eucherius sighed. "No, hardly." He shaped a wan smile. "At best, a camp follower, stumblefooted and starveling, always homesick."

"I hear it is lovely at Neapolis," Bodilis said low to Budic. "Hills behind and a bay before, utterly blue; the old Grecian city nestled between; and that Italian light and air about which we can only dream here in our gray North."

"We must forsake this world and seek our true home, which is Heaven," Eucherius reproached. Another spell of coughing racked him, more cruel than the first. He put a cloth to his mouth. When he laid it down, the phlegm on it was streaked red.

3

Eppillus having given them leave, Cynan and Adminius set off to see a little of Ys and sample its pleasures. For guide they had Herun, a young deckhand in the navy. They had made his acquaintance at Warriors' House, where the legionaries were quartered together with men of the professional armed service. Those of the latter who were not on duty or standby generally stayed at home, but for the present the Romans had no place else to sleep than the barrack.

While at liberty one wore civil garb, and no steel save a knife whose blade length could not exceed four inches. Adminius thoughtfully tucked a cosh under the tunic he hung on his wiry frame. Cynan was gaudier in the clothes of his native Demetae, fur-trimmed coat, cross-gartered breeches, saffron cloak flapping in the gusty air; from his left shoulder a small harp hung in its carrying case. Herun was attired in Ysan male wise, linen shirt, embroidered jacket open to display a pendant on his breast, snug trousers. The predominant Celtic strain in him showed on big body and freckled face; the beard trimmed close to his jaws and the hair drawn into a horsetail down his neck were coppery.

"Methought we'd go around by Aurochs Gate and Goose Fair, thence wend north for the Fishtail," he said, slowly and carefully so as to be understood. "Thus will you pass some things worthy of a look ere we settle down to carouse."

"That sounds well." Adminius turned to Cynan and translated into Latin. Meanwhile the three dodged through the traffic on Lir Way and took a street quiet and narrow which wound among the abodes of the wealthy.

"You've seized onto a mickle of our language in the short span you've had," observed Herun.

Adminius grinned his snaggle-toothed grin. "A cockroach scuttling about the docksides of Londinium 'ad better be quick, if 'e'd not get stepped on," he replied.

"Mean you that yours was a hard life?"

"Well, my father's a ferryman on the River Tamesis. Early on, the count of 'is brats began to outnumber the count of 'is earnings. From the time I could walk, I scrabbled for whatever I wanted, over and above my mother's boiled cabbage. That was a lawless as well as a poor quarter, but on the same account, chances would come now and then. To snatch them, I 'ad ter be able ter understand men from around 'alf the world, it seemed. So I got a sharp ear and tongue."

Herun frowned, laboring to follow. As yet, Adminius perforce spoke haltingly, with a thick and unique accent, using many words that might be common elsewhere in Armorica but were strangers here. It helped that the mariner had encountered some of them on his travels. Patrolling widely around the peninsula, sailing convoy in periods of special danger, Ysan warcraft often put in to rest or resupply. They usually chose small harbors where there were no Imperial officials to encumber transactions.

"At length you enlisted?" Herun guessed.

Adminius nodded. "I'd made enemies in Londinium. Besides, the legionary's life is no bad one, 'speci'lly when you're good at scrounging and at slipping through cracks in the rules."

"What are you gabbling about?" demanded Cynan.

Adminius returned to his kind of Latin: "Aow, nothing but my biography. Don't fret. You'll soon be slinging the lingo too."

Cynan's dark features stayed fixed in a scowl. "Maybe then those warlocks won't strip my purse—when I've learned how to counter their spells."

"Now, now, don't sulk. It was an honest game. The dice just weren't friendly ter yer. I took my share." Adminius jingled his own pouch. Like Rome's, the Ysan armed services were paid in coin as well as in kind. Most of what he had were sesterces, of depleted worth but preferable to bagsful of nummi. They would serve for such minor dealings as an evening on the town. "And I'm not the chap that won't stand a chum a treat."

Cynan bridled. "I ask no alms."

Adminius ran fingers through his sandy hair. "Mighty near a 'opeless case, ain't you? Why'd you come along if not for a bit o' fun? Consider it a loan. Let the next bout be yours." He slapped the other on the back. "Barracks too dull for yer, eh? Well, you'll feel cheerier after you've 'ad a drink and a wench."

The street passed a walled enclosure, within which rose a domed habitation. Four sentries stood at a grillwork gate: on either side, an Ysan marine and a Roman legionary. Herun saluted in his fashion, Adminius waved at his friends, as they passed by. "Is this the royal palace?" Cynan asked.

"Got ter be. You know we don't assign anybody anywhere else, so far. You and I'll be drawing this duty soon."

"I understand how the centurion—the prefect—wants men of his on guard. But why not more? And why have natives at all?"

"Eppillus was explaining that ter me. Gratillonius ain't just the prefect now, 'e's the flinking King. It'd be an insult if 'e didn't let 'em watch over their King. And we wouldn't like if 'e didn't let us 'elp."

Cynan pondered. "That feels true in me," he agreed after a space. "He's a wise one, no?" Resentment flickered afresh. "At least when my turn comes I won't be cooped up indoors."

"Easy, lad, easy. Are you really that eager ter start in again on drill and digging latrines? Never fear. Give 'im time ter get the lay of the land, and 'e'll find plenty for us ter do, 'e will."

Terrain began dropping fast. Except for the residential towers, buildings grew less lavish and more old. Ever higher did the rampart rear in view and, under a declining sun, fill the ways with shadow. The last sellers, buyers, brokers, and hawkers were leaving Goose Fair. Its stones boomed beneath hoops and wheels; echoes rolled hollowly. The Brothers at Aurochs Gate were outlined black athwart heaven.

Herun turned right, through streets that became mere lanes, half-roofed by overhanging upper stories between which they twisted. Cobblestones lay lumpy underfoot. More people were about than in New Town —sailors, workmen, housewives, fishwives, children in skimpy tunics, individuals less easily recognizable. Their garments might be flamboyant, rough, or sleazy, but were always cheap. They themselves bore marks of toil and sometimes of past sickness. Yet there was no sign of hunger or alley-cat poverty as in Londinium, nor did the quarter smell sourly of refuse and unwashed bodies. Sea air blew through all Ys, tinged with salt and kelp, chill where walls blocked off sunlight. Gulls cruised white overhead.

The three men halted before a small, rudely cubical structure of rammed earth on a patch of ground defined by four unshaped boundary stones. Between wooden roof and door was inset a solar emblem of polished granite. Despite repairs and replacements which had been made as need arose, the wear of centuries was plain to see. Herun genuflected in reverence.

"What's this?" Cynan asked; his Ysan was sufficient for that.

"The Shrine of Melqart," Herun said. "Thus did the founders of the city name Taranis when first they came hither, long and long ago. Later He got temples more grand, and now this is only open on solstice days, with but a single man to make sacrifice. Elsewhere in Old Town, and not unlike it, is the Shrine of Ishtar—Belisama—which opens at the equinoxes. We honor our Gods in Ys."

He conducted his followers onward. Adminius paraphrased his explanation for Cynan. The Demetan traced a sign in the air. "Well might they honor their Gods," he said low, "they who live on the sufferance of Ocean . . . But you're a Christian, you don't understand."

"I ain't that good a Christian," Adminius confessed.

Farther on was another reserved space, this for a megalith man-high, lichen-spotted, darkling. "Menhir Place," Herun said, again bending his knee. "The pillar was here before the city. Out in Armorica have I seen works of the Old Folk that Celts have chiseled their glyphs into, and lately Christians likewise. But our forefathers, and we, ventured not to trouble this that was raised to a God unknown."

Adminius shivered a bit. As if continuing his earlier sentence, he muttered, "I know when somewhere is 'aunted. . . . Wish I'd brought my cloak. It's gotten futtering cold."

Beyond the harbor end of Lir Way and the respectable buildings there, the Fishtail began. It was quite a small slum, less mean than any counterpart in the Empire. Nevertheless dwellers went ragged, slinking or truculently swaggering. Beggars wailed, decrepit whores gestured weary invitations, children shrieked mockery, narrow stares out of hard faces followed the strangers. " 'Tis less grim than you might think," Herun said, "and the inn we're bound for is easy on the purse."

It occupied what had once been a fine home. Plaster was mostly gone from bricks, few good tiles remained among cheap newer ones, mere bits were left of relief sculptures beside the entrance. Within, the former atrium, now the taproom, showed fragments of mosaic in its clay floor. The soot and grease of centuries hid nearly all fresco color, but a stain going halfway up the walls was unmistakable.

"Wotever 'appened 'ere?" Adminius wondered.

"Ancient damage done by the sea, I think, before the rampart was raised," Herun said. He gestured at a table. Four men sat benched there, drinking. They were weather-beaten, knobby-handed, coarsely clad. "Greeting," Herun called to them, and they grunted a response. He and his comrades took the opposite end, ten or twelve feet from them. "Fishers," he whispered. "Decent in their way, but given to overweeningness. Best we leave them be."

Candles added what they could to light that seeped in through thin-scraped membranes stretched across windows. The air was acrid with smoke, heavy with odors from tallow and an adjoining kitchen. A man who must be the landlord sent a boy pattering over to ask what the newcomers wanted. "The mead is not bad," Herun recommended. "Beware the wine." He gave their order, and paid when the goblets arrived. "Be this round on my reckoning. Hail and haleness."

A woman emerged from an inner room and made hip-swaying approach. She was comely enough, aside from greasy hair and shabby gown. "Why, Herun, dear," she warbled through a broad smile, "welcome. Where have you been all this time? Who are your friends?"

"Mayhap you've heard the Romans are back amongst us," the mariner replied. "They came with the new King. Here are two of them. Adminius and Cynan."

She widened her eyes. "Romans! Ooh, how *won*derful!" She sat down opposite them, next to Herun. "Be you welcome too, you sightly fellows. If 'tis a romp you'd have, you've sought the right place. I am Keban."

"Where are the others?" Herun asked. "This is seldom a busy hour for you."

"True." She cast a surly glance at the fishermen. "They *say* the catch was poor and they've naught to spend on more than a stoup or two. Well, as for the girls, Rael is under the moon; says she feels too badly to do *any*thing. Silis got pregnant and has not yet recovered from having that taken care of. So I'm by myself." Suggestively: "I long for company."

"You shall have some," Herun laughed. "But first let's give you the drink you expect." He signalled the potboy.

Adminius told Cynan more or less what he had heard. The youth's nostrils flared. He gripped his cup till knuckles stood white above the wood, drew shaky breath, and said deep in his throat: "By the Hooded Three, but I've gotten a need on that march we made! What would they say if I laid her down right on the floor?"

"They'd say you were a fool, wearing out yer knees when a straw tick goes with the rental. 'Old it in a bit, lad. You'll enjoy it the more."

The door opened and banged shut again. A man strode in with a sailor's rolling gait. His garb was rough too, and bore a slight smell of fish. Medium tall, he was broad and powerful; his shoulders, chest, and arms might have fitted a bear, his hands were like capstans which had each raised five anchors. Rugged features and green eyes stood within hair and beard whose blackness declared him still fairly young, however much wind and sun and spindrift had turned his skin to leather.

The fishers rose, reseated themselves, and made gestures of invitation. He smiled and waved but steered for the Roman end of the table. " 'Oo's that?" Adminius asked.

"I know him a little," Herun murmured. "His name is Maeloch."

"Why do they defer to 'im? I thought you said their sort make way for no one."

"He is a Ferrier. A Ferrier of the Dead. No bad wight, no bully, but have a care of his pride."

"Mead!" the man roared in a voice to carry through gales. He reached the table, looked down at Herun, and touched his breast. The navy man did likewise. It was the formal Ysan salutation between equals. "Well met," Maeloch rumbled genially. "Who be these strangers?"

"You'd not heard?" Herun replied.

"Nay, I've been at sea this sennight past. Great run of mackerel off Merrow Shoals, if ye can ride out the weather. Now I've a raging thirst and a rampant stand."

"Your wife—"

"Ah, Betha nears her time again. Another mouth to feed; but still, I'd not risk harming the sprat by pounding on her." Maeloch went to rumple Keban's hair. She purred and rubbed her cheek against his thigh. He planked himself down beside her. The mead came for the two of them. "Hail and haleness, all!"

Goblets lifted, except for Cynan's. He glowered, and angrily asked Adminius for translation.

Meanwhile Maeloch's right hand fondled Keban, his left wielded his drink, and he drew from Herun an account of what had happened. It did not quite seem to please him. "A new King, aye, that's long overdue," he growled. "Colconor was offal. Were it nay that no Ysan may, I'd've challenged him myself—well, nay, I suppose not; that would've meant forsaking my Betha." He nodded stiffly at the legionaries. "But if this King is a swab for Rome— Well, we can hear ye out, ye twain, after I've done my first tupping."

"I want her now," Cynan exclaimed. "Adminius, you said you'd help. Make her price good while I—" He scrambled to his feet, swung past the table end, and tugged at Keban's gown. "Where do we go?"

Surprised, she could only titter. Maeloch tensed. "Hoy, what's this? Let her be!"

"The soldier's want seems more urgent than yours," Herun said hastily. "They were many days on their way hither, these guests. Come, drain your cup and let me buy you another."

"What, me betread wet decks . . . after a Roman?" Maeloch heaved his bulk up like a spyhopping whale. He stepped over the bench. His right hand closed on Cynan's tunic and cloak, under the throat, and hauled the Briton around. His left fist drew back. "Belay that and begone!"

Cynan whitened. He hissed. His knife came forth. "Let me go, you filthy fishmonger!"

Herun and Adminius exchanged glances. They leaped, Ysan to Ysan, Roman to Roman. From behind, each threw a lock on the arms of his man. Neither could have held it long, but their voices prevailed: "Stop, easy, easy, are you mad, would you bring the watch down on us, let's talk, let's be civilized—" When they felt thews slacken a little, they released their grasps. The antagonists backed a few steps apart and stood with heads thrust out between shoulders, breath harsh in mouths.

Herun: "Maeloch, hold. He's scarcely more than a boy. Believe me, I knew these wights, they've not come to oppress or levy on us. Fain would they be our friends. In the names of the Three, peace!"

Adminius: "Get yer 'ead out o' yer arse, Cynan! If the centurion 'eard you'd started a brawl over a 'ore, this early in the game, 'e'd 'ave yer flogged till beetles could dance on yer ribs. Sit down. We'll call for a new round, and maybe toss a coin to see 'oo goes first."

Everybody eased—also the fishers at the far end, who had sprung clear and made ready for general turmoil. A much relieved landlord offered a free serving. This brought men together. In the beginning they laughed too loudly and slapped each other's backs too heartily, but soon they felt fellowship. Maeloch and Cynan could do no less than swap a rueful handclasp in the Ysan manner. Between Herun and Adminius, the full story of the legionaries came forth, from the war at the Wall and onward. It fascinated the fishers, and required more mead for soothing of gullets. If most purses were lean, Herun and Adminius stood ready to buy. The tale reminded Maeloch of a song about a boatman who had lured a shipful of marauding Saxons onto a reef. He sang it for his Roman mates. Not to be outdone, Cynan unlimbered his harp and offered a ballad from his homeland. He did it well. The company shouted for more.

Keban sat by herself, waiting. One hand cradled her cheek, the fingernails of the other drummed the table.

4

Soon after Imbolc, Niall maqq Echach, King over Mide, left Temir accompanied by his body servants, warriors, learned men, and eldest son Breccan. He did not follow the Queen and their children to that one of his halls which she sought. Instead, he made progress around his realm—sunwise, as he must under gess—and was more than a month about it. This was not very commonly done after the first time, when a King was newly consecrated; but Niall said he had been so much away at war that he should get to know his folk better and right any wrongs they were suffering.

Indeed he listened, and not only to the powerful men who gave him lodging. Although he never gainsaid the judge in any district, which was not within his right, he heard disputes brought to those worthies, and sometimes offered advice in private before settlement was decreed. His gifts were generous to the poor as well as lavish to the mighty. He was grave or boisterous as occasion demanded, thus making friends among men; and after a night or three, many a young woman came to feel a warmth for him which glowed from her into her father, brothers, or husband.

Some people murmured that he was being shrewd. Although the

weather was fair for this time of year and there was no reason to expect
lean months, sooner or later they came. The blame for it was less likely to
fall on the King if he was well-beloved. Restless Niall might not be at
home then to defend himself against charges of evildoing that had angered the Gods. Moreover, his repulse last summer, while not inglorious,
called for explaining if he would have warriors follow him willingly on his
next adventure.

That he planned one was beyond doubt. Already at Temir he had been
in secret talk with men of several different kinds. While his train made its
slow way through the countryside, messengers often came speeding with
word he did not reveal. Thereafter he was apt to ride off, gazing afar, with
none but his guards along and they forbidden to speak to him.

Gossip buzzed. It swelled to a tide when Niall entered Qóiqet nUlat
without asking leave of any lord therein, sought Mag Slecht, and made
blood sacrifice to Cromb Króche and the twelve lesser idols. Although he
wended back peacefully enough, word of this caused swords to be whetted.

And so in due course he reached the sea, rode down to Clón Tarui, and
took lodging at the public hostel there. Day after day he abode, still
meeting quietly with men who came and went, but still keeping his own
counsel. Since the River Ruirthech that emptied into the bay just south of
this place marked the border of the Lagini, the idea arose that Niall had
in mind to enforce the Bóru tribute. It had gone unpaid for many years.
True, his following here was too small to overcome a whole Fifth of Ériu;
but was he making a threat, or was he sending forth scouts and spies to
gather knowledge for a campaign in summer? When hints or questions
reached him, Niall simply smiled.

The day came at last when he and Breccan had gone hunting, and
returned toward eventide. They had started a red deer in the woods
northward and chased it down in a breakneck halloo; Breccan's sling had
knocked half a dozen squirrels from their trees; everyone was weary and
happy. Through cleared lands they now rode, broad and gently rolling
acres of pasture and field, bestowed on the hostelkeeper so that that person might give free guesting to travelers. The small round houses of tenants huddled here and there, wattle-and-daub beneath cones of thatch
through which smoke seeped into the wind. It had been a day for rain-
squalls and continued blustery, although a low sun struck rays like brass
through the wrack that scurried overhead. Horses and hounds plodded in
the mire of the road. But when the bay gleamed in sight, and the great
oblong of the hostel, whinnies and bellings arose, hoofs and feet pounded,

the huntsmen forgot how wet and cold they were and lifted a shout of their own.

Suddenly Niall stiffened on the horseblanket. Out of the brume upon the eastern sea, a pair of sails had appeared, above a lean hull—a currach, bearing down on Clón Tarui. "It's reckless early in the year they've been abroad," said a guard.

"It . . . is . . . not, I am thinking," Niall answered slowly. *"Hai!"* He struck heels against his mount. The beast plucked up strength and broke into gallop. Breccan's alone could keep pace; the warriors fell behind. Niall did not heed. Nor did he stop until on the shore.

By then the currach was near. It was large, two-masted, the leather of it holding a dozen men. Sails rattled down on their yards, oars bit water, and the craft drove up onto the strand. One man leaped forth first. Niall sprang from horseback. They ran to each other and embraced.

"Ah, welcome, welcome, darling!" the King cried. "It's grand you are looking—and all the lads home alive, too! How went the quest?"

The newcomer stepped back. He was bony, sinewy, auburn hair and beard slightly grizzled around a face that weather had seamed and bedarkened. Despite that and his drenched garb, he bore himself with an easy arrogance. "Bucketing over the sea and trudging over the land," he laughed. "Yet well worth the trouble. What you thought might come to pass has done so indeed, indeed. The Roman soldiers have hailed Maximus their lord, and he has left for Gallia with the most of them."

"Ha-a-ah!" Niall roared.

"Slow, dear master, slow. It does not seem they will be stripping their defenses bare for this—not soon—and I'll be giving you some news about the Saxons, also."

Niall smote fist in palm. "Nonetheless—!"

The skipper arrived to pay his respects. Niall greeted him well and spoke of venison at the feast tonight. Meanwhile the thin man's glance fell on Breccan, who stood aquiver. "And might this be your son, my lord?" he asked. "It's long since I saw him last, and he a babe in arms."

"It is he," Niall replied. "Breccan, my dear, you will not be remembering, but here is Uail maqq Carbri, a trusty man who has gone on many a mission for me—though never, maybe, one that needed as much boldness and wiliness as this."

"Och, it was not that hard, so don't you be daunting the lad about such things," Uail said, cockily rather than modestly. "I know my way about over there, and the speech—a bit of the Latin, too. It was mostly to wander as a harmless pedlar, watching, listening, sometimes getting a soul drunk or furious till his tongue ran free. There was no big secret."

Niall's look blazed across the waters like the last stormy sun-rays. "Maximus withdrawn," he breathed. "We'd likely not be wise to strike Alba this year, at his heels—not yet—but southward, Roman will be at war with Roman—" Again he bellowed. "Ha-a-ah!"

Breccan could hold himself in no longer. And he saw his chance. He seized Niall's hand. "Father," he cried, "I am going along, am I not? You promised! I shall help you get your revenge!"

Niall swept the slender form to his breast. "You shall that!"

He let go, stood for a heartbeat or two, frowned, then shrugged. "It seems Medb will have it so," he muttered. Straightening, he turned to Uail and the sailors. "Come," he said, "make your boat fast and let's be off to the hostel. The keeper is the widow Morigel, and a fine table she sets. Afterward . . . I will be querying you about everything you have learned."

Breccan danced and whooped.

X

1

The chamber in the basilica where the Council of Suffetes met could have held many more than it did this day. It was ornamented only by its stone paneling, but that was superb, mica-sparked granite, veined marble, mottled serpentine, intricate onyx. Large windows admitted ample greenish light. Under the barrel-vaulted ceiling, sound carried extraordinarily well. On either side of a central passage, padded benches in tiers looked down to the farther end. There stood a dais whereon rested a throne. Behind it, the wall curved to form a bay. Against that wall were statues of the Triad, ten feet tall, Taranis on the right, Belisama in the middle, Lir represented on the left by a mosaic slab out of which stared a kraken.

When everyone else was seated, Gratillonius entered, magnificently robed, bearing the Hammer, the Key in view on his breast, but his head encircled by a fillet rather than the royal crown. His legionaries followed in full armor. The crash of hobnails resounded along the passage. At the dais they deployed right and left and came to attention behind it, in front of the towering Gods. Gratillonius mounted the platform and took stance before the throne. Silence thundered down upon the gathering. He raised the Hammer and intoned as he had been taught: "In the name of Taranis, peace. May His protection be on us."

The Nine sat together in blue gowns and white headdresses at the left end of the foremost benches. Vindilis rose, spread out her arms with palms downward, and responded: "In the name of Belisama, peace. May Her blessing be on us."

By this Gratillonius knew that today she would lead the Gallicenae, speaking for them except when some other had reason to enter the discussion. He wondered why they had elected her instead of, say, wise old Quinipilis. In Vindilis's hatchet features he read an intensity that might prove troublesome. But the Queens moved in their own ways, which it was not for anyone else to question.

Vindilis reseated herself. At the right end of the interrupted arc, Hannon Baltisi stood up. The gray beard flowed from his furrowed countenance over a robe worked to suggest a heavy sea, white manes on green waves. He was not a priest, for the God Whose worldly affairs he guided had none, unless one reckoned every skipper of Ys. But his it was to say, as Captain, "In the name of Lir, peace. May His wrath not be on us," and bring the butt of a trident booming down on the floor before he too sat.

Gratillonius handed the Hammer to Eppillus, whom he had designated his Attendant, and stood for several pulsebeats looking the assemblage over. Besides the high priestesses, it numbered thirty-three, all male and all drawn from the thirteen Suffete clans. (He had learned that those corresponded somewhat to the Roman senatorial rank, save that nobody could buy or wheedle or even earn his way into them. Entry was strictly by birth, marriage in the case of a woman, or adoption in the case of a child.) Soren Cartagi was conspicuous among them in the red robe and miter of his role as Speaker for Taranis. Like Hannon, he represented the corporation of his temple, though he had no ritual part in the proceedings today. He could also, if he chose, argue on behalf of the Great House of Timbermen which was his.

Three men belonged ex officio to the Council—Adruval Tyri, Sea Lord, head of the navy and marines; Cothortin Rosmertai, Lord of Works, who oversaw the day-by-day administration of city business; Iram Eliuni, Lord of Gold, whose treasury function had become almost nominal. The Sea Lord wore ordinary Ysan clothes of good material, his colleagues had decked themselves in togas.

A few more togas were visible among the rest. The majority had selected robes, or else shirt and trousers. Not every garment was sumptuous, for Suffete status did not necessarily mean wealth. The delegates from guilds had themselves been fisher, sailor, wagoner, artisan, laborer, or the like. Even some heads of Great Houses had been poor in their youths. However, most had not, for these firms generally stayed in the same families through many generations.

Thirty-three men. Gratillonius's gaze searched across them. No two were alike; and yet— The aristocrats of Ys had consciously set barriers to inbreeding. None could marry within his or her clan. Brides from outside were usually made welcome. A couple might adopt a promising youngster from among the commons or the Osismii, in hopes of invigorating the bloodline. Nonetheless, again and again he met the "Suffete face," nar-

row, high-cheeked, aquiline, a memory in flesh and bone of lost Phoeni-
cia.

Well. Best to start. He remained standing but assumed an easy posture.
"Greeting," he said in Ysan. "First will I thank you for your forbearance.
This honorable Council meets four times annually, I hear, around equinox and solstice. Thus you've but lately completed a session, and have
affairs of your own awaiting your attention. Although the King possesses
the right to order a special assembly when he sees fit, I have striven to
make clear that mine today is for the welfare and safety of Ys, and not
capriciously in future will I call you back. Rather will I hold frequent
private conference about our shared concerns as these arise; and ever will
you find me heedful of you."

He smiled. "I trust we can finish within a few hours. You know why we
are here. 'Twould expedite matters if we, or at least I, used Latin. Else
must I slowly mangle my way through your language, which does it no
credit. My hope is that soon I shall be in better command of it. Meanwhile, has anybody aught in disfavor of Latin?"

Hannon lifted a hand. Gratillonius recognized him.

"Myself, no," he said in an Armorican seaman's form of that tongue.
"There must be some who've not wielded it since school days, but if they
may talk Ysan, well enough. My lord King, when you've trouble understanding something, I suggest you ask for translation. Likewise for whoever don't follow you very readily."

"We need a single interpreter," Soren pointed out, "or we will be babbling into each other's mouths."

"I propose Queen Bodilis," came from Vindilis.

"She's both learned and quick-witted. Are you willing, Sister?"

"That I am," replied Bodilis in scholar's Latin.

Gratillonius regarded her. An attractive woman, he thought, seems to
be in her mid-thirties, best years of a woman's life, my father always told
me. The knowledge that he would bed her stirred him—unexpectedly,
when Dahilis sat right beside her. Bodilis returned his glance with calm,
candor, and a slight smile.

He cleared his throat. "Thank you," he said. "Let me begin by explaining my purposes. I've already done that as best I was able, to several
among you. But for the rest, it could be that what you heard at second or
third remove has suffered in transmission. Afterward we can discuss everything, and I hope at the end you'll formally ratify my program, and
then take a share in it."

Increasingly, he felt sure of himself. This did not seem too different
from addressing the soldiers of his century on the day of a mission. He

wondered for an instant if, somehow, the fact of cooperation with Bodilis had heartened him. However brave a front he presented, when he first entered this chamber the strangeness of all that was around him had been daunting.

"I realize you've had well-nigh every sort of man for King in Ys," he went on. "As for myself, you know I am a legionary: Gaius Valerius Gratillonius, centurion, hitherto serving in Britannia. There, last year I helped kick the Scoti and Picti back from the Wall. I've heard what pests the Scoti are to you also. I'm a Briton, Belgic, of curial family; and I've visited Armorica in the past.

"Now you should be quite clear about this, that I did not come here with any intention of making myself your King. It happened. Frankly, I'm still not sure just how it happened. But we've got the fact of it before us, solid as your headlands. And . . . it may be through the favor of the Gods. Not many people seem to have liked Colconor." That drew a few chuckles. "I don't know if I can be another Hoel, but I mean to try."

He took up earnestness as he would have taken up his shield: "My task was, and is, to be the prefect of Rome in Ys. You haven't seen my like since time out of mind. Nevertheless, the treaty—the Oath—remains in force. Ys is a foederate of Rome. It has duties toward Rome, which it may be called upon to fulfill. And Rome has duties toward Ys, which I am also here to see fulfilled. To that end, it may prove valuable that I've won the powers of your King.

"Not that I intend to abuse them, nor throw my weight around as prefect. My assignment is simple. There is reason to fear trouble in the Empire. Gallia in particular may well be in upheaval. I cannot imagine you'd want Ys drawn into that. As far as possible, your city has always kept aloof. My task is to lead you in staying at peace. No more, no less. For that, we cannot sit passive. If Roman Armorica—western Armorica, at least—if it becomes embroiled, Ys can hardly stay out. And Rome, which I serve, will take yet another wound, a wound that could prove hard to staunch.

"What Ys must do is lend its aid to the cause of peace, of order. Legates and governors elsewhere may wish to take sides in the fight. We need to keep them home. A word here, a bribe there, a show of naval strength yonder—that should suffice. What exactly shall we do? I plan to work that out in concert with the leaders of Ys, and then get it done.

"That's all. Later we'll consider together what else we can undertake, in the better day that I believe lies ahead. But first we must weather the storm that's brewing. I want your agreement to this, followed by your best efforts—under me, the prefect of Rome and now your King—to carry out the mission. For the welfare of Rome and of Ys!

"Thank you."

He folded his arms and waited. After a hush, Soren said, "My lady Bodilis, could you put that in Ysan for the benefit of any who may not have caught every word?"

"I can paraphrase," replied the Queen. "Meanwhile let each of us be thinking of what this portends."

She stood and spoke. Gratillonius admired her handling of the matter; she seemed to express things more clearly and compactly than he had himself.

When she finished, a buzzing went along the benches, until Sea Lord Adruval declared bluntly, "We can't navigate in a fog. And foggy you've been, O King, when we talked before. What is this menace we're supposed to prepare against?"

"I have not said, because I am not party to secrets of state, nor am I a prophet to read the future," Gratillonius answered. "What my commander gave me to understand was that great events will soon happen, and they may get violent. I pray it be less bad than the Magnentian War, and the outcome better. But we must wait for word, and hold ourselves ready to act on it."

Vindilis did not signal request to be recognized. Silence fell immediately upon all others when the spokeswoman of the Gallicenae announced in a steely tone: "I can tell you more than that. Gratillonius's superior, who dispatched him to us, is Magnus Clemens Maximus, Duke of the Britains. The legions in that diocese have hailed him Augustus. They have crossed over to Gallia and are warring for the purple. Gratillonius,"—her eyes burned at him—"you are not stupid. I suppose he never told you outright, but you must have understood; and you are Maximus's man."

The Suffetes gasped. Thundersmitten, the King of Ys cried, "How can you know?"

"By the same means we knew of your coming." Vindilis gestured toward the woman on her left. "Forsquilis went in a Sending."

"What's this? Priestess, we've only your naked word."

Soren's ruddy visage darkened. "Do you call the Gallicenae liars?" he shouted. A growl as of shingle under surf lifted around him.

Quinipilis rose, leaned on her staff, raised her free hand for attention. "Be not hasty," she said in Ysan. "Gratillonius is new among us. He means well. And he *is* King and prefect. Give him a chance to learn."

The centurion wet his lips. "I'm certainly willing to listen," he said. "Do explain."

"That were best done in private," Vindilis answered, "between Forsquilis and yourself."

"Well—that is, if the lady agrees—" Gratillonius's look went to the Pallas Athene face of the seeress. No expression relieved the coldness of its lines when she nodded. But Dahilis, even in this moment, flashed him an impish grin and jerked a thumb upward.

"Aye, this is no place to reveal a mystery," said Bodilis in Ysan. "The Power reaches beyond speech. Let us go on with the business of our assembly. At eventide Forsquilis can show the King what she chooses."

A mollified Soren agreed: "Very well. Shall we stipulate that the Empire is again at civil war? Since Maximus could not arrange to rally Armorica behind him as he has the Britannic legions, it is to his advantage that Armorica stay neutral while he campaigns east and south of it. Gratillonius's orders are to assure this. He may be right about it being best for Ys too, provided we do not provoke resentment in the Imperium, should Maximus fail. Let us discuss it, and then go on to ways and means."

Gratillonius stood soldierly and helpless while debate began.

2

He could not guess what awaited him at the house of Forsquilis. They walked there in silence, unaccompanied, after the meeting dissolved. Dusk lay blue upon the world; the earliest stars trembled forth. From this high part of the city he could see over the battlemented bowl of night which it had become, to a mercury glimmer in the harbor basin and the vast sheening of Ocean beyond. Right and left gloomed the headlands; out on Cape Rach, fire burned atop the pharos, red, unrestful as a seeking eye. Air was cool, slightly sweetened by a lilac in a stone basin at her doorstep, and wholly quiet.

Lamplight spilled yellow across the paving as a manservant bowed the two inside. "Dinner is ready, my lady and lord," he said. Savory odors confirmed it.

Forsquilis glanced at Gratillonius. He saw that her eyes were gray, like those of the Minerva—the Athene whom she so much resembled. No, he thought confusedly, that Goddess wears a helmet and carries a spear and shield. But what Gorgon's head may this woman bring forth, to turn men into stone?

Her Latin was fluent: "I sent a messenger during the day, directing a repast be prepared. Does this please the King?"

He attempted a jest. "Can't you read the answer in my mind?"

Her solemnity reproved him. "No, unless by strong magic, which might not work; and without dire need, it would be no decent thing to do."

Flushing, he gave his cloak to the servant, as she did hers, and they went directly to the triclinium. Atrium and corridor showed bucolic scenes that he suspected she had never bothered to have altered, nor had those who lived here before her, for they looked old. The dining room likewise was antique; but perhaps she found jarring whatever pattern was on the floor, since reed mats covered it. The furnishings were table and chairs, Ysans never having reclined at their meals. On a richly decorated cloth stood costly ware. He wondered if this was on his account and ordinarily Forsquilis ate austerely. Her slenderness suggested it.

He wondered, as well, just why she reverted to her mother tongue while they settled opposite each other: "Difficult has today been for you. Shall we now take our ease and refresh ourselves?"

"You are . . . considerate," he responded, deciding to stay with Latin. Why burden himself needlessly in a taut situation? "I'll try. Though it has for certain been difficult. Pardon me if I can't put matters aside at once."

It was not that the Council had, in the end, denied him support. It was that that had been considered, and finally given, almost as if he, the prefect, were a mere courier—at most, an ambassador: as if Ys were not subordinate to Rome but deciding independently that its interest lay in emerging to some degree from the secrecy it had kept around itself.

For the first time, he saw Forsquilis's lips curve upward. "Think you 'twas my fault? Well, in a way. But would you not have done the same if you could, for Rome?"

A servant in livery of black and gold brought bowls and towels for the washing of hands. Another poured unwatered wine, a third set forth appetizers, boiled shrimp, pickled eggplant, raw fish, sauce of garum and minced onion. They ate well in Ys who could afford it, not gluttonously but well.

Gratillonius lifted his beaker. Relief swept through him. "Right! And there's no real conflict between us. I admit being, m-m, surprised. It's hard to believe you'd know what Maximus is doing before I myself have heard. I held back the information about his intentions because, frankly, I wanted the upper hand, if anything untoward happened. But you'd have gotten it as soon as I received whatever word he sends. He will be good for the Empire, and that means he'll be good for Ys."

"We trust so, we of the Sisterhood. We called on the Three to give us the right king, and you are the one They brought."

Gratillonius felt a shiver. He was of Rome, a soldier, a civilized and educated man. Maximus had ordered him here for excellent, logical reasons. He must not believe it had really been the work of alien Gods, and witches, and—He might have dismissed the idea if Forsquilis had raved at him or made mystical passes or done anything but sit there, more and more fair to behold, talking quite evenly— No, not that either. In her tone, in her eyes, there went ghosting something else. He could imagine that she lived on the fringe of the Otherworld.

He snatched after ordinariness. "Well, let's see if we can slack off as you propose. You've heard about me, but I know nothing about you. Tell me."

Her look dwelt long and seriously upon him. "Dahilis spoke true," she murmured at last. "You are a kindly man. You may well prove a second Hoel." And then it was as if a shudder of her own went beneath the controlled exterior. "Although the omens were obscure," she whispered. "But we live in such an age of breakup—"

He *would* not peer into those dim and lawless depths, not yet, not yet. He took a fragrant gulp and a pungent bite. They brought him back to the understandable earth. "You were wife to Hoel?" he asked.

She nodded. "The Sign came upon me when Quistilis died, a year before he did. I was fourteen. He was gentle. But I was bearing his child when he fell. What Colconor did, that caused me to lose it."

A red lump on the floor or in bed or the privy, that might have stirred for a minute, Gratillonius thought. Freezingly: She tells it in such calm, as if it happened to somebody else long ago. Her soul was withdrawn. Will it ever return?

"May I ask how old you are?" he said.

"Twenty winters."

Dahilis was not much younger. . . . "You are wise beyond your years, Forsquilis."

"I had nowhere else to go but into the arcane," she told him quietly.

—She showed him a little after the meal, during which they had discussed safe matters. (Not that that was dull; each had endlessness to talk about.) A curtained chamber, dark save for a lamp made out of a cat's skull, held within its weaving shadows a shelf of scrolls and codices, a female figurine in clay that she said was from ancestral Tyre, inscribed bones, herbs dried and bundled, flints that perhaps had been shaped by the Old Folk as some said or perhaps were thunderstones as others said. . . . "These things are not needful in themselves, Gratillonius." Her eyes glistened huge in the murk. "They are but teachers and helps. As I wait entranced, my spirit fares forth. It is a power that once belonged to every Queen. But in this age when the very Gods are troubled and faltering, it has only come to me. Do you remember an owl, of the great sort called eagle owl, at midnight above a glade in Armorica—?"

—In the bedroom she said gravely, "Let us hallow ourselves. Belisama be with us." When she unwound her headdress, he saw that her hair was golden-brown. When she let her gown fall, he saw that she was shapely.

The Bull arose. Fleetingly he remembered Dahilis. But this would be her wish.

All at once Forsquilis laughed aloud and pointed. "Oh, but the Goddess has been generous!"

Ugliness stabbed: how could she tell? She had known just Hoel and Colconor, had she not? Maybe, during the reign of the beast King, maybe her Sending had prowled into homes more happy?

No. He would not think further. He could not. The Bull was in him, the Bull was he.

Astonishment followed. With Dahilis he had gone slowly at first, soothing her fears, finding his way toward what pleased her. He had looked for this Athene to be likewise, if she did not simply lie there and accept. But she was hastily up against him, her hands seeking and urging. When he laid her down and entered her she yowled. In the morning he recalled the changeableness and unknown depths of the sea. His back was clawed red.

XI

1

A light rain turned the world cool and horizonless on the afternoon when Gratillonius came to call on Bodilis. She admitted him herself. "Welcome, lord King." Her tone and her smile made him believe she meant it.

Entering, he threw back the cowl of his cloak and undid the brooch. Beneath, he wore everyday Ysan garb lately tailored for him. Raindrops sparkled in the auburn curls of the beard he was growing. It still itched sometimes, but he had decided he should show his people every sign he could of his oneness with them. "I am sorry—" he began.

"O-oh, mother! Is *he* the King?" An eight-year-old girl darted from a doorway, tawny locks flying about an elven countenance.

"Now, Semuramat, bow like a proper lady," Bodilis said. Although warmth pulsed in her voice, the child obeyed at once, whereafter she stood staring out of enormous eyes.

"Greeting," the man said in Ysan. "I am . . . in truth your new step-father. For this is your mother, is she not? What is your name?"

"S-s-semuramat," the girl whispered. "My lord."

He saw her tremble. The Queens had kept their daughters away from Colconor as much as possible, which became nearly all the time; but there would have been an aura of hatred and terror. "Be not afraid, Semuramat," Gratillonius urged. "I expect we shall be happy together. Hm. Do you like horses?" She nodded twice and thrice. "Well, suppose you come for a ride on my saddlebow as soon as I have a free hour, and we'll get to know each other. Afterward we may perchance look into finding you a pony."

Bodilis laughed. "Don't overwhelm the poor creature!"

"I'd fain be the friend of this household," he replied earnestly. "As I was about to say, I'm sorry to have let seven days go by since the Council, ere sending word I would visit you now if you desired. You may have heard how I've been at work, getting to know the city's defenses above all. Three of those days I wasn't even in town, but riding around the hinterland on inspection. At night I'd fall asleep as if into a well." Alone. Not that purely male companionship and concerns were unwelcome, however much he missed Dahilis.

"Go back to your work, dear," Bodilis directed. When Semuramat had pattered off, she explained to Gratillonius, who was hanging his cloak on a peg: "My servants are presently out to fetch what's needful for a worthy supper. I've ever made my daughters help in the house. Princesses should have skills too."

"And discipline, of a loving sort," he approved.

She regarded him for some while before murmuring, "So you understand that also. Few are the men who'd show your regard for a woman's feelings. Oh, mine were never hurt; well did I see why you must stay absent. Yet it gladdens me what you have revealed of yourself."

The compliment made Gratillonius flush. He had been returning her look with pleasure. She was simply clad, in a gray-blue gown with silver stars embroidered on the neckline and sleeves. A belt of crimson mesh snugged the cloth around fullness of bosom, hip, and thigh. He admired the strong bones in her face, and her eyes were like those of Dahilis, her half-sister. There seemed to be no tensing, no qualms in her. She took his hand as naturally as if they had been man and wife for years. "Come," she said, "let us talk."

They passed from the entryroom to the atrium. He saw that, while its floor was antique Roman, the frescos were not. Their colors bright and fresh, they depicted a vividness of dolphins in waves, sea birds skimming overhead. The style was not quite representational; elongated lines and curves hinted at more than this world knew. Seeing him notice, she said with a touch of diffidence, "Mayhap I should not have covered up the old art. I did first copy it onto vellum, that future generations may have a record. But it was tedious stuff. Whoever inherits this house from me can get rid of mine if she dislikes it."

"What?" he exclaimed. "You painted it yourself?"

"I dabble at things. But come onward. 'Twould be most honorific to receive you in this chamber, but 'twill be more—real—if we seek to my scriptorium." Bodilis laughed. "Besides, Semuramat is not allowed there, not till she grows older and more careful. She's a darling, but she'd pester the life out of us."

"I gather you've other daughters."

Bodilis nodded. "Two. They are both wild to meet you, of course. But

Talavair is standing vigil at the Nymphaeum, and Kerna is at her studies in the temple. She'll be home for supper."

"The girls are . . . Hoel's?"

"All three. The Sign came upon me in Lugaid's reign, but he fell almost immediately afterward. Talavair will finish her vestal term this year. She has a young man picked out for herself. A year hence, I may well be a grandmother!"

"What of—Kerna, is that her name?"

"Oh, she's just fifteen, and studious. She intends to renew her vows at age eighteen and become a minor priestess. Not that that debars marriage. However, most men are reluctant to take a wife whose duties will often have her away from home. Former vestals who enter the priestess-hood most commonly do so after having been widowed."

They had left the atrium and gone down a hallway beyond. The layout of this house was similar though not identical to that of Dahilis's or Forsquilis's, and unlike the usual Roman. Bodilis opened a door and led Gratillonius through. He found a room nearly as spacious; later she would explain that she had had the wall removed between two former bedchambers. Lamps of a shape as graceful as her gait brightened the dullness that today seeped through windowpanes. One burned on a table, beneath a legged small pot that it kept warm. The oil was olive, nearly odorless. Flagons of wine and water stood beside it, glass goblets and earthenware cups, a plateful of titbits. Shelves around the walls held scrolls, codices, the portrait bust of a woman solemn and beautiful, ivory and bone miniatures of fleet animals. A much larger table filled the far end of the room. Writing materials littered it, open books, brushes and paints, botanical specimens, shells, rocks, a flute, a cat asleep in the middle of everything.

"Pray be seated," Bodilis said. "Would you thin your wine according to your taste?"

"What's in the pot?"

"An herbal infusion. I seldom drink wine save at supper, and then little." Bodilis smiled. "I fear you'll find me drab company."

"Contrariwise, I think." They took chairs. "I'm no heavy drinker myself, most times. May I try a cup of your brew?"

The tisane was fragrant and sweet-acrid, good on a chilly day like this. "I heard aright; you are a scholar," he remarked.

"Well, I enjoy learning things. Also out in the open—I love to ramble about the countryside or go forth in a boat—but nearsightedness does somewhat hinder me there."

"You seem at work on something literary."

"Translating the *Agamemnon* into Ysan. A pity that scarce any of us today read Greek, but better my poor words than no Aeschylus at all."

"How did you learn?"

"I taught myself, from a textbook and lexicon I had sent me. Eucherius, the Christian minister, gave me more instruction, and corrected my pronunciation. They still use Greek where he hails from in Italia." She grew quietly ardent. "Oh, Gratillonius, you have so much to tell too! What the folk of Britannia are like, their tales and songs and— For me 'tis twice wonderful that you are come."

He dropped his glance downward, into his cup, as if to seek an omen in its murkiness. "I think you will be mainly the teacher," he mumbled. "The Ysan language—"

"Already you handle it rather well. I might be able to help with vocabulary. We make much use of synonyms, for example."

"And the history, the lore, everything below the surface. That is why I —I wanted to visit you first."

"Ask me what you will," she sighed, "but remember I lack the wisdom of Quinipilis, the forcefulness of Vindilis, the witchcraft of Forsquilis, the charm of—Well, I'll try my best."

He heard pain in her voice, raised his eyes, and saw lines at the corners of her mouth, as if she struggled not to show what she felt. It came to him: I'm a blundering ass. She thinks I don't see anything in her but her mind. I never meant that. Jupiter thunder me, no! But if I instantly say she's lovely, she may suppose I'm only snorting after yet another new female body.

He groped his way forward. "Ah, let's talk a while like ordinary human beings. I want to know you, Bodilis. Tell me of your life."

She shrugged. "Naught to tell. 'Tis been well-nigh eventless."

He guessed that, of the Nine, she had had the most resources, the broadest reaches of escape for her spirit, during Colconor. He did not care to think about it. Instead—He tugged his chin. The whiskers were still too short, but he oughtn't scratch his face. Slowly, he said, "You remarked on your middle daughter's wish to remain with the temple after she's free to leave. Was that yours too, when you were a girl?"

The glance she gave him was startled. Then, inch by inch, she leaned back, smiled on him, finally found words. "Aye. The Sign did come upon me when I was the age that is Kerna's now; but ever had I been a child moody and solitary."

"Was that because of . . . the circumstances of your birth?"

Again she regarded him closely for a spell. "Gratillonius," she breathed at length, "you are a remarkable man. You truly are."

"Nay," he tried to laugh, " 'tis but that a military officer must needs gain some skill in guessing about people." He sobered. "Would you liefer not talk of this? I shan't press you."

She reached to stroke his hand. "Why should I hang back? Dahilis must have told you things, and . . . and if the Gods are willing, we will be together, you and the Sisterhood, for many years." Her look drifted off and came to harbor at the bust. "You know my father Wulfgar begot me on his daughter Tambilis. It was the will of Belisama, no sin among the Gallicenae, but I am told he fell to brooding, and within a year lay dead at the hands of Gaetulius. Certain it is that this left a shadow on my mother, who did not regain gladness until Hoel came. By him she had Dahilis-to-be, you recall. But hers had been a somber house for me to grow up in. I fled into my books and my walks and—all you see around you. My wish was to become a minor priestess, for life."

"Instead you became a Queen," he said low.

She colored. "Hoel made me, too, happy. Not that his was any great intellect. He confessed I could bewilder him. But he was gusty and kind and well knew how to make a girl purr. And his friends, his visitors, how they could talk of marvelous things and mighty deeds! He loved to invite foreigners to the palace; they blew in like winds off the sea. Later I began to frequent Star House—"

She broke off, snapped after air, finished bleakly: "Under Colconor, the Symposium kept my soul alive."

"Oh, my dear!" he said in pity.

She shook herself, confronted him, and retorted, "I ask for no balm, Gaius Valerius Gratillonius. My life has been better than most on this earth, despite everything." Her tone softened. "And now you are King."

Silence fell. He drained his cup and filled a goblet with wine, undiluted. Once more she looked away from him. Blood went in and out of the cheek he saw, like drumbeats. He knew what she was thinking of, and surely she knew that he did.

He cleared his throat. "Well. I see. Um-m . . . whose is yonder bust?"

"Why, Brennilis," Her relief was plain to hear. "Brennilis of the Vision, Brennilis of the Veil. 'Tis uncertain whether the portrait was done in her time or is imaginative, but I like to believe this is indeed how she appeared."

"Who was she?"

"You know not?"

"I am an ignoramus, remember."

"Well, then," she said cheerfully, "what better way to pass the hours ere we dine than for me to relate a little of the history of Ys?"

2

The oldest records were fragmentary, but tradition held that the site was discovered by Himilco when he came exploring up from Carthage some eight and a half centuries agone. Returning, he recommended that a colony be founded there. What Carthage required was a way station and naval base for its trade with the far North. Britannic tin, Gallic furs, German amber, honey, hides, tallow, timber, walrus and narwhal ivory, together with the Southern goods which paid for them, needed protection as well as transport.

No mere outpost could long be maintained at such a remove. Hence it must be a town, capable of feeding and defending itself. Since few of the then prosperous Phoenicians were willing to leave home, they recruited widely about the Mediterranean lands. Prominent among those who immigrated in the early decades were Babylonians fleeing the Persians who conquered and destroyed their city, and Egyptians resentful of Persian rule.

Legend said that when Himilco was first investigating the region, men of his were slain in their camp every night. At last he tracked down the monster that was doing this thing, and the sailors put an end to it. The creature had laired in a passage grave. The Old Folk whose bones lay there, grateful to be at peace again, promised that settlement here should flourish as long as the dwellers were likewise at peace with the Gods; but if ever there was a falling out, the sea would reclaim its own.

Perhaps because of this, the city was consecrated to Ishtar, for She was powerful over all the elements and was the Star of the Sea. Soon afterward the mixed colonists identified Her with Isis and established an order of priestesses to serve Her.

Otherwise the community was subject to Carthage, though at its distance this was nominal, amounting to little more than a governor from the motherland. As it grew and enlarged its own trade, wealthy men began to chafe under even so light a yoke.

More or less at the same time as the founding of the city, the Celts had arrived, overrunning the aboriginal population and intermingling with it to produce the Gauls. The aristocrats of the new tribes were generally descended from the invaders. It was natural for the city to make alliance with neighbor natives against further newcomers. Wars and raids had harmed those nearby folk enough that they were willing to accept Punic leadership.

By now the name "Beth-Ishtar" or "Beth-Isis" had become shortened to "Ys."

The city was often endangered, more than once besieged. Yet, supplying itself by sea, it outwaited the enemy Celts, who never were very good at sitting still. Water was the worst problem, a fact that may have enhanced the sacredness of its sources in the minds of the people—although the Gauls venerated springs and streams too. The constant need for fighters and workers, in a commonalty still small, bred repugnance for the practice of sacrificing children to Baal Melqart, and eventually its discontinuance. However, prophecy and tradition agreed that from time to time some great blood offering must be made the Gods.

Gradually warfare eased off. While rivalry with the seagoing Veneti remained strong and occasionally flared into battle, Ys developed ties to the Osismii, as that mingled breed of Old Folk and Celts called themselves. Intermarriage became frequent, deities were identified with each other, rites and institutions conjoined, the very language of the city Gallicized.

In Ys the Triad became paramount among Gods. Ishtar-Isis most often bore the name Belisama, which meant "the Brightest One." Melqart assumed the name and attributes of the Celtic sky God Taranis. Lir, Whose cult was more ancient than colony or tribe, took unto Himself the awe and dread of the sea.

These evolutions were not barbarizations. They went hand in glove with political changes. Increasingly occupied against Rome, Mother Carthage gave Ys ever less consideration. Finally the magnates expelled the governor and established a Council of Suffetes on the Phoenician model. For the head of state, they took from various Gauls the idea of the King of the Wood—who was ordinarily no more than a figurehead, and whose death in battle replaced the former sacrifice of children.

The Sisterhood of the Nine grew from both Punic and Celtic roots. It was recruited from among the daughters and granddaughters of Queens, albeit most of the latter were born to ordinary men. Such a girl took holy orders at age seven and served as a vestal until age eighteen. She generally lived at home, but went to temple school and, when old enough, spent days and nights on end in religious duties within the city or at the Nymphaeum. At the close of her term, she was free to do whatever she liked—unless first the Sign had appeared on her and she had been wedded to the King and enrolled in the Gallicenae. After the third generation a given line of female descent was released from all obligation, for then the blood of Incarnate Taranis was thinned down to mere humanness.

If she chose, upon completion of her vestalhood a princess could renew her vows, or at any later time, and become a minor priestess. The temple would also accept other volunteers who qualified, train them, advance them according to what abilities they showed; but of course no such outsider would ever become a Queen.

Ys looked upon vestalhood as a divine privilege. It had its worldly benefits as well. Besides an excellent education, a maiden received a generous stipend. On going into civil life she got additional gold and goods, as a dowry for herself or investment capital if she did not elect marriage. The temple could well afford that, for much of the wealth of the state flowed into it from holdings, offerings, and bequests.

Ysan commerce waxed. The city commanded only meager natural resources, other than what it wrested from the waters, but skilled workers turned imported raw materials into wares that, exported, won high prices. Merchantmen on charter and adventurers among the barbarians brought in wealth of their own. When Rome finally sowed salt where Carthage had been, it made no large difference to Ys . . . although some folk wept.

For a hundred or more years afterward, the city prospered. It had no imperial ambitions; it was content with its modest hinterland and outlying island of Sena. Nor did it need more than a small, efficient navy, chiefly for convoy and rescue duty—when its Gallicenae could raise a storm at will. Its ships went trading and freighting throughout the North; likewise throve its manufactures, brokerages, entrepôts; and its poets, artists, dreamers, magicians.

Yet the sea at whose bosom it lay was ever rising. . . .

The Veneti had always been troublesome. When Julius Caesar came conquering, Ys gave him substantial help against them. When he had crushed and decimated those foes, he visited the city in person.

What happened then would be hidden from the future. Brennilis of the Gallicenae had had a vision while in a prophetic trance, and somehow she prevailed upon the tough and skeptical Roman. He actually appointed a soldier to slay the King of the Wood and succeed in that office—a young favorite of his, thus a sacrifice on the part of them both. Other things which were done required eternal silence: for Belisama had revealed that a new age was come to Ys. Archivists of the city believed that this was why Caesar made no mention of it in his writings.

The upshot was that Ys became a foederate of Rome, paid a reasonable tribute, accepted a prefect and his staff, enjoyed the benefits of the Roman peace, and otherwise continued its wonted life.

To be sure, as Armorica was Romanized, there were effects upon this city too. On the whole they were benign. Indeed, Rome saved Ys from destruction. The vision of Brennilis warned that sea level would mount and mount until waves rolled over everything here, were measures not taken. As defensible as it was between its headlands, this site ought not to be abandoned; but already people were moving to higher ground.

From the time of her revelation, onward through her long life, Brennilis was the effective ruler of Ys. In her old age she won for her people the help of Augustus Caesar. To her he sent his best engineers, that they erect a wall against the waters. They did much else while they were there, but the wall and the gate were their real accomplishment, for which the city gave them a triumph.

That labor did not go easily. Besides the sea to contend with, they had the folk. The Romans thought it ridiculous that the wall be built as high as Brennilis demanded; they did not live to see tides eventually surge where she had foretold. Nor could they understand why they must not use enduring concrete. They insisted on it, and not until storms had repeatedly wrecked their work and snatched lives from among them did they yield. True, they then wrought honestly, in dry-laid blocks of stone so well shaped and fitted that a knife blade could not slip between. But they never understood why.

Brennilis and her Sisters did. In her Vision, Lir had told her that Ys must remain hostage to Him, lest it forsake its Gods in the eldritch days to come. He would only allow a wall that He could, at need, break down, for the drowning of a city gone faithless.

The gate was no defiance of this; Ys required one if it would receive ships as of yore. Sealed in copper, oak endured for many a decade. Sometimes the doors must be replaced—machinery and multitudinous workers doing it in a few hours of the lowest tide and deadest calm, followed by three days and nights of festival—but the necessity came seldom, and Ys abided.

Yet also, as lifetimes passed, it drew ever more behind the Veil of Brennilis. This too had been part of her apocalypse, that the Gods of Ys were haughty and aloof, that They would not demean Themselves to plead for worshippers against a new God Who was to come, but would, rather, hold Their city apart unto Themselves. For all its splendor and prosperity, Ys grew obscure. Chronicles which described it gradually crumbled away without fresh copies having been made, burned in accidental fires, were misplaced, were stolen and never recovered, were scraped clean so that the vellum might be reused for a Gospel. Curiously few Roman writers ever referred to it; and of those who did, their works had a similar way of becoming lost.

A part of this may simply have been due regained autonomy, as Roman commerce and government began to fall apart. Longer and longer grew the periods during which the Emperors saw no reason to send a prefect; at last, none came. Payment of the tribute was more and more often delayed by bad communications; at last, Septimius Severus remitted it altogether, in thanks for help the city had given him against his rival Albinus. That was the final intervention of any consequence that Ys had made. Thereafter it looked to its own.

But it was not totally isolated. The storms that racked the Empire inevitably troubled Ys as well. Trade shrank, Scotic and Saxon raiders harried the waters and the coasts, inland barbarians pressed westward, evangelists of Christ led men away from the Gods of their fathers. Among the Gallicenae arose a feeling that they had come to the end of still another age. What would the new one bring? None could foreknow. Like a creature of the sea, Ys drew into its shell and waited.

3

By candlelight in the bedroom, Bodilis showed no mark of being past her youth, save for maturity itself. Smiling, she went to Gratillonius. "How can I best make you welcome?" asked her husky voice.

She responded to him, in movement of loins and hands, in soft outcries; but always there was something about her that cared more for him than for herself; and before they slept, she murmured in his ear, "I pray the Goddess that I be not too old for bearing of your child."

XII

1

Suddenly fog blew out of the west. Then wind died while cloud thickened. *Osprey* rolled to the swell, the eyes painted on her bows as blindfolded as eyes in the skulls of the men aboard her. Barely did sight reach from stem to stern, and the masthead swayed hidden. It was as if that formless gray also swallowed sound. There was nothing to hear but slap of waves on strakes, slosh in a well where the live part of the catch swam uneasily about, creak of timbers and lines and of the sweeps where crew toiled—and dim and hollow, at unknown distances and in unsure directions, those boomings which betokened surf over the rocks around Sena.

Maeloch drew his hooded leather jacket tighter. Leaving the prow of his fishing smack he went aft, past the four starboard oarsmen. Sheeted fast, the lugsail slatted to the rocking. Despite chill, air was too dank for breath to show. As Maeloch neared, the helmsman slowly changed from a phantom to a mortal like himself, beard as wet as the sail, leathery face stiffened by weariness.

"How fare ye?" Maeloch asked. "Need ye a relief?"

Usun, his mate, shrugged. "Not so much as the deckhands. Might be one o' them and me should spell each other."

"Nay. While we keep sea room, their task is but to maintain steerage way. Should we find ourselves drifting onto a skerry or into a snag, aye, they'd better row their guts out. But worse will we need an alert steersman. My thought was ye might want to change with me and go stand lookout for'ard."

Usun sagged a little over the tiller. "If ye, who captain us through this passage on those nights, if ye be lost—"

"Who'd nay be, as long as we've wallowed in this swill?" Maeloch snapped. "Would Lir fain destroy us, why couldn't He ha' sent an honest gale?"

"Ha' ye gone mad?" Usun exclaimed, shocked. "Best we join in vowing Him a sacrifice if He spare us."

"He got His usual cock ere we set forth."

"I—I've promised Epona—"

"As ye wish." Maeloch's rough countenance jutted on high. "Myself, I'll deal with the Gods like my fathers before me, straightforwardly or nay at all."

Usun drew back. Ever were the Ferriers of the Dead an arrogant lot, not only because they enjoyed exemption from tax and civic labor but because—the source of their privileges—they met the unknown, on behalf of Ys. But Usun, who was himself along on such crossings, had not thought the captain's pride would go this far.

Maeloch filled his lungs and shouted: "D'Ye hear me, out there? Ahoy! Here I stand. Drown me if Ye will. But remember, my eldest living son be a stripling. 'Twill be years till he can help bring Ye your wayfarers. Think well, O Gods!"

The fog drank down his cry. Louder snarled the surf, and now there was in it a hiss of waves as they rushed across naked rock. Two crewmen missed a beat. The vessel yawed. Usun put the steering oar hard over. His own lips moved, but silently.

Something passed alongside. A splash resounded. Maeloch trod to the rail and peered downward. Foam swirled on darkling water. Amidst it swam a seal. Twice and thrice it smote with its rear flippers. The front pair kept it near the hull. It raised its head. Great eyes, full of night, sought toward Maeloch's.

For heartbeats, the skipper stood moveless. Finally Usun saw a shiver pass through him too. He turned about and said, well-nigh too quietly for hearing: "Stand by to give what helm I call for."

But striding off, Maeloch trumpeted: "Pull oars! Full stroke! We're going home!" The seal glided beneath and beside him.

When he reached the bows, the creature swam on ahead, until he could barely see it through the swirling gray. Once it glanced back at him and made a leap. Thereafter it started off on the larboard quarter.

"Right helm!" Maeloch roared. "Stroke, stroke, stroke! Give it your backs, ye scoundrels, if e'er ye'd carouse ashore again!"

Dread was upon the men, they knew not what this portended, nor knew what to do save obey. To and fro they swayed on their benches. Their breath loudened. Sweeps groaned at the tholes, throbbed in the waves. "Steady as she goes," Maeloch ordered. The seal swam on.

Surf crashed to starboard. On the edge of sight, a reef grinned. Yet *Osprey* had clearance enough. "Might that be the She-Wolf?" Maeloch muttered. "If 'tis, we've tricky navigation before us." The seal veered. "Left helm! . . . Steady as she goes."

Stroke, stroke, stroke. The waters bawled, seethed, sank away and sighed.

—The sun must have been low when the mainland hove in view, shadowy at first, later real, solid, the southside cliffs of Cape Rach. Men dared utter a ragged cheer. With their last strength they brought the battered and tarry boat into her home cove and laid her to at Ghost Quay. Oars clattered inboard. Feet thudded on close-packed stone as sailors climbed onto the dock, caught mooring lines, and made fast to iron rings set in boulders. The hull rolled, rubbing against rope bumpers hung on a log secured to the wharf.

At the stempost Maeloch slowly lifted his hand, waved, let the arm drop again and watched the seal depart.

Usun sought him. A while they stood in silence. Fog seemed thicker still, or was it only that night drew near? They could make out a pair of companion smacks at the quay, rowboats drawn onto a strand which had become cobble-hemmed and tiny at high tide, nets across poles. A track wound up the steeps, to join roads toward the pharos and Ys. A second trail went under the scarp. At its end, a deeper dimness showed where those few rammed-earth cottages were that bore the name Scot's Landing. A hush had fallen. Cold gnawed in through garments and flesh.

"Ye men'll sleep aboard," Maeloch said at length. "We've our catch to prepare for market in the morning, ye know." Only he and Usun among them dwelt here, where some were boatowners like him and all were haughty—however poor—and a little strange, concerned less with affairs of the Fisher Brotherhood and the city than with things that were their own. "But I'll dispatch boys to tell your kin ye came back safe."

"How did we?" one sailor whispered.

"I know nay."

"You . . . a Ferrier of the Dead . . . know not?"

"What I do those nights is a mystery to me too," Maeloch answered starkly. "Ye've heard what folk tell, that Gallicenae who've died may return in the shape o' seals, abiding till those they loved ha' fared out to Sena. No dream has told me if this be so or nay. But when yon swimmer appeared, I had a feeling we should follow her.

"Goodnight."

He left the craft and trudged toward his home. There his wife Betha kept vigil, among their living children and the babe that was great within her. For his sake she was invoking Belisama, Our Lady of the Sea—and, silently or by secret tokens, beings about whom the fisher women never told their men.

2

The day was bright when Innilis came to the house of Vindilis; but within lay dimness and quiet. "Welcome," said the older Queen, with a smile such as was rarely seen on her gaunt countenance. She took both hands of Innilis in her own. To the servant who had admitted the visitor: "We twain have matters of discretion before us. Let none disturb."

The servant bowed. "Never, my lady." This was not the first time he had been so commanded. As half-sisters, both daughters of Gaetulius, unlike though they were in aspect, this pair might be expected to cherish one another. In any event, it was not for him to question what the Nine did, or even wonder.

Vindilis led the way. Innilis must hurry to match her strides. They passed through the atrium. Like Bodilis, Vindilis had had the walls of hers painted over; but these now bore only spirals and Greek keys, black on white.

Beyond was what she called her counsel chamber. Light fell greenish through leaded panes to reveal mostly bareness: a table, a few chairs, a broad and backless couch upholstered in red. A niche held a statuette of Belisama. On a shelf below it were a lamp and an offering of evergreen. Refreshments waited on the table.

Innilis bowed to the shrine and signed herself. After a moment, Vindilis did likewise. The image had nothing about it of serenity. Rather, it showed the Goddess spear in hand, dress and unbound hair flying, astride a night wind like a stream or a snake—Her persona as the Wild Huntress, leading through the air the spirits of women who died in childbed.

Vindilis turned to Innilis, laid hands on her shoulders, kissed her on the lips. "How went it?" she asked, more softly than was her wont.

"Oh—I—" Innilis looked away. Her fingers, fragile as reeds, twisted together. "He was not unkind. Not knowingly." In haste: "I'm sorry to arrive this late. Three people begged my help at the same time."

"You could not well refuse, if you had no duties more urgent," said Vindilis. "Nor would you ever. Be seated. Here, let me pour you some wine. 'Tis that sweet Narbonensian you like." As she bent to pick up the flagon, light sheened on the silver streak in her hair and the raven coils around it. "What were their needs, those people? Illness?"

"For two." Innilis settled herself. "One is a man I've seen erenow. His dropsy was coming back. I gave him foxglove; that helps. But, poor soul, he has scant strength any more to earn his living. I think soon the temple must consider him and his family deserving of aid."

"You may be too tender-hearted, as often erstwhile." Vindilis sat down opposite her guest. "Go on. You need talk for easing of your mind. Let me be your physician and prescribe it."

Innilis shook her head, drank unsteadily, and replied: "The second was the worst. A girl with a raging fever, none knew why, least of all myself. I could but give her tisane of willow bark, for cooling of her poor little body, and invoke the Mother."

"If any of us can heal any longer by the Power of the Touch, 'tis you, Innilis. You She still heeds. As well She might."

The younger priestess reddened. "I am not worthy. Yet I pray that She will. . . . The third was an old man on his deathbed. He wanted a blessing."

"*Your* blessing."

"Oh, but 'tis only a rite of comfort."

"That is just why 'tis best coming from the one of us whom everybody loves."

"I . . . I spent a while more at his bedside. That is what really delayed me. I had my harp along, and gave him some songs he liked. If only my voice were better." Innilis's was high and thin.

Vindilis regarded her for a spell that lengthened, her own chin cupped between hands. After fourteen years of consecration, Innilis hardly seemed changed from the thirteen-year-old girl on whom the Sign had appeared in the reign of Hoel—not even by the daughter she had borne him. Short, slight, ivory-skinned, lips always parted beneath a tip-tilted nose, eyes large and blue, she let her hair flow freely, a light-brown cascade down her back, like a commoner maiden, save when occasion demanded she dress it. Her gown today was glowing saffron, but jewelry lay nowhere on her.

Vindilis, clad in silver-accented black with a Gorgon's-head pendant, lifted goblet. "Drink again, darling. I know 'twill not be easy for you to tell me about yesterday."

Innilis's lashes fluttered wildly. Red and white pursued each other above the fine bones. "There is, is naught to tell," she stammered. "I said he . . . was courteous, told me he re-re-regretted he'd not been able sooner to . . . pay me his respects, and—" Her words trailed off.

"What further?" Vindilis asked sharply.

Innilis spread her hands, a gesture of helplessness. "What could there be? What know I to talk about with a man? We both tried, but long silences kept falling, until supper came as a release. Then he suggested—What better had we to do? I told you he meant well."

Vindilis sighed, considered, abruptly set her vessel down hard and inquired, "Should I tell you first about my time?"

Innilis nodded, mute, staring down at the tabletop.

Vindilis leaned back, crossed her legs, frowned into space, crooked a finger as if summoning memory to report in full. Her tone was impersonal:

"Well, he arrived at the hour agreed, mid-afternoon. That was earlier than with you, but we knew we had much to discuss. He'd taken the trouble to ask about me beforehand, and actually said he was sorry I'd dismissed Runa for the day; said he looked forward to meeting another daughter of Hoel, who must have been a good father. And he said he'd gotten a feeling that Quinipilis paid me less heed when I was a child than she did her older girl—since Karilis-to-be was by Wulfgar, whom she liked, and I by Gaetulius whom she did not care for—and Gratillonius wondered if this was why I was reckless and rebellious in my school days. But when he saw his prying was offensive to me, he stopped, and after that our discourse became intelligent.

"He started by asking what we priestesses, both high and minor, *do,* other than conduct our rites and the affairs of our temple corporation. Naught boorish in that question; he begged pardon for his ignorance and said he hoped to remedy it. So I talked of counselling the troubled, healing the sick, teaching the young, taking part in the public business day by day as well as when the Council meets—everything, save that he sheered somewhat away from our spells, the thought of those making him uneasy. Ha, this may be a whip wherewith to chastise stout drayhorse Gratillonius, if he gets over-frisky!

"But now he was merely appealing for my help. Nay, wrong word. In soldierly wise, he put it to me that he and I, all the Nine and their lesser Sisters, should work with him for the safety and well-being of Ys. That talk went on for hours. When at length we took a repast, neither of us noticed what we ate or drank. Yea, methinks I could come to like Gratillonius, as much as lies in me to like any man."

Silence entered and pressed inward. Finally Innilis breathed, "Also after he—he spent the night?"

Vindilis laughed, with neither mirth nor bitterness. "We went to bed, of course. I'd told him the Goddess would be angered were not the sacred marriage consummated, except with a Queen like my mother who's so old the moon no longer rules over her. He was taken aback, but then smiled a bit and said, 'I carry out my orders.' When he began to feel of me, I asked that he mount at once. He did. He took a time about it, as busy as he'd been with others, but wrought no harm, and was satisfied with the single doing. At least, he lay straight down to sleep. In the morning I told him men do not arouse me; Hoel tried often and failed, Colconor was disgusting, Gratillonius might do best to leave me in peace. Could we not be partners, aye, and friends? Dahilis, or anyone, would be welcome to all such honors due me. He laughed and kissed my hand. We parted amicably."

Vindilis's brow darkened. "Although," she said in a harshened voice, "I must needs conceal what I felt, knowing that the same evening he would seek you."

Innilis lifted her gaze. "Oh, but I told you he was kindly." Her speech wavered.

"Once and no more, as with me?" pounced Vindilis.

"Nay—but—"

Vindilis sucked air in between her teeth. "Ah, well might I have foreseen. 'Tis my fault, I should have taken more of his goatishness on myself . . . for you. Though you are too beautiful—"

"I, I never besought him. He might have stopped, but I never thought to ask. And he was so eager, and between times he looked at me so mildly, stroked me and murmured. I—it seemed not to matter that it had hurt."

Vindilis reared in her seat. "Badly?" she grated.

Innilis made fending motions. "Nay, nay. Be not angry. Please. 'Twas but that he is big and I was, well, dry at first . . . and later, when I was not, I remembered how Hoel sometimes gave me some pleasure, and I thought mayhap Gratillonius—"

Vindilis rose, came around behind Innilis, stood smoothing the long brown tresses and crooning, "Poor sweetheart, poor little sister-wife." In Hoel they had shared a father for the child that each bore. "You were very brave. Now rest, be at peace, be happy. 'Tis over and done with. Presently we'll find a way to take the burden off you too. He may well have been inflamed because you reminded him somewhat of Dahilis. And surely she will be our ally, whether she know it or not."

Vindilis bent over to pass lips across Innilis's cheek. Her fingers plucked at the silken cord and amber button which closed the neck of Innilis's gown. The younger woman turned her head. Mouths met and lingered. In Colconor they had shared misery which brought them together.

Afterward on the couch, Innilis said through tears, "This *must* be right. The Mother *must* smile on us."

"She has not cursed us, throughout these years, has She?" Vindilis replied drowsily. They had been over this ground before.

"Nay. She has kindled love in us." Innilis clenched a fist. "But oh, if only we need not keep it secret!"

3

Wind whooped above glittery waters, made sails dance, drove white pennons across a vast blue field. It stung tears from the eyes of Gratillonius when he squinted into it. Between that and the glare, he could just make out a low, dark streak in the west: Sena, where again today Dahilis stood her lonely watch.

"Uh, you were saying, sir?"

Eppillus's rusty voice recalled Gratillonius to himself. He grinned, half abashed. "Pardon. My mind wandered."

"Well, the centurion has a peck o' things to think about. And they don't sit still neither, do they? Wriggle around like worms, I'll bet."

"The more reason to use this chance. Come." The two men resumed their walk atop the wall. Passing the Gull Tower, where a sentry saluted, they went above the harbor basin toward the gate. "The seaward defense is holding a practice. I wanted you to watch, and tell me what you think."

On the bastions, rain shelters had been dismantled and removed. The war engines crouched amidst the men who served them, spaced at intervals, three bolt-shooting catapults to each great stone-throwing ballista. Gratillonius and his deputy stopped at the first they encountered, which was of the former sort. Light by comparison, it did not require the recoil-absorbing wall reinforcement of the latter kind, and was much easier and faster handled. "Heed us not," the King told the team officer. "Get on with your business."

"Aye, my lord," said the Ysan. "We're about to start. 'Twill go quicker for the following rounds, but skeins get slack in damp weather—as my lord knows, being a soldier."

He called for winding. The men at the lever arms threw their weight into the work, twisting two vertical strands which, with the frame, flanked the trough. Meanwhile others were bringing ammunition and stacking it. "Hold," the officer ordered. The winders withdrew their levers from the sockets. Pawls clicked into notches. For a moment the wind alone gave tongue.

With a small hammer, the officer tapped the right skein. It sang, a deep bass note. Into the sinew and horsehair of which it was braided had been woven something resonant. Head cocked, the officer listened until the sound died away, before he struck the mate and heard it out. "Hm," he said, "not quite balanced yet. Give this'n a half turn more and we'll try again."

Equal tension was necessary so that the missile, when loosed, would not rub against the groove, and when free would fly straight. Eppillus whistled to behold such a method of gauging. Gratillonius smiled wryly. He would never command Ysan artillery. His ear was too poor; at home, his fellow centurions had requested him to refrain from singing in their presence.

Satisfied, the chief had the casting arms inserted in the skeins. The strong bowstring linking their opposite ends was to propel a slide which in turn pushed a long, iron-headed bolt down the groove. The machine had already been laid for elevation and direction. Now a windlass creaked, drawing the string back against the resistance of the skeins, until the slide engaged a locking mechanism at the base of the slotted beam. The chief undid skein pawls. "Would my lord like to send the first shot?" he asked. "Methinks 'twould bring us luck."

Gratillonius nodded, stepped forward, pulled the trigger that released the engagement. The catapult whirred and thumped. The bolt sprang forth, nearly too fast to see.

Other engines had likewise begun to shoot. Their targets were several rafts anchored at varying distances. Boats rested nearby on their oars, bearing scorekeepers, eventually to haul rafts and spent missiles back. But the exercise would go on all day while tide ebbed and flowed. Afar, a naval galley stood by to warn off any merchantmen that might appear.

Eppillus's small eyes bulged with fascination. These designs and procedures had countless differences from the Roman. Gratillonius must nudge him twice to get his attention: "Move that paunch of yours, you. We want to inspect every emplacement on this arc."

They did, walking to the gate and back to the tower, where they descended. Thrum, shouts, horn signals rang in their ears till well after they had passed the temple of Lir. "I don't think we need look the south side over," Gratillonius decided. "They're quite satisfactory, wouldn't you say?"

"I would. Oh, a funny style they've got, but I've seen Romans shoot worse. Naming no units, by your leave, sir. I'd say between their engines and their warships, they're plenty secure to seaward."

Gratillonius frowned. "That's a thing I want to talk over with you. We may have very little on hand in the way of navy, from time to time. Remember, our mission is to make sure not only of Ys, but this whole end of Armorica. That may call for a show of force at certain places. I'll send discreet letters to their officials as soon as I know what the situation is in the east, but those may not be enough. Meanwhile, what's keeping me busy is preparing for contingencies here." His chuckle was rueful. "Ysans can be as stubborn and slippery as any Imperials."

Eppillus rubbed his bald spot. "Hm, well, I'm no seaman, o' course, but I'd still hate to row up at that artillery. And I suppose the city infantry would be on the wall too. Plus every civil mariner in town, eh? Not that a sailor who's never been on a parade ground would be worth too much if a real army hit him."

They walked on by the ancient sanctum of Ishtar and through the mean streets of the Fishtail. Gratillonius had said he wanted to go by an obscure route, where he would less likely be recognized and detained by petitioners, gawkers, or Suffetes. Eppillus was the guide through this quarter. His familiarity with it amused Gratillonius—although doubtless the old roadpounder spent more tavern time gabbing about his past life than in gambling or wenching.

"That's the main business before us today. I've been dismayed at how little I've gotten to see of my own men. But with everything else besieging me— How are they doing?"

"Haven't your honor guards been smart, sir?"

"They have. And when I've asked them the same question, they say, 'Fine, sir.' What would you expect them to tell me under those circumstances? I'm counting on your honesty."

Eppillus stroked the broken bridge of his nose. "Well, we've had our problems, but they're mostly behind us and I needn't pester the centurion with 'em. Sitting around in barracks wasn't good for the boys. The centurion will understand. Now that we're busy again, not just drill but patrols and field exercises, why, they're shaping up fast. Give me another ten, twelve days and I'll have them back in crack condition."

"Splendid!" Gratillonius felt it would do no harm if he slapped the burly shoulder beside him. "We'll proceed to the royal palace and talk at length. I've things to tell you. Between us we can work out the right ways to use our troops. When we're done, I'll see to it that you go back to Dragon House with a bellyful of the best food and wine Ys has to offer. Which is plenty good, believe me." For the sake of Roman prestige, Gratillonius had insisted that his deputy be lodged among the marine and naval officers.

"I know. Thank you, sir." Eppillus gusted a sigh. "Though I got to admit those fine things are kind of wasted on me. I'll settle for a stoup o' Dobunnic red, a roast o' pork, a heap o' cabbage, and a slice o' bread— fresh from the oven, if my wife was baking that day."

"When you return home and retire to your bit of a farm, eh?"

"Mithras willing. I'll stick with the centurion till he leaves here. When will that be, sir?"

"Mithras knows. In two or three years, let us hope. The trick will be to stay alive till then."

—At the palace, a stranger waited.

A Roman. A military courier. He bore the first communication Gratillonius had received, other than rumors out of the hinterland. It was a letter directly from Maximus.

4

When Forsquilis heard what the King wanted to speak of, she raised a palm. "Nay, not here. Come with me to the secretorium."

In her chamber where flamelight flickered through the eye sockets of a cat's skull, shadows made the small female image from Tyre seem to stir, herbs sharpened the air with their memories of wildwood, she sat down facing him. Her hands rested quietly on her lap, her visage bore the calm and pallor of Pallas, but the gray gaze was darkened in this dusk and stars of red fire-glow moved within it. "Now say," she commanded.

In his mind Gratillonius clung tight to the handfast world outside. "Maximus reached Gallia on the day you declared. His legions have swept all resistance before them. Not that there was much. His opposition had little more to set against them than poorly trained auxiliaries. Some legionary units did arrive, hastily called from the eastern frontier or out of Hispania, in time to give battle—but of those, whole cohorts went over to the eagles of Maximus. He writes that he was in danger of outrunning his supply train, and this was among the reasons he had no chance to dictate a message earlier. Flavius Gratianus, co-Emperor, was in Lutetia Parisiorum. Maximus marched on that city. When he got there, the garrison rebelled and foreswore Gratianus. Maximus entered without hindrance. Gratianus had fled. Maximus is—was—making ready to pursue, defeat him decisively, lay grip on the whole of Gallia and Hispania."

"What will he have you do?" she asked low and tonelessly.

"Oh, I'm to send back a report by his courier, continue in my mission, keep him informed. We'll soon have a new and better Augustus, Forsquilis."

"And what will you have me do?"

"I think you know already." Gratillonius must moisten his lips. His armpits were wet enough. "Ys looks well prepared. Aye, not only to defend herself but to carry out the task Rome has given her. Yet . . . 'tis unforeseeable what may happen. The Empire is in turmoil. Its legions guarding Britannia and the East are stripped to the bone. Beyond the frontiers prowl wolves."

"You said we can stand off attack. Not that I think any barbarians would be so mad as to try."

"But Rome, Rome—"

"Ah." Forsquilis sat quite still. Misshapen glooms danced in silence. At last: "You ask that the owl fly forth again."

"Aye."

"And, if need be, the Nine take a hand, seek to order the tides of time."

He mustered courage. "You did it with me."

"That was for Ys," she answered sternly.

"If Rome falls, can Ys long endure?" he pleaded. "Bethink you how alone she will stand, while darkness deepens and the sea rises higher."

She was mute another while.

"This is a strange thing you seek," she then said, like one who talks in her sleep. "But these are strange years. I must think. Later I must meet with my Sisters. I will call you here when we have decided." Her eyes came back to him and focused. "Go."

He left. Not until he was outdoors did he let himself tremble.

5

The temple of Taranis was a majestic edifice on the west-northwest edge of the Forum—Roman-built on the colonnaded Roman model, save that it enclosed an open courtyard, its temenos. Only the south wing of the building was given over to worship. The rest held offices, treasury, a hall with sumptuous kitchen nearby for the sacred banquets of the seasons, and a conference room for the Speaker.

There Soren Cartagi privately received Queen Lanarvilis. On the wall behind his chair of state, under an inlaid Sun Wheel, hung weapons of war, surrounding a gold-trimmed Hammer. On the wall to his right a mosaic depicted the God victorious over Tiamat of the Chaos; windows, above a writing table, occupied the left side; bookcases flanked the entrance which he faced. For Lanarvilis, a throne of equal dignity had been brought. However, this day he and she wore plain silk with simple embroidery.

His fist lay knotted on the chair arm, his mouth was stiff, he must wrench the words out: "Thank you for coming, my lady. Believe me, I've no wish to ask about . . . what concerns you yourself. But for the good of Ys—after you have spent time alone with our King—can you tell me aught new?"

Faintly, she flushed, although she held her own voice level. "Those before me spoke truth. He is a well-intentioned and able man."

"For Rome."

"The cause of Rome is the cause of civilization: which means that 'tis equally Ys's."

Soren shook his head. "Always have you thought more highly of Rome than it deserves, my dear. You dream of a greatness, a grandeur of soul as well as domain, that has long since died, if ever it truly lived. I've dealt with the Empire; I know."

"Soren," she said quietly, "let not your resentment speak for you. Whatever you think—and I myself am not so dewy as to believe in any human perfection—still, the fact is that Gratillonius has our welfare at heart, is moving strongly to assure it, and seeks our advice, inquires about our wishes. He spent hours talking with me, and listening, too, as if I were a man."

"What was the drift of this?"

"Well, he . . . he'd heard you and I often confer and work together on behalf of our temples. Thus much of his querying concerned you. You've been polite but aloof, he said. And he needs your active help, the more so when the Lord of Works is in opposition to him."

"Indeed?" Despite everything that roiled in his breast, Soren's interest awoke. "How is this?"

"Gratillonius wants fortifications on the headlands. Immediately."

"Hm." Soren tugged his beard. "Little can be done that fast."

"Well, he spoke just of mantraps, with here and there a dry-laid piece of wall to protect archers and slingers. He fears an assault from the sea while our navy is off supporting our envoys to the Roman governors." Lanarvilis laid finger to chin. "Nay, 'fear' is wrong. He wants precautions taken. They will require a work levy."

"Ah. Does he understand what that means?"

"He does. I had him describe it to me."

Soren hesitated. "I intend no offense, dear, but in your desire to think well of him, you may have credited him with a better grasp of matters than he has. Would you tell me what he said?"

"Why—" She paused, shrugged, and recited: "Taxes to Ys may be paid in money, in kind, or in labor. The labor is limited to public works, to a short maximum period in any year, and to times when it will inflict no undue hardship. Since most construction was completed long ago and needs little maintenance, no such levy has been imposed on the poor for generations."

Soren smiled grimly. "I can see why Cothortin Rosmertai digs in his heels. 'Twould upset his administrative routine. Does Gratillonius realize that?"

"Certes. And he's not such a fool as to ride down a Lord of Works whose future friendship will be worth having. He asked me if I could lend my good offices—and prevail upon you—to persuade Cothortin. I agreed. I'll speak to my Sisters also." Warmth: "Glad will they be to have this additional token that the Gods meant well by us when They answered our call."

Soren winced. "You admire him, then. And not only because he is Roman."

Again she flushed, but lifted her head and replied proudly: "Aye. Had the Sign come upon my daughter"—by Lugaid—"while Colconor reigned, I would have made her kneel, and with this hand slashed her throat, lest he get her. Yestereven Gratillonius cleansed me of him. As he is cleansing all Ys."

Soren scowled. "He may yet scrub too hard, he with his foreign God. 'Twould not be the first time the Three withdrew Their favor from a man."

Pain crossed Lanarvilis's face. She rose and reached toward him. "Oh, Soren! Close that wound in you. Speak no ill omen. Bethink your sons and the city that shall be theirs."

He hunched his shoulders. "So be it," he growled. "I'll help. For Ys. And for you who wish it."

6

"**A**h-h-h," Maldunilis breathed. "That was good. You wield a mighty sword." She giggled. "How soon will you sheathe it anew?"

Gratillonius lifted himself to an elbow and looked down at her. Afternoon sunlight came through the windows to glow across an expanse of sprawled flesh. They had gone to bed shortly after he arrived, for there seemed nothing else to do. Innilis had at least, shyly, proposed a game of draughts. . . . Maldunilis was tall and plump, with brown eyes and reddish-brown hair now lank from sweat. Although her father had been Gaetulius, the heavy features recalled grandfather Wulfgar. Yet she was by no means ugly, and had shown her new husband a certain lazy sensuality which made the Bull roar loud within him.

"Give me a while," he laughed.

She raised herself too. The copious breasts slithered around as she reached for a bowl of sweetmeats on a stand beside the bed. Their fragrance blended into the closeness of the room. No matter that she kept the largest domestic staff of the Nine, always a measure of slovenliness prevailed in this house.

She offered him a confection. "Thank you, nay," he said. "I've small tooth for such." She fluffed up pillows to lean against and munched it.

"Aye, maybe best you keep your appetite," she answered. "The cooks are preparing a feast." Archly: " 'Twill take hours. How shall we spend them?"

Well, he thought, *since I've set aside the time till sunrise, why not dawdle about? Gods know I need a rest, a little freedom from responsibility. She's a simpleton, but amiable and a pretty good lay. Unlike some.*

The tiny crescent on her bosom seemed abruptly to burn. How had the Sign come to Maldunilis, of all Gallicenae daughters? he wondered. The ways of Mithras could be mysterious, but the ways of Belisama—of the Three Who brooded over Ys—were those of the wind, lightning, the sea deeps, falling stars, death in the night.

He sat straight in the rumpled bedding, crossed arms over knees, and suggested, "Shall we get to know each other better? Tell me of yourself."

She yawned, scratched, fumbled after a second sweetmeat. "Why, naught's to tell. I was never a, a scholar like Bodilis or a seeress like Forsquilis or a politician like Lanarvilis or—I am only me. I do what I am supposed to, and harm nobody." She smirked. "Command me, my lord."

"Oh, surely something," he protested, while observing that she did not even ask for his story.

She put a hand on his thigh and slid it along an insinuating path. "I can tell you that I love to futter. Hoel enjoyed me."

He could not forbear to bark, "Colconor?"

"Aye. He wasn't very heedful, but nor was he as bad as they said. Once he saw I liked having him on me, and I'd willingly do *whatever* he wanted —as I would for you, O King—he did no worse than spank me sometimes, and that only made this big bottom of mine tingle. He'd have treated me better yet had I given him a child. And I did open my womb, I left off the Herb, but the babe dropped out of me early." Maldunilis nuzzled Gratillonius. "I'm sure you can give me one that lives."

He froze.

"What's the matter, my lord?" She sounded plaintive.

His breath came hard and harsh. "That day—in the House of the King, ere I arrived—"

She nodded. "Vindilis and Forsquilis and I were keeping him there. Waiting for you."

"But—but for them it was a necessity—like Brutus striking down Caesar because he hoped to save the Republic. You—"

She smiled. "Why not enjoy? That was why my Sisters picked me for the third. Colconor would know I wasn't feigning. Instead it doubled the pleasure to know I helped prepare the way for you, his conqueror."

The most horrible thing, he thought in a distant part of himself, the ghastliest thing was her innocence.

It thundered in his head. He rolled around and sprang to the floor. Tiles felt cold beneath his feet. Somehow he could chatter, "Pardon me, this is not courteous. Of a sudden I've remembered pressing affairs of state. I must begone."

Her face screwed up. "But my feast!" she wailed.

"Eat it in health. Invite somebody else. Do what you will. I must away." He scrambled into his clothes.

She blubbered a bit. However, she made no effort to keep him, just sat in bed watching while her hand traveled absently between bowl and mouth.

He strode out into the street. A clean wind blew off the sea. He would go to his palace, he decided, take a hot bath, don fresh raiment. Only there in Ys was it permissible to keep horses. He would have one saddled and gallop off across the hinterland, alone.

His Queens—Nobody remained but Fennalis, and she was the mother of Lanarvilis. Flat-out against the Law of Mithras, to lie with both daugh-

ter and mother. He would explain that to Fennalis sometime soon as
kindly as he was able. They said she was a friendly sort, usually cheerful,
bustling about upon charitable works. Besides, with seven living children
by Wulfgar, Lugaid, Gaetulius, and Hoel, she might well be past the rule
of the moon. Dismiss Fennalis. He had carried out his duty by the lot of
them.

It didn't matter which had known beforehand of that whore-hearted
conspiracy to entrap a man. Dahilis had not. She had merely appealed to
her Gods for deliverance.

Ignoring persons who hailed him, Gratillonius stalked through Ys. He
would ride the roads above the sea until his horse could go no more. Then
he would return, bathe anew, dress well, and seek the house of Dahilis.

With her he would abide as long as the Gods allowed. Let people say
whatever they chose. Was he not the prefect of Rome?

XIII

1

The word had gone forth around Mide: again this year would the King at Temir carry a spear abroad. Let ships and currachs gather at the mouth of Boand's River. Let those noble landowners who owed him warlike service make ready themselves and their men, to meet well-provisioned once seed was in the ground and cattle on their way to upland pastures. Let any other man who was free to do so and wished for adventure, glory, and plunder come too. Niall maqq Echach would await them and lead them—this time not to Alba, where fighting and loot had been splendid but where the Wall of Rome still stood—this time south to golden Gallia!

First there must be the rites of Beltene, welcoming in the summer and striving to make it fruitful. Throughout Ériu, folk would rise before dawn to gather the dew for its powers of cure. Women washed their faces in it to make themselves fair, men their hands to make themselves skillful. Women then drew the magical first water from the well and left flowers behind; men set up a bush before the house, and prepared to defend it against whoever might steal it and the luck it carried; youngsters plucked healing herbs, together with blossoms for shrines, horse bridles, every place that might please the Goddess. Later in the day came exchange of gifts, balls bearing the signs of sun and moon, followed by hurling-games played with these, which could well lead to brawls and bloodshed. Youths and maidens went in procession around the countryside, singing, acting out Her coming, celebrating Her gifts of life and light. Families made no marriage pacts, because that would have been as ill-fated as it was to be born this day. However, many couples plighted troth of their own for the year to come or renewed it, and made love upon the earth.

Food was cold, for all household fires had been put out the evening before. At sunset the dwellers in each neighborhood left their revels and solemnly gathered on the highest ground nearby. While bards or poets sang and druids watched for portents, a chosen man kindled new flame with flint and steel, to make twinned bonfires. Into these folk cast their festival bushes and whatever they had that seemed unlucky, so that fortune might consume misfortune. Farmers drove their cattle between the blazes, for protection against murrains. Those who thereafter went home carried along some of the needfire to relight their hearths. The hardier stayed on till sunrise, for doings that left them weary and a little dazed the next day.

In these observances, every king of a tuath and his queen took a leading part. The King and Queen on Temir must do so on behalf of the whole land. Niall had foreknown he would have no time to himself on the day and night of Beltene; and immediately afterward would come the whirlwind of busking for his expedition. Yet he had felt the need of some calm counsel.

Therefore he had walked out upon the eve preceding the holy dawn. He went in company with his druid Nemain maqq Aedo and with Laidchenn maqq Barchedo, who had become chief among his poets.

As busy as he had been, this was late in the day. Weather had brought rainshowers, though free of the cold east wind or frost that would have boded ill for the coming season. Now clouds drifted low and leaden beneath an overcast that quite hid the sun and laid an early twilight in the valley. Breezes plucked fitfully at grass and leaves. Odors of growth had given way to dankness. Homebound rooks cawed afar, otherwise silence abided the night.

Niall took the northward road, between the Rath of Gráinne and the Sloping Trenches, thence downhill. Well-kept, it was not unduly muddy or rutted; but at this hour it stretched empty, nothing bordered it save meadow and coppices, no firelight gleamed from houses in view. The sole brightness, and it wan, came off the spearheads of Niall's four guards, who encompassed the three great ones at a respectful distance, and off a golden torc around the neck of the King. Although he was still magnificently clad, after receiving guests who arrived during the day, dusk was fading all colors.

"Best we not linger outside overly long," counselled Nemain. "The síd will soon be opening and letting their dwellers loose." The eve of Beltene was second only to that of Samain as a time when unhuman beings went abroad through the dark.

Niall tossed his bright head. "We can turn our cloaks inside out and bewilder them," he said.

"So do people suppose," Laidchenn answered; "yet I could tell you many a story, my dear, about those who put overmuch faith in that trick. Even washing in one's own piss is often not shield enough. For Those Beyond may have deeper ends than leading us astray or altogether out of the world."

"Well, what I have to say is quickly said," Niall snapped.

"Then say it," murmured the druid.

The King's mood gentled. He stared before him, down into the gloom toward which he walked. Trouble freighted his tone: "This I could not utter in the hearing of others, lest they think I was afraid and so, themselves, falter. But to you two, my hearts, I can speak without misunderstanding. And what I have to ask of you is whether you can read any warning signs, in this night before us when sorcery reigns, or whether you can cast any guardian spells—for my warfare after I am off upon it."

"Have you cause for dread?"

"I have not. Would I of my free will take men who trust me on a venture I deemed unwise?"

"Nevertheless you are uneasy," said Laidchenn.

"It is about my son, my son Breccan. He burns to prove himself. A while ago, in a gladsome moment, he lured me into a promise that he could come along on this voyage."

"Surely you, of all men, will not begrudge your boy his chance to win fame."

"But he is so young—"

"No younger than yourself, when you returned from Torna's house to claim your birthright."

"I was stronger than he is. Och, he will grow to be a goodly fighter if he lives. But at present he has still his mother's slimness." Niall's voice wavered, seemed to speak of itself, as if he could not stop it. "And, O Ethniu, your face—"

"You loved her."

"As Diarmait loved Gráinne. I do yet, though she be fourteen years in her grave. Breccan is all that remains of her." Niall's hand slashed swordlike through the air. "Enough!" he barked. "This grows unmanly. I, your King, am calling on you two for your counsel and help."

"Is that right for Breccan's own honor?"

"Hold!" said the druid. "Our lord simply asks, Laidchenn—asks what may be done to stave off needless woe. Had King Conaire been better advised, he would not have broken the gessa upon him and thereby come to perish in Dá Derga's hostel. Let us take snares from the path of the young stag; wolves he can battle himself."

His staff thumped the ground as they trudged on mute. Ahead of them an oakenshaw enclosed the road. Its outer trees stood limned against heaven, branches reaching like the arms of gnarled giants, while between them gaped darkness. Wings ghosted overhead and vanished among those shadows. Somewhere a belated cuckoo called.

Laidchenn started. "That cry! An evil sign at just this time."

"It is not evil for us," Niall replied, "for it came from the right, which means luck."

"Before we can take thought and cast the yew chips for divining," said Nemain, "we must know more of what you intend. You have not given out much."

"Lest word somehow reach the Romans and warn them," Niall explained.

The druid nodded his white head. "That is clear. However, with us two you can feel safe, darling, else why have you sought us? Now tell us where in Gallia you mean to raid."

"From the supplying you have ordered," observed the poet shrewdly, "I doubt you plan on the north coasts."

"You are right," Niall answered. "They have been well picked over. Besides, I seek no clash with Saxons, like two flocks of carrion crows quarreling over some bones."

"Have a care," warned Laidchenn. "Those are birds of the Mórrigu that you bespeak."

Niall laughed, which shocked his friend afresh, before he asked, "Sure, and may not a man jape a little within his own family?"

The druid nodded, though his demeanor had turned solemn. Niall's claim to lordship rested on more than his having often fed the flocks of the Triple Goddess of war. Many men believed that the hag with whom he had lain as a youth had not only been the Sovereignty of Mide, but Herself.

"Well," said the King, "it's of more than Saxons I am thinking. Foremost, there is Ys."

They went under the oaks. It was not quite so dark there as it looked from outside, but murky enough, the sky a blue-gray glimmer behind barricading leaves, boles and boughs heavy in shadow. "Ys!" exclaimed Nemain. The name cracked through stillness. "Heart of mine, you are not thinking of attacking Ys, are you, now?"

"I am not," Niall declared. "That would be madness. That wall and those guardian witches—Indeed I have no wish to fall on Armorica at all, at all. Ys is a Roman ally. War among the Romans should cause it to reach a protecting hand over its whole end of the peninsula. We will steer wide of Ys. And this is one thing I am hoping you can help me do, keep the favor of Manandan while we are that far out at sea."

"Where do you mean to go?" Laidchenn asked.

"Around and southward, to the mouth of the Liger and up that river. There lie rich farmlands, towns, a city. With strife drawing men away, they should be thinly defended—worse off than Alba, where last year's fighting will have left the Romans wary and prepared." Despite that which gnawed in his breast, exultation made Niall laugh. "Oh, fine shall our harvest be!"

The trees thinned out. Not much more light straggled through, when dusk had been deepening. Sufficient remained for the men to glimpse an eagle owl depart from the shaw: sufficient to flicker across great wings and glisten on great eyes before the bird disappeared from sight, southbound.

Nemain halted and stood staring after it. Uneasily, his companions drew close to him. "What is the matter, wise one?" breathed Niall at last.

The druid bent his thin shoulders. "I do not know. I felt something uncanny there. Come, best we turn about at once and get into shelter before full night has fallen. It will be very dark."

—Obedient to his gess, Niall rose at the dawn. Fireless, the hall was dolmen-black. Straw rustled dryly under his feet. He groped at a bolt and pushed the shutters from a window. The sky had cleared; the first silver flashed through drifting mists and back off dew; though chill, the air already smelled green. He took a long draught of it.

Suddenly he stiffened. From a beech tree nearby he heard the melodious cry of a cuckoo—too early, too early in the morning, and a harbinger of death if heard from within a house at Beltene.

Yesterday the cuckoo had promised better. Well, signs were often unsure. Niall turned from the window. Nemain would be taking omens and Laidchenn making a powerful song, for the sake of Breccan. The King must remain undaunted.

XIV

1

From the harbor and the markets, through the Forum and over the high ground where the wealthy dwelt—from the philosophers at Star House to the marines in Warriors' House—from Scot's Landing under the cliffs to the noisy workshops outside High Gate—from mansions on the heights above the canal to the hamlets of the valley floor—the whisper flew around Ys and its hinterland. Something tremendous was afoot. This morning the state barge bringing a Queen back from her Vigil on Sena had not, first, taken another out to replace her. All the Nine were gathered together in the temple of Belisama.

In various ways, a few men knew that this was at the behest of the King. None but he knew why.

When Gratillonius left the palace he went alone. A King here could do that if he chose, could walk about or ride abroad, be a man among men. It was the Emperors who sat in a shell of splendor, god-kings with humanity under their feet, those who were not merely gloves on the hands of ruthless real men. Through Maximus, when his victory was complete, Rome would gain back her soldier-Emperors of old.

In a plain, hooded cloak, Gratillonius followed the streets as they wound down to Lir Way and upward on the other side. Traffic had begun to bustle along the thoroughfare. Some persons recognized him and touched fingers to brow; when he noticed, he acknowledged with a nod and passed on. Two or three approached, clearly hoping to ask favors. His dismissing gesture sent them off. The King might be on sacred business.

It was not the practice for him to hear petitioners or give alms, anyhow. Such things were handled by the Suffetes, Great Houses, guilds, temples. Occasional rulers in the past had distributed largesse or heard complaints . . . occasionally. Thus far, Gratillonius had not, if only for lack of time. Besides, it was not what a centurion did. Lately, at odd moments, he had wondered if he should institute a regular court—twice a month, perhaps—open to whoever had found no better recourse. But he would be unwise to rush into that, without more knowledge of the city and its customs than he yet possessed. Magnates might resent what they felt as an intrusion on their ancient functions. His mission required that he keep them cooperative, and already there was friction aplenty.

Such children as had tagged after him at a distance gave up when he, seeking calmness, entered Elven Gardens. A wall with guarded portals kept the general public out of these exquisitely contoured and cultivated grounds. He found himself alone. If any else were present, the intricacy of paths, hedges, bowers kept them well off, despite this preserve being less than a hundred yards across.

Stillness underlay birdsong. Flowerbeds were hallways, hedges, walls, trees, roofs; each petal and leaf seemed in its perfect place, as though sculptured. Nowhere were trails, staircases, arched bridges wider than for two people to walk abreast, and nowhere could he see more than a few paces before their curves went out of his view. Yet he had no sense of crowding. Sunlight and shadow made secret depths. A statue of a nymph or faun, or a fountain where stone dolphins played, or the chiming of a streamlet would leap out at him. The forenoon coolness was full of fragrances.

At the farther end he came forth before the staircase to the temple. It climbed steeply, unrailed, from surrounding flagstones. There he had an overlook across much of the city, its towers agleam between shouldering headlands which had turned emerald and gold, the sea beyond whose daughter Ys was, sails like wings beneath the burning Wheel of Taranis. It was not the first time since his arrival here that beauty had taken him by the throat, and he a hardened roadpounder.

He mounted to the building. It resembled the Parthenon of Athens, in smaller size, though a close glance showed aliennesses—columns more slender, with capitals suggestive of kelp and surf; a frieze of women, seals, cats, doves, blossoms, sheaves, in a style that flowed like water or wind; the marble left bare, weathered to the hue of pale amber.

Bronze doors stood open. Gratillonius entered into a foyer radiant with mosaics of the Mother's gifts to earth. Attendants waited, minor priestesses—who were mostly in their later years—and young vestals. Among the latter he noticed one he had not seen before. Therefore she could be no child of any of his wives. Her mother must be dead; judging by her apparent age, her father had been Hoel. She was of plain appearance and seemed a little dull-witted. He gave her no further thought.

The women greeted him ceremoniously. He replied as he had been taught to and let a maiden take his cloak. Beneath, in deference to this place, he wore a scarlet robe trimmed with ermine, the Wheel embroidered in gold upon the breast. Above it, out in view, hung the Key. That last was as much emblem as he really needed.

A senior led him through a corridor around that great chamber where the threefold image of the Goddess oversaw services. At the rear was a room for meetings. It was amply impressive. In somber stonework, the four walls showed Her leading Taranis back from the dead to His reconciliation with Lir; present at the act of generation, while dandelion seeds blew and bees flew past the bed; triune as girl child, woman, and crone; in the van of the Wild Hunt. Windows above illuminated the high white headdresses of the Gallicenae. Blue-robed, they sat benched in a half-circle before the dais onto which Gratillonius stepped. His guide closed the door and departed.

Gratillonius looked down into the faces of his wives. Briefly, he was daunted. What strangeness was it that had fallen over them? Wry old Quinipilis; lean, intense Vindilis; Forsquilis, half Athene and half she-cat; sensuous, indolent Maldunilis; shy Innilis; stout, kindly, gray Fennalis; her daughter Lanarvilis, earnest and in some hidden way sorrowful; Bodilis, beneath whose warmth and learning he thought he had sensed steel; darling Dahilis—

No, *she* had nothing but love in her gaze. And as for the rest, he must not let his feelings about them, especially about certain of them, unduly influence him. In their own view they had acted righteously, after intolerable provocation. Seemingly they knew things and wielded powers that were beyond him—that was why he was calling on them—but he should not stand in awe of them, either. He had knowledge and abilities of his own.

Muscle by muscle, Gratillonius relaxed. He smiled. "Greeting," he said. By now his Ysan was adequate, and daily improving. "My thanks for heeding my summons. I think you understand 'tis for the good of the people. I, a man and a foreigner, am still ignorant of much. If we ought to begin with a prayer or a sacrifice, tell me."

Fennalis stirred on her seat. "We cannot," she snapped, "with you in this house, you who follow a God Who does not hear women."

Startled, Gratillonius grabbed after a handhold within himself. What possessed this generally cheerful little person? Offense at his never having slept with her? She had seemed to accept his awkward explanation that it was against his religion—ruefully, he suspected, but no more than that, for she was in fact past childbearing age. Usually bustling about on her charitable works, carelessly dressed, she was the last of the Nine whom he would have expected to show intolerance. Her snub-nosed features had stiffened.

"I . . . I revere Belisama, of course," he tried to respond, "and all the Gods of Ys."

"They sent him to us!" Dahilis cried. Appalled at her own brashness, she covered her mouth; but her eyes still shone defiant.

Quinipilis laughed. "Shall we save the squabbles for long winter evenings when there's naught else to do?" she said. "This council has business more interesting. At the same time, nay, Gratillonius, we need no rite. Such may come later. Today we are but met to reach a decision."

"It is a very grave decision, however," Lanarvilis replied. "Questions of statecraft. . . . We should have other men on hand, the Speaker for Taranis, Lir Captain, the Sea Lord—"

"I will certainly be in conference with them," Gratillonius promised. "I'll have them out to the Wood when, shortly, I stand my full-moon Watch there. But first I must have the willingness of the Gallicenae."

Vindilis scowled. "That turns on the willingness of the Gods. Who dares to try to read Their minds?"

"Aye," said Bodilis softly. "And even without hubris, what may stem from a terrible deed? Agamemnon did not truly sacrifice Iphigenia for a fair wind—the Gods wafted her away to safety—but Clytemnestra knew this not, and so murder led to murder until the curse on the house of Atreus was fulfilled."

"Hold on," Quinipilis admonished. " 'Tis no delicate balancing of ifs and maybes we have before us, 'tis a practical question not unlike the last such that we Nine faced. Meseems we came rather well out of that one."

Bodilis smiled a little. "I agree. My inclination is to do what the King asks. Without Rome, what is Ys? I only urge that we think first."

Maldunis looked bewildered. "What is this? Nobody has told me," she complained.

"You didn't trouble to listen," Dahilis said in scorn.

"I—I think—no, wait—" After Innilis had tried several times, her Sisters realized that she hoped to utter a word, and indulged her. "That's . . . not fair to Maldunilis. Did anybody ever seek her out and ask what she thought? I've no real understanding of it myself. I don't. Gratillonius wants us to raise a tempest . . . against some barbarians who aren't our enemies. . . . Well, why?" She sank back in confusion. Vindilis gave her hand a reassuring clasp.

The man saw that matters were getting away from him. He cleared his throat. "It may be the best to lay everything out in plain sight, no matter how much you already know," he said. "Forsquilis, will you explain what you have discovered?"

The seeress nodded. All eyes turned her way. Though she remained seated, it was as if she had stood up, tall and prophetic.

"You remember Gratillonius asked me to make a Sending, widely about," she told them. "The Empire is at war with itself. Our fleet is off to keep western Armorica at peace. But might barbarians, then, take the chance to strike at Ys? Or might a Roman faction? We needed forewarning.

"With your consent, I agreed. My spirit flew forth over land and sea, to look and listen. What it found, I have reported to him but not erenow to every one of you. Hark ye."

The centurion was still unsure what truth lay in her. He believed her sincere; but lunatics as well as charlatans infested the world. Nevertheless he had gotten his glimpses of the unexplainable; and his duty was to use every possible weapon for Rome. After sleepless nights, he had decided to try this.

If Forsquilis could really send her ghost abroad and understand what it heard, no matter in what language, then it might well be that the Gallicenae had those other powers they claimed.

She was so calm about it! "There are no plans against Ys. The Armorican Romans mean to stay quiet. Some resent our show of naval strength, regardless of its being made as a polite hint rather than a threat. More of them, though, find in it a godsend, the very excuse they longed for to avoid the risk of taking sides; and they have prevailed on the rest. Barbarians are astir along the denuded eastern frontiers, but that is remote from us.

"It is in Hivernia that I found fresh grief being prepared for the West. A chieftain—a king, a great king, the master behind last year's attack on Britannia—means to take advantage of civil war in the Empire and launch an onslaught up the mouth of the Liger—very soon."

She ceased. Stillness descended while each priestess withdrew into herself.

Then: "Oh, wonderful!" Maldunilis piped. "The River Liger, 'tis well south of us, is't not? Won't the Scoti sail far around Ys?"

Forsquilis nodded. "They've abundant respect for us."

" 'Tis a piratical raid, you told me, not an invasion," Lanarvilis said. "Is it then any concern of ours?"

" 'Twill be a massive raid."

Gratillonius regained the word: "That's my fear. Portus Namnetum lies not far upstream, a vital harbor for this entire region. Because of the war, 'twill be poorly defended. If the barbarians take and sack it, as well they may, not only will shipping around Gallia Lugdunensis suffer. The whole Liger valley will lie open to later attacks." His forefinger tried to draw a map in the air. "Can you not see Armorica, Ys, cut off, and Rome suddenly bleeding from a huge gash of a wound? I ask you to defend the well-being of your children and grandchildren."

"Or that of Maximus?" Fennalis challenged. "You'd have us wreak harm on folk who wish us none."

"But who intend doing hideous damage elsewhere to those who never harmed *them,*" Bodilis retorted.

Quinipilis nodded. "We need to kill them where we can as we need to kill foxes in a chickencoop, though the chickencoop happen to be our neighbors'."

Bodilis laughed. "You might have found a metaphor more dignified, dear. But I agree. I cannot believe the Gods of Ys would forbid a strategy of defending civilization itself."

"Under our King!" Dahilis shouted.

"The Nine alone cannot—" Lanarvilis began, and broke off. "Well, you said you would consult with Soren, Hannon, the leading Suffetes ere anything is decided."

"I am aware I must have their support," Gratillonius answered. "But I cannot speak meaningfully with them unless first I have yours."

Forsquilis shivered. "My Sending has felt cold winds blowing out of the future," she mumbled. Aloud: "The Gods have granted Ys a proven leader. Let him lead."

"We should . . . give him his chance . . . this time," Vindilis said slowly. A dark fire burned in her. Innilis clung to her hand.

Fennalis made a slight shrug. " 'Twould be foolish of me to cross my whole Sisterhood. Very well. You may be right."

"Pray somebody tell me what 'tis we're to do!" Maldunilis begged.

Gratillonius gave her, and all of them, his reply.

2

An eerie thing happened as Niall maqq Echach was leaving Ériu.

His warriors were gathered where Boand's River met the sea. Tents, which had settled over the hills like a flight of wild geese, were now struck. Grass would soon heal campsites, for the season was well on; it had taken a while after Beltene to finish work and then trek here. Wagons and chariots stood ready to rumble home. Banners lifted above bright spearheads where men surrounded their tuathal kings. The currachs that would bear most of them were still beached, but several ships lay anchored in the shallows. Everyone waited for the Temir King to board his.

Racket and brawling were silenced, clangor was hushed. Rain misted. The cool smells of it came from earth, growth, cattle, smoke out of wide-strewn shielings, the waters that beckoned ahead.

Niall strode forth. The grayness around could not subdue the saffron in his tunic, the woad in his kilt, the gold at his throat, the steel on his spear, least of all the locks that streamed from brow to shoulders. His left fist gripped a shield painted the color of fresh blood. Behind him came his son Breccan and his guardsmen, hardly less brilliant. Beside him on the right walked his chief poet Laidchenn maqq Barchedo, on the left his chief druid Neimain maqq Aedo.

His ship lay before him. She was a galley of the Saxon kind, clinker-built, open save for small decks fore and aft, seats and thole-pins for rowers along the bulwarks. Oars lay ready across the benches. Down the middle stretched mast, yardarm, and sail, bundled together on two low racks, not to be raised unless a following wind should arise. The stempost lifted proudly, carven and gilt, a Roman skull nailed on top. Black the hull was, rocking and tugging at its stone anchor, eager to be off to war. Cargo filled the bilge, supplies and battle gear laid down on planks.

Niall had come near enough to hear eddies rustle and chuckle, when the thing came to pass. Out of the gray rain flew a raven. It was the largest any man there had ever seen, its wings like twin midnights. Arrow-straight it glided, to land on the upper rim of Niall's shield and look into his face.

Heavily though that weight struck, the shield never wavered. Not for one step did the King falter. The point of the beak was an inch from the bridge of his nose and could in two pecks take out his eyes; but their blue looked straight into the jet behind that beak, the while he said low, "Hail and honor, if this be She Whom I think."

A gasp and a moan blew through the host. Breccan yelled and stumbled back before he mastered his terror. The guardsmen milled in confusion till their captain spoke a command and got them back at their lord's heels. Laidchenn raised the chiming rod that proclaimed him a poet, inviolable, before he went on along beside Niall. The knuckles were white where Nemain clutched his staff.

Niall stopped at the water's edge. "I promise You many slain," he said, "but this You know I have given and will give. Is there anything else that you are requiring?" The bird did not stir nor blink. "Is it that You have a word for me, darling? I listen. Ever have I listened, and when at last You call me, I will not be slow to come."

The grisly beak moved, touched him lightly on the forehead. Wings spread. The raven went aloft. Thrice it circled low above Breccan maqq Nélli. Then it flapped back up into unseen heaven.

Men were casting themselves to the ground, making signs against evil, vowing sacrifices. Niall and his company stood firm. He did shift the spear to the crook of his right arm, and laid that hand upon the shoulder of his son.

After a time Nemain said softly, "This is a wonder and an omen. I am thinking that that was the Mórrigu Herself."

"As Medb, She has . . . favored me," Niall answered. "I remember tales of how She has thus appeared to armies before a battle."

Breccan clenched his fists. "What happened to them afterward?" he cried. His voice broke in a squeak. At that, a blush drove the pallor from his face, like rage overwhelming fear.

"Why, some won the day and some fell," Laidchenn told him, "but always it was a battle from which fateful issue welled."

Niall regarded Breccan. "Her message was for you too," he said.

"Choosing him for undying fame," Laidchenn offered.

"Choosing him, at least," Nemain muttered into his beard.

Niall shook himself. "Enough of this. Quickly, now, before the lads give way to terror. Sing some heart back into them, poet!"

Laidchenn rang his chimes, took forth his harp, smote the strings. Men roused from their bewilderment when they saw and heard, for he commanded unseen dominions of his own, whence words came forth to blast, blight, or bless. The trained throat spoke from end to end of the hundreds:

"Well may it be that this means
Mighty ones at work,
Willing we all gain honor.
I invoke victory!"

Niall raised his spear on high. His call rolled out: "The Mórrigu is with us! Rejoice!"

The kings who were gathered saw their King run into the water. It sheeted white about his knees. One-handed, he grabbed the ship's rail and swung himself aboard. There he immediately seized a red cock which lay trussed in the prows. With his sword he cut those bonds, so that the bird fluttered and cawed wildly in his grasp. "Manandan maqq Leri, you will be granting us the passage of Your sea, that we may bring You glory!" He put the victim against the stempost. A sweep of his blade beheaded it. The death struggle laved the Roman skull with blood. "Onward!" he roared to his men.

A cheer lifted, ragged at first, but ever louder and deeper. Weapons flashed free. Standard bearers whipped their poles to and fro until banners were flying as if in a gale. Breccan shuddered in exaltation. Laidchenn and Nemain kissed him on the cheeks, then stood waving farewell as he embarked and the guards followed. Readymaking went swiftly. The anchor came up, the oars bit, the King's galley stood out to sea.

That was the signal for the rest to start. They swarmed. The fleet was on its way.

Even in this weather, that was a grand sight. The ships were not many, and aside from Niall's had no more crew than needful. They were meant mainly to carry home loot and captives. But the currachs were everywhere, lean and low, coursing like hounds around horses. Some of those leather hulls could hold only four or so warriors, but in others were better than a dozen. As they got away from land and met real waves, they no longer simply spider-walked; they danced, they skimmed, they soared. Chants of oarsmen went back and forth across unrestfulness, surf-sounds.

Those not at this work were busy getting things shipshape. By the time they were done, the salt was in their nostrils to whip their blood alive. They agreed that the raven had been a marvelous vision, a holy vision, foretelling slaughtered foes, plundered lands, and return to fame. Breccan was so rapt in dreams of it that Uail maqq Carbri, skippering the royal ship, relieved him of duty just to keep him out from underfoot.

Dim on the right, Ériu would be Niall's guide for the first few days. At eventide, whenever possible, his folk would camp ashore. Given their numbers, they need not fear attack by the Lagini, since it would be clear that they were peacefully passing by. However, wind, fog, seas, or rocks might sometimes force them to lie out overnight. After crossing the channel where it was narrowest, they would use Alba the same way—more or less; there was no sense in anything but a straight dash across the Sabrina firth, and safe campgrounds would be hard to find in Roman country.

At the southwestern tip of Dumnonia the men must either hope for a spell of fair weather or settle in and wait for it. Ahead of them would be days and nights on the open sea, as they steered clear of Armorica and its Ysan she-druids, then turned east for the Liger mouth. True it was that they could be rowing that whole while, watch and watch, or sailing if Manandan was kind. But they must see sky well enough to hold a course. Otherwise—"We might blunder our way to Tír innan Oac," Niall had laughed. "Likeliest, though, we'd only gladden the gulls and sharks, and they have not any great name for the returning of hospitality."

The plan was quite sound, he went on to say. Armorican fishermen regularly worked farther out than he proposed to go. Jutish traders and pirates regularly made trips as long, also beyond sight of land, between their homes and Alba. And had not his Milesian ancestors sailed the whole way up from Iberia?

The voyage met no worse trouble than kept men on their mettle—until the first night beyond Dumnonia, in the very Ocean.

Heaven was clear, the moon full, so that vessels need not keep dangerously close together to stay in sight of each other. This was twice good, because they had gotten the wind for which rowers longed and were under sail. It crooned low and not too cold, when you ran before it; waves whooshed and gently rumbled, gleams and silvery traces swirling over the obsidian of them; ships rocked, surged, talked to themselves in creak of timbers and tackle. Niall, who stood a lookout himself, had finished his turn and was about to go join the crew who slept nested together down the length of the hull. Muffled in a cloak, he took a moment of ease on the foredeck. Starboard, larboard, aft, his fleet came along like leaping dolphins. The eye sockets of the trophy skull gaped toward Rome.

Something caught his gaze. He turned his head upward. Broad wings slipped by. An eagle owl . . . at sea?

It swung away and vanished eastward. Niall said nothing to the other man, who had not seen. That night the King slept ill.

3

In the morning Eppillus took the legionaries out on Redonian Way to the far side of Point Vanis. The whole thirty-two were present. Gratillonius had relieved the honor guard of duty, observing that he would not be at the palace for a while. After his required stay at the Wood, he would be busy in and around Ys, and lodging in Dragon House so he could readily confer with officers of the armed forces.

The Romans tramped smartly off. It was a clear, calm day. Sunlight glared on their metal. A few fleece-ball clouds drifted overhead as lazily as bees droned about wildflower blossoms. On the promontory the grass was thick and intensely green, studded with shrubs and boulders. Under Northbridge, the sea churned and roared among rocks between the headland and the wall of Ys; but everywhere else it reached in sapphire brilliance, its calm broken only where it went white over reefs. Far and far away, a streak of darkness marked Sena. The pharos at the end of Cape Rach, beyond sky-striving Ys, seemed in its loneliness to be calling to the isle of the Nine.

Where Redonian Way bent east, Eppillus barked: "Halt! Fall out." He turned to face the men. "You've been wondering what this is for. Well, I didn't know myself till yesterday when the centurion told me. We're going to do a little drill, boys, a little war game. That's how come I ordered you each to bring a baton. Save your real swords. You might be needing 'em."

"Eh?" said Adminius. "D'you mean we're expecting an attack? Why, just last night, down in a 'ore'ouse, I was talking with a chap back from Condate Redonum, and 'e was telling 'ow it's all serene. Maximus is way off south by now, driving the opposition before 'im."

Eppillus squirted a jet between his front teeth, to spatter on a breast-high wall of dry-laid stone about ten feet long. A couple more were nearby. Already they looked as ancient as a beehive-shaped rock shelter for shepherds in the distance. "This wasn't built against no Roman troops," the deputy said. "What use in that? It's to protect archers and slingers from enemy coming up out o' the water. One thing you'll do today, my fine fellows, you'll learn and learn well where the lilies are."— as Romans called mantraps of the kind that Ysan laborers had here dug for them. "Wouldn't want a stake up your arse, would you?"

"Saxons!" Budic exclaimed.

Cynan shook his head. "No such rovers anywhere near," he replied. "The fishers know. I was talking myself—with Maeloch; you remember Maeloch, Adminius—he and I've gotten to be pretty good friends—"

"As broody as you both are, I can see that," the man from Londinium said with a gap-toothed grin. "Wot d'you do, sit around arguing whether Lir or Nodens is 'arder ter please?"

"Silence!" Eppillus rasped. He planted his legs well apart, put hands on broad hips, and glowered at the troops. "Now listen close, you braying jackasses. I don't want to have to say this twice. Ask your stupid questions today. Later on, each one costs an hour's pack drill. Got me?

"Well, then. Maybe once in a while one or two o' you's come up for air out o' his beer and noticed how the centurion's got work started on land defenses. The city could stand off any barbarians that might land, sure; but he don't aim to *let* them land and go around scorching the country-side. That'd make a hungry winter for us, wouldn't it? Did any such thought ever stir in your dim little minds?"

Having captured their full attention, he relaxed his stance and lowered his tone. "Ah, the centurion's a deep one, he is. But I didn't understand how deep, myself, till yesterday, when he called me in. Brace yourselves, boys. This is uncanny.

"Somehow, he didn't say how, he knows there's a big fleet o' Scoti at sea. It's bound for the Liger mouth, to loot and lay waste that whole fine country. The garrisons there are stripped because o' the war. Gratillonius don't figure he can allow this, not at the back o' Maximus Augustus." He drew breath, hunched forward, dropped his voice close to a whisper. "Well, somehow, and believe me, I didn't ask how—somehow he knows a great storm's going to come out o' this clear blue sky, and blow the Scoti onto the rocks around Ys and drown them!"

Rocking back on his heels, thumbs hooked in belt, he let the men mumble their amazement, clutch their lucky charms, speak their hasty prayers. When he judged the moment right, he grinned and said:

"Easy, now. You've got nothing to be scared of, less'n you're a Scotian. After last year on the Wall, I don't suppose any o' us in the Second Augusta bear those headhunting devil-cats much love. Our job is to make sure o' them. You see, all their boats may not be wrecked. Some crews may make it ashore. If we let them go, we'll have a dangerous nuisance on our hands, or worse, for months to come. If we don't—if we cut 'em down as they straggle up from the water—why, not only will we be saving ourselves future trouble, we'll be doing Mother Rome a whopping big favor. Every Scotian we nail is one that won't ever go raiding again."

Cynan cleared his throat. "Question." Eppillus nodded. Cynan turned and pointed over Ys, toward Cape Rach. "I mentioned I've become friendly with a fisher captain. I've visited him and his family in that tiny village down under the southern cliffs. They don't call it Scot's Landing for nothing, deputy. It's the only good place to put in hereabouts, aside from Ys itself, and pirates have used it in the past."

"That was long ago, wasn't it?" Adminius protested.

"What matters," Cynan snapped, "is that Scoti still use it now and then. Not for hostilities, no. But small traders from Hivernia drop in to do business without paying Ysan duties. Or Scotic fishers blown off course come to refill their water casks."

"I know," Budic interposed. "They are from the south of Hivernia. Many are Christian. Father Eucherius was telling me about them."

Cynan sneered. "Is it impossible for a Christian to be a pirate? Besides, surely, if he's not a fool, the chief of this Scotic fleet that Gratillonius . . . foresees—surely he's provided himself with information about these waters and pilots who know them, even if he doesn't intend anything against Ys."

Adminius rubbed his chin. "M-m, you've a point there, chum."

Cynan's somber stare challenged Eppillus. "This is my question," he said. "Why are we being assigned here? Why not down at Scot's Landing?"

A smile relieved the heaviness of the deputy's features. "Ho, a damn good question, soldier. I'm going to tell the centurion you asked it. He's said he needs leaders from among us. You might make vinestaff someday."

Cynan did not return the smile, simply folded his arms and waited.

"Well," Eppillus explained, "the centurion knows what you do, and more. He's made ready. The fishers are a tough lot, nobody you'd care to meet in a brawl. Ysan marines will be on hand too, to help them hold Cape Rach. The centurion himself will stand by in town, at the head of a striking force which'll go wherever it's needed the most. But that leaves this place."

He pointed. What had once been a path, worn away by neglect and weather to a poor excuse for a trail, dropped down between brambles, over the edge of land and out of sight. "That goes to the ruins o' the Roman maritime station," he said. "Possible place for boats to put in. Maybe not likely, but possible. The centurion wants to cover all bets. He's decided to place a few men here, few but good. That's us, and you'd better measure up. We'll have Ysan sharpshooters with us, and we can send for reinforcements if we need them—like I told you, he'll be standing in reserve—though I hope we won't."

"With luck," said Adminius, "we won't get any custom."

Eppillus laughed. "Oh, I'd like some, not too big for us to handle by ourselves, but enough to look good when the centurion writes his report. Bonuses, promotions, and such, you know. I expect Maximus will be generous to them as deserve it. New-made Emperors always have been, I hear." He rubbed his hands. "Maybe extra acres for my bit of a farm when I retire?"

Straightening: "All right! If there are no more questions, let's get cracking."

4

No barge of state took the Gallicenae out to Sena. That would have been too dangerous—after dark, when few sailors dared come near the rocks around the island, and on a mission as dread as was theirs. None would do to navigate but Ferriers of the Dead.

Just past the full, the moon stood low above the cliffs. It threw a shuddery bridge over waters otherwise dark as heaven, closer to hand flecked by foam-gleams that were like fugitive stars. Quiet though air and sea were, whiteness snapped its teeth across the reefs strewn everywhere about. The stillness seemed to deepen the chill that always followed sunset, out away from land.

A pair of boats could carry eight women with sufficient rude dignity. Oars creaked, not loudly, almost the sole human sound. The smack *Osprey* went first. Two of her passengers sat silent in the bows near the lookout, two in the stern, where Captain Maeloch had the helm. He knew this passage so well that in fair weather he would merely need warning of something unexpected, a driftwood log or a piece off a wreck.

Dahilis had settled closest to him, legs curled beneath her on a cushion, at the larboard rail. She could not have been altogether lost in meditations, for from time to time she glanced up to where his beard jutted athwart the Bears. For his part, he stole some looks at her. Very fair she was with her cowl thrown back, hair aglow in the dimness. Above her reached those stars called the Maiden. Finally their glances chanced to meet, and turned aside in confusion, and she smiled at herself while he scowled at himself.

Low and flat, the island drew nigh in sight. A small stone building with a squat tower made blackness behind a dock where a lantern glimmered red. The lookout finally did call soft words as he gestured, and Maeloch gave orders and put his helm accordingly. The boat thudded against rope bumpers. The lookout sprang off with a line which he made fast to a bollard. Maeloch tossed him another line for the stern and lifted and secured the steering oar. Flamelight showed that it was old Quinipilis who had had today's Vigil and now stood waiting.

Dahilis rose. Maeloch offered his arm. "Let me help you, my Queen," he said softly.

"Thank you," she answered, which many of the wellborn would not have troubled to do.

He guided her over the deck, jumped to the wharf, and gave her support as she followed. No matter the unknown deed in which she was about to take part, impishness broke forth and she whispered, "That was needless. I'm no cripple. But I enjoyed it. I hope you did."

"My Queen—" For one of the few times in his life, he was taken aback. Hastily: "Um, 'tis not for me to do aught but obey here. However, best will be if ye ha' done ere moonset. The tide will've gotten tricky—nasty rips. But we'll abide your pleasure."

"I think not 'twill take very long, that which we go to," she replied, serious again. "Remember, you and every fisherman, sail not out tomorrow, nor till the King gives you leave."

"We'd no thought of that," he said, "after being told how all ye Nine will come back with us tonight."

Quinipilis beckoned. Dahilis went to join her Sisters. Slowly, in single file, they walked off. Harsh grass, gray under the moon, wet kelp, pools where strange small creatures scuttled, were the other signs of life upon Sena. But three seals followed along the shore till the trail went inland, then lay afloat as if awaiting the high priestesses' return.

At the Stones Quinipilis set her lantern down and lifted her arms. She led the women in their prayer to the Three and in the sacraments of salt and blood. They kindled no wood this time, for their doings were apart from the element Earth. Rather, they sacrificed Fire to Air by raising the lantern hood and blowing on the flame till it burned furiously, then to Water by quenching the candle in a bowlful of brine. Hands joined, they danced solemnly around the menhirs while they chanted:

"Wind of the West, awaken! The wolf is again a-prowl.
The ravening reaver of sheepfolds has lifted his head to howl,
And the watchmen shudder in summer to hear those wintry sounds.
Wind of the West, awaken! Unleash now on him your hounds.

"Calling on Lir, we loose you to harry our enemy
That dared to depart from the heathlands and hunt upon His sea,
And His waves shall answer your whistle, and come to course the
      beast
Wildly through brakes of spindrift, relentlessly to the East.

"Calling on Lord Taranis, the Guard of the city wall,
We order up horror and havoc, lest what is worse befall,
And we lend your hand His hammer where storm-flung squadrons
      go
Onto the waiting skerries, that heavy may be the blow.

"Calling on Belisama, Our Lady of Life and Death,
Whose kisses put warmth in the newborn and stop the old man's
      breath,
And Whose stars betoken Her peace in the dawn and the sunset
      skies,
Doom will we deal to sea wolves. O Wind of the West, arise!"

XV

1

On his second and third nights at sea, Niall again glimpsed the owl. It came out of the eastern darkness, swung silently above the Roman skull, turned back and vanished in empty distances. Other men saw it too, and muttered of it to comrades who had not. Before fear could spread through his fleet, the King commandeered a currach and had himself rowed to the nearer vessels. "It is nothing to frighten us at all, at all," he declared to them. "No natural bird, surely; but it's done us no harm, has it, now? Maybe a poor wandering ghost, such as we've charms against. Maybe a scout for the witches of Ys, but if so, it's telling them we mean no harm to their country. You'd not be letting a single fowl scare you, would you, my darlings?"

The bold beauty of him, as he stood spear in hand and seven-colored cloak about his wide shoulders, breathed courage into everyone. What further thoughts he had, he kept to himself.

It had been easy to get about thus on the water, for the airs had turned crank, foul when any whatsoever blew, and craft crawled forward on oars. Everywhere stretched Ocean, barely rocking beneath a cloudless sky, and sunblaze blistered fair skins. Niall could only guess where he was. However, he said, one more day must certainly put them well south of the peninsula, after which they could seek land. There they would get their bearings and, hugging the shore, proceed to the Liger mouth.

But on the night before this change of course—the third night, some hours after the owl had passed by—clouds began piling up in the west. Like black mountains they were, and ever more tall they grew, while stronger and stronger became the wind that skirled from them. By dawn it was a full storm.

No man saw that sunrise. There was naught but a faint lightening of what had been utter murk. Heaven was hidden. Wrack flew beneath like the smoke of burning houses. Monstrous were the waves, towering over hulls as they rushed and rumbled by, their backs white with foam, the hollows of them shading from green on top to abyssal black in the troughs. Their crests blew away in blinding froth. Wind filled the world. It struck fangs of cold into the bones of men, it lashed them with bitter scud, it grabbed their garments and sought to drag them leeward to their drowning. Often a burst of rain and great hailstones flew down upon it and streaked across the fury round about.

Niall's folk could do naught save hold their galley head on to the seas. Those who were not at the oars were bailing—buckets, cups, helmets, boots, whatever might keep the water a-slosh no higher than their ankles. The ship pitched, bow down till the stempost flailed amidst spume, bow up and a flood of tears from the eye sockets of the skull. Timbers groaned in anguish. Otherwise the warriors were helpless, driven before the tempest toward wherever it would have them.

Niall went back and forth, balancing himself against the surging as a lynx would. Labor was gess for him, the King; his part was harder, to keep heart in his followers. "Good lads, brave lads, it's fine you are doing. Sure and Manandan is proud of you. And what a tale you'll have to tell by your hearthfires!"

But once when he was aft, he let himself falter. Nobody was in earshot, in this tumult, besides Uail maqq Carbri at the helm, and he a close friend and indomitable. His back to the blast, Niall peered right and left. He made out a few currachs, riding better than the galley but no more able to hold a course. The rest of the fleet was lost to sight in gray chaos, scattered, perhaps much of it already broken and the crews sunk. His shoulders slumped. "I wonder if we should give a Manandan a man, that He soften his anger at us," he croaked.

Uail, the old mariner, shook his head. "We should not," he answered through the racket, "for I am thinking this is no work of His, but of Lir, His father. And Lir is the truly terrible—no handsome charioteer but a Force that will not be swerved by anything in human gift."

Niall shuddered. "Who raised Him?"

Uail shrugged, squinted into the storm, devoted himself to his tiller.

Niall started forward again, bench to bench. His son Breccan was among those bailing. Without the brawn to row, bare-legged under a kilt, the prince kept on somehow when grown men had crumpled up, worn out and numbed by the cold. He looked aloft at the King. His golden hair was plastered to his cheeks, as sodden as the shirt that clung to his lanky frame, and his eyes seemed enormous, dark-shadowed by weariness, in the face that was his mother's. The rhythm of his pail checked. He flashed a grin and a thumb-sign of defiance at his father, before he bent back to his task and sent another load of water over the side.

"Medb with us!" Niall shouted. "I did well to bring you!" After that he was cheerful—

—until the first white spurtings and bestial growls told how the fleet had drifted in among reefs.

Uail bawled orders which the roars of Niall passed onward against the wind. Regardless of the danger of getting swamped, the danger of tossing about was worse. Oars churned. Many a wave dropped away from a blade, hissing in mockery, and the stroke smote air. Yet the ship did get turned around. She could not fight her way west, but she could wallow along under some measure of control, claw off the rocks that surrounded her, seek to keep alive.

Save when rainsqualls whooped by, the skies had paled somewhat and Niall could see farther than erstwhile, through a weird brass-yellow light. The gale had slackened just a bit too, so that there was less spindrift to whip his eyes. Yet whistling and bellowing and deep sucking noises filled his ears, while the seas ran even heavier. He witnessed currach after currach dashed against a skerry and its ribs smashed to splinters. Men would tumble out of the wreckage, flop for a ghastly moment, and go under, unless the surf rolled their bodies onto a ridge. Flotsam from a second galley, sundered, her crew and cargo spilled, went swinging past. At the edge of vision he spied a low-lying duskiness which he knew from mariners' accounts was the island Sena.

More craft were getting through than lost. Let them understand the King was too, and rally after they had passed these shoals! Niall fetched men from the bailers, Breccan among them, and had them step and secure the mast. That was long and perilous toil. Once the pole fell, caught a man's arm against the rail, made mush and shards of it. He swooned from the pain. Coolly, Breccan cut a strip of clothing and bound the hurt lest he bleed to death. Meanwhile his fellows got the mast in place. Raising sail would have been madness, but the King's banner fluttered aloft, color streamed in the spray, a hoarse cheer lifted through the hull.

Though the sun remained withdrawn, Niall reckoned the time as late afternoon.

Standing lookout in the bows, he was the first to make out the shadow ahead. It grew as the storm-clouds had done, rising, solidifying, until ruddy cliffs and the turmoil at their feet were unmistakable. The mainland.

Chill struck Niall in the breast. Then wrath leaped on high. He raised a fist. "I see. It is you yonder who have done this to us," he said between clenched teeth. "Why, why, why?

"Well, you shall mourn for it."

Wind continued to slacken, clouds to thin, the range of eyesight to stretch. The seas were still enormous, impossible to go against, but at least men could work partly across them, could pick the general direction in which a vessel was to be forced landward. Niall saw what he supposed were all the survivors of his fleet, or most of them—less than half the grand host which had sailed from Ériu, battered, awash, the strength wrung out of their crews, but alive, alive.

He saw which way they were setting. If only he could yell across the waters! His flag was a forlorn signal which few would likely fathom.

He could merely do what seemed best, or least bad. Niall moved aft. Amidships, he squatted, tapped Breccan on the shoulder, and said to the dear face: "Lay off that. Tell everybody to stop, take a rest, try to get warm. I think soon we'll be fighting."

"Oh, father!" It was a joy to see the joy that flamed in the youth. Breccan caught Niall's hand between both his. Niall rumpled the wet hair and went on to Uail astern.

"You've a plan, master," said the steersman.

Niall nodded. "I wish I had a better one. It seems the witches of Ys have been working for our destruction. How likely would it else be that we were blown straight onto this deadly ground? Medb, come help us get revenge."

He swept a finger around. "Look," he said. "We cannot beat back west. Seamanship would have us bear as much north as we may, try to round Armorica and win to the Alban Channel. With her weight and draught, this ship is able. But wind and waves are opposed, and overwhelming to the currachs. . . . Have we any more galleys left us? I see just the poor currachs, riding on top of the sea and thereby debarred from making more than a little way across it. . . . One by one, they are bound for yonder headland."

"For Scot's Landing beneath it."

"I know. Remember how much I inquired before we left home."

"Since they are forced onto a lee shore, those with men aboard who know it pick the only safe spot. The rest follow."

"It is not safe," Niall said grimly. "I think Ysan fighters are waiting there to slay them as they debark."

"That could well be." Uail regarded his King. "You've a plan, master," he repeated.

"I do that. *We* can work north. Never would I willingly forsake men who've trusted me. Have you not told me of another landing beyond the city?"

"I have. It is on the far side of Point Vanis, as they call that part. The Romans had a station there, but Saxons destroyed it and nobody has used it since."

"We will. If the Ysans plotted this, as I do believe, then they expect that whoever came through the reefs alive will seek haven at Scot's Landing. There they'll stand prepared. Now our lads, however wearied, should give a good account of themselves. But I doubt they can force a passage to the heights and refuge in the hinterland. The Ysan aim must be to kill most and drive the rest back to the hungry waters. We, though—here we've a shipful of the finest warriors in Ériu. We'll dock at the old station, hurry overland around the city, strike the Ysans from behind, scatter them and join our comrades. After that, the enemy should sit earthed behind his defenses till the weather clears and we can fare homeward."

"Homeward? . . . Well, it took Lir Himself to make Niall maqq Echach retreat. We'll bring back our honor, if nothing else." Uail hesitated, even while he strained at the oar. "But what if the other approach is guarded also?"

Niall's head lifted haughty as his banner. "Why, we'll cut our way through."

"Row, you scuts!" Uail cried. "Stroke, stroke, stroke!"

Four currachs, which happened to be far enough north, managed to follow. Doubtless the foe was watching and would guess the intent; but given his need to man the southern harborage, could he stem *this* tide? The hope of rescue, vengeance, and glory swelled higher in Niall than ever did lust for a woman.

Passing the headland, where the pharos stood like a sinister phallus, he was almost unaware of the white fury of water churning between it and the city wall. This was his first sight of Ys. He caught his breath.

The rampart shot up sheer, a cliff itself, topped by crags that were turrets. The very smoothness of that height, the marshalling of battlements above, even the frieze of playful, colorful shapes aloft in the granite, made it more awesome than the ruggedness which abutted on it. The gate was shut—barred and locked, Niall had heard—and the floats that opened it at low tide dashed back and forth, up and down, on waves that ramped and foamed. When one of those padded balls struck stone or metal-sheathed wood, a drum-boom rolled huge and hollow through the wind, with an iron rattle from the chains.

Behind the wall rose towers like frozen cataracts, rainbow-hued; and on the slopes beyond were terraces, gardens, gracious dwellings; and suddenly, briefly, Niall thought he saw why the Romans in Alba had given him such stubborn resistance.

He had his men to save. The galley drove onward.

2

Another cloudburst struck, fiercer and longer than any before. Rain slanted down in sheaves of spears; hail skittered off stones and made hoar the grass it had flattened; wind shrilled till a soldier's head rang in his casque. At last, as quickly as it had come, it went. The gale was dropping too. Through a brief rift in heaven, a sunbeam smote out of the west, from low above the waves, and shattered dazzlingly on them.

Eppillus trudged to the path and a little way through its mud and cascades, for a look below. When he saw, he stopped and whistled softly. Somehow, during the squall, a ship of the Saxon kind and four boats had made fast at the ruins of the wharf. They were vomiting warriors.

"Son of a bitch," he muttered to himself. "More than we bargained for." Slipping and swearing, he climbed back up and trotted across to where his legionaries stood ranked. Native archers and slingers stared over their defensive walls, read his visage, and readied their weapons.

"If we wanted a fight, Mithras has been mighty generous," he rasped. "We can't hold the path against as many as are coming. Scoti are like goats anyway. Most o' them 'ud scramble around and take us from the rear. Budic, boy, hit leather." He jerked a thumb at a horse tethered nearby. "Go tell the centurion we got a hundred or worse bandits on our hands here and could use whatever reinforcements he can spare us."

The Coritanian snapped a salute, leaped to the saddle, and was off. To the rest, Eppillus continued: "What we'll do is deploy in a half circle beyond the barriers. I drilled you in the maneuver; now let me stir those pea soup memories o' yours. It breaks the line, but just the same, man for man you're better than any two unarmored barbarians. Besides, the idea is to let the lilies and the sharpshooters take some o' them first. I expect they'll get together after that and go hooting away inland. Whoever they've happened to point themselves at, stand firm. Everybody else watch me. When I swing my sword over my head, like this, you run to me, around any enemy. We'll take tight formation while he's busy with those first few of us and hit him wherever he looks ripest for it. Got me? All right, to your posts. Hang in there for Mother Rome, not to speak o' your flea-bitten necks."

He stumped to his place at the middle, directly opposite the trailhead. Though the wind was falling off, its chill bit through metal, wool, and flesh. Drenched, grass moved sluggishly under its flow. A second sunbeam pierced the tattered, flying gloom and lit wildfire over the wetness. He remembered such weather from his boyhood in Dobunnia—but there the countryside was tamed, neatly kept, graced with trees along the roads and in the paddocks where cattle grazed red, farmsteads such as the one which waited for him—not bleak and open above a city where sorceries laired; and the storms came in honest wise, of themselves. Eppillus swore, spat, planted his flat feet firmer on the ground, and loosened blade in sheath.

The Scoti appeared. Leading them was a very tall man. His shield was blood-colored. The sea had not dimmed the brightness of his steel, garish clothes, beard, or the locks that streamed yellow from under a helmet. His billowing cloak half concealed a younker who bounded on his right. Behind him spilled his followers. Their weapons whirled, their yells resounded, thinned but sharpened by the wind.

Before drawing his own sword, Eppillus dropped hand to a pouch at his wrist and squeezed it. The shape of the thunderstone within was comforting. "Sweat us out some luck, will you?" he said. "Mithras, Lord o' Battles, into Your keeping I give my soul. Come on, stone, I know you can do your job."

As he observed, his heart bounded for joy till he thought it must be making the hair on his chest quiver. The foe had forgotten even such schoolboy discipline as their sort had shown in Britannia. They swarmed forward any old way, howling at the wide-spaced Romans.

Bows twanged. Slings snapped. Barbarians lurched, stared and scrabbled at arrows in them, fell to earth and lay writhing while blood pumped forth. Skulls shattered in a gush of brains where lead smote. Beneath other men turf collapsed, pits opened, their screams rose faintly from the stakes at the bottom whereon they were skewered. Why, this alone may panic them, Eppillus thought.

No. Their leader shouted. His sword flared aloft, a beacon. The wild men heard, and saw, and rallied to him. He has the magic, Eppillus thought. I've seen it before. The centurion has some, but this fellow got all there was to get.

The stripling loped ahead, probing for traps with a spear. In a loosely gathered pack, the Scoti came after. They were too fast for missiles to inflict many more casualties. Reaching the wall on their right, they overran it and butchered its Ysans in passing. The tall man stayed in their van. His sword flickered back and forth like lightning. Drops of blood dashed off it into the wind. He turned left and made for the center of the defense.

He's aiming straight at *me*, Eppillus realized. He knows what he's doing. It's like last year over again.

The deputy waved his blade on high. From the corners of his eyes he saw his men leave their posts and converge on him. Good soldiers, good grumbly roadpounders. But here came the Scoti.

Roman javelins flew. They stopped too few of those bastards.

Still ahead of his warriors, the tall man reached Eppillus. His blade whirred. The deputy's shield caught the blow. Its violence tore through hand and arm and shoulder to rattle his teeth. He shoved the boss forward. The Scotic buckler intercepted that. Eppillus brought the top rim of his shield upward, trying for the jaw. The tall man swayed easily aside. His sword swung underneath.

Eppilus felt the impact as something remote, not quite real. Abruptly his left knee gave way. He shifted weight to the right foot and stabbed. His point went into red-painted wood. The barbarian cut him across the forearm. His hand lost its grasp, he let go of his sword. His shield overbalanced him on the crippled left leg. As he fell, another blow took him in the neck.

Battle thundered over him. Armor or no, he felt ribs break. It didn't hurt, nor was the blood that ran out of his wounds anything but warm. He was afar, a boy, lying at ease in a meadow where honeybees buzzed. Dimly he heard shouts, clash of iron, thud and grunt and saw-edged shriek. He tried to think what it meant, and could not, and gave himself up to sleep in the great summer.

3

Those of the Scoti who put their currachs alongside Ghost Quay and sprang onto it made a mistake. Ysan marines stood there, full-armored, shield by shield in the Roman manner. From that fortress the laurel-leaf blades darted out. Archers and slingers on the path above sent a steady hail. Soon the close-packed stones were buried under corpses and entrails, while the water beneath foamed red.

Others among the incomers sought east of the wharf. They could beach their leather boats under the trail that led to Scot's Landing, though time was lacking to secure these and most soon drifted away. Meanwhile the crews must climb a steep and rocky slope to the path—where poised the sailors of Ys. That became a desperate battle.

Holding the high ground, the shellbacks finally prevailed. Such of the barbarians as survived withdrew to the water's edge, panting and snarling. A lull fell over the combat.

The wind was likewise dying down. Waves still ran gigantic, casting whiteness yards aloft where they burst on reefs and cliffs, but their ferocity was spending itself. The storm had done its work; now nature would fain rest.

Maeloch wiped his ax on the shirt of a dead foeman. Rising, he leaned on the weapon, drew long breaths, stared outward.

"What be ye thinking about so hard, skipper?" asked Usun at his side.

"I wondered what'll become of the enemy fallen," Maeloch answered.

Usun was surprised. "Why, I suppose the funeral barge'll take them out and sink them, save as with anybody else but a King."

"Aye. But after that, what? Will they knock on our doors and call us to ferry *their* spirits off—and to where?"

Usun shivered, he who had lately filled edged metal with furiousness. "Gods, I hope not! They'd find scant welcome on Sena. Can we cast a spell to keep them down, d'ye suppose?"

"Not ye nor me, mate. Let's ask our wives to try. 'Tis the women that stand closest to death, like they do to life."

4

Dahilis had never altered the house she inherited from her mother. To her its softly tinted pastoral frescos had once been signs of love and peace, afterward of refuge, lately of joy. She did fill vases with flowers in season; and in her bedroom she had replaced an ivory image of maternal Belisama with a wooden one. It was crude, but it had been carved for her when she was a child by an adoring manservant.

In dimness scented by roses, she knelt before the niche, raised her hands, and begged:

"All-holiest, ward him. If he must go to the fight, ride before him, Wild Huntress. Keep him safe, Protectress. And if he is hurt—he is so brave, you know—make him whole again, Healer. For the sake of Your people. Who else is more wise and good? Oh, let him live many, many years. When time comes for the Sacrifice, may it be me who goes instead of him. Please."

Her voice dropped to a whisper. "But not ere—well, you know."

The last few days, while Gratillonius was too busy to visit her, she had been sick in the mornings; and for more than a month, she had had no courses. She could hardly wait to tell him.

5

The King's reserves were standing by at Warriors' House, with horses bridled and saddled just outside High Gate. Thus when Budic delivered his news they were on their way immediately.

Galloping up the road onto Point Vanis, they saw the Scoti swarming down. What was left of the legionaries, about two dozen, followed closely but no longer pressed the attack. Maybe if Eppillus had been in command —but he wasn't. The knowledge rammed into Gratillonius. Indeed an overwhelming force had landed here. It must have been more skillfully led than barbarians usually were, too. Plain to see was that, in spite of their losses, the Scoti had outflanked the Romans before those could dress ranks, killed several, and held the remainder off by rearguard action. Since they were not bound east toward safety but south toward Cape Rach, their intention must be to aid their fellows at Scot's Landing. If they took the Ysans there in the back, they might well clear that whole area and evacuate every raider who was alive.

"By the Bull," said Gratillonius, "it shall not be. Ghost of Eppillus, hear me." He cast reins over his horse's nose, a signal to the well-trained beast that it must not stray, and jumped to the ground. In their strange bright armor, his marines did likewise. They assumed formation and quick-marched to intercept the Scoti.

There was no mistaking the enemy chief, a tall, golden-haired man, like some pagan God of war. I'm going after him first, Gratillonius decided. Once we've taken him out, the rest will be dung to our pitchforks.

Now it was the Scoti who were outnumbered—and unarmored, fatigued, many among them already wounded. As the marines advanced, the legionaries did too, from behind. The chief shouted and beckoned. His follower rallied around, formed a primitive shield-wall, started chanting their death-songs. They would not perish easily.

Gratillonius at its center, the Ysan line made contact. Everything became delirium, as always, except that the marines and the legionaries worked in coordinated units. Gratillonius could see his target man over the heads of others, but in the chaos that man had gotten elsewhere and was hewing away at Romans. "Ha-a-a! Ha-a-a!" Clang and bang, tramp and stamp, thrust parry, Gratillonius pushed inward.

A last, violent gust of wind went over the headland. A raven flew upon it.

Gratillonius was never sure afterward what had happened. He remembered a woman, titanic and hideous, lame, swarthy, sooty, a cast in her left eye, who wielded a sickle that mowed men like wheat. But that could not be right, could it? Surely the truth was just that somehow the Scoti battled their way through the onslaught, heaped casualties in windrows, won back to the trailhead and thence to the sea. Gratillonius had taken a blow on the head which, helmet or no, left him slightly stunned for a while. He must have suffered an illusion. That others had had the same was not uncommon in combat.

In the end, after they had done what they could for their own injured and cut the throats of whatever foes lay crippled, he and his troop stood at the brink, looking down. They saw the galley beating along the point on oars. The coracles trailed after. "That remnant is not in simple retreat," Gratillonius deemed. "They still aim to give reinforcement below Cape Rach. Well, we'll see about that."

He almost regretted the killing. If Rome had civilized Hivernia, long ago when that was possible, what soldiers for her its sons would be!

6

Hulls rolled, pitched, yawed, shuddered. Spray sheeted over the bows. Yet close in to land the seas were no longer too heavy to row against, with the currachs in the galley's pathbreaking wake. The reefs farther out took most of their rage. It would have been mortally perilous to venture there. Niall had another reason as well for staying near the cliffs. "The shortest way is the swiftest," he explained to Breccan. "The sooner we reach our people at the harbor, the fewer of them will die."

The boy hugged cloak around shoulders. Legs braced and hands clutching rail, they were standing together on the foredeck. Bailing was not immediately needful—a boon, when the crew were dwindled and so exhausted that turns taken on the benches were brief indeed. "Can we truly help them?" Breccan wondered.

"We can, if the Mórrigu be with us still." Awe tinged Niall's voice. He had seen the Mother of the Slain at work on the battlefield. "This game is not played out, darling. I think that not all the players are human." His gaze brooded over the waves. "What we'll do is engage the enemy yonder while those of our men ashore who've lost their boats—the which they'll have had no chance to make fast—come aboard. Thereafter we'll stand out, escorting what currachs are left. With more men, this ship can get about readily again. The currachs may want towlines from us to escape the maze of rocks we must thread; or if any get wrecked, we can try to rescue the crews."

"Will not the Ysans pursue? I've heard tell of their war fleet, and they know these waters as we do not."

"Those ships are elsewhere, my heart. Otherwise they would have attacked us before ever we could make any landings. For the masters of Ys knew we were coming. It can have been none but their she-druids that caused us to be blown here." Niall's fist smote the rail. "May each be raped by a demon, and may the whelps he gets on them tear them apart in the birthing."

Breccan looked troubled. "Father, always you told me to honor a worthy foe. And they've been bonny fighters here. They have."

"They set on us with their magical tricks when we meant them no hurt whatsoever." Niall sighed. "Ah, but Ys is fair and wonderful. Let us escape, and I'll forgive the folk if not their rulers." A smile crossed his lips. "Why, someday I'd like to come back, in peace. Behold. Let your eyes revel."

They had rounded the point and were about to pass the city at a distance of several hundred yards. High and high the walls gleamed, and the towers beyond; it was as if the voyagers had truly crossed Ocean and come to Tír innan Oac. The very rowers stared and marveled as they toiled.

Breccan shaded his brow from the spray. "Father, something is different. See, there on top. The little sheds are gone, and—what *are* those things?"

"You've the eyesight of youth," Niall said. "Let me try—Cromb Cróche!" ripped from him. "Those are killing machines! Helm over, Uail! Get us away!"

The air had gone quiet and cold. Waves ran noisily, but not so much as to smother the deep drone and thud which sounded from either side of the sea gate. Boulders the size of half a man came flying, tumbling, arching over with a horrible deliberation. Six-foot shafts, their iron heads murderously barbed, flew straight between them.

A splash erupted alongside. The galley rolled on her beam ends. Aft, Niall saw a direct hit on a currach. And it was no longer there, merely bits of it afloat, and two men who threshed about for a small span until they went under.

"Row!" Niall bellowed. "Pull out of range before they target us!"

Two bolts smote the larboard planks. Their points protruded into the hull. Their shafts dragged, waggled, got in the way of oars. Another pierced a currach, which filled and drifted useless. Men of the third boat drew close and tried to save those who clung to the wreckage. A ballista stone sank it.

"We cannot help," Niall groaned. "We'd only die ourselves." Nor did any chance remain of giving aid at Scot's Landing. The galley must now get so far from Ys that her crew would have all they could do to keep her off the skerries. By the time she could labor around to the south shore, that battle would be over.

"Manandan, I offer You a bull, white with red ears and mighty horns, for every lad of mine who comes home," Niall cried. Surely some could win back to such vessels as had not floated away, and thereupon ride it out, maintain sea room, finally steer for Ériu. Oh, let it be so!

Niall drew sword and shook it at the city. A sunset ray broke through clouds to glimmer along the iron, and to make brilliant the armor of the Ysan artillerymen. Tears mingled with salt water beneath the eyes of the King.

"Father, don't weep," Breccan said. "We did well—"

A bolt took him in the stomach, cast him down into the bilge, and pinned him there. His blood spurted forth. For a moment he struggled, flailing arms and legs, like an impaled beetle. He choked off a scream. Then he mastered himself and forced a smile.

Niall reached him, knelt, and tried to pull the bolt free. It was driven in too hard for even his strength. Useless, anyway. Breccan was sped. "Father," he gasped, "was I worthy?"

"You went that, you were, you were." Niall hugged him and, again and again, kissed the face that was like Ethniu's.

Soon Breccan lay quiet, save that the ship made limbs and head flop. His blood and shit sloshed about in the bilgewater.

Niall rose. He clambered back onto the foredeck. Three splashes in the waves, followed by no more, showed that he had drawn beyond reach.

He raised the sword he had dropped when Breccan was hit. He lifted it by the blade, in both hands, letting the edge cut his right palm till red flowed down the steel. None was in his countenance, which was as white as the eyeballs of his dead boy. Looking toward the beautiful city he said, low and evenly:

"Ys, I curse you. May the sea that you call yourself the queen of rob your King of what he loves the most, and may what he loves afterward turn on him and rend him. May your sea then take yourself back to it, under the wrath of your Gods. And may I, O strange and terrible Gods, may I be he who brings this doom upon you. For my revenge I will pay whatever the price may be. It is spoken."

Trailed by the last of its currachs, the ship went in among the rocks. Three boats got away from Cape Rach to join them, but one was presently ripped open and the men drowned. Darkness fell. The survivors found anchorage of a sort. In the morning they started home.

XVI

1

Ys jubilated. That evening the Fire Fountain was kindled in the Forum. Its jets and cascades of flame would make luminous the next six nights, for which the Nine had promised fine weather—part of the celebrations, both solemn and sportive, that would give thanks for victory.

In certain houses happiness was absent. Among them were those which had lost a man in battle. Some other people had their different misgivings.

At sunrise Gratillonius left the palace. He did not seek the gate for its ceremonious unlocking; the waves were still running too high. Instead he went alone, in a hooded cloak, unrecognized by such few persons as were abroad this early, to the Forum. Oil to the fountain was turned off just as he came onto the plaza; a little smoke lent acridity to remnant mists.

Mounting the west stairs of the former temple of Mars, he heard the voice of Eucherius the Christian pastor quaver out of the bronze door left ajar. He frowned and halted. Evidently the daily Mass was not over yet. He recognized the blessing that followed Communion, having caught snatches of Christian liturgy throughout his life. A coughing spell interrupted it. Well, then, they'd soon be done in there. It would be bad manners to enter just now. Gratillonius composed himself.

Half a dozen worshippers came out. The catechumens, who did not number very many more, had already heard the part of the service that was permitted them and gone off. These, the baptized, were four women and two men, of humble station and getting along in years. They didn't notice him. When they had passed by, he went into the vestibule. At the inner door he looked beyond, into the sanctuary, where Eucherius and old deacon Prudentius were occupied. Softly, he hailed.

"Oh—the King!" The small gray man was astonished. They had been introduced, but as hastily as Gratillonius felt was halfway polite. He had

had too much pressing business. Eucherius left Prudentius to put away the portable tabernacle of the Host, which in Ys was little more than a wooden box in the usual turret shape. The chorepiscopus trotted forward to take his visitor by the forearm. "Dare I hope—?" His shy smile faded out. "No, I fear not. Not yet. Were you waiting outside? You would have been warmer in this room. It's open to everybody."

"I don't belong," Gratillonius answered. "But I thought I should give you a sign that I respect your faith."

The pastor sighed. "You wish I would respect yours. Well, I do. From everything I have heard, it is an upright creed. I am sorry—I should not be, but I am—that I may not concede you more than this."

"I've come on a matter touching yours."

"I can guess what. You are indeed a virtuous man. Let us go talk." Eucherius led the way through the corridor around the sanctuary to his quarters. There he offered bread, cheese, and water; he had nothing better. Gratillonius partook sparingly.

"Eight of my soldiers died yesterday," he said. "Seven were Christian. Their legion and funeral society are away off in Britannia. It behooves me as their commander to see that they get the kind of burial they wanted. When I inquired, I learned that no Christians are ever laid in Ysan soil."

Eucherius expressed sympathy before he nodded. "True. Any burials near the city have long been forbidden, since men decided the necropolis should spread over no more valuable land. Not that the faithful could well rest there. And pagan sea funerals—" He grimaced, as if in actual pain. "Ah, poor souls! Father, forgive them, for they know not what they do. They mean well, too, but—but even Queen Bodilis, who has been so benevolent to me—My son, you have at least seen the outer world. How can you partake in these gruesome rites?"

"It's not forbidden me as a Mithraist. The Lord Ahura-Mazda created many beings less than Him but greater than men. Besides, I don't agree the Ysan practices are bad. They sacrifice no humans, like the Germans." Gratillonius drew aside from the combat in the Wood. "Nor do they sanction those obscene things that get done in the name of Cybele." Irritation roughened his tone. "Enough of that. Graves are allowed inland. Some farmers and shepherds, who'd rather keep their dead close by, bury them on their own property. Why doesn't your church maintain a plot?"

"None has been granted us. We have nothing but this building. I doubt anybody would sell us an ell of ground to consecrate, supposing I could raise the money. They would be superstitiously afraid of offending their Gods."

"I see. What do you do, then?"

"There is a churchyard outside Audiarna, the Roman town at the southeast border. It's not too far, about a day's journey by wagon. I have an arrangement with a carter, and with my fellow minister yonder." Another fit of coughing racked the thin frame. Concerned, Gratillonius noticed how bloody was the sputum. Eucherius gave him a sad smile and murmured, "Forgive me. I should not detain you, who must have much else to do. Send one of your soldiers who is a brother in Christ, and between us he and I will take care of everything."

"Thank you." Gratillonius rose, hesitated, and added, "If you have any needs in future, ask. I don't think you'll find me unwilling to help."

"Save where it comes to propagating the Faith?" replied Eucherius gently. "Regardless, yours is a noble spirit. Do you mind if I pray to my God that He watch over you and someday enlighten you? As for—charitable works or the like—oh, Bodilis may have some ideas." His eyes burned fever-brilliant in the gloom. "Give her my love."

2

Soren Cartagi sent an urgent message to the royal palace. The king should promptly meet with the Nine, as well as with Lir Captain and the Speaker for Taranis. "No surprise," Gratillonius snapped. He set the hour of noon and dispatched the courier to inform everybody named. At the time, he escorted Dahilis to the basilica. Twenty-two legionaries followed them. Some limped, some displayed bandages. Eight more lay dead, and two were an honor guard on the last journey of their seven Christian comrades.

The king wore a robe of splendor; the Key hung out in sight on his breast. He had better cut a potent figure. When he had mounted the dais before the eidolons of the Triad and, having formally opened the session and heard the invocations, gave the Hammer over to his attendant, he was much too aware that that man was not Eppillus. Recovering himself, he nodded gravely at the eleven faces that looked up into his.

"Well met, I trust," he said. "Though belike 'tis matters of import you would bring forth, let us strive to move them expeditiously. We all have many urgent duties, both secular and religious. The Gallicenae should resume their cycle of Vigils, while those in the city attend not only to the Gods, but to the hurt and the bereaved among our folk. My lords, your Great Houses and those who serve them have many calls on your attention in the wake of recent events. As for myself, I must see to public business that has gone neglected, as well as re-establishing communication with our navy and with Roman officials throughout Armorica."

Hannon Baltisi stirred his rawboned length on the bench. "Well may you do that last, O King," he growled, "as heavily as we've paid out for the benefit of Rome. Can you get us any reimbursal of the debt?"

Gratillonius had expected this. Lir Captain was devout to the point of fanaticism. In his days as a shipmaster, he said, he had often encountered the Dread of Lir. He had also seen, spreading through the Empire, a Christianity from which he awaited nothing but evil. "Methought we'd talked this out beforehand," Gratillonius replied mildly. "Ys dare not let barbarians lay waste the civilization which nurtures her also. We had the means to prevent it, and did, at remarkably small cost for the harvest we reaped."

"Nonetheless, cost! And never have I agreed that our action was necessary. While Ys remains true to Him, Lir will guard her. Why should we make enemies among tribes with which we could very profitably trade?"

"We may do that, now that we have chastened them. I know their kind; they respect naught but strength." Gratillonius drew breath. "If we are to discuss policy, we should have summoned the whole Council of Suffetes."

"Nay," rumbled Soren. "That's for later; and in honesty I must say I think you, lord King, are more nearly right. But you are wrong in other ways. You have forgotten the primal charge laid upon the King of Ys."

Gratillonius nodded. "He is the high priest and in a sense the Incarnation of Taranis. Aye. But you know that *this* King is also your prefect."

"And he is no Colconor!" Dahilis cried. Glances turned to her. She reddened, touched her lips, then squared shoulders and gave back a defiant stare.

Gratillonius smiled. "Thank you, my dear," he said. "Let me remind this honorable assembly, 'twas understood when first I mounted your throne that I'd have much on my hands, things too long ignored that must be set aright, new things for which there is an aching need. 'Twas with your consent that I devoted myself to them. What's happened since shows that you were wise to go along with me."

"That's past," Soren declared. "The time has come when you should in earnest assume your sacral duties."

"Gladly will I, insofar as Mithras allows."

Teeth flashed in Soren's beard. His burly form hunched forward. "Then why do you refuse to lead the thanksgiving sacrifice today?"

"I explained that to the priest who asked me yestereven." That had been one of those Suffete men who, otherwise occupied with their own everyday affairs, were initiated into certain mysteries and therefore authorized to conduct the rites of Taranis. The Speaker was among them, but tradition decreed that once he had taken that office he no longer acted as a flamen.

"He should have approached me earlier," Gratillonius reproved. "Then I would not have committed myself to be elsewhere at the time set. 'Tis a holy commitment which I cannot break, just as it appears the hour for your ceremony is now unchangeable. Well, my presence is not absolutely required. Choose a priest to take my place. As for me, surely the God will think Himself best served by a man who has first honored the claims of manhood."

"And what, pray, mean you by that?"

Here comes the crisis, Gratillonius thought. Beneath his robe he tautened himself like a soldier before battle. He kept his voice calm: "You may have noticed that Quintus Junius Eppillus, my deputy, is not here. He fell in defending Ys. As do I, he worshipped Mithras. This day he shall have the burial he deserves."

Soren scowled. "The necropolis was closed lifetimes ago."

"He should not lie there in any case, nor be cast to the eels. Such is not the way of Mithras. I'll leave him on Point Vanis, looking toward the Britannia to which he longed home, but forever guarding this land."

A gasp went among the Gallicenae, save for Dahilis, who had already been told, and Bodilis, who was clearly perturbed. "Nay!" shrilled Vindilis. "Forbidden!"

"It is not," Gratillonius retorted. "That's grazing commons. A headstone will do no harm. Rather, 'twill recall his bravery on behalf of Ys."

Hannon bit off word after word: "It seems my lord King is misinformed. The necropolis was not closed merely because 'twas encroaching on land needed by the living. 'Twas draining down into the sea. Why think you we haul away our sewage from pits, 'stead of letting cloacas open in the bay? Corruption of His waters is a mockery of Lir. Men at sea must beg His pardon ere they relieve themselves. Let Ocean have clean ashes of a fallen King; let His fish otherwise have clean, undecayed flesh."

"One grave high on a foreland will not—"

"The precedent!" Lanarvilis interrupted.

Quinipilis raised her staff and suggested, "Could you not lay your friend to rest inland, Gratillonius? I'm sure almost any landowner would allow, aye, believe 'twas lucky and pay honors ever afterward to the dead man."

That was the sticking point, precisely because it was reasonable. Gratillonius had picked the gravesite on impulse, out of sentiment, a wish to give good old Eppillus some small compensation for the farm he would never return to. Only later, when he explained to Dahilis why the priest had left with such a scandalized expression, did she remind him of the prohibition. He had quite forgotten it until then.

Now he could not compromise. His authority had been challenged at its foundation; if he failed to maintain it, he would soon fail as the prefect of Rome.

"I fear that would be to break a vow I made before my God," he stated. "Moreover, with due respect, 'twould be wrong if Eppillus—the memory of Eppillus—became a yokel godling. His soul has earned more. Nay, he shall lie in earth which his blood has hallowed. It will not be a precedent. I will proclaim that this memorial is unique, revering every man who ever gave his life for Ys."

He folded his arms just beneath the Key. "This is my will," he told them most quietly. "Bethink you, my ladies and lords." He made no least gesture at the motionless iron rank of his men.

Not much further was said. Hannon himself had no more desire for a confrontation than did Gratillonius. One by one, the gathering mumbled assent.

Still, success was exhilarating, giddying. Gratillonius wanted to make them happy too, make them again his well-wishers. He raised his palms. "Let me give you the glad tidings," he said. "Queen Dahilis is with child."

A murmur, not really surprised, went among the women. Bodilis and Quinipilis, at her sides, embraced her.

Goodwill rushed over Gratillonius. Let bygones be bygones. If Colconor had been wronged, the swine wasn't worth avenging. Certainly that incident should no longer encumber the King in his politics and his daily relationships.

"Hear more, O Sisters of hers," Gratillonius continued. " 'Tis true I've perforce postponed many of my tasks; but as her time approaches and she is hampered, why, we shall all get to know each other better."

Vindilis flushed as if struck. Fennalis sneered. Quinipilis frowned and shook her head slightly. Bodilis bit her lip. Lanarvilis and Forsquilis stiffened. Maldunilis and Innilis seemed to accept, and Dahilis was radiant—she had felt so guilty about having him to herself when he was with any woman whatsoever—but he realized in some dismay that somehow he had said the wrong thing, and it could not very well be unsaid.

3

Sunset cast scarlet and gold over the half of heaven that reached above Ocean. Water glimmered and glowed beneath the cliffs. Sounds of surf came muted. A breeze ruffled the grass on Point Vanis. It came from the north, cooling the day's warmth, bearing a smell of salt and maybe, maybe, of fields in Britannia.

Six legionaries bore the freshly made coffin of Eppillus to the grave that had been dug and lowered it down. Then they saluted, wheeled, and marched back to the city in formation. As Christians, they could give no more honors to their officer. Four stayed behind: Gratillonius, Maclavius, and Verica, the Mithraists in their vexillation, together with Cynan, who had offered his help. Funerals were not forbidden to noninitiates; after all, wives, daughters, mothers, young sons, companions had farewells to make.

Not before had the believers held a service. That might have been disruptive, on the march and during the settling in and the preparations for war. They had contented themselves with private prayers. This evening they stood together in the presence of eternity.

The three rankers took the spades they had carried and filled the hole. At first clods fell on wood with a sound like footfalls; afterward the noise was muffled, until the low mound had been patted down to await wildflowers. A headstone would come later. Gratillonius had not yet decided what the epitaph should be. Name, position, unit, of course—and, perhaps, the old Roman "STTL. . . . *Sit tibi terra levis.* . . . May the earth lie light upon you."

Meanwhile he spoke the sacred words. Holding the grade of Persian within the faith, he could do that, though best would have been if Eppillus could have had his valediction from a Father. "—Since this man our comrade has fared from among us—"

The soul was surely bound for Paradise. How long its trek would be, no mortal could tell. Eppillus had talked of feasting with Mithras; the God must set a grand table! But seven gates stood on the road to the stars, each guarded by an angel who would only let the soul pass when it had undergone a further purification. To the Moon it would leave its vitality, to Mercurius its voracity, to Venus its carnality, to the Sun its intellectuality, to Mars its militancy, to Jupiter its pride, to Saturnus the last of its selfhood; thus would it attain the eighth heaven and the Light, to be forever One with Ahura-Mazda. Gratillonius found the thought of Eppillus trudging on that pilgrimage peculiarly lonely.

But farewell, farewell.

Colors died in the sky. It shaded from silvery in the west to royal blue in the east. The earliest stars trembled forth.

"Let us go back," said Gratillonius.

Cynan plucked at his sleeve. "Sir," he murmured, "may I have a word with you, apart?"

Surprised, the centurion looked into the somber young visage a heartbeat or two before he nodded. They went off to the trailhead above the cliff, up which the enemy had stormed. Peace breathed around them.

"What do you want, Cynan?" Gratillonius asked.

The Demetan stared outward. His hands wrestled each other. "Sir," he forced from himself, "would it be . . . possible . . . for me . . . to join in your rites . . . hereafter?"

"What? But you're a Christian."

"It means nothing to me," Cynan said hurriedly. "The centurion knows that. Else why would I be here? I offered to my tribal Gods, they seemed more real, but—I always wondered, and then the other day—" His tongue faltered.

"What happened?" Gratillonius prompted.

"You know!" Cynan exclaimed. "That ghastly giantess who entered the battle."

A prickling went through Gratillonius's skin. "What? Did you too have that, that delusion?"

"Not me alone. I've talked with others."

"Well," said Gratillonius carefully, "I suppose the Scoti may by some kind of magic have called in some kind of creature to help them at the last. Little good did it do them."

Cynan clenched his fists and twisted about to face his leader. "Sir, that isn't it! I'm not afraid of Halfworld beings. But I saw . . . I saw an old, animal horror, and it lives inside me, inside everybody, and . . . and nothing can keep it from us but a God Who is not mad. Will you teach me about yours?"

Gratillonius forgot military discipline and hugged him.

Stepping back, his wits restored, the centurion said, "You'll certainly be welcome to worship with us if you'll accept the discipline. But just as a postulant, a Raven. If you do well, I have the power to raise you to an Occult. No more. Initiation into the true Mystery needs a Father."

"Someday I'll find one," Cynan replied ardently.

It burst upon Gratillonius like sunlight through clouds: Why not?

Votaries of Mithras were scattered through the Empire, their congregations isolated, often persecuted. There must be some in the cities and barracks of Armorica, not to speak of Britannia and the rest of Gallia. In Ys they could find tolerance, the Brotherhood free and open. Not that they could settle here as a general thing, but they could come for prayer, elevation, heartening upon earth, strength for the wayfaring afterward. Moreover, most being soldiers, such ties with them would help him draw together a defensive webwork for the whole province.

He could not found or lead a Mithraeum. That required a Father. But he could cherish the dream and work for its attainment.

4

With the round of the Vigils broken, Bodilis volunteered to be the first who started afresh. The order of rotation was not important. What mattered was to have a Sister on Sena—always, apart from special circumstances—in communion with Our Lady of the Sea and the souls whom She had taken unto Herself.

Bodilis thought she might be the best of the Nine to go forth after the gale, simply because of having both strength of body and an orientation toward natural philosophy: for she did not expect that the cycle could in fact be immediately resumed. She proved right.

Though morning seas rolled as gentle as rocks and riptides allowed, the barge of state that bore her could not make land. The wharf was gone, except for a few splintered bollards. It would have been dangerous for a vessel of any size to approach. Instead, a jollyboat carried the high priestess to shore. Its oarsmen waited while she walked to the building and, afterward, around the entire island.

That took a pair of hours, during which the sailors kept reverent silence. From time to time they glimpsed her, in a cloak of the blue that was Belisama's color, moving over rocks and treeless flats. Before them was the sight of the building and the damage it had suffered. It was a small, squared-off structure of dry-laid granite from which a tower jutted, on the east end of Sena. Billows dashing over the low ground had displaced several blocks at the bottom, visibly though not enough to cause collapse. On the frontal western side, window glass was shattered, shutters torn off, the oaken door a-sag on its hinges.

The calm of this day became a chilling reminder of what had passed. Waves lapped, chuckled, glittered green, azure, white, streaked with dark tangles of kelp. A few seals cruised to and fro, close in the shore; it was as if their gazes too followed Bodilis. Gulls, guillemots, puffins, cormorants winged beneath cloudlessness. Through the air went a current of summer's oncoming warmth.

She returned and had the men bring her back to the barge. There she nimbly climbed the rope ladder to the deck and sought the captain. "We go home at once," she told him. "The place is unfit. It needs restoration."

The officer was bemused, a little shocked. "How, my lady?"

Bodilis smiled. "Be at ease. This is not the first time over the centuries that that has happened. The worst was in the era of Brennilis, when Ocean destroyed everything. It was among the warnings by the Gods against making the wall around Ys otherwise than according to Their will. These repairs ought take no more than some days. Furnishings and holy objects shall be replaced as well, likewise stocks of food and water—aye, in particular the cistern must be emptied, cleansed of salt, supplied with fresh sand and charcoal. The Stones abide as always. However, the hearthsite there would benefit from attention."

The captain tugged his beard. "But what of the House itself, my lady? Restoring yon blocks will be hard labor, impossible for women to do, if the Queen will pardon my saying so." A thought struck him. "Could the King's soldiers lend their skills? The Romans are the greatest engineers in the world."

"Nay. Even Brennilis's Romans were only permitted to draw up plans and give advice. Among men, none but husbands or sons of former vestals may ever betread this island above high-water mark, and then only when the necessity is beyond doubt and after they've been blessed in certain ancient rites. At that, once they are done, all we Nine must come out and reconsecrate everything. Gratillonius is a good man, but he would never be able to understand—" Bodilis broke off. "Come, unship the sweeps, let us begone."

XVII

1

After the victory celebrations, Ys settled back down into the ways of peace. Those did not mean idleness. Besides workaday tasks and repair of storm damage, there were preparations for the great midsummer festival. However, folk no longer tensed themselves against the morrow. The Scoti were broken, the Saxons would surely heed that lesson, the Romans of Armorica stayed quiescent, and—word trickled from the palace, to which couriers brought letters—Maximus was campaigning, successfully, in the South. A person dared again take a certain amount of ease.

Even Gratillonius did. Most of the time he kept busy. He must confer with the individual Suffetes, try to win their confidence, wrangle over ends and means, defense, outside relations, how to refill city coffers that Colconor had emptied, what reforms were desirable in a civil service ossified with age, countless petty details. Without compromising the status of King or prefect, he also tried to make the acquaintance of ordinary people, their needs and wants, strengths and failings.

Still, he could now take some recreation, set up a woodworking shop for himself, go riding, hunting, sailing. He could devote more attention than erstwhile to Dahilis. (As yet, aware that he had blunderingly given umbrage to his other wives, but unsure how to make amends, he met them only publicly, when at all. Dahilis too kept silence about the matter. He knew, and knew that she knew, that to some extent they were selfishly grasping what time remained to them before her fruitfulness was so far along that they had better sleep apart.) He and his soldiers, Mithraist and Christian, could properly observe that Sunday whose holiness they shared.

He could instruct Cynan in the Faith.

He received the Demetan in a room of the palace meant for private talks. On the upper floor, it was small and plain save for frescos of pastoral scenes, narrow-windowed, sparsely furnished. The first day when Cynan came happened to be rainy, which cast a dimness as if this were indeed a crypt of the Mystery. A servant showed the visitor in, closing the door after him. Cynan snapped a salute. In Roman tunic and sandals, painstakingly barbered and scrubbed, he could not altogether hide surprise at sight of his chief.

"Greetings," said Gratillonius from his chair. "At ease. What's the matter?"

"The centurion is . . . very kind," replied the newcomer huskily.

Gratillonius studied the darkly handsome face, the muscular body, the hillman beneath the civilized shell, before he murmured, "At ease, I said. Outside this room we are legionary and officer. But here—the first thing for you to learn is that in Mithras are no worldly ranks. No high or low, rich or poor, free or slave." He smiled. "So what's bothering you?"

Trembling, Cynan blurted: "You aren't like before, sir! I didn't really see it till now, but you aren't."

Gratillonius considered. He wore Ysan shirt, jacket, and breeches, as he usually did except when overseeing his troops. Though close-cropped, auburn mustache and beard had reached their full growth. As yet his hair was too short to draw into a horsetail, but it fell beneath his earlobes and was confined by a fillet. Aye, he found himself thinking in Ysan, the lad may well wonder what sorcery beyond the sea gate has flowed its tide over me.

"I have to be King oftener than prefect, remember," he said in his plainest Latin. "Remember also, Mithras doesn't care about your outside. Only your inside, your spirit, counts. Do sit down." When his guest had obeyed, he himself poured wine for them both. "Let's talk."

He couldn't lighten the mood. Cynan wasn't that sort; and, of course, this wasn't that kind of occasion. Gratillonius could, though, seek to penetrate the bashfulness—and the fierce pridefulness—that stood between them. "Before we start," he went on, "we should know each other better. I picked you to come along, back in Isca, because I'd seen you fight like a demon beyond the Wall. But why did you volunteer?"

Cynan stiffened. "It was an adventure, sir."

"Can you look me in the eye and smile when you say that? Listen, son, if you're afraid to be honest, Mithras will not make you welcome. And if I punished you for your honesty, He would disown me."

Blood pulsed up into the young countenance. A fist clenched. "Very well, sir!" the Demetan cried. "I wanted to travel and fight, not do drill at headquarters. But I did not want to travel with Maximus and fight Romans. My home village was near the coast. I came back from hunting in the glens and found the Scoti had been there. What they hadn't plundered, they'd burnt. They killed the men, my father, my older brother. They gang-raped my mother. They bore off my young brother and two sisters for slaves. I swore I'd live for revenge. I lied about my age and my Gods, to join the army. I gloried when we cut down the vermin in the North, and again here—oh, sir, you were Vengeance itself! Then that troll-thing on the battlefield—and afterward, when you gave Eppillus his honor—*That's* why I've come to your God!" He covered his face and wept, long, coughing sobs: no Roman now, a Celt.

Gratillonius let him have it out, and comforted and calmed him, and could finally begin:

"I'm not the best of a long shot to explain the Faith. A lot I don't understand myself. I only rate as Persian, the fourth grade. But maybe it's good for you to hear about it first in simple soldier lingo.

"Persian. . . . The Faith came from Persia, Rome's old enemy, but a worthy foe. Often a man learns more from an enemy than a friend. And, of course, it wasn't always war; and others than Persians were believers; and as the ideas moved into the Empire, Greek thinking, and later on Roman, worked them over.

"Before and above all, forever, the One from Which Everything comes —" He checked himself. The concept of Time—Aeon, Chronos, Saturnus, the Source, the Fountainhead—was for the higher ranks, those allowed into the sanctuary. You didn't pray to the Ultimate anyway.

"Above all Gods," Gratillonius said, "is Ahura-Mazda. He's also called Ormazd, Jupiter, Zeus, many names. Those don't mean much; He Is, the High, the Ever-Good." He found himself slipping into the words of the Lion from whom he had received instruction. Well, they were doubtless better than any he could put together. "Below all Gods is Ahriman, Evil, Chaos, maker of hell and devils and misery. The story of the world is the story of the war between Ahura-Mazda and Ahriman. So is the story of your soul, lad. They war for it the same as they do for the whole of Creation. But you don't have to stand by helpless. You can be a soldier yourself.

"Then your Commander is Unconquered Mithras.

"He is the God of light, truth, justice, virtue. Because these come into being, suffer, and die—like mortals, or like the sun that rises and sets and rises again—you'll see Mithras shown with two torchbearers, the Dadophori. One torch is upright and burning, the other is turned down and going out.

"Our Lord Mithras was born from a rock, which some say was a cosmic egg. It was on the banks of a river, underneath a sacred tree. Only shepherds witnessed this, and came to adore Him and bring offerings. But Mithras was naked and hungry in the cold winds. From the fig tree He plucked fruit and from its leaves He made Himself garments. Then His strength came to Him."

Gratillonius paused before saying slowly: "This happened before there was life on earth. I don't understand that myself. But why should a man be able to understand the Eternal?

"The first battle of Mithras was against the Sun. He overcame His noble foe, and received the crown of glory from Him. Thereafter He raised up the Sun again, and They swore friendship.

"His second battle was against the Bull, the first of living creatures that Ahura-Mazda made. He seized It by the horns and rode It, no matter how much He was hurt, till It was worn out and He could drag It to His cave. It escaped, and the Sun sent the Raven as a messenger, bidding Mithras kill the Bull. Against His will, He did this. He and His dog tracked It back to the cave where It had returned, and He took It by the nostrils with one hand while with the other hand He plunged His knife into Its throat.

"Then from Its body sprang life upon earth, from Its blood the wine of the Mystery. Ahriman sent his evil creatures to destroy this life, but in vain. A great flood covered the world. One man, out of the humans alive in those days—one man foresaw it in a vision, and built an ark that saved his family and some of every kind of being. Afterward Ahriman set the world afire, but this too it survived, thanks to the labors of the Lord Mithras.

"Now His work on earth was done. With the Sun and His other companions, He celebrated a last supper before He ascended to Heaven. Ocean tried to drown Him on His way, in vain. He is among the immortals.

"But He's still our Commander in the war against evil, that shall end on the Final Day when Ahriman is destroyed, and the righteous are resurrected, and peace reigns eternal."

For a while was silence. Unaccustomed to speaking at such length, Gratillonius had gone hoarse. He didn't think it would be impious to take a long drink of wine, not much watered.

"I have heard a little of this before," Cynan said low. "But you make it . . . real."

"If so, I'm glad," Gratillonius answered, "though it's no credit to me. Thank the Spirit. You think about this. Ask questions. I'll have more to tell, the next few times we meet. After that, if you still feel you want to join—and mind you, if you don't, I won't hold that against you, because every man has to find his own way—if you still do, I'll initiate you as best I can."

2

Dahilis wished to visit the Nymphaeum and seek a special blessing upon her unborn chid. To her delight, Gratillonius said he would come along. The distance was less than ten miles, so no servants or provisions were needed, other than a basket of food for a light midday meal. He did take three of his legionaries, explaining that, while there was nothing to fear, they maintained the royal dignity. Dahilis laughed and clapped her hands in glee. She had long hoped to know the Romans better, her husband's trusty men. These were Maclavius, Verica, and Cynan.

On horseback, the five of them went out High Gate. Beyond the smithies, tanneries, and other clangorous or malodorous industries forbidden within town, they turned off paved Aquilonian Way onto a path running due east along the middle of the valley, beside the canal. This cut through the southern edge of the Wood of the King. Though the day was glorious and the leafage all green and gold, Dahilis shivered in the shadows of the oaks and reached to take Gratillonius's hand. She recovered her merriment as soon as they were again in the open.

"Isn't it beautiful?" she exclaimed. "Aren't the Three good and kind, that They made this for us?" She gestured around. Beneath a vault of light where a few clouds wandered and many wings beat, the valley sides lifted intensely verdant. Pastures were starred with wildflowers. Orchards stood rich near farmhouses thatched, earth-walled, but snug and neatly whitewashed. Groves and gardens framed mansions—red-tiled, tawny-plastered, glass agleam—on the heights. Dwellings of lesser size and luxury but in the same pattern, wide-strewn over the slopes, radiated a sense of well-being. A breeze lulled warm, bearing odors of blossom, growth, soil. Canal water glittered and chuckled above its bed of fitted stones, between its narrow banks where moss made softness; frogs leaped, dragonflies hovered lightning-blue. High and high overhead, a lark caroled.

Gratillonius smiled on her. "No doubt," he answered, "but it suffers by comparison with you." Indeed she was lovely. Her head was bare and she had not piled her hair in the elaborate coiffure of a noblewoman but let it flow free, like a maiden's or a commoner bride's, past the pert features and down her back, as yellow as the loosestrife nodding in the grass. A gown of silver-worked samite was belted close around a slenderness which the life within had, thus far, not changed. Skirts hiked up for riding astride, her legs might have been turned on the lathe of a master craftsman who was also a Praxiteles, save that they seemed about to start dancing. How tiny were her sandals!

"Oh, my," she laughed, "you're becoming quite the courtier, darling. Beware lest you lose your proper Roman bluntness."

The path climbed leisurely, leaving homes behind and passing through rail-fenced meadows where cattle grazed. Ysan territory held scant plowland; the city got its grain from the Osismii. An occasional boy or girl dashed to gape at and hail these remarkable passers-by, the big man in his fine tunic and breeches, the three in flashing metal, the fair lady. Dogs clamored. Dahilis waved and warbled greetings.

They stopped in a shady place to eat and rest. Dahilis served forth the bread, butter, pickled fish, hard-boiled eggs, wine. Cynan shook his head, walked off, stood gazing into the distance. "Isn't he well?" the Queen asked, concerned.

"He practices certain austerities before a religious rite," Gratillonius replied.

"Oh." She shied from the subject. Verica and Maclavius were nothing loth to entertain her. Seeing that she winced at mention of war, they talked instead about their Britannic homelands. Her eyes grew still more huge. "I do hope we can go there someday, Gratillonius, beloved, you and I—to *your* country." The centurion refrained from saying how unlikely that was, or how risky and wretched.

The unguarded frontier was not far when path and canal bent north and wound steeply upward. The waterway became natural, a string of small, chiming falls and whirly pools. Forest grew thick, casting sun-flecked duskiness, and the air turned cool. When at last he came forth and saw the Nymphaeum, which he had done just once before and then briefly, Gratillonius was almost startled.

This was no mere pergola. The grounds occupied a couple of acres, the nearly flat bottom of a hollow under the hilltops, open to the south. North, east, and west the terrain rose somewhat higher, slopes and crests covered with wildwood. On the east side the holy spring welled from a heap of boulders whereon stood a statue of the Mother in Her serenity, shaded by a giant linden. All the waters flowed together to make a broad, clear pond, whence issued the stream that fed the canal. Swans floated upon it. Around it, and in a swathe leading to the building on the west side, a lawn reached silk-smooth, aglow in the afternoon light; peacocks walked there. The grass was bordered by flowerbeds, hedgerows, bowers,

laid out with a sweet simplicity. The Nymphaeum itself was of wood, as
befitted these surroundings, but on colonnaded classical lines, painted
white. Modest in size, it was nonetheless large-windowed, airy, exquisite.
A pair of cats, sacred to the Goddess, lay curled in the portico, while Her
doves cooed above.

Here, said belief, the female spirits of nature came, to bathe on moonlit
nights and flit frolicsome among the trees by day. Here too would stag-
horned Cernunnos often come, drawn by their beauty, to this one place in
the world where the forest God was not terrible; it was said that breezes
at dawn and sunset were His lovesick sighs. No few wedding parties
sought the Nymphaeum, and mothers-to-be like Dahilis, and folk weary
of spirit, beseeching benison. Gratillonius's band dismounted, secured
their horses, and approached in a reverence that was joyous.

Priestesses other than Queens, and descendants of Gallicenae serving
their vestalhoods, occupied the house by turns. Seven, robed in plain blue
and white, they came out while the newcomers went up the stairs. The
girls among them gasped and squeaked as they recognized the King. The
aged leader bade him a welcome grave but not awed. When Dahilis spoke
her desire, the old one smiled and laid a gnarled hand on her shoulder.
"Verily shall you have a blessing, child—at once, or as soon as you have
rested from your journey if you need that." The leader looked at Gratillonius. " 'Tis a solemnity not for men. Could you absent yourselves an
hour or two? You may like to accompany your steeds to the guardhouse;
that's a pleasant stroll in this weather, and the warders would be glad of a
chat. Afterward you shall sup with us and spend the night. Aye, you may
stay as long as you wish."

"I thank my lady," said Gratillonius. This was exactly what he had
counted on. "Duty demands return to Ys tomorrow, but until then we
gratefully accept the hospitality of the Goddess."

"Guide them, Sasai," directed the leader, took Dahilis's elbow, and led
the Queen inside.

A girl of sixteen or seventeen advanced awkwardly and, mute, proceeded down the stairs. Gratillonius recalled her; she had been at the
temple of Belisama when he came to ask a storm of the Nine. She was
tall, heavy-hipped, thick-ankled. Her head was small, with stringy brown
hair, thin lips, underslung chin, and too long a nose. When he drew
alongside her, she reddened and cast her glance downward.

His men led the horses behind him on a woodland trail that began at
the rear of the Nymphaeum. Quietness brooded. He wanted to be
friendly. "Sasai, is that your name?" he asked the maiden.

"Aye, lord," she mumbled, always watching the ground.

"Who is your mother?"

"Morvanalis. She is dead."

Gratillonius swore at himself. Of course. He had met all the children of his wives. With an effort, he remembered who Morvanalis had been, the full sister of Fennalis, both born to Calloch and Ochtalis. As for the girl, judging by her age—"Your father was Hoel?"

"Aye, lord."

Silence stretched. He searched for words. Finally: "Are you happy, Sasai?"

"Aye, lord," said the monotone.

"I mean, well, do you think you will continue in service of the Goddess after you turn eighteen?"

"I don't know, lord."

Gratillonius sighed and gave up. The poor creature must be dull-witted as well as homely and ungainly. He doubted she could catch a husband or shift for herself. So let her take the vows of a minor priestess; Belisama would shelter her.

The walk was short to the guardhouse and its stable. A dozen marines were barracked there, in case of danger—not that misfortune had ever stricken these hallowed precincts or the wildest of men dared to violate their peace. The warders were indeed pleased to have company and broke out the mead. Gratillonius had already met some and convinced them that the new King could be a comradely sort. Romans and Ysans sat yarning longer than he had expected, until he must hurry back.

Dahilis sped down the lawn to hurl herself into his arms, never mind stateliness. "Oh, beloved, it was so wonderful, and the omens—the omens —She'll be like none ever before her—*your* daughter!" She stood on tiptoe and crammed her lips against his.

—Supper with the women was simple but savory. Once grace had been said, talk became animated. Soon Verica and Maclavius were at their ease too. Cynan, fasting, had gone straight to the guestroom he would share with them.

At sundown the other three soldiers left the triclinium and went forth. The superior had given them permission to pray to Mithras, if they did it off the grounds. They found a glade where the last rays streamed level between boles. On the way back, despite piety, Gratillonius felt cheerful enough to be jocular: "Don't oversleep, boys."

Again Dahilis waited outside for him. "Shall we take a walk ere we retire?" she proposed. He was willing. Hand in hand they sauntered about through the dusk, under the early stars. No nymphs appeared, but she was amply sufficient.

In their own chamber she slipped off sandals and belt, pulled gown and undergarments over her head, let everything fall and reached toward him. A single lampflame cast glow on cheekbones, eyes, the dear vessel that was her belly. Elsewhere shadows caressed her. She smiled. "Why stand you there like that?" she breathed. "See you not how I want you?"

"Is it . . . seemly . . . here?"

"You marvelous fool!" she trilled. "Where is it more right to make love?"

When they did, he felt as though Belisama were truly present.

3

Gratillonius had told his dreams to wake him at dawn, and they obeyed. Windowpanes were gray; the room brimmed with murk, chill, and silence. He could barely see Dahilis beside him. On the pillow, in its flood of tresses, her face looked like a child's. How long were those lashes. Babywise, she was curled up under the blanket. He rose as easily as he was able, but the leather webbing under the mattress creaked aloud.

Her eyes fluttered open. He stooped to kiss her. "Hush," he whispered. "I go to my sunrise prayers, and maybe afterward a jaunt in the woods. Sleep on." He had not told her his real intent, because he knew it hurt her to be reminded that his faith debarred her. If he did now, she would be too excited to rest, and that might not be so good for the unborn. She smiled and closed her eyes again.

He had clean garb in a bag, which he donned, but when he was shod and combed he took something additional and threw it over his arm. Soft-footed, he left the room and groped his way to a rear door. None of the priestesses or vestals was awake; their services were at noontide, full-moon midnight, and the heliacal rising of Venus. His men awaited him outside. They also wore white tunics, together with military cloaks against the cold. Wordless, they gave him the Roman salute and formed single file, Cynan last. Stars glimmered yet in the western heavens, but the east was lightening. Mists drifted over pond and turf. Dew laved sandaled feet. Only the clear ringing and clucking of water had voice.

The day before, scanning the heights, he had decided to go northeast. The trail was barely a trace, gloom loured between the trees, men rustled through underbrush and stumbled on roots, but the rivulet they followed sang and glistened for a guide. It took a while to find the sort of place for which Gratillonius had hoped, but then it was perfect, as if Mithras Himself had chosen it. The hillside broadened to form another hollow, like the one where the Nymphaeum stood save for being tiny. Issuing from a spring a little farther up, the stream ran bright, here a whole three feet wide and better than ankle-deep. Beech, hazel, thorn crowded around, night still in the depths among them but crowns silvery under the dawn. They did not grow too close for free movement. Instead, masses of convolvulus twined stems and lifted white chalices. Dew was brilliant on those leaves.

"We are come," said Gratillonius. "Let us prepare ourselves."

Following an invocation he gave, he was first to strip and wash himself in the purifying water. Maclavius and Verica went in next, then stood on either side of Cynan while the postulant did likewise. These three resumed their tunics, heedless of being wet and cold, but Gratillonius had donned a robe and Phrygian cap.

"Kneel," he said, laid hands on the head of the recruit, and asked for divine favor.

Radiance burst forth. The sun cleared the eastern treetops. Gratillonius, Maclavius, and Verica said the morning orison; Cynan stayed aside.

The Mithraist legionaries had brought flint, steel, tinder, dry wood, and an object which Gratillonius had had a smith make for him. As they, whose rank in the Mystery was Soldier, started and blew on the blaze, Gratillonius the Persian led Cynan through memorized responses. They rang firm into the quiet.

The bed of the fire was soon hot. Maclavius took the branding iron by its wooden handle and held it in the coals. "Kneel," ordered Gratillonius again, "and receive the Sign." Cynan obeyed. Gratillonius accepted the iron from Maclavius. Cynan watched unflinchingly. Verica came from behind to brace him by the shoulders. Gratillonius strode from the fire with the iron red in his right hand. His left brushed back a lock that had fallen over Cynan's brow. For an instant, looking down into those eyes, he recalled how he had slashed this face on shipboard. The weal was long gone. The brand of the Sun would never go, quite, though in time it would fade to as pale a mark as was on him and the other two men. Speaking the Word of Fire, he put the iron to the forehead. Breath hissed between Cynan's teeth, the sole token the Demetan gave. A roasting smell marred the air. Gratillonius withdrew the iron, gave it to Maclavius, and bent to help Cynan rise. "Come," he said. Together they went back to stand in the stream. Gratillonius scooped a handful of water and let it run over the angry red sigil. "Be welcome, Raven, to the Fellowship," he said. He embraced the new brother and kissed him on both cheeks. They returned to earth, wading through the convolvulus. "It is done," Gratillonius said.

A cry ripped across his awareness. Swinging about, the men saw Dahilis under the trees. Her hair was disheveled, her gown mud-stained. Tears coursed down her countenance.

"What are you doing?" Gratillonius roared in his shock, and heard Cynan snarl: "A woman, at this holy hour?"

"I couldn't sleep, I followed your tracks in the dew and went on upstream, I thought we—O-oh," she wailed, "oh, I'm sorry, I'm sorry, but 'tis dreadful what you've done. I dared not speak till now—" She lifted arms and gaze heavenward. "Belisama Mother, forgive them. They knew not what they did."

As ever in crisis, Gratillonius's mind leaped to action. He confronted the men. "She has not profaned the ceremony," he said in Latin with all the authority he could muster. "This is no Mithraeum, just a site that was suitable, open to anyone, and she did not interrupt. Mithras is satisfied. You be too." Inwardly, he could only hope he was truthful. He himself had not been instructed in the deepest lore of the Faith.

When he saw them glowering but calm, he went to stand before Dahilis. His arms longed to hold her close and dismiss her despair. Instead he must fold them and say levelly: "We have done no harm, no sacrilege. We held an initiation. That requires flowing water, and there is none in Ys." A sardonic part of him remembered that city Mithraeums commonly drew it from a tank. But of course there was no Mithraeum in Ys.

"Don't you . . . don't you *see?*" she stammered. "This stream—from Ahes—it flows to join Her most sacred water—and, and you, your male God—"

He decided that it would not be unwise to close his fingers gently on her forearms, look straight into the lapis lazuli eyes, and say, quite sincerely: "My dear, in the end all Gods go back to the One; and as for me, I am the high priest and avatar of Taranis, Her lover. If I have done wrong, on my head be it; but I deny that I have. Ask your Sisters. Meanwhile, fear not."

She gulped, shuddered, straightened. He wished he could console her. Abruptly her smile kindled, however tremulous. "Why, I am, am with you always, Grallon—Gratillonius, beloved," she said. "Cynan, I'm sorry if I . . . disturbed you . . . at a wonderful moment . . . and belike naught was profaned. And, and here is the spring of Ahes, *my* nymph, my patroness. Surely she'll listen when I ask her to intercede with Belisama—Shall we be friends again, we five?"

The King thought in a leap of joy: With so high a heart, she may well fulfill the omen she spoke of, she may well bear us a daughter who'll be remembered when Brennilis herself is forgotten.

Dahilis looked about. "Why, see the convolvulus," she exclaimed as vivaciously as might be. "Is't not fair? Could you wait a little, kind sirs, while I gather some?" She became busy doing so. Her chatter went on: "'Tis medicinal, but we grow it not in the city or nearby, for 'tis apt to overrun gardens. My Sister Innilis has told me her supply's run short, for ever does she go about as a healer among the poor in Ys. Belisama's Cup, they call this flower. Know you why? The story is that once, long, long ago, a wagon was hopelessly mired. She came by in the guise of a mortal and told the carter She would help him free it. He laughed and asked what payment She wanted. 'I give My gifts for love,' She answered, 'but now I thirst. Would you give me some of your wine?' Said he, 'Well, I'd not grudge a woman that, but alas, I've no cup with me.' She plucked a convolvulus flower, he filled it, She drank, and thereupon the wheels rolled onto firm ground. Aye, the Goddess can be tender."

And terrible, Gratillonius thought. Dahilis loaded her arms. The dew on leaves and blossoms was cool, almost cold, like moonlight.

4

Innilis needed pretty things around her. The house that she inherited she had had painted rosy pink on the outside; within, the walls became pale blue trimmed with gold, where they did not carry paintings of blooms and birds. Delicate objects filled the rooms, statuettes, crystal, silver, as well as gauzy hangings. Most she had not bought, for she lived quietly and spent much of her stipend on alms and charitable works; she had received it from people who rejoiced to behold her joy. Two servants, man and wife, sufficed her. They were apt to go about their work he smiling, she singing.

Ocean sheened as if polished beneath a late sun when Vindilis arrived. Innilis let her in. They two could merely exchange salutation and looks while the woman attendant stood by. "Welcome, oh, welcome," Innilis whispered. She drew breath and turned to the servitor. "Evar, the Queen and I have m-m-much to discuss. We'll sup—after dark, I suppose. I know not when, I'll tell you at the time, it need only be a light collation. Come." She hastened from the atrium. Vindilis strode at her side.

In the conference room, they closed the door and curtained the windows. Thereafter the kiss went on and on. " 'Tis been so long," Innilis half sobbed, her cheek upon Vindilis's small bosom.

"Aye," Vindilis replied into the fragrant brown hair. Nobody else in Ys had heard her croon. "But this time is ours. We've done our duty, now we may have our reward."

Innilis stepped back, keeping hands linked with hands, stared up into the gaunt visage before her, and said sadly, "Not yet may I take much ease, dear darling. Those men worst hurt in the battle—many wounds have become inflamed—men lie tossing on their beds, sometimes raving, while their wives and children know naught to do save pray."

"And call on you," Vindilis added. " 'Tis ever thus. You, the Sister of mercy."

Innilis shook her head. "Nay, you know better. Bodilis, Fennalis, Lanarvilis—"

"They do what they can, but the grace of the Goddess is in your touch."

Innilis flushed. "You've had your work too."

"In truth." Vindilis's tone hardened. "Our King would fain turn everything topsy-turvy. Along with much else, he wants changes in management of the public treasury, starting with inventory of every coffer, religious and civil alike. I must agree 'tis not necessarily a bad thing. I'd no idea how slipshod record-keeping had become in the Temple. Yet the Nine shall retain control of its finances. Quinipilis and I are overseeing the work. Her strength flags early in the day, so most of it falls on me." She laughed. "That's why my note said we should meet here. At my house, some female prothonotary is like to burst in at any moment with a question."

Innilis's smile lighted the chamber. "Well, you *are* here," she sighed, and swayed close again.

They undressed each other with many endearments and little jests. There was a broad couch. They sank onto it. Hands, lips, tounges went seeking, caressing. Time passed unheeded.

The door opened. Dahilis came through. She carried a basket full of Belisama's Cup. "Innilis, dear," she called happily, "Evar told me you—" She dropped the basket and choked off a scream.

Vindilis bounded to her feet. "Shut the door!" she hissed.

Numbly, Dahilis did. Her glance went from the lean, crouched form with fingers crooked like talons, to Innilis huddled back on the couch, an arm across her breasts, a hand over her loins, mouth parted, eyes widened till the blue was ringed in white.

Vindilis stalked forward. "You meddlesome witling." Her fury was like the iceberg that flays a ship. "How dared you? How dared you?"

Dahilis retreated. "I didn't know."

"Vindilis, darling, she couldn't have," Innilis quavered. "I should have told Evar . . . not to let anybody in, not even a Sister. . . . I forgot. I was so glad y-you were coming . . . I forgot. 'Tis my fault, mine alone!" She cast herself down on a pillow and wept.

Vindilis halted. "Well, I might have noticed and seen to it, but I didn't," she said. "Whatever the blame, we'll share it, as we've shared our hearts."

Dahilis squared shoulders, "Belike this was . . . the will of the Goddess," she said. "Certes 'twas never mine."

"I'll yield you that." Vindilis picked up her cloak and covered her nakedness. Grimly: "What we must decide is how to cope with the matter."

Dahilis went to the couch, knelt beside it, threw arms around Innilis. "Cry not, little Sister, cry no longer," she begged. "I love you. I love you best of all of my Sisters. Never will I betray you, nay, not to my lord himself."

Vindilis let her continue murmuring, soothing, stroking hair and brow, while she reclad herself fully. When at length Innilis was quiet, save for gulps and hiccoughs and nose-blowing, Vindilis fetched a nightgown from the bedroom. Dahilis helped Innilis draw it on. Its fluffiness made her seem a child. She sat up near the head of the couch, the other two sat on the foot, and they looked back and forth through dimming light.

"I thank you for loyalty, Dahilis," said Vandilis.

"Well, you were kind to me in the past," responded Dahilis.

"Less kind than I might have been. I see that now. But 'tis not my nature." Vindilis paused. "Nor is it my nature to care for men."

Dahilis cast a troubled regard at Innilis, who faltered, "I, I know not what my nature is. Hoel and Gratillonius—but they never taught me!"

Dahilis bit her lip. "That may be my doing. I've been . . . greedy . . . about him. I fear that's offended the Goddess."

Vindilis bridled. "Think you *this* has?" she challenged. "Nay, we twain gave each other the strength to endure Colconor. Thus we could carry out our duties, and not go mad. Love is the gift of Belisama. Should we spurn it, for a man who cares naught?"

"You wrong him," Dahilis protested. She clenched her fists. "Aye, there I think is your sin, that you turn your back on the King the Three sent to deliver us. Innilis—you, at least—oh, do!"

"I can try," came the whisper. "If he will. But never can I forsake Vindilis."

"That may perhaps be—Who am I to say? Who are we?"

Slowly, Dahilis unclenched her hands. She stroked them over her belly, once, and calm flowed after them. Rising, she looked straight at the two and said:

"I promised I'd keep faith with you, and I will. But we must find what is right. Let us think where we may seek. Tell me when you feel ready. Until then, farewell, my Sisters."

She walked out. The hem of her skirt scattered the spilled flowers.

XVIII

1

A short way north of Warrior's House where fighting men on duty had barracks, the Water Tower raised its great bulk higher than the adjacent battlements of Ys. A conduit under city wall and pomoerium led the flow of the canal there; ox-turned machinery pumped it to chambers near the top, whence pipelines redescended beneath pavement and carried it off to certain temples, important homes, fountains, and baths. The pipes were ceramic, because people here had a notion that lead was slow poison. Otherwise, and mainly, they depended on catchbasins and storage tanks with sand filters; rainfall kept those well enough filled.

The roof of the Water Tower held an observatory. Many Ysans did not trust in astrology, but many others did. In any case, stars and planets were vital to timekeeping, navigation, religious rites. Moreover, there was an ancient tradition of gathering knowledge for its own sake. This work required a building hard by to contain instruments, library, scriptoria, auditorium. The Romans who remodeled Ys gave it a new Star House, in an Athenian style modified for the Northern climate. It came to be the meeting place of philosophers, scholars, poets, artists, visitors who had interesting things to tell, citizens whom the Symposium voted into membership.

A King could not be denied. Few had availed themselves of the privilege—more than once or twice, at any rate. Gratillonius wanted to, but had not hitherto found time. Now he could go.

A supper would be followed by free conversation, which might well outlast the night; but first the afternoon was for formal discussion. Word that the King would attend had brought well-nigh everyone who belonged. Decently clad though never sumptuously, most wearing togas, they reclined like the ancients on couches arranged in a circle, a couple of

dozen men and Queen Bodilis. Between each pair, a small table bore
dilute wine, raisins, nuts, cheese, which barefoot youths—noiselessly, always listening—kept replenished, not for the gratification of stomachs but
to maintain clear heads while the drink lubricated tongues. The room was
austere unless one considered the beauty of its marble and onyx or the
extraordinarily clear, almost color-free window glass.

Today the president of the symposium was Iram Eliuni, otherwise Lord
of Gold. A short, bald-headed, fussy man, he was not without humor as
he said, "Fain would I begin by lodging a complaint against our distinguished guest, Gratillonius the King. For generations my office was a
sinecure, and I have had leisure to cultivate learning. Of late, he insists
the treasury *do* something."

He cleared his throat and proceeded: "However, that is not the topic
chosen for this gathering. 'Twas agreed by the committee that faith—that
which men believe is the nature of God and Spirit, the meaning and
destiny of Creation—that this is the highest and deepest question to
which our souls can aspire. Moreover, if men be sane and righteous, belief
will determine how they think, how they behave. In sooth, if you know
not the faith of a man—or a woman, of course, my Lady Bodilis—then
you understand that person not at all. Is this stipulated? Aye. Accordingly we shall in mutual respectfulness investigate each other's religions.
Gratillonius?"

Forewarned, the Roman could answer readily: "You wish me to explain
mine? Well, to be frank, I doubt I can say much which this group knows
not already. Mithraism was widespread when Ys was close-knitted to the
Empire. You must have descriptions. I'll be glad to talk about whatever
you want to hear, as long as 'tis allowable for me, but I really think 'twill
suffice to assure you afresh that I can and do honor the Gods of Ys . . .
barring minor matters of ritual which count for naught . . . and if I've
overstepped my bounds, 'tis been for lack of information, not of good
will." He looked around the circle, face to face. Bodilis, in a gray gown,
wore perhaps the gravest expression. "Let me make a request," said Gratillonius. "Let me ask you first about your religion. I pray you, enlighten
me."

"Where'd we begin?" asked a hoarse voice. Several men smiled. The
inquirer was among the four regular members who belonged to no Suffete
family—an artisan, but in his free time an experimenter who studied the
behavior of material objects.

"Perhaps by starting with history, which you recall we've talked about,
Gratillonius," suggested Bodilis.

"We have," the centurion replied. "Sirs and my lady, I've knocked about in the world. I know how often the Romans of old were mistaken when they reckoned a foreign God to be the same as Jupiter or Neptunus or Whoever. Thus far I've not been able to make entire sense of your Ysan pantheon. No disrespect; I simply haven't."

"For example?"

"Oh . . . some of your Gods appear to come from the South or from Asia, but some are Gallic. And yet not Gallic. Taranis Himself—here in Ys He has taken the primacy from Lug and the hammer from Sucellus, neither of Them having any cult among you as far as I know—" Gratillonius ventured a smile of his own. "Help me understand what I have become!"

Esmunin Sironai said, almost inaudibly out of his thin chest: "I trust you realize that we, at least we who are educated, do not take ancestral myths for literal truth, as if we were Christians. They are symbols. As different languages, or different words in one language, may denote the same thing—albeit with subtle variations of aspect—so, too, may different Gods represent the same Being. They change with time as languages do, They develop, according to the evolving needs of Their worshippers. The very heavens change through the eons; nevertheless, the reality of Heaven endures." He was the chief astrologer, once tall, now frail, white-bearded, nearly blind. Under his direction his students, who loved him, continued his researches: for he was not satisfied with Ptolemaeus's depiction of the universe.

"Mayhap 'twould help if the chronicle of the Gods were set briefly forth," propounded Taenus Himilco. "Parts you will have heard, Gratillonius, but not the whole, nor in orderly wise."

A murmur of assent went around the circle. "Do you do this," Iram Eliuni decided. "You are best qualified among us." Of aristocratic appearance and bearing, with a seat on the Council of Suffetes, Taenus was also a landholder near the Wood of the King. He knew not only what city dwellers thought, but what countryfolk did.

At Gratillonius's urging, he commenced:

"In the beginning, Tiamat, the Serpent of Chaos, threatened to destroy Creation. Taranis slew Her. But She was the mother of Lir, Who therefore waylaid Taranis and killed Him. Heaven and earth were plunged into darkness, until Belisama descended into the underworld. At a fearful price, She ransomed Taranis and brought Him back; and She made peace between Him and Lir. A condition of this peace was that Taranis must die over and over, until the End of All things, though He would ever be reborn. This mystery we enact in Ys. Formerly 'twas by yearly human sacrifice. Today 'tis in the person of the King. He dies in battle, he is resurrected in the victor, who fathers new life upon the Gallicenae, the chosen of the Goddess.

"In a sense, therefore, every daughter of King and Queens is divinely engendered. Only nine at a time are actual avatars. The rest live common human lives. Likewise do persons born of congress between other divinities and mortals. We have families claiming descent from, say, Teutatis, Esus, Cernunnos—mine—or from female deities by mortal lovers, Epona, Banba. . . . 'Tis mere ancestry, unattested save by legend. More meaningful, mayhap, though vague as sea-fog, is a tale that in the Ferriers of the Dead flows blood of cold Lir. . . ."

Silence fell. Gratillonius nerved himself to break it: "The Ferriers. I've heard of them. But nobody wants to speak of it. What does happen to the dead?"

"That no one knows. The stories are many, many. Ghosts haunting their homesteads, barrow-wights, the Wild Hunt—dim Hades or utter oblivion—Here in the city and along the coast, we bury our dead at sea, as you know. Their bodies. The Ferriers have the task of bringing the souls out to Sena, for which terrifying reason they are exempt from tax or civic labor. Yonder, 'tis thought, Belisama judges those souls, though some say Lir shares in it. Many say that certain are reborn—that dead Gallicenae, especially, may become seals, which linger until they can accompany their own beloved into the Beyond—But we do not pretend to know."

"As you Mithraists do," Bodilis said coolly.

Gratillonius flushed. "I know not what will become of me," he snapped. "A man can but strive to earn salvation."

"A *man*. Is it denied to any who are not washed in the blood of the Bull? That would admit only the wealthy to Heaven."

"Nay!" exclaimed Gratillonius, doubly stung that she should be the one who gibed. "The Taurobolium—that ugly business where the worshipper stands in a pit and the blood bathes him—that's for Cybele. The Great Mother, they call her."

"You were sanctified by the blood of a King. Why should others not be sanctified by the blood of the bull?"

"As you will. 'Tis not required among them either. The rites are open to women." Gratillonius stopped himself from admitting how closely the Temples of Mithras and Cybele had often cooperated. He had never liked that cult, where men driven hysterical had been known to castrate themselves. Let women follow Christ, Who was good enough for his mother. "When we slay a beast to Mithras, we do it with dignity, as He did."

"I pray you, I pray you!" Iram cried. "This is a comparison of views, an exchange of cognizances. Debates, if debates are desired, must be arranged separately."

Gratillonius suppressed his temper. "Well, about human destiny," he said, "many of my fellowship believe 'tis controlled by the planets, but I confess to doubts about that. Could the learned Esmunin enlighten us?"

"I am not in the least sure of the horoscopes I cast," replied the old man, "although I do my best as duty demands. If there is fate, then methinks 'tis on a grander scale, the forces of it all but incomprehensible to us. The apparition of comets, enigmatic eclipses, precession of the equinoxes—"

It became fascinating.

2

Gratillonius would happily have stayed as late as the last philosopher, but soon after the meal Bodilis plucked his toga and said low, "Come away with me. We've things to talk about."

Despite lingering resentment, he knew she would not request this idly, and made his excuses. No armed guard was necessary hereabouts; a lantern bearer sufficed, a boy who did not know Latin.

"I'm sorry I angered you," Bodilis said in that language. "But given the opportunity, I thought I must."

Astonished, Gratillonius glanced at her. Stars threw more light on her face than did the glow bobbing ahead. He studied its strong molding as if for the first time until, confusedly, his gaze roved off, past the towers to the vast glimmer of Ocean. The night was cool. Footfalls rang.

"You see," she said presently, "you do not understand free women. If you're to reign as we both hope, you need to. I gave you a taste of what you've been giving us."

"What do you mean?" he protested. "My mother, my sisters—no slaves they. Nor most of those I've known."

"But not equals either," she retorted. "We Gallicenae are. Never forget that."

"What have I done wrong?"

She sighed, then smiled and took his arm. "Not your fault, really. Everywhere else, unless perhaps among some of the barbarians, women are underlings. The Romans honored their matrons, but gave them no voice in affairs. The Greeks shut theirs away in houses; no wonder that became a nation of boylovers, as dull as they made their poor women!

Your cult won't admit them. The Christians will—but subservient, looked at askance as vessels of temptation, denied any possibility of ever administering the sacraments. How could you know?"

The Great Mother—no, She was a screeching Asiatic. Tonight, around him, Gratillonis felt the majesty of Belisama, to Whom belonged moon and stars.

He swallowed. "Did I insult you Nine? I didn't mean to. Dahilis said nothing."

"She wouldn't. She's too loving. Nevertheless I suspect she has urged you pay more heed to her Sisters."

"Well—she has—but—"

"Ah, I speak of pride, of what is due, not of lust, though the flesh does have its just demands. Think back, for example. When you announced Dahilis was pregnant, and this would release you in due course to service the rest of us—Do you like being patronized?"

"No! But—but—"

She laughed softly and held his arm the tighter. "Dear Gratillonius. You've never been a man more than now when you flounder helpless. Do you imagine I'd have bothered trying to teach Colconor? Why, Hoel himself could not understand. He might have—he was not stupid—but he would not make the effort, he would not patiently listen. In you there is hope."

"I will . . . listen, as long as seems reasonable . . . and try to do what's right," he said carefully, "but I will not humble my manhood."

"Nobody asks that of you. It's simply that we will not humble our womanhood."

They went on in silence until they reached her home. There Gratillonius tipped the boy and dismissed him. Inside, servants had gone to bed, as short as the nights were now growing, but had left a pair of lamps burning in the atrium. Light fell amber upon Bodilis. She whirled about and seized him. "Come," she said huskily, "don't wait, the hours are wearing away."

She had been good before. This time she was magnificent.

3

Rain came misting out of the sea, to hide the towers of Ys and make its streets twilit ravines. Dahilis and Innilis felt it on their faces, like the kisses of a thousand ghosts. They drew their cowled cloaks as tight as they were able while walking. Despite the apprehension in them, they were glad to reach the house of Quinipilis.

The high priestess let them in herself. She had thrown a shawl over a gown often patched; wool stockings and straw slippers were on her rheumatic feet. Carelessly combed, her hair made a white lion's mane. "Welcome!" she hailed. "Stand not there getting wetter, come inside where 'tis halfway warm. I've mulled wine on the brazier, or I can brew up some tisane if you'd liefer." She waved them through and rocked after them. "Pardon my appearance. Your note asked for a private talk, so I gave the staff this day free. Ordinarily I do not meet folk until I've gotten my jowls neatly tied up against my ears."

"We, we meant not to cause you trouble," whispered Innilis.

"Nonsense, child. You've given me unassailable cause to stay away from the temple and slop about here. Toss your cloaks anywhere." Quinipilis led the way to a room off the atrium. Like the rest of her establishment, it was somewhat garishly decorated. The furniture was battered but serviceable. "Be seated. At ease, as our good centurion would say. We've the whole day if we want, not so?—and a kettle of soup cooking. Made it myself. My cook's no slattern, but she *will* put in too few leeks."

They sat down and, for a space, sipped mutely from their beakers. Across the rim of hers, Quinipilis squinted at the guests. When she deemed the moment ripe, she said: "The trouble is yours, plain to see, and a bitter grief in you. Tell me whatever you wish."

Twice Innilis tried to answer, and could not. She shrank back in her chair, clutched her cup, and fought against tears.

Dahilis squeezed her hand before taking the word, low but almost steadily, looking straight into the eyes of Quinipilis: " 'Twas my thought that we seek your counsel, you, the oldest and wisest of us. We wanted Vindilis along, but she refused—sought to keep us from going—If you find her more aloof and haughty than ever, that will be the reason."

"Age in itself brings no wisdom, dear. But I have seen a thing or two in the past. Say on."

"This is a thing that could destroy. Yet I d-dare not call it wrong. I found out by sheer chance, unless 'twas the will of the Goddess. . . . Innilis and Vindilis are lovers."

Quinipilis bared what was left of her teeth in a soundless laugh. "Ho, is that all? I've known for years." Innilis gasped. The wine splashed from her cup and stained her lap. Quinipilis ignored that, smiled at her, and said kindly. "Fear not. I'm sure none else has suspected. Me, I'm curious about people. Their bodies speak more honestly than their tongues. I've learned a bit of the language."

"But what shall we do?" Dahilis pleaded.

Quinipilis shrugged. "Need we do aught? This cannot have been the first time in the centuries. Nine women to one man may be sacred, but 'tis not natural. Yet Ys has done rather well throughout its history. 'Tis only that its folk have inherited, from their Carthaginian forebears, an abhorrence. I believe Belisama understands."

She gazed afar. Her voice dropped. "Poor Innilis. And poor Vindilis. I was never the mother I should have been to her, my Runa, Vindilis-to-be. There was Lyria, you remember, my daughter by Wulfgar whom I'd been so fond of. Aye, 'tis fair to say I loved Wulfgar; and you cannot remember, being too young, what a bright, beautiful child Lyria was. Then Gaetulius slew Wulfgar, and on me begot Runa. Oh, I never hated the little one; she could not help having the father she had. I did my duty by Runa. But to Wulfgar's daughter Lyria I gave my love. And then in the reign of Lugaid the Sign came upon Lyria, and she took the name Karilis, and she died in giving birth, and to this grandchild who is now Forsquilis I passed on the love I had borne for her mother. . . ."

She shook herself. "Enough. 'Twas long ago; and who can command her heart? Do your duty as a Queen. Whoever else may be in your life, provided 'tis not adulterously another man, that person is your own."

"But I hate keeping a secret like this from Gratillonius," Dahilis mourned. "It touches him so deeply, though he know it or not. And, and he is the King we prayed for. We owe him our loyalty."

"What loyalty has he shown us?" demanded Quinipilis.

"Why, why, he has been—kind and sage and strong—" Dahilis's cheeks burned. "Aye, certain things he's neglected, but that's my fault as much as his, and Bodilis told me she's spoken to him and he paid close heed—"

"That is well," said Quinipilis. "Mistake me not. I like him very much. I fear lest he lose the favor of the Three. Mayhap this . . . between you and Vindilis, dear Innilis—mayhap 'tis Their punishment of him, even though it began ere he arrived. If They do no worse, we should give thanks for mercy."

"That's my terror too," Innilis forced forth. "That the Gods are affronted as They were by . . . the earlier King. When Dahilis discovered us—could that be Their sign, Their warning?"

Quinipilis came to attention like an old hound that has caught wolf-scent on the wind. "Eh? What's this? Meseems you've more on your minds than you've yet told."

"We do," Dahilis answered. Struggling for every word, she related how Gratillonius had held his Mithraic rite in a stream hallowed to Belisama, and afterward been unrepentant. "He swore 'twas no harm; and he *is* so strong and clever that, that I made myself believe him—but then this next thing happened, and I cannot sleep for fright—Counsel us what to do!"

"Hm. Hm." Quinipilis tugged her chin. "This is bad, I think. He's already defied Lir, d'you see, by burying that soldier of his on Point Vanis. And I scarce imagine Taranis is pleased that Gratillonius has dawdled about getting Him daughters on the rest of the Nine. The Gods are patient, but—"

She rose and paced, hands clasped behind her back, though an occasional wince showed that each step cost her pain. The younger women sat dumb, their stares following her to and fro. Finally she halted, loomed above them—her tall form against the window seemed to darken the room—and said:

"He is worth saving. The best hope, I swear, Ys has had in my long lifetime, or longer than that. Wulfgar and Hoel were good men too, but they lacked the skills of war and governance that seem to be Gratillonius's, nor, in their day, did such storm-driven tides beat on our gate as are now rising. If he refuses to expiate his sins, we Nine must do it for him. Is that not ever the lot of woman?

"How? I cannot tell. In matters like this, I'm a simpleton: too much earth in me, too little fire, air, or seawater. Let me ask of Forsquilis. Young though she be, that grandchild of mine is deep into strange things. Well do we know."

Dahilis and Innilis shivered.

" 'Twill take time, doubtless," Quinipilis went on. "Meanwhile, we'll do what we can to make amends and fend off divine anger. First, I'd say, Gratillonius *must* rightfully honor and make fruitful those of the Gallicenae who are able. If he'll not take the first step toward that, they—we —shall have to."

Dahilis bowed her head. "I've tried," she mumbled. "And, and Bodilis says she did reproach him, and afterward he and she—How glad I was. He keeps telling me, though, he keeps telling me he'll . . . see to the matter . . . when I've grown heavier. What else can I do?"

Quinipilis rasped a chuckle. "What, need the Crone instruct the Wench? Your blood knows the answer." She sighed. "You've been too proud, all you lasses. You've concealed your hurt. Have you thought that that might have overawed him? Belike he's unaware of this, he tells himself he only wants Dahilis, with whom he's in love. But underneath—he knows you have powers—and . . . every man dreads failing with a woman. Which he never will with any of you; but does he truly realize that?"

She laid a knotted hand on the head of Innilis. "Seek him out," she urged. "Set fear aside. Open yourself to joy. Ah, I remember."

"I w-w-will do my best." The words came high and thin.

Quinipilis stood a while looking down at Innilis. It was as if that look went past clothes and the skin beneath, to flesh which had been torn and knitted poorly, to frail ribs and narrow hips. Whatever of the restorative Touch that had once belonged to every Queen lingered in Innilis, it sufficed not for the healing of herself.

Finally the old woman said low: "I was forgetting. The birth of your child by Hoel nearly killed you; and Audris is sickly and not quite right in the wits. Aye, a strong reason for you to seek where you did." Stooping, though the motion wrenched a groan from her, she hugged the other. "Take what time you need, girl. Nerve yourself. Let others go before you. Dahilis will be your ally. And there is the Herb. If the Gods did not smite the Nine for bearing Colconor no child, why, surely they'll condone you safeguarding your health, mayhap your very life. But when you feel ready, go to him. Never be afraid of loving him."

XIX

1

Festivals surrounded Midsummer. In part they were religious. On the Eve, bonfires blazed around the countryside after dark, while folk danced, sang, coupled in the fields, cast spells, asked welfare for kith and kine, house and harvest—across Armorica, across Europe. In Ys, day after day processions went chanting to rites at every fane of the Three. Most were parades as well, where the Great Houses, the Brotherhoods, the Guilds turned out in their best, where the marines marched smartly and, this year, the King's legionaries outdid them. There were traditional ceremonies: the weavers presented Belisama with a brocaded robe, the horsebreeders gave Taranis a new team for His wagon, the mariners sailed forth and cut the throat of a captured seal that Lir might have the blood—the single seal that Ysans were allowed to kill throughout the year. There were other offerings to other Gods, deeds ancient, secret, and dark.

Midsummer was likewise a season of secular celebration. It was a lucky time to get married in. It was a time for family reunions, grandiose feasts, youthful flings that elders winked at. The short, light nights were full of song, flutes, drums, dancing feet, laughter. Green boughs hung above every door. People forgave wrongs, paid debts, gave largesse to the needy. Few slept much.

Yet Midsummer was also worldly, political. The day after solstice was among the four in the year when the Council of Suffetes always met.

Often this had been scarcely more than an observance, soon completed. Behind its strong wall and, belief went, the subtle Veil of Brennilis, Ys had been free of many things that aggrieved the earth. But nothing is forever.

On the dais of the basilica chamber, Gratillonius raised the Hammer and said: "In the name of Taranis, peace. May His protection be upon us."

Lanarvilis rose to say: "In the name of Belisama, peace. May Her blessing be upon us." So the Nine have chosen her for their principal speaker at this session. Gratillonius thought. Why? Because she's a good friend of Soren Cartagi, who generally opposes my policies?

Hannon Baltisi stood. "In the name of Lir, peace. May His wrath not be upon us." The trident butt crashed on the floor.

Gratillonius gave Adminius the Hammer to hold. A while he stood watching the faces before him—long, narrow Suffete faces for the most part, but not altogether, certainly not on stout Soren or craggy Hannon or, except for traces, any of the Gallicenae. They returned his reconnaissance. Stillness deepened. Best get started, he thought.

"Let me begin by thanking you for your patience and support in these past difficult months," he said. Flashing a grin: "Today we can talk Ysan." A few lips flickered upward, not many. "We've weathered a mighty storm. The seas still run high, but I know we can reach safe harbor if we continue pulling together." Don't remind them how they quibbled and bickered and sometimes came near rebellion. They never quite went over the brink. That's what counts.

"We broke the Scoti. They'll not come again soon, if ever! We kept ourselves from embroilment in the Roman civil war, and kept Armorica out of it too, by our direct influence on our near neighbors and theirs on people farther east. For this, Magnus Maximus is grateful. I have letters from him, which some of you have read and all are welcome to. Having served under him, I can tell you that he rewards service; and he is not far now from winning his Imperium.

"But we have work yet undone, we in Ys. I think the Gods have laid a destiny upon us. We have become the outer guard of civilization itself. We must not fail in our duty."

Hannon barely signalled for recognition before he stood up, graybearded patriarch, and snapped: "Aye, we know what you want, you. To keep our whole strength marshalled, however the cost may bleed us. For what? For Rome. King, 'twas I who showed you the mystery of the Key, and loth I am to clash with you—for you are at least an honest man —but why should Ys serve Rome, Christian Rome who'd forbid us to worship our Gods—and yours, Grallon, yours?"

Adruval Tyri, Sea Lord, heaved his burly form erect. As head of the navy, and a former marine, he could say: "Hannon, with due respect, what you speak is walrus puckey. A grandmother of mine was Scotic, my mother was half Frankish, I've traveled about both trading and fighting, I *know* the barbarians. What d'you want? That we haul in our warships, keep none in commission save the usual coast guard, and thereby avoid offending the Saxons? I tell you, if you buy the wolf off with a lamb, next twilight he'll be back wanting the ewe. The Gods have given us a King who understands this." He ran fingers through thinning red hair. "Heed him, for Their sake!"

Hannon glowered and growled, "What do you wish in truth, lord?"

They returned to their benches. Gratillonius cleared his throat. "This," he said. "We've a Heaven-sent opportunity. Armorica has been spared war, thanks largely to Ys. 'Twill accept our leadership, eagerly, at least until such time as the Imperial issue is decided. I'd have us work with the Roman authorities throughout the peninsula. We can help them rebuild signal towers and establish a line of beacon fires ready for ignition. We can keep our fleet on standby for them, who have almost none—for, if the Scoti are no longer a menace, the Saxons remain, and are worse. In exchange, the Romans can defend our landward frontiers."

Soren stirred. "What need have we of that?" rumbled the Speaker for Taranis. "What on land endangers Ys?"

"The threat to Rome, if naught else," Gratillonius replied: "which is the threat to civilization, I tell you. Sirs and ladies, Ys cannot feed herself. Trade is her life. Let Rome fall, and this your city will starve."

Lanarvilis rose. Grace had never imbued her long body or heavy haunches; but the blond hair lifted on high like a helmet as she said quietly: "I would not gainsay the King—not at once, on a single point of issue—but mothers must needs look further ahead than fathers. So I ask this assembly, although we may indeed find some cooperation expedient —ultimately, does Ys the free want to rejoin that Rome which has become a slave state? Had we not better keep our distance and trust in our Gods? Bethink you."

She sat down. Gratillonius swallowed hard. The worst was, he couldn't deny to himself that her question was quite reasonable. If it had not happened that his own Mother was Rome—Clearly, his rampart for her would be years a-building. Well, a mason necessarily went brick by brick. Today he might lay two or three. He cleared his throat for a response.

2

In ancient times, the King had stayed always at the Sacred Wood, whither the high priestesses sought by turns, and whatever men he invited. Gradually it came to be that he visited the city to preside over various ceremonies; and these visits lengthened. When Julius Caesar's man won the crown and refused to sit yawning in the primitive House, he merely confirmed and completed what had been the case for several reigns before his. Thereafter the Kings moved freely about and inhabited a proper palace in Ys.

Yet while Taranis thus allowed His law to be lightened, it could not be abolished. The King must return to meet every challenger, slay or be slain. Moreover, save in war or essential travel or when a major ritual coincided, he must spend the three days and nights around each full moon out in the Wood. His presence there being the sole requirement, most sovereigns had taken a wife or two along, and sent for friends, and passed the time in recreations which ranged from decorous to debauched.

Dahilis felt horror of the place. Beneath those shadowing oaks Colconor had killed her father and might have killed Gratillonius, whose blood would also someday nourish their roots. After she confessed this, just before his initial Watch, he had kissed her and gone off to sleep alone.

The duty was otherwise not irksome. Free of distractions, he studied material from the archives, practiced the language, conferred at length with magnates he summoned, pondered the tasks before him, and maintained his regular exercises to keep fit. About the underlying finality he was unconcerned. He awaited no rival soon. Such advents were, in fact, generally years apart. Any fighters who did come, he felt confident he could handle. Eventually his strength and speed must begin failing; but he did not mean to be here that long, although at the present stage of things he saw no sense in planning his departure.

The morning of his third moon dawned already hot. Clouds banked murky in the east and rose higher hour by hour, while a forerunner haze dulled the dwindling western blue; but no breeze relieved the wet air or freshened its musky odors. Soren and the priests who officially escorted Gratillonius sweated beneath their robes so that they stank. They were as grateful as dignity permitted when he offered them beer at the House. He, who had tramped and fought in armor, suffered less, but was glad to strip down to a tunic after they were gone.

Servants had carried along pens, ink, parchment. That last was costly stuff for the letters he meant to write to various Imperial officers of the region, but papyrus was not to be had, as disrupted as trade routes were on both land and sea, while wood was simply too plebeian. Well, he thought, this material should be impressive, emphasizing the capabilities latent in Ys and, by the bye, offsetting his awkward style and vagrant spelling. Only afterward was it to occur to him that Bodilis could have corrected those.

The hall was the most nearly cool place to be. He ordered a table and chair brought in and settled himself down to work. It went slower and harder than he had expected. After a while his jaw and back ached from tension. He wasn't sure why. Maybe a ramble in the grove would help. He set off. That was about noon.

At once he was alone. Utterly alone. Around him the trees brooded, huge boles, twist-thewed branches, claw twigs. Their leaves made a gloom through which a weird brass-yellow light struck here and there, out of a sky gone sooty and steadily darkening further. Silence weighed down the world, fallen leaves too sodden to rustle underfoot, brush stiff as though straining after any sound, never a bird call or squirrel chatter or grunt from a wild boar whose blood was to wash the corpse of a King, nothing astir save himself; but fungi glimmered like eyes. Even the canal, when he reached it, seemed to flow listless, tepid, forbidden to quench his thirst.

Gratillonius scowled. What was the matter with him? He was no superstitious barbarian, he was a Roman. . . . But Romans disliked wilderness. It was beyond their law. In its depths you might meet Pan, and the dread of Him come upon you so that you ran screaming, blind, a mindless animal, while His laughter bayed at your heels. . . . A Presence was here. He felt It as heavily as he felt the slugging of his heart. It might be of Ahriman. Best he return.

As he did, he heard the first muttering of thunder.

He breathed easier after he got back to the Sacred Precinct, its courtyard flagged and swept, open to heaven and onto Processional Way, with a view beyond of the heights, garden-garnished homes, pastureland above the cliffs of Point Vanis where Eppillus kept his long watch. Yet he was still beset by portents he could not read. As he stood there, clouds covered the last western clarity, gray yonder, blue-black where they mounted out of the east. Summer's verdancies were discolored, bruised. Dominant in the courtyard reared and sprawled the Challenge Oak, shield hanging from it dully agleam with brass that the hammer had smitten over and over. Between its outbuildings loomed the House, crimson hue somehow bringing forth the brutal mass of timbers, grotesqueness of images that formed its colonnade. When Gratillonius looked away toward Ys, the city at its distance appeared tiny, fragile, a fantasy blown in glass.

Suddenly as a meteor flash, he became aware of the three on the road. How had he overlooked them? They were almost here. He forced steadiness upon himself. A wind sprang up, soughing in the treetops and tossing them about. The hammer swung on its chain, hit the shield, belled in a mumble. Lightning flickered afar. Thunder rolled more loud.

The three halted before their King. Under their cowls he saw Forsquilis, Vindilis, Maldunilis. He could not quell a shudder.

"Greeting, lord," said Forsquilis. "We have come to attend you during your sentinel stay."

He sought to moisten his lips, but his tongue had gone dry too. "I thank you. . . . However, I did not ask for . . . your company."

Vindilis's look smoldered in the bony face. "You hardly would," she replied. Did a whiplash of spite go through her tone? "Not of us three out of the Nine."

Forsquilis lifted a hand. "Peace." Calm, resolution were upon her Athene countenance. The gray eyes took hold of Gratillonius's and would not let go. "Aye," she said, "just we three, who held Colconor here until his doom could find him. That was needful evil. The hour has come to set it right."

Maldunilis sidled close to tug Gratillonius's sleeve. "We'll be sweet to you, yea, very sweet," she said, and giggled.

Lightning flared anew, brighter; thunder boomed; the shield rang. Gratillonius felt a surge of anger as heartening as the wind. "Now look you," he snapped, "I accept your intention as good, and mayhap I have been neglectful, but we'll settle all this in rational wise, later."

"We will not," Forsquilis answered. While her tone was level, she had let go of her cloak, and it flapped at her shoulders like great wings. "This is something that must be, lest the time-stream flow still worse awry. I have made a Sending. It did not reach the Gods, that is not in my power, but it did come near enough to hear Them whisper. Follow me." She strode toward the House. Numbly, Gratillonius obeyed. Vindilis and Maldunilis flanked him.

Beyond the doorway, the hall gaped cavernous. The staff had lit fires in the trenches against the approaching storm, but their light only bred shadows which seemed to make move the carven pillars and wainscots, the tattered banners from battles long forgotten. Smoke stung nostrils and blurred vision. The crackling of wood was merely an undertone to the halloo of wind outside.

"Go," Forsquilis ordered the assembled manservants. "Be off to town, fast, ere the downpour catches you. Come not back till the moon has waned."

Gratillonius confirmed with a stiff nod. What else could he do?

"We'll see to you," Maldunilis tittered in his ear. "Oh, we will." His flesh crawled at her touch.

When they were alone with him, the three shed their cloaks. Underneath, they were royally dressed. As one, they confronted him. "Lord King," said Forsquilis gravely, "in us—you and your Queens—the Gods are on earth. We are seed and soil, weather and water, the cycle of the year and the tides, of the stars and the centuries. We engender, we give birth, we nurture, we protect, we dream, we die, we are reborn in our children at the springtime and we die again in the harvest at autumn. If ever in this we fail, Ys perishes; for we are Ys.

"Therefore let that which was done here in hatred be now done in love. Let the wombs that were shut be opened. Let the dead quicken. Taranis, come unto Belisama."

Lightning burst. Its flare through doorway and smokehole made wan the fires. Thunder wheeled after, down and down heaven. Hailstones rattled before the wind, whitened the ground, clamored on the shield. In a mighty rushing, the rain arrived.

It was as if Gratillonius stood aside and watched another man go into the arms of Forsquilis. Then there was no Gratillonius, no woman, there was only that which happened, which was everything that there was.

—Lamplight glowed throughout the bedchamber, but its Roman accoutrements seemed unreal, infinitely remote; and the light was not soft in the eyes of Forsquilis, it turned them yellow, like a hawk's. Her visage had become Medusa's, gold-brown locks spread snakish over the pillow, she wrapped long arms and legs about him and cried out as her hips met his plunging.

—"I did wrong to bid you go away," Vindilis breathed in the dark. "Give me another daughter, a new babe to cherish."

"But you told me you liked not—"

"I should have told you what I do like. Hoel could not understand, but Bodilis and Dahilis say that you listen."

"I do. For I want you—you, not just a body lying still—"

"Let us try, let us see. Give me your hand to guide—"

—The sleepy noontide sun cast richness over Maldunilis where she lay. "We're going to drain you dry, you know," she laughed, and somehow that was not impious, for the Gods have humor too and it is not always ironic or cruel; love and death have their ridiculous moments, that the spirit may be refreshed. With Forsquilis and Vindilis playful on either side, Gratillonius saw that Maldunilis honestly desired him and was quite ready to adore him. His ardor torrented.

—The Bull was in him, he was the Bull, rampant among his cows, although in glimpses of self-awareness he knew it was a bull seal he had been thinking of, out on a rookery reef near Sena.

—The last night ended as dawn paled the sinking moon. All four were so weary and sore they could barely drag themselves to their feet. Nonetheless Gratillonius and Vindilis, aye, Vindilis went forth to stand in dew and wildflowers across the road. "Now do you believe?" she asked quietly.

"I seek to," he answered.

Across her dark head, lifted against the sky, the white streak gleamed like a warrior's plume. "We have been Gods. Belike 'twill never happen again. Flesh would burn to ashes. Nay, we shall return to what we were, perhaps a little wiser, a little stronger, but always mortal. Yet we have been Gods."

The sun rose, bearing the glory of Unconquered Mithras. Gratillonius gasped.

He was silent when Speaker and priests led him and his Queens back to Ys. Dahilis met him at the palace, kissed him, said in tender mirth that he had earned a good long rest. She took him to a room curtained and cool, and left him by himself.

A sunbeam struck through. Gratillonius went to that window, opened it, leaned out, holding his palms and his branded brow up to the light. "Nay, I do *not* understand!" he cried. "What came upon me? What was it?" He heard, surprised, that he had called in Ysan. He fled to Latin. *"Tene, Mithra, etiam miles, fidos nostris votis nos!"*

XX

1

Adminius was the new deputy to Gratillonius. Few would have thought the lean, snaggle-toothed scrounger and japester a wise choice, but he quickly vindicated the centurion's judgment, laid his authority firm upon his remaining twenty-three fellows, kept them in sharp form, maintained cooperation with the Ysan regulars and popularity among the Ysan folk.

The municipal theater at the Forum operated, on grants from the Great Houses, during the four months around Midsummer, when daylight could provide illumination after working hours. For the most part it offered classical drama, music, readings; dance, gymnastics, and sports were for the amphitheater outside of town. Not until a month after solstice did the soldiers have leisure to go. Gratillonius kept them too busy strengthening defenses and executing joint maneuvers with the marines.

Finally, though, Adminius announced a party. "We'll march down in formation, 'spite of being civil dressed, impress everybody proper, and take in the show. Don't be afraid. It's the *Twin Menaechmi,* lots of fun—dirty jokes in there too, if you're quick enough on the uptake. I sneaked inter a performance once when I was a brat in Londinium. Afterward we'll 'ave a banquet at the Green Whale. Some of you already know 'ow good a table Zeugit sets. The city's paying, by way of a bonus for our services in the late unpleasantness. And then you're free to go waste yer substance in riotous living—but I want you back in barracks and fit for duty at sunrise, d'you 'ear?"

It was therefore a shock when a spokesman for the patrons announced that the theater was proud to present the *Agamemnon* of Aeschylus in a new Ysan-language translation by the most gracious Queen Bodilis.

"Wot the Sathanas!" Seated on the right of his contingent, Adminius turned to his neighbor opposite, a portly and patrician Suffete. "Excuse

me, sir," he said in the vernacular, "aren't they doing Plautus this eventide?"

"Nay, that is tommorrow." The man smiled superciliously. "I daresay
our way of counting days straightforward, rather than backwards from
ides and nones, is confusing to Romans."

"Oh, bloody Christ." Adminius addressed his men in Latin: "Sorry,
boys, I got the date wrong. Wot we'll be seeing is . . . m-m, I think it's
an old Greek tragedy."

Scowls and growls went among them. Cynan, beside the deputy, started
to rise. "Well, let's go," he said. "I'm in no mood for—"

Adminius grabbed his arm. "We stay. This is a civilized country, and
we owe it ter Rome and the legion ter make a good impression on the
natives. You'll take in some culture, s'welp me 'Ercules, if I've got ter 'old
yer noses and pour it down yer flinking gullets."

A disapproving buzz went along the close-packed benches. Sullenly,
the men resigned themselves. At least they would be able to follow the
lines, more or less; none of them knew Greek.

The theater was of the Roman kind, a semicircular bowl before a stage,
roofless although with arrangements for spreading a canvas top in wet
weather. However, differences were many, most of them more subtle than
its comparatively small size. The upper gallery was point-arched, supported on columns slim, unfluted, their capitals in the form of breaking
waves. A box aloft there was empty, reserved for the Gods. Female roles
would be taken by women, not prostitutes but honored artists. In a well
below the stage sat an orchestra with horns, flutes, syrinxes, sistrums,
cymbals, drums, harps, lyres. It played for a while, a heavy, moody music; then, as the cloth-of-gold curtain was rolled down, it fell silent, until a
lone trumpet call resounded.

Scenery portrayed the front of a cyclopean palace, altars before it. A
backdrop showed night, slowly brightening to day as layers of gauze were
withdrawn. An actor stood peering outward. He bore spear, shield,
archaic armor; the great helmet descended to make his mask. After a
space motionless at his sentry post, he sighed and sighed and began: "O
Gods, relieve me of this weary watch, this year-long waiting like a guardian hound with no more rest than elbow 'gainst the roof above the hall of
the Atreides! Too well I've learned to know the midnight stars—"

Cynan's eyes widened. "Mithras!" he whispered. "That's the way it *is.*"

"Shh," Adminius cautioned. But when the beacon fire blazed afar to
proclaim the King's return, he himself let out a cheer.

Thereafter the soldiers spoke never a word; but often they drew breath or smote knees with fists.

When finally Clytemnestra had scorned the chorus and starkly told Aegisthus that they twain would rule; and another trumpet call died away; and the audience applauded and went out into the sunset street— Adminius said, "Wow!"

"Those women, those poor brave women." Budic was not ashamed to shed a few tears.

"What happened next?" Cynan wanted to know. "That Orestes they spoke of, he must have done something. Are there more plays?"

"I've heard Greek plays go in threes," Verica answered. "Maybe Queen Bodilis has translated the rest. Or maybe she will."

"Well, anyhow, she did a damn good job on this one," Maclavius declared. "Especially seeing she's a woman. Only a man who'd been a soldier could've written it."

"He understood more than soldiering, I can tell you," said Budic with the loftiness of youth.

"That was a lucky mistake you made, deputy," remarked Guentius, and general agreement murmured from the rest.

Adminius laughed. "Fine, fine! We might as well appreciate wot's around us. I've a notion we'll be 'ere quite a spell."

2

Summer advanced in triumphal procession. Colts, calves, lambs, kids grew long in the legs and full in the haunches. Apples, plums, cherries burgeoned in orchards. Freshly cut grass filled hayfields with fragrance. Bees droned about heather, clover, gorse, replacing the tribute men had exacted from them earlier. Carts laden with produce trundled out of Osismiic lands, to return full of wares from workshops and the sea. Poppies and cornflowers bejeweled roadsides. Children grew scratched on the hands and purple about the lips, gathering wild blackberries. Young storks, geese, ducks flopped overhead, in training for the trek south. On clear nights the Swan, the Eagle, and the Lyre stood high.

While he still had much to do, most of it of his own making, Gratillonius began discovering time for himself. More and more Ysans, great, humble, and ordinary, were coming to accept him as a man when he was not being the sacral King. He could poke around town, ask people about their work, listen to legends related by granny or gaffer, put a child on his knee and tell it a story while dinner was cooking in some house where he was a guest. He could whistle up his crew and take the royal yacht, a trim and swift little galley, off for a day on the water. With a few bodyguards he could go a-horseback, hunting or simply exploring, well past the frontier. He could sit up late over wine, talking with scholars, philosophers, men of affairs, visiting skippers, everybody who had something worth listening to; and Bodilis was not the sole woman among them. He could participate in sports, watch contests and shows, hear music and readings, wander into books, lie on his back in the open and look at the clouds and find images in them until he drowsed off. He could practice his handicraft.

That last was especially precious to him, because so long denied. As a boy on his father's villa, he had been forever making things. As a soldier, he became the one in the cohort to see when some job of repair was tough or some tricky apparatus needed devising. However, this was limited, since the engineers and other specialists had their pride. Mostly Gratillonius had whittled, cut leather, that sort of thing. Now he had his own workshop, a shed by the stable behind the palace. (None but the King was allowed to keep horses inside the city.) He filled it with hand tools, lathe, whatever he ordered. Although no joiner—he hoped eventually to teach himself that fine art—he fashioned furniture, household oddments, items for garden and travel, serviceable and not bad-looking. From the royal hands, they made welcome gifts.

He had been thus busied all day, a while after the inland Celts had celebrated their feast of Lug. Evening closed in. Smiling, pleasantly at ease, he put things in their places and left the shop. Outside, the sun was down and dusk settling in. Swallows darted after mosquitoes, shadows against violet. Most flowers had finished blooming, but trees and hedges made the air sweet, while rose mallow stood pale against walls. Before him, he thought, lay supper with Dahilis, just the two of them, and whatever might follow. He divided half his nights among the other five Gallicenae who expected it, Bodilis, Forsquilis, Vindilis, Maldunilis, Lanarvilis, when they were not having their courses or he was not elsewhere. It was never tense with them anymore, and sometimes it was very good, and they seemed content to let him be with Dahilis otherwise, at least until such time as it would endanger her child. The fullness upon her made her, if anything, more dear to him than ever, if that was possible.

Entering by a back door, he smiled at a servant who saluted and went down a hall lit by wax candles in bronze sconces, to the bedroom and its adjacent bathing basin. There he would cleanse himself and change into fresh clothes, not formal but colorful, cheerful, matching her spirit.

He entered and halted. She was there, dressed for the street. Beside her was Innilis, clad in a gown of sheer silk richly bordered with floral patterns. A star in gemmed silver gathered it low above her breasts, so that the Sign of the Goddess was plain to see. The women stood hand in hand. Lamplight darkened the window but gleamed off the rich brown hair of Innilis, delicate features, teeth white between lips always slightly parted.

"Uh, greeting," Gratillonius said, taken aback.

Dahilis came to him. "Darling, I go home this eventide," she told him. "Today did my Sister here seek me and give me the joyful news that she feels ready to be your true Queen."

Gratillonius stared across her shoulder at Innilis. "What a surprise!" he blurted, and noticed he was embracing Dahilis. "I had no wish, well, no wish to force aught on anyone."

"I know." Innilis clasped fingers together. "You were kind to wait while I . . . while I sought the Goddess within myself."

" 'Twas not easy for her," Dahilis murmured against Gratillonius's collarbone. "Help her. I'll call again tomorrow. But we Nine, we've agreed Innilis should have time, days, in your company. Be good to my little Sister. Oh, but I know you will."

Strange, passed through Gratillonius, strange that Dahilis thinks of Innilis as her little sister, when Innilis is—what?—a decade older, and has borne a child, and—But she does look so vulnerable. No, more than that, she already carries a wound that has never healed. I'm sure of it, though I can't think what it might be.

"Well, my lady, you honor me," he found his way to saying.

Dahilis drew him forward until the three of them stood with arms entwining bodies. She kissed Gratillonius and Innilis. "Goodnight," she said between laughter and tears. "Have a splendid night." She departed.

"Um, uh—" Gratillonius searched desperately for words.

Innilis raised eyes that had been downcast. "Do as if I were Dahilis," she suggested.

"Why, why—" The Bull awoke. By Venus, she was beautiful! "Aye, indeed," Gratillonius exclaimed. "First let's have a bit of wine, and then maybe you'd like to share my bath, and later, we'll dine and talk—"

—And hours afterward—he had been as heedful and patient as he was able, until she began astounding him with passion—she whispered through the dark: "I was afraid. But now I love you too."

"Me *too?*" he asked.

She caught her breath. "Have we not all of us . . . others . . . we love?"

"Ah, well." He slid a hand down her flank and laid it to rest. "I'll inquire no further if you'd liefer I didn't."

"Oh, dear Grallon." She kissed him fleetingly, wearily, happily. For a moment, before sleep overtook her, resolution spoke: "No more am I afraid. I will leave the Herb aside, in hope of your child."

XXI

1

Summer welled forth in its final great warmth, light, and greenness. Fields stood ripe, sickles labored, wagons creaked behind oxen. Osismiic villagers brought in the last sheaf, gave it a name and the place of honor at festival, next day burned it and buried the ashes, that no witch might use them to wreak evil and that the God might come back to life at springtime. Soon asters bloomed defiant purple; but it would not be long before the first tinge of yellow was on the birches, and already the storks were leaving, while other migratory birds gathered to make ready in clangorous flocks on hills and at meres.

There was less observance of the season in Ys, but folk were nonetheless aware that another year was passing away. Though business bustled for a term at Goose Fair and the Cornmarket, where the Osismii brought foodstuffs to trade, and at Epona Square, where the horse dealers came, and in flour mills, breweries, bakeries, smoking and pickling establishments: Skippers' Market stood empty, windswept, no further merchant ships awaited. Fishermen drew their boats ashore and settled down to caulk, pitch, mend; most also sought odd jobs in town. Housewives polished lamps and saw to oil supplies. Those who could not afford this increasingly expensive commodity dipped wicks into tallow. Husbands stored away firewood bought from lumbermen. Suffetes who were well-to-do, which not all were by any means, prepared for a round of social events, now that work in the Great Houses would be damping down. Poor people looked to them and to the temples for help during the cold months, not that many in Ys ever knew dire want. The temples themselves made ready for rites immemorially old.

The full moon before autumnal equinox came early that year, in the middle of these happenings. It was the night when Forsquilis went forth alone, as the vision granted to her Sending had enjoined.

She left Ys by Aurochs Gate on the south. None of the sentries there or in the flanking towers called the Brothers challenged her; portals stood open in times of peace. They recognized her, though, cowl thrown back to bare those sharply pure features to the moon, silver coronet around her brows, hair blowing loose; they dipped their pikes in awed salute, and when she had gone they dared not mutter about her mission, whatever it might be.

Wind prematurely whetted and skirling drove clouds in tatters across the sky. The moon seemed to fly among them. It touched their darknesses with ice. Water swirled and snarled as she crossed the shouldering rock between city wall and headland. Beyond, along Pharos Way, rime glimmered on grass; gravel scrunched underfoot, a sound small and lonely and soon lost in the wind. Forsquilis followed the road west. The gap sundering rampart and promontory grew wider as she fared, until the western arc swung north and waves ran unhindered. Cape Rach reached somewhat farther. At its end, the lighthouse fire flickered and streamed like a candle flame. Ocean rolled beyond, around, out past Sena to the edge of the world. The crash and long-drawn rumble of surf on rocks came faintly.

She stopped short of the pharos. Here the road passed through the necropolis. Long had that stood forsaken. Headstones leaned crazily or lay hidden in weeds, names and remembrances blurred off them by centuries of weather. Tombs bulked and gaped. Some were made like miniature Roman temples, some like the dolmens and passage graves of the Old Folk. All were lichenous and eroded, gray beneath the hurtling moon. Forsquilis sought among them, stumbling over the gravestones, until she found the one she needed. It was the largest, a small mausoleum, the entrance Grecian-pillared; but no one could now make out what friezes had been carven above.

Forsquilis stopped. She raised her arms. The cloak fluttered at her shoulders as if trying to flee. "O Brennilis who sleeps within," she called, "forgive that I trouble your rest. It is the whisper of the Gods that sent me hither upon this night. No other sign has been granted me, save omens unclear and portents darkling, which say that your Ys is again at the end of an age. The Old is dying. Time travails with the New, and we fear Its face which we have not seen. For Ys, Brennilis, your Ys that you saved when you walked in sunlight, the sunlight you have forgotten—for Ys, Brennilis, I, Forsquilis your successor, beg a bed for the night with your dust, that in dream I may behold what must be done so Ys may live after I too am gone from the sun. Brennilis, receive your Sister."

She went to the door. If ever it had been locked, the lock was long corroded away. Bronze flaked off beneath her fingers. The door groaned and sagged open. Lightlessness waited. Forsquilis went in to the dead.

2

Rain blew out of hidden heaven and sea. Its noises and its bright gray engulfed the city. Water blinded windowpanes, drummed on roofs, swirled and gurgled in streets. No fire seemed able to fend off a raw darkness. It seeped through walls into lungs and marrow.

In what had been the temple of Mars, the Christian pastor Eucherius lay dying. His bed was a straw tick on the floor of the chamber which he had made his cell. A lamp guttered nearby; everywhere else the too-large room was full of the dark. Light touched eyeballs, bridge of nose, grizzled beard stubble. It lost itself in the hollows under his cheekbones. The Chi Rho and fish he had drawn in charcoal on the wall, to see above his feet, were swallowed up in thick, swaying shadow; but they were crude anyhow, barely recognizable. He had been no draftsman.

He plucked at the blanket. Slime rattled in his lungs and bubbled red on his lips. Bodilis must bring her ear almost to that mouth before she could hear him. "My lady Queen—" He stopped and struggled for air. "You are wise." Again he must toil to fill what was left of his lungs. "You are pagan, but wise and virtuous." He coughed and gasped. "Aristoteles, Vergilius—

"Maybe you know—

"One hears so many . . . tales of ghosts—

"Do souls . . . on their way . . . to judgment—

"Ever linger a while—

"Only a little while?"

She wiped away the sputum and stroked the thin gray hair. "I know not," she answered in the same Latin. "Who does? But in Ys, many of us believe Gallicenae can be reborn as seals, to lie off Sena waiting for their own dear ones, watching over them. Do you want more water?"

He shook his head. "No, thank you. . . . I feel I am drowning. . . . But I . . . must not . . . complain." Coughing shook him. "Gratillonius, . . . you have seen . . . enough men die, . . . worse hurt . . .

than me." This time his fight was lengthy. "If I am being . . . contempt-ible, . . . please tell me, . . . and I'll try . . . to do better."

"No, no." The centurion squeezed the minister's hand, very carefully, so frail it was. "You are a man, Eucherius."

He had come in answer to Bodilis's summons, after she had heeded the plea of the deacon, who found the chorepiscopus lying swooned, with blood caking down the front of his coarse robe. It was not certain how long Eucherius had been thus alone. She washed him and gave him a fresh gown and tucked him into bed. Presently he regained awareness and courteously refused the healing Touch that Innilis might possess. Most likely Innilis would have failed regardless, as she did oftener than not in desperate cases. Hot infusions gave some brief strength. A courier was on the way to Audiarna. Gratillonius doubted the chorepiscopus would sur-vive a trip over the mired road for Christian last rites. Meanwhile old deacon Prudentius, exhausted, had perforce tottered off to his rest. Bodilis and Gratillonius kept vigil.

Eucherius twitched a smile. "You are good too," he said. "As for me, . . . it would be very pleasant . . . to see Neapolis again, . . . dream-ing before the blue bay, . . . my mother's house, . . . the small crooked streets, . . . a garden where . . . Claudia and I—But God's will be done."

Of course it shall be done, Gratillonius thought. What else? Ahura-Mazda reigns, and beyond Him, inexorable Time. Well, people babble in their death throes.

"Look after my poor," Eucherius begged. "Get Prudentius . . . home to Redonia . . . to die . . . with his kin . . . and in Christ."

"We will, we will," Bodilis promised, weeping most quietly, keeping sight of it from him.

He scratched at her hand. "My congregation, . . . they who thirst for the Word, . . . who shall comfort them now?"

Gratillonius recalled his own mother at her prayers. The remembrance overwhelmed him. "I'll bring in a new shepherd for your faithful as soon as possible," he heard himself declare.

Eucherius lifted his head an inch off the pillow. "Is that a promise?"

"It is. Before Mithras, it is." What else could Gratillonius say, with the deep eyes of Bodilis turned on him?

"Good. Good. . . . Also for you. . . . Not only your chance of salva-tion, . . . my son." Eucherius cawed. "Could a . . . totally pagan Ys . . . hope for much alliance . . . with Rome?"

Startled, Gratillonius thought: But he is not maundering!

Eucherius sank back. "May I . . . pray for you two . . . by name, . . . as I do . . . for all Ys?"

Bodilis knelt on the stone floor and embraced him. Abruptly a measure of resonance was in his voice: "Our Father, Who are in Heaven—"

The cough that seized him shivered every bone. Underneath it was a hideous rattling, gurgling noise. With each convulsion, blood gouted from his mouth. Bodilis ignored it, held him close.

He slumped back. Waxen lids fell half over his eyes. He answered no call or sign; he seemed barely to breathe; to the touch he was clammy and cold. Bodilis cleansed him again as best she could. She and Gratillonius stayed at their post. Eucherius died shortly before his confessor arrived from Audiarna.

3

"The military season draws to a close. A winter campaign would be possible, of course—you have read your histories—but is not really feasible, for either Theodosius or myself. Why dare the unpredictables of weather, supply, and sickness? Instead, by tacit consent, we withdraw to our headquarters and govern the territories we hold, pending spring. After all, in this game the prize is the Empire. Neither of us wants to dissipate it.

"I could almost wish that Gratianus were not a victim of the war. More than vengeance for his fallen colleague, Theodosius has prestige to consider. Else he might have made agreement already. As matters stand, he has given to his eldest son Arcadius the title of Augustus to which I aspire. We shall have to see what God desires.

"He helps those who help themselves. Christ keep me from sinful pride. Yet I cannot but feel that our successes to date show that the ultimate victory of our cause is in His plan for our Mother Rome. While campaigning may have ended for the nonce, we must not relax our efforts on every possible front. To do so would be sacrilegious.

"You have done remarkably well, C. Valerius Gratillonius. I have commended you for it before, and I will not forget it in future. However, as a soldier you know that duty has not ended until the enemy has passed beneath the yoke.

"I thought I had assigned you a minor station on the periphery. I was wrong. You yourself have shown your importance. Now a great part of my strategy for the coming year turns on you.

"Armorica must remain stable, fending off any barbarians or other in-

*vaders but else quiescent. I know better than to call troops from it, but I
cannot permit my opponents to try. Moreover, in view of your success
against the Scoti, I want you to extend a webwork of defensive cooperation
not only north along the Saxon shore, but south as far as the Liger estuary.
In these past months, wittingly or unwittingly, you have through your negotiations and shows of force, and the secondary effects of these, drawn an
outline of it across the peninsula. Now I order you to begin on the actual
structure.*

*"The Duke of the Armorican Tract has consented to this. Herewith his
letter of authorization to you. His agreement was given reluctantly and
under pressure. You will understand that no such official enjoys handing a
crucial commission to an unknown quantity such as you. I also suspect he is
less than enthusiastic about the cause of Magnus Maximus. He is, though,
intelligent enough to realize what an opportunity this is for Rome. The
attention and strength of his command have been concentrated in the east
and the interior, and he feels this must remain so. Terrible though the
devastations wrought by pirates have been, an overland invasion of Germans would be worse, as experience has shown. Therefore he has scamped
the coast defenses. Now at last, God willing, something can be done about
them. Do it well, and you will make your mark—"*

Gratillonius laid down the letter. While he had it well-nigh memorized,
he had thought he would do best to read it aloud to Soren Cartagi. "I
could go on," he said, "but certain details are confidential, and surely you
see the general drift."

The speaker of his cult, otherwise head of the Great House of Timbermen, nodded heavily. Outside this conference room of the palace, the day
reached bleakly bright. Wind whooped. "I do," he said. "You'd fain leave
Ys."

"I must," Gratillonius replied. "To Condate Redonum and elsewhere
—a circuit with my soldiers, to carry my warrant and knit the region
together as it should always have been."

"Ah. You'd not be content with couriers as hitherto?"

"Nay, I cannot be. The Romans are unorganized and demoralized.
They have responded to my calls for a united front against the barbarians
with assent but little action and no vigor. Where it comes to choosing
sides in a conflict for the Imperium—And yet Rome must have one master, and he an able man. Can you not see?"

Soren stroked the beard that fringed his massive countenance. "Well do
I see. Ys shall serve the ambitions of your war lord."

"For the common weal—" Gratillonius left his chair, prowled the
room, stood for a while staring out at the wind, turned about and thrust

his gaze against that of Soren. "Hark," he said, "I called you in to talk about this not only because of your position in *my* Temple. You are a leader among the Suffetes. They listen to you closer than to most. Help me, and together we may do as much for Ys as Caesar did."

"I have wondered how much that truly was," Soren murmured. He straightened where he sat. "No matter; too late. But you, the King of Ys, propose to go faring about, abandoning your sacral duties, for two or three months, on behalf of Rome. This has never been."

Gratillonius gave him a tight grin. "I do not propose to do it, good sir. I am going to do it. What I have hoped for is your support, your explanation to the Suffetes and public that 'tis for their own welfare."

"And if that support is not forthcoming?"

Gratillonius shrugged. "Then I go anyway. How do you plan to stop me? But I should think you'd liefest not rive the state asunder."

Soren glared. "Be careful. Be very careful, my lord. 'Tis happened erenow that Ys has had Kings who overreached themselves. Suddenly challengers appeared at the Wood, one after the next in rapid succession, until those Kings fell." He raised his hand. "Mistake me not. Here is no threat, simply a warning."

Gratillonius's temper, never the strongest part of him, flew into flinders. Somehow he kept their heat from igniting him; but he planted fists on hips, loomed over Soren, and ground out of his teeth: "Enough, sir. 'Tis you who are reckless. Not yet have my Gallicenae called down on me the curse they did on Colconor, whom I slew. Nay, I have spoken with them, and they are willing for me to go. A new age is upon Ys, upon the world.

"Enough of provincial selfishness and dragging of feet. My sword and the swords of my men lie sheathed. We will draw them for Rome, when and as necessity dictates. Bethink you how many blades you can summon on that day."

Soren's breath rasped. I must not drive him into a corner where all he can do is try to fight his way free, Gratillonius comprehended. Again he turned away to the window and the wind. After a moment he said, quite low:

"Sir, we really should not lie in strife as too often we've done. I know not why you've been hostile to me; myself, I've ever wished for friendship. But in your words, no matter. What does matter is the lives of our Mother cities. They are conjoined. Let us set aside any bitterness, yea, any pride, and seek to serve them."

It took an hour or more, but he won grudging acceptance.

XXII

1

At equinox all the Nine must be in Ys, attending the Council and carrying out certain rites. They took advantage of it to meet by themselves in the temple of Belisama.

Quinipilis opened proceedings. Through the greenish light from the windows, between the four walls whereon were depicted aspects of the Goddess, the old woman limped to the dais. Her staff and her breathing rattled loud in the stillness. Painfully she climbed up, turned about, leaned on the stick and peered down at her Sisters. In blue robes and high white headdresses, they looked back, each in her own way. Bodilis sat calm and expectant, Lanarvilis alert, Dahilis wide-eyed, half afraid and half defiant. The crisis had aroused some excitement in Maldunilis, but in Fennalis largely the indignation that had frequently seized her these past months. Innilis huddled close to Vindilis, who held her hand. Forsquilis kept a distance aside, her countenance unreadable. She had been very quiet since the last full moon.

"Ishtar-Isis-Belisama, Your presence be with us, Your peace dwell within us, Your wisdom speak through us," Quinipilis prayed. Ritual response murmured from the benches. When the invocation was finished, she began:

"This is a grave matter, perhaps more than the cursing of Colconor; for it concerns that new King whom we ourselves, under the Gods, did summon to slay him and join with us in holy wedlock. Yet the first thing I would say is this—do not be daunted, my dears. We will find our way."

"The same way as erstwhile?" asked Fennalis.

"What mean you, mother?" exclaimed Lanarvilis, appalled. "Not to bring early death on Gratillonius!"

"Nay!" shrilled Dahilis. She curbed herself. "You, you cannot mean that, Fennalis, you who are ever so kindly and helpful."

The little plump woman stiffened. "I did not counsel it," she declared. "However, somebody must needs set the thought forth. Else we'll slink around it terrified, as we did when it touched Colconor, far too long."

Quinipilis stood stoutly above. "Well, then, let us clear the air," she directed. "Why should we even consider ridding Ys—and ourselves—of Gratillonius? He's able, forceful, honorable, and better prepared to cope with the outside world than any other King in living memory. *I* think him Heaven-sent. But say on, unabashed. This is the hour for plain speaking."

"Understand me," replied Fennalis, "I hate him not. In truth he is all you maintain. But his soul is harnessed to Rome. Bodilis, you've told the tale of the Atreides, how a curse may hound generation after generation, bringing woe on whole peoples. Is there a fatal flaw in this King? Think only of his leaving Ys."

"Not till after Council and festival," Dahilis said quickly. "And we agreed!"

"What choice had we, as suddenly as he put it before us?"

"There is naught absolutely requiring his presence throughout the autumn," Bodilis reminded them. "A King has always been excused from his Watch in the Wood when a great holy time is on hand, or a great necessity such as war—and who judges the necessity but himself? We can safely assume no challenger will appear. If any does, well, we can house him in the Red Lodge to await Gratillonius's return. He promised us he'd come back before solstice."

"Nonetheless I'm uneasy," Lanarvilis admitted. "What if he perishes on his travels?"

"Ys has met contingencies erenow in her history," said Bodilis. "The Key remains here. Not that he'll likely encounter any mischance he can't cope with."

"Be that as it may, this journey of his is but a single violation of ancient ways," Fennalis pursued. "We have heard, secretly between us, how he insulted a stream consecrated to Belisama. Everyone knows how he buried a corpse where its rottenness would drain down into Lir's sea. And—" She reddened, gulped, plowed ahead: "And he made mockery of the sacred marriage."

"He did not!" Dahilis cried.

"That . . . breach . . . has been healed," Innilis whispered. "Has it not?" Her glance strayed downward. No doubt remained that she was with child.

"Indeed he has been filling gaps," said Maldunilis smugly.

Fennalis flushed deeper. "Has he?"

"You and I are too old for more children," Quinipilis stated.

"Just the same—" Fennalis choked on her words.

Bodilis leaned over to stroke her hand and murmur, "We know. We feel the hurt to your pride and, aye, your loneliness every night. But Sister mine, remember Wulfgar—my father, who died of my birth as surely as my mother could have done—because she was his daughter. And Wulfgar was sheerly heathen, a sacrificer of horses to Thor. How much more does a civilized man with a stern faith, like Gratillonius, look on incest as deadly sin? He knows, too, how of old it brought damnation on Grecian Oedipus and plague on his kingdom, innocent of wrong intent though he and his mother had been. Why, in Ys, too, 'tis abhorred."

Fennalis's features worked. "The royal marriage is different. The Gods Themselves choose the Gallicenae. They know what They do! Oh, aye, since I am no longer under command of the moon, he may claim lawfulness in shunning me." She forced a smile. "And I hope you'll agree I've no large vanity to wound. I was ever homely and dumpy and, once past girlhood, resigned to it." She paused. "But what if, in future, when some of us here have passed on . . . what if then the Gods confront Gratillonius with the full meaning of Queenship?"

"They wouldn't!" Dahilis wailed.

A shiver went among the rest. "Will They, ever?" Innilis asked desperately. "What would make Them that angry at him?"

"He has already affronted Them," Fennalis said. Now her tone held pity; she might almost have been speaking to one of the poor families to whom she ministered, telling them that their breadwinner's illness could prove mortal. "That is why we are gathered—true, my Sisters? We've bespoken the burial and the misuse of Belisama's waters and his forthcoming journey. Can we be too quick to forgive his treatment of us?" Still more gently: "Dahilis, darling, I'm sorry. I blame not you, as young and loving as you are. But he did, for months, deny his other wives. If he has lately become more dutiful, he has not repented the past, nor done penance for any of his transgressions." Her voice lifted, ragged. "Will the Gods bear with that?"

"Aye," said Quinipilis, "there is the real question. You've done well, Fennalis, to force it thus out into the open. What shall we do? Disown the King?"

Dahilis's denial was merely the loudest of those that arose from seven pairs of lips and, after a moment, the eighth.

Quinipilis nodded. "Good." Strictness descended. "If he will not do expiation—and in the conscience that is his, he cannot—then we must do it for him. But hear me, Gallicenae. We are not ourselves without guilt. *You* are not."

Innilis caught her breath. Vindilis let go her hand, flung that arm around her waist, and lifted the free hand for attention. Her visage turned from side to side along the tier, eagle-proud. "You have heard what is between us twain," she said. "We will not forsake it. We cannot. I even believe we may not."

"I think, I hope we have all come to understand, since hearing yestre'en," answered Bodilis. That had been at a rite of purification for the Nine alone, when they made confession of everything they knew that might stand between them and the Goddess. Thus had Forsquilis ordered. "We shall keep your secret because we must. Yet is this not itself a faithlessness toward the King our husband?"

"I wonder, too, how many of you besides Innilis have opened your wombs to him," said Quinipilis. "Oh, the Herb is yours to use as you see fit, Her gift to Her high priestesses. But to refuse Gratillonius children, as though he were horrible Colconor—"

"I haven't," piped Maldunilis. " 'Tis but he's not futtered me often enough."

Laughter jerked through the room, less mirthful than startled.

"I have not either," said Bodilis. "But after each of us has decided—for herself—'tis the Goddess Who disposes. Thus far only Dahilis and Innilis —" She sighed. "Let us search our souls. Meanwhile, how can we set right that which has gone wrong?"

Silence lengthened. One by one, gazes sought Forsquilis.

She rose and, through the deepening twilight, approached the dais. There she helped Quinipilis down and guided the dowager to a seat before taking the high place. A while she stood beneath the Resurrection of Taranis, like an eidolon, before she said, low and slow:

"You know what I did in our need, that I sought the tomb of Brennilis and slept next her bones. You know that hitherto I have kept silence about what dreams came to me; for they were weird and ambiguous, and still am I unsure whether I have seen through to their meaning. But this is what I believe they foretold.

"The Gods are troubled, even as are we mortals. Therefore They will stay Their anger and at Their appointed time make peace with us, that Ys may abide and keep holy Their names.

"This is the sacrifice They require. At the Turning of the Sun, one among the Nine shall not be here as always erenow, but must keep Vigil on Sena. She will receive a hard test. If she endures it well, then shall she be purified, and with her the sacred family, Queens, King, and daughters. Thus did I hear the Word."

Ere anyone else could speak, Vindilis called: "I will go!"

Forsquilis shook her head. "I fear not. For the Word was that she must bear the morrow beneath her heart. I can only think this means she must be heavy with child."

To and fro went their looks. Winter solstice was but three months hence; and for most of that span, Gratillonius would be gone.

Dahilis swallowed twice or thrice, thereafter said almost merrily, "Why, that is myself. Of course I'll go."

"Oh, nay, darling, nay!" protested Fennalis. "You'll be too near your lying-in. You know how apt we are to be weatherbound yonder, in winter perhaps days on end."

"Fear not. As close as I can reckon it, my time will be half a month or more after solstice."

"Hm. I've consulted records. Both Bodilis and you surprised your mother Tambilis, despite your having different fathers. Early births run in that bloodline."

Dahilis had attained calm. "The Goddess will care for me."

Hesitantly, reluctantly, Bodilis said, "Remember the tradition."

"What tradition?" Dahilis asked, bewildered.

"You may never have heard. 'Tis a story ancient and obscure. I sought it once in the archives, but too much is missing after centuries, and I could neither confirm nor disconfirm. The story is that Brennilis was born out on Sena. Thereupon a seal gained human voice, to prophesy that any so born thereafter would bring the end of the age which Brennilis was to make begin. It may be a mere folk tale."

The others hearked back. The law was simply that one and only one from among them must be on the island, save on the high holy days or in periods of peril. She could be any of the Nine; and more than weather worked to keep Vigils out of orderly cycle. There could be strong obligations elsewhere, illness, the frailities of age, advanced pregnancy, evil omens— In spite of every precaution it had happened a few times in the past that a high priestess was dead when her relief arrived; and this called for the same hecatomb against disaster as when a King died in bed.

Sight converged on Innilis. Vindilis held her close, close. She stared out of that shelter and said in a thin tone, "I've been chosen. Have I not?"

"It seems you have," answered Forsquilis. Compassion stirred beneath steeliness. "Take courage. It may be hard, but it shall be glory unto you, and unto your new daughter."

Innilis blinked back tears. "Well, I will go. Gladly."

Vindilis's lips brushed her cheek.

"I have a word further," said Forsquilis as though it hurt to talk. "In my dreams was a sigil, white-hot from the fire, and it sealed a book with wax made not from honeycomb but from the fat and blood of sacrificed humans." To horrified exclamations: "Nay, the grisly rites of old are long behind Ys." She smiled, briefly and bleakly. "Moreover, such a seal would not hold in this real world. 'Twas a sign for me."

She braced herself before continuing: "I have thought, I have sought, I have prayed and offered; and this is how I read the vision. We must pledge our faith beforehand. We must take the Great Oath—by the Ordeal—that we will indeed hold a Vigil at Midwinter, which never was before, and that none shall stand it but she whom the Gods have marked out. Then shall all again be well with Ys."

Anew the Nine fell mute. They had undergone the Ordeal when they plighted fealty to each other and to their purpose ere they went forth on Sena and cursed their King. That had not happened for generations earlier. They fasted and thirsted and scourged. . . .

Dahilis gripped her belly. Light-boned as she was, the unborn swelled and burdened her. "Oh, please," she implored. "Not me. I could lose her."

Quinipilis stood up and made a gesture of blessing. "I daresay 'tis uncalled for in your case, youngster," she said. "And in Innilis's. Your situations are patent." Her wrinkled countenance went from side to side, haughtily. "As for the rest of us, we can very well endure it again. We *are* the Gallicenae."

2

His last night in Ys Gratillonius spent with Lanarvilis. This was not by chance. Dahilis was now forbidden him, save for a kiss and a promise, until after she became a mother. The remaining six out of the Nine he had begun visiting in turn, at their homes so that he might at least have Dahilis freely about in the palace during the day. Everybody concerned realized that, for any of numerous reasons, a turn must occasionally be postponed or exchanged. His forthcoming absence was just the first and most obvious example. Still, he had been surprised and somewhat dashed when the message came that it would not be Forsquilis who received him, but Lanarvilis.

He put on civil garb and his best face, to seek her house about sunset.

She met him in the atrium sumptuously clad in a low-bosomed scarlet-and-gold gown that flattered her figure, the blond hair coiled about her head and caught by a garnet-studded silver frontlet. "Welcome, my lord," she said, and held out a hand.

He took it, as was Ysan style. "Thank you, my lady. I regret I could not arrive sooner. Preparations for departure tomorrow sunrise—"

She chuckled. "I foresaw, and ordered a supper that would take no harm from waiting. Shall we to it? We've much to talk about."

They went side by side through this most luxuriously appointed of the Queens' dwellings, past drapes of Oriental opulence, big-eyed Egyptian portraits, exquisite Grecian figurines, and—somehow not incongruous—Roman busts, Marius, Caesar, the first Augustus, Hadrianus, they whose workmanship had shored up, enlarged, repaired their state. Although the food and wines served in the triclinium were no Lucullan feast, they were excellent. A boy stood in the background softly playing a lyre.

"My lady is most generous," said the King after they were settled.

"The Gallicenae desired a worthy sendoff for you," Lanarvilis answered. "We discussed it, and the choice fell on me."

He sipped from his goblet, a taste rich and tart-edged, as cover for his close regard of her. The countenance—green-eyed, slightly wide in the nose and heavy in the mouth, past the freshness of youth, withal by no means bad-looking—was amply mobile but told him nothing. Best might be if he took the initiative. "You do it elegantly," he said. "However, methinks you were elected for more than the table you set."

Unsurprised, she nodded. "Can you guess why?"

"Well, you are the closest of the Nine to the mundane affairs of the city. Quinipilis doubtless was once, but her years are upon her. The rest have their special interests. For yours, you occupy yourself with business of the Temple corporation. You are often in conference with Soren Cartagi, who's not only Speaker for Taranis but a power in the economy and politics of Ys. Hannon Baltisi, too, Lir Captain—you've taken a lead in reconciling them with me, or to me. In that it's helped that you have more knowledge of the Roman world than perhaps anyone else among your people. Were you a man, Lanarvilis, I'd call you a statesman."

"You cannot, simply because I am a woman?" she said in an undertone. Promptly, aloud: "Your words do me honor, my lord. Aye, the Sisterhood did feel I might best represent them this eventide—not least because I am, as you know, favorable to Rome. Rome has given civilization so much—the Roman peace—"

As her voice trailed away, he added, "That peace which is falling apart, but which I hope to help restore."

"True. Therefore 'twas felt we should talk freely, you and I. Tell me, for you've been taciturn about it, what your plans are for your journey."

"If I've said little," he replied carefully, " 'twas on account of there being little to say. How can I lay plans ere I've learned, in detail, what the actual circumstances are? 'Twould be scant use sending Ysan agents unaccompanied. No matter how honest their intentions, they could never quite see, quite understand."

She smiled. "I do, at any rate to the extent of agreeing 'tis a Roman military man who must go. But can you say somewhat of your aims afterward?"

He had no hesitation about that, and the meal passed in conversation as good as with Bodilis—not the same, largely down-to-earth, but scarcely less intelligent. The wine flowed more readily than either of them noticed.

—Her bedchamber adjoined a room of blue carpeting, crimson drapes, furniture with inlays of walrus ivory and upholstery of leather. There they went for dessert—honeycakes, spiced fruit, a sweet Falernian to drink— and private talk prior to retiring. They sat together, leaning against the cushions on a couch that had a back, the refreshments on a low table before them. He rested an arm across that back, hand on the warmth and smoothness of her shoulder. She leaned close to him. Several beeswax candles burned; their light picked out the fine lines in her brow and radiating from her eyes, the mesh across the skin beneath her throat; and the flesh under her chin had started to sag; yet she was a handsome woman.

"Your scheme looks sound to me," she said softly. "I will so tell my Sisters, and we'll ask the Gods to favor your enterprises."

"You can do better than that," he responded. "You can work on the secular powers, Suffetes, Guilds, aye, common folk. If Ys is to take the lead in Armorica that duty calls for, and reap the rewards that faithful service calls for, Ys must be whole-hearted about it."

"What can I . . . we . . . do?"

"Persuade them. Make them see 'tis their destiny. You, Lanarvilis, you could begin with Soren Cartagi—" He felt her stiffen. "Why, what's wrong?"

"Oh, naught." She leaned forward, took up her goblet, drank deep. Staring before her: "Soren is an honorable man."

"Did I say otherwise? Look you, I've always regretted it when we've been at odds. I cannot think why. He learned, able, aye, and a patriot. He should know where the real welfare of Ys lies. For myself, I'm willing to yield on many matters. But if I seek discussion, he soon breaks it off.

What is it that makes him clash with me, over and over? Can you, his friend, milden him?"

"I can try." Again she took a long drink, before turning her head and saying, eye to eye: "But you do us, your Queens, an injustice. You never trouble to imagine how we already labor for you."

Caught short, he had no better return than, "What? Well, I know you pray, and . . . and you tell me 'tis your doing I am here, although—"

"Nay, more than that, and more. But I verge on secrets." Lanarvilis brought her attention back to the cup. Her laugh was uneven. "Desist. We've been political quite long enough, and morning comes far too early, and you must be away and I to my penance. Let us be happy while we may."

"Your penance?" he asked sharply. "What mean you?"

She bit her lip. "I misspoke me."

Concern rose in him. During these past difficult months she had been steadfast, neither toadying nor accusing, just quietly going about her work on behalf of the city and its Gods. Her spirit was a soldier's. "Dear, tell me. Is aught amiss?"

"Yea!" she flung forth. "And we must set it aright, we, the Nine. As soon as you are gone . . . certain austerities begin."

"But what *is* the matter?" he pleaded. "I should know, that I may help. I am the King."

Metal rang: "You are the King. A man. Do you admit me into your mystery of Mithras? Then ask no more about this."

He took a while to say, unwontedly humble, "So be it. However, here I am, and here I will be again. Always feel free to call upon me."

"Oh, Grallon—Gratillonius!" She put down her cup and cast arms about his neck. Her breath was heady with wine. "Enough, I said. Let's forget all else and be only ourselves. Surely we've earned that much."

—Very late, as lamps were flickering low, he raised himself on an elbow and looked down at her where she lay half asleep. Drowsiness crept over him too. But the thoughts, the images stole by behind his eyes, before his soul. Of the seven who were fully his wives, might this be the strangest?

Dahilis, of course, was purely loving. Maldunilis enjoyed, in her lazy and slipshod fashion, and was in truth not a bad person. Bodilis was . . . comradely, altogether a woman when they embraced but otherwise a friend who had a great deal to impart; between him and her he felt bonds of loyalty growing like those between him and his father or him and Parnesius or—With Innilis he came to the frontier of enigma. She was sweet, acceptant, sometimes responsive, delighted to be bearing his child . . . and beyond her defenses he glimpsed a shadow, a thing which he could not bring himself to ask about because he was afraid of hurting her. Vindilis seemed (though what was a seeming worth?) a little more comprehensible, whatever wounds she bore being encased in armor, out of sight and never bespoken. About anything else she talked with him like man to man; that included their joinings, where they had found ways which suited him sufficiently and left her, well, not disgusted. Forsquilis —He had looked forward to spending this night beside Forsquilis. Whether or not it was true that a King was powerless except among the Nine, Gratillonius must needs keep abstinent on his coming travels, since Ysans as well as legionaries would accompany him. Forsquilis might actually have made him welcome such as a rest. He knew she was the deepest into the unknown of all the Gallicenae; but whenever they were alone, that soon ceased to make any difference.

Lanarvilis, though—He lowered his head to brush lips across the down that covered her cheek, as soft as moonlight. She had learned how to take her pleasure with him, as she took it with her home, art collection, food and drink, the spectacles and recreations and social occasions which Ys so abundantly offered. As for her work in administration and statecraft, doubtless she had a strong sense of duty, but doubtless it was also something she enjoyed, perhaps in the same way as he enjoyed making a piece of craftsmanship grow between his hands. Then what was lacking in her life? From time to time Gratillonius had caught a sense of terrible emptiness. This, too, was a thing about which he did not venture to ask.

She stirred beneath his caress. "You *are* a good man," she mumbled. "I'll do my best, for you and your Rome."

XXIII

1

The Black Months were upon Armorica. As Midwinter drew nigh, day shrank to little more than a glimmer between two huge darknesses, the sun wan and low and oftenest lost in leaden clouds or icy rain. Weather slowed the last stage of journeying, and dusk had fallen when Gratillonius saw Ys again from the heights of Point Vanis. It sheered sharp athwart the tarnished argency of the sea. Beyond, mists drifted past the pharos flame, the sole star aloft.

He reined in to give the headstone of Eppillus a Roman salute. Metal clinked, leather creaked, horses snorted wearily at his back. "Dress ranks!" he heard Adminius bark. "We'll enter in style, we will." With a rattle of shields and stamp of hobnails, the soldiers obeyed, also the Ysan marines who reinforced them. The deputy had extended his authority over those, not overtly as against their own officer, but by sheer weight of example on the march.

If there had been no trouble, quite likely that was thanks to the sight of disciplined troops. Saxon pirates had ended their raiding till spring, but the woods housed Bacaudae the year around—ever more numerous, it was said, and certainly apt to be desperate in this season.

Gratillonius turned downhill. The horse of Bomatin Kusuri came alongside. He had represented Ys before the Imperials of Armorica. Well qualified he was, Mariner delegate to the Council of Suffetes: more than that, a man reasonably young and entirely vigorous, himself a skipper whose trading and occasional slaving voyages had made him the familiar of folk from Thule to Dál Riata. Gratillonius and he got along well.

"Ha!" he said in his bluff fashion. "Is it a true parade when nobody's out to watch? Well, I'm as glad of that. Best to arrive quietly."

Gratillonius glanced at him. In the murk he saw only the hulking body, the flamboyant sweep of mustaches; barbarian-bestowed tattoos were shadowed. "I daresay you're eager for hearth and bed."

"Well, now, my lord, between the twain of us—mind you, I say naught against my wife, she's a fine woman, though I could wish she'd nag me less to put on her kind of airs—but as long as we are coming in unheralded—Should she ever ask, would you tell her I had work to clear away, and therefore lodged this night in Dragon House?"

"But there's nothing we can't take care of tomorrow."

"Save for a bit of sport, without getting jawed for it afterward. We've been going hard, this trek. For safe return, methinks I should make a thank offering to Banba." That fertility Goddess had, in Ys, become the patroness of harlots. "Pour Her a libation or two, haw!"

Gratillonius frowned. Lying went against his grain as well as his faith. However, the chance was slight that Bomatin's wife would ever inquire of him, no matter how much she tried to shine by reflection from the King.

"You, my lord, have a choice ready for you—" The seaman checked himself. "Forgive me. I meant no disrespect. 'Tis but that we've fared and worked shoulder by shoulder all this while, you never throwing your weight around more than necessary. I've sometimes forgotten you're also the Incarnation of Taranis."

"I understand," said Gratillonius, relieved. He would have hated to give a reprimand or, worse, a cut of the vinestaff. Yet if he did not maintain the dignity of the King, could he remain effective as prefect? He had two dozen legionaries to support his governance of a city ancient, proud, and secretive. It was not what he had awaited when he left Isca Silurum, ages agone.

"We did a good job," Bomatin said. After a silence broken just by clopping hoofs and thudding feet, surf on reefs and cliffs as they neared the water: "Did we not?"

"The future will tell," said Gratillonius, which ended talk.

Riding onward, he found his own mind less on what had happened than on what lay ahead. Immediately ahead. Had he entered by daylight he would have gone straight to Dahilis. No, the dear lass would have come forth to meet him, running as fast as the weight within allowed, laughing and weeping for joy. But she was doubtless asleep, or ought soon to be, and rousing her might be a little risky, now when her time approached. . . .

The sentries at High Gate, and up in the Gaul and the Roman, cried hail. "Quiet," Gratillonius ordered. "No sense in a tumult. Everything went well. Tomorrow in the Forum I'll tell the people. Tonight we're wearied and need our rest."

He left his horse to the military grooms, bade his men farewell as became a commander, and walked off, still in wet cloak and muddied centurion's outfit. Windows gleamed here and there, out of surrounding houses or aloft in towers. Even nowadays, when oil had become costly, Ysans liked to keep late hours; they would burn tallow if they must. Despite gloom rapidly congealing to night, broad Lir Way was easy to walk on, and when he turned off in the direction of Elven Gardens, Dolphin Lane was so known to him that he walked its narrow, wall-enclosed twistiness with never a stumble.

Glass was aglow at the house of Bodilis. He banged the knocker, which was in the form of a fouled anchor, blurred by centuries of hands (and what had each of those callers been seeking?). It was no surprise that she opened the door herself. She usually let her servants go home when they had cleaned up after a supper simple and early. Then she was likely to stay awake far into the night, reading, writing, creating.

What caught at Gratillonius's throat was how beautiful she was. A blue robe, wrapped around and held by a sash, hugged the full but still graceful figure. Her hair fell in soft and lustrous waves past the broad, blunt, alive countenance and eyes that were like Dahilis's. Lamplight and bees-wax candlelight from behind could only touch a curve, a tress, the hands that reached forth, but somehow he saw. "Oh, you, you," breathed the husky voice, "welcome home, beloved!"

He embraced her, mouth to mouth, till he heard a slight gasp and realized he was straining her breasts too hard against his coat of mail. He eased his grip, let palms rove across shoulders, back, hips, while the kiss went on.

"Come in," she said finally, let him by, and closed and barred the door behind them. "How are you? What have you . . . what have you accomplished, King?"

"I am well." He glanced down at himself and snorted a laugh. "Though mired and sweaty and, in general, unfit for polite company. . . . Dahilis! How fares she?"

"Excellently."

"A-a-ah-h-h."

Bodilis hesitated. "I took for granted you'd seek her first."

He felt his face grow warm. "We arrived later than we foresaw. Best leave her undisturbed. I knew you'd tell me the truth."

Bodilis laughed, low in her throat. "And once any fears for her were allayed—why, you've been long on the road."

He gave her a crooked grin. "I have that."

Her eyelids drooped. " 'Tis been long for me too."

He strode forward. She fended him off, playfully, seductively. "Nay, wait half a heartbeat! Would you not like refreshment first? You wouldn't? Then let's at least remove your armor and wash you clean. I'll enjoy doing that."

—They lay on their sides, close together, each with a hand on the haunch of the other. As yet they felt no need to draw up the blankets. Recklessly many lamps illuminated her in gold. Outside, rain had begun, a susurrus against the shutters.

"Aye, on the whole, things have continued as erstwhile in Ys," she said. "Well, poor Innillis has been having a bad time, as she did when carrying Hoel's child. Sickness, pains—but no worse than before, if we remember aright, and the first birth is commonly the hardest, and we Sisters have been taking care of her. I think—if you seek her out tomorrow as a friend, simply a friend . . . that will cheer her much."

"Of course I will."

"Of course. You are you." Bodilis's expression intensified. "She needs every help she can get. This solstice she takes Vigil on Sena."

"What?" asked Gratillonius, bemused. "I thought . . . on the quarter days . . . all you Gallicenae were here."

"Hitherto true. But the age born of Brennilis is dying, and—" Bodilis laid fingers across his lips. "Search no further. This is a thing that must be, that Ys may live."

Chill struck through him. She sensed it, smiled, flowed nearer. " 'Tis well, not ill. A duty to carry out, like standing on the Wall. Surely you've overcome worse hazards this trip. Tell me."

He hung back. She nibbled his earlobe. "Oh, do, Gratillonius. I'm afire with curiosity."

He became eager to oblige. It was a line of retreat from that which had no name. And this was Bodilis whom he had sought, Bodilis, because she was the one who could both meet his body's needs and then discourse widely and deeply—more so than he could always follow, but that was itself a rousing challenge—He set Innillis aside.

"The tale goes on and on, like the miles," he said. "I've kept a daily record which I want you to read, if you'll overlook my lame language. For now, though—you're not sleepy?—well, let's bring in some wine and lie at ease while we talk. Interrupt me whenever you wish."

She did, in questions and comments that heightened his own understanding of what he had seen and done; but mostly she led him on. The story came forth of his march to sad Vorgium, which had once been prosperous as Ys; to Condate Redonum, where he privily broached ideas for putting the Frankish laeti in their place; south as far as Portus

Namnetum and Condovincum, to consider mutual assistance between the hinterland resources of those neighboring cities and the navy of Ys; back north to Ingena and thence along the route he had followed earlier, until he branched off it to visit the tribune in charge at Gesocribate— "On the whole, we reached agreements in principle. 'Twill take years to build the machinery and get it working properly, I know. Still, we've made a fair start."

"*You* have," she murmured, and again her caresses went seeking.

2

Vindilis had moved in with Innilis. None thought the worse of this, or even of their sharing a bed. The younger woman was so often ill and in pain; she should not be left to servants who loved her but were ignorant and clumsy about such matters. In truth, nothing untoward happened, as weak as Innilis had become, beyond kisses, and those grew to be as between mother and child.

A cry in the night or a feverish tossing would wake Vindilis. She then did what she could. All vestals studied the elements of medicine, and priestesses of every grade who showed any gift for it were trained as full physicians. Vindilis practiced little. Her hands were cunning enough, but the Touch of the Goddess was not in them, nor had there been comfort in her manner. This last had changed of late.

The worst attack thus far ended a fitful sleep. Vindilis bounded onto a floor cold beneath her feet and bent over the other. Shutters blocked off any light from outside, but she always left a lamp burning when they retired. The untrimmed wick streamed smoke and a purulent, guttering flame. She could just see that Innilis lay hunched, arms and knees drawn against a now swelling belly. Her hair was lank with the sweat that studded a face blotched, yellowish, sunken in around the bones. The reek drowned any woman-fragrance. Sobs and hissings went between cracked lips. Vindilis put a hand on the brow and felt heat, though Innilis shuddered as with chill.

"Darling, darling!" Vindilis hurried to pour water from a jug, lay arm under neck, raise mouth to cup. "Here, drink." Innilis gulped and retched. "Nay, slowly, sip, sip, oh, my poor sweet."

Eventually she could ease the patient back onto the pillow. She went after her cloak. Both slept nude, for whatever warmth and consolation that might give. "Don't go, please don't go," Innilis moaned. "Stay. Hold my hand. It hurts so."

"Abide a little minute or two. I go to fetch powder of mandrake I've had brought. 'Twill give you some ease."

Innilis's eyes widened to ghastly white. "Nay! No drug. It might hurt the babe."

Vindilis bit back a curse upon the babe. "I think not. In any case, you can't go on like this."

Innilis clutched herself below breasts that were ripening to full loveliness but too sore for fondling. "Nay, Grallon's child, and, and she and I together on Sena. I can endure. I must." Her face turned toward a niche where a small image of Belisama was barely visible in shadow. "Mother of Mercies, help me."

Vindilis threw the cloak over her shoulders and fastened the brooch. "Well, you can at least quaff a pellitory infusion. That's never hurt you, and it should cool you off." She took the lamp. "I'll need this. Be not afraid in the dark."

Innilis shook her weary head. "I am not." Vindilis suspected she lied. "Please come back soon."

"Very soon." Vindilis kissed her cheek and went out.

A door opened and Innilis's daughter Audris came into the corridor. "What is the matter?" she asked. "Is Mama sick again?"

"Aye," said Vindilis. "Go back to bed."

The girl's face screwed up. "I want to see my Mama!"

This child of Hoel was ten years old, two more than Vindilis's Runa by the same King. So unforeseeably did the Sign come upon a maiden. Runa, though, was already as tall, and bright and lively. Audris had something of her mother's looks, except for being towheaded, but still talked like an infant, seemed unable to learn much, and fell into occasional fits. Hers had been a frightful birth. Vindilis had wondered over and over how her half-sister's next would fare.

"Back, I said!" the high priestess yelled. "Back to your room or I'll hit you! And stay there!"

Audris gaped at the snarl above the lampflame, whimpered, and fled.

Dawnlight stole down the smokehole in the kitchen. Vindilis stirred up a fire banked under the hob and fed it with dry sticks and chips to hotten it fast. She kept decoctions readymade, but needed warmth to dissolve honey. That would hide the taste of the willow bark she added to the pellitory. It was supposed to endanger the unborn and Innilis would have refused it on that account; but she required a strong febrifuge—and, yea,

a pinch of mandrake. Vindilis paced from flames to wall and back, to and
fro, to and fro, while the dull light sharpened and the potion heated.

When she returned, Innilis had slipped partway into unconsciousness.
"Here, beloved, here I am, always, always," Vindilis whispered. She
raised the head and urged the liquid down. Thereafter she laid herself in
the bed, damp and stinking though it was from sweat, and held Innilis in
her arms and crooned lullabies until sleep came.

The lamp was nearly burned dry, but no need to refill. The servants
would arrive shortly and throw back the shutters. Vindilis knew she
would get no more rest until nightfall. She might as well wash and dress.
Not enough hot water was left for bathing, but she preferred it cold.

The most direct way took her through the adjacent room, where Innilis
had spent much of her leisure in happier days. A large bronze mirror on
the wall caught what light there was and sent it off silver bowls, painted
vases, bright draperies, bits of artwork. Another image of the Goddess,
standing in a niche, was pretty too, benign, perhaps a trifle vapid; but
abruptly, as the light struck ivory, it seemed to leap forth in the terrible
majesty that was Hers.

Vindilis caught her breath. She turned, went to the niche, threw herself
bruisingly hard prostrate on the floor. "Ishtar-Isis-Belisama," she begged,
"spare her. Take whom else You will, how You will, but spare Innilis, and
afterward I will seek only to serve You."

3

On the road, Gratillonius had promised the legionaries and marines leave
for a homecoming feast. Preparations took several days. They included
reserving a favorite tavern down in the Fishtail, where prices were low
and rowdiness expected; providing it with a couple of pigs to roast and a
barrel of better wine than the landlord dispensed; engaging musicians,
entertainers, a few strumpets to help out the regulars; inviting friends
from the city and environs. This depleted the company fund, but that
didn't matter much. Ys furnished the Romans, as well as her own fighters, necessities and services for which they had been wont to pay in
Britannia. Furthermore, it gave them a wage, modest but in honest coin.
The King had insisted on that, pointing to their proven value as guardians
against foes and patrollers against crime. The move was popular with
merchants, since it got money out of the city coffers and back into circulation.

On the appointed day, Adminius led the troops forth. Otherwise he set his rank aside, and the passage was no march but a roaring romp. This was in the afternoon, in order to have daylight for the jugglers, acrobats, dancers, prestidigitators, and dancing animals. The weather was overcast but cold and dry: a blessing, as performances would have proper space in Skippers' Market rather than being crammed into the tavern. "Did the Nine arrange it for us?" joked Guentius.

"Quiet!" said Budic. "Don't mock sacred things. You know they never cast spells like that except at the most awful times."

"What? You, the superpious Christian, defending pagan faith?" Cynan gibed.

Budic's young countenance flushed like a girl's. "No, of course not. Although it is a decent sort of paganism. Queen Bodilis—But you don't want to insult our comrades, I hope."

"I was talking Latin," Guentius retorted. "Didn't you notice?"

"Some of them know it," Cynan decided. "Budic's right. Lay off."

Cheerfulness prevailed. When the show ended, as the early dusk was falling, men flocked to the inn and settled down to await the meal whose smoke and savor enriched the air. Goblets thumped, dice clattered, women squealed and giggled, voices lifted hoarse in talk and, presently, song.

—"Ah, 'tis fine to be 'ome again," sighed Adminius in Ysan. His left hand hoisted a beaker, his right gave the girl Keban a preliminary feeling over.

Herun of the navy raised brows across the table. " 'Home,' said you? We're happy to have you amongst us. However, yearn you not for your Britannia?"

Adminius shrugged. "God knows when we'll get back there, if ever. And frankly, 'tis no great loss. I could end my days 'ere quite contented. Might do so regardless, when I'm discharged."

"Hm." The sailor stroked his gingery beard. "If you truly mean that, you'll be looking about for a wife. I've a sister you might like to meet."

"Not so fast!" laughed Adminius, while Keban looked miffed.

"Nay, nay. She's young, hardly more than a child. Our parents will want to know any suitor well ere they give consent. For that matter, no girl in Ys may be married against her will, unless a vestal—Um, but a worthy man with Roman connections would be a welcome visitor."

—Said Maeloch the fisher to his friend Cynan: "Aye, do come stay with me when ye can get furlough. Ye know the house is small but snug, and though we're not rich, my Betha be a spanking good cook. The boys as well as myself—not to bespeak our neighbors—we'd love to hear ye yarn about your trip. We can promise to keep your whistle well wetted the while."

"Thank you," said the soldier. "It cannot be till after the Midwinter Council. The centurion wants the whole two dozen of us for a guard."

Maeloch's rough countenance tightened. "What, looks the King for trouble?"

"Oh, no threat, surely."

"Better not be. They'd have us, the whole folk, the seamen 'fore all, to reckon with, did they lay finger on our King or little Queen Dahilis."

Cynan's usual dourness broke in a smile. "You've grown fond of him, then?"

"With reason, with reason. He's brought honor back to the Key, order back to the holy family; he's rid us of the Scotic pirates and strives to get something real done about the Saxons; he's dealt fair and square with commoners like me, and now, I hear, he means to hold a court every month where anybody can bring a plea; and . . . he's made Dahilis glad, Dahilis who ever talks kindly."

"Well, 'tis good to hear you say so. As for the Council, I think he just wants his legionaries for an honor guard, same as before, to help overawe opposition there."

"Aye, even down under the cliffs we hear as how some magnates, Soren Cartagi of the Timbermen foremost, mislike the way he'd link us back to Rome. *I* say, when a storm is rising, break out your sheet anchor and make fast the rode." Maeloch's fist thudded down on the table. Its thick planks trembled. "Enough. Let's drink!"

XXIV

1

There was no wind on the night before Solstice Eve, nor was the air unduly cold. A swelling moon frosted thin, feathery clouds, among which a few stars blinked. Ashimmer like polished obsidian, Ocean heaved slowly, as if breathing in sleep. Sounds of surf rolled faint through deserted streets. The pharos light might have been a candle flame.

Then hour by hour a haze began drawing over heaven out of the west. As the moon sank toward it, a ring came aglow up there and stars withdrew from sight. Shadows blurred, lost themselves in the general darkness.

The moon was low beyond hidden Sena when abruptly a clatter and banging arose. It seemed thrice loud and harsh in this quietude. A cat on the prowl squalled and fled. Had the dead swarmed in from the necropolis to rattle their bones through Ys?

"Open, help, open, ow-w-w!"

A maidservant unbarred the door on which the knocker had beaten. Ghostly in nightgown, she peered at the small figure which jittered on the cobbles. After a moment: "Oh, but 'tis Audris. What are you doing here at this hour, child?"

"Fennalis come quick!" the girl keened. "Mama sick, Aunt Vin'ilis tol' me get Aunt Fennalis, quick!" She herself wore merely a shift pulled over her head. The paving must have numbed her bare feet.

The high priestess was swiftly awake. Unlike most of her Sisters, she kept an attendant always in her house, because she had become hard of hearing and might not be roused by a belated appeal. Aside from lacking the Touch that Innilis seemed, erratically, to have, Fennalis was the best physician in the city, responsive to the great and the lowly alike.

She paused for no more than sandals, gown, cloak, and medical kit.

"Audris, stay," she ordered the yammering visitor. "Blodvin, tuck her into my bed, warm her some milk, sit beside her. If she throws a fit—drools, rolls her eyes, strains backward—put a towel in her mouth lest she bite her tongue, but panic not." Fennalis took a lantern that the maid had kindled from the nightfire and trotted forth. Wan light wavered across snub-nosed features, gray bristle of hair.

The way was short but steep to the home of Innilis. Its door stood open. Fennalis passed through. Candles burned everywhere. She set her lantern down and stood panting and wheezing.

Vindilis came into the atrium. She was naked. Blood bespattered her, dripped from her hands. "At last," she rasped. Heedless of stains, she gave Fennalis support while she well-nigh dragged the older woman along.

"A thump, a scream. She may have started out of bed to go to the pot. Or mayhap—Her mind has sometimes wandered. I suppose she fell off the edge onto the floor. There she lay, writhing and screaming. I saw the waves going down her belly. Somehow I got her back into bed, and lights lit to see by. The waters gushed forth. They were tinged red. Blood followed. I've tried to stanch it. Small success."

They reached the bedroom. Splotches and footprints went crimson across the floor. Sheets, blankets, mattress were soaked. Innilis half sat against a heap of pillows. Her jaws were wide, straining for air, making a Gorgon mask. Eyes stared, blank with pain and terror.

Fennalis regained her breath. She bustled to the bedside, kissed the brow beneath her, and murmured, "How goes it, Sister?" while she removed the cloths Vindilis had tucked between the thighs.

"Oh, it hurts, it hurts," moaned Innilis. Vindilis clenched fists together but kept aside, out of the way.

"Hm. Naturally it would," said Fennalis. "I think you did succeed. No issue now to speak of. Blood always looks like more than it is."

"But too much nonetheless," Vindilis replied in the same grating monotone as before.

Fennalis nodded. "To be awaited. The suddenness and all. I daresay injuries from the first birth never healed aright."

Innilis reached to scrabble after her. "Help me!" she cried. "Save me. I don't want to ride in the Wild Hunt!"

"You shan't."

"Certainly not you." Vindilis came around to lean over the head of the bed, stroke the face that was bent away from her, drop kisses and tears down into the hair. "You are a Queen. Whatever happens to us, Belisama takes us home to Her sea, She, the Star of it."

"Stop that nonsense," Fennalis snapped. "We can get this over fast if we go about it rightly. Vindilis, curb yourself. Stand yonder. Help her kneel. . . . Now, child, bear down."

Innilis shrieked. *"Nay!"*

"Yea," said Fennalis. "Harken. You're not going to lose it. You've done that already. Your task is to get rid of it."

"Oh, my babe, the King's babe!"

Fennalis slapped Innilis on the cheek. "Stop that. Get to work. Vindilis, support her while I unpack my kit."

—When at last Innilis lay simply weeping, Fennalis made her drink from a vial. To Vindilis the physician said: "Opium. Scarce as cocks' eggs nowadays, but I've saved out some for special cases. 'Twill ease her, and can do no harm now."

"Nay." Vindilis stared at that which lay on the floor, quiet after a brief stirring. "It can do no harm now."

"When Innilis is soundly asleep, we'll sponge her off and shift her to the couch in her receiving room. Ease your mind. I don't believe our Sister is in further peril, though belike she'll be slow to regain strength. The servants will be here before dawn." Fennalis yawned mightily. "Then at last we twain can go tumble into bed and sleep till noon."

"Nay," said Vindilis again. Weariness barely dulled the iron in her voice. "Not till well afterward. Have you forgotten?"

2

The state barge daily set forth at sunrise, or as soon thereafter as ebb tide had started opening the sea gate. This time, fetching Maldunilis back, it carried no replacement. For the next three days, all the Nine would be in Ys, attending to rites and Council. Or thus it had been hitherto.

The last feather-clouds departed. By afternoon the sun shone in a sky gone milky; shadows stretched pale from the south. A breeze sprang up, cold, gradually strengthening until it whittered in streets and raised whitecaps on a darkly greenish-gray sea.

Seven of the Nine met at the temple of Belisama. They dismissed the vestals and minor priestesses, save for one who was to stand outside and admit Dahilis when she arrived, and went on into the main chamber of worship. Chill and dimness lay within, barely lighted by windows whose glass was the hue of underwater; for lamps and candles had been extinguished. They would be rekindled at midnight—would shine from every observant house in the city—to welcome home the returning sun. Grain of stone and mosaic scenes of myth were vague in vision. At the far end, behind the high altar, the images of the triune Goddess towered pallid and stern. Silently, each in her own way, the Gallicenae prayed for mercy.

After a while Dahilis slipped in, clad like the rest in sacral blue and white. Tears gleamed below the tall headdress. Her voice came thin: "I'm sorry, I beg pardon I'm late, but—but—"

Quinipilis approached her, looked close, and said, "Come, best we seek our meeting room at once."

"Nay, I m-m-must make my devotion—"

"You shall, for the whole Sisterhood and people."

"You don't understand! Listen!"

"Hush. This is no place for news. Come."

Numbly, Dahilis followed the old woman, while the others trailed after. They went down the corridor to the chamber behind the sanctuary and entered. It was scarcely warmer, but better served by its windows; the Four Aspects on the walls stood forth in vividness.

Several cried out. On the dais, red-robed, Key in view on his breast, Hammer against hip, Gratillonius waited. He had used the rear entrance —not that anyone would have dared refuse him admission after a single look at his countenance.

Vindilis first got her wits back. Her words attacked like a stooping hawk. "My lord, what is this? Arriving without right is sacrilege. Begone!"

The square, massive visage hardened still further, the powerful body seemed to take stance as if readying for an enemy charge. Rougher than had been his wont, his answer rolled forth. "I have every right. I am the King of Ys. He Whose avatar I am is Belisama's lover."

Dahilis stumbled forward to stand under the dais, confronting her Sisters. They could see how her breath labored, almost how her heart galloped, beneath the child-bulged gown. She raised her palms. "Hear me," she beseeched. "I never intended—But 'tis my fault. Mine alone. When the m-message came to the palace . . . about poor Innilis—I was so shocked I blurted unthinkingly—"

"And I sensed something more behind that, and thundered it out of her," Gratillonius said. "She strove to hold back, but she'd already let slip she must go hither at this time, about a matter more grave than the loss of an infant. I said I would come too, my legionaries at my back if need be, and have the truth. That—" He faltered. For a moment he stood gnawing his lip, then whispered, "That broke her will."

"Nay, wait, wait," exclaimed Quinipilis. She rocked up to hug Dahilis to her ample bosom. "There, dear, there, 'twas indeed no sin of yours. You were helpless."

"She was sensible," declared Fennalis. "Better give the man his way, and a while to calm down, better that than an open breach, right in the sacred building."

"True," growled the centurion. "She has a wiser head on her, young though she be, than some I could name. Now can the lot of you sit down and we talk this over like reasoning beings?"

"I fear 'tis too deep for reason," said Bodilis; but she took the lead in urging that they try. To Maldunilis she must utter a stiff "Be quiet or I'll throw you out" before that Queen controlled her dread of what these events might portend. The rest won sooner to a stoic peacefulness.

"Well." Seeking to ease things a little, Gratillonius leaned on the long haft of the Hammer. "I hope you understand my wish is to do my duty as your King. But I have other duties too, as the prefect of Rome . . . and as a man. It grieves me to hear what Innilis has suffered. If I have not hastened to her bedside, 'tis because of this business. To be frank, I am yet unclear about it. I know only that she was supposed to spend the solstice day and night on Sena, but the task has fallen on Dahilis."

"I will fulfill it, oh, I will," Dahilis vowed.

Gratillonius's anger burst forth anew. "Alone, in your condition? Have you seen the sky? Foul weather's on the way, if ever clouds gave signal. You could be trapped out yonder for days, no boat able to live through the waves and reefs. Madness!"

It was as though fire flickered behind ice in the gaze of Forsquilis. "Nay, Roman," she said to the man with whom she had made love this past night. Intensity caused her to tremble. " 'Tis the command of the Gods. To learn it I have guested the dead; to carry it out we have thirsted, fasted, and scourged; no more may we deny or defy it than you may spit on the sacrifice of your Mithras. Or less—for He would send you alone down to hell, whereas the wrath of our Gods would fall upon all Ys. It is required that a Sister take Vigil at this Midwinter while bearing within her a child. That was to have been Innilis. Now it must needs be Dahilis."

"You went behind my back." Gratillonius raised the Hammer. "Why, why, why?"

"To expiate the sins against Them, among which yours, O King, wax rank," said Lanarvilis quietly, almost sorrowfully; and she explained.

"But—but that is—See here!" Gratillonius roared. "If I've erred, I'll make whatever amends you want . . . if they be seemly. . . . *I* will!"

Silence answered, save that Forsquilis shook her head. Dahilis had gone dry-eyed. She sat straight, hands serene in her lap, resoluteness upon her.

"Mithras will protect you! He is just, and He is above—" Gratillonius stopped. He knew implacability when it stared at him.

He had two dozen soldiers. Most ordinary Ysan men would recoil from assaulting him, he trusted; even some of the marines might hang back. In any event, given speed and determination, his company could fight its way clear and on to safety in Audiarna, bearing Dahilis along—

No. He foresaw what that would do to her. And it would irretrievably wreck the still frail structure of defense he was building. His mission was to save Armorica for Rome, not tear it asunder.

"Forgive me. I meant no insult to the Gods of Ys." A while he stood, head bowed, both hands on the butt of the Hammer to upbear his weight, which seemed to have grown boulder-huge. The Key dangled free from his neck.

Finally he shook himself, squared his shoulders, and said, "Very well. So be it. But Dahilis shall take no needless risk."

"Do you doubt that the Goddess will look after her?" Vindilis challenged. "Or if not, who shall fathom Her ways? That which has happened may indeed have been Her will making itself manifest."

"Then do you doubt its fulfillment, whatever we mortals may do?" Gratillonius retorted. "I ask merely that one or two of you—or somebody—accompany Dahilis, and stand by against . . . troubles such as we have had already."

"None of us may," answered Quinipilis. "Gratillonius, my dear, you're a kind man in your fashion, and I feel what wound is in you. But 'tis a condition of this sacrament, and we are bound to it by the Great Oath, that none among us may betread Sena tomorrow, other than the chosen high priestess and her unborn. And of course nobody else ever may."

Gratillonius pounced. "Ha! What of the workmen—*men*—who repaired the storm damage?"

"That was a holy necessity," Lanarvilis replied. "First they underwent rites of purification and consecration. Afterward the entire island was rededicated. Think not we can evade Belisama's commandment by falsely praying over anybody at this late hour."

His response came as no surprise to himself. It had been rising like a sea tide. "*I* am sanctified," he said.

Horror hissed around the room.

"I am the King. I am Taranis on earth," he followed. "If the King's presence on Sena is unheard of, why, likewise is a Midwinter Vigil."

"The King—in Ys—must preside over the festival," Fennalis protested.

Gratillonius fleered. "Are they backwoodsmen here, to believe their celebrations rekindle the sun? Nay, those are but celebrations. I've asked about them. All I'm supposed to do is take part in a ceremony. Somebody else—a priest or Soren, my Speaker—he can do it as well. Has naught like this ever happened erenow in your history?"

"There have been two or three times," Bodilis confessed. "A King was ill, or at the frontier when invasion threatened, or—"

"You see?" Gratillonius cried. He drew breath. "Fear not," he said in a level tone. "I've no wish to profane anything. I'll keep away from the mysteries. But . . . come worst to worst, I am a good man of my hands, a farm boy who has helped birth many an animal, a soldier who knows how to treat many a hurt. The sailors who ferry you there set foot on the wharf, at least. Would you refuse your sacral King what you grant them?" Most softly: "I am going. I have spoken."

Bodilis stirred, raised her hands, gazed beyond the walls as her mind felt its way forward. "Hold, wait," she said. "Sisters, a God does dwell in our King. Who can be certain that Belisama wants not him also? . . . I told you, Gratillonius, the matter is too deep for reason. Yet while sunlight never reaches the ocean depths, it illuminates the waves. . . . Aye, listen. 'Tis true that outsiders may walk on the wharf. Indeed, the ground below high-water mark is allowable. That law is for the sake of mariners who may be driven onto a lee shore, but does not explicitly ban others." She met his glance. "Can we, together, find a compromise?"

Hope blazed in him. "I think we can."

The face of Dahilis was like sunrise.

XXV

1

The barge of state was impressive not in size, for its length was a bare sixty feet, but in appearance. The graceful hull was blue with silver trim. At the prow lifted a carven swan's head, at the stern a fishtail, both gilt. A deckhouse amidships, though wooden, was built and painted to resemble a Grecian temple in miniature. While the vessel was oar-driven, she bore a pole for the flying of a flag—heavy silk, gold-fringed, dolphin argent on azure, the annual gift of the Needleworkers' Guild. The crew were navy men, periodically chosen by their captains as an honor.

She departed Ys somewhat late on solstice morning because seas were running heavy, causing a chop in the very basin. When ebb had swung the doors safely wide, a trumpet sounded, men ashore cast off lines, the galley stood out. From quay, wall, towers, folk watched this unprecedented faring in awe.

Beyond the shelter, the craft rocked, pitched, shuddered. Wind drove strong, hollowly hooting, thrumming the stays, making waves roar white-maned along until they burst in a crash and a fountaining on the rocks everywhere about. It harried a wrack low and wolf-gray out of murk rising ever higher in the west. Spindrift flung salt onto lips. Chill slashed.

The galley toiled onward, picking a way through the safe lanes. Lookouts strained their vision overside, the steersman and his standby poised taut, rowers changed frequently so as to keep at peak strength. Slowly the shining spires of Ys sank away aft, until flying brume swallowed sight first of them and then of the mainland. No birds were aloft except a cormorant that followed afar, a hovering and soaring blackness. As the barge approached Sena, a score or more of seals appeared and accompanied it.

The interior of the deckhouse was a cabin, snug and well-appointed, dim today when windows perforce were shuttered. Gratillonius and

Dahilis shared a seat. Most of the time she leaned close and he had an arm about her, bracing her as the vessel rolled and plunged. Whoosh and boom of waves, creak and groan of timbers, occasional shouts of the men filled the room. Yet they could talk. They needed to, for yesterday he had spent the evening on his preparations, whereupon she passed the night at the temple, in purification as well as sleep.

"How much may you tell me of what you shall be doing?" he asked.

" 'Tis to be a Vigil like any other—in form, at least," she replied. Earnestly: "You do understand what that means, do you not? On behalf of Ys, communion with the Goddess, prayers for the people; and, yea, devotion to Lir, since 'tis Taranis Who is with Her everywhere else. At the House of the Goddess I drink Her wine and eat Her bread; more than that I must not say. I then walk to the two Stones that the Old Folk raised near the middle of the island, and perform certain rites. Thence I go to the far western end and give Lir His honors. After that I return to the House for orisons, meditation, another sacred meal, and rest until sunrise. After dawnsong I am free, and soon the barge comes to bring my Sister and take me home." She squeezed his hand. "To you. This time, with you."

"Hm!" He scowled. "I mistrust the weather."

"Oh, but we're not supposed to endanger ourselves. We do whatever looks safe, and are excused from the rest. The House is stoutly built. Its tower is for refuge when a storm dashes the waters clear across land. I am sure, though, I'm sure the Gods want a full sacrament at this of all Vigils. They will provide."

Her faith tugged at his heart. He almost wished he could share it. But in the Gods of Ys was too much of the ancient darkness from which They had risen. "When can I see you?"

She turned her countenance up toward his to give him the gift of her smile, which she thought of as a present to herself. "Well, the door of the House is in view from the wharf. You'll have sight of me as I go in and out. And I of you. I don't think Belisama will mind if we wave at each other."

How dear she was. Hair tumbled in a golden cataract past features whose fine bones might be of the Suffetes but whose flared and tip-tilted nose, wide and soft mouth just parted over flawless teeth, fair skin and underlying liveliness were belike from her father Hoel. The great dark-blue eyes she shared with Bodilis; the light that danced within them was her own. Her voice was likewise low: not husky, however; its music, again, uniquely hers. Never before had he known a woman could be so merry and still so loving. He leaned down toward her. The sweetness of tresses and flesh dizzied him.

She blocked his lips with gentle fingers. "Nay, darling, we musn't, not till we're back home." Laughter purred. "But I don't think She will blame me, either, for looking forward."

He sighed. "Suppose we're weatherbound."

"Then the priestess must carry on the round of services as best she can until she is relieved. I mustn't come to you. We'll make up for that after our girl is born."

"But what if that happens meanwhile?" he fretted. "That's why I'm here, you know. Unless worse befall. I will not stand idly by if you need help, Dahilis. I will not. Afterward let the Gods fight it out with me."

"Hush!" she said, scandalized. "You . . . you shouldn't be . . . hostile like that, darling. The Mother loves us. I know She does. And I am not due quite yet. Oh, aye, if bad trouble strikes, of course I may seek your tent. My Sisters and I talked this out last night. This Vigil is not for, for punishment. 'Tis to set things aright, that the Gods may again be free to bestow blessings on Ys."

He cleared his throat. "Umf, I meant no offense. Certainly not. . . . But the House will be better shelter for us."

She shook her head violently. "Nay! A man would desecrate it. 'Twould have to be purified and consecrated anew, as 'twas after the carpenters and masons had finished. Meanwhile the poor dead had to wait in the Twilight." Dahilis drew a sharp breath. "The workers were there by divine consent. If you broke in unasked—Nay, I dare not think what vengeance the Gods might take on you. On *you*. Please, beloved, nay, promise me you'll not!"

"Ah, well, we speak of what we trust is unlikely," he evaded. In haste to change the subject: "But what's this about the dead? I remember the funeral barge went out more than once while the repair work was going on."

He could barely hear her whisper through the din: "That was only their bodies. Later the Ferriers bring their souls to Sena for judgment. On such a night the Queen in the House must stay wakeful till morning to pray for them."

"Have you?" Instantly he regretted his heedlessness.

She nodded. He couldn't tell whether she had gone pale, but her eyes were more big than ever, staring straight forward. "Surely. At sundown I have suddenly *known* there would be the landing, and the whisper of the names, and—and been glad to have light around me after I lit lamps on the altar—This is a mystery."

"I'm sorry," he mumbled. "I'd not cause you distress for the world and Heaven."

She embraced him, carefully chaste but altogether forgiving. Her spirits soon lifted afresh. His did too, somewhat.

2

The barge came in with difficulty through the wild water. Watching on deck, Gratillonius admired the skill of captain and crew. Rowers strained: the master gauged wind and waves, gave hand signals; a stentor bellowed the orders. They caught a billow and rode it. As it crested, the steersman put his helm hard over; larboard oars snapped up out of harm's way while starboard oars brought the hull about; the steersman's partner disengaged the left rudder oar and hauled it free; strokes boomed against rope bumpers suspended from bollards. Immediately sailors leaped off onto the wharf, lines in hand, and made fast. Two aboard ran out a gangplank which their fellows ashore secured.

The captain gave Dahilis the salute of deference. "Thanks be to Lir that He brought us here in safety, and to Belisama that She gave us you, O Queen, to convey hither," he said formally. The wind tattered his words.

She inclined her head to him. "And I thank you on behalf of the Gallicenae and Ys," she replied likewise, then could not resist laughing: " 'Twas a pretty show!"

Gravity returned: "The hour is late, on this shortest day of the year. I must commence at once. Farewell."

Gratillonius escorted her to the wharf. Small and alone she looked against the gray-green tumult that battered the island, the dreariness of rock, scrub, and sere grass beyond. Sacral gown and headdress were woolen for winter, as was the cloak she hugged to her, but cold sought inward. A moment her gaze dwelt on him. "Fare *you* well," she said, "forever well."

Turning, she walked off, over the planks and along a short path to the House of the Goddess. From her left hand dangled a bedroll, from her right a bag of other necessities. Despite the burden and even through the garments, he was aware of how dancingly she moved. Her unborn had never dragged her down much. She had often, delightedly, said what a quick and easy delivery should be hers, and what a fine, healthy babe— "Come, Gratillonius, put your hand here, feel her kick, already she wants out. Oh, she'll make the world remember her!" And only a few days ago, Dahilis had felt the lightening.

She glanced back and waved, as she had promised, before she disappeared in the somber bulk of the House. Rushing rags of cloud brushed past its towertop. The western half of heaven had become a cavern.

Someone diffidently touched Gratillonius's arm. "Your pardon, my lord." The King glanced around and recognized a young man named Herun. "We have to set up your camp without delay."

"Oh . . . oh, indeed," said Gratillonius. "So you can start back. Trying that after dark would be deadly in this weather, I'm sure."

"In truth, lord. As 'tis, likeliest the gate will be shut, or too narrowly open to attempt. But given such a tide, we can make Ghost Quay if we've light to see by. It happens often enough."

Gratillonius must oversee the work and take a hand of his own, as newly invented as it was. None less than Bomatin Kusuri, Mariner Councilor, had helped him devise his shelter yesterday, and gotten craftsmen to prepare what extra parts were required. In effect, a Roman army tent went up on the wharf, tethered to bollards and piles. Meant for eight men, it would be less warm for one, though roomier. However, its leather would fend off any blast that did not tear everything loose; a rug would lie beneath; he was well clad, in fisherman's tunic, trousers, boots, with jacket and gloves and ample changes in reserve; he had candles, lantern, oil, tinder, punkwood, flint, steel.

Nevertheless it was a swine of a job to erect the tent. Leather flapped into faces, cords flew about like slavedrivers' whips. Men said no profane word, but obscenities were plentiful. Afterward, watching for Dahilis, Gratillonius realized she must have gone out again, inland, while he was thus engaged. He had not seen her greeting to him.

Finally the task was over. He said his appreciative goodbyes. The crew embarked, cast loose, fended off, departed. He stood watching the galley dwindle: a brave sight, but how fragile amidst the surges and surfs, like Dahilis beneath this sky.

Having sadly given up on seeing her again for hours, he busied himself settling in. There were things to stow, food such as didn't need cooking, water, wine, bedroll, towels, washbasin, comb, teeth cleansers—the list went on, ending with what he had brought to pass the time. A book could have been too easily blotted, ruined; and he possessed no musical gift whatsoever. He did, though, have waxed tablets and a stylus, for noting down any thoughts that occurred to him about Ys and Armorica. Mainly he had brought pieces of wood, and tools to carve them into ornaments for furniture and toys for his stepdaughters. And why not for his own

daughter as well, his and Dahilis's? She'd not appreciate more than a rag
doll at first, but later she would enjoy, say, a tiny wagon. . . .

Gratillonius smiled as he crossed his legs on the rug. He reached for a
whetstone. Several of his blades needed sharpening, and no servant of his
had quite the right final feather-touch.

Wind gusted, screeched, noisily flapped the doorfolds, which had been
tied back to admit light. His pleasure drained from him. He should not be
doing work as mechanical as this. It freed his mind to wonder how
Dahilis was, alone with her Gods at Midwinter.

3

Gratillonius did not notice her. He and the sailors were struggling to put
up his tent. Dahilis wished she could linger till his glance wandered her
way. But already she had had to be hasty in the first communion rite.
More than half the short day was gone, while clouds drew downward,
ever darker, and wind grew still more fierce. She must be back before
nightfall was complete, so she could see to kindle fire—on the hearth for
herself, in lamps for herself and the Goddess.

"Belisama, Queen and Mother, watch over him," she whispered, and
started forth.

For a space the footpath followed the shoreline. Castoffs of the tide lay
strewn, kelp, shells, dead fish, pieces from the many wrecks that these
waters had claimed over the years. Beyond churned and foamed the sea
itself, nearly black save where it burst in gigantic whiteness. Growl and
roar were like drums beneath the war horn of the wind. Seals swam in the
turmoil. They kept turning their heads inland—toward her? The path
bent that way, then west again; she lost sight of them.

It hurt to turn her back on the Kindly Ones. It hurt to leave Gratillonius behind. It hurt!

Dahilis halted with a gasp. The pain started at the small of her back
and came around to grip her in the belly. It was like the pangs of lightening, but those had been brief and mild. This laid hold of her inmost
depths. She barred a cry behind her teeth. Dear Isis, had the birth begun
so early?

The cramp passed. A while she stood shivering. Best return, start the
fire, wait. If this went on, seek Gratillonius.

Nay. Dead Brennilis, speaking through the mouth of Forsquilis, had
warned that the trial would be severe. This was not worse than she,

Dahilis, could endure. The pains might well be false. In any event, likelihood was that she could move about freely, most of the time, for hours and hours yet. Let her do so, and win her man forgiveness.

And the Sisterhood and Ys, of course.

She strode on. The wind was now straight in her face. She tasted the salt spray that it flung the length of Sena. It sought to tear the cloak from her shoulders. She could barely hold the garment together; it fluttered and snapped frantically. The cold probed through every opening. Her gown made valiant defense, but the wind flattened it against her and her babe, jeered as it lifted the hem, swirled up from underneath. The low, scudding clouds had given way to a roiling leadenness above, a monstrous gloom ahead. Leafless bushes flicked their twigs above stones and patches of withered grass. Hoot and howl streamed around her.

But there were the two menhirs, where she had helped bring Gratillonius and, later, bring him the aid he needed against the reavers out at sea—A second spasm coiled through her. She waited it out.

Shakily, she approached the Bird and the Beast. She said the words, she danced the sunwise dance, she ate the salt and gave the drop of blood, she asked leave to depart and peace on the Old Folk. It seemed a good omen that the next attack held off until this was all done.

After that, though, she lost count of how many stops she must make on her way west. Belike the wind slowed her, she thought: thrusting, battering, chilling, as if Lir had sent it to keep her away from Him. The flat landscape seemed everywhere the same. As she went on, it grew vague in her sight. The wind was lashing such tears from her eyes. Spray flew ever thicker. Its bitterness caked on her lips. Snow that was half sleet began drifting against her. Horizon and sky were lost.

"Lir," she appealed, "Lir, are You really angered that he buried his friend, in the name of their God, above Your sea? You can't be. You are Captain and Helmsman. You understand what manhood is."

But Lir had nothing of humanity about Him. He was the storm that whelmed ships, the lightless depths that drowned men, the waves that flung them onto rocks for gulls to eat what the eels had not. Well did He nourished great whales, and dolphins to frolic about sailors and seals to watch over them. Well did He raise great shoals of fish and the winds that bore rich cargoes homeward. But He was Ocean, the Son of Chaos, and Ys lived only on sufferance of His, only because it had made itself forever a hostage to His wrath.

Let her appeal and appease—She sank to knees, to all fours, and could not quite hold back a cry. Some births came fast. This, her first, too early at that, this birth ought not to, but, "Belisama, Mother, help me."

Dahilis lurched back to her feet. The drift around her grew more white as everything else grew blacker.

Then ahead, at endless last, she spied the tip of the island. Surf ramped beyond it; she heard the boom and long, withdrawing snarl, she could well-nigh feel them through her bones. That was farther out than she must go. She need only descend a few tiers of rock to one that jutted out above high-water mark. Upon it stood an altar, a block of stone, sea-worn until ledges and carven symbols were nearly gone. There she must give Lir His honor. Afterward she could return to the House of the Goddess.

She picked her way down carefully, half blinded as she was. Wind raved, snow and spindrift flew. Her womb contracted. She bent herself around the anguish. Her heel slipped on wetness. She felt herself toppling, helpless. It seemed to go on and on, while she stood aside and watched. Shock, pain, those too struck somebody remote.

—They waited patiently until she crawled back from wherever she had been. That was a slow battle. Often she slid back downward. A birth pang would drag her up again. The agony in her right leg resisted this, as the wind had resisted her walking. But when she did break free, it became her friend. It was something other than a confusion of wind, snow, water, darkness, and noise. Her mind clung to it. Don't let go, she begged. If you do, I'll slip away from this, and I mustn't.

Scrabbling, her fingers hoisted her gown. The right foot was bent awry. Fractured ankle. She would dance no more, not soon. How long had she lain unaware? Not long; her head was unhurt, mayhap saved by the cloth wrapped around it, though that had come loose. Nonetheless, thought fumbled through drift of snow and scud. Her garments were drenched, weighting her when she tried to raise herself on her hands. Water sheeted. The tide was coming in swiftly. With the wind behind it, surf would reach around the altar of Lir. It might pull her off to Him, or it might simply kill her and the child.

She must find shelter before the chill reached her womb. Already she felt numbness stealing inward. She tried to get up on the sound foot and hop. That knee buckled. She fell on the broken ankle. Bright lightnings cast her back into the dark.

It was closing in on the world when she next regained herself. Another cramp pulsed through her. She felt it more keenly than she now felt the broken bones. "Hold," she muttered. "Abide. We'll go to him." His right name eluded her. It was lengthy, Latin, unmusical. Her tongue remembered how Ysans sometimes rendered it. "Grallon. Oh, Grallon."

Dahilis began to crawl.

When she had hitched her way over the terraces, onto the flatland, she could not find the path. Whiteness lay thin upon rock and soil. It flowed along in the air, on the wind, through the deepening dusk. The crash and rush of the sea behind her filled her skull. She must get away from the sea. Somewhere yonder were Grallon and Belisama. "Be not hasty," she told her daughter. "Wait till he can help us." She knew little else, but she did know that she must creep onward, each time that the pains allowed.

4

As twilight fell, Gratillonius grew more and more uneasy. Ignoring cold, he sat in the entrance of his tent. It opened toward the building. He did not see her, he did not see her. By every hell of every faith, she ought to be back. Ought she not? The island was small. Any healthy person could walk it from end to end in an hour or so. Allow as much for the return. She did have her duties along the way, but they couldn't be too elaborate, could they? A slight snow had begun, dry flakes borne nearly level out of the west. It hindered vision. He might miss sight of her. He didn't want that.

His woodcarving forgotten, he waited. Thoughts tumbled through him, memories, mother, father, the farm, camp, girls who seemed to have gone unreal, the Wall, Parnesius, combats that no longer mattered—where *was* Dahilis?—Maximus's will to power, the march to Ys, Dahilis, Dahilis, things he needed to do, also among her Sisters—what in Ahriman's name was keeping her?—how he might disengage himself from Ys after his work in Armorica was done, but not from Dahilis, no, he must win her over to Rome, and where *was* she, what was keeping her? The snow streaked denser than before.

Finally he realized he'd better start fire while he could still see. That meant closing the tent against the gusts that had been whirling about in it. The consequent gloom, and his own impatience, cost him several failures before he had ignited the tinder, blown it to life, kindled a punkstick, and brought that to a candle. Then it took a while more to get his lantern going. It was a fine big one, bronze with glass panes, but awkward in the ignition. He'd be stupid not to use it, however, for a naked flame might well die when he reopened the tent flaps.

It did. He blinked at night. Not dark already! He should stand outside and let his eyes adapt. The wind savaged his face. Waves bawled unseen; he felt the wharf tremble to their blows. With the slowness of a torturer, some vision came to him. He discerned the House not as a mass but as an abyss, blacker than black. If Dahilis had entered it while he wasn't look-ing, she must be asleep in there.

The knowledge struck into him like a swordthrust. "Asleep?" he yelled. "Can't be!" Not as early as Midwinter nightfall was. She had spoken of an evensong; surely that required lamps. And she would have lighted a hearthfire. But never a glimmer—

He fought himself till the breath sobbed in his gullet. He'd missed sight of her. Shutters and door blocked light. If he went there, she would be aghast. She was supposed to seek him, should necessity come upon her. Stand fast, Gratillonius, stand your watch, keep your post.

Snow hissed. Blindness deepened. He raised his hands. "Mithras, God of the Law, what shall I do?"

A still small voice replied: Look for the smoke.

Gratillonius's heart stumbled. The smoke of sacrifice, the smoke of the hearth, it rose. However swiftly wind snatched it away from its outlet, firelight from beneath should glimmer on it . . . and on the flying snow . . . but there was no light. None whatsoever.

A faraway part of him recalled moments of commitment to battle. In them had been a certain eerie bliss. You had no more thinking to do, nor hoping nor praying. You only drew sword.

He fetched the lantern and carried it by the lug, as low down as might readily be so that he could pick his way up the path. Wind, snow, night had receded to remoteness; he barely heard the sea. The door of the House bore a knocker formed like a triskele. He thudded it as hard as he was able. "Dahilis, Dahilis, are you within?" The noise disappeared.

"The sacrilege is mine," he said, mainly for her sake, and opened the door.

Shadows wavered misshapen around a single room. From the Roman-tiled floor a wooden staircase led up into the tower. But that was for refuge. Here he saw a hearth, an oven, utensils, chair, stool, table, cabinet . . . rug on the floor, lamps and candlesticks on a shelf, hangings to relieve the bleakness of stone walls . . . at the far end, what might be an altar . . . closer by, a single bed, and tossed onto it the rolled sheets and blankets he knew.

"Dahilis!" he roared. Echoes laughed.

So, he thought.

She would need a fire, but he didn't know when he would come back with her. He laid out the nicely stacked kindling and sticks. From a jug he drenched them with lamp oil. Let that soak in, that he might be able to start a blaze immediately when he had brought her here to shelter.

Fire. . . . He could be a long while searching. Best that he take several

tallow candles to recharge the lantern. He snatched them off their shelf
and stuffed them into the pouch at the belt of his Ysan garb. Down with
them he put flint, steel, tinder, and punk, just in case—though he'd need
some kind of windbreak before trying to start anything burning. Across
his left arm he slung a wool blanket, while he took a firm grip on the
lantern, ready to keep it level should he trip. Then he set forth.

"Dahilis!" he cried. "Dahilis!"

The wind whistled, the waves resounded, his voice was lost. As he left
the House behind, he glimpsed a seal that had come ashore to lie on the
strand. Its gaze followed him till he was gone into his darkness.

He didn't know this damned island at all. There should be a footpath of
some kind, but where? Snow had laid enough veil over the ground that he
couldn't tell by looking. He only knew that it wasn't under the hummocks
and tufts of winter grass or the bare, snickering bushes; but those grew
sparsely. Besides, she might be anywhere.

It would do no good to run around yelling like a scared pup. Best he
weave his way to and fro across the narrow land, guiding himself as best
he was able by whatever clues there might be, such as the noise of the
waters north and south. At that, he could easily miss her, if she didn't
hear him and call an answer. Well, if so, he would work back again. Come
daylight he could see farther than by the feeble glow he carried.

But it would be a long night.

—"Dahilis, Dahilis!"

—He came upon a pair of menhirs. Much taller than he, close together,
one bluntly pointed and one with a beaklike projection near the top, they
must be the Stones about which he had heard words let slip. They might
be something toward which she would seek. At least they were things,
here in the middle of nothingness. He cast around and around. She was
not there. His voice was giving out.

—The snowfall ended in a last, spiteful sleet.

—He could only croak, like a crow with a bad cold.

—When he replaced the candle, fatigue made his hand shake so that he
nearly dropped it.

—The wind slackened, but chill strengthened. Heaven was lightless.
Gratillonius began to hear the surf at the western end of Sena.

—He came upon her quite suddenly. Another shadow he wasn't sure
of; a turn for a closer look; he stubbed his toe on a rock; and there she lay.
Ice had formed in crackly little patches on her drenched garments. She
was huddled around her unborn. Her face was bloodless and peaceful.
The lids were not entirely shut, lantern light flicked off eyeballs. As he

stooped above, he saw the wrecked ankle. O Mithras! Belisama, why did You let this happen?

He knelt beside her. His hand sought beneath her gown, his ear to her nostrils. Faint, faint . . . but she lived, the weather had not yet killed her. . . . Almost as faint was the throb farther down. What, was her daughter trying to be born?

You will have to wait your turn, child.

It was less that strength came back to Gratillonius than that he ceased to feel weariness. He got the blanket around Dahilis, both arms under her, thumb and forefinger crooked again at the handle of his lantern. Rising, he began to walk. Meanwhile he, or someone inside him, laid plans. He must know his every move beforehand, for time would be short. His father, in mariner days, had instructed him about death from cold, what the danger signs were, what to do for a victim. An army surgeon on the Wall had similarly lectured to young officers from the South, as winter approached. Dahilis was far gone.

Belisama, Belisama, help her. Surely you love her too.

Did an owl swoop overhead? The merest glimpse—

The House loomed forth. He supported part of her weight on a thigh while he got the door open. As he entered, his light sent shadows bounding hunchbacked around the room. He kicked her stuff off the bed and laid her on the mattress. Wind whined outside, found the door ajar and skirled through. Water dripped from Dahilis's cloak and hair. He had set the lantern on the floor. To start a fire, oil or no, would take longer than he could afford. She must have warmth at once. His fingers flew, stripping the wet garments from her. Dahilis flopped like a jointed doll.

Now, off with his own clothes. The bed was as narrow as a grave, but that was all right; she needed him, the heat of his body, close against her. He grabbed a couple of dry blankets and threw them over both while he found a place for himself. He must cling, and the frame dug painfully into his hip, but no matter, no matter in the least.

His lips touched her cheek. It was like kissing ice.

A change went through her, a shivering, a dewiness on the skin. The breath he could barely sense turned irregular and faintly, faintly, infinitely remotely, labored. He stamped on the horror that wailed within him and reached under her jaw, seeking the pulse. The jaw fell. He heard sounds and caught smells that were much too familiar.

It was so weak a death struggle that it was almost a surrender. (Belisama, Your will be done.) Gratillonius rolled from the bed, found the floor, bent over her. Again his fingers searched for the pulse in her throat. He couldn't find it. Eyes rolled back and half shut, blank, her face gaped slackly at him. He laid a palm over a breast and caught the slightest of motions. She was still breathing just a little.

The hand went down to her swollen belly. Did he feel a beating, as if against a door? He wasn't sure. He was no physician. Yet he remembered slaughtered beasts and slain barbarians. Caesar himself had made Roman law of what was olden practice: in cases like this, one must try to save the child.

Maybe she wouldn't have wished it, had she known what it was going to cost him. He couldn't ask her.

Time hounded him, closer even than before. The unborn were quick to follow their mothers into death. He had heard of some that were delivered but became defectives, worse than poor Audris. He could stay here and fight for Dahilis's life and almost certainly lose; and then her daughter was best left at peace in the dark. Or he could try for the rescue of her blood, not herself. The odds against that looked long also, but not hopeless. As fast as she was going, he must make his decision *now*.

He took the lantern again and went out, down to his tent, unaware of the wind and the cold.

When he came back, he used the flame to start candles, and thereafter kindled fire. Often he interrupted himself to attend Dahilis. His ministrations had no effect. When he ceased to feel her breathe, he used a bronze mirror he had found in her kit. Of course she had a mirror along, like any woman who wants to please her man.

At first it misted over. Soon that was so little that he crouched holding it in place below her nostrils. When it dried, he flung it clanging across the room.

He would have liked to kiss her farewell, but this was not Dahilis. He dropped a towel over the face. As for that which lay naked, he would not think about what it had been. He hoped he would not think about it. He hoped his farmer and craftsman skills, his rough knowledge of anatomy, would serve. A man could only try.

He had—how long? Three minutes, four, five? No more. Arrayed on the table, which he had dragged to the bedside, lay his small sharp knives.

5

Seas ran high on the morning after solstice, but wind had fallen off and skies were clearing. Dawn was barely a promise when Forsquilis and her companion came down the cliff trail to Ghost Quay and along the path to

Scot's Landing. At Maeloch's door she smote the wood with her staff, whose iron finial was in the shape of an owl. The knock, knock, knock sounded loud amidst the clash of waves on rocks.

The door opened. The fisherman stood unclad, battle ax at the ready. "What the squid-futter—" he growled, and then saw. The lantern that the other woman bore cast glow across the austere features of the high priestess, hooded in her cloak. Behind them, water gleamed under the first thin light in heaven.

"Oh! My, my lady Queen!" He shifted the ax blade to cover his loins. "I thought—'twasn't the Summons—pirates? My lady Forsquilis!"

"We have not met," she said levelly, "but you know me by sight and I you by repute. They call you both the boldest and the most knowing among the fishers. I command you to a faring as momentous as any of yours with the dead—or more, because on this hinges the morrow of Ys."

"What?" Behind his shaggy beard, he gulped. "My lady, that's plain recklessness. Look." His free hand gestured at the chopping and leaping.

The eyes beneath the cowl would not let him go. He saw how haggard she was, as if she had been awake this whole night. "Go we shall, Maeloch," she said, "and faster than ever you traveled erenow."

He thought before he answered: "I've heard as how Queen Dahilis went out to Vigil yesterday, like none ever did before. And the King at her side. Will you relieve her?"

"One might say that."

"Why . . . why, I'll go, be sure I will, if little Queen Dahilis needs help. But the others may balk."

"Are they Ferriers or not?"

Maeloch squinted past the lantern at her who bore it. "This is Briga, of my household," Forsquilis explained. "She goes too."

She was a sturdy, blond young woman, clearly an Osismian. Such often came to the city and worked a few years, earning dowries for themselves. Sometimes they got married there, or seduced. Briga's free arm nestled a very new babe against her large bosom. Her countenance declared both fear and a doglike trust in her mistress the witch.

"Make haste!" said Forsquilis's whipcrack voice.

Maeloch mumbled excuses, retreated to get dressed, came forth again to beat on neighboring doors and bawl men off their pallets. When they saw the Queen, their grumbles quickly ceased, though she stood in place like an eidolon. Enough of them heeded the call to make a crew for *Osprey,* as they did at a Summons. Most of the regular deckhands lived elsewhere.

The smack lay beached under a roof for the winter; but the Ferriers of the Dead kept gear and supplies always aboard their boats, and were swift to fetch rollers and launch this one. She was off soon after the sun had cleared the Bay of Aquitania. The passage went better than the sailors had feared, though amply difficult. The tide was with them and the wind cold but easy, swinging around widdershins until after a while they could raise the sail to help them at their oars. Sundogs danced in a crystalline heaven. Given such brightness, the helmsman readily kept off reefs.

Briga huddled under the bows, miserably seasick, caring for her infant between trips to the rail. Forsquilis sat nearby, impassive. None ventured to address her. A sailor even forgot her when he pissed over the leeward side a short distance off. His ritual apology to Lir reminded him. "Hoy, my lady, I'm sorry!"

She gave him the phantom of a smile. "Think you me a vestal?"

He wrung his calloused paws. "I should've taken the slop bucket aft. But this crossing, we know not why, 'tis got me all muddled. . . . We do head straight back home, don't we, my lady?"

Forsquilis nodded. "I shall abide. The rest of you will return."

"Ye—?" He looked down at his feet, braced wide upon the pitching deck. "But 'tis festival time."

Her own look went beyond the horizon. "There are signs to seek, rites to begin. In another day or two the barge can safely come fetch me."

He saw that she wanted to be by herself, saluted awkwardly, and went about his duties.

—The rocks around Sena made approach so tricky that perhaps no skipper but Maeloch could have accomplished it today. When at last he brought *Osprey* to the wharf, his men slumped exhausted on their benches.

Forsquilis rose. "Rest a while," she said. "We drove relentlessly west. You can go easier eastward, homeward. Wait here."

She sprang ashore, no need for a gangplank, and made for the House of the Goddess. Her cloak rippled blue. Gulls dipped, soared, creaked through the salt wind. Out amidst the skerries, where waves crashed and foam burst, were many seals.

—The door stood open, the windows were unshuttered, the room was bright and barren. On the bed lay a form covered by a blanket. The floor had been scrubbed clean. Gratillonius sat in a chair next the bed. In his arms he rocked a newborn girl. Her crying was loud and furious.

Forsquilis entered, darkening some of the light. Gratillonius looked up. Auburn hair and beard seemed doubly vivid against a face drained and congealed, nothing behind it but weariness. "I have brought a nurse for her," said Forsquilis. "Come down to the boat. I will see to all else."

XXVI

1

He came awake believing it was Dahilis who roused him. Happiness filled him like sunshine. His heart felt bird-light. Oh, my dear darling!

He opened his eyes. Bodilis withdrew the hand that had been shaking him. Gratillonius remembered. He cried out and sat up in bed.

Dim day entered the chamber through its panes. Bodilis stepped back. She was clad entirely in white, no jewelry, a coif over her hair. "I'm sorry," she said low. "But you must arise. You've well-nigh slept the sun through a round."

He recalled vaguely that Fennalis had given him a potion after he reached the palace. Earlier than that, sailors had borne a wrapped form on a litter from the quay toward Wayfaring House. Earlier than that he had been at sea, a rough passage. . . . His memory was full of jagged gaps where mists and fragments drifted.

"We cannot delay further," Bodilis urged gently. "You are the King. The Gods require Their due. And then there is the infant."

Dahilis's daughter. "How is she?" grated out of him.

Bodilis smiled a tiny bit. "Lustily yelling and kicking, the last I saw. Amazing, in view of—" the smile died—"the circumstances. But yours is strong blood, and her mother was no weakling. Now do get up, Gratillonius. You have your duties."

His whole body ached, as if he had spent a night in combat. His mind moved heavily. His spirit wanted to go away, home to Britannia or off to war or anywhere else. But he was the King. He was the prefect of Rome and a centurion of the Second.

Bodilis guided him to a hot bath. While he lay in it she brought him bread and wine. He had no appetite, but partook and gained strength. A massage afterward by his burly body servant pummeled some sluggish-

ness out of his muscles. Bodilis stood by as attendants arrayed him in
crimson robe and royal finery. "Where are we bound?" he asked.

"To the temple of Belisama," she replied. "It was decided to have both
sacraments together, inasmuch as the mother is gone and you soon have
your Watch to stand."

"Both?"

"First the naming and hallowing of the child."

He nodded. Dahilis and Innilis had told him about that while they were
expecting theirs. "I am to do what the mother would have done?"

"This is custom when a Queen dies in childbed."

He remembered thoughts he had had while he waited in the House of
the Goddess and afterward aboard ship. "Very well."

Side by side, he and Bodilis went forth. The day was overcast, a silvery
gray deepening toward lead as the unseen sun declined. The air lay quiet
and raw. His legionaries stood marshalled to escort him. They saluted.
"Oh, God, sir, I'm sorry," Adminius said. His lean features worked. "We
all are."

"Thank you," said Gratillonius, and walked on.

" 'Bout face!" Adminius shouted. "For'ard march!" Hobnails hit paving like a roll of drums.

Traffic stopped when people saw who was coming. Nobody ventured to
draw near or even utter a greeting. Gratillonius and Bodilis moved within
a shieldwall of quietness.

"We know almost nothing of what happened," she said softly. Her arm
was tucked in his. "From what the fishers and the maid Briga and . . .
others here in the city . . . had to tell, we can guess at some of it. What
do you wish to relate?"

In faint surprise, he noticed that talking didn't hurt. It was merely a
task he performed. Most of him was trying to understand what the thing
itself meant. He could not yet really realize that he would never see
Dahilis again, and that his last sight of her must forever be—what it had
been. "When she had not returned by nightfall, I went in search. It took
hours to find her. She lay with a broken ankle, in labor, unconscious,
nearly frozen to death. I carried her back, but I could not *bring* her back.
As soon as she died, I did my best to save the child. Any sin, profanation,
blasphemy is mine alone. She was entirely innocent."

Bodilis's grasp tightened. "We shall purify and dedicate the island over
again. As for your deeds, I dare hope—we Sisters have decided we dare
believe—the justice of the Gods is satisfied. They need but look into your
spirit. And as for the sacrifice They demanded, we believe Dahilis must

have made that. It was not what the Nine awaited, and mayhap not what the Three intended, but surely it was an offering precious enough."

Bitterness seared his gullet. He wanted no part of any such Gods. He refused the load of guilt They would lay on him. Let Mithras be his witness. But he would keep silence, he would duly go through Their rites, for Rome, and because he did not want to wound Bodilis. She must already be inwardly bleeding.

They reached the temple. The soldiers clanked up to form a double line on the stairs. King and high priestess went on in. "The ceremonies will be brief and simple," she reassured him. "It is not like a Bestowal of the Key. A new Queen is presented to the people, and they make merry, only after the soul of the former Queen has crossed over."

"What?" he asked, startled out of reverie. Before she could dispel his confusion, they were inside.

Vestals were ranked along the aisles. Their clear young voices lifted in a hymn. It chimed through the twilight of the sanctuary. Minor priestesses flanked the altar at the far end. From under her coif Bodilis pulled a gauzy veil across her countenance and went to join her Sisters. They waited behind the altar, beneath the tall strange images of Maiden, Mother, and Hag. Lamps on the marble block threw gleams off a golden basin which rested there. The white vestments everywhere around made the temple ghostly.

Gratillonius paused a moment before he concluded he should advance. He did so at a solemn pace. In front of the altar he halted and stood empty-handed, bareheaded. Neither Hammer nor crown had been laid out for him. Here in the holy place of Belisama, he bore just the Key.

A high priestess came forward to face him across the stone. Veil or no, he recognized Quinipilis. Though she spoke steadily, the youthfulness that had hitherto lingered in her voice was gone. "King and father, we are met to consecrate your child. Because her mother has departed, yours is the benison. Let her be brought unto us, and do you give her name and First Sign."

A senior underpriestess approached carrying the infant, which slept, red and wrinkled and how very small. You would not have thought that anything so small was hard to bring into the world. Quinipilis whispered: "Do you know, Gratillonius? Dahilis was Estar."

He knew, and knew that generally the first-born of a Queen received the name that she herself had borne as a vestal. But he had known her as Dahilis, and this creature he had cut from her body was all that remained to him of her. Alone with the dead on Sena, he had pondered the question. It had been something to fill the hours.

Quinipilis took the blanket-wrapped babe and held her out. "Draw a crescent on her forehead," she directed low. "Say: 'Ishtar-Isis-Belisama, receive this Your servant Estar. Sanctify her, keep her pure, and at the last take her home to Yourself.' "

Gratillonius dipped his right forefinger into the water that glimmered in the basin. He traced an arc on the diminutive brow. His voice rang loud: "Ishtar-Isis-Belisama, receive this Your servant Dahut. Sanctify her, keep her pure, and at the last take her home to Yourself."

The hymn faltered. Breath rustled and hissed among the priestesses. It was overriden by an angry scream from the awakened child. She struggled to get free of her swaddling.

Gratillonius met the unseen stares of the Gallicenae and growled in an undertone, "I want her mother uniquely remembered in her. 'Tis lawful, I believe."

"Ah, aye," answered Quinipilis. "Contrary to usage, but . . . the law is silent. . . . Be you Dahut." She returned the babe to the elder, who took it away to soothe.

Gratillonius's intent was clear. Dahilis had taken her sacral name from the spring of the nymph Ahes, to whom she had had a special devotion. The prefix "D" was an honorific and could be retained. The suffix could not, but "-ut" formed a commemorative ending. Thus did Dahut come to Ys.

The hymn ended. Quinipilis straightened as much as she was able, raised her arms, and cried: "Let the divine wedding commence!" Echoes flew around the hush.

Wedding? Gratillonius stood hammerstruck. Now?

But of course. How could he have forgotten? He must have wanted to forget. When a Queen died, the Sign came immediately upon a vestal. Eight women stood before him; and Forsquilis was on Sena.

He would not! Dahilis was not even buried yet!

The spectral forms came from behind the altar to surround him. Quinipilis stayed where she was. One of the others moved, stumbling a little, next to Gratillonius.

"Kneel," the old priestess commanded.

He could go. They were nothing but women here. Outside waited his Romans. Thus easily could be betray his mission. Gratillonius knelt beside his chosen bride.

As if from far away, he heard a prayer. A new hymn swelled. More orisons followed, but they were mercifully short. He and she were bidden to arise. He obeyed the order to lift her veil. At the same time, his wives threw back theirs. The song soared triumphant.

He had seen the homely, timorous face before, but he could not recollect when or where.

"Gratillonius, King of Ys, in homage to the Goddess Who dwells in her, and in honor to the womanhood that is hers, receive your Queen Guilvilis—"

2

There was a modest banquet at the palace, which the Gallicenae shared. Directly afterward the seven each kissed the new Sister and left. Servants requested her benediction and reverentially escorted the pair to a bedchamber swept, garnished, and lighted by many lamps and wax candles. Celebrations would come later, when the spirit of the former Queen had departed.

Talk had been scant at the table. Gratillonius said nothing whatsoever. She sat by her husband, eyes downcast, eating as little and as mechanically as he did. While goodnights went on, Bodilis had drawn Gratillonius aside and whispered in Latin: "Be kind to her. Poor child, she never wished for this. Nobody imagined it. The ways of the Goddess are a mystery."

"What is her lineage?" he asked hoarsely.

"Her father was Hoel, of course. Her mother was Morvanalis—full sister to Fennalis, but that makes her no closer than a cousin to Lanarvilis. Morvanalis died a few years after this girl was born. The child was good-natured but dull. I remember how she suffered the teasing of brighter classmates uncomplainingly, and sought her few friends among menials and animals. Everyone took for granted that when she finished her vestalhood—that would have been next year—she would take vows as a minor priestess, unless some man of humble station offered to marry her for the dowry the Temple provides. Instead—Don't blame her, Gratillonius. Treat her gently." Bodilis's gaze went deep into him. "I believe you have the strength to do that."

I believe I shall often be drawing on the strength that is in you, he thought.

Incense sweetened the air in the bridal chamber. The flames gave warmth as well as amber light. Beyond the shutters, a night wind lulled. Guilvilis stood in her white gown at the middle of the floor, hands clasped above her loins, head bowed. It was a small head with rather thin, dull-brown hair and a protruding nosetip. Her figure was tall, bosom low, hips and legs heavy; her movements were awkward.

I have to say something, Gratillonius decided. "Well."

She stayed mute. He began to pace, back and forth in front of her, his own hands clenched together behind him. "Well," he said, "fear not. I shan't hurt you. Indeed, tell me what would please you."

He could barely hear: "I know not, lord."

His cheeks heated. Without meaning to, he had asked that which it took an experienced woman to answer, and every vestal was a virgin. He cleared his tightening throat. "Might you like something in the way of comforts, pleasures, enjoyable tasks, freedom from uncongenial ones? Anything?"

"I know not, lord."

"Um-mf. It seems . . . nobody told me what your name was before."

"Sasai, lord." She had not moved an inch from her passive stance.

"Ah!" It came back to him. "Aye. You were at the Nymphaeum and guided me to the guardhouse when—"

When Dahilis and I went there to ask a blessing on her babe, and that night we made love.

I will not *hate this person here.*

Gratillonius moved to a nacre-inlaid table where stood cups and carafes. He poured wine for himself without adding water. "Do you care for drink?" he asked. "Make free."

She glanced up, and hastily away. "Thank you, nay, lord."

He tossed off the cup in a few draughts that lit fire in his stomach. He'd need help getting to sleep. At least this was not the same room, the same bed where Dahilis and he had taken their joy. "How came you to pick the name Guilvilis?"

"It . . . oh . . . Queen Lanarvilis said I could. 'Tis from a hamlet in the hills, she said. The house of Suffete Soren owns p-p-property there."

"Hm." Gratillonius rubbed his beard, refilled his vessel, drank more slowly. A thawing had begun to spread through him. "I take it . . . when the Sign appears . . . you tell somebody, and word goes to the—the rest of the Nine—and they meet with you?"

"Aye, lord." A finger strayed up to touch her gown above the shallow curve of breasts. "I woke from sleep, from a flash like fire, and, and—" She swallowed. He saw tears. "I was so afraid."

A certain pity touched him. He took another swallow, set the cup down, went to stand before her. His left hand he laid on her shoulder, his right he put beneath her receding chin, to raise her face toward his. "Be not afraid," he said. " 'Tis the grace of the Goddess."

"They . . . were good to me—but—Oh, why was it me?" she quavered. "Naught do I know."

"You'll learn," he said. "Belisama must have known what She was doing." Inwardly, he wondered. He patted her back. "Be of brave heart."

She half moved to put her arms about him, but withdrew them, a jerky, frightened motion. "My lord is kind. O-o-oh. . . ." She gulped, snuffled, somehow kept from sobbing.

He let her go and sought the wine. It gave him the courage he had been needing. His back to her, he said, "Well, 'tis been a hard day for you, Guilvilis. Shall we to our rest?"

"Aye, lord."

Still looking away and drinking, he said, after a space: "You must understand something. I have had a great sorrow. All Ys has, but . . . as for myself . . . take it not amiss—we'll simply sleep this night, and . . . for a while to come."

"Aye, lord."

Perhaps the Goddess had shown him a mercy. This mooncalf would make no demands on him, ever.

He finished his wine and turned about. She had undressed and stood naked at the bedside. There was more paunch than he had seen on most young women, but her complexion was clear, but her buttocks were huge and her legs like tree trunks, down through the ankles to the big feet. Ankles—The crescent above her breasts smoldered red.

She ventured the faintest of smiles. "Whatever the King wants," she said tonelessly.

"We'll sleep," he snapped. He went about blowing out the lights as if he were the bride, not the groom. The bed creaked and rustled when she entered it. In the dark he removed his own clothes, left them on the floor, and felt his way.

He lay down and pulled sheet and blanket over him. Wine or no, he feared lying awake through the night. The incense cloyed. He turned on his side. It had been toward her, he suddenly knew—sheer habit. She stirred. He felt her nearby warmth. A scent of clean hair and flesh pierced the sweetness. His hand fell upon hers.

His member awoke. No! he cried, but it swelled and throbbed. No, this isn't decent! Heat boiled in him. She sensed his restlessness and, herself, turned. He made a motion to keep her off. His palm encountered a breast and closed over its softness. The nipple hardened and nudged.

O Dahilis! The Bull shook horns; Its hoofs tore the earth. Blind though he was, Gratillonius knew how Guilvilis rolled over onto her back and spread her legs. He was not Gratillonius who mourned, he was he who cast himself between her thighs, thrust straight through her maidenhead, heard her cry aloud and took delight, hammered and hammered and hammered. Gratillonius stood aside, at his post of duty, hoping that afterward the Gods of Ys would allow him to sleep.

3

The funeral barge was fifty feet in length, goldtrimmed black, with a low freeboard and a broad flat deck. Stempost and sternpost terminated simply in spirals. A staff amidships bore an evergreen wreath.

When possible, she went out every third day, bearing the dead of Ys from their homes or from Wayfaring House. Often that was not possible, and sometimes their hostelers must lay them to rest in the brine vats. Always, though, in the end, they went to sea.

This morning was bright and calm, sun frosty in the south. Wavelets glittered sapphire and emerald, marble-swirled. They lapped against cliffs, wall, hull. Oars chirked and splashed as the barge passed the gate on an ebbing tide. Gulls dipped and hovered. Seals glided among the reefs.

The dead were laid out shrouded, each on a litter with a stone lashed to the feet. Deckhands went quietly about their work. The loudest noise, and it low, was the ringing of a coxswain's gong, timing the slow strokes of the rowers. Passengers stood aside or sat on well-secured benches. For the most part they were kinfolk who wanted to say a final goodbye, clad in more subdued fashion than was ordinary. Three were ever on hand: a trumpeter, a drummer, and some of the Gallicenae.

Upon this faring the whole Nine were aboard, and likewise the King, to follow their Sister. They stayed in a group near the bows, mute, looking inward or else far outward.

The barge traveled no great distance, because the bottom dropped rapidly. When the captain deemed they were over the deeps, he signaled. The trumpeter blew a long call, the gongbeat died away, the rowers merely held their vessel steady.

The captain made ritual request of the high priestess in charge. This time she was Quinipilis, who because of frail health had not come along in years. Blue-clad, her headdress tall and white, she trod forward, lifted her hands, and spoke with more strength than anyone had awaited. "Gods of mystery, Gods of life and death, sea that nourishes Ys, take these our beloved—"

Having finished the invocation, she received a tablet from the captain and read the names aloud. They were in order of death, as were the bodies. At each, sailors lifted that litter and brought it to a chute on the larboard side. "Farewell," said the high priestess, and the men tilted their burden. A shape slid down. The water leaped a little and closed again.

—"Without a name." Innilis caught her breath and reached after Gratillonius's hand. He took hers. "Farewell." Still weak, barely able to go through with the parts that had been hers, she sat down again.

—"Dahilis." He felt his other hand taken, glanced aside, and saw Bodilis. The shape dropped from sight. "Farewell." The men carried back its bed.

—A trumpet call flew forth over Ocean. The drum marched underneath. There was a silence, save for the waves and mewing gulls. "About and home!" the captain ordered. Oars toiled, the gongs resumed, the galley turned landward.

—The declining sun changed the waters to molten gold whose light sank into the wall and the towers of Ys and radiated back. Shadows had begun to lengthen. Their intricacy made sculpture of the brutal headlands, made a weaving of mystical signs, while the city glimmered between like a dream.

When the boat had passed through a now narrowing gateway, it found the harbor basin full of mist and blue shadings. High and high overhead, an albatross caught sunlight on his wings. A murmur stirred in the coolness, traffic noises muted to a single sound, the breathing of a woman about to go to sleep.

The barge docked and passengers got off. On the quay, under a proud, time-crumbled façade, stood a few men in robes of office. Among them were Soren Cartagi, Speaker for Taranis, and Hannon Baltisi, Lir Captain. A touch surprised, Gratillonius accompanied his Gallicenae to meet them.

Soren offered salute. "My lord," the Suffete said, "not hitherto have I had opportunity to bespeak my sorrow."

By immemorial law, neither he nor Hannon were permitted on the barge until their own final journeys. "Aye," said the gray skipper, "she was dear to everybody, but most to you."

Soren's gaze traveled to Lanarvilis, then back to Gratillonius, and held steady. His heavy features gave less away than his voice. "You will have memories, King," he said. "They burn you, but may you later warm your hands at them on cold nights." He cleared his throat. "Enough. What I— what we here wish to tell you is this. We think the Gods have worked Their will and are at peace with Ys. In a certain measure you've bought that, lord. And you *are* a good King. We'll fight you no more."

Lanarvilis smiled as though she had foreknown.

Soren lifted a finger. "Mind you, lord," he said, "we may well find you wrongheaded in future and ourselves in opposition to you. We must stand fast for what is right. But 'twill be loyal opposition, for the welfare of Ys."

Gratillonius took a moment to marshal words. "I thank you," he said. "More than you know, I thank you. We'll go on together."

Abruptly he realized that he meant it. Despair was for cowards. He still had work to do, battles to wage, dreams to dream. The life that had been in Dahilis flowed on in Dahut. Her tomorrows, which he must make sure of, were his renewal.

His next Watch would begin on the Birthday of Mithras.

XXVII

Maeloch awoke. Night engulfed him, save for fugitive red gleams from the banked hearthfire. The single room of his home was full of chill and odors, woodsmoke, salt, kelp, fish, humanity, sea. Again it knocked on his door, a slow one, two, three.

He sat up. His wife Betha stirred beside him. The straw tick rustled. He heard a child of theirs whimper, terrified.

Knock, knock, knock. "I come," he called.

"The Summons?" she breathed.

"Aye, what else?" he replied, lips close to her ear. "The island's been hallowed anew, I hear. And 'twas a while in the doing; we'll have a load this trip."

He always kept seagoing clothes where he could find them in the dark. Best not to light a torch at these times. You mustn't linger. Nor did you want to see too well.

"Who has the Vigil?" he muttered as he fumbled. "Queen Bodilis? Meseems I've heard 'tis she. Pray hard, Queen Bodilis."

The command had gone on down the row of cabins that was Scot's Landing. Clad, Maeloch gave Betha a quick, rough kiss and went out. The moon was full, the air mild. Light glittered and torrented on small inshore waves, flickered and shimmered across the swells beyond, made flags of the foam on skerries. Only the brightest stars were clear in sight. Orion strode opposite the hulking murk of the cliffs, thence the River of Tiamat flowed across heaven past the North Eye and back into unknownness. Frost glistened on thatch roofs. A breeze wandered from the southeast, winter-cold, not strong, but you could lift sail and get help for your oars on the way to Sena. Well, They made sure before They called the Ferriers of the Dead.

Among the men gathering by moonlight, Maeloch recognized two fellow captains. Three boatloads, then. So many had not crossed over since the battle in summer.

Fishing smacks were soon launched. *Osprey* and the others lay alongside Ghost Quay. Gangplanks thudded forth. The wind and the sea murmured.

Maeloch spied nothing but moonlight on shingle, cliffs, and waves. He heard nothing but the sounds of the night. Yet he felt a streaming across the planks, and saw how hulls settled down into the water. They would bear a full cargo tonight.

The stars wheeled in their silence.

Osprey rode no lower. "We are ready," Maeloch said. His breath smoked white. "All hands aboard."

The three boats stood out. Sails blundered aloft. The trimming was tricky, and oarsmen must keep their benches, but it gave a little more speed for passengers who had waited long. Maeloch walked around issuing low-voiced orders as needed. Otherwise nobody spoke. The companion craft were like swans afloat.

Moonlight sleeked the coats of seals.

—The boats maneuvered in among reefs whose treachery the moon betrayed, and made fast at Sena dock. The House of the Goddess loomed black, apart from glimmers of lamplight where the high priestess was praying. The island stretched ashen.

Men who had been securing lines came back aboard and stood aside. Maeloch drew back the hood of his leather jacket, to uncover his head, and took stance near the gangplank. The moon shone, the stars gleamed.

As the souls debarked, *Osprey* rocked ever higher in the water.

Maeloch heard them blow past, breaths in the night, bound for he knew not where. "I was Dauvinach," came to him barely. . . . "I was Catellan. . . . I was Borsus. . . . I was Janatha. . . ."

The sea and the wind sighed.

—"I was Rael," he heard. "I was Temesa."

—A whisper went by without a name.

—"I was Dahilis."

—When it was done, the Ferriers of the Dead cast loose and made for their homes.

Historical Background

By the late fourth century, the Roman Empire was disintegrating, but scarcely anyone was aware of this. After all, daily life continued as it had done for generations. Times had grown hard and were growing harder; contests for power had become frequent and fierce; corruption and banditry were rife; territories were being lost or abandoned to foreigners; barbarians harried the coasts and the landward frontiers, sometimes breaking through and wreaking havoc, sometimes founding unruly colonies on Imperial soil. Nevertheless, Rome held sway from Britain to North Africa, from the Atlantic to the Rhine, throughout southern Europe and much of hither Asia. Early Christians had denounced it and prophesied doom, but now Christianity was the state religion and the Emperors ruled under God, as sons of the Church. It was unthinkable that this could ever pass away.

Yet "Rome" no longer meant a city-state which had acquired an enormous hinterland. All free subjects were citizens, regardless of national origin; but freedom and citizenship were concepts almost as fictitious as the Republic that the Empire still pretended it was. It had split into two parts, Eastern and Western. The Emperors of each—usually a so-called Augustus and a Caesar, his colleague and heir apparent—were supposedly partners, sharing the governance of a realm that was supposedly one. In practice, they were most often bitter rivals. The seat of the Eastern power was Constantinople (now Istanbul); that of the Western was Rome no more, but wherever its ruler chose, with Milan the capital during most of the time of our story.

As they had done in the past and would do again and again in the future, taxation, inflation, and regulation had well-nigh destroyed the economy. The privileged senatorial class battened on what remained of the mercantile and productive classes. These latter were being strangled between the decay of commerce and the inordinate demands laid on them by an increasingly desperate state. The proletarians, when not outright slaves, were impoverished city rabble or virtual serfs on the land, locked into what amounted to a caste system. Increasingly, the great estates and their dependencies were making what they needed for themselves, because that was the only way they could obtain it.

As for the military, the old yeoman army was long extinct. Soldiers served for pay, ever more of them not even citizens but barbarian mercenaries. Nearly all the legions had shriveled to mere holding forces as cavalry increasingly took dominance over infantry. While technological developments had something to do with that, the basic reason was not that infantry was inherently inferior—it would prove otherwise centuries later, at such battles as Morgarten and Bannockburn—but that Rome by this time could not afford to maintain it at effective strength. (We have reason to think, and assume in our story, that the situation in Britain had changed less. If so, this was a lonely exception, soon to end.)

Thus the barbarians could press inward. They were not entirely wild men. Many, notably the Visigoths and Ostrogoths, were at least nominally Christian, though sectarian differences exacerbated relations with the Romans. Such people did not want to pull down the Empire. They just wanted a share in it, as large as they could seize and hold.

Much of their migration was under pressure from others who were truly alien. Among those on the Continent were the Huns—who, however, were occasionally allies of one or another Roman faction. Likewise pagan and warlike were the Germanic Franks and Saxons farther north. The former thrust overland, the latter came in large part by way of the sea. In Britain there were the Picts beyond Hadrian's Wall, which guarded the frontier of the Roman part. In Ireland there were the Scots, who made piratical raids and would eventually send numbers of settlers to the Pictish country and bestow their own name on it.

So is the picture as we are apt to see it today. But it is a picture sketchy at best, falsely colored by hindsight, altogether oversimplified. The decline of Rome was not only long-drawn, it was endlessly complex, with rallies as well as routs. The date of 476 for the fall is quite arbitrary. That was simply when the Germanic warlord Odovacer displaced the last

Western Emperor. He immediately assured Constantinople of his loyalty and submissiveness. Indeed, the Eastern Empire would endure for another thousand years. Western Europe entered the Dark Ages but never forgot what had been. When at last Charlemagne made his mighty attempt to bring it back together, he called his dominions Roman.

Throughout, the vast majority of people went on with their daily lives, making the best of the situations in which they found themselves. To them events on the world stage were only of secondary interest, if any, unless catastrophe broke over them. In other words, they were like all ordinary folk before or since.

Herewith we offer a brief chronology of major happenings in the time of this novel. Some of the dates that we give are uncertain or controversial.

382: Theodosius, Emperor in the East, makes allies *(foederati)* of the Visigoths. Gratian, co-Emperor in the West, issues a decree banning paganism. Magnus Maximus, military commander in Britain, repels a massive onslaught by Picts and Scots.

383: Maximus leads troops across the Channel, trying to win supreme power in the West. Gratian is defeated and murdered. His co-Emperor Valentinian and Emperor Theodosius recognize Maximus as an Augustus with rule over Britain, Gaul, and the Hispanic peninsula.

385: Maximus has the heretic Priscillian and his principal disciples put to death. For this St. Martin, Bishop of Tours, denounces him.

387: Maximus breaks the treaty with Valentinian and Theodosius and invades Italy.

388: Defeat and death of Maximus.

390: St. Ambrose, Bishop of Milan, forces Theodosius to do penance for a massacre, thereby advancing further the authority of the Church as against the state.

392: The Frankish count Arbogast has Valentinian murdered and sets up Eugenius as his puppet Emperor.

394: Theodosius overthrows Arbogast and Eugenius and reunites the Empire for what will be the last time.

395: Death of Theodosius. The Empire is divided between his sons Arcadius in the East and Honorius in the West. The Visigoths, under their new king Alaric, revolt and invade Greece. Stilicho, soon to be the ruler of the West in all but name, brings about the fall of Arcadius's energetic praetorian prefect Rufinus.

396: Stilicho launches a campaign against the barbarians in Britain.

397: Death of St. Ambrose. Stilicho drives the Visigoths out of Greece.

398: Alaric is made a governor in Illyricum. Stilicho marries his daughter Maria to his ward Honorius. He concludes his British campaign and withdraws troops to help quell Gildo's revolt in Africa.

400: Death of St. Martin.

401: Alaric and his Visigoths invade Italy.

402: Honorius moves his court to Ravenna.

403: Stilicho defeats the Visigoths but lets them depart peacefully and settle in Illyricum.

404: Honorius abolishes gladiatorial shows and closes the Colosseum.

405: Under Radagaisus, a mass of barbarians, chiefly Ostrogoths, invades the Empire.

406: Radagaisus's horde enters Italy. With herculean effort and the aid of allies, Stilicho annihilates it. Meanwhile other barbarians ravage Britain and northern Gaul. The army in Britain proclaims one of its men Emperor. At the very end of the year, another swarm of barbarians enters Gaul from the east.

407: The barbarians devastate northeastern Gaul but then turn south. Constantine takes control of the revolt in Britain. He brings the last of the legions to Gaul to support his bid for supremacy. The Armoricans and certain other Gauls secede from the Empire.

What happened thereafter is described in the Notes at the end of the fourth book.

Notes and Afterword

Although our aim has been to make the text of this novel self-explanatory, certain historical details may surprise some readers, who may thereupon think we are in error. Other readers may simply wish to learn a little more about the era. Nobody has to look at these notes, but anybody who wishes to is welcome.

A word about nomenclature. In the story we generally give place names the forms they had at the time, rather than use their English versions. This is for the sake of accuracy as well as color. After all, the boundaries of most cities, territories, etc. were seldom quite identical with those of their modern counterparts, and the societies occupying them were entirely different. There are a few exceptions, such as "Rome" or the names of famous tribes, where insistence on the ancient rendering would have been pedantic.

As for personal names, the story uses original forms throughout, again with a few exceptions. Most are attested, a few represent conjectures by us. Ysan names are imaginary but not arbitrary; they are supposed to show the Celtic and Semitic roots of the language, plus later Graeco-Roman influences. "Ys" itself is pronounced, approximately, "eess," though the vowel is pure, not a diphthong of the English sort. The French *"ice,"* as in *"justice,"* comes close.

A discussion of the Breton legend follows the notes at the end of the last book.

ROMA MATER

I

Mithras (or Mithra): A deity of ancient Aryan origin, whose cult reached Rome by way of Persia. Especially popular among soldiers, it became for a time the most important rival of Christianity, with which it had much in common.

The Birthday of Mithras: 25 December. Formerly it had been celebrated on the winter solstice, but precession of the equinoxes caused the latter to move backward through the calendar. About 274 A.D. the Emperor Aurelian fixed the birthday of Sol Invictus as the 25th, a date which the related Mithraic faith adopted. The Christian Church would not settle on it for the Nativity of Christ until much later; in the fourth century, that event was still considered of secondary importance.

Gaius Valerius Gratillonius: Throughout the lands that the Empire ruled, inhabitants belonging to the upper and middle classes, and often persons more humble, generally imitated Roman nomenclature. Here "Gaius" is the given name—which, however, men did not much use, if only because the selection was small. "Valerius" belongs to a Roman *gens,* and indicates that at some time in the past someone of that tribe patronized, adopted, or freed a British ancestor. "Gratillonius" is the cognomen, the family name, and is a Latinization of a native one (in this case, postulated rather than historically attested, in order to account for the later form "Grallon"). Admittedly, by the time of our story, the system was breaking down and there were many exceptions to it; but provincials would tend to be conservative.

Borcovicium (also recorded as *Vorcovicium, Vorcovicum,* etc.): Housesteads.

Mail: Heavy infantrymen of this period generally wore coats of mail, not the loricated cuirasses of an earlier day. A centurion was outfitted differently from those under him. The crest on his helmet, detachable for combat, arched side-to-side rather than front-to-back; greaves protected his shins; his sword hung from a baldric, and on the left instead of the right; he did not carry the two javelins, light and heavy, but did bear a twisted vinestaff as emblem of authority and instrument of immediate punishment for infractions.

Cliff: Where nature had not provided such a barrier, a deep ditch paralleled Hadrian's Wall on the north. Another, with earthen ramparts, ran at some distance to the south.

Fifteen feet: Post-Roman quarrying has much brought down what is left of the Wall, but this was its original height, more or less, along most of its length. As for that length, from Wallsend on the Tyne to Bowness on the Solway it is 73 English or about 77 Roman miles.

Eboracum (or *Eburacum):* York.

Other legions in Britain: Besides the Sixth, those permanently stationed there were the Twentieth Valeria Victrix, based at Deva (Chester), and the Second Augusta, based at Isca Silurum (Caerleon). Evidence indicates that a vexillation, a detachment, of the latter was called to Housesteads in the emergency of 382 A.D. As elsewhere throughout the Empire in its later days, legionary regulars were outnumbered by auxiliaries from all over, equipped and operating in their native styles.

Duke: At this time the *Dux Britanniarum* commanded the Roman forces in northern England, with his seat in York.

Vindolanda: This site is today occupied by the farm Chesterholm.

Tungri: A tribe in the Low Countries.

Basilica: Originally this word meant an administrative center, civil or military.

Base: Contrary to modern popular impressions, Hadrian's Wall was not intended as a line of defense, and hardly ever served as one. It provided a means of controlling peacetime traffic between Roman Britain and the tribes to the north; in the event of hostilities, it was a base out of which soldiers operated, taking war to the enemy rather than waiting for an attack.

Highlanders: The country of the Picts (a name loosely bestowed by the Romans) lay well to the north of Hadrian's Wall. Another common misconception makes them dwarfish; they were actually a rather tall people.

Warriors from across the water: The Scots were at this time living in what is now Ireland, except perhaps for an enclave on the Argyll coast. As the Empire declined, they came more and more to raid it, much in the style of the vikings centuries later.

Praetorium: The commandant's house in a legionary fortress. It doubtless had other uses as well.

Principia: The headquarters block, generally comprising three buildings around a courtyard.

Isca Silurum: Caerleon in southeastern Wales.

Hispania Tarraconensis: A Roman province occupying a large piece of Spain, in the northeast and east.

Clean-shaven: To judge by contemporary portraits, many Roman men of this period were, though closely trimmed beards may have been a little more common.

Cunedag: Better known as Cunedda, but that is a later form of the name. His move to northern Wales with a following of his native Votadini (sometimes rendered "Otadini") is historical; there he drove out the Scots and founded the kingdom of Venedotia, which eventually became Gwynedd. The Roman intention was that this should be a foederate, a closely controlled ally, but when the Empire receded it naturally became independent. Most authorities take for granted that the move was at the instigation of Stilicho, not Maximus. However, this is not certain; and Maximus himself did enter Welsh legend as Maxen Wledig, a prince who did something wonderful though unspecified for that country. Could it have been providing the leadership and organization from which the medieval kingdom developed?

Ordovices: The people occupying northern Wales. Roman practice was to convert native tribes into local units of government, somewhat like Swiss cantons.

Dumnonii: The people occupying, approximately, Cornwall and Devon.

Language: It is not quite certain, but it is not unlikely that there was a single Celtic language, with mutually intelligible dialects, throughout England and southern Scotland.

Stools: Chairs were not in common use. People ordinarily sat on stools, benches, or even floors.

Hivernia (or *Hibernia*): Ireland.

Wine: The Romans favored wines so sweet and thick that they were best watered.

Mediolanum: Milan.

Augusta Treverorum: Trier.

Arians: Christians following the doctrine of Arius, which the Council of Nicea had declared heretical.

Silures: The people occupying southern Wales.

Belgae: These folk held a broad territory in the South, ranging approximately from Somerset through Hampshire. They were the last Celts to reach the island, just a couple of centuries before the Roman conquest, and their Continental kin retained the same name. The Belgae claimed a strong Germanic strain in their ancestry.

British soldiers: For reasons uncertain today, auxiliaries of British birth, unlike most such, seem hardly ever to have been stationed in their home country. However, probably this was not so general a rule for regular legionaries.

Aquae Sulis: Bath.

Dacia: Approximately, modern Romania. In the later fourth century, the Empire had almost entirely abandoned this province.

Nervii: A tribe in the Low Countries.

Abonae: A small town on the River Avon (Latin *Abona*) in Somerset, near the meeting of this stream with the Mouth of the Severn (Latin *Sabrina*), which gives on the Bristol Channel and thus the sea.

Armorica: Brittany.

Gesoriacum: Boulogne.

Condate Redonum: Rennes.

Vorgium: Carhaix. In Roman times, until it was sacked, it was the most important city in western Britanny . . . except Ys!

Caledonians: A confederacy in the far North. However, the name was often given generally to the peoples beyond Hadrian's Wall.

Temenos: The hallowed ground before or around a temple.

Parnesius: Kipling makes him a centurion of the Thirtieth Legion, which was stationed in the Rhineland; we have found no confirmation of T. S. Eliot's assertion that it, or a vexillation of it, was on Hadrian's Wall at any time. Rather than leave Parnesius entirely out of the story, we suggest that he actually belonged to the Twentieth.

Serfs: Latin *coloni* (singular *colonus*), tenant farmers and their families whom the "reforms" of Diocletian had bound to the soil they cultivated, as their descendants would be bound for the next thousand years and more.

Ahura-Mazda: The supreme god of Mithraism.

Pronaos: An entrance hall above or adjoining the inner sanctum of a temple.

Tauroctony: A representation of Mithras slaying the primordial Bull.

II

The history of Ireland from the earliest times through the heroic age, and even the beginnings of the Christian era, is obscure, often totally confused. Such sagas, poems, and chronicles as we have were written down centuries after the events they purport to describe. Taken as a whole, they are full of contradictions as well as anachronisms and out-right impossibilities. Moreover, it is clear that the medieval recorders misunderstood much, deliberately changed much else as being too pagan or otherwise unedifying, and supplied numerous inventions of their own. Foreign historians are of small help, because Ireland never came under Roman rule. Archaeology supplies some clues, as well as data about everyday life. One can also extrapolate backward from the oldest extant documents, notably the Brehon Laws, and from customs and beliefs reported by observers almost until the present day. Anthropology, with parallels to draw from other parts of the world, gives many hints as well.

In general, for this novel we have chosen those interpretations and hypotheses which best fit our story. Various authorities would disagree with us on various points. We will try to discuss briefly the most controversial matters as we go along.

The Irish still have no unanimity on how to spell Gaelic. The basic problem is that this is a language which does not lend itself well to the Roman alphabet. Besides, historical and dialectical variations are great. Our characters speak a forerunner of the language known as Old Irish, which itself is at least as different from modern Gaelic as Old Norse is from modern Danish. For a single example, the medieval and modern "mac," meaning "son of," was earlier "maqq," pronounced approximately "makw." We are indebted to Celtologist Alexei Kondratiev for what knowledge of the ancient forms we have, but he must not be held responsible for our mistakes and deliberate modifications. Notably, we use the name "Niall," although the older version is "Néll," because its bearer looms so large in Irish history and tradition.

Imbolc: In the modern calendar, 1 February. The pagan festival must have taken place approximately then. Our guess is that it, like others, was determined by the moon. The customs mentioned flourished as late as the early twentieth century. They look very ancient, only slightly Christianized.

Manandan (maqq Leri): Later called Manannan mac Lir; a major Irish god, associated with the sea.

Brigit: Originally an Irish goddess. She appears to have been tripartite, as many Celtic deities were. Her name passed to a Christian saint—nowadays Brighid or Bridget—who was especially popular and whose feast day was 1 February. The spring tide nearest this date bore her name and was believed to be the greatest of the year.

Condacht (or *Olnegmacht):* Connaught, west central Ireland, still a recognized division of the country. We will presently discuss the Fifths.

Mumu: Munster, southwestern Ireland. Like "Leinster" and "Ulster," the modern form of the name traces back to the Danes, as does, for that matter, "Ireland" itself.

Tuath: This word is often rendered "tribe," but that is somewhat misleading. A tuath, consisting of families with an intricate social ranking, was a political unit occupying a definite territory, but not otherwise especially distinct from others of its kind. Each tuath had a king *(rí)*, who owed allegiance to the King of the Fifth, about which arrangement there is a later note.

Temir (later *Teamhair):* Now called Tara, this hill is located about 15 miles northwest of Dublin (which, of course, did not exist in our period; early Ireland had no towns). It had been used, if not continuously occupied, at least since megalithic times, and was regarded as especially charged with *mana.* However, tradition says that it was not until a few generations before Niall that a dynasty from Connaught established itself here.

King: The institution of the High King *(Ard-rí)* of Ireland did not exist even in theory until a much later date, and was never really very effective. In ancient times, at best the principal king of a Fifth commanded the allegiance of various lower-ranking kings, each of whom led a tuath or an alliance of several tuaths. (More grades of royalty eventually developed.) The King of a Fifth might, though, have additional powers or claims outside its borders. Allegiance amounted to little more than the payment of tribute—with the overlord expected to give a smaller amount of goods in return—and military service on strictly limited terms. Basically, any king lived off the proceeds of his own holdings, off certain payments from those beneath him, and off whatever he could plunder in wartime. His function was at least as much sacral as political.

Niall maqq Echach ("Echach" is the genitive of "Eochaid"): Later famous as Niall of the Nine Hostages, ancestor of the Uí Néill dynasties. On the whole, we have followed traditional accounts of his life and exploits. Certain modern scholars maintain that these date him a generation or two too early; a few doubt that he is historical at all. It is true that many contradictions and other puzzles in the medieval chronicles can be resolved by some such theory, and we do not venture to say this is mistaken. Yet perhaps it gives certain annals more weight, at the expense of others, than they deserve. There are authorities who think so. Discounting the fabulous elements that have crept in, the old stories about Niall look plausible enough. The real problems arise with some about his successor Nath Í, which are scarcely to be taken seriously. For that matter, the chronology and the very identity of St. Patrick are in confusion. Given all this, we have felt free to choose, from among the different accounts of Niall, those parts that accord with our story. Of course, we have added inventions of our own, beginning with his son Breccan, but these are not incompatible with our sources.

Ollam (or *olave):* The highest grade of any profession considered learned or skilled.

Free tenants: Land was held in ancient Ireland under a system too complicated to describe here. Briefly and incompletely put, however: land was inalienable from the tuath, which held in common the nonarable parts suitable for rough grazing, peat and wood gathering, etc. Farmland and the richer pastures were usually the property of some "noble"—whether the king, a *flaith,* or a learned man such as a judge, poet, physician, etc.— who, though, basically held the acreage in trust for his family. Otherwise real estate belonged to a sept, who subdivided it from time to time among different members. Land not directly used by the owner(s) was rented out to tenants, who paid in kind and in services, since the early Irish did not coin money. A free tenant *(soer-céli)* supplied all or most of his own stock, paid moderate rent, enjoyed a good social standing, and might often be wealthy. A bond tenant *(doer-céli),* to whom the landlord must furnish "starting capital," paid a much higher rent and ranked much lower. Both classes had other obligations, but those of the free tenant were lighter, and his rights and privileges under the law were far more. Nevertheless, the bond tenant was in no sense a serf; the relationship was contractual, and either party could terminate it. Indeed, there appears to have been social mobility, with poor men occasionally bettering their lot. Slaves, without rights and set to tasks nobody wanted, were generally captives taken in wars or raids, or children of these.

Mide: Occupying approximately modern Counties Meath, Westmeath, Longford, parts of Kildare and Offaly, it is supposed to have been carved out of Connaught, Leinster, and Ulster by the upstart Tara dynasty. Whether or not it actually existed as such an entity in our period is uncertain, but we assume that it did.

The Lagini: The people of Leinster, southeastern Ireland. Their territory was known as "Qóiqet Lagin," i.e. "the Fifth of the Lagini." The later form is "Cóiced Laigen."

The Ulati: The people of Ulster, northeastern Ireland. Their territory was Qóiqet nUlat.

Fifths: According to tradition, Ireland was anciently divided into five parts, the Fifths. Though their inhabitants had much in common with each other, four of these regions had quite distinct histories and, in some particulars, ways of life. Those were Ulster, Leinster, Munster, and Connaught, which retain a meaningful existence to this day. The medieval chronicles state that Mide was formed out of parts of them, mostly Leinster, by a dynasty originating in Connaught. This dynasty took possession of holy Tara and eventually produced the High Kings who theoretically were supreme over all lesser kings throughout Ireland. Boundaries were ill-defined and often variable, not identical with those of the four modern provinces. Thus, at times Munster was divided in two, and Ulster shrank under the impact of the Uí Néill. As we have remarked above, at best the Fifths corresponded only roughly to separate kingdoms, as limited as royal powers were; and the High Kingship, which did not appear until well after Niall's time, was more a legal fiction than a working institution. (Some modern scholars argue that the chronicles must be wrong and that Connaught actually developed out of Mide. It may be so; but as far as possible, we have chosen to follow the traditional accounts.)

Emain Macha: The seat of the Ulster kings, near modern Armagh.

Hill fort sacred to Medb: The ruins of this are now known as Ráth Maeve (a later form of the name "Medb"). They may or may not be contemporary with the main earthworks on Tara; our guess is that they are older, but were maintained. The attribution to Medb may well be right. She has been identified with the wife of Airt the Lonely, father of Corbmaqq (later called Cormac), but we suspect that originally the dedication was to Medb, tutelary goddess of Mide.

Forest: Unlike the country today, ancient Ireland was thickly wooded.

Boand's River: The Boyne, of which Boand was the goddess.

Great Rath: The remnants of this are now called the Ráth na Ríogh, or Royal Enclosure, but that is pure guesswork. "Rath" means such an enclosure, surrounded by an earthen wall—usually circular—which was originally topped by a palisade and often ringed by a fosse. It might protect anything from a single farmstead to a whole group of houses.

Pigs: The early Irish kept swine not only for food and leather, but occasionally as pets.

Heads: Like their Continental cousins before the Roman conquest, the Celts of Ireland were headhunters until they became Christian.

Flaw: No man could be king who had any serious deformity or disability. Some kings abdicated after suffering mutilation in war or accident, rather than risk expulsion.

Hostages: Alliances, subjugations, etc. were cemented by exchange of hostages, generally from leading families—unless a victor took his without giving any in return. As a rule, provided the terms of agreement were observed, they were well treated.

Bodyguards and champion: Besides his retinue of full-time warriors, an Irish king had several bodyguards—the number four is in the annals— who were with him whenever he went forth, as much for his dignity as his protection. For similar reasons, he kept a champion to deal with challenges to single combat, as opposed to war. Incidentally, aggrieved parties could not bring lawsuits against him, but could do so against his steward. In case of adverse judgment, naturally the king put up the compensation. The British monarchy preserves a version of this custom.

Equipment of the warriors: Contrary to Giraldus Cambrensis, the Irish used battle axes before the viking invasions; but they did not wear armor, except occasionally helmets or greaves.

Royal Guesthouse; King's quarters: It is merely our suggestion that these may correspond to what are now dubbed, respectively, the Forradh and Teach Cormaic. Some scholars question whether Tara was ever actually occupied, proposing instead that it served just for meetings and ceremonies. But not only are there raths, there are traces of actual buildings. Our idea is that, at least after the establishment of a dynasty centered here, a maintenance staff lived permanently on the hill, while aristocrats and their retainers came for short periods during the year.

Mound of the Kings: Today called the Mound of the Hostages, because of a story that a dormitory for hostages stood upon it. This is impossible; it is far too small. Another story says that hostages who died while in captivity were buried here; but excavation has turned up only a few post-Neolithic skeletons. Undeniably, this mound had some kind of sacredness from of old. Archaeology has revealed that it consists of earth heaped over a megalithic passage grave. Our guess is that this led to a reverence for it which grew over the years, until it was the site chosen for consecrating new kings at Tara.

Phallus: The Lia Fáil, Stone of Destiny. It stands on the Teach Cormaic, but was moved there in the eighteenth century; earlier, it seems to have been on or near the Mound of the Hostages. The name "Phallus of Fergus" was local in recent times, and probably well-founded. Certainly this upright pillar could not have been a stone on which kings stood at their consecrations, as they did throughout early Ireland. The legend that it roared upon contact with a true king is ancient; we have borrowed a modern idea that in fact somebody swung a bullroarer. The "coronation" stone on top of the mound is our own notion; nothing of the kind is there now.

Rath of the Warriors: Today called Rath of the Synods. More guesswork on our part: if kings stayed on Tara for any length of time at all, their military retinues would have needed some shelter, and this earthwork could have enclosed their barracks.

Dall and Dercha: The names of these two small burial mounds may or may not go back to our period.

Druid (actually the plural, *drui* being the original singular): Unlike their Continental (and probably British) counterparts before the Romans, Irish druids were not priests. Rather, they were repositories of knowledge, tradition, and wisdom, who had undergone a long and arduous education. Some were female; women had a high standing in this society. Druids served as teachers and counselors. In the earliest times they were also poets, judges, physicians, etc., but these gradually became separate specialists. They were believed to have powers of divination and magic. We might note that they did not collect mistletoe—a plant introduced into Ireland much later—nor pay any special regard to the oak; the trees that the Irish considered powerful were the hazel, yew, and the rowan.

Ogamm (later *ogham*): A primitive alphabet, its signs consisting of strokes and dots along a central line. It seems to have been used almost entirely for memorial and magical inscriptions.

The Mórrigu (or *Morrigan*): The goddess of war. She seems to have had three aspects or avatars with different names. It has been suggested more than once that Morgan le Fay of Arthurian legend is a later version of her.

Taking valor: Ancient Irish of the warrior classes often put their sons through a ceremony of "knighthood" as early as the age of seven.

Poets: A top-ranking poet *(Fili)* was an awesome figure; in some respects, he was more powerful than any king. Like a druid, he had survived a relentless course of training and commanded incredible linguistic and mnemonic skills. His words could make or break a reputation; if he was angered and composed a satire, its effects were believed to be physically destructive. Probably the worst crime in old Ireland was to offer violence to a poet, druid, or other learned person. There was a lower class of versifiers, whom we may as well call bards, but they, although respected, were essentially just entertainers.

Senchaide (or *shanachie*): Today, simply a storyteller, albeit often a delightful one. Very few remain active. In ancient times he was historian and genealogist to a basically illiterate society; he carried the annals of the country in his head.

The Feasting Hall: More guesswork on our part. What is now called the Banquet Hall (Teach Miodhchuarta) is the remnant of a great oblong earthwork, of approximately the dimensions that old stories ascribe to the hall where the Kings of Tara held their feasts. Some modern scholars think this was merely an open-air meeting site—but then why the ramparts? Others say the banks were formerly higher, which they doubtless were, and roofed over—but then why no traces of wood, when these have been identified elsewhere on Tara? Now it is attested in later history that the Irish could and did raise quite impressive temporary buildings, e.g., on one occasion to receive the King of England. Therefore we suggest that anciently they would erect such a hall within the elongated rath, demolishing and rebuilding it every three years for the triennial fair.

The feast: Unlike many peoples, the Irish generally took their principal meal of the day in the evening.

The cookhouse: Because of the fire hazard, cooking was usually done in a separate structure.

Battle-scarred women: Celtic women not uncommonly fought side by side with their men.

Laidchenn's verse: The syllabic prosody and interknit alliterations attempt to suggest one of the numerous early Irish poetic forms. Laidchenn himself figures in the sagas.

Lúg: A primary god of all the Celts, remembered in place names as far off as the south of France (Lyons, which was known to the Romans as Lugdunum).

Magimedon: A nickname meaning "servant (or slave) of Medon," who was presumably a god. Another interpretation is "master of slaves."

Carenn (or *Cairinn):* Laidchenn is relating the legends about Niall's early life that have come down to us today. It is not implausible that these would have cropped up almost at once; examples of the same thing are everywhere around in our own era, usually less close to the facts than tales of him may have been. We have modified them only slightly, in order to rationalize the chronology. Our assumption is that listeners, including Niall himself, accepted even the most fantastic parts as being metaphorically if not always literally true; moreover, there could well have been a considerable amount of selective recall and actual self-hypnosis, phenomena which are also common enough today. As for his mother, the medieval account calls her a Saxon princess, but this is most unlikely. On the other hand, if we take her name to be an Irish rendition of "Carina," she could have been Romano-British—perhaps the daughter of some tribal chieftain, or even a princess.

Succession of kings: Kingship, whether over a tuath or a larger polity, was inherent in a particular family: that is, a particular line of descent on the male side. Otherwise it was elective, and illegitimacy was no barrier.

Marrying the land: Well into Christian times, Irish kings at their inaugurations went through a ceremony of "marrying the tuath" or "the realm." This was purely symbolic; but the earlier pagans doubtless enacted it literally, choosing some maiden to embody the goddess, with whom the new king spent a night. The patron deity of the Tara line, and so presumably of Mide, was Medb. Thus legend says that Niall coupled with her, despite her disguise; and whether or not he believed this happened in fact, he did with her mortal representative.

Dál Riata (or *Dalriada):* A kingdom of eastern Ulster which founded a colony of the same name in Argyll, the first important settlement of Scots in what was to become Scotland. The date of the founding is quite uncertain. Since the colony enters into the traditional story, we perforce assume that it was already in existence by Niall's time. This is debatable but not impossible.

Gess (later *geas;* plural *gessa):* A kind of taboo; a prohibition laid upon an individual or a class. It might be traditional or might be imposed by one person on another. Sometimes the gessa look very strange. For example, another of those on the King at Tara was that he must never travel widdershins around North Leinster; and the hero Finn mac Cumail (Old Irish form) was forbidden to sleep more than nine nights running at

Allen. To break a gess was thought to bring disaster, and would certainly be disgraceful unless one was forced to it by trickery or circumstance, as various legendary figures were.

Burdigala: Bordeaux.

(Gallia) Narbonensis: A Roman province incorporating part of southern France.

Wine: This was produced in southern Britain under the Romans, and well into medieval times, after which the climate became too severe. With conditions now again milder, some is once more being made.

Fish and Chi Rho: These ancient Christian symbols were still in common use, whereas the crucifix was not yet so, and the cross not often.

Villa: To the Romans, this word meant a farm, not a house—especially a farm of some size.

Solidus: A gold coin, one of the few that had not been debased, therefore valuable and hard to come by.

Saddles: It is not certain whether the Mediterranean civilizations had yet adopted the Asian invention of stirrups; but improved saddles were already making cavalry more important than it had ever been before.

Cataphracts: Heavy-armored cavalrymen. Such a corps may have been the historical original of Arthur's knights, half a century or so after our story closes.

Ard: A primitive plow, wheelless, and possessing merely a pointed end. The moldboard plow appears to have been a Celtic invention, not much employed by the Romans except in areas where heavy soil gave it the advantage. Since no effective horse collar existed, an ox was the usual draft animal.

Curials: The curials, also called decurions, were those men of a city and its hinterland who had a certain amount of property. That is, they corresponded more or less to the middle class of modern Western civilization. They were expected to be active in local government and to meet various public expenses out of their own coffers. The caste system imposed by Diocletian froze them into this station, while the decay of the economy and the inordinate taxes of the state gradually ruined them.

Londinium: London. Its official Roman name, Augusta, was falling out of use.

Senators: In the late Empire, senatorial rank was conferred as often as it was inherited, carried privileges and exemptions rather than obligations, and was frequently attained by corrupt means.

Theater: Despite the generally moralistic atmosphere of the late Empire, performances—supposedly of classic stories—were apt be as raw as anything on our contemporary screens.

Navicularius: A shipowner. Such persons were tightly organized into a guild. Theoretically they were born to their status and could not get out of it, but in practice there must have been exceptions.

Dubris: Dover. Rutupiae (Richborough) had supplanted it as a major military base, but being a fort of the Saxon Shore it must have kept a garrison, and it was still an active seaport.

Navigation: The ancient mariners generally avoided sailing in autumn and winter less for fear of storms than because weather was too likely to hide the landmarks and heavens by which they found their way.

(Gallia) Lugdunensis: A Roman province incorporating much of northern and part of central France.

Wives: In contrast to the practice of earlier times, soldiers of the later Empire were allowed to marry during their terms of service. Doubtless this was meant as an inducement to enlist, for conscription was seldom resorted to any more, and when it was, oftenest out of subject peoples. Wives and children lived near the base, husbands joining them when off duty.

Gesocribate: It is not certain whether this town developed into the modern Brest, or was simply near the site of the latter.

Count (Latin *comes*): An official in charge of the defenses of a particular area. Best known to English-speaking moderns is the Count of the Saxon Shore, who governed the fortresses along the southeastern coast of Britain.

Foederate (Latin *civitas foederata*): A nation allied with or satellite to Rome. The word was also used for troops recruited from such peoples.

Gratillonius and his men: The army of the late Empire was organized differently in some respects from that of the Republic or Principate. Eight men of a legion formed a *contubernium,* sharing a tent and pack horse; in barracks they also shared two rooms, one for equipment and one for sleeping. Ten such parties made up the usual century *(centuria),* commanded by a centurion: thus numbering 80 rather than the original 100. Six centuries were grouped in three pairs (maniples) to form a cohort, and ten cohorts comprised a legion. The first cohort was larger than the rest, being made up of five double centuries, because it included all the technicians and clerks of headquarters. Hence the legion contained about 5300 infantrymen. In addition there were 120 horsemen—orderlies, scouts, and dispatch carriers rather than cavalry—distributed among the various centuries; there were also higher officers and their staffs, specialists, etc. Altogether a legion was from about 5500 to 6000 strong. As political, economic, and military conditions worsened, the actual total often became less.

The backbone of the legion was its centurions, most of whom had risen from the ranks. The senior centurions *(primi ordines)* were in the first cohort, whose first century was commanded by the chief centurion *(primus pilus),* a trusted and honored veteran who, after a year, might go on to become camp prefect *(praefectus castrorum),* in charge of the legion's internal organization and operations—or might take some equally responsible post, if he did not simply retire on his savings and a large gratuity given him.

Originally the commandant of the legion was the legate *(legatus),* who was a political appointee of senatorial rank, although he was expected to have served before as a military tribune—staff officer—and so to have learned generalship. Since the reign of Gallienus, the camp prefect had supplanted him. There is no need here to describe other functionaries.

Many legions had existed for hundreds of years, and some had been based at their sites for almost as long. Strangely enough, considering the vital function of the centurions, they were quite commonly assigned and reassigned to different legions, sometimes across the width of the Empire. Probably the government did not want too close bonds of mutual personal loyalty between such career officers and the enlisted men. Gratillonius had not held the rank sufficiently long for this to have happened to him, but likely it would have if Maximus had not entrusted him with a mission that brought him to an unforeseen fate.

Or perhaps it would not have happened. What we have just been describing no longer existed in the eastern part of the Empire. There infantry was largely made up of *limitanei,* reservists who were called on to fight only in the areas where they lived, while the core of the armed forces was the cavalry, composed mostly of Germanic mercenaries. By the end of the fourth century, the strength of a legion was no more than 1500 men, set to garrison and other minor duty.

However, though these transformations were also taking place in the West, they were much slower, and quite likely had scarcely begun in Britain or northwestern Gaul. For one thing, there the principal menaces to Rome—Saxons, Franks, Alemanni, etc.—were not yet horsemen. Military reforms like those enacted at Constantinople were indeed imperative, but the enfeebled government of the West was incapable of doing anything quickly or efficiently.

Thus a soldier such as Gratillonius could have begun his service in a unit in a legion not very different from, say, one of Marcus Aurelius's— aside from the large number of auxiliary troops—and ended it in an army not vastly different from, say, William the Conqueror's.

IV

Sails: Roman transport ships did not use oars, except for steering. Warcraft generally did, making sails the auxiliary power. It is worth remarking that the rowers were free men, and rather well paid. Galley slaves did not appear until the Middle Ages.

Pharos: Lighthouse. The beacon was a fire on its top after dark; by day, the tower was a landmark helpful to navigators. The Dover pharos, of which a part still exists, was about 80 feet high.

Dobunni: A tribe occupying, approximately, Gloucestershire, Herefordshire, and some adjacent areas.

Deputy: Second in command of a century, chosen by the centurion himself, hence the Latin name *optio.*

Regnenses: A tribe in Sussex.

Demetae: A tribe in the western part of southern Wales.

Coritani: A tribe occupying, approximately, Lincolnshire and adjacent territories.

Navy: The *classis Britannica* that guarded the coasts around the Channel and the North Sea approaches disappears from history about the middle of the third century. Its former base at Dover, abandoned even earlier, was converted to a fort of the Saxon Shore. However, Dover remained a seaport, and surely the military still needed some ships of their own.

Prefect of the cohort (praefectus cohortis): Commander of a unit of infantry auxiliaries. The word *"praefectus"* was used in a number of different contexts.

Lanterns: These, with panes of glass or thin-scraped horn, were known to the Romans. Some were quite elaborately made.

Hostel (Latin *mansio):* Accomodations for persons traveling on business of the state were maintained at rather frequent intervals along major routes. It seems reasonable to us that the one closest to a small city such as Gesoriacum would be outside rather than inside the walls, to save valuable building space and for the benefit of persons who arrived belatedly. On the other hand, there would probably have been at least one hostel near the center of any large and important city.

Candles: The Romans had both wax and tallow candles. The latter, at least, were considered much inferior to lamps, if only because of the smell, while the single material available for the former, beeswax, was too expensive for any but the richest people. Nevertheless tallow candles were much used, especially in areas where oil for lamps was scarce and thus costly.

Publican: The publicans of the Bible were not jolly taverners, as many moderns suppose, but tax farmers. Only Jesus, among decent people, could find it in his heart to associate with them. Their circumstances and practices changed as the Empire grew old, but not their spirit.

Tax in kind: This had become especially important as debasement made currency increasingly worthless. Diocletian and Constantine had reformed the coinage, but honest money remained scarce.

Couriers: The Roman postal service must still have been functioning reasonably well in most areas, since we have a considerable volume of correspondence among clergy and other learned men. Graffiti show that literacy was not confined to the upper classes, either. However, in regions as distressed as the northern Gallic littoral now was, the mails had surely deteriorated.

Massilia: Marseilles.

(Civitas) Baiocassium: Bayeux.

Hoofs: Horseshoes had not yet been invented, but a kind of sandals or slippers was sometimes put on the animals when ground was bad.

Standard bearer: The *signifer* wore an animal skin of a sort traditional for his unit. In a small detachment like this, it would make sense to rotate the duty. The standard was not the legionary eagle but a banner.

Rations: Archeology has revealed that the legions enjoyed a more varied diet, with more meat in it, than historians had thought.

Beans: Broadbeans (fava), the only kind known in Europe before the discovery of America.

Lent: As yet, the formula for calculating the date of Easter had not been finally settled upon, but varied from area to area and was the subject of much controversy. Nor was there agreement on how long a period of abstention should precede it, or on what austerities should be minimally required. For that matter, there was no standardized weekly practice of self-denial, such as the meatless Friday of later centuries. One may presume that even soldiers who were devout would not trouble themselves about that, at least while on duty. However, Easter, the holiest day in the

Church calendar, and observances directly related to it, would be of concern. Strictly speaking, therefore, our use of the word "Lent" is anachronistic—but it conveys, in brief, approximately what Budic had in mind.

Sunday: The week as we know it had not yet been officially taken into the Roman calendar, though of course it was ancient in the East. One may well wonder how many ordinary soldiers were conscious of it, especially when in the field.

Nodens: A Celtic god, especially revered at the Severn mouth, in which flow great tidal bores.

Leagues: The Gallic *leuga* equalled 1.59 English or 1.68 Roman mile.

Rhenus: Rhine.

Caletes: A tribe in northeastern Gallia Lugdunensis, occupying approximately Seine-Maritime, Oise, and Somme.

Osismii: A tribe in the far west of Brittany, occupying approximately Finistère and part of Côtes-du-Nord. Place names and other clues seem to show they were not purely Celtic, nor were neighboring tribes. Rather, Celtic invaders probably imposed an aristocracy which interbred and became identified with the people. Meanwhile the language, too, became largely Celtic. The earlier race was not necessarily descended straight from the megalith builders; there could have been more than one set of newcomers over the centuries. Yet nothing appears to forbid our supposition that the Armoricans *believed* the "Old Folk" were among their ancestors. An analogous tradition exists in Ireland.

Honestiores: Great landholders, virtual feudal overlords.

Alani: An Iranian-Altaic people, originally living in what is now southern Russia. Under pressure from the Huns, the western branch of them mingled with the Germans and joined these in that great migration into Roman territory which was just getting well under way at the time of our story.

Ingena: Avranches. Today it is Norman rather than Breton, but of course neither of those peoples had yet reached France.

Vorgium (later *Osismiis)*: Carhaix. Folk etymology derives the present name from "Ker-Ahes" ("Stronghold of Ahes," the latter name being given to Dahut in some versions of the Ys legend), but this is false.

Mauretania: Approximately, northern Morocco.

Condate Redonum: Rennes.

Veneti: A tribe in south Brittany, occupying approximately Morbihan.

Fanum Martis: Corseul. The tower is still there, in remarkably good condition.

Garomagus: There was a Roman town of some small importance—as we describe later—in the area of modern Douarnenez, but its name is not known. "Garomagus" is our conjecture, referring to its production of *garum,* a fish sauce which was a major item of Armorican trade.

Passage grave occupied by refugees: A case of this is known. There were probably more.

Ahriman: The supreme lord of evil in the Zoroastrian religion and its Mithraic offshoot, as Ahura-Mazda (or Ormazd) was the lord of good.

Franks in Condate Redonum: Those tribes lumped together as Franks (Latin *Franci)* originated in western Germany and the Netherlands. As yet they had not overrun Gaul, but some had entered and settled in various areas. The laeti at Rennes and their open paganism, including even human sacrifice, just at the time when Gratillonius passed through, are attested.

V

Sena: Île de Sein. Archeology shows it to have been occupied since prehistoric times, but we suppose that for several centuries it was reserved exclusively for the use of the Gallicenae—as the first-century geographer Pomponius Mela says was the case in his own period.

House: There are traces, now submerged, of what is believed to have been a Roman building at Île de Sein. Was this actually the sanctuary of its priestesses, remodeled under Roman influence?

Stones: These two megaliths are still on the island.

Cernunnos: A major Celtic god, represented as a man with stag's antlers.

Yes, yea, aye: You may have noticed that hitherto no person in the story has used any of these words. This is because Latin and the Celtic languages have no exact equivalent. We suppose that Semitic influence on the evolution of the Ysan tongue, otherwise basically Celtic, produced such words in it, just as the Germanic example would cause the Romance languages to develop them. Latin and Celtic do not employ a simple "No" either when giving a negative response. However, we have supplied it in rendering the former, in order that that may seem colloquial to the modern reader, and have also provided Ysan with it.

VI

Astrology: Belief in this prevailed throughout the late Roman Empire, along with countless other superstitions. Since it appears to have been part of the Mithraic faith, Gratillonius was heterodox in his reservations about it.

Book: The codex may go back as far as the first century. Toward the end of the fourth it had displaced the scroll except for legal and other special purposes. Elaborate illumination of the medieval sort was not yet done, but illustration of a simpler kind was, and it seems quite likely that the binding of some religious manuscripts was ornate and costly.

Twenty miles: Roman miles, of course.

Gobaean Promontory (Promontorium Gobaeum): The Cap Sizun area.

AVC: Anno Urbis Conditae ("V" was habitually used for "U" in inscriptions), year after the founding of Rome, for which the traditional date corresponded to 753 B.C. The Romans themselves rarely counted time from this baseline, but the reference was not unknown.

SPQR: Senatus Populusque Romanus, "The Roman Senate and People," proud motto of the Republic, long borne on standards of the legions.

Fortress and maritime station: The remnant of the fortress can still be seen on Pointe de Castelmeur. There must have been more of it extant in Gratillonius's day. The station is rather conjectural.

Key: By Roman times, locks had developed into bolt-and-pin types not too unlike modern sorts. Their keys had corresponding prongs. When a key was inserted, these prongs pushed up the pins, whereupon a sidewise pull drew back the bolt.

VII

Fresh-made laurel wreath: The laurel is an evergreen.

Cape Rach: Pointe du Raz (hypothetical reconstruction of the aboriginal name). The *ch* is supposed to be as in modern Scottish or German.

Refusing the crown: While today our knowledge of Mithraism is scanty, this detail is attested.

VIII

Point Vanis: Pointe du Van (hypothetical reconstruction of the aboriginal name).

Nummus (plural *nummi):* A coin of the late Empire, minuscule and debased. It took more than 14,000 to equal one gold solidus. Archeology shows that Gresham's Law was as operative in Roman times as it is now.

Thule: It is not certain what the Classical geographers meant by this name. Iceland and Norway are among the more common suggestions. We incline toward the latter.

The sea gate of Ys: Today one would solve the problem of protecting a harbor from overwhelming tides by constructing locks. These, however, were not developed until much later.

Saxons (Saxones): This name did not distinguish any single tribe or kingdom. Rather, it was a general term used by the Romans for all those robbers and invaders who came across the North Sea from the northern Netherlands, the German littoral, Jutland, and possibly regions still more distant.

IX

Soap: This appears to have been a Gallic invention, regarded by the Romans more often as a medicinal for the skin than as a cleansing agent.

Basilica: In this period and earlier, the word referred to a building for public business—administration, trials at law, etc.

The layout of the church: Private homes were frequently converted for this purpose, but it is clear that no one in Ys who might be willing to make such a donation possessed a suitable one; so, as happened elsewhere (for example, to the Parthenon), this pagan temple was expropriated by Imperial decree. Normally there would be a baptistry, but in Ys there was no resident bishop, and a chorepiscopus had no authority to administer this sacrament—which was not usually given children anyway. *Vide infra.* Believers who had not received it could enter no farther than the porch or vestibule, and were dismissed before the Communion service began in the sanctuary. Even in the great churches, furniture was basically the same as described here. Such amenities as pews were for a later era.

Redonic: Of the tribe of the Redones, around Rennes.

Audiarna: Audierne, on the River Goyen, some nine English miles east of the Baie des Trépassés. There are traces of Roman occupation. Our Latin name is conjectural, and we assume the name of St. Audierne comes from the town rather than vice versa.

Consecrated bread and wine: At this period, only a bishop could consecrate the bread and wine for the Eucharist, or perform several other important functions. This consecration was generally of large quantities at a time, which were then distributed among churches. Eucherius would seldom have to restock. Not only was his congregation tiny, but the majority of it were unbaptized, having only the status of catechumens and therefore unqualified to partake of the Lord's Supper. Baptism was a rite regarded with great awe. It must be done by a bishop or, at least, under the supervision of one; as a rule, this was just once or twice a year, notably at Easter. Most believers received it comparatively late in life, not uncommonly when on their deathbeds—as in the case of Constantine I. After all, it washed away prior sins, but was of no avail against any that might be committed afterward, which indeed would then be the deadlier.

Eucherius's heresy: It anticipated that of Pelagius, in some small degree; such ideas were in the air.

The appointment of Eucherius: At this time the Church organization that we know today, including the Papacy itself, was still nascent. Originally each congregation had had its own bishop, the priests and deacons being merely his councillors and assistants, but eventually the numbers of the faithful were such as to require something more elaborate, which naturally came to be modeled on the Roman state. The process was under way in the decades around 400 A.D., but as yet there was a great deal of local variation, arbitrariness, and outright irregularity. For example, St. Patrick may well have consecrated himself a bishop. The chorepiscopus served most of the functions later assigned the parish priest, but by no means all of them.

Neapolis: Naples.

(Gallia) Aquitania: A Roman province occupying, approximately, the part of France south of the Loire, west of the Allier, and north of the Pyrenees.

Tamesis: The Thames.

The Hooded Three: The *genii cucullati*, a trio of gods (?) in Britain about which we have little more information than some representations and votive inscriptions.

Handclasp: The handshake as we know it seems to be of Germanic origin, but might have appeared independently in Ys, or been observed by travelers and become a custom at home.

Niall and the women: In sleeping with women of various households, the King was not exerting any special prerogative nor giving any offense. Early Irish society gave a great deal of freedom to women other than slaves, including the right to choose which of several different forms of marriage or cohabitation they wanted. Wives often took lovers, with their husbands' knowledge and consent.

Mag Slecht: In present-day County Cavan. Cromb Cróche (later Crom Cruach) and the twelve attendant divinities were probably pillar stones, sheathed in gold and bronze. There will be more about them later.

Ruirthech: The Liffey.

Clón Tarui: Now Clontarf, a district of Dublin on the north shore of the bay. It became the site of a famous battle in the year 1016.

Public hostel: There were several classes of these in early Ireland, endowed by kings or communities with enough land to support the provision of free food and lodging to all travelers. Such hospitality was required to maintain honor; and, to be sure, it encouraged trade. The innkeepers were usually men, but sometimes women.

Border of the Lagini: The River Liffey does *not* mark the border of present-day Leinster. It did, though, come to form one frontier of lands subject to the southern Uí Néill. Given the enormous uncertainties about conditions at the time of their great ancestor, we think it reasonable to suppose that Mide extended this far. After all, Niall could scarcely have ravaged Britain as repeatedly and thoroughly as the chronicles say, did he not have at least one port of embarkation on the east coast of Ireland.

Bóru tribute: About this, more later. Imposed of old by Connaught on Leinster, it came to be claimed by the Tara kings, but more often than not they had to collect it by force, and oftener still it went unpaid. In large part this was because it was exorbitant (though one need not take literally the traditional list of cattle and other treasure). King Brian, eleventh-century victor at Clontarf, got the nickname Bóruma—now usually rendered as Boru—because he did succeed in exacting it.

Smoke: Modern experiments have shown that primitive Celtic houses could not have had vent holes as more elaborate halls did. Instead, smoke simply filtered out through the conical thatch roofs, killing vermin on the way.

Horseblanket: The ancient Irish seem to have used merely a pad when riding. It is not certain whether they had saddles by the time of our story, but if they did, the use of these could not have been common.

X

Greenish light: Even the best Roman window glass had such a tinge.

Diocese: A division of the Empire. In our period there were fifteen, of which Britain constituted one. Each was governed by a vicarius, who was responsible to a praetorian prefect. The praetorian prefect of Gaul, residing in Trier, also administered Britain and Iberia. A diocese was subdivided into provinces, whose governors, called praesides, had civil but not military authority.

Triclinium: The dining room in a Roman house. However, the basic layout of an Ysan home was different from that of a typical Roman one.

XI

Ishtar: The recorded Carthaginian form of this name is "Ashtoreth" or something similar, but we assume "Ishtar" was the older version; and Babylonian immigrants to Ys would have reinforced its use.

Sea level: This has varied considerably in historical time, presumably because of melting and refreezing of polar ice as climate passes through cycles of warmth and cold. In the late fourth century it was at, or not long past, a peak. Western Brittany, where the tidefall is always great, would be especially affected—above all in small bays with steeply shelving bottoms between sheer headlands.

XII

Lutetia Parisiorum: Paris.

Draughts: Board games of various sorts were popular in antiquity, though none seem to have been identical with any played nowadays. However, versions of what we now call draughts or checkers go back to Pharaonic Egypt.

XIII

Noble landowners: A *flaith* was a man who actually owned land, normally by right of inheritance although subject to the claims of his kindred and tuath. He rented out most of it to others, for payment in kind and in services.

Beltene (also spelled *Beltane, Beltine,* etc.): In the modern calendar, 1 May. In pagan times the date may have been set according to the moon, but would have fallen approximately the same. Most lunar calendars count from the new moon, which is the phase most readily identifiable, but we assume that the Northern Celts, at least, wanted a full moon at their great festivals, to help light ceremonies held after dark. They could have added fourteen or fifteen days to the time when they observed the new one—or they may simply have taken advantage of the fact that the full one is less often completely lost to sight in the wet climate of their homelands. Second only to Samain in importance, Beltene carried with it many beliefs and customs which survived, somewhat Christianized, almost until the present day. We have extrapolated backward in order to suggest what various features may originally have been like.

Marriage: In ancient Ireland this had several different forms. Among them was not only the usual arrangement negotiated by parents with an eye to advantageous alliance between families, but unions for a limited span, freely entered into by the individuals concerned. While women did not have all the rights of men, on the whole they enjoyed—if freeborn—more liberty than their sex would again, in most of the world, until the twentieth century.

Needfire: Before the invention of matches, kindling a fire was a laborious and ofttimes precarious task, therefore a serious matter. If a hearthfire went out, it was generally easiest to borrow coals from a neighbor to restart it. Deliberately extinguishing it, in order to begin quite afresh, was an act fraught with religious and magical significance.

Rath of Gráinne and Sloping Trenches: These are present-day names of ruined works on Tara which were probably burial rather than dwelling sites. People in Niall's day may already have been telling much the same stories about them that we now hear.

Síd (later *sídhe):* "Fairy mounds" or, in general, underground habitations of supernatural beings, to whom the same word is applied as a name. They appear to have been originally megalithic tombs, although later they included natural hills. When Christianity had prevailed in Ireland, the síd folk became largely identified with the Tuatha De Danaan, tribes possessing magical powers who had retreated into these fastnesses after suffering defeat in war, but still came forth on occasion for good or ill. It is clear that those were, mainly, the old gods themselves, slightly disguised. To the pagan Irish, the síd folk were presumably ghosts and other such night-wanderers.

Conaire: The story of this king and his death at the destruction of Dá Derga's hostel appears to be so ancient that it was already a myth among the Irish of Niall's time.

Samain (today usually spelled *Samhain):* In the modern calendar, 1 November. It was the most important and awesome of the Celtic festivals. Many beliefs and practices associated with it continued through the Christian era virtually to the present day.

Diarmait (later *Diarmuid)* and *Gráinne:* A legendary pair of lovers, with whom folklore associates the Rath of Grainne.

Liger: The Loire.

XIV

Bare marble: The classical Greeks generally painted their statues and buildings. The Romans did likewise for sculpture, but as for buildings, at least in the later part of their history, they were more apt to make the stone itself the decoration, frequently as a facing on a concrete structure.

Portus Namnetum: Nantes. Condovincum, uphill, was later incorporated.

Shield grip: Celtic and Nordic shields were not held by loops for the arm but simply grasped by a handle. The Romans added a shoulder strap.

Breccan maqq Nélli: Breccan son of Niall, "Nélli" being the genitive.

Tír innan Oac: The Land of Youth, one of several paradises which Celtic mythology located afar in the western ocean.

Milesians: In Irish legend, the last wave of invaders (prior to the vikings). A number of tuaths, especially in Connaught, claimed descent from them, and looked down on "Firbolo" who could not.

Following wind: It is not clear whether Germanic galleys and Irish currachs (or "curraghs" or "coracles") could tack at all. Roman square-riggers could get no closer than seven points off the wind, and had the advantage of comparatively deep draught, in that era when the keel was not yet designed to help. Sprit-riggers did better. As for currachs, Tim Severin put leeboards on his *Brendan* but admits this may be an anachronism, since there is no evidence for them until well into the Middle Ages. We therefore suppose that they did not exist in our period. Under sail, doing anything but running straight downwind, crews would have used their oars for lateral resistance to keep on a broad reach, which was probably the best they could achieve; without a wind from astern, they struck their sails and rowed. It must have been likewise for Germanic galleys. Certain archeologists doubt that those even had sails until just before the viking era, but we think that at least some had primitive rigs in imitation of the Romans.

Christian Scoti: It appears that there was a significant Christian community in Munster, if not in the rest of Ireland, well before St. Patrick.

Wolf: We know that the bad reputation of this animal is undeserved. However, until recent times most people dreaded and hated it, and there is reason to believe that wolves did occasionally attack humans—especially in hard winters when they could get no other food—as well as raid livestock. Firearms have changed that; the wolf is quite able to learn a lesson and teach its young.

XV

Maze: Intricate sets of paths had been laid out in northern as well as southern Europe since neolithic times, probably for religious or magical use.

XVI

Funeral societies: A Roman legionary was expected to belong to a military funeral association, the dues of which were stopped from his pay. When he died it gave him a proper burial.

Sena: Implicit are various topographical differences from today's Île de Sein. It is most unlikely that so low and small an island, constantly battered by waves which storms sometimes dash clear across, would remain for centuries unchanged.

XVII

Mithraism: Little is known today about the doctrines of this religion. We present those which are reasonably well attested. Their parallels to Christianity were remarked upon at the time, in writings which survive, and are presumably due to common origins of the ideas in question. As for the rites, there is virtually no record, aside from some propagandistic Christian references. Out of these we have taken what looks plausible, and added thereto a good deal of conjecture.

XVIII

Planets: In classical astrology and astronomy, the sun and the moon counted as planets, making—with Mercury, Venus, Mars, Jupiter, and Saturn—seven in all.

Carthaginian abhorrence: It is not certain what the actual attitude of the Carthaginians was toward homosexuality. The Mosaic prohibition suggests that they may have tried to ban it like their fellow Semites the Jews, if only as part of a general reaction against the Graeco-Roman world, but this is perhaps a mistaken idea. However, in any case Ysans who did disapprove—conceivably as a legacy from the Celtic side of their descent —would naturally attribute the same feeling to the founders of their city. As for contemporary Romans, although bisexuality among men, especially in the form of pederasty, had been widespread in the late Republic and the Principate, under the Dominate Christian influence and a generally puritanical mind-set eventually drove it underground.

XIX

"Tene, Mithra," etc: The line is adapted from Kipling's poem "A Song to Mithras"—"Mithras, also a soldier, keep us true to our vows!"

XX

Theater: Where there was a curtain in a Classical theater, it was generally deployed from below rather than above, since the building was roofless. The Ysan theater is unique in several respects, perhaps most notably in allowing women—perfectly respectable women—to perform. Among the Greeks and Romans, they only did so in pornographic shows; otherwise female roles were played by boys.

Feast of Lug: Known to the Irish of recent times as Lugnasad, it is now fixed at 1 August, although we are again assuming that originally the date varied. We also suppose that the Continental Celts named the god slightly differently from their insular cousins.

XXI

C. Valerius Gratillonius: The name "Gaius" was abbreviated "C.," a relic of times before the Roman alphabet possessed a letter "G."

XXII

Guilt and expiation: Some modern Christian apologists have maintained disapprovingly, and some neo-pagans have maintained approvingly, that the ancients had little or no concept of sin, few sexual inhibitions, etc. This is utter nonsense, as even a superficial study of their writings, onward from the oldest Mesopotamian and Egyptian texts, will show. For that matter, anthropologists have found that the concept of any noble savages living anywhere in happy innocence and harmony with nature is equally ludicrous.

Dahilis forbidden to Gratillonius: Present-day medical doctrine allows sexual intercourse, if there are no complications, practically to the end of pregnancy; but this is a very recent idea, as your authors can attest with some ruefulness. In most societies, abstinence has been urged or commanded for expectant mothers during the last several weeks or months. Given the limited capabilities of physicians and rudimentary knowledge of sanitation in the ancient world, this was probably wise then.

Falernian wine: Renowned in Roman times, it came from an area within Campani, which was a region including modern Capua and Naples. Today's Campania, in turn, includes ancient Campani in a larger territory.

XXIII

Black Months: The Breton expression for this time of year may well have ancient origins.

Dál Riata: A kingdom in Ulster, or its colony of the same name, across the North Channel on the shore of what is now Scotland.

Mandrake: Besides its alleged magical properties, mandrake root was anciently used as an emetic, purgative, and narcotic. The *Encyclopaedia Britannica* (11th ed.) observes, ". . . it has fallen into well-earned disrepute."

Pellitory: Pyrethrum parthenium, Shakespeare's "feverfew," related to the chrysanthemum.

Money in circulation: The economic depression in the Roman Empire, with more and more trade being in kind, inevitably affected other states.

Coins, especially those least debased, tended to accumulate in hoards such as later ages have unearthed. However, a society whose institutions were still basically sound would respond to any stimulus given its businesses.

XXIV

Opium: This was known to the ancients in the forms of extract from either the whole plant or the capsule, but apparently used only as an analgesic. The source being Asia Minor, where the opium poppy was native, supply to Western Europe must have cut off as trade declined.

XXV

Teeth cleansers: The Romans had versions of toothbrushes and dentifrices.

Toys: If Gratillonius appears unsentimental about Innilis's miscarriage, one should remember that attitudes toward such things, and toward infants, were different then. Prior to modern medicine and sanitation, mortality was so high that parents dared not invest much love in a child until it was old enough to have a reasonable chance of living further.

Snow and ice: These are not especially common in Breton winters, which are oftener rainy, but do occur sometimes.

Caesar: The Caesarian section gets its name not because Julius was thus born—he wasn't—but because he re-established the old Royal Law that when a woman died in late pregnancy, a surgical attempt should be made to save her child. The first recorded operation on a living woman occurred in the sixteenth century, and until recent times the fatality rate was so high that it was a last-choice procedure. Nowadays, of course, it is almost routine.

Bay of Aquitania: Sinus Aquitanicus, the Bay of Biscay.

Wet nurse: For a newborn infant, it would naturally be preferable to have a woman who had herself given birth very recently.

The Birthday of Mithras: As we have stated before, this was fixed at 25 December—but in the Julian calendar, which was already out of step with astronomical time. Hence the date of the full moon following was earlier than a modern ephemeris for the fourth century, using the Gregorian calendar, indicates. Throughout the writing of this novel, we have tried to be as accurate as possible about all verifiable details.

GALLICENAE

1

The child knew only that she was upon the sea. It was enough to overwhelm her with wonder. That this was the Blessing of the Fleet lay outside her understanding as yet, like nearly all those sounds her father made: "—And how would you like to come along, little one?" What spoke to her was the strength of his arms and the laughter rumbling in his breast as he took her up and held her close.

Already fading out of her were the marvelous things that happened at the docks, people in bright robes, deep-chanted words followed by music that sang, chimed, whistled, quivered, twanged, boomed, as the procession went from hull to hull. The gray-bearded man in the lead was frightening to see, with his long pole and its three sharp spikes that he held on high, but behind him came the Mamas—nine of them, though she was too small to have the use of numbers. Some carried green branches that they dipped into pots that others bore, and then sprinkled oil on the prows. The first had a bowl that swung from gold chains and gave off smoke. When the wind shifted and brought the smoke to the child, it smelled sweet. She and her father stood aside, watching. He was very splendid in his own robe, a great sledge hammer at his side, on his breast the Key that usually hung inside his clothes; but she had no words for any of these things.

Afterward he picked her up again and carried her on board a ship that led the rest forth. The water in the harbor basin was lively, for the gate stood wide and a fresh breeze blew yonder. As her father's yacht passed through, the deck started to roll beneath her. Keeping her feet became a delightful game. The air was shrill and cold. It flung salt spray that tingled on her lips. The planks she stood on were still sun-warmed, giving off a fragrance of new pitch.

Everybody was jolly, men and women and such children as they had with them, none of those as young as the girl. From aft resounded the coxswain's drum, setting time for the rowers, whose oars cracked against the holes. Between strokes they often tossed words back and forth that made them grin. The ship creaked too, stays thrummed, a ruddy pennon at the masthead went *snap! snap!* Gulls mewed, hundreds of them, a snowstorm of wings, dipping and soaring. Other birds were likewise out in their darker throngs, aloft or afloat, and sometimes their cries also cut through the wind.

The craft that followed spread formation into a half-moon. Many were bigger than this, whether low and lean or high and round-bellied. Many more were smaller, duller-painted, and the men in them weren't so finely dressed. Some had raised sails, the rest continued under sweeps. Behind them rose the city wall, sheer, murky red save for the frieze under its battlements, and its towers, and the still taller spires inside, whose copper and glass and gilt flung light blindingly back at the sun. The headlands bulked rugged on either side, surf tumultuous underneath. The valley and hills beyond were turning green.

But it was the sea that captured the girl child, the sea. At first she clapped her hands together and shouted. Later she stood silent, aware of nothing else, for this was everything, this was the forever changing boundlessness that she had not known was within herself.

The sky reached pale and clear, only a few clouds scurrying at the edge of the world. Waves rushed and rumbled, long, maned, foam-swirled, wrinkles dancing in webs across their backs. Colors played over them, through them, gray-blue, grass-green, purple-black. Where they broke on the rocks and reefs that lay everywhere about, they bellowed hollowly and sent milkiness fountaining. Torn-off strands of kelp moved snakishly in their troughs. Creatures swam, tumbled, darted, at one with the waves, not only fowl but the sleekness of seals, a few times the silver leap of a fish or the frolicsome grace that was a porpoise. The child did not recognize a piece of driftwood as being off a wreck.

Time was no more, nothing was except the miracle that had taken her unto itself. She did not come back to anything else until the helmsmen put their steering oars over and the yacht turned again landward. The parade was done.

Most vessels headed the same way, wanting their berths prior to commencing the season's farings. A few bore southeasterly, toward fisher hamlets along the coast. The child realized that her adventure neared an end. She did not weep, such was not her nature, but she made her way to the side, the better to watch while she still could.

This was on the foredeck, above and forward over the rowers' benches. The bulwark was too high for her to lean over. When a seal drew alongside, she had just a tantalizing glimpse. Nearby squatted a bollard, the anchor rode coiled around it, the hook leaning massive against it. An active creature since her birth, she got a purchase on the hemp and climbed to the top. There she glanced widely around.

Aft she spied a streak of land low in the water, from which rose a single building, dark, foursquare, surmounted by a turret. But she had already seen that. What she wanted to do was look at the seal.

It swam close, easily matching the speed of the oarsmen. The amber-brown of its coat was warm amidst the brilliance of the waves. It did not move like its fellows, intent on prey or whatever else they sought. Rather, as much as possible, it kept gazing upward. Its eyes were big, beautiful, as soft as sleep. Enchanted, the child stared back into them.

A grown-up noticed her on her precarious perch, exclaimed, and hastened to pluck her off it. He was too late. The yacht rolled heavily. It was nobody's fault—these were notoriously treacherous waters—and had happened several times today. The girl was pitched loose and went overboard.

As she fell, the yells from above reached her faintly, unreal, lost in the welcoming noise of the sea. It received her with a single enormous caress. Her thick garments drew her under. A lucent yellow-green blindness enfolded her. She felt neither chill nor fear, merely surprise, a sense of homecoming. The sea tossed her about much like her father bouncing her in his arms. A humming began to fill her head.

Before she could gasp a breath, solidity struck, gripped, whirred her away. Held between the front flippers of the seal, she drank wind and salt scud. And then her father was there, threshing clumsily but mightily through the billows. Somehow it became he that clutched her, kept her face in the air, roared for a line. Scrambling and confusion overran them; and they were back on deck. She released her shock and bereavement in a wail.

He hugged her close to him. She felt his heart slugging behind the iron Key. His voice shuddered. "Are you well, darling? Are you all right, my little Dahut?"

2

The summons came to Gaius Valerius Gratillonius in the third year during which he had been Roman prefect and King of Ys. Having read it, he told his majordomo to arrange accomodations for the courier, because he would need a few days to find out precisely what his reply must be. Thereafter he sent for Bodilis and Lanarvilis.

Bodilis arrived first. It was raining. In the upstairs conference room where he received her, a brazier did somewhat to relieve cold, but a couple of lamps mainly cast unrestful shadows that made the pastoral frescos on the wall dim and unreal, like memories of the summer that was waning. She had left her cloak with the palace doorkeeper. Though it had a cowl, drops of water sparkled in the dark-brown waves of her hair and misted the strong-boned countenance. Two graceful strides brought her to him. He took both her hands—they were warm beneath the dampness —and smiled down into the deep-blue eyes—not very far down.

"It's good to see you again," he said, and brushed his lips across hers, a kiss quick and cool but aquiver. "How have you been, and the girls?" He spoke Latin, and she replied in the same tongue. They ordinarily did when by themselves; she wanted to maintain proficiency in it.

"Oh, Kerna is all agog, planning a feast to celebrate when she finishes her vestalhood, and Semuramat is wild with envy and insists the eight years still ahead of her might as well be eternity," she laughed. Of the three children she had by Hoel, Talavair had completed Temple service and was married, with one of her own on the way. "Una was sound asleep when your messenger came." That was the daughter Bodilis had given Gratillonius last year.

He sighed. "If only I could spend more time in your household."

"No," she said earnestly, "don't think like that."

He nodded. Had Dahilis been less beloved by her Sisters than she was, his lavishing of attention on her would have created stresses he could ill afford. Since her death, he divided his nights as evenly as feasible among the seven Queens with whom he slept, and his days among all the Nine— or, rather, what remained of his nights and days after royal duties and masculine recreations. "Well, we'll have tomorrow, you and I, if the moon be willing. Keep it clear for me."

She smiled. "I've been preparing. But why have you called me here today?"

"Best we wait for Lanarvilis. . . . No, you may as well read this at once." He pointed to a papyrus sheet on the table. It was curled from having been carried as a sealed-up roll. She spread it between her hands and brought it close to a lamp. As she lowered her head, nearsightedly, to scan the writing, she murmured, "Lanarvilis too, and none other? Are we to compare notes on your youngsters? Then why not Guilvilis?"

The jape fluttered forlorn. She had spied the grimness upon him. "It's not that you two—well, you three—among the Gallicenae have happened to bear me offspring this soon," he explained in his methodical fashion. "Although I well know it's no chance pure and simple. You and Lanarvilis took most thought for the future. You both saw that after what . . . happened with Dahilis, my fathering of more princesses would strengthen my shaken standing in Ys."

"Also," Bodilis said, "we are neither of us young women. Time is at our heels."

"Well, because you are what you are—yourself learned and wise, she versed and shrewd in the politics of the city—I want your counsel before I tell anybody else about this matter."

"Whereas you think poor Guilvilis is neither," remarked Bodilis sadly. "She has nothing to offer you but her utter love."

He bit back a retort that any dog could do as much. It would have been unkind, and not quite true. He must not blame the newest of the Nine for supplanting Dahilis; that had been no wish of her own. Guilvilis was dull, true, but she was humble and sweet and helpful; the first infant she had brought forth, Sasai, was healthy and seemed bright enough; she was carrying a second. "Read," he said.

While Bodilis did, Lanarvilis came in. Blue gown and tall white head-dress showed that she had been taking her turn as high priestess at the Temple of Belisama. Nothing less than the wish of the King would call such a one away, and it had better be business vital to the city or the Gods.

Gratillonius greeted the big blond woman courteously, as was his wont. Between them was little of the warmth he had with Bodilis or the wildfire with Forsquilis. Even when they coupled, she held back her inmost self. But they had become friends, and partners valuable to each other in the governance of Ys. "What betokens this?" she asked briskly in her native language.

"A moment," he requested in the same speech. "How fares Julia?" Her sixth and most likely last living child, the babe was frail, often ill. Some-times, when it fell out that the King visited Lanarvilis while she was keeping Dahut, the beauty, vitality, and willfulness of Dahilis's daughter seemed almost inhuman by contrast, elflike—no, catlike.

"Her fever grew so fierce yesterday that I sent for Innilis, who laid on hands and gave her medicine," replied the mother. "Today she's much better."

"Ah, good. Will you be seated?" Gratillonius gestured at a chair. After two and a half years in Ys, he had come to take that article of furniture for granted, well-nigh forgetting that it was not commonplace elsewhere.

Lanarvilis settled down. He joined her. Bodilis finished reading, passed the letter to her Sister, and likewise sat. For a while, silence took over the room, apart from the susurrus of rain outside.

Then Lanarvilis, whose lips had been moving and forefinger tracing, lowered the papyrus and said with a rueful smile, "I find my Latin worse rusted than I knew. It seems the Augustus commands you to report. But you've been sending him news of your stewardship whenever he required it."

"He wants me to come in person," Gratillonius said.

She drew a sharp breath. "Where?"

"Augusta Treverorum. You may remember hearing how he entered it in triumph early this year"—after he, Magnus Clemens Maximus, scattered the army of co-Emperor Gratianus, who was presently murdered; and Valentinianus made a peace that gave Maximus lordship over Britannia, Gallia, and Hispania, while Valentinianus retained sovereignty over Italy, Africa, and part of Illyricum. The Eastern half of the Empire stayed under Theodosius in Constantinople.

" 'Tis understandable," Gratillonius went on. "The issues are settled, the weapons fallen silent, the task no longer to seize power but to wield it. He can learn more, and better, of Ys in interviews with me than from any amount of my clumsy writing."

"And what will he do with the knowledge?" Bodilis wondered.

Gratillonius shrugged. "We shall see. Yet I have ever maintained that Maximus Augustus is the stern physician whom sick Rome needs. He'll heed my advice, if it be sound. This is among the things I'd fain discuss with you two, what my recommendations ought to be."

"He may forbid you to return here," Lanarvilis fretted.

"I doubt that. True, he need no more fear a hostile Armorica at his back. But you know how much is left to do, putting down piracy and banditry, reviving trade, weaving the whole peninsula back together. I'm in the best position to lead that work, and I've proven my loyalty to him."

"You may be gone for a long while, however."

Gratillonius nodded. "Belike so. Even on Roman roads, 'twill be more than half a month's journey, unless I kill horses. And though the conference should not fill many days, I want afterward . . . to use the opportunity."

"They'll not like it—Suffetes, votaries, commoners, all folk in Ys—having the King take leave of them."

"I've been away erenow. Granted, this may prove a lengthier absence. But no military leader will be called for, and our interior affairs prosper. As for my ceremonial and sacral tasks, they can either await my return or be delegated. I want your thoughts on all this."

Bodilis's gaze grew intent. "What else have you in mind to do?" she asked.

"Well," he said uncomfortably, "you remember that when the Christian minister Eucherius lay dying, we promised him a successor in his church. That's two years gone, and the pledge still unfulfilled, as busy as we've been. I'll seek a man we can get along with."

"That's a small matter, to Ys and in your own head," she responded. "I've come to know you, my dear. What is your true intent?"

"Very well!" he blurted. "You know how I've wished to found a Mithraeum, for the worship of the God Who is mine. I cannot, unless first I've won the rank of Father in the Mystery. My hope is to find a temple where this can be done."

Lanarvilis looked shocked. Bodilis remained calm: "You may search through a vast territory, if I've heard aright about the persecution of that faith."

"Oh, I wouldn't. Mithras is a soldier. First and foremost, He expects a man to do his duty. But if I went as far south as, say, Lugdunum—I'd need permission, but I suppose I can get it—I should at least learn whether any such congregation is left within my reach."

"Would your elevation take long?"

"I trust not. Once, aye, years; but there are so few of us these days, and our needs are so urgent. I promise I'll not seek consecration if it demands more time than Ys can spare."

"I see." She glanced away, thoughtful.

"This is unwise," said Lanarvilis nervously. "Your breaking of traditions has already caused discord in abundance. If now the King, high priest and Incarnation of Taranis, openly gives allegiance to a foreign God—"

"I've made no secret of my prayers," Gratillonius answered. "Never in aught that matters have I failed to give the Gods of Ys Their due. Nor will I." He felt an emptiness as he said that. In his soul he had forsworn Them. "Have we become Christians here, to deny respect to everything divine other than the Lord of our narrow sect?" He forced a grin. "Or sects, rather. They might as well have a dozen different Christs, the way they quarrel about His nature."

Dubious, she yielded. "Well, we can be tactful."

"Aye." Bodilis leaned across the table and laid her hand over his. "Dear, if you are going to Lugdunum, and not terribly belated, would it be too much farther for you to come home through Burdigala?"

"What?" he asked, startled.

Her smile was wistful. "You remember how for years I've been in correspondence with Magnus Ausonius, the poet and rhetor. He's retired to his estate there. If you could bring him my greetings, and carry back an account of him as a person, it would be—almost like meeting him myself."

Pity touched Gratillonius. Her life was not impoverished. More than the perquisites of a Queen, she had the riches of her spirit. But she had never traveled beyond the island of Sena in the west and the frontier of the Ysan hinterland in the east, a few leagues away. The glories of Greece, Rome, all the great civilizations of the Mediterranean and the Orient, existed for her only in books, letters, and the conversation of an occasional visitor. Bound by Imperial law and military discipline, he nonetheless had freedoms she could but dream of. "Why, indeed," sprang from him, "if I can, indeed I will."

3

Again the King stood on the dais in the council chamber of the basilica, at his back the twenty-four legionaries remaining to him, behind them the eidolons of the Triad, and before him the Gallicenae and magnates of Ys. He wore a robe inwoven with gold-threaded tapestry figures to represent the eagle and thunderbolts of Taranis. In sight upon his breast hung the Key, and to his right, deputy Adminius had received the Hammer.

The garb was a part of his message, for at the quarterly meetings he had not dressed quite this grandly, and in everyday life he picked clothing simple and serviceable. It told the assembly that today he was not the blunt-spoken soldier with whom they handled the affairs of the city; he was embodied Power, secular and sacred. Several of the councillors must have anticipated this, for they too were in antique vestures or in Roman togas.

Still, after the invocations, Gratillonius used plain language. Oratory was not among his gifts, and while he had become fluent in Ysan, a number of its subtleties would always elude him, First he summarized the situation in the Western Empire and the reason why he hoped for a better future, at least in those parts where Maximus had control.

"What are the Augustus's plans for us?" growled Soren Cartagi.

"That we shall learn," Gratillonius told them. "I am bidden to his presence."

The news drew the storm of protest he had expected. He let Lanarvilis and Bodilis do most of his arguing for him. Although unprepared, a few joined in on their side, such as Sea Lord Adruval Tyri and Mariner Councillor Bomatin Kusuri. Their grounds were practical. "In Roman eyes, our King is an officer of the army and the state," Adruval reminded. "If he goes not when ordered, that's insubordination. D'ye want a legion coming to winkle him out of here?"

Vindilis's lean features whitened. "Let them dare!" she cried.

"Nay, now, be wise, my Sister," Quinipilis urged. Her voice was unsteady; in the past year or so she had much weakened. "How could we stand them off?"

"The Gods—"

Forsquilis the seeress interrupted in a tone low and carrying: "I think the Gallicenae may no longer be able to raise the Gods in aid; and They Themselves are troubled. For the heavens have moved from the Sign of the Ram to the Sign of the Fish, and the old Age dies as the new comes to birth." Her gaze dropped and her hand passed across her robe, under which a life swelled toward its own forthcoming.

"Will the Emperor let our King return?" asked Innilis. She sounded terrified.

"Why not?" said Bomatin. "He's been doing a masterly job here."

"Doing it for Rome," Hannon Baltisi, Lir Captain, snarled. He raised his arm. "Oh, I agree he's served us well. I don't believe he'd willingly do us an evil turn. But what will he have to say about things?"

"Aye." Soren nodded his massive head. "When Rome was caught up in its tribulations and forgot Ys, we stayed free. Now there's a strong Emperor, the kind who always wants more power—and more cash—and he's become aware of us. What's next?"

Gratillonius decided he had better assert himself. "Hold!" he boomed. "Hear me!" Having gotten silence, he adopted an easy manner:

"My Queens and worthies, bethink you. What's to fear? I served under Maximus when we cast the wild men back from the Wall. I know him for a man able and well-intentioned. He'll listen to me.

"Consider what Ys has done for him. We kept Armorica quiet. We saved Gallia from what would have been a ruinous barbarian attack. We have taken the lead in rebuilding defenses throughout the peninsula. Commerce begins to revive as the risks diminish. Folk should soon start reconstructing what's been destroyed. Maximus must be a madman to wish this changed; and he is not. That's the more so when he still has to reckon with the untamed Germani and Alani and, it may be, his fellow Emperors in the South and East. Far from helpless, Ys is in an excellent bargaining position.

"I'd liefer not brag, but this and more we have done under my guidance. And I have been not only your King, but also the prefect of Rome."

"Then be glad if we can renew our ties to Rome the Mother!"

There was some discreet applause, some reservation, several faces that stayed troubled. Hannon Baltisi scowled, cleared his throat, and rasped:

"Well and good, O King, save for this, that Rome has long since become whore to Christ. Need I recall to you how they mock the Gods there, violate temples, smash images, hound worshippers? Will Christ dwell in peace with the Gods of Ys, those Gods who alone hold Ocean at bay?"

Mumbles and whispers passed among the forty-two. The legionaries who formed Gratillonius's honor guard kept still, but he could virtually feel resentment radiate from most of them at such a denunciation of their faith. He weighed his reply carefully. The old man's travels, in his days as a sea captain, had if anything reinforced his fanatical hatred of the Church; but persons more moderate were uneasy, and for cause.

"This is a question among many that I hope to take up with the Augustus," Gratillonius said. "It touches me too, not only in my royal office but in my heart." He congratulated himself on the subtlety of this reminder that he was a Mithraist. Before ground could be broken for the temple of his dreams, foundations must be laid in the minds of men. "But I'm unafraid. The fact is that the Empire continues full of people who are not Christians, a number of them in high positions. Maximus knew my beliefs when he appointed me your prefect.

"Clergy are few and far between in these parts. The Augustus should be satisfied with a new minister here for the Christians among us, just as we had before. That was a harmless man. Fate willing, I'll have a voice in choosing his successor. Rest assured, 'twill be no Ambrosius!"

Bodilis and three or four others recognized the name of the forceful bishop of Italian Mediolanum, and smiled. Relief spread visibly through the rest.

Gratillonius pursued his advantage. "To that end, I may have to search a while," he warned. "Also, 'twould be well that I make myself familiar with conditions throughout Lugdunensis, aye, and in Aquitania—" he saw Bodilis kindle, and tipped her a wink—"so that we'll be ready to cope. This will keep me away for a period of months. I'll be absent at the equinox and mayhap at the winter solstice, as well as other occasions. Yet I'll leave the city in order, fully able to steer itself that long. Surely the Gods will take no offense, when this is for the well-being of Their people."

He knew himself for a hypocrite. But his ultimate purpose was honest, and as a soldier he had never objected to ruses. He sat down on the throne, resigned to a theological dispute. Bodilis and Lanarvilis were primed to conduct it for him. Afterward would come practical topics. What should he say and seek in Treverorum? He sincerely wanted suggestions. If need be, let discussion go on for a few days.

Only a few, however. He must not keep the Emperor waiting.

4

It chanced that this was his night to spend with Innilis. Knowing how he felt, and remembering the mother, his wives tried to shift custody of Dahut so that he could see her when he visited each of them. The effort failed more often than not, since strict rotation was impossible. He might be preoccupied, perhaps out of the city altogether, in the hinterland or on the water or standing his monthly Watch at the Wood. He might have been working hard or late, and in sheer weariness bedded down alone at the royal palace. For her part, a Queen might likewise be overbusied, or having her courses, or sick. Pregnancies and childbirths had been intervening too, and bade fair to increase. Forsquilis was now fruitful, Guilvilis was again, and Maldunilis had finally decided to trouble herself about it. Moreover, the two Gallicenae with whom he did not sleep, aged Quinipilis and aging Fennalis, claimed a share in the upbringing of Dahilis's daughter, which for the sake of harmony could not be denied them.

Fortune did have Dahut at Innilis's house when King and Queen arrived on that evening. "Oh, my lord, my lady, how good you're back!" exclaimed the maidservant Evar as they entered. "The little one's been that fretful. She threw such a tantrum I feared she'd hurt herself, I did, and restrained her."

Dread struck. "Is she ill?" Gratillonius demanded.

"Nay, lord, I think not. Like a crazed ferret she's been, for dashing about and throwing things—oh, my, ferrets don't throw things, but my lord knows what I mean—'Tis but that kids are troublous in their third year. Well, she's not quite in that yet, is she? But ever so far ahead of her age, already speaking, and so much alive. With my lady gone all day—Does my lord want to see her?"

"I do." He brushed past the woman and strode to the room that had been designated a nursery.

When he opened the door, he saw the debris of small destructions strewn about, a broken toy chariot, stuffing ripped out of a rag doll, general chaos. The chamber pot stayed upright; in certain things, Dahut had a feline neatness. The child was curled on the bed, brooding over her wrongs. She had stripped off her clothes. Sunset light, striking through a windowpane, turned her skin to ivory, hair to gold, eyes to lapis lazuli. O Mithras, how she recalled Dahilis!

She gathered her limbs beneath her, again like a cat. "Father," she hissed.

"Ah," he blustered, "we've been having a mutiny, have we? What for? Why have you been such a bad girl?"

She struggled for words. "I wos . . . wos . . . *me.*"

Did she mean "all alone"? How could he tell? He hunkered down and spread his arms. "Well, well, little rebel, let's make it right again, hey?"

She uncoiled and sped to him. He hugged her withy-slimness. How sweet she smelled! "You mustn't do this, you know," he said into the warmth between her throat and shoulder. "It's not kind to your Mamas, or their poor servants who have to look after you."

"You di'n' come," she gasped; but she shed no tears, she hardly ever did.

"Oh, you were awaiting me? I'm sorry. Your Papa had work to do. Let's get you nicely dressed, and then before Evar brings you dinner we'll play horse and I'll sing you a song—because you're the single human being who does not flinch when I sing, and too soon will that end."

—Innilis ate lightly and simply. Gratillonius liked the fare her kitchen offered, after the frequently elaborate meals he got in Ys. She had learned to give him portions of adequate size. Ordinarily they made small talk over the table and retired early, for although she often showed him affection, they had few interests in common. This evening she spoke earnestly. The glow of beeswax candles lay over the delicate features and in the big eyes.

"Sometimes I fear for Dahut," she said. He could barely hear. "There is something about her."

He harked back to a night on Sena, and a day when a seal had saved the child from drowning, and incidents more fugitive. It took courage to reply, "Mayhap we see the beginnings of a destiny. Or mayhap not. Who can say? I've scant faith in astrologers or fortune tellers. Let's take each day as it comes. We must anyhow."

"Oh, I thought not of the occult. I meant only—well, I've fretted about this, and talked with Vindilis—Vindilis and others—Do we do right, shunting her from household to household, with never a den where she can snuggle down? Is this why she's wild?"

He frowned. "I know not. How could I? She's my first-born." Unless he was the casual begetter of a brat or two in Britannia, of which transgression he hoped Mithras had absolved him. "And the King of Ys can't be a real paterfamilias. Has not the Sisterhood always shared in the raising of a princess whose mother died?"

"Aye, but I think never like this. You are different. And Dahut is. I cannot put it in words, I'm too weak and stupid to understand it, but Vindilis says—You *are* the bringer of a new Age, and you did father Dahut."

Different, he thought, indeed different. The daughter of Dahilis is so spirited, so intelligent and beautiful.

—After Innilis miscarried, he had agreed with Vindilis that henceforward she should use the Herb. The next stillbirth could kill her, or the next live birth give another pitiful Audris. Six fertile Queens were ample.

She had not asked him to refrain from making love to her. He had found his way to what was best: much kissing and caressing, then much gentleness, for a single time. About half such joinings seemed to give her pleasure, and the rest no distress. At least, she cuddled close afterward.

This night she stayed awake a while, which was unusual. He could feel how she tensed and faintly shivered against him. "What vexes you?" he asked. When she grew evasive, he pressed the query. In the end she confessed:

"Oh, you, Grallon, fear about you." She seldom gave him his proper name any more but, like an increasing number of Ysans and Osismii, softened it. "You're bound away."

"I'll return," he said.

She drew a ragged breath. "Aye, since you've promised it. But how long will you stay? You surely yearn back to your homeland."

He lay for a spell, unspeaking. The question haunted him too, but nobody else had raised it. He was astounded that this meek person should. And what in Ahriman's name was the answer?

Of course there was a great deal yet to do in Ys, and he hated leaving a task unfinished. The challenge here called him beyond himself. The making of a useful thing in statecraft was muddled and never really complete, unlike the making of a thing in woodcraft. Just the same, the satisfactions bore no comparison to each other. He had shaped history and law, he had raised bulwarks for the lives of people. . . . What would come of it all? A barbarian wave had broken itself against Ys, but the tide of barbarism was still at the flow, over land as well as sea. Could he abandon the defenses he had been building?

And yet, never to have a son, if it was true what chronicles and belief said. To abide among aliens until the last death-fight in the Wood made an end of him—

And meanwhile, would those duties truly have been so important? Once the rule of Maximus was firm, his peace would soon reach this far. Likewise, in due course, would his law. What then would be left for the King of Ys? Ceremonies; routines; judgments that made a difference to the parties concerned but were yawnfully tedious for the judge, and as readily rendered by somebody else.

Even now, calm was descending. Though northern Britannia seemed again troubled, the rest of that diocese lay secure. Communications had redeveloped to the point where Gratillonius had had three letters from his father, and sent back replies. To visit the villa once more! Not that he'd accept the wretched curial existence of his free will; but he shouldn't have to. Given the tiniest hint, Maximus Augustus ought to confer senatorial rank on a man who had served him well. And mighty work remained to do in the outer world, reform of the state, subjugation of the barbarians, binding of wounds upon Mother Rome, winning of fame immortal.

Was that his wish?

If not, why not? Ys would never consentingly let its King depart for good. In the past he had wondered about cutting his way free, he and his legionaries or a rescue expedition from outside. But that thought was obsolete—which gladdened him, because he recoiled from any idea of killing his subjects. Come the time, he need merely make a pretext for another journey, and fail to return. It wouldn't hurt the city's institutions too badly. Precedents existed; not every king had died in the Wood. The Suffetes would get somebody—until, no doubt, the Christians came to power here also, and made an end of those bloody successions.

Three years hence, let us say, what reason would Gratillonius have to dwell in Ys?

Well, status, friends, his wives, or certain among them, and Dahut, whom he could smuggle out but would that be the best thing for her?

Innilis nestled against him, weeping most quietly. "Nay, I will abide," he said, and wondered how much of a liar he was, "as long as the Gods allow."

II

1

"Again the tuba, the tuba calling:
'Come, legionary, get off your duff!'
The hobnails rising, the hobnails falling,
We're bound for glory, or some such stuff.
Farewell, dear wenches! There's time to kiss you
And gulp a beaker before we go.
The Lord on high knows how we will miss you,
So give us memories that will glow."

It was one of the old, interminable, nonsensical songs that men had sung as they marched from Pontus to Hispania, from Egypt to Caledonia, and beyond, in the service of Rome. Footfalls crashed rhythmically beneath its beat. Words rang into the woodlands bordering the highway, until they lost themselves among trees and shadows. This was mostly second-growth forest, beech, elm, hornbeam, though here and there gloomed a huge oak, hallowed perhaps since before the first Caesar, until cultivation died away a hundred or more years ago. Leaves were still thick, full of greenish-gold light, but some had begun to turn color. The air below was windless, cool, scented by damp earth. Overhead were fewer wings than last month; many birds had, by now, departed south.

Riding at the front of his two dozen infantrymen and their pack animals, Gratillonius saw stone pavement run straight before him until, at a dim distance, it went from sight in one of those curves that had been the engineers' reluctant concession to terrain. Behind him lay turbulent Condate Redonum, where soldiers of his had nearly gotten into a fight with members of the Frankish garrison. Ahead, he had been informed, was the Liger valley, rich and well populated as of yore. At Juliomagus he would swing east and follow the great river for a while. His route was not the shortest possible, but almost entirely, it followed roads like this. Spared slogging through mud in the wet season, and most often spared the toil of preparing a walled and ditched camp—because well-secured official hostels stood along the way, near which they could simply pitch their tents—the men should make their best time to Augusta Treverorum.

They were eager too. While they had all become fond of Ys, and several had formed strong ties, the hankering to be back among things Roman was only natural. That had been a large part of his reason for taking the whole twenty-four as his escort, and nobody else. As for the rest of his reason, he wasn't quite sure, but he had a notion that Magnus Maximus would not take kindly to a spokesman native to witchy Ys.

Otherwise his feelings were happy. He also was bound home to his people.

"I'm getting old and my joints are creaky,
The lentils grumble within my gut,
My tentmates snore and the tent is leaky,
And come a combat, I might get cut.
But never mind, we have got our orders.
So cheer up, fellows, for I do think
When we have crossed over foreign borders
There will be wenches, and lots to drink!"

" *'O-old!'* " Adminius cried. The deputy could bring a surprising volume out of his narrow chest. "Battle ranks!"

Gratillonius heard clatter and scramble. He drew rein. Gravel scrunched to silence on the shoulder where he rode. Glancing back, he saw the vexillation quickly bring the animals together and themselves in position either to protect or attack. He'd kept them in crack training.

Adminius trotted over to him. "Being cautious, sir," he said. "Wot does the centurion want we should do?"

Gratillonius peered ahead. No danger was obvious in the mounted man who had come around the curve and was galloping their way. As he spied them, he waved and shouted frantically, and kicked his horse to go faster. The beast was sweaty but not yet lathered; it hadn't carried him far. The man was portly, with black hair cut short and a close-cropped fringe of beard in the Roman style, but tunic and trousers showed him to be a Gaul. Soon Gratillonius made out a dull-red splotch on his left thigh, from which edges of cloth flapped back. A flesh wound. That went with the condition of the horse.

"No pursuit," Adminius deemed. " 'E's escaped. Didn't seem worth chasing, I s'pose." He squirted a gob of spit from a gap between teeth. His thin, sandy-stubbled face crinkled in a grin. "Well, they didn't know anybody like us was anywhere near, eh, sir?"

Beneath Gratillonius's calm went an ugly thrill. "We'll wait and hear what he's got to say."

The Gaul halted in front of them. For a moment the only sounds were the whickering breath of the horse and the man's gasps. His eyes rolled. At length he got out, "Romans! Legionaries! God be praised! Quick, and you may yet save us!"

The Latin was fairly good, with an accent that Gratillonius recognized as that of the Namnetes. He had come as far south as their seaport two years ago, when he was trying to link the cities of the littoral in cooperation against barbarians and neutrality in the civil war. "The sooner you make sense and tell me what the matter is, the sooner we may be able to do something about it," he snapped.

"Bacaudae—" The man groaned.

"That's no news. Let's have facts."

The stranger gulped, shuddered, mastered himself in some degree. "My wagon train . . . goods out of Armorica and Britannia . . . left Redonum. . . . Bishop Arator and his attendants joined us there, bound for a conference in Portus Namnetum. We'd been told the route was safe. I b-b-brought guards anyway, of course. But now, in th-th-this forsaken stretch . . . suddenly, there they were, scores of the vilest robbers springing out of the woods and—" He plucked at Gratillonius's wrist. "God aided me to flee, because I found you. Don't delay! It's only two or three leagues. The guards will fight. You can get there in time. God calls you!"

The centurion spent a flash considering. His mission took primacy. However, his squadron should be a match for any plausible number of outlaws; banditry required suppression; and if word got about that he had been less than zealous in the cause of a prelate, he might as well turn land pirate himself. Worse could be the consequences to Ys.

"On the move!" he barked. Adminius shouted commands. Metal gleamed as the formation reshaped itself and started off.

The Gaul kept his horse alongside Gratillonius's. "Can't you go faster?" he pleaded.

The centurion shook his head. "Three or four miles at a dead run in full armor wouldn't leave the boys fit for much. We'll do what we can. I promise nothing. We may find everybody in your convoy lying throat-cut, and your merchandise gone with your animals. In that case, I can't pursue. We're on urgent business of the state. I can only ask the garrison commander in Juliomagus to try for vengeance."

He felt no great excitement. If he could save yonder folk and kill marauders, that was fine. It depended on how long the guards could hold
out. The steady, relentless tramp at his back had carried Rome's eagles
across the world.

"Tell me what to expect," he said. "First, what strength did you have?"

The merchant swung his hands and sometimes keened over the loss he
might suffer, but piece by piece, the tale came forth. He was one Florus, a
dealer in fabrics. With money what it was these days, he most commonly
traded rather than bought and sold, which meant he handled a variety,
not just cloths but leathers, furs, raw materials. "This trip my best acqui-
sition was a consignment of those wonderful weavings they do in Ys, that
have scarcely been seen for many years, oh, priceless. . . ." The train
consisted of four mule-drawn wagons; their drivers; the reverend bishop
with two priests and four deacons; Florus himself; and six guards, toughs
who hired out for this kind of duty despite the law frowning on it. Two
were Gauls, three were Frankish laeti, and one was a brown-skinned
person who said nothing about himself but might well be a deserter from
the army. "We take what we can get, right, centurion? We make do." The
guards had sword or ax, plus a few spears. Their armor amounted to
boiled leather jackets, cheap kettle helmets, shields of barbarian type.
Then, to be sure, the muledrivers possessed knives, cudgels, whips. And
three of the deacons were young and sturdy, equipped with stout walking
staffs. "They should be able to fend off the evildoers a while, don't you
think? But hurry, hurry!"

"How did you get away?" Gratillonius inquired.

"Oh, I was mounted, by the mercy of God, and when they swarmed
out it was clear what they intended, and by God's grace they didn't close
a line across the road to the north before I'd gone past. They almost did.
You can see where a spear hurt me. Do you have a surgeon with you? Or
at least poultices? This kind of injury inflames so readily. It hurts me
abominably."

"We're not stopping for anything just yet, friend. Why did you flee?
One more *man* defending might make all the difference."

"But I had to get help. God saw to it that I could get help." Florus's
voice sank to a mutter. "That means the goods will be safe, doesn't it, O
Lord? You'd not let Your faithful servant be ruined, almighty God Who
delivers us from evil."

Gratillonius snorted and sent his horse a little ahead.

Slowly the tumult became visible from afar. Noise drifted thin. Gratillonius signalled for double time. He was tempted to speed in advance for
a better look. It was getting hard to see any distance as the sun declined

and dusk began to seep out of the earth. He resisted the impulse. He had no right to take unnecessary risks. Solitary heroics were for barbarians and fools.

Yonder they grew aware of his approaching force. He saw the struggle die down, like a wave that smashed itself on a reef outside Ys, recoiled in foam, and dwindled away. The next wave was coming. . . .

He reined in and jumped to the ground. The men saw his intention and needed but a minute to tether the horses. "You, keep out of the way!" he told Florus. He unslung his shield from the harness, slipped the retaining strap over his neck, gripped the handle, drew blade, and took his place as leader. The squadron advanced.

Nearing, he saw that the battle was almost done. The travelers had given a good account of themselves. Somehow they'd gotten three wagons on the sides of a square, cutting loose the mules, which might well panic. There hadn't been time to bring the fourth around, it stood off where the robbers must have led it, but a crude little fort existed. While three guards held fast at the open side, their comrades and certain of the other men repelled foes who sought to climb over the vehicles or crawl underneath.

Yet they could not long keep off assailants whom Gratillonius estimated to number thirty. As he guessed at once, they were still alive—some of them—only because the bandits lacked proper training and discipline. After being cast back with losses, the outlaws milled around, none wanting to be the first to meet that steel again. They tried to bargain. Gratillonius learned afterward that the bishop had strengthened the will to resist, calling on divine help, while he cleverly strung the talk out. At length the brigands lost patience and made a fresh charge. It failed likewise, though at heavy cost to the defenders.

After that, the attackers resorted to slings. Kept up, the bombardment would have done its job. The travelers took wounds and a couple more deaths. However, they had enough protection to be difficult targets, and eventually the supply of missiles was exhausted. Yet the defense was now so weakened that the bandit leader could egg his men on to a third assault. It broke through and was in among the wagons when the legionaries arrived.

Gratillonius took his troop toward chaos. The outlaws were Gauls, in ragged, filthy garb, pieced out with hides or old blankets or whatever else came to hand. Hair and beards were matted, greasy manes, out of which glared faces gaunt, scarred, weatherbeaten. Shoes were agape, rudely mended, or mere bags of skin stuffed with grass. The barbarians who raided Britannia were better off. Weapons were spears, knives, pruning hooks, firewood axes, a few swords acquired somehow. The wielders screamed hatred and defiance at the Romans. At the same time, those on the fringe were pulling back, making for the trees, in disorderly fashion. They knew that if they stood their ground they'd be butcher's meat.

Which was exactly what they ought to be. "Right and left!" Gratillonius called. "Circle them!" He leading a detachment, Adminius its mate, his men hastened to bag as many as they could.

Those inside the laager could not readily disengage from opponents who, heartened, fought furiously. It had never been a proper battle at all, but more like a riot. It pushed combatants apart, flung them against their fellows, sent them tripping over each other. Somebody fallen but alive might grab at an ankle or cling to a spearshaft. Wrestlers on the ground further impeded everyone.

First from the soldiers went the terrible flight of javelins. Meant for use against shields, here they struck unprotected flesh. Men fell, writhed, shrieked. Those who tried to help them to safety were themselves delayed. And then the legionaries were upon them.

A fair-haired youth with downy whiskers attempted to dodge past Gratillonius. The centurion gave him the sword between rib cage and pelvis, forcing the blade right and left to make sure of the liver. Flesh resisted softly, heavily, helplessly. The lad went down. Before Gratillonius could pull his weapon free, a full-grown man was at him, weeping, howling, belly wide open as he swung his arms back for an ax blow. Gratillonius rammed the boss of his shield into the solar plexus. Breath whooped from the Gaul. He dropped his ax and fell to his knees. Gratillonius crashed the bottom rim of his shield against the man's temple. The Gaul crumpled.

Gratillonius had delivered a knockout blow he hoped wasn't fatal. He wanted prisoners to bring to Juliomagus for beheading, or whatever the judgment would be—examples. He withdrew his sword. Blood pumped forth. A stump end of gut protruded past the tattered shirt. "Mother," the youth wailed, over and over. Gratillonius went on. The whole episode had taken just a minute or two, scarcely interrupting the rhythm of onslaught.

He saw a cluster of men pass under the trees, disappearing amidst boles and brush. They bore along a figure robed and struggling. He had no chance to think about it. He only had a fleeting perception of one who seemed in charge, slender, swift of motion, uniquely well-clad. After that, Gratillonius was busy finishing the engagement.

—The legionaries had suffered no harm worth mentioning. Of the travelers, besides Florus, there survived, slashed and battered but reasonably hale, two Frankish men-at-arms, three drivers, a priest, and a deacon. The rest lay stretched out on the roadside, blood wiped off as best might be, dead or dying. The clergyman had already prayed over them.

And Bishop Arator was missing.

As for the robbers, a full twelve had fallen in battle or, hopelessly wounded, received the mercy stroke. Their bodies were stacked on the opposite side of the road. Nobody had cleansed them, closed staring eyes or tied up fallen jaws, but the kindly shadows were well on the way to covering them. Six captives sat bound to the wagons.

Nobody said much. Most of the survivors were still too stunned. Now and then pain made somebody moan. Otherwise they huddled, shivered, looked emptily before them, clutched the bread and wine that had been passed out. The soldiers were in full self-possession but occupied with making a safe camp, since they would spend the night here. An occasional sentence, grunt, oath sounded beneath the thud of axes, the sucking noise as spades turned wet humus.

Gratillonius and Florus had drawn aside at the latter's request, away from the dead, wounded, captured, the thickening blood puddles. As yet, the sky and the crowns of trees were bright overhead. A few rays slanted golden through the westside gloom. Only a hint of chill was in the air. Crows cawed.

"But the bishop is gone," Florus wailed. "A holy man, a lord of the Church, borne off by a gang of sacrilegious murderers! I'll never live down the scandal, never. And my mules, my well-trained carters, lost! Why could you not make better speed?"

"I told you," Gratillonius said wearily. "If you mean to complain at the garrison, spare your breath. Any competent officer will understand. Be glad we saved what we did and can help you finish your journey."

His command would have to do that. The chances of some other group coming along, whom he could dump the chore onto, were slight, as feeble as traffic had become. He couldn't leave these people without escort when a dozen outlaws were still at large. The delay in his own progress would be excused him. Though the Christians would be aghast at what had happened to a veritable bishop—

"*Hs-s-s,*" whispered from the brush. "Roman, listen."

Gratillonius spun about. He saw nothing but tangled green, murk behind it. Helmetless in the aftermath of battle, the breeze cool upon his brow, did he hear a rustling?

"Hs-s-s," went the voice again. "Hark'ee."

"What's this?" yelped Florus. "Are the murderers back? Help! To arms!"

Gratillonius caught him by the nape and squeezed till he whimpered.

"Be still," the centurion said, never looking away from the forest. "Go back to your wagons and say nothing. I'll handle this."

"But—you can't—"

"Begone and shut up, or I'll have you flogged."

He let go. Florus stumbled off, half sobbing. Gratillonius spoke softly: "Who are you?"

"The Bacauda chief. Make no move, if you want your bishop back alive."

Something eased in Gratillonius. He heard himself chuckle. "Very well," he said. "Now how shall we go about bargaining?"

2

The centurion's tent was large enough for two men to sit in, on its floor which kept out the dampness of the soil. Its walls likewise withstood autumnal cold. Outside, a wind had arisen after nightfall, to rush through branches, whirl dead leaves away, rattle the leather of the tent and make its poles tremble. Within, a lantern threw dull highlights onto faces, against monstrous shadows.

"Your price is high," Gratillonius said.

Rufinus shrugged and grinned. "One bishop for six Bacaudae. Take it or leave it. Myself, I think I'm being swindled."

Gratillonius peered at him. His invited visitor was young, about nineteen or twenty he guessed, though the spirit behind the green eyes seemed as old as the night wind. Rufinus was of medium height, much of it in his legs, and wirily built. Features otherwise sharp and regular were marred by the scar of a cut, poorly treated, puckering his right cheek and giving his mouth the hint of a perpetual sneer. Though his beard was still scanty, he kept it trimmed in an unconventional fork. His black hair was also short, and reasonably clean, as were the rest of his person and his clothes. Faded, many times patched or darned, shirt and breeches were of stout material. A deerskin jerkin gave additional protection, and he had doffed a cowled cloak. His footgear was clearly from no shoemaker's shop, but just as clearly made to his measure with a degree of skill. At his belt were a pouch, a knife, and a Roman sword.

"You put me in a cleft stick," Gratillonius said. "Unless I let dangerous bandits go free, what will become of the bishop?"

"He'll be butchered like a hog," Rufinus answered coolly. "Before then, maybe some of the boys will use him."

"What?"

"Well, we seldom see a woman, you know. Though in this case, it'd be revenge more than lust. *I* wouldn't want that withered prune."

Fury thickened in Gratillonius's throat. He could barely stay where he was, and not assail the other. "You rotten snake!"

Rufinus lifted a palm. "Hold on," he said. "I'm only warning, not threatening. I'd forbid such a thing if I could. But I'm no army officer. We're free men, we Bacaudae. We choose our leaders ourselves, and follow their orders if and when we want to. My gang is enraged. If they don't get their friends back—if, instead, those fellows go off to death, maybe first to torture—I can't stand in the way of their justice. They'd kick me aside."

He leaned forward. His Latin flowed easily despite rough accent, sloppy grammar, and idioms strange to Gratillonius. "As is," he said, "I'll hear curses aplenty when they learn they won't get a ransom besides the exchange. I wonder how you dare hold back stuff that could make you sure of your holy man."

Gratillonius returned a grim smile. "He's not my holy man. I'll have to answer for whatever happens. Leave me this much to show. If you won't, well, I need just report that no meeting took place." He didn't know if he could bring himself to that. Certainly he could not if put under oath. However, he needn't reveal his vulnerability. "Besides, think. You'll have to go far and fast, before the garrison comes after you. This wood isn't too big for them to beat. Four of our prisoners are too hurt to walk much. They'll encumber you enough, without adding boxes of goods."

Rufinus laughed. "Right! That's how come I gave in on that point. I did hope for some solidi, but you win."

He grew serious, with an underlying liveliness that never seemed to leave him. "How's this sound? We meet at sunrise. You keep your men in camp. We're woodsrunners; we'll know whether you're honest about that. We'll show up half a mile south with the bishop. One of us'll stand by him —me—ready to kill if anything goes sour. You release our four disabled buddies and give time for us to carry them well away. Then two of you bring our two hale down the road. You can have their hands tied and leashes on them, and you can have swords, but no javelins. We stop a few yards apart and let our hostages go, both sides. The bishop's slow on his feet, so I'll release him first, but you've got to release ours while he's still near enough for me to dash up and stab him. Naturally, you can pay us back in kind if I play you false. We scamper off into the woods and you return to camp. Satisfied?"

Gratillonius pondered. This was a quick intelligence he dealt with.

"The leashes will be long, so your fellows can't bolt off after we let go," he decided. "When they reach you, you can cut the cords."

Again Rufinus laughed. "Done! You're a workman, Gratillonius. Be damned if I don't like you."

In his relief, the centurion couldn't help smiling back. "Aren't you damned already?"

Mercurially, the Gaul turned somber. "No doubt, if it's true what the Christians say. But then I expect the fire for me won't be so hot as what they keep for the great landowners and senators. Do you really know the masters you serve?"

Memories crowded on Gratillonius. He scowled. "Better them than outright banditry. I've seen enough places looted and burnt, women who'd been raped over and over, children and oldsters killed for fun, that I've no lost no sleep after striking down what reavers I could—be they barbarians or Romans."

Rufinus gave him a long look before murmuring, "You aren't from hereabouts, are you?"

"N-no, I'm a Briton. But these past two years and more I've been in Armorica. Osismiic country, that is."

"I don't believe there're any Bacaudae that far west."

"There aren't. Most of it's been picked too clean. Ys alone has stayed well off, because it's got ways to keep the wolves out."

Rufinus sat straight. His eyes caught the lantern light as they widened. "Ys," he breathed. "You've *been* there?"

"I've operated in the area." Gratillonius's instinct was to reveal no more to an enemy than was unavoidable. "Now I'm on a different mission. I planned no fight with you. Nor did those wayfarers you attacked. For whatever you've suffered, blame yourselves."

"Ys, the city of fable—" Rufinus broke off, shook himself, spoke sharply. "I've never been yon way, of course, but I can guess what kind of 'wolves' you're thinking of. Saxons and Scoti for the most part, hey? And some Gauls who took the chance to go looting around after everything was wreckage—though I'll bet a lot of those were driven to it by hunger. Where was the Roman state that taxed them and ordered them about, where was it when they needed it? But anyhow, they were not Bacaudae."

"Do you mean you're something else than marauders?"

"I do." With bitterness: "You wouldn't care to listen. I'll go now. See you in the morning."

"No, wait!" Gratillonius thought for a moment. "If you'll stay a while, I'll hear you out."

"How's that?" Rufinus asked, surprised. He had gotten up. His movements were apt to be quick, nervous, but deft.

"Well, you see," Gratillonius explained, "I am a Briton, and my time in Gallia has all been at the far western end, except for a march there from Gesoriacum. But I may be, well, in future I may be having business elsewhere. I can handle it better if I know how things are. All I know of the Bacaudae is that they're vagabond gangs of runaway serfs, slaves, every sort of riffraff. I mean, that's all I've heard. Is there more to it?"

Rufinus stared down at the big, blunt-featured, auburn-haired man. "You're a deeper one than you make out," he said low. "I'd give a bit to learn what your business really is. But—Look here. What I've got to tell won't please you. It'll be the truth, but the truth about Rome. I'm not after another fight."

"I don't want any either. Say what you will, and if I get angry, I'll hold it in. I may or may not believe you, but . . . I've had worse foes than you."

Rufinus's smile glistened forth, bad though his teeth were. "The same right back at you, Gratillonius! Let's." He lowered himself.

The centurion rose in turn. "How about some wine to help our tongues along?"

—The tale came out in shards. Sometimes Rufinus japed, sometimes he struggled not to weep. Gratillonius plied him with drink and questions, and meanwhile tried to fit events together in his mind. Later he would try to understand.

Rufinus was born to a smallholder near the latifundium of Maedraeacum in the canton of the Redones, about twenty miles northwest of Condate Redonum. Albeit impoverished, the family was close-knit and had its joys. Rufinus, the youngest, especially liked herding swine in the woods, where he taught himself trapping and the use of the sling. Yet even before his birth, the vise was closing. The best of the land had been engulfed by the manors. Imperial regulation made needed goods costly when they were available at all. Such transactions were generally furtive, while farmers had no choice but to sell their produce openly, under strict price control. Meanwhile taxes climbed out of sight. Rufinus's father more and more sought refuge in the cup. Finally, his health destroyed, he coughed himself to death one winter.

Rather than let children of hers be sold into slavery for back taxes, the widow conveyed the farm to Sicorus, owner of Maedraeacum, and the family became his coloni—serfs. They were bound to the soil, compelled to deference and obedience, required to do labor for their lord and, after working for themselves, pay more than half the crop over to him. Their grain they must have ground at his mill and at his price. There were no more forest days for Rufinus. Thirteen years old, he was now a field hand, his knees each evening ashake with weariness.

The following year his pretty older sister Ita became the concubine of Sicorus. She could not be forced, under the law. However, he could offer easements for her kin—such as not assigning her brothers to the most brutal tasks—and for her it was a way out of the kennel. Rufinus, who adored her, stormed to the manor house to protest. The slaves there drove him off with blows. He ran away. Sicorus coursed him down with hounds, brought him back, and had him flogged. The law permitted chastisement of contumacious coloni.

For another year, he bided his time. Whispers went along the hedges and in the woodlots; men slipped from their hovels to meet by twilight; news seeped across this narrow horizon. It came oftenest on the lips of wanderers who had made their lifework the preaching of sedition. The Empire had rotted to worthlessness, they said; Frankish laeti at Redonum sacrificed human beings to heathen Gods; raiders harried the coasts, while war bands afoot struck deep in from the East. Meanwhile the fat grew fatter, the powerful grew ever more overbearing. Had not Christ Himself denounced the rich? Was not the hour overpast to humble them and take back what they had wrung from the working poor? The Last Day drew nigh, Antichrist walked the world; your sacred duty was to resist him. Righteous men had sworn themselves to a brotherhood, the Bacaudae, the Valiant. . . .

Ita's death in childbed was the last thing Rufinus endured. After that, he planned his next escape carefully, and found his way to the nearest Bacauda encampment.

—"We're no saints, oh, no, no," he hiccoughed. By then he was fairly drunk. "I learned that soon enough. Some amongst us are beasts of prey. The rest're rough. I give you that. But the most of us, the most of us, we only wanted to live in peace. We only wanted to till our plots of ground, and keep the fruits of our work, and have our honor under the law."

"How do you live?" Gratillonius asked. He had matched the Gaul stoup for stoup, but he was larger and not half starved.

"Oh, we hunt. What a pleasure that is, when we know we're poaching! We raise a little garden truck in the wilds. We rob when we can, from the rich, like that futtering smug trader today, but we swap the loot in honest wise for what we need. And merchants who pass through sections, regular-like, where we are, they pay toll. They're not s'posed to, but they do, undercover, and save 'emselves trouble. And our own people, serfs who've not fled and what few small freehold farmers are left, they help us out, for love."

"For love. Indeed." Gratillonius made his voice heavy with sarcasm. "I'm a farm boy myself. I know farmers. What you say sounds exactly like them."

"Well, we're fighting their war," Rufinus declared. "It's only right for them to pay their share. Food, clothes, that sort of thing. Besides, we protect 'em against bandits."

Gratillonius shrugged. He could well imagine what their protection consisted of. Cotters who declined it were apt to find their roofs ablaze or their throats slit.

Rufinus read his thought and said defensively, "It *can* be for love. How d'you think I got this outfit of mine?"

By charm, Gratillonius imagined. This young man had an abundance of that. Let him enter the drabness that was the life of some isolated, poverty-stricken wife—in and out of it, like bursts of sunshine when wind drove clouds across heaven, like an elf by moonlight— If every Bacauda were as glib, the band today would have looked a great deal less scruffy.

Still, said Gratillonius's stubborn mind, Rufinus was in fact as neat and clean as possible in his kind of existence: which revealed something about him.

The centurion shifted the subject toward matters of more immediate interest. "Well, then, have you Bacaudae a secret kingdom that considers itself at war with Rome, the way the Persians usually are? That doesn't square with what I've heard. But tell me."

"M-m, no, not really," Rufinus admitted. "We do have emperors—an emperor for each region—but he doesn't do much except lead his own group and be at the head of the gatherings, when several groups meet. We call the head of any other band its duke." His sardonic tone implied that the title didn't mean "leader" but was a deliberate parody of Roman organization. "I'm the duke of mine."

"A bit young for that, aren't you?"

"There are no old Bacaudae," Rufinus said quietly. Gratillonius remembered Alexander of Macedon. For that matter, he himself was twenty-five when he became King of Ys.

"We do make our deals," the Gaul went on in a rush, as the wine sent another tide through his head. "I've heard of bargains struck with Scotian or Saxon. Our folk'd guide 'em to a manor, they'd sack it but in return let the serfs be. And I got friendly with a Scotian—fled his homeland, he did, on account of a feud, and came to us—he told me 'bout Hivernia, where Rome never ruled, where they've always been free—"

Rufinus started, stiffened, once more shook himself. "I'd better not go on," he said. "I might let too much slip out. You're a good fellow, Gra— Gra—Gradlon. But I can't let you in on any secrets of the brothers, could I, now?" He picked up his cloak and lurched to his feet. "G'night. I wish we could be friends."

"I'll take you past the sentries," the soldier offered, rising too. He would have liked to continue the conversation, but it verged on questions that might suddenly make this two-legged wildcat lash out, and his duty was to get the bishop back unharmed.

They walked together into the windy dark, mute. As they parted, they clasped hand to arm.

III

1

About fifteen miles west of Augusta Treverorum there was an official hostel where Gratillonius decided to spend the night, even though sundown was still a couple of hours off. This was doubtless the last such place till he reached the city. Starting at dawn, with nothing to do except swallow breakfast and strike tents, the soldiers should reach their destination early enough next day that he would have no trouble getting them settled in and word of his arrival borne to the Emperor. Besides, he might find no suitable campground between here and there. The hills roundabout were largely given over to vineyards, with scant room between rows. Hazed and dreamy under the declining sun, this country seemed to lie in a different world from Armorica, as did most of what he had passed through. It was as if wars, brigands, and wild men had never been, save in nightmares.

As was common, the hostel maintained an open space for military parties. Having seen his established and supper cooking, Gratillonius sought the house. The dignity of his mission required that he avail himself of it, whether or not it was the kind of fleabag he had found too often along the way.

A man stood outside. He had come forth when the legionaries arrived and watched them set up. As Gratillonius neared, he lifted a hand and said, "Greeting, my son. Peace be with you." His Latin had an odd accent; he could not be a native Gaul, though it shortly turned out that he used Gallic idioms with ease.

Gratillonius halted. Dignity also required he return courtesy, no matter how poor and unkempt the person was who offered it. This one didn't cringe or whine, either. He stood straight, spoke levelly, and looked you square in the eye. "Greeting, uncle."—what soldiers usually called an elderly man who had a bit of respect due him but not too much.

The stranger smiled. "Ah, that takes me far back. I was in the army once. Let me compliment you on the smartness of your squadron. Sadly rare these days. Not many units of old-fashioned regulars left, are there?"

"Thank you," Gratillonius looked closer.

The other carried his years well. While slenderness had become gauntness, the shoulders were wide and unbowed, and if his gait was no longer lithe it remained firm. A snub nose marked a face pallid, lined, and gaptoothed, which you barely noticed after meeting its brilliant blue gaze.

Puzzlement rose in Gratillonius. Why should somebody like that, clearly well-educated, go in a coarse dark robe, hardly fit for a slave, belted with a rope underneath a camel-hair cloak—when his footgear was stout though well-worn, bespeaking many leagues of use? Had he fallen into poverty? Then he should at least have had the pride left to keep himself clean. Streams, ponds, and public baths weren't that scarce. He had in fact laved hands and feet, but Gratillonius could smell him. Pungent rather than sour, declaring that he spent much time in the open, the odor nevertheless demeaned him . . . did it not? He shaved, but probably seldom, for white stubble covered jaws and cheeks. Likewise it bristled over the front half of his pate. Behind, hair rose wildly; it would have waved in the breeze if he had washed it.

"Well, you'll want to inspect your quarters before we eat," he said. "Shall we go in?"

Gratillonius stared. "You're lodging here?"

The old man smiled. "I'd rather sleep under God's stars or the roofs of His poor, but—" he shrugged—"a bishop traveling a main highway isn't allowed that."

Gratillonius stood a moment in his neat Roman outfit, confronting the beggarly figure, and wondered whether he had heard aright. Arator had been bedraggled when the Bacaudae released him, but his clothes were of the best, and it didn't take him long after reaching Juliomagus to reappear bathed, barbered, and resplendent. "A bishop?"

"Unworthy though I be. Martinus of Caesarodunum Turonum, at your service. May I ask your name, my son?"

Gratillonius stammered it forth, together with his rank and his legion, scarcely hearing himself. His head was awhirl.

"You are a long way from your home base, eh? I think we shall have considerable to talk about. Come." Martinus took him by the elbow and led him inside.

While he changed clothes in his room, Gratillonius tried to put his thoughts in order. Only recently had he first heard of yonder person, but what he had heard was extraordinary.

Passing through the Liger valley, he had observed that the small pagan temples that elsewhere dotted the landscape were absent, or made into heaps of stone and charred timber. Occasionally he went by the stump of a tree that had been huge and ancient; occasionally he spied, afar, a hut raised by a spring or on a hilltop which must have been a sacred site, where now a single man dwelt. Curious, the centurion had inquired among people he met when he stopped for a night. He learned that the bishop of Turonum and a troop of monks had been going about for years, not only preaching their Christ to the rural population but destroying the halidoms of the old Gods and rededicating these to the new.

"A great and wonderful work!" cried devout young Budic. At last his faith was marching out of the cities.

"Hm," said Gratillonius. "The wonder is that the people stand for it."

Well, he reflected, this Martinus did have the Imperium at his back. Gratillonius himself was technically violating the law when he worshipped Mithras. Had the heathens killed the churchmen, they would have risked terrible punishment. Still, they might have resisted in other ways. Gratillonius well knew how stubborn and sly rustics could be.

It seemed as if Martinus overwhelmed them, simply by being what he was. Gratillonius was unsure how much belief to give stories of miracles wrought by the holy man. They said he healed the sick, the lame, and the blind by his touch and his prayers, that he had even recalled a dead boy to life. They said that once, demanding a hallowed oak be cut down, he had accepted a challenge to stand, bound, where it would fall; as it toppled, he lifted his hand and it spun about and crashed in the opposite direction, narrowly missing and instantly converting the clustered tribesfolk. Maybe so. Gratillonius had seen strange things wrought by his Gallicenae.

He thought, though, most of the force must lie in Martinus himself. The bishop was humble as well as strong. He dwelt outside the city, in a community of like-minded men whom his reputation had drawn to him. Mainly they devoted themselves to worship and meditation. When they went forth evangelizing, Martinus never ranted or threatened. People told Gratillonius that he spoke to them in their own kind of words, quiet, friendly, sometimes humorous. They told of an incident: he and his followers had torched a Celtic temple, but when the flames were about to spread to the landowner's adjoining house, the bishop led the firefighting effort.

He had never desired his office. When it fell vacant, a trick brought him from his peaceful monastery elsewhere, and a crowd fell upon him and carried him off, willy-nilly, to be consecrated. That was the second time he had been conscripted. The first was long before, he a lad in Pannonia who only wanted to enter the Church, borne away at the instigation of his pagan father and enrolled in the army. Not until the twenty-five-year hitch was up could he give his oath to his God. Thereafter he had been clergyman, hermit, monk— Had that God chosen this means of training him for his mission?

Or was it only, or also, that the Gods of the land were failing, that in some secret way folk knew they had no more reason to honor Them? Gratillonius remembered what Forsquilis had said in Ys. . . .

He re-entered the main room as the kitchen help were bringing out supper. Martinus's entourage sat at table. They amounted to four men, younger than their leader but tonsured and dressed like him. The bishop sat offside, on a three-legged milking stool he had evidently taken along, and ate from a bowl on his lap. The food he had ordered for them consisted of vegetables, herbs, and a few scraps of dried fish stewed together. Prayers preceded the repast. A reading from the Gospels, by a brother who fasted that evening, accompanied it. Gratillonius ate his robust fare in silence.

Afterward Martinus beckoned him over, proffered a bench, and said cordially, "Now, centurion, do you care to tell us what you've been doing? You must have many curious adventures under your belt."

Gratillonius dug in his heels against liking the man, found himself dragged toward it anyhow, and settled down. "I am . . . on business of the state, reporting to the Emperor," he said.

"I thought so. And we are bound home after business with him. Maybe we can help each other, you and I."

"Sir?"

"I can give you an idea of what to expect. There's been trouble at court, a most cruel strife. God willing, it nears its end, but you'll do best to avoid certain topics. For my part, I'd be very interested to learn more about how things are in Armorica . . . and Ys."

Martinus laughed at Gratillonius's startlement. "Obvious!" he continued. "In Treverorum I heard incidental mention that Maximus Augustus's prefect at the mysterious city was coming. Who else would you be, you who identified yourself as belonging to a Britannic legion? Take your ease, have a fresh cup of the excellent local wine, and yarn to us."

He and his companions did not join in, sipping merely water, but Gratillonius got from them a sense of cheer, the sort that men feel when they have completed a hard task. He used his own call for more drink to buy time for thought.

How much dared he relate? He had shaded his dispatches to the Emperor, omitting details of religious and magical practices. He had spent hours on the road rehearsing in his mind how he should reply to various possible questions. He would not give his commandant any falsehood. But if he provoked outrage and cancellation of his commission, what then?

"Well," he said, "you must be aware that we're getting matters under control in our part of the country. We'd like to help with that over a wider range." The tale of his brush with the Bacaudae and the deliverance of Bishop Arator, augumented by the exclamations and thanksgivings of the monks, took a usefully long while. He went on to remarks about the revival of trade that was beginning, and finished quickly:

"But it'll soon be dark, and I want to start off at daybreak. You mentioned things I might need to know. Will you tell me?"

Martinus frowned. "The full story would take longer than till bedtime, my son."

"I'm a simple roadpounder. Can't you explain enough in a few words?"

The ghost of a smile crossed Martinus's lips. "You ask for a miracle. But I'll try." He pondered before he started talking.

Nonetheless Gratillonius was bewildered. He could only gather that one Priscillianus, bishop of Avela in Hispania, was accused of heresy and worse. The centurion knew that "heresy" meant an incorrect Christian doctrine, though it was not clear to him who decided what was correct and how. In a vague fashion he was conscious of the division between Catholics, who held that God and Christ were somehow identical, and Arians, who held that They were somehow different. Mithraism was an easier faith, its paradoxes a part of the very Mystery and in any event nothing that directly concerned mortals.

This Priscillianus preached a canon of perfectionism which Martinus felt went too far; fallen man was incapable of it without divine grace. Yet Martinus also felt that this was no more than an excess of zeal. Certainly it spoke against those charges of fornication and sorcery that the enemies of Priscillianus brought. There might have been no large stir had not people by the hundreds and perhaps thousands, despairing of this world, flocked to the austere new creed. As was, Bishop Ambrosius of Mediolanum got the then co-Emperor Gratianus to issue a rescript banning its adherents. They scattered and concealed themselves.

Priscillianus himself and a few followers went to Rome to appeal to the Pope. Among them were women, including two friends of the consul Ausonius. This gave rise to nasty gossip.

The Church had adopted a rule that when internal disputes arose, the final appeal would be to the bishop of Rome. Pope Damasus refused to see Priscillianus. The accused proceeded to Mediolanum, where through an official who was an enemy of Ambrosius they got a rescript restoring them to their churches.

Then they took the offensive, getting charges of calumny levelled against their principal persecutor, Bishop Ithacius of Ossanuba. He fled to Treverorum and found an ally in the praetorian prefect. Intrigues seethed. Maximus revolted and overthrew Gratianus. Ambrosius traveled north to help negotiate the treaty that divided the West.

Ithacius brought his allegations against Priscillianus before the new Augustus. Maximus ordered a synod convened at Burdigala to settle the matter. Much ugliness ensued, rumors of immorality, a noblewoman stoned by a rabble. In the end, Priscillianus refused to accept the jurisdiction of the synod and appealed to the Emperor in Treverorum.

Prelates flocked to the scene, Martinus among them. While he did not say so, Gratillonius got the impression, which later conversations confirmed, that he alone did not fawn on Maximus. Rather, he argued stiffly for what he held to be justice. When the Augustus had him at table and ordered the communal wine cup brought first to him, Martinus did not pass it on to Maximus, but to the priest who was with him; and the Augustus accepted this as a righteous act.

Ithacius saw his religious accusation of heresy faltering, and against Priscillianus pressed the secular, criminal charges of sorcery and Manicheanism. Martinus took the lead in disputing these.

He won from Emperor Maximus a promise that there would be no death penalties. However much the Priscillianists might be in error, it was honest error and deserved no worse than exile to some place where they could meditate untroubled and find their way back to the truth. Gladdened, Martinus started home. The whole wretched business had caused him to neglect his own flock far too long.

—" 'Wretched' is the right word," Gratillonius muttered.

"What?" asked Martinus.

"Oh, nothing." Gratillonius's glance went to a window. Deep yellow, the light that came through it told him that it was time for his sunset prayer to the Lord Mithras. Besides, after what he had heard, he needed a few lungfuls of clean air. "Excuse me if I leave," he said, rising. "I've duties to see to before nightfall."

The monks took that at face value, but Martinus gave him a look that held him in place like a fishhook before murmuring, "Duties, my son, or devotions?"

Gratillonius felt his belly muscles tighten. "Is there a difference?"

"Enough," said Martinus. Was the motion of his hand a blessing? "Go in peace."

2

The squadron entered Augusta Treverorum by one of two paved ways passing through a gate in the city wall. That gate was a colossus of iron-bound sandstone blocks, more than a hundred feet wide and nearly as high, with twin towers flanking two levels of windows. Behind it, structures well-nigh as impressive showed above roofs closer to hand, basilica, Imperial palace, principal church; and approaching, the men had noticed an amphitheater just outside that was like a shoulder of the hill into which it was built.

Façades reared grandly over streets, porticos gleamed around marketplaces, where people in the multiple thousands walked, rode, drove, jostled, chattered, chaffered, exhorted, quarreled, postured, pleaded, vowed, were together, were alone. Feet clattered, hoofs thudded, wheels groaned, hammers rang. The noises were a veritable presence, an atmosphere, filled with odors of smoke, food, spice, dung, perfume, wool, humanity. Litters bore a senator in purple-bordered toga and a lady—or a courtesan?—in silk past a Treverian farmer in tunic and trousers, a housewife in coarse linen carrying a basket, an artisan with his tools and leather apron, a porter under his yoke, a guardsman on horseback, slaves in livery and slaves in rags, a pair of strolling entertainers whose fantastical garb was an extra defiance of the law that said they must remain in that station to which they were born—

Gratillonius had seen Londinium, but it could not compare with this. Abruptly Ys seemed tiny and very dear. He got directions and led his soldiers in formation, giving way to nobody. Before their armor the crowds surged aside in bow waves and eddies.

Space was available at the metropolitan barracks. Maximus kept a large household troop and a substantial standing army. Their cores were legionary regulars, drawn from border garrisons as well as from Britannia. However, more men, auxiliaries among them, had departed for the South with Valentinianus. Thus total Roman strength in Gallia was much reduced. Echoing rooms and empty parade grounds, in the midst of civilian wealth and bustle, roused forebodings in Gratillonius. The Mosella had only about a hundred miles to flow from here before it met the Rhenus, and east of that great river laired the barbarians. Many were already west of it.

He made arrangements for his men. Several whooped joyously when they recognized acquaintances from Britannia, and everybody was chafing to be off into town. "Keeping them taut won't be easy," Gratillonius warned Adminius. "Temptations right and left, starting with booze and broads, leading on toward brawls."

The deputy grinned. "Don't you worry, sir," he answered. "I'll let 'em 'ave their fun, but they'll know there's a 'and on the tether." He cocked his head. "If I'm not being overbold, maybe the centurion'd like 'is own bit o' fun? I'll soon find out where that's to be 'ad."

"Never mind," Gratillonius snapped. "Remember, I want you reporting to me regularly at my lodging."

He proceeded alone to the government inn where he would stay. Temptation—aye, he thought, it simmered in him too; and he realized he had been thinking in Ysan, while certain of his wives stood before him, unclad and reaching out, more vivid than the walls and traffic around.

The room he took was clean and well-furnished, if a little time-faded. He unpacked and got busy. First he must notify the palace of his arrival. He had already prepared a note to that effect—writing never came easily to him—and now tied it together with a commendation that Bishop Arator had given him. That letter was embarrassingly fulsome, but explained his not coming sooner and, well, should do his career no harm. Escape from the curial trap—

After he was finished in Ys, if ever he was—

He didn't want to pursue that vision. Hastily, he sought the manager of the house, who dispatched a messenger boy for him.

As Gratillonius then stood wondering what to do, a uniformed centurion entered from the street, stopped, gaped, and shouted his name. "Drusus!" he roared back at the stocky form—Publius Flavius Drusus of the Sixth, whose unit had side by side with his fought its way out of a Pictic ambush. They fell into each other's arms, pounded each other's backs, and exchanged mighty oaths.

"I'm staying here too," Drusus explained, "waiting to deliver a report. Since we won his throne for the Augustus, my vexillation's been stationed at Bonna. Reinforcement for the Fifth Minervia. The war whittled that legion pretty badly, not so much through casualties as because most of it stuck with Valentinianus. The Germani got so uppity that at last we made a punitive expedition. I've been sent to tell how that went; pretty good. Come, we've daylight left, let's go out on the town."

"I'm supposed to report, like you," Gratillonius demurred. "I'd better be here when they call me."

Laughter rattled from Drusus. "Your heels will freeze if you just sit waiting, old buddy. I thought today I'd finally gotten my summons, but no, they told me there the Emperor was suddenly too busy again. You'll be lucky if you're called inside this month. And if the word happens to come when you're out, no sweat. Everything's scheduled hours and hours in advance, because whenever some backlog of state business can get handled, there's so much of it. Enjoy while you've got the chance. I'll go change clothes and be right with you."

Gratillonius sat worrying till his friend returned, and asked as they went forth: "What's happened? Maximus didn't allow this kind of shilly-shallying in Britannia."

"Not entirely his fault," Drusus replied. "You remember how he always oversaw as much as possible personally. Well, he's the same now that he wears the purple. And it worked for a while. Name of Christ, how we sliced through Gratianus's ranks! But being Emperor is different, I guess. He keeps getting interrupted by new problems."

"Why does he want a direct account of a border clash?" Gratillonius wondered.

"M-m, don't quote me. I could get in trouble."

"I wouldn't do that to you, Drusus. D'you imagine I've forgotten that day in the rain? All the puddles were red."

Hand squeezed shoulder. "I remember too. Well, nobody's told me anything officially, understand, but when a smell comes downwind I can usually tell whether it's from a rose or a fart. After Gratianus died—and he was murdered, make no doubt of that, murdered when he'd been promised safety at a feast with an oath on the Gospels—" Drusus glanced about. They were anonymous in a throng of people intent on their own lives. "Maximus put the blame on his cavalry commander, but never punished the man. . . . Anyway. While negotiations were going on afterward, Maximus got the Juthungi to invade Raetia. He had connections to them. Pressure on Theodosius to make a settlement. Valentinianus is only a kid, under the thumb of his mother. But her Frankish general in his turn got the Huns and Alani to harry the Alemanni so close to the Rhenus that Maximus had to move troops to that frontier.

"Which is why I'm still posted yonder, and the Augustus is anxious about whatever the barbarians may be up to, and why. They've gotten a taste of playing us Romans off against each other."

Gratillonius raised a dam against the words that rose in his throat.

What was this fellow saying about their Duke, the man who rolled midnight back from the Wall?

Gratillonius told himself that a commander could not always control what his subordinates did, and statecraft unavoidably had its dirty side, and Drusus was a solid sort who might be misled but who should be heard out before any arguments began. "Well, however that is," he said, "why aren't things better organized here? It doesn't sound a bit like Maximus. Can't he get competent officers any longer?"

"It's the Priscillianus mess," Drusus answered. "Before then, we had a pretty smooth mill running. But since that rift spread this far—"

He paused before he sighed and added, "I don't understand any miserable part of it. This town's full of jabber about the First Cause, the Sons of God and the Sons of Darkness, Spiritual Man, mystical numbers, and I don't know what else, except I was there when a man got knifed in a tavern ruckus that started over whether or not the age of prophecy is over. I think Priscillianus has to be wrong when he says men and women should stay apart, never get together. If that is what he says. I don't know. But why all these fights about it? I wonder if Christ in Heaven isn't weeping at what they're doing in His name. Sometimes I almost envy infidels like you."

They had wandered down toward the river. Through an open portal they saw the bridge across it, and vineyards and villas beyond. A fresh dampness blew off it. Leaves blazed with autumn. Gratillonius remembered Bodilis reading to him a poem Ausonius had written in praise of this stream; the author had sent her a copy. *Like a girl-child playing with her hair before a mirror, fisher lads sport with shadowy shapes underwater.* Sudden laughter welled up in him and he pitched away the cares of the world. They'd climb back onto him soon enough. "Not our department," he said. "How about we find us a place where we can have a drink and swap brags?"

3

Four days later he was in the presence of Maximus Augustus, but as a prisoner.

News had exploded through the city. The Emperor, who had promised clemency for the Priscillianists, was rehearing the entire case. Bishop Ithacius withdrew as prosecutor. It was said that he feared the wrath of such powerful colleagues as Martinus and Ambrosius.

Earlier, the bishop of Mediolanum had come back this far north, ostensibly to see the bones of Gratianus returned to Italy for burial, actually to attend the first trial. Maximus refused him a private audience but received him in consistory, where he in his turn declined the Emperor's proffered kiss of peace and accused the latter of being a lawless usurper. Maximus responded in the course of proceedings with a denial that Valentinianus was his equal; if nothing else, the boy-Emperor and his mother were known to have strong Arian leanings.

Though Ambrosius had since gone home, the qualms of Ithacius were natural. In his place, Maximus appointed Patricius, an advocate for the treasury. Did the Augustus want the property of the heretics?

Gratillonius found a military tribune who was a reliable conduit of information, rather than rumors. What he learned about the goings-on within the Church perturbed him less than what he learned about Maximus. How long must he hang around this cursed city? Most of his time he spent sightseeing, or talking with chance-met men. They were a varied lot, many of them trading up and down the rivers or overland. There grew before him a vision, clearer than ever, of the Empire, how vast it was and how troubled.

The detachment came for him toward evening, when he had lately returned to the hostel after a day's ride in the hinterland. A vintner had hailed him and invited him home for a cup and a gab; there the pretty daughter of the house smiled upon him. Now he sat in the common room prior to supper, more content than he had been, thinking back over the small experience. The door opened. Four soldiers in combat gear tramped through, and at their head a centurion.

"We seek Gaius Valerius Gratillonius, of the Second Legion Augusta," that man announced.

"Here he is." Gratillonius's heart leaped up as fast as his body.

"In the name of the Augustus, come."

"At once. I'll just outfit myself—"

"No. Immediately."

Gratillonius stared into faces gone hard. A prickling went over his scalp. "Is something wrong?" he asked.

The centurion clapped hand to sword. "Silence! Come!"

Household staff gaped, shrank aside, and saw their guest depart surrounded by armed men. Folk outside likewise fell silent as the group strode down the streets to the basilica.

Guarded gates led to a cloistered courtyard where dusk was rising: for the sun had gone below the outer walls. Light still glowed on the upper courses of brick and red sandstone that made up the great building within, and flared off glass in its windows. Numb, Gratillonius accompanied his escort into this citadel of his hopes, past several checkpoints and thus at last to the audience hall where the Emperor was.

The soldiers clanked to a halt and saluted. Gratillonius did too. That was his old commandant there on the throne, the same Hispanic hatchet features and lean body though purple be wrapped around and a golden wreath set above. He hardly noticed the splendor of the room or the several councillors who sat or stood beneath their master.

The officer waited for the Imperial nod before reporting that he brought the person required. "Ah, Gratillonius," Maximus said low. "Step forward. Let us look at you."

The King of Ys posed for what seemed a long while, until he heard: "Know that we have been told such evil of you that we have ordered your arrest. What have you to stay for yourself?"

Despite foreknowing he was somehow in danger, Gratillonius felt as if clubbed. "Sir?" Breath sobbed into him. He braced his knees, gave Maximus eye for eye, and declared, "My lord, I have served you and Rome to the best of my ability. Who's spoken ill of me?"

Maximus straightened and clipped, "Your own men, centurion, your own men. Do you call them liars? Do you deny having trafficked with Satan?"

"What? Sir—my lord—I don't understand. My men—"

"Silence." Maximus nodded at a pinch-lipped person in a drab tunic. "Calvinus, read the report."

That one took up a set of papers and began what soon became a sing-song, like a chant to his God. It developed that he was high in the Imperial secret service. His agents were everywhere, in every walk of life, with instructions to keep alert for anything the least suspicious and follow it up until they had sufficient clues to warrant full investigation. As if across a sea, Gratillonius heard how his legionaries, innocently talking in barracks and around town, had spoken of him. There was no need to interrogate any of them; all were ready to boast about their leader and about the wonders of Ys.

Gratillonius heard how he, in a pagan ceremony where the images of devils were brought forth, had wedded nine women who were avowed witches. He heard how he had accepted and openly borne the emblems of a sea demon and a demon of the air. He had sent forth a spirit in the form of a bird to spy upon his enemies. He had ordered magic to raise a storm. He had betrodden an island that was from time immemorial the site of the blackest sorcery—

Courtiers shivered and made signs against malevolence. Lips moved in whispered prayer. The squad that had taken Gratillonius kept martial stiffness, but sweat came forth; he saw it, he smelled it.

At the end, Maximus leaned forward. "You have heard the charges," he said. "You must realize their gravity, and the necessity we are under of finding the truth. Sorcery is a capital offense. The powers of darkness have reached into the very Church; and you are a defiant unbeliever, who bears upon himself the mark of it."

What mark? He had left the Key of the gate behind in Ys, as being too vital to risk anywhere else. He'd grown a beard there, but it was close-cropped like a Roman's. He did wear his hair in Ysan male style, long, caught at the nape to fall down in a tail. . . . He clawed out of his bewilderment and thought Maximus must refer to the brand of Mithraic initiation on his brow, though it had faded close to invisibility and—and Mithraists were loyal Romans.

"You may speak," the Emperor said.

Gratillonius squared his shoulders. "Sir, I've practiced no wizardry. Why, I wouldn't know how. The Duke—the Augustus always knew what my religion is, and it doesn't deal in magic. They believe differently in Ys, true. Well, given my job, how could I keep from showing respect to their Gods? I did—I did ask help from whatever powers they might have, but that was against barbarians who menaced Rome. As for that time on Sena, the island Sena, I wasn't supposed to set foot on it, but my wife—a wife of mine was dying there—" His throat locked on him. His eyes blurred and stung.

"You may be honest." Maximus's tone was steady; and did it hold a slight note of regret? "We had cause for confidence in you, and therefore entrusted you with your mission. But if nothing else, you may have been seduced by the Evil One. We must find out. God be praised, now that the Priscillianus matter nears an end, we have had a chance to hear this news of you. And we have given it prompt consideration as much for your sake —Gratillonius, who did serve valiantly on the Wall—as for Rome's. We will pray that you be purged of sin, led to the Light, saved from perdition." Abruptly the old military voice rang forth. "If you remain a soldier, obey your orders!"

He issued instructions. The squad led Gratillonius away.

4

In the early morning he was brought from the cell where he had spent a sleepless night. On the way down the gloom of a corridor, he met a procession under heavy guard. At its front walked a gray-haired man, skeletal, eyes fixed luminous upon another world. Four men came after, and a middle-aged woman and a younger who held hands. All were in coarse and dirty garb. They moved stumblingly, because they had not only been half starved but severely tortured. They stank. Lanterns burned smoky in the dank air around them. Hoarsely, they tried to sing a hymn.

"The heresiarch and those followers of his who've been condemned," said one of Gratillonius's guards to him. "They're off to the chopping block. Have a care, fellow, or you'll be next."

—Light was dim also in the interrogation chamber. Gratillonius could just identify scenes of the Christian hell painted on its plaster. How neatly the instruments and tools sat arranged. This could have been an artisan's workshop. Nothing felt quite real, except the chill. Two men waited, the first skinny and wearing a robe, the second muscular and in a brief tunic, ready for action. They studied the prisoner impersonally. He heard through a buzzing in his head:

"—by command of the Augustus. Cooperate, and this may be the only session we'll need. Otherwise we will be forced to take strict measures. Do you understand? We're coping with none less than Satan—"

Surprised at his meekness (but resistance would have been of no avail, when he was so alone), Gratillonius undressed. His nudity made him feel twice helpless. The torturer secured him in a frame so that he stood spread-eagled and took a lead ball off a shelf. It dangled at the end of a thong. Meanwhile the questioner continued talking, in an amicable voice. "—your duty to help lay bare the work of Satan. We do not wish to harm you. Simply as a warning—"

Snapped by an expert hand, the ball smote Gratillonius's elbow. Agony went jagged up that arm. He strangled a scream. He *would* not scream.

"—now tell me, in your own words—"

Whenever he resisted or equivocated, not that he meant to play games but often he wasn't sure how to respond, the blow landed, on joints, belly, the small of the back, until he was a single slab of pain; and worst was that the next attack might come between his sprangled thighs. Weirdest was that, from time to time, the proceedings would stop, they would bring him water, the torturer would sponge the sweat off him while the questioner chatted about everyday things.

Mithras, Who hates a liar, give me to cling to the truth! "—I did n-n-no such deed, ever. Others may have, I don't know about that, I'm just a soldier, but it was for Rome, everything I did was for Rome."

"He might want a taste of the hook," said the torturer thoughtfully. The questioner considered. "Once."

When the barbs went into his thigh and out again, Gratillonius knew what it was like to be raped.

"But I cannot tell you more!"

"You've said a good deal already, boy."

"All I could. All." And never screamed, Gratillonius thought blurrily. Never screamed. That much pride is left me. But I don't know if I can keep it after my arms and legs crack out of their sockets on yonder rack, or when he starts hitting me in my manhood.

"Well," said the questioner with a smile, "that will do for today. Please remember how much the state needs your cooperation, you, a soldier; and think what it means to your salvation." The torturer fetched salves and bandages and set about dressing open wounds. "You haven't suffered any permanent damage, you realize. I pray God you don't, dear soul." The questioner stroked the prisoner's wet hair. "But that depends on you."

He called the guards to bring Gratillonius back to his cell.

5

After two days and nights, wherein nothing happened except diminishing soreness and horrible expectations, suddenly he was brought forth. The person in charge was unctuous though uncommunicative. Gratillonius would see the Emperor! First he must needs be bathed, groomed, properly attired. . . .

This time Maximus sat in a room small and plainly furnished, himself simply clad, behind a table littered with papers and wax writing tablets. Apart from two soldiers at the door and the two that led Gratillonius in, he was unattended. Gratillonius gave him a salute, noticing with faint annoyance how awkward it was in his condition. "Sit down," the Emperor directed. Gratillonius lowered his weariness onto a stool.

Maximus observed him closely before saying, "Well, centurion, how are you today?"

Something grinned within Gratillonius. Aloud he answered, "All right, thank you, sir."

"Good." Maximus ruffled the beard over his craggy chin, stared into space, and proceeded: "You came through interrogation rather well. We've no reason to doubt you were innocent of any criminal intent. Your rescue of Bishop Arator argues in your favor, too. Not being of the Faith, you failed to see the wiles of Satan before you. Meditate on that! But your intentions were patriotic. I expected they'd prove to be. You understand we had to make certain."

Gratillonius spared himself a reply. It would have been too much effort, for no clear purpose.

"Now." Maximus's gaze swung back to stab at him. "Let us hear what you have to relate about Ys."

Surprised, Gratillonius stammered, "The Augustus . . . has my dispatches—"

"If those sufficed, I needn't have brought you here." Maximus barked a laugh. "Since time is lacking, and you're in no shape to take the initiative, I must. Listen well and answer clearly."

His questions were shrewd. At the end, he nodded and said, slow-toned: "Aside from your mistakes—and we pray you've learned your lesson—aside from those, you've done a creditable job. We're minded to keep you at your post. But." He raised a finger. "But we set restrictions on you. You will not further abet the practice of sorcery in Ys. Do you hear? You will not. Instead, you, as the prefect of Rome, will do everything in your power to suppress what is diabolical."

A smile quirked his lips. "I know that won't be easy. You're set among pagans, and they seem to be especially obstinate. I'm not sure any Christian could handle them at all, and certainly I've no Christian officer available with anything like your capabilities." He sighed. "I must use whatever God sees fit to send me."

He grew stern: "We shall not let witches live. Once the last of this Priscillianist obscenity is behind us—we'll be sending agents to Hispania to root it out, down to bedrock—once that's done and the West is secure, look for us to enter Ys and inquire into your stewardship. Therefore be zealous. To drive the lesson home, you'll be led from here to receive five strong lashes, one for each wound that Our Lord suffered upon the Cross. No more, and with an unweighted whip. We are disposed to be merciful."

Gratillonius mustered strength to say, "I thank the Augustus."

"Good," replied Maximus. "Thereafter you may return to your quarters and recuperate. Use the time well. Think about your errors, seek counsel, pray for the grace of the Holy Spirit. Then, whenever you are fit to travel, you may do so."

Dulled though Gratillonius's mind was, a flickering went through it. He dared not wonder if he was being wise before he said, "Augustus,"—how weakly his voice resounded in his skull—"you tell me to get advice . . . from learned men. Well, may I search for it elsewhere than here?"

"What? Where else?" Maximus scowled. "No, do not linger in Caesarodunum Turonum. They're devout there, but you might become confused about certain things."

"I meant farther south, sir. To Lugdunum, Burdigala, places where . . . where many sages live."

"Are you quite right in your head? You're no student, to sit at the feet of philosophers."

"The Augustus knows . . . we need a new Christian minister in Ys. That calls for searching. Not just anyone will do."

Maximus fell into thought. "His appointment is not yours to make," he said at length, "but the Church will take your recommendation into account, I suppose. You may prove mistaken. Still, the idea is to your credit." Again he paused. "And as for your personal request—well, why not? It should do your soul good to see more of the Empire, of Christendom, than this Northern fringe. And clergymen who were not involved in the affair here, they may appeal better to your heart." Decision came. "You may travel freely, provided you stay within Gallia, conduct yourself properly, and take no longer than, oh, six months until you return to duty. My secretary will prepare a written authorization."

Wistfulness brushed him. "After all," he said, "we were soldiers together, you and I, soldiers on the Wall. Go with God."

"Thank you, sir," Gratillonius made himself utter.

Maximus's glance went back to the documents before him. "Dismissed."

Gratillonius's guards led him off to the whipping post.

6

Four-and-twenty legionaries, fully encountered, marched out of the rain into the common room of the hostel. They shooed the help away and came to attention, ranked, before the couch where Gratillonius lay on his side to spare his back. Lamplight made their metal gleam against the shadows that had stolen in with eventide. As one, they saluted. "Hail, centurion!" rolled forth.

He sat up. The blanket fell off him. "What's this?" he demanded.

"By your leave, sir," Adminius replied, "we're 'ere for yer judgment."

"What do you mean?"

The deputy must wrench the words out: "We 'eard wot 'appened, and 'ow it was our stupid fault. Word's got around, you see. Sir, w-w-we wants ter make it good, if we can. Only tell us wot ter do."

Budic's lip quivered. Uncontrollable tears ran down his cheeks. "That *I* should have betrayed my centurion!" he nearly screamed.

"Quiet, you," Adminius snapped. "Bear yerself like a soldier. Sir, we await yer orders. If you can't tell nobody ter flog us, we'll do it ter each other. Or anything you want."

"We haven't yet found out who hurt you," said Cynan starkly, "but when we do, they're dead men."

Shocked, Gratillonius got to his feet. "Are you a Roman?" he exclaimed. "I'll have none of that. They did their duty, under orders, as Rome expects you will. If anything rates punishment, that notion of yours does. Kill it."

A part of him noticed that he hadn't gone dizzy this time, rising. Anger was a strong tonic. But he was recovering pretty fast, too. That knowledge went through him in a warm wave. He looked upon his men in their misery, and suddenly had to blink back tears of his own.

"Boys," he said with much carefulness, "you're not to blame. I never instructed you to keep silence, because I never expected trouble myself. Who would have? And let me say, this show of loyalty damn near makes me glad of what happened. It hasn't done me any real damage anyway, aside maybe from a few extra scars. Give me three or four days more, and I'll be ready for the road."

"To Ys, sir?" Adminius blurted.

Gratillonius shook his head. "Not at once."

"Well, wherever the centurion goes, all 'e'll need is ter whistle us up. Eh, lads?"

The squadron rumbled agreement.

"I'm not likely to require much of a troop in the South, where I'm bound," Gratillonius said, "and as for Ys—Shut in here, I've had time to think. Some of you are very likely homesick, after all your while in foreign parts. I can probably dispense with a Roman cadre, the way things are now set up in Armorica. Before leaving Treverorum, I can try to arrange reassignments for you, to your proper units in Britannia."

"Wot, sir? No!"—"Not me."—"Please, I want to stay."—"We're *your* men, sir."

"You're Rome's men," Gratillonius reminded them sharply. Behind his mask of an officer, he wondered. Barbarian warriors gave allegiance not to any state but to their chieftains. Was the Empire breeding its own barbarians? He thrust the chilling question aside. He could not penalize love.

Also, he could not be entirely sure that there would be no further use in Ys for these roadpounders of his.

"Well, think it over, and quickly," he said. "I told you, I'm starting off soon, and whoever comes with me will be gone a long time." He drew breath. "Thank you for your faithfulness. Dismissed."

" 'Bout face!" Adminius barked. "Off ter barracks. I'll follow shortly. Want a private word with the centurion first."

When the rest had tramped out the door, Gratillonius reseated himself and looked up at the thin face. He saw brashness abashed. "Well, deputy, what do you want?" he asked.

"Um, sir, I don't mean ter get above myself, but—could I speak freely, like? Man ter man."

Warmth rose afresh in Gratillonius. He smiled. "Go right ahead. If you overstep, I'll simply tell you."

"Well, um—" Adminius wrung his hands and stared downward. "Well, sir," he said in a rush, "the centurion *is* a man, very much a man, but 'e's been through a 'ard time, after driving 'imself so 'ard, and now means ter begin again, sooner than wot a medic might call wise. It's not for me ter tell yer 'ow ter be'ave. But we in the troop do worry about yer. You're getting your strength back, seems. But where's any pleasure? A man can't go on forever with no fun, no little rewards ter 'imself. Not unless 'e's a flinking saint, 'e can't. Could I, or anybody, 'elp the centurion to a bit of re-cre-ation? I'd be that glad, I would."

"You're kind," Gratillonius said, "but the food and drink are tolerable in this place, and—I am a marked man, who'd better watch his step. Enough."

"No, not enough! Listen, sir. I know it wouldn't do ter bring a woman in 'ere, or anything like that. But if you go out, would a spy follow? I don't think so."

Gratillonius chuckled. "I haven't made your acquaintance with the sort of house you have in mind."

"No, sir, you're a very serious-minded man. But listen, if you would like a bit of sport, let me recommend the Lion's Den inn at the end of Janus Way. Can't miss it. It's safe, draws a nice class of customer, the drinks and the games are honest, the girls are clean, and right now they've got the damnedest bank of musicians you ever 'eard. That's if you want, of course. I've said my piece. If the centurion 'as nothing else for me, goodnight, sir, and do be good to yerself." Adminius saluted and bolted.

Gratillonius laughed. He hadn't done that since his arrest. It was a grand feeling. What a dear bunch of mother hens he led!

At that, he thought, the deputy had a point. Before setting off on what was, after all, business of the most serious, he'd be well-advised to refresh his spirit, get out of this dull dwelling, to where winds could blow the lingering horrors from his head. A vintner who'd been hospitable, and his pretty daughter—

The girl was doubtless chaste—

Gratillonius felt the stirring in his loins. And that had not happened either, following his imprisonment, until now. Fear about it had begun to nag him. . . .

By Hercules, but he'd been long deprived! And he'd spend additional months before coming back to his wives. Into his wives. The visions flamed up. Oh, he'd been told that some or other spell made it impossible for a King of Ys to possess any but the Gallicenae. That was in Ys, though, hundred of leagues away at the far, lonely end of Armorica, Ys whose Gods he had in his heart forsworn and Who were fading away into myth. What power had They left Them? As he recalled the comfort that lay in a woman's arms and breasts, the forgetfulness of self that lay between her legs, his rod lifted fully. When he regained his feet, it stayed firm.

He cast hesitation aside, fetched his cloak, and went forth into a fine rain that he thought really should steam off his flesh.

—She was a big young blond whose guttural accent somehow excited him the more. He didn't quite make out her name, but she told him she was from east of the border. Hard pressed these days, many half-civilized Germani drifted across the Rhenus in search of employment, and often women trailed along. Roman authorities usually looked the other way, what with a labor shortage acute and worsening. While she talked and her right hand raised the cup of mead he had bought her, her left began to explore his person.

He paid the fee for two turns and they went upstairs. None of his Queens would ever know if he could help it, but if perchance they found out, surely most would understand that a man has needs.

A couple of tallow candles burned in the cubicle where her bed was. Their rankness was exciting too, like animals in rut. His member throbbed. She pulled off her gown and stood smiling at him. Her bosom was heavy above a rounded white belly and a patch that the wan light shaded but that gave off brass glints. He scrambled out of his clothes.

Then he felt the coldness and the shriveling. His knees shook, his pulse rattled.

They lay down and she tried this and that. Nothing availed. Finally she said, "Vell, too bad, but I got to go vork, you know?" He sighed and nodded. There was no mention of a refund.

—He groped his way through night, back toward the hostel. It had been foolish not to carry a lantern. The rain fell heavier than before, with a wind to dash it into his eyes and hoot between the walls. Chill sneaked under his cloak.

So, he thought. I am once for all the King of Ys. Anywhere I may be, as long as we both shall live.

Despite himself, he smiled a bit. Then maybe they're not mistaken about other things in Ys, he thought. Maybe the soul of Dahilis is still somewhere thereabouts, waiting for me.

He could almost believe that something of hers had watched over him. He was in search of the highest consecration to Mithras. His hypocrisy before Maximus still tasted nasty in his mouth, necessary though it had seemed. At least now he was, like it or not, free of any further impurity.

IV

1

Even without the need to make fortifications each afternoon and demolish them next morning, the march to Lugdunum took half a month. It might have gone faster, but Gratillonius wanted to assure himself of complete recovery. He had seen what could happen when men overtaxed their healing bodies. Also, he had been unable to obtain sufficient rations for his squadron in Treverorum, but must needs get them piecemeal at way stations. Several were out of commission, which meant delay while soldiers searched and dickered. Maximus's war had caused some of the damage. More was due to incursions of Franks and Alemanni. The Romans had succeeded in driving those barbarians out ten years ago, then lacked funds and labor for complete restoration.

The countryside was beautiful, but autumn traveled south with the troop, bearing downpours and shivery winds. Journey's end and roofs overhead felt good indeed. Gratillonius gave his soldiers and himself a few days to rest, see the great city, and take what pleasures were available. He knew they would be close-mouthed, and in any event he had not confided his real purpose to them, except for Adminius. The deputy's Christianity was nominal, and his boyhood in the Londinium slums had taught him how to learn much while revealing nothing.

Gratillonius felt it best to keep his own inquiries about Mithras worship incidental to those about possible clergy for Ys. The latter questions were the merest token. He knew full well that such an appointment could only be made in the North. However, if secret agents demanded a report on him, this should satisfy them.

Whatever guilt he felt had left him as he sat hour by hour in the saddle or lay alone in his tent at night. It was Maximus who was the betrayer. He had not strengthened the Empire, he had split it asunder as Roman slew Roman. He had not given it peace and prosperity, he had raised persecution and fear. He had broken pledge after pledge, to Gratianus, to Martinus, to poor old Priscillianus, to the Senate and the People of Rome; how long would he keep his to Valentinianus? He proposed to violate the ancient compact with Ys. Gratillonius disliked practicing deception, but such knowledge about his commandant had eaten away his resistance to it.

Seeking a better mood, he wandered around Lugdunum and found marvels, stately public buildings, baths, theater, and, outside its walls, sculptured tombs, magnificent aqueducts, an artificial lake for mimic sea battles. While many warehouses stood hollow, commerce still flowed along rivers and roads. Though poverty lurked in tenements and alleys, joviality flourished in taverns, foodstalls, bawdyhouses, odeions, the homes of the well-to-do. Few folk seem to worry about much besides their private lives, unless they be devout Christians intent on the afterworld.

No Mithraeum survived here, but presently Adminius heard that one was left in Vienna, some twenty miles south. Gratillonius's spirits lifted. He ordered departure the following day. None of the twenty-four asked why, or what else he had in mind.

A considerably lesser city on the left bank of the Rhodanus, Vienna nevertheless possessed its splendors, including a large circus and a temple that Claudius Caesar had erected four hundred years ago. More to the point, military accommodations and civilian amenities were adequate. The troop might be staying for some time.

Adminius had ferreted out the name and location of Lucas Orgetuorig Syrus, a wine merchant. Walking thither the day after his arrival, Gratillonius found a house with a moderately prosperous shop. Syrus proved to be an old man whose features, despite generations of intermingling, bore traces of his family's Asiatic origin. When Gratillonius gave him the initiate's grip, his dim eyes widened, then filled with tears, and he came near collapse. Rallying, he took the newcomer to a private room, where Gratillonius made the signs of reverence before speaking those secret words that identified his rank in the Mysteries as Persian.

"Be welcome, oh, very welcome, my son," Syrus quavered. "It's been so long since any of the faithful appeared who were young and strong. Are there more like you?"

Gratillonius nodded. "Three, Father, men of my company. Two have the rank of Occult. The third joined us a couple of years ago. He's only a Raven, of course."

"He has not been advanced? Why not? Advancement should be swift, when we are so few, so few—" The voice trailed off.

"How can it be, Father, with none superior to me where we've been? That's why I've sought you, that, and the hope of your blessing."

"The blessing you have, my son, but . . . but let us be seated. I'll call for refreshment and we'll talk. Or am I being selfish? Should I first send for Cotta? He's our Runner of the Sun, he deserves to hear. Oh, I must share these glad tidings with him."

"Later, Father, I beg." Gratillonius assisted the frail form to a bench. "Did you wish drink? Permit me to call a servant."

Conversation went haltingly. Syrus had not lost his wits, but they were apt to wander, and twice he dozed off for a few minutes as he sat. Gratillonius learned this congregation existed on sufferance, provided it stay discreet and refrain from any hint of proselytization. It might have been banned altogether, as the Imperial decree required; but Syrus's family had money and his son carried weight in civic affairs. Although himself a Christian, the younger man did not care to see his father's heart broken. Death would close down the Mysteries soon enough.

Gratillonius explained his desire as best he could. "I know it's a great deal to ask, such a promotion, especially when I can't stay here long. It may be impossible. If so, I ask forgiveness for presuming. But if it can be done—if I can be raised to your rank, Father—why, Ys will have a temple of the God, and full celebration of His rites, proper instruction for the young, elevation of worshippers. The faith will live!"

"A wonderful vision, my son," Syrus whispered. "Foredoomed, I fear, but wonderful. Mithras, sentry at the frontier of the dark—" His head drooped, snapped back up; he gulped air. "I must think, study, pray. It *is* irregular. But, but I wish—how I wish—Can you come to services tomorrow sundown? Bring your fellow believers. It will be a common rite, they too may take part, and welcome, welcome—"

Gratillonius gave him an arm and upbore half his weight when he shuffled off to bed.

—Mithraeums had never been large. The one in Vienna consisted of a single room in Syrus's house. Its windows had been boarded up and plastered over to simulate a cave. Benches along the walls left just a strip of aisle between. A cord at the entrance end marked off the vestibule. Neither font nor image of lion-headed Time stood there, only a basin for holy water. At the sacrificial end, the Bullslaying and the Torchbearers were merely painted above a table that did duty for an altar. Nothing was squalid; wax candles gave light, incense sweetened the air. But of the handful of regular attenders, every head was gray or white.

Yet after the feverish chatter beforehand had stopped and men entered this sanctuary, solemnity brooded over it. The lesser members took stance behind the cord and made reverence as the higher—two Lions, two Persians (Gratillonius the second), the Runner of the Sun, and the Father, all in minimal vestments—passed by. The offering was simply wine raised before the Tauroctony. The re-enactment by the two seniors—of Mithras overcoming the Sun, then crowning Him to be forever after the Unconquered—was bare-bones simple. The liturgy was brief. Subsequently those forward reclined on the benches while Ravens, Occults, and Soldiers brought the sacred meal and served them. That food, at least, was of the best, within the limits of prescribed austerity. Gratillonius savored it, as being like a sign unto him of the soul's ascent Heavenward . . . when he had tasted nothing holy but prayers for nigh on three years.

Thoughts tumbled through him. Why was he doing this, why was he feeling this? He knew he was not a deeply religious person—no spiritual kin to, say, Martinus of Turonum. Well, but what else had he to cleave to? The Gods of Achilles, Aeneas, Vercingetorix were dead: phantoms at most, haunting glens and graveyards and the dusty pages of books. The Gods of Ys were inhuman. Christ was a pallid stranger. Rome the Mother was a widow, her husband the Republic and their tall sons long since dead in battle, herself the booty of every bandit who came by. Mithras alone stood fast, Mithras all alone.

2

When they consecrated Gratillonius a Father, he felt weariness drop off him like a cloak of lead unclasped, and himself momentarily victorious.

There had been too much he must learn, in too brief a span. He had no gift for acquiring doctrine, words, gestures, arcana; he must hammer them into his head, toiling till dawn grizzled his window and he fell into a few hours of sleep wherein his dreams gibbered. Meanwhile he must ever strive to keep chaste and pious. That was not hard for the body, requiring little more than exercise, cleanliness, and temperance. But his mind was a maniple of barbarian recruits, raw, rebellious, slouching off every which way the instant that the drillmaster's glance strayed off them. He should have had years for his undertaking and done it openly, while the rest of his life went on in everyday wise. Instead, he rammed his way through the teachings, hoped for godliness, and took precautions against the authorities.

Probably no one would ever denounce him. He had entered Vienna quietly, stayed inconspicuous, responded to questions with evasive phrases about a confidential assignment. His men knew nothing and were content to enjoy themselves—aside from Maclavius, Verica, and Cynan, his fellow Mithraists, and Adminius. Those would not give him away. Syrus's congregation had learned silence. However, somebody else might notice how often Gratillonius visited that particular house.

No matter! he told himself. By the time such gossip reached Treverorum, if it did, he'd be back in Ys. Maximus would look upon his establishment of a Mithraeum there as an act of rebellion, which it was, but could scarcely do anything about it for another two or three years, during which anything might happen. Live each day as it comes, like a soldier in the field.

They raised him to Runner of the Sun and he concelebrated the Mystery with Syrus. In his exhaustion, he felt only that he had passed a mark on an endless uphill road.

But when Syrus and Cotta together had finished the rite that made him Father, and for the first time he—with his own hands, farmer's, soldier's, woodworker's hands—lifted the chalice before the Tauroctony, and drank the blessed wine—then abruptly, blindingly, the sacredness of it came upon him. Did the Sun lift out of the night in his spirit, to blaze in terrible majesty from his heart? He knew not. As he spoke the words, he wept.

Everyone embraced him. "The grace of Mithras be with you always, beloved brother," Syrus wished.

That was impossible, of course. After he left the sanctum, he was merely Gratillonius. What had happened within, he could barely remember.

Maybe You will reveal Yourself to me again, God of my fathers, he thought. Or maybe not. I am unworthy of this much. But I will serve You as steadfastly as lies in the power of mortal flesh and grimy soul.

—The Birthday was not far off. Syrus asked Gratillonius to join him in honoring it. The old man cried a little when he heard that that would be unwise. The legionaries had lingered suspiciously long as it was and must be off straightaway. Gratillonius gave him the kiss of peace, and received it.

In the morning the squadron started west toward Burdigala. Gratillonius had another promise to redeem.

3

Decimus Magnus Ausonius smiled. "You show me the lady Bodilis as still more fascinating in person than in correspondence," he said. "You see, she's had so many questions for me that I failed to question my own assumptions. Thus I came to regard her as a brilliant human being, but one condemned to existence in a stagnant backwater. My mistake. What you have had to tell makes me wonder if Ys may not hold the world's highest civilization. Were I capable of the journey, I would accompany you there, Gratillonius, and explore it. 'Oh, that Jupiter might restore to me the years that are fled!' " His quotation and the sigh that followed were rueful, though quite without self-pity.

"But I talk too much," he went on. "Better to listen. In a sense, Ys is more distant than the farthest land we know of. That mysterious force which has worked for centuries to erase its name from our chronicles— You can remain a while, can't you? Please."

"I should be returning soon, sir," Gratillonius answered.

"You are restless. You hunger for achievement. Well, let us work some energy off you before we dine." Ausonius guided his guest to the door.

Gratillonius went along gladly. Inclement weather had kept people indoors these past two days, during which he—after getting his men barracked in the city—had stayed with the poet. Not that he hadn't enjoyed himself. Ausonius was delightful company. Still erect and lively in his mid-seventies, he had been more than a famous teacher of rhetoric; he had been tutor to ill-fated Emperor-to-be Gratianus in Treverorum, afterward prefect of Gallia, Libya, and Italy, eventually consul. In retirement since Maximus took the throne, he remained active among colleagues, students, civic leaders, a large household and its neighborhood, while from his pen streamed verses and epistles to friends throughout the Empire.

Nevertheless it was a special pleasure to step forth on the portico of the rural mansion, flush lungs with fresh air, and look widely around. Rain and sleet had yielded to sunshine which, although slanted from the south, gave January a pledge of springtime. Grounds swept darkling with moisture down to the bank of the Garumna; mist smoked off the river, roiled by a breeze, half obscuring the vineyards beyond. On a paved path that the men took, doves moved aside from the sapphire arrogance of a peacock.

"A slave told me you have several scrolls in your baggage," Ausonius said. "May I ask what the texts are?"

Gratillonius hesitated. They were from Syrus, aids to his memory of doctrine and rites that a Father must know, and none of lesser rank. When he had no more need of them in Ys, he was to destroy them by fire, with certain prayers. "I'm sorry. It's forbidden me to tell."

Ausonius gave him a close regard before murmuring, "You're not a Christian, are you?"

"I follow the Lord Mithras."

"I suspected as much. Well, I'm Christian myself, but hold that to be no grounds for scorning the ancients or any upright contemporaries who believe otherwise. Surely God is too great to be comprehended in a single creed, and we mortals do best simply to pay our due respects and cultivate our gardens."

Gratillonius recalled poems of Ausonius that Bodilis had shown him. They were concerned with everyday matters, sometimes humorous, sometimes grave, sometimes—as when he mourned the death of his wife or a child—moving, in a stoic fashion. *"Gather you roses, girl, whilst they and you are in flower, remembering how meanwhile time flies from you. . . ."*

Hoofbeats drummed. The men turned to look. Up from the riverside galloped a mud-splashed horse, upon it a boy of eight or nine years. "Why, yonder comes Paulinus," the rhetor exclaimed happily.

Gratillonius had met the lad, Ausonius's grandson, born in Macedonia but now here to get the finest possible education. Being shut in by the rain had made him miserable, despite the elder's unfailing kindliness. The ride had evidently refreshed him, for he drew rein at his grandfather's hail and greeted the men in seemly wise. "Are you ready to go back to your books?" Ausonius asked, smiling.

"Please, can't I ride some more first?" Paulinus begged. His Latin was heavily Greek-accented. "Bucephalus, he's just getting his second wind."

"Discipline, discipline, you must break yourself to harness before you dare call yourself a man. . . . But in indulging you I indulge myself. Go as you will. 'Good speed to your young valor, boy! So shall you mount to the stars!' " Ausonius quoted with a chuckle. "Meditate upon that line. It should make Vergilius more interesting to you."

"Thanks!" Paulinus cried, and was off in a spatter of wet earth.

Ausonius clicked his tongue and shook his head. "I really must become stricter with him," he said. "Else a rhetorician of considerable potential could go to waste. But it isn't easy when I remember his father at that age."

Gratillonius thought of Dahilis and Dahut. "No, it isn't easy," he said through sudden, unexpected pain. Hastily: "Still, he ought to keep in shape. He may well find need for a set of muscles."

"Oh? Why? We moderns don't revere athletes like the Greeks in their glory. His career should resemble mine, writing, teaching, public office."

Gratillonius's gaze went eastward, toward the Duranius valley through which he had come on his way to Burdigala. Those thickly wooded steeps and hollows lay no great distance hence. Yet little traffic moved there any more, for fear of the robbers who haunted them. "How long do you suppose that sort of life will stay possible?" he asked harshly. "Why, already—when was it?—about twenty-five years ago, the barbarians cut the aqueducts of Lugdunum itself."

Ausonius nodded. "I remember. It caused the taxes to fail that year."

"Didn't it mean any more to you than that?"

"Oh, these are troublous times, admittedly." The furrows of the old countenance turned downward in sorrow. "My friend Delphinus was fortunate in passing away before his wife and daughter met their fate at the hands of the tyrant Maximus." Ausonius gripped the arm of Gratillonius. "You've intimated that you were a witness to the evil done in Augusta. If you've spoken no more about it, I can understand. But the martyrs are safe in heaven—we must believe—and a measure of justice has since prevailed."

"Really?" asked the centurion, surprised. "How?"

"You have not heard? . . . Well, I suppose you scarcely could have, on the road as you were." (Or immured in Vienna, Gratillonius did not add.) "I have received letters, including one from a colleague who is in correspondence with Martinus, the bishop of Caesarodunum."

Gratillonius's pulse quickened. "I've met that man. Tell me what happened."

"Why, Martinus was on his way home when he learned of the executions of the Priscillianists, a breach of Maximus's promise to show them mercy. He burned up the road back to Augusta and demanded to see the Emperor. That was denied him. But Maximus's wife, a pious lady, grew terrified, begged Martinus to dine alone with her and discuss it. They say he had never done that with a woman, but consented, and she laved his feet with her tears and dried them with her hair. The upshot was that Maximus did hear Martinus out, a thunderous denunciation, and agreed not to send inquisitors to Hispania, heretic-hunting, as he had planned. In exchange, Martinus celebrated Communion with the bishops who had been active in the prosecution. So you see, civilization, tolerance, common decency won in the end."

A glow awoke in Gratillonius. "By Hercules," he exclaimed, "that Martinus is a soldier yet!"

At the back of his mind went the thought that this boded better for Ys, and for the hopes he cherished, than hitherto.

"Be less pessimistic," Ausonius urged. He gestured. "Look about you. The foundations hold firm. Broad, fertile, well-cultivated acres; flourishing cities; law and order, which reach into the very palace of the usurper. True, the Empire has its difficulties. But the life of the mind goes on, and that is what matters. That is what is eternal."

The mood of the younger man changed as he listened. He wanted to be away, immediately, back into action. He curbed himself. Best he abide a few days more, for his own sake as well as Bodilis's, maybe also for the sake of Ys and Dahut. Let him gather what roses he could and bring them home. If ever he returned here, the flowerbeds might well lie trampled by the hoofs of warriors' horses.

V

1

Ever was there something strange about Mumu, something apart from the rest of Ériu. To this southernmost of the Fifths, it was said, the Children of Danu withdrew after their defeat by the Children of Ír and Éber; now their King dwelt within the Mountain of Fair Women, the síd beyond the plain of Femen. Folk gave more sacrifices to Goddesses than to Gods, and believed that by mortal men certain of These had become ancestresses of their royal houses. Female druids, poets, and witches practiced their arts as often as did males, or oftener. Here above all it was terrible to be out after dark on the eves of Beltene and Samain, when the doors between the worlds stood open—so swarmed the dead and every other kind of uncanny being.

Highlands walled Mumu off. Traffic did go back and forth, but less than elsewhere, and war with men of Condacht, Qóiqet Lagini, or Mide seldom became more than a season of skirmishes. The Ulati were far in the north; one scarcely even heard of them. The men of Mumu bore ample spears against each other. At the same time, safe harbors brought about overseas trade in a measure unknown to the neighbor realms. Roman goods arrived from as far as Aquitania: wine, oil, glass, earthenware, in exchange for gold, honey, beeswax, furs, hides. Likewise did the sumptuous fabrics of Ys. Scot's Landing, below that city, took its name not from pirates out of Ériu but from the frequent, peaceful visits of Mumach fishers. The Christian faith got its first foothold on the island among their kinfolk, who claimed that some of the Lord's own apostles had been there.

Missionaries had not yet reached the rugged country about the Mountain of Fair Women when Lugthach maqq Aillelo was king over its allied tuaths. Afterward poets told how Fedelmm, daughter of Moethaire of the

Corco Óchae, fought him. Not only did she have warriors at her beck, she was a mighty witch. The story went that she had a friend in the female warrior Bolce Ben-bretnach from Alba. Perhaps as a way to making peace, Bolce sought out Lugthach and laid upon him the demand that he bed her. He could not refuse one with her powers, and thus Conual maqq Lugthaci was begotten. At the birth, the father was away but Fedelmm was present, and to her the mother gave Conual for fostering.

Fedelmm took the infant home. The next night a coven was to meet in her house. Lest harm befall him, she hid Conual in a hole beneath the hearthstone. One of the witches sniffed him and said, "I do not destroy anything save what is under the cauldron." At that, the fire flashed downward and burned the ear of the boy.

From this, some say, came his nickname Corcc, the Red; but others say that was the color of his hair. He also became known as Conual maqq Lárech, because his foster mother bore the nickname Láir Derg, the Red Mare.

To her came a seer, who read the child's hand and told him: "Always set free any captives you meet, if you are able. Do this, and your race will grow great and your fame endure." Conual could scarcely have understood, then, but throughout his life he strove to obey the commandment.

So went the stories. They did not say why Fedelmm soon gave the fostering over to Torna Éces. She may have wished the lad to be free of the dark forces around herself.

Torna was the foremost poet of his day, a man who saw deeply into things and knew promise when he found it. Already he was raising Niall maqq Echach, son of the King of Mide. He had rescued the child from the murderous spite of the King's new wife, Mongfind, the witch-queen out of Mumu.

Conual was only three or four years old when Torna deemed Niall of an age to return to Temir, show that he was not dead as everybody there believed, and claim his rights. Mongfind could wreak no further harm upon him. However, after his father died, she succeeded in having her brother Craumthan maqq Fidaci hailed King.

A better person than his sister, on the whole he reigned well. His grief was that he was childless. When he heard about Conual, who was his cousin, he sent for the boy, meaning to make him an adoptive son. Torna let Conual go, counselling him to remember the kindly duty given him.

The newcomer was soon a worshipful friend of the older Niall and, when big enough, accompanied him to war. Fighting in Qóiqet Lagini, they took a prisoner who proved to be a learned man. On that ground, Conual persuaded Niall he should be released without ransom.

The closeness between the princes aroused all of Mongfind's malignancy. Niall was by then too strong, with too many handfast men, for her to seek his overthrow. It would take very little to break the uneasy peace and let him avenge the wrongs she had done him and his mother Carenn. But she could poison Craumthan's mind against Conual, word by sly word. At last, sick of soul, the king decided he must be rid of the youth.

He could not well have his fosterling slain at home. Instead, Mongfind whispered, he should entrust Conual with a message for a Pictish chieftain in Alba who was tributary to him. As a leavetaking gift, Craumthan gave Conual a shield whereon stood words engraved in ogamm. Conual took them for a good luck charm.

Having crossed the North Channel and being wearied, he made camp on the beach. Who should chance by but the scholar he had set free? Conual welcomed him, and presently fell asleep. The guest read what was on the shield, as the Pictish lord would also be able to do. The bearer was to be killed. The scholar changed the inscription. Hence, when Conual reached his destination, he was lavishly received, and soon got a daughter of the chieftain in marriage.

Thus the story, and few men would be so rash as to gainsay a poet. Yet naked truth may be garbed in many different words. This tale might be a profound way of relating that Conual Corcc got in trouble at Temir and perforce departed with what small following he could muster, but won high standing in his exile.

Of Niall, the poets told that he became King in Mide after Craumthan and Mongfind destroyed each other with an envenomed drink. Erelong he was warring abroad as well as in Ériu and gaining a mighty name.

Conual Corcc dwelt four years with his wife among her people. He gathered men sworn to him and led them in battle through the great onslaught Niall masterminded and Magnus Maximus repelled. Afterward he brought them and their women down to the country of the Ordovices and Silures. A good many Scoti had settled there as Roman power ebbed out of the hills.

Slowly that tide turned. Before leaving the Wall, Maximus had sent an ally, Cunedag of the Votadini, to take charge in that part of Britannia. Between him and the Second Legion, stationed at Isca Silurum, the Scoti found that they could no longer seize land as their numbers increased, but must fight to keep what they had. Conual Corcc became a leading war chieftain of theirs, who often raided deep into regions the Romans had supposed were safe. Loot made him wealthy.

Yet he was, in his way, a thoughful man. Torna may have put that into him. Wherever he went, he looked keenly at things, and he turned the memories of them over and over in his head. He considered the farms, manors, towns, fortresses—the tools, machines, books, laws, the sense of a dominion and a history vaster than they could imagine in Ériu. Captives whom he let go spoke well of him upon returning home. In the course of time, truce and trade with Conual became just as possible as war. When he visited a Roman center, he asked endless questions; and to Romans who ventured into his purlieu on peaceful business, he gave hospitality and protection.

It was not that he had any wish to become a subject of their Empire. He understood too well what it was doing to itself. Besides, more and more he yearned for his homeland. But the riches and the knowledge he was gaining here would let him return in strength.

2

It was noon when the legionaries again saw Ys. Sun and sky stood winter-wan, but light gleamed off the few clouds and many wings aloft. Grass on the headlands was, as yet, sere above their stern cliffs. Glimpsed from these heights, the water below ran in amethyst, beryl, flint, silver. Its noise growled through a shrillness of wind, air alive with salt, kelp, and frost. And there between the steeps rose turreted ruddy walls, soaring and flashing towers. At high tide the sea gate was closed, surf battering under the battlements, and that too was utterly right, a part of coming home.

The soldiers raised a cheer. Riding in front of them, Gratillonius signalled for double time. Hobnails crashed on paving. Westbound along Aquilonian Way, the men saw ahead to the end of Cape Rach, where the pharos loomed beyond clustered tombs. But soon their road swung north and downward, into the valley. Folk began to spy them and flock forth shouting from homes, farms, orchards nestled in the hills. Sentinels observed afar and sounded their trumpets. Aquilonian Way turned west again at the amphitheater, whose walls barred sight of the sacred grove. Thence the track ran straight between smithies, tanneries, carpenter shops, all the industries required to be where people did not live, until it entered High Gate.

"The King, the King!" Crowds jubilated. Gratillonius's eyes stung. He swallowed hard. Did they truly love him like this? He recognized an occasional face among those that swirled around, Herun the navy man, Maeloch the fisher, several marines who'd been escorts of his or fighters against the Scoti, a wineseller for whom he had once gotten restitution from a swindling wholesaler in Condate Redonum, a woman whom he had once given a judgment against an abusive husband, lesser Suffetes—the magnates would seek the palace for a more formal reception— "Company dismissed!" he rapped. His men broke formation and flung themselves into the throng, searching for comrades and sweethearts.

Gratillonius rode on. An impromptu guard formed, burly commoners who cleared his way for him, genially if not always gently. The press eased off as he turned from Lir Way into the crookedly rising streets along which the wealthy had their houses. Nobody was forbidden to go there, but most Ysans had a feel for what was becoming, an ancient dignity he had never encountered elsewhere.

At the main entrance to the palace he dismounted, gave his horse over to the excited servants, and strode in his armor through the garden—winter-bare, but trees and shrubs awhisper in the wind—to the modest-sized building. Up its staircase he went, between the sculptured boar and bear, under the gilt eagle on the dome, the creatures of Taranis. Bronze doors, intricately figured, were flung wide for him, and he passed the entryroom and came into the atrium.

There they stood, his Queens and their daughters—and Dahut, next to Quinipilis, O Mithras, how the child had grown, and how solemnly she stared from under a golden mane! Also present were the men of the Council, attendants hovering in the background. He halted with a military stamp and clang, raised his palm, intoned, "Greetings, my ladies and worthies," while his heart thuttered and he forced his eyes to swing around, away from the girl who looked so much like Dahilis.

The male grandees didn't matter. Not yet. But what of the Gallicenae? Bodilis smiled at him in unchanged serenity. Tears shimmered on the thin cheeks of Innilis, who huddled close to expressionlessly saluting Vindilis. Lanarvilis's ceremonial gesture showed more warmth. Maldunilis squealed in delight; she was very pregnant. The gaze of Forsquilis smoldered out of her Athene countenance above the infant she bore, whose age must be about two months. How Quinipilis had grown old, the hands trembling that clutched the staff on which she leaned, flesh dried away from the knotted, painful bones, though her grin crinkled wicked as ever. Fennalis too seemed less plump than erstwhile, like an apple that has begun to wither. Guilvilis stood timidly to the rear, her own newest babe clutched to her bosom, her older daughter by Gratillonius clinging to her skirt.

Three stepped forward and confronted him: Soren Cartagi, Speaker for Taranis; Hannon Baltisi, Lir Captain; Forsquilis, whom the Nine serving Belisama must have chosen to be their voice today. "Welcome, King, thrice welcome to Ys, your city," they said together. "May you hence-forth long abide in our midst."

"I thank you," said Gratillonius out of an unreasonably dry throat. Seeking to lighten the atmosphere: "And I so intend. You seem well prepared for my arrival."

Forsquilis nodded. Her glance caught his. He nodded back. On the previous three nights, when his band made camp for lack of other accommodation, a great owl had ghosted by.

"How have you and the city fared?" he asked.

Soren shrugged. "There's little to tell, save that— No matter now, no large matter at all."

"What mean you?" Gratillonius demanded.

"Ah, we'd not spoil this hour," Hannon said. He was seldom that cordial. "It can wait. You're the one with the real news, whatever it be."

"News indeed," Gratillonius drew breath. "Too much for telling at once. When I do, I think you'll agree my journey's borne fruit we had need of, knowledge, though some of it be bitter on the tongue. Bodilis, I did visit Ausonius." She grew radiant. "As for the rest of what I have to convey, it will require much time and thought of us. Best we wait until tomorrow or the day after."

Soren opened his mouth as if to protest, but Forsquilis cut him off. "We understand," she said. "With no immediate danger, 'twould be foolish to rush into complexities. Come, let's proceed to the banquet we've prepared for our King."

3

When the others departed after the festivities, she stayed.

In his secret self, Gratillonius had hoped for that. After celibate months, the Bull ramped through his blood. A phantom went there as well, memory of failure in Treverorum, fear of new punishment for his sin. Forsquilis was both the most passionate and the most artful of the Nine.

In a candlelit bedchamber, he invested a few moments of extravagant admiration, bent over the cradle of little Nemeta. (After all, he had been unable to keep from hugging Dahut.) The mother ended that herself, pouncing and clutching, purring and mewing.

They well-nigh ripped the clothes off each other. Her beauty flamed at him. He never knew whether he cast her down or she pulled him down. He entered her with a roar, and her hips surged beneath him like the sea.

After the second time they were satisfied to lie talking while strength regathered itself. He half sat, propped on pillows against the headboard that was usual on Ysan beds. She lay curled in the curve of his left arm, her hair spilling amber-brown across his chest. The odor of her was warm and wild.

"Ah," she crooned, "I've missed you, Grallon."

"And I you." His free hand strayed over her breasts. Milkful, they jutted proudly from her slenderness. How golden the light was upon that white skin.

"I'm sure you did," she answered, "especially after—" The words turned into a laugh. Appalled, he felt her fingers on his lips. "Nay, we need speak naught of that. Stallions will be stallions, for which I thank our Lady of the Lovetime."

"Is there aught you don't know, you witch?" he gusted in his relief.

She sobered. "Much. The politics of men and their God—" Her look sought a shuttered window . . . the night wind beyond? "You have returned a sadder man than you went, my darling. Why?"

Strangely, it was not strange to blurt to this cat-female, as if she were a man or wise Bodilis: "Maximus, Emperor Maximus, I misjudged him. He lives not for Rome but for power, and for power not only over bodies but souls."

From him stumbled the story of what he had seen and endured. Forsquilis held him close.

"So you see Ys is in danger," he ended. *"You* are, your whole Sisterhood. He means to destroy what he calls witchcraft, rip it out by the roots and cast it on the fire."

"And you're to do his weeding for him, eh?" she said low, again looking elsewhere.

"I won't. I am the King of Ys, as . . . I finally, truly discovered on this faring. . . . But I cannot rise against Rome!" he yelled.

That roused Nemeta, who began to cry. Forsquilis flowed from the bed, took up the babe, soothed and nursed her, the eidolon of young motherhood, while she asked coolly, "What then do you propose to do?"

"I know not." Gratillonius smote fist into palm. "I've thought and thought. I suppose we have two or three years' grace. Maximus must secure his frontier along the Rhenus and make a lasting settlement with Valentinianus—aye, still more with Theodosius in Constantinople."

"And meanwhile," she said, smiling down at her child, "much can happen."

He nodded violently. " 'Tis my hope. Already Ys is central to the defense of Armorica. If we can weave such a net of alliances that we are vital, with so many powerful friends in the Empire that he must keep his hands off us—"

"I was thinking of what might happen to Magnus Maximus," she said. A shiver went through him.

Forsquilis straightened and gave him a level regard. Her tone turned brisk. "Well, these things can await the morrow. We've a third celebration to carry out, I trust, you and I. It should be soon, for you'll need a good night's sleep."

Her words roused fresh lust and gladness. "Oh, we can lie abed late."

She shook her head. "Nay, that would not be meet. You must be up betimes, O King. Too long has your duty been undone."

"What's this?"

"Ah, no large task. 'Tis only that postponing it further would dishonor Taranis." The Queen frowned. "Hm, I'd forgotten, we never told you. Well, soon after you departed, a challenger arrived at the Wood. We've perforce housed him there, fed him, supplied him with harlots and amusements and whatever else befits one who might become King, these past months. High time to end the farce."

Gratillonius sat upright. His muscles tautened. "A fight to the death?"

Forsquilis laughed anew. "Nay, merely a chore, albeit a sacral one. This is a pitiful shrimp of an Osismian. Clear 'tis, he heard the King would be long away, and knew what a challenger is entitled to, and came to take advantage, with the intent of sneaking off ere you returned. But I divined as much and warned Soren, who ordered a surreptitious watch kept on him. When news of your advent blossomed today, he tried to flee, but was promptly seized. Tomorrow morning you'll kill him, and there's an end of the business, aside from the rites that follow."

She tenderly laid her babe, now drowsy, back in the cradle; turned about; glided toward the bed, arms wide. "I believe you are ready now." she whispered. "Come, let's make love. A long, long love."

4

Rain blew up during the night. By dawn its chill drizzle engulfed sky, sea, hills. At the Wood of the King, it dripped off bare oak branches and runneled down trunks and made soggy last year's leaves on the earth. The blood-colored house at the border of the grove was dulled, as if the blood were starting to clot.

There waited Soren in his sacerdotal robes, together with six marines, their horses and hounds. They were the guards over Hornach, who had dared strike the Hammer to the brazen Shield that hung in the yard outside.

His centurion's battle gear moved easily on Gratillonius's frame as he mounted the steps to the portico. Grotesque idol-shaped columns grinned at him. Underneath the roof lay shadowiness through which he peered at his opponent. Hornach was not quite the weakling of Forsquilis's comtempt, but he was scrawny; the mail into which they had stuffed him draped limp over knocking knees, the helmet threatened to slide down his nose. Even in this cold, his fear stank.

"Hail!" boomed from the seven men and the household staff to the King.

Hornach reached out. "Oh, please," he croaked, "please, I've made a horrible mistake, I'll surrender, abase myself, do anything—"

"Shall we accompany you, sir?" asked a marine. "Wouldn't do to make you chase him. Heh!" he snickered.

"Nay, that were unseemly. 'Tis never been done thus," Soren declared. "We'll put a leash around his waist for you to hold, my lord." A snarl: "Unless you, you wretch, can find the manhood to die as Taranis wills."

"I have an old mother, sir, I've been sending her coins from here, she'll starve without me," blubbered the Osismian. A trouser leg darkened and clung to the shin; he was dribbling piss.

Gratillonius had expected a straightforward fight against somebody like a Bacauda—had deceived himself into expecting it, he suddenly understood. His gullet thickened. "This is no combat, 'tis butchery," he got out. "Unworthy of the God. I accept his surrender."

Hornach went on his knees, weeping, and scrabbled to hug the King's. His guards yanked him back. "That may not be, lord," said Soren, shock clear to see beneath his implacability. "This creature issued the challenge. Worse, he did so in falsehood. Strike him down, in the name of the God."

Gratillonius remembered Priscillianus.

But he was the King of Ys, and here was a rogue who had taken an impudent gamble. "Well," he said, "let it at least be quick."

After praying to Taranis, they hitched a cord around the waist of Hornach. Gratillonius led him on his wabbling way through the brush, until they stood alone in a glade. Rain mumbled in the trees around, washed away tears, sought past armor. Dead leaves squashed underfoot.

Gratillonius undid the leash, stepped back, drew sword and brought up shield. "Make ready," he said.

Hornach shuddered, once. His blade jerked forth. It was of the long Germanic sort, and either he had refused a shield—unlikely—or no one had thought to offer him it, or he in his terror to voice the request.

"Have at me," Gratillonius invited. Do! screamed within him. "You might win, you know. You might become the next King of Ys." He gagged on his lie.

"Let me go," Hornach pleaded. "I meant no harm. I never did. Let me go, and the Gods will love you."

Not the Gods of Ys, Gratillonius thought. In a moment's confusion: But I in my heart give Them no honor any longer. Why should I do this thing?

Iron answered: Because I will destroy myself, my Kingship, everything that is left me to care about, if I openly flout Their will.

Hornach wailed and half turned to run. Get it over with! thought Gratillonius, and advanced. His opponent twisted around, raised sword, chopped wildly. Gratillonius caught the feeble blow on his shield. The other throat was open to him. He smote.

The trouble then was that Hornach did not die. He flopped on the ground, spouting blood and screams. When Gratillonius bent down to give a mercy stroke, hands tried to wave it off.

Abruptly Gratillonius must vomit.

When he had finished, Hornach lay still.

Gratillonius stood in the rain, plunging his blade into the earth, over and over, to cleanse it. The image of Ausonius said: *"What you have had to tell makes me wonder if Ys may not hold the world's highest civilization."*

I *am* no knacker! he cried into the nothingness and the cold. I am a soldier. Threefold Gods Who robbed the world of Dahilis, will You not send me honest enemies? If You make sport of me, why should I pour out blood for You? Taranis, Lir, Belisama, be warned. I am calling on Mithras to come end Your day, Mithras, Lord of Light.

VI

1

Up from the South wandered spring, and as she breathed upon naked boughs and wet earth there leaped forth blossoms, leaves, new grass, tender herbs, across the length of Armorica. Sunbeams and cloud shadows pursued each other, with rainsqualls and rainbows, till the wind lay down to rest and whiteness brooded huge in the blue. Lambs, calves, foals explored meadows, amazed by brilliance. Wives reopened their homes to air while they scrubbed away winter's grime; farmers hitched ox to plow, mariners bent sail to yard.

Little of the day had entered the house of Queen Vindilis, unless it be a certain bleak freshness. When Fennalis arrived, she gave her brief greeting and led her straight through the austerely ornamented atrium to the private room. Refreshments did wait on its table, nothing more than wine, bread, cheese, and, to be sure, oysters in their opened shells.

Having closed the door, the women made reverence before the image that occupied a niche, Belisama in Her aspect of the Wild Huntress. "Be seated," said Vindilis then. "Avail yourself. How fare you?"

"Oh, you know my rheumatism plagues me in changeable weather, and we get so many bad colds among people at this season that I've scarce had time to think." Fennalis was much in demand as a healer, second only to Innilis. She lacked the Touch that sometimes came to the latter, but she had the sympathy, together with more practical skill. She lowered her dumpy form to the couch, reached for a bite and a sip, chuckled. "*I* know you've not asked me here to put polite questions."

Humor died away as she looked up at the one who stood over her. As usual, Vindilis was plainly clad for a person of rank in Ys: today a gown of pearl-hued wool bordered with a procession in blue of the Goddess's cats and doves, a massive garnet brooch at her throat. Hair drawn back in tight, coiled braids made doubly vivid the white streak through its blackness and emphasized the aquilinity of her features. In the greenish light from the window, her eyes seemed enormous, full of night.

"I thank you for coming," she said, with no softening of her tone. "I believe you'll agree 'tis on a matter of moment."

Fennalis's pugnosed countenance registered puzzlement. She ran fingers through the snowy mane that bristled out of the pins and comb wherewith she sought to control it. "Why me? I'm not wise or strong or, or anything. Oh, if I can help you, dear, of course I'll try."

"I am with child," Vindilis told her.

Fennalis half rose, slopping wine from cup. "What? Why, wonderful!"

"That remains to be seen. Yesterday Innilis examined me and confirmed what the signs had said. The birth should come about winter solstice."

Fennalis sank back and was quiet a while before replying low, "Why are you troubled? 'Twas your choice to leave off using the Herb. Aye, you're not youthful, but you've kept yourself as fit as a lynx. Fear not."

Vindilis snapped forth a laugh. "Does the smith who is forging a sword fear it will cut him down? Nay, what frets him is that it may prove weak in the wielder's hand."

"What mean you?" Fennalis asked, not quite steadily.

Vindilis began pacing, to and fro before the couch. Her skirts whispered. She stared before her as she said:

"I confide in you because you are the only one I can. And you are neither weak nor foolish, Fennalis, underneath those flustery ways of yours. Six children have you borne to three different Kings, and all are still alive. Under Colconor, you could have drawn yourself into the background—he had little yen for you—but instead you stood up to him, again and again, took his abuse, fended the worst of his cruelties off Dahilis as well as your own daughters. And in the end, if you were not the first, neither were you the last who dared call on us to curse him. Since then—"

Fennalis waved her hands. "I am not hostile to King Grallon."

Vindilis laughed anew. "Nor intimate of his, either. You made no secret of your displeasure when he would not truly take you for his wife, and in Council you've opposed more than one proposal of his."

Fennalis sighed. "That's past. He's true to his faith, and so meant me no insult. Whatever dreams had stirred in me have quietly gone away. I am content."

"Are you?" Vindilis swung about and stood confronting her. "The rest are, more or less, aye. Think them over. Bodilis is his favorite, his . . .

his friend. Lanarvilis has her disagreements with him, but not very often any more. To her, he is Rome, the Roman virtue and the Roman peace she imagines once existed. Quinipilis surely has her doubts, but she enjoys his company and is, anyhow, too old and weary for dispute. To Maldunilis, he has a big cock and is kindly. Guilvilis is his adoring brood mare. Forsquilis—who can ever tell what Forsquilis thinks? I dare not yet be frank with her. That leaves you."

"And Innilis."

"Innilis . . . will follow my lead." Suddenly the voice of Vindilis had a lullaby sound. "But what shall it be? She also looks on him as a good man, and . . . sometimes his attentions give her pleasure. The Lady forbid that I ever put Innilis in danger or distress." She signed herself.

"If you are embittered, why are you bearing his child?" Fennalis asked as softly.

Vindilis smiled slightly. "I am not aggrieved. He slew horrible Colconor. He does his best for Ys and for his Queens, and his best is generally excellent." She drew breath. " 'Tis not his fault that Innilis and I can snatch only stolen, secret moments. 'Tis not his fault, even, that that aborted get of his almost killed her. Nay, we could be far worse off. I doubt we could be better off."

"But still you oppose him."

"Because he *is* what he is!" Vindilis cried. "I've not come lightly to this. I've watched, questioned, listened, pondered. I've prayed to the Mother of Stars for guidance. No clear answer came to me, but—what dreams I had, what signs I read in the sea-foam and heard in the sea-wind, all seemed to call me forward."

Fennalis occupied herself as prosaically as might be with slicing the cheese. "At last you decided to have his child," she said.

Vindilis nodded. "What other hold on him can be mine?"

She went to the window and stood staring into it, as if able to see clearly through the small, leaded panes, out beyond the city and across Ocean. " 'Twas no easy decision," she said to the woman at her back. "A wish for this was never vouchsafed me. In my vestalhood I meant to renew my vows and become a minor, virgin priestess. What hopes I cherished ran toward things like founding a gymnasium for girls. Understand, Fennalis, I do not hate the minds or the deeds of men. 'Tis their sweaty, hairy bodies that repel me—that, and their supposition that because of what's between my legs, I should forever stay within walls."

Fennalis forbore to mention the freedom that most Ysan women enjoyed. "I remember," she said. "The Sign came upon you and—You were lucky that Hoel was King then. He too was decent."

"Just the same—did you know?—'twas Quinipilis, my mother, who forced me to open my womb to him. Forced me, I say, by endless arguments and browbeatings and—" Vindilis shrugged, grinned. "She was a formidable character in her day, she was. At last I gave in and produced the grandchild she wanted. One. You know well I never paid Runa more heed than I absolutely must. Poor little brat. I hope I'm shrewder these days, more in control of myself."

There was a silence, apart from a *whoo-oo* of springtime wind under the eaves.

"Why do you tell me this?" Fennalis asked at length.

Vindilis turned about. "Is it not clear? I want your counsel, your help. For Ys and its Gods."

The older woman put aside the food with which she had toyed and took up her wine instead. It was more fitting. "You want influence on Grallon beyond your mere persuasions."

"Aye. I need it. We all do."

Vindilis resumed her caged pacing. "Think," she said. "Because he has done so well, authority flows more and more to him. Now he's put the final seal on his Kingship, his halidom, by slaying a challenger in the Wood. That wipes out, from the minds of the people, any last fear that he may not yet have settled his account with the Gods. And he's young, strong, skilled. Surely he'll make short work of any future contestants.

"But he is a Roman!

"What about this new Emperor Maximus, who sent him to us?"

"Grallon explained he won't let Maximus in," Fennalis ventured.

"So he says. Belike he means it. But can he, can Ys hold off the Romans without the help of our Gods? And in spite of the outcome of that fight, I do not believe he is friends with Them. Why, he intends building a temple to his Bullslayer. What will Taranis feel when His priest and avatar bows down to Mithras?"

"That may—I know not—"

Vindilis pressed on, like a hunted toward wounded quarry: "Also, what may happen, what will he do, when next the Sign descends? Have you never lain awake wondering, you whom he refused because Lanarvilis is your daughter? Quinipilis has few years left her—mayhap only hours. Which of the vestals will the Gods then choose?"

"It could be any."

"Are you so hopeful?" Vindilis compressed her lips. "Myself, I doubt They will make the matter easy for him. I think They will give him a daughter of one of us. And not your Amair. Not when They have Lanarvilis's Miraine and Boia. Or . . . soon Innilis's sad, weak-witted

Audris will be of marriageable age; and not long after that, Bodilis's Semuramat or my Runa. The Gods have Their sport with us, don't They, Fennalis? You're old too, after all. Or any of us could die unexpectedly. What *then?*

"I say to you, whatever peace is between Grallon and the Gods is as uneasy as peace between Rome and Ys; and it will erelong be put to the test. We Gallicenae must make ready for that, as best we are able. Therefore I am bearing the King a child. A lure, a hostage, a talisman? I know not. Help me, my Sister."

The energy seemed to go from Vindilis. She lowered herself to a chair opposite the couch, lifted a wine cup, drank, and stared into emptiness.

"I see," Fennalis breathed. "Yours is a noble soul."

"Nay," Vindilis mumbled. "Only one that would fain stay free."

"Belike that's the same thing. . . . Well, you're right. We must seek to steer the King away from what he might otherwise do. I mean all the Nine, once you and I have found the ways to explain this to them. And, yea, motherhood does confer power, if used wisely."

Vindilis nodded. "As small a touch as proposing a name."

"What?" Fennalis asked. She considered, and nodded in her turn. "Aye. Though 'twas he who wanted the three Roman tags we have."

"Our Sisters were clever enough not to speak against it."

What they thought of were not Maldunilis's Zisa, Guilvilis's Sasai, or Forsquilis's Nemeta. The custom was that the first-born of a Queen should carry her mother's vestal name onward. But Guilvilis now had Antonia, called after a sister of Gratillonius afar in Britannia; and Lanarvilis had borne Julia, honoring his mother; and Bodilis had Una, though whom that commemorated had not been declared.

"I expect he'll like my suggestion," Vindilis said.

"What is it?"

"Augustina. From the legion that was his."

2

In the two years following his disaster at Ys, Niall maqq Echach waged war over and over in his own land of Mide. Tuaths that thought him weakened, or in disfavor with the Gods, would refuse him his due, and take arms when he fared to demand it. The first several such battles were desperate, for he had indeed suffered heavy loss, the finest of his warriors. Yet he blazed his way through, won victory, made stern terms of peace, brought heads and hostages back to Temir. As word got around, rebelliousness slacked off, while a new crop of young men began dreaming of glory and booty to be gained in the host of this lord.

It was Éndae Qennsalach, King over the Lagini, who had egged on much of this revolt. Bad blood was ancient between his folk and Niall's. Some three hundred years before, Tóthual the Desired had founded Mide, carving the largest part of it out of Laginach territory. Nevertheless, the King of the latter wedded a daughter of Tóthual—but, wearying of her, confined her in a secret place, gave out that she was dead, and got her sister's hand. When the second wife chanced to discover the first, both died of the shame this incest had put on them. Tóthual thereupon raged through Qóiqet Lagini, slaying, plundering, burning, till he got abject surrender. His price was the paying, every second year, of that tribute which came to be called the Bóruma.

So vast was this sum of cows, pigs, cloaks, bronzeware, and silver that it would have beggared the Lagini. Hence the time was not long until they refused. Since then, those Condachtach and Mide Kings who had the claim seldom got it satisfied, and only by collecting it at sword's point after a bitter war. Thus did hatred build up over many lifetimes.

Éndae, always a maker of trouble for Temir, took what he thought was a chance to bring ruin on his enemy. In the third summer, Niall came looking for revenge.

The armies met south of the River Ruirthech. That was a day when clouds blew like smoke, low above the valley, underneath a sky the hue of lead. Rainshowers rushed out of them, drenched men, washed their wounds and their dead, passed away on the keening wind. All colors were dulled except those of blood and gold. Shouts, horn calls, hoofbeats, footfalls, clamorous wheels, clash and rattle of weapons, were somehow muffled. But blows fell as heavy and sharp as always.

Niall's chariot boomed ahead. Grass was thick but slippery beneath its iron-shod fellies; it took all the skill Cathual the driver owned to keep onward full tilt. Behind him the King stood cat-balanced against the rocking and jouncing. Niall roared, stabbed with his spear, smote with his blade, lifted their reddened points on high for a sign to his followers. He himself was a banner, a guiding comet. Above the height of him, hair and beard fell primrose-yellow from the helmet, seven-colored cloak fluttered back from the wide shoulders, gold and amber shone upon the saffron tunic. The handsomeness of his face was twisted into battle fury, wherein eyes glinted lightning-blue, teeth bone-white. Hounds ran alongside, to leap, bay, slash, tear, howl. He seemed as much beast as they, as much war-god as Lúg come to earth. Many a brave man saw what approached and fled, casting his arms from him, wailing the same blind panic into his comrades.

Withal, Niall remained a leader, a part of him watchful and aware. He kept track of the other chariots in his van, right and left. Nearest was that of Domnuald, son by the second of his Queens. This was the lad's first combat, he no more than fifteen summers of age. Hard practice rewarded itself; Domnuald poised easily and struck keenly. Hair like his father's hung wet down cheeks still girlish. O Brigit, Mother of Love, how he recalled Breccan, who died in Niall's arms outside the wall of Ys!

Older sons drove in the wings, themselves already blooded men, restless as stallions, toplofty as eagles. Several nobles had chariots too. More chose to come behind afoot, leading their tenants, with swords, spears, axes, bills, slings, while bows twanged and arrows hissed. The din cut through wind and rain, on up to the hasty clouds. There cruised scaldcrows and ravens, birds of the Mórrigu, gathering at Her feast.

Before Niall, and soon around him, the Lagini fought back. They were equipped and marshalled like his men, and maybe numbered the same. Most of them battled wolfishly well. But they could not make headway. They could not even hold fast. Day had not much dwindled when they were all fled, or captive, or sprawled and emptily staring corpses.

3

Éndae sent a herald to ask for truce. Niall received him as was fitting for one whose person was sacred, and sent him back with word of agreement.

The meeting place they set was near the battleground, a house of the king of the tuath that lived thereabouts. While they waited, Niall and his chieftains took it over and made merry. Dark as the afternoon was, they burned lamps and links without stint. Breaths smoked white athwart shadows crouching, dancing, changing shape, filling every corner and the smoky spaces under the roof. Highlights gleamed, an eye, a smile, a lifted beaker. This was no mead hall, with benches along the walls and a flock of servants. The highest ranking men sat on stools, the rest on the clay floor, and drink passed from hand to hand. Nonetheless, merriment rang.

"Have you a song for us, Laidchenn, dear?" Niall called.

"I have that," answered the poet. As was the custom, he had accompanied the army to watch what happened and afterward put it in words. That was as honorable as to fight, or more so; for what was the use of mighty deeds, did they not live in memory and the fame of them travel afar? "But I ask leave to wait a while."

"How is this?" wondered Niall. The buzz of talk died away until rain sounded loud on the thatch overhead.

Laidchenn gestured. He was a burly man with fiery, bushy hair and beard, carelessly dressed, but a man to command awe—chief singer to the King, former pupil of Torna Éces in Mumu. "You know that I, like you, have brought a young son of mine along for the experiencing of his first war, though Domnuald is to become a valiant fighter whereas Tigernach is studying my art under myself. Would you be so kind as to hear the lad's piece? A maiden effort, but burning within him it is, and I think not unworthy of you."

"He is very welcome," said Niall graciously.

Tigernach stood up. He was about the same age as Domnuald, and growing toward his father's body form. Brown-haired, his countenance was plain, somewhat marred by skin eruptions beneath a fuzz of whiskers. He did not shake a chiming rod, for he was, after all, a novice in the craft. Yet melody rippled clear and true from his harp, and boldness—brashness, almost—rose in his tones.

"Lord who harried Lagini,
Star-brilliant in the battle—"

His verse lacked subtlety, the tropes were sparse, and older men winced a bit at its fulsomeness. However, it was properly composed and showed high promise, as spirited as it was. Niall thanked him and gave him a silver brooch. Tigernach blushed so it could be seen in the dimness, mumbled his own thanks, and sat down. Laidchenn glowed with pride.

Of course, there was no comparison to the father's words. They soared, they cried, they sent ghosts shivering up and down backbones. Tears rolled over leathery visages, fists clenched, eyes stared outward beyond the world, as Laidchenn wove his magic.

Meanwhile King Éndae drove up with a dozen well-born attendants. Guards made them wait until the chant was finished and the reward given. A youth at Éndae's side protested. "Hush," said the King. "This is meet and right. Never show disrespect to a druid or an ollam poet. That is a gess upon all men."

He stared glumly into the gloomy day. Rain and mist made vague the encampment of the invaders, though he heard their boisterousness loudly enough. Closer by, servants of the dispossessed labored at the cookhouse to prepare a magnificent meal, or at the pens to feed cattle that would doubtless be herded away.

At last the guards let the newcomers in. When Éndae's champion announced him, and the Laginach King himself entered, Niall did not rise, nor even lift a knee. However, he did in seemly words offer a few seats he had reserved, and call for full cups that the guests be refreshed. Attendants bore off their overgarments and brought dry cloaks for them to wrap themselves in against the chill.

"Well," said Niall presently, "shall there be peace between us or shall there not?"

"That we must see," answered Éndae. He was a lean man, gray of hair and beard.

"Let us begin by knowing each the other," Niall said, and beckoned Laidchenn to name the Mide men on hand, with their honors.

"No such show have I this mournful day," Éndae said, "but myself I will tell you who accompanies me." He gestured. "Here are my sons—"

He came to one about the same age as Domnuald and Tigernach, also clearly a war-virgin until now: slim, comely, intensely black of hair, white of skin, blue of eye. "Eochaid, youngest who has followed me; but younger still are brothers he has at home, and they growing."

"Why, that is the name my father bore," Niall said with a smile. "Well met, Eochaid, I hope."

He got back a glower. Cruel it was that defeat make rank a lad's first taste of battle.

Éndae hastened on with the introductions. "Now, then," he concluded, "the Gods this day have seen fit to grant you the victory, Niall maqq Echach; but you will be acknowledging that it was dearly bought, and the valor of the Lagini abides. What offer do you make us, that we swear peace with you?"

Niall tossed back his bright locks. "No offer, Éndae Qennsalach. Why should I pay for that which I have won? Henceforward you shall keep your spoon out of my stewpot; and, obedient at last to oaths given long ago, you shall deliver the Bóruma."

Breath hissed between teeth, but men sat still, not altogether surprised —save young Eochaid, who leaped to his feet and howled, "What, would you gnaw us bare, you maggots? Never!" His voice cracked across, which enraged him the more. "We'll pull you from our flesh and stamp you flat!"

"Quiet," Éndae commanded. He reached to pluck at his son's sleeve. "You disobey."

Eochaid was unaware. "Maggots, blowflies, beetles you are!" he raved. "Wait, only wait, and we'll seek your nests and smoke you out!"

Laidchenn surged erect. The bulk of him loomed huge in the flickering gloom, a touch of flame in his beard. He rang his poet's chimes. Men shrank into silence. "Have a care, boy," he warned. "Overwrought or no,

you slander honorable foes, like some mad crone in a ditch. Behave yourself."

Eochaid wept. His arms flailed. "Crone, am I? Go back to your sheep-
fold, old ewe, and let the rams tup you again!"

Horror ran around the room. Before anyone else could rally the wit to
speak, Laidchenn's son Tigernach was up also. In him, fury was a winter
storm.

"You fling filth like that at my father, at a poet?" he hissed. "Go down
in the dung yourself." He made a twin spike of the first two fingers on his
left hand and thrust it toward Eochaid. As if something inside him had
foreseen, brooded, prepared, the verses snarled from him:

"Listen, you light-witted youth!
For that you thus dared speaking
Words unwise and without truth,
We shall soon hear you shrieking.

"Bellowing your bluster out
As if you'd gnawed a nettle,
You'd be shrewder not to shout
But kick an empty kettle.

"Shame there shall be on your face.
It is of your own earning.
Curs will cringe when in disgrace.
May likewise you be learning!"

Eochaid screamed, stumbled backward, fell to his knees, clutched at his
head. On cheeks and brow three great blisters were springing forth,
blood-red, sleet-white, mould-black. He groaned in his pain.

4

Toward sundown the rains blew over and the wind lay down to rest.
Laidchenn and his son walked from the house, away from others who
likewise came forth, off toward the river.

Clouds still towered in deepening blue. Light, pouring level through the
valley, reached to a rainbow. Grass drank those rays and gave them back
in glitter and green glow. They made treetops smolder, water glimmer.
The air was cold and quiet, save as shoes scuffed and slithered over wet-

ness or voices came faint across distance. Most of those cries were
sounded by carrion birds, scared into darkling clouds by men who
searched the battlefield for kin and comrade.

"You should not have done it," said Laidchenn softly. "I did not reproach you then, for that would further have undermined King Niall; but
now I tell you, a satire is a weapon more fearsome than knife or poison."

Stubbornness made Tigernach thrust out his lower lip, though it
quivered. "How did it harm our King, if one who behaved thus in his
presence suffered punishment?"

Laidchenn sighed. "It was too harsh for a grieving, bewildered boy. His
insults diminished none but himself. Surely his father was about to send
him outdoors with a heavy penance to do. Now—The blisters will heal.
They may or may not leave disfiguring scars. But the wound in the soul
will fester for aye. Niall saw this—I could tell—and softened his demands. Else the damaged, unappeased honor of the Lagini would have
forced them into war to the death. After Ys he can, as yet, ill afford that.
You have cost him dearly, my son."

Tigernach's will broke. He shuddered, covered his eyes, wavered on his
feet. "If the King wants my head for that," he choked, "here it is."

"Not so." Laidchenn squeezed the shoulder beside him, and kept his
hand on it as the two walked along. "We understand each other, himself
and I. His feelings were clear to me from his glances my way and the
words he used. Folk should certainly avenge injuries done their darlings.
He is not angry because of your anger on my behalf. He is only . . .
rueful. After all, he did win the day; he did exact good terms; the Bóruma
was really too much to hope for, unless in some later year."

Still Tigernach sorrowed. "Indeed, my heart," Laidchenn went on after
a moment, "none was more surprised than me at what happened. Who
would have thought that you, as far as you are from being an ollam poet,
that you could already cast a destructive satire? Did a God seize you, or
do you have it in you to become at last as powerful as Torna? Whichever,
clear is to see that you have been marked for a fate that will touch many
lives."

Tigernach drew an uneven breath and straightened.

Laidchenn gazed toward the river. Mysterious flittings and rustlings
went through the reeds along the bank. "Beware," he said. "Henceforward be always careful, and never use your art but on those occasions
when you feel sure you must. This day you have made us an unforgiving
enemy. Do not do it again without sore need. Your fate will be famous,
but perhaps it will not be happy."

VII

1

At high summer, the rain sometimes fell nearly warm through unmoving air. It was heavy upon the day when Queen Lanarvilis received Lir Captain and the Speaker for Taranis. Sight quickly lost itself in that iron-colored cataract; it found no more sky, no more sea, only dim walls along streets where water rushed and gurgled. What filled the world was the noise of the downpour on roofs and paving, and below this, remote and eternal, waves a-crash against the rampart of Ys.

The men gave their hooded cloaks over to the servant who admitted them and proceeded directly to the room where the priestess waited. For them, its numerous candles did not truly fend off gloom, nor its red-blue-ivory-crystal sumptuousness offer comfort. She had attired herself in a loosely cut dress of white silk whose folds and drapes joined with a silver headband to make a timeless dignity. The visitors were in plain civil tunic, trousers, half-boots. Besides the weather being unsuited for robes, they had not wanted to draw notice on their way here.

"Welcome," she said, touching her breast in the salutation between equals. The gaze of Soren Cartagi followed that hand. "Be seated, pray. I've naught set out but wine and water, for your message asked I receive you on grave business. Gladly, though, will I call for better fare, and afterward have you be my guests at supper."

Taking the couch that faced her chair, Hannon Baltisi shook his craggy head. "I thank you, my lady, but best we not linger, the Speaker and me," he said. "Folk might wonder why, and this needs to be secret."

Soren joined his companion. For a moment, play of light tricked the eye, and Soren's hair and beard seemed as gray as Hannon's. As he settled down, they regained their darkness around his broad, beak-nosed visage. It was just the scattered white in them, more of it all the time. He and

Lanarvilis regarded each other, forgetting that a third party was present, until she said slowly: "This concerns the King, does it not?"

"Who else?" Soren growled.

Her voice wavered a little. "What's wrong? I read trouble, anger on you, but—but he's done naught that he shouldn't." Flushing, compelling herself to look steadily into the faces, both the faces: "It happens he spent last night with me. After three years wedded to him, I'd have known if aught was awry. Did it touch the city, he'd have told me."

"What had he to say, then?" Soren asked impulsively.

The color mounted in her cheeks. "No affair of anyone else!" She regained self-possession; she had had much practice at that. "Oh, mainly small talk. We played a while with Julia, and he babbled about the latest wonderful thing Dahut has accomplished, and we went on to discuss his journey in autumn. Naught new. His plans remain the same that he set forth at the Solstice Council."

Hannon nodded. Tension gathered in his lank frame. At that meeting he had led the opposition to the King's proposal to make yet another circuit about western Armorica and down to Portus Namnetum, weaving tighter his web of alliances. Gratillonius had been far too much away, neglecting his sacral duties to the point of contumely before the Gods. In the end, a compromise had been reached. Gratillonius would go, but not until after the equinox, and he pledged himself to have returned by winter solstice.

Before Hannon could speak, Soren did: "I beg my lady's pardon. No intrusion—no discourtesy intended. The more so when we are here to seek your counsel and help."

Lanarvilis leaned back in her chair and let her hands lie quietly crossed on her lap. "Say on."

"Tis this, this temple of his foreign God Mithras he means to build." Soren choked and coughed.

"Why, I thought that was agreed on. Reluctantly by a number of Suffetes, aye. But when we, the Gallicenae, having searched our hearts, our books, and our dreams, could find naught forbidding it, as long as he stays dutiful toward the Gods of Ys—"

"How long will that be? At the combat in the Wood—" Soren curbed himself. "No matter that. 'Tis Lir Captain who bears the word today. I simply came along to give my support, my own plea for yours. You and I have worked together often over the years, Lanarvilis." He hunched where he sat.

The older man's voice rolled forth as if once again he trod the deck of a ship. His look commanded, too.

"Forgive me if I'm curt, my lady. You know 'tis my way.

"Ill did Grallon's wish strike me. Bad enough having a Christian priest mewling amongst us again. The King can't help that, I give you, and no true man or woman 'ull pay any heed. But this Mithras, now—well, in my seafaring days I learned somewhat about Mithras. Mind you, he's no bad God like yon Christ. He stands for uprightness, manliness, and He'll let other Gods abide. But He *is* the Bullslayer, the Comrade of the Sun. He sets Himself above the rest and lays a law of His own on His worshippers. Remember how Grallon must needs refuse the crown after he won Kingship. Not a great thing in itself, maybe, but a sign of . . . what else?

"In storm, in fog, in dead calm and sea-blink through endless silences: I have known the Dread of Lir, my lady. Ys lives on His sufferance. No disrespect to Belisama or Taranis, nay, nay. We live by Them too. But the Pact of Brennilis made Ys forever hostage to Lir, did it nay?"

Quietness deepened until the rainfall sounded torrential. Lanarvilis nodded and signed herself. Soren knotted his fists.

"And Lir wears no human face," Hannon said.

After a heartbeat, he went on: "Well, Grallon aims to take a warehouse down by the harbor, unused since trade went to hell ere we were born, he'll take that and make it into a temple of Mithras. You remember this was after the Council wouldn't let him buy land and dig a cave out in the hinterland."

They could barely hear Lanarvilis: "The earth is Belisama's. And Mithras will have no women devotees."

"Taranis makes fruitful the earth," rumbled from Soren.

"Therefore Grallon needs a house in town," Hannon said. "Now that arrangement seemed to me just as wrong. What gave it Lir for His honor, Lir Who's so quick to wrath?" He paused, filled his lungs, stared past the Queen. "Well," he said, "people don't pray to Lir, you know. We sacrifice, we obey, but He'll have none of our cries, none of our tears. His sea is already salt enough.

"And yet—well, sometimes He does make His will known, 'stead of whelming those who go against it. He did for Brennilis, long ago. If now we're at the end of the Age she birthed, might He again? I went forth by myself, in a boat, beyond sight of land. I fasted, I thirsted, I held myself sleepless, till—"

He surged to his feet. "Nay, no vision, no voice, only a remembrance. But when I uttered it aloud, soon there came a breeze blowing me back home, and seals and dolphins gamboled all about under the moon."

He placed the big, scarred sailor's hands on his hips, stood astraddle next to the second servant of Taranis, looking down at the high priestess of Belisama, and said: "This is my simple thought. That Lir be honored, let the temple of Mithras also be hostage to Him. When the Romans built our wall, the waters didn't come so high as they do today. In the seaward towers are rooms which're below the waves, abandoned on that account. I've been to see, and one at the bottom of the Raven Tower would do fine. 'Twas never meant for more than a storage cellar; no windows. Dripping wet, but that can be fixed. 'Tis lower than anything he could dig ashore, so 'tis a cave, better than trickery with a warehouse. And—I met Mithras folk when I was young, abroad—the raven is a holy bird to them. What happier sign could Grallon ask for? Or we?"

Again silence, but for the rain. Air slithered, candle flames guttered.

"I see," Lanarvilis finally murmured. Her head was bowed; Soren could no longer read her face.

"You understand, don't you?" the Speaker asked eagerly. "If Gratillonius will accept this, every faction should be satisfied. We'll have interior peace, and peace with the Gods."

She lifted her glance to confront his. "You want my help," she said, flat-voiced, "because you know he is no fool. He'll know that this means placing Mithras under Lir."

"Nay, not really. A gesture of respect, and should there not be respect between Gods? Lir gives Mithras this fine site. Mithras, in turn, acknowledges that Lir, that the Three are the patrons of Ys."

Soren leaned forward. Impetuously, he reached across the table between couch and chair. Blindly, Lanarvilis did likewise. Their hands met and clung. Hannon sat back down, folded his arms, rested like a reef outside Sena.

"You want me to . . . persuade the King," Lanarvilis said.

"First, we suppose, persuade your Sisters," replied Soren. "Make the Gallicenae work together on Gratillonius till he agrees."

"I expect we can," Lanarvilis said.

"You can do so much with him, you Nine," rushed from Soren. "The power that lies in women!"

She withdrew her hands, sat straight, and told him, "Most of that power comes from patience, Soren, from endurance."

He snatched a cup and half emptied it in a gulp, though the wine had not been watered.

2

Some thirty miles east of Ys lay the head of navigation on the River Odita. Thence the stream flowed south for about ten miles to the sea. These were birdflight distances; it was longer for a man, whether he went by land or water through the winding valleys of Armorica. There a Roman veteran had taken the lead in founding a colony, three hundred years ago. It was actually a little below the farthest north a ship could reach when tide was high; that point was just above the confluence of the Odita with the lesser Stegir. He chose the site because of its handiness to a Gallic settlement and hill fort on the heights behind. Those had long since been abandoned, leveled by man and nature until only traces remained. Houses and small farms replaced them, though for the most part Mons Ferruginus was unpeopled, a woodland through which a few trails wound.

The Roman named the colony Aquilo, from the Aquilonian district of Apuleia in Italy whence he hailed. Sufficiently inland not to fear surprise attack by pirates, it became a minor seaport. Here entered wares of metal and glass, olives, oil, textiles. Out went mainly products of the heavily forested hinterland, hides, furs, nuts, pigskin, preserved meat, tallow, honey, beeswax, timber—but also salt, beneficiated iron ore, preserved fish, garum sauce, and the marvelous things they wrought in gold, silver, ivory, shell, and fabric in Ys.

The fortunes of Aquilo waxed and waned with those of the Empire. However, its leadership stayed in the hands of the founder's descendants. These Apuleii intermarried with their Osismiic neighbors and folk of other cantons until by blood they were almost purely Armorican. In their lives they stayed Roman, even claiming that their ancestor had been kin to the famous writer. They sent their elder sons to be educated at such centers of learning as Durocotorum, Treverorum, and Lugdunum. Eventually they won elevation to senatorial rank. As such, they were no longer supposed to engage in trade; but they had ample relatives to serve as their agents while they devoted themselves to civic and—increasingly of recent decades—military affairs.

Gratillonius had passed through three years before, on his mission of keeping the western end of the peninsula quiescent while Maximus warred. Now, when he returned, Apuleius Vero made him heartily welcome. They had struck it off at once, in spite of the host being a devoted Christian.

After all, the centurion served Rome too; he had fascinating things to tell of the city in his charge; he was making possible a revival of commerce. For his part, Apuleius was well-traveled, well-read, experienced in the ways of the world. After his student days in the South he had dreamed of a public career, and begun by becoming a confidential amanuensis to the governor of Aquitania. But the death of his father laid on him the duty of coming back and taking over a post in which Gratillonius considered him wasted. Likely Apuleius would have agreed, save that Roman virtue and Christian piety both forbade him to complain against fate.

"You wish to strengthen further the ties between Ys and the Gauls?" he asked when they were alone. "Why? Not that the resumption of dealings hasn't profited everybody. It has, and nowhere more than in my poor Aquilo. However, the Empire is again tranquil, and the barbarians have drawn in their horns since that disaster the Scoti suffered. Can trade not grow of itself?"

He was a slender man in his mid-thirties, of medium height, dark-haired, straight-nosed, clean-shaven, with large hazel eyes whose near-sightedness caused him to wear an appearance of intense concentration. Somehow he seemed to Gratillonius more Hellenic than Roman, perhaps because in his quiet fashion he took pride in a bloodline going back to Magna Graecia. As the man sat, his wife Rovinda came softly in and replenished the wine and nuts they had been enjoying. She was young, comely, the daughter of an Osismiic headman. Since their marriage two years ago, Apuleius had been teaching her the manners of a senatorial matron; but she had never lacked inborn gentility. They had a single child thus far, a girl, and another swelled within her.

Gratillonius weighed his reply. He had rehearsed it in his mind, for he would need it repeatedly, but this was the first time.

"I'm afraid that tranquility is only on the surface, and can't last much longer," he said. "You've heard of the Priscillianist business last year?"

Apuleius grimaced. "Ugly, from what little I know. Unworthy of the Faith. But it's behind us now, praise God. Isn't it?"

"I'm not sure." Gratillonius frowned into a lampflame. The floor of the house was warm from a hypocaust, but the air kept a chill, and outside the shuttered windows an autumn wind wuthered. "The Church stays divided, and it and the Empire are woven together. Maximus accuses Valentinianus of heresy. It may be just a pretext. But what a dangerous pretext! No, I don't think we've seen the end of civil war."

"God help us," Apuleius said sorrowfully. "But what can we do, you and I? We're nothing but minor officers of the state. How can you bypass the Duke of the Armorican Tract?"

Gratillonius smiled. "You think I might take too much on myself? Well, I am the prefect of Rome, not of Maximus Angustus but of Rome, in Ys, which is not a province but a sovereign ally and has made me its King. I read that as meaning I've got discretion to act in the public interest as I see it, and answer for my actions afterward . . . to the proper authority."

"That would be the Duke, wouldn't it? How will he feel about you making his policies for him?"

"I may be cocky, Apuleius, but I'm not crazy. I wrote and got his leave to, m-m, 'do what seems best to develop further those good relations between Ys and the Roman communities on which a start has lately been made.' The Duke's no dunderhead either. He recognizes the facts, no matter how he has to gloss them over. First, he's necessarily most concerned with the eastern and inland parts of the peninsula. I can do in the west what he cannot, and he knows it. Second, he never was happy about Maximus's rebellion. He hinted pretty strongly, in writing to me, that my aims please him."

"I see. . . . But what are they?"

"This: that western Armorica, and as much else of it as I can reach, not get embroiled in any new fighting. That we refuse demands on us to come help kill our fellow Romans, in anybody's cause."

"Which means the cause of Maximus, you know."

Gratillonius nodded. "I think, if we do stand together in this resolution, I think he'll know better than to order us to break it. Later, if he prevails—well, at least we Armoricans will be strong enough to have some say in what happens to us. And he might not prevail."

"Valentinianus is weak," Apuleius mused, "but if Theodosius should take a hand—"

A tingle went through Gratillonius. "It could be. Who knows? In which case Armorica might expect quite favorable treatment. A daydream, maybe. I don't tell myself any nursery tales about us making the difference in what happens. I just think our chances will be better, and Rome will be better served, if Armorica looks after its own, unitedly."

"Under Ysan leadership."

Gratillonius shrugged. "Who else is taking the initiative? Besides, Ys is the natural leader of this whole region." He grew earnest. "Believe me, though—I give you my word of honor—I've no ambitions for myself."

Inwardly, fugitively, he wondered. The world groaned in its need for a man who could set things right. Why could nobody else see what must be done? It was so simple. Government firm, just, obedient to its own laws; military reforms and the taming of the barbarians; honest currency; reduction of taxes, of every burden that was destroying the productive classes; liberation of the individual man from bondage to the estate to which he was born; religious toleration—nothing else, really, than what he had hoped Maximus would enact.

But Gratillonius had no legions to hail him Emperor. He would do well if he could save Ys for Mithras and Dahut. If he was very fortunate, he might save Armorica. Give him that and he would lie down contentedly on his deathbed, knowing he had been a good son of Rome.

Apuleius considered him a while before saying, "I think I'll believe you. To be frank, I also think you talk too vauntingly. What do you and I really know—" a hint of bitterness—"in these backwaters where we sit?"

"I've been out," Gratillonius replied. "Last year, for months, over much of Gallia. I spoke with men as various as Maximus himself in Treverorum and Ausonius—well, an old, learned man in Burdigala."

Apuleius sat straight. "What?" he exclaimed. "Ausonius? Why, I studied under him. How is he?"

Gratillonius gladly let conversation go in that direction. Apuleius's admiration for Ausonius was not unalloyed. Arriving in Burdigala while Julianus the Apostate still reigned, himself at the vulnerable, combative age of twelve, he had—as he wryly admitted—changed from an indifferent to a prayerful Christian largely in reaction against the coolness or outright paganism he encountered everywhere around him. Ausonius, he felt, was a man of antiquity, born out of his time, who accepted Christ with the same impersonal politeness he would earlier have accorded Jupiter. And yet, and yet, Ausonius had such riches to give. . . .

The evening ended a trifle drunkenly and altogether cheerily.

3

Morning was lucent. Gratillonius made it an excuse for staying another day. He would take advantage of the weather to do what he had not had time to do on his previous visit, ride around the countryside and get a little familiarity with it—for purposes of military planning if that need should arise, he told Apuleius.

His host smiled, and declined to accompany him. Apuleius was no outdoorsman. He kept fit with methodical exercises, as a duty, but gave his leisure to his books, correspondence, religious observances, family, and whatever intelligent conversation came his way. He offered to assign Gratillonius a guide, but the latter refused in his turn and rode off alone.

The fact was that he wanted solitude, as a man does now and then. It was hard to find when he must always be either the King of Ys, the prefect of Rome, or a centurion of the Second. Therefore he likewise left behind the legionaries who were escorting him, to take their ease with the Aquilo garrison. This consisted of some infantry recruited mostly among the local Osismii and a few horsemen. Younger men of the civil population formed a reserve that would augment it in times of emergency. The Duke had never felt that more strength was needed here. True, pirates often ravaged the estuary—a few years ago they wrecked the lovely villa of the Pulcher family—and occasionally rowed upstream; but to date they had always been driven off short of the city. Ruinous though Vorgium was, the main force in these parts continued to be stationed there.

Gratillonius was soon out of Aquilo. On the left bank of the Odita, it amounted to a few hundred homes—cob, timber, brick, the elegant but small town house of the Apuleii—together with such establishments as a church, a smithy, a marketplace, and a couple of warehouses down by the harbor. Smoke seeped from thatch roofs or curled out of holes in tile coverings; wives went about their tasks with pauses to gossip; wheels creaked; an anvil rang. This late in the year, no merchant vessels lay docked, and Gratillonius did not go out that gate and over the bridge to the west. Instead, he took the eastern portal. The walls around the city were of the old Gallic sort, earth over interlocked logs reinforced with rubble, wooden blockhouses at the corners.

On his right, as he followed a dirt road upstream, was a narrow strip of lowland, behind which rose that long, high hill called Mons Ferruginus. Dwellings dotted it, well-nigh lost to view among the reds, bronzes, golds of autumnal woods. Most migratory birds had departed but heaven was bewinged by crows, sparrows, robins, a falcon afar.

After a short distance, he saw the lesser Stegir flow from the north and join the Odita on the opposite side. Past that was a bridge to cross, whose planks boomed underhoof. On the farther shore the land rolled gently. He left behind him the Odita, which here ran from the east before it bent south, and took a rutted road paralleling the Stegir. It led him through cultivated land, the estate of the Apuleii. He saw the cottages of three tenant families. Beyond them he passed the manor house. Its owner used it mostly as a retreat. Sere weeds and brambles filled much former plowland, with saplings as outrunners of the wildwood in the offing. Lack of markets, lack of labor—how much of this had he come upon!

His spirits revived after the road, becoming scarcely more than a path, took him into the forest. That began about where the channel of the Stegir shifted west. It walled in the farmland on two sides. Mainly it was oak, though beech, maple, ash, and other trees made it at this season a storm of color. There was scant underbrush; deer kept that down, as well as the swine that boys herded. The ground was a softness of soil and old leaves, with fallen boles on which moss grew smaragdine. Squirrels frisked about, small red meteors. Vision faded off into sun-spattered shadows. The air was cool, moist, smelling like mushrooms.

He rode on for a timeless time, letting his thoughts drift. And then, abruptly, a stag stepped into view ahead of him, a glorious beast with a mighty rack of antlers. He reined in. It stopped and stared down the path at him. He had brought a bow along in case of such luck. His hand stole down to unsling it, take an arrow, nock, aim. The stag bounded off. The shaft missed. "Harroo!" Gratillonius shouted, and urged his mount into gallop.

A while the chase thundered over the ruts. Gratillonius's big gelding narrowed the gap. The stag veered and went off among the trees. Gratillonius followed.

Of course it was in vain. He dared not keep on at full unheeding speed where a root or a burrow might cause his horse to snap a leg. The quarry soared now right, now left, until presently the splendid sight glimmered away. Gratillonius halted and swore. His mount whickered, breathed hard, stood sweating.

The man's oath was good-natured. He hadn't really expected to take the prey. The challenge had merely been irresistible, and he'd gotten a grand run. Best he return to his route. He wanted to reach cleared country on the far side of the woods and survey it before he must start back.

He had ridden for a spell when it came to him that he should already have been on the road. How could he have missed it? Every direction looked the same, and a haze had drawn over the sky to obscure the sun. What he sought was no spear-straight Roman highway but a track that twisted to and fro like the ancient game trail that doubtless underlay it. He could cast about for hours, randomly seeking a random goal.

He swore with more feeling. The anger was at himself. He had imagined that in the past few years he had learned to control a quick temper, an impulsiveness, that used to get him into unnecessary embroilments. Well, apparently that thing was not dead in him; it had been lying low, biding its chance to spring forth.

"Gone astray, lured off by a deer, like a chieftain in a folk tale," he muttered. "I'll never hear the end of this."

To be sure, if he could get back before dark, he needn't confess. . . . When he studied the sky carefully, bearing in mind the time of day and year, he established which way was south. The Stegir was certain to be somewhere yonder. Having reached it, he could follow it till it met the Odita.

The quest proved long. The forest floor was only partly clear. Often he must work through or around brush, logs, or pools. When at last he found the stream, the going along it was no better.

The sun went out of sight. Murk and chill welled from the earth. He realized that night would overtake him. To struggle on would be foolhardy. Best he halt soon and make himself as little uncomfortable as possible while he waited for dawn. He had taken with him just a piece of bread and cheese, long since eaten. His belly growled.

The Stegir gurgled around a thicket. Having passed this, he suddenly came upon a hut. A trail, narrow but clear, went thence, doubtless toward the road. Gladness jumped within him. He would still have to spend the night, but here was shelter, and a quick journey come morning. He drew rein and dismounted. His horse's head drooped, as exhausted as the poor beast was.

The hut was tiny, a cylinder of wicker and clay, moss-chinked, under a conical thatch roof. A hide hung from a stick in place of a proper door. He had seen better housing among the Picti. However, the oak whose boughs arched above was magnificent. "Hail," he called. "Is anybody home?" The gloomy depths around blotted up his voice.

The hide crackled aside and a man stepped out. He was tall, powerfully built in spite of gauntness. A crag of nose and headland of chin jutted from a long, hollow-cheeked face; the black eyes were set deep under shaggy brows; the stiff black hair and beard, roughly haggled, were shot with white. He wore a coarse linsey-woolsey robe, belted with a rope. The bare feet were calloused and begrimed. Clearly he had not bathed at any recent time, if ever, although an outdoor life made his odor pungent, a bit smoky, rather than sour.

"Peace be with you," he said in Latin. His voice was rather harsh. "Are you lost?" He smiled, showing large teeth. "You seem to be a stranger to these parts, and at this hour I doubt you've come for counsel."

"I am Gratillonius, a soldier, and I have certainly missed my way. Is Aquilo very far?"

"No, but too much for you to reach before nightfall, my son. May I offer you my humble hospitality? I am Corentinus, a hermit." The man looked up between boughs to gray-purple heaven, sniffed the air, and nodded. "We'll have rain in a while. At least my roof is tight."

"Thank you." Gratillonius hesitated. He didn't want to impose on poverty. "Could I, in return, help or—or make a donation?"

"You may make an offering to the Church if you wish. I myself have no needs that God and these two hands cannot fill." Corentinus regarded him. "You must be famished. It's not my habit to eat more than once a day, but I'll prepare you something and—" the laugh rang—"he would be a rude host who didn't share with his guest."

Gratillonius led his horse to drink, unsaddled and rubbed it down, tethered it nearby to graze on some herbage that kept a few withered leaves. Meanwhile he cast mind back over what he knew about hermits. That was hearsay. A practice, said to have originated in Egypt, was spreading northward through Europe, devout Christians going off to be alone with their God, away from the temptations of the world and even the distractions of the Church. Believers, including otherwise pagan countryfolk, often sought out such holy men, who must surely have wisdom and powers beyond the ordinary.

This Corentinus didn't seem quite to fit the picture. If nothing else, he looked too robust; and he must once have been fairly well educated.

Turning from his chores, Gratillonius saw him, robe hiked over knobbly knees, squatting in the burn. Its iciness made no visible difference to him. He murmured—a prayer?—and reached underwater. After a moment he rose. A large trout lay in his hands. Lay! Eeriness touched Gratillonius. The fish was alive; its sheen in the fading light showed it to be healthy; but it did not flop, and it had come straight into that grasp.

"God provides, you see," said Corentinus calmly. He waded ashore and went into his hut. Half stunned, Gratillonius followed. The interior was dark, save for a small, banked fire on the dirt floor, which gave just enough light to work by if you knew where everything was. Corentinus took a knife that rested on a slab with a few other objects. "Be you blessed, little brother," he said, "and be God thanked for His manifold mercies."

With a deft motion he sliced the flesh from one side of the trout and tossed the piece down. Gratillonius sucked in a breath of astounded outrage. He had never condoned cruelty to animals, and this was wanton. Yet the fish only waved its tail. Before Gratillonius could speak, Corentinus had gone back out. Gratillonius came after, automatically. The hermit cast the half filleted creature into the stream and signed the air with the Cross. Gratillonius gasped again. The trout was swimming off as if unharmed—and was it in fact whole, healed?

He grew aware that Corentinus had laid a hand on his shoulder and was speaking in a low tone: "Fear not, my son. What you beheld is no sorcery. It happens daily, unless I am fasting. Thus God keeps me fed. Why He should vouchsafe such grace to me, a wretched sinner, I know not, but He surely has His purpose. Now let's go settle ourselves and talk. You look like a man with good stories in him, and I must admit that in my weakness I can grow weary of seeing nobody except an occasional rustic."

Gratillonius mustered will. He had witnessed things stranger than this, in and around Ys, and some of them had been malignant, whereas Corentinus seemed wholly benign. "Remarkable," he heard himself say.

"A miracle." Corentinus waved. "And yet is not all Creation a miracle? Look around you, my son, and think." He led the way inside and urged his guest to take the stool that was his single item of furniture.

In quite everyday fashion he laid the piece of fish across a mesh of green twigs and hunkered down to roast it above the coals. "It's better baked," he said, "but as hungry as you must be, I won't make you wait for that. You'll find hardtack in yonder box. Dried peas and things too, but, again, I don't want you to endure the time it would take to cook them. No wine or ale available, I fear." He grinned. "Who dines with a hermit must take short commons."

"You are . . . very kind." The fire, poked up into sputtering flames, picked sights out of shadow. He saw a towel, a spare robe, a blanket hung from pegs in the sooty wall. No bed. Well, he had his horse blanket and cloak, with the saddle for a pillow. The implements he glimpsed were of the crudest, except for that excellent sharp knife. (Corentinus must not want his wondrous fish to feel pain at being carved.) A stone pot, an earthen jug, a grass basket, a couple of wooden bowls and spoons—No, wait. As far as possible from the hearth was a second slab. Upon it, wrapped in fine linen, rested what Gratillonius recognized as a book, doubtless a Christian Gospel.

Through the smoke-tang he began to smell cooking meat. His mouth watered. Corentinus looked across at him and grinned anew. Highlights traced the big bones of his face, ruddy amidst murk, and the whiteness of his teeth. "Brace up, lad," he said. "We'll soon have some cargo down your hatch." The Latin had turned accented and ungrammatical, commoner speech.

"How long have you lived here?" the centurion asked.

Corentinus shrugged. "Time ceases to have meaning after a few seasons of seeking eternity." Again he talked like a schooled man. "Um-m . . . five years?"

"I hadn't heard of you, though I visited Aquilo three years ago."

"Why should you? I'm nobody. You must be far more interesting, Gratillonius."

"What, when you can do magic like this?"

Corentinus scowled. "Please! I said it is no sorcery, no pagan trick. *I* don't do the thing. When I had first fled my sinfulness, an angel of the Lord appeared to me in a dream and told me of the divine favor I was given. I didn't know what it meant, I was bewildered and frightened. After all, the Devil had come in the same guise, no, in the guise of the very Christ, to my holy father Martinus, and tried to deceive him." His tone softened. "Oh, I had to rally my nerve, I can tell you. But what could I do except obey? And behold, my little brother swam quietly into my hands, just as you saw; and I understood that God's mercy is infinite."

Gratillonius wrestled with his honor and lost. He cleared his throat. "I'd better be frank with you," he said. "I'm no Christian myself."

"Oh?" Corentinus seemed no more than mildly surprised. "You, an officer who goes around on what must be important missions?"

"Well, I—All right, sir. I follow the Lord Mithras."

Corentinus looked long at him. "It's well for you that you didn't dissemble, my son. I don't matter, but God doesn't like false pretenses."

"No. My God doesn't . . . either."

"You may wish to reconsider, after what you've seen this evening."

Gratillonius shook his head. "I don't deny your God has powers. But I will not deny mine."

Corentinus nodded. "I'd begun to suspect you were not of the Faith. Your behavior, your stance, everything. I knocked around in the world before coming here."

"If you don't want me under your roof, I'll go."

"Oh, no, no!" Corentinus raised his free hand. "God forbid! You're a guest. A most welcome one, I might add." He smiled a bit wistfully. "I've no hopes of converting you in a single night, and know better than to try. Let's just swap yarns. But . . . you spoke of making me some return for hospitality. If you really mean it, then what you shall do is think. Look around you at God's world and ask yourself how it could have come to be and what this life of ours is all about. Think." He paused. "No, I'll not ask that you pray for guidance. You couldn't, if you're as true a worshipper of Mithras as you seem to be. I do ask that you open your mind. Listen. Think."

After a brief silence: "Well, I believe supper is ready; and you haven't yet gotten out the flatbread!"

He insisted Gratillonius take nearly the whole of the food. His share was only a token of friendliness. There was nothing but water to drink. Regardless, the two men soon fell into talk that lasted through the rain till the sunrise.

Corentinus took fire at what Gratillonius told about Ys. He had been there once, as a crewman on one of the few outside ships that called; he had toured its wonders and, he admitted without breast-beating, its resorts of sin. That Ys was coming back into the Roman sphere struck him as a happy portent.

Indeed, despite his isolation, he was astonishingly well-informed. Mention of Priscillianus grieved but did not surprise him; he had known. It turned out that he still got occasional letters from his mentor Martinus.

As for his past, he was the son of a Britannic immigrant to Osismia, born on the fundus of a well-to-do, thoroughly Romanized family. There he received a good basic schooling, though he was more interested in ranging the woodlands or galloping the horses. (He and Gratillonius found kindred memories to chuckle at.) But meanwhile his father's fortune was declining: between the general ill health of commerce, the depredations of the barbarians, and the grinding down of the curials. (Now the two could be grim together.) At the age of fifteen, Corentinus got out from under the ruin and went off on his own. Through what connections remained to him he obtained a berth on a ship, the law being winked at, and spent the next several years as a sailor, a rough man in a rough life.

Finally a storm blew his vessel so far out to sea that the crew despaired of winning back. Most perished miserably in the attempt, in spite of forgetting whatever Christianity was theirs and making horrid sacrifices to other Gods. Corentinus saw visions in his delirium. When at last he reached the Liger mouth, once he had regained strength he made his way to Pictavum, where Martinus then was, Martinus of whom Corentinus had never before heard from any human mouth.

This man gave him instruction while he settled into the monastic community. Its books added to his learning. In time he grew restless, and was delighted to accompany Martinus when the latter went to Turonum; to take baptism at the hands of Martinus after Martinus became the bishop; to aid in the effort to evangelize the countryside—until he fell from grace with a heathen woman. Aghast at himself, he asked leave to seek forgiveness through penance, and returned to Osismia to become an anchorite. There it was revealed that, despite everything, God had not cast him off.

—Gratillonius re-entered Aquilo full of thought.

4

As closely as it followed winter solstice, the Birthday of Mithras at Ys gave a glimmer of daylight, barely more than six hours, in a cavern of night. Before sunrise, walls on either side made the pomoerium brim with darkness. Air was bitterly cold. Beyond the rampart growled the sea, and above it skirled the wind. Yet Gratillonius dared hope he saw a good omen in the stars flickering overhead.

Lanterns bobbed, brought faces half out of shadow, made grotesqueries flutter across stone. Buskins clicked, raiment rustled, men kept mute as he led his procession up the stairway. The Raven Tower bulked four-square out into the surf, its battlements like shields raised against heaven. Sentries, who had been told what to expect, saluted and stepped aside. Lantern-glimmer showed awe on one countenance, misgiving on another, stiffness on the third and fourth. The door stood open. Gratillonius and his followers entered the turret. A stairwell gaped before them. They mounted, came forth on top, looked across the parapet to the dawn.

It whitened above inland hills, turned their ridges hoar, crept down the valley, while stars went out. The towers of Ys caught it in a flash of copper, gold, and glass. The roofs of Ys rose from murk like whales from the sea. Beyond them Point Vanis reared and brightened. Closer by, Cape Rach thrust ruggedly forth. Shifting illumination made it seem as if the old dead were stealing back to their sleep in the necropolis. The pharos smoked briefly—its keeper had snuffed the flame—then gleamed of itself. Ocean sheened, wrinkled, spouted off reefs, out to Sena and on across the curve of the world. Drifts of kelp darkened it here and there; seals tumbled about in the waves.

There were a few minutes to wait. Men stood contemplative or talked in low voices. Gratillonius and his father drew aside, until they looked down on the finger of sea that reached between headland and city wall, east toward Aurochs Gate. Thus confined, the water dashed noisily against stone and a strip of beach. Gloom still dwelt in that gap, but glints went like fire.

"The moment draws near," said Marcus Valerius Gratillonius.

"At last," answered Gaius his son.

Marcus smiled one-sidedly. "I never believed those historians who put ringing periods in the mouths of leaders when a great event is about to happen. Real people mumble words worn smooth of meaning."

"Well, we can keep silence." Gaius's gaze strayed west toward the seals and Sena. Did the shade of Dahilis really linger somewhere yonder? Did she watch him now?

Marcus summoned resolution. "Except for this. It's not too late to turn back. Not quite."

Gaius sighed. "It always was. I'm sorry, father."

Since a delegation of Ysan marines, and the legionary Cynan for spokesman, sought him out at the villa in Britannia this past summer and brought him here in the royal yacht, Marcus had questioned the wisdom of establishing a Mithraeum—so lavish, too—in this of all cities. True, the King had overcome opposition, but he had not quelled it in many hearts, and those were only the hearts of men.

Nonetheless Marcus had accepted the instruction and ultimately the consecration that raised him to Runner of the Sun. How strange it felt to Gaius, to be the guiding Father over this man who had brought him into being.

"I understand," Marcus said, almost meekly. He had aged much in the past few years. "Forget my croakings. We'll build Him His fortress."

On the frontier of the night—Day was advancing.

"Good for you, sir!" Gaius blurted.

Marcus plucked at the sleeve of the hierophantic robe. "Afterward we'll have time for ourselves, won't we?" he whispered.

Gaius squeezed the bowed shoulder. "Of course. I promise."

Between royal and Roman duties, the King had had small opportunity thus far to be with his palace guest, and then it had mostly gone to preparing the latter for his role this morning. Fortunately, Marcus had been glad to explore the city and enjoy his grandchildren, Dahut the foremost.

Come spring, he must return home, lest that home crumble from the hands of the family. He and his son did not suppose they would ever meet again. But first they could lighten the Black Months for each other. That was why Gaius had sent for Marcus.

He could more readily have elevated somebody else. Soon he must do so. By issuing invitations during the year, he had gained a congregation for the hallowing of his temple: three Ravens, two Occults, a Lion, two Persians. Additionally, he had seen Cynan through to the rank of Soldier, Verica and Maclavius to Lion. That was all he had.

Light flared. The sun rose over the hills. Gaius Valerius Gratillonius led his men in hymn and prayer.

Before they went below, he raised a hand in salute to Point Vanis, where rested the bones of Eppillus.

Candles in holders of gilt bronze waited inside the tower. With these the party descended. The uppermost room was a watchpost and rain shelter, the next pair were given over to storage. Farther on they echoed empty; those times were past when the treasures of Ys had overflowed into them. Walls sweated, air grew dank, flames streamed smoky, as the stairs went down below the surf.

Finally came a space refurbished. Hidden ducts ventilated the fires of a hypocaust that kept it warm and dry. Statues of the Torchbearers flanked a doorway. A mosaic floor in black and white showed emblems of the first three degrees in the Mysteries. On plastered walls glowed frescos of the tree that nourished infant Mithras and of His reconciliation with the Sun. Benches stood beneath, and a table bearing food, drink, and utensils for the sacred meal. A new wall with its own door shut off the sanctum. With holy water sprinkled off pine boughs, with incense of pine cones, with wine and honey upon each tongue, the Gratillonii led the dedication.

Thereafter it was time to go back above and hymn the noonday sun. It glimmered wan, low in the south. Clouds were gathering, wind shrilled, seas ran white-crested.

The men returned to the Cave of Mithras. Only Father, Runner, Persians, and Lions passed through to the sanctuary; the rest had their lesser devotions to perform in the pronaos.

The King of Ys could well honor the God from the East. Here the Dadophori were sculptured again, in their faces, eyes, postures something not quite Greek or Roman, fluid and sleek, like a wave or a seal. Lion-headed Time stood stern in His own marble, serpent-enwrapped. The font was the carven calyx of a flower. The four emblems in the floor led the gaze onward, past benches above which glistened symbols of the planets, to the twin altars at the far end, where Mithras arose from the Rock, and to the high relief of the Bullslaying that filled yonder wall. The ceiling was deep blue, with golden stars. Candles stood ready in sconces, lamps in niches, to give brightness once they were lit. Soon here, too, resin sweetened the air, along with incense.

Pater and Heliodromos trod forward. Together they led the rites.

Afterward came the Sacrifice, for all initiates. On this unique occasion it began with blood. Cynan, having been duly purified, brought in a caged dove which he had gone to fetch in the course of exercises outside. Marcus Gratillonius took it forth and held it tight while Gaius cut its head off with a clean slash and let it bleed into a golden bowl. Cynan bore this and the remains into the pronaos. Tomorrow he, the Occults, and the Ravens would immolate them. Meanwhile the Gratillonii enacted the subjugation and coronation of the Sun by Mithras.

Finally they officiated over the divine meal which the lower ranks served the higher, a foretaste of the soul's ascent after death. Upon this great occasion it was fare less frugal than was customary: beef, subtle seasonings on the vegetables, honeycakes, the best of wines drunk from silver cups. When it was finished, Gaius Valerius Gratillonius gave benediction, and the men departed for the upper earth.

Weather hid the sunset. Nevertheless they said their prayers atop the Raven Tower before they bade one another farewell.

Gratillonius made his voice hearty as he did. Inwardly there remained a wistfulness. He had seen the Spirit enter certain of the worshippers; from Cynan it had fairly flamed. Nothing had touched him akin to the divine fire that lighted his consecration.

Or had it? The God revealed Himself in forms as infinitely various as the forms and signs of love. Was the feeling of completion, of rightness, that Gratillonius did have—was it Mithras's "Well done" to His soldier, while also reminding him that the establishment of a lonely outpost was not in itself any victory?

Night fell upon son and father as they made their way back to the palace. Wind yelled, drove rain and scud before it, filled streets with chill. Under the sea wall, tide ramped and snarled.

VIII

1

The equinoctial gales blew out of Ocean like longings, to wake the soul from winter drowse. When a milder air had borne Marcus off, Gaius Gratillonius felt a redoubled need to be away himself, in action. Luckily —perhaps—there was a call upon him that neither Gallicenae nor Suffetes could deny was urgent. A letter from Maximus had scathingly denounced him for founding a new temple of Antichrist; it had been inevitable that word of that would eventually reach Treverorum. Were it not for pressing demands on his attention, the Augustus wrote, he would recall his prefect, occupy Ys, and extirpate demon worship. As it was, he must content himself with requiring the prompt installation of a new Christian pastor.

The centurion had an idea of what those demands were. Indeed he had better mend fences, both temporal and ghostly. Writing to the Duke of the Armorican Tract, he requested a conference. The reply was that that high official would be in Caesarodunum Turonum for the next several months, and receive him there. It was the civil if not military capital of Lugdunensis Tertia; the Duke doubtless had fence mending of his own to do.

With a few soldiers at his back, all mounted, Gratillonius set forth. He allowed himself and them two days' rest at Aquilo. Otherwise they pushed hard, down to Portus Namnetum and up the Liger valley.

That was lovely country, freshly green and blossomful. Riding through, he felt cheer reborn in him. Why yearn for the barracks in Britannia or hope for a precarious prominence in the Empire? Ys was his home. Its people had become his people. He could see his work on their behalf grow beneath his hands. If he could have no woman besides his Queens, weren't they sufficient and then some? If none of them could bear him a son, did he not have Dahut? The little darling was so bright, so headstrong. She might very well grow up to be another Semiramis, Dido, Cartimandua, Zenobia, but happier fated; her father would lay the foundation for that! And, of course, his other daughters were sweet.

Danger prowled around Ys, but so it did everywhere in the world. As Quinipilis was fond of saying, to borrow trouble was stupid, considering the interest rate on it.

Crossing a bridge from the military highway to the left bank, his party passed through the gate of Turonum and found quarters. He was both relieved and perturbed to discover that the civil governor was absent, summoned to the Emperor along with his counterparts throughout Gallia. At least now he could confer straightforwardly with the Duke.

They got along well at their first meeting. It was privately agreed that neither would send forces to any internecine conflict. They would explain that defense against the barbarians must take precedence. It was true.

As for Gratillonius's need of a clergyman, the Duke recommended him to Bishop Martinus. "He comes into town once a week, usually, from that monastery of his, to lead services at the main church. M-m-m, I know what you are, but it'd be wise of you to attend them then."

Always scout ahead if you can. Gratillonius went for a preliminary look, and was shocked. The church was larger than most, and rather handsome for a building erected in recent decades. However, it was filled with madmen—the sick of mind and feeble of mind, ragged, filthy, some roaring, some shivering, some posturing, some taking attitudes absurd or obscene, while mutters went through the dimness. "San, san, san. . . . I am Jupiter, but they have me locked in hell. . . . Fintharingly and no, no. . . ."

A deacon explained upon being asked that this was at the order of the bishop. Elsewhere energumens, as such persons were called, wandered starveling, shunned for fear of the demons supposed to possess them, when they were not whipped off with curses, beaten, tormented, sometimes raped or killed. Martinus decreed that they be fed and sheltered in the house of God. Each Saturday he came in among them, clad in sackcloth and smeared with ashes; he lay full length on the floor in their midst, and hour after hour implored mercy for them or wrestled with the Fiend who afflicted them. His touch and his prayers had seemingly freed a number to return to the human world. The rest adored him in their various weird fashions.

Gratillonius thought of his Gallicenae. They too, Innilis especially, had had a measure of luck in coping with insanity. But when they failed, the law of Ys was that the sufferers must be expelled. "It's well done of the bishop," he said.

"Oh, his is a loving soul, sir, underneath the strictness," replied the deacon. "He served in the army, did you know? Conscripted, and spent twenty-five years before he could have the baptism he longed for, but never did his charity falter. When he was stationed at Samarobriva, I've heard—not from him—how one freezing day he saw a near-naked beggar. He'd already given away most of what clothes he had, but he drew sword, cut his cloak across, and let this man have half. No wonder he has power to heal. Of course, he had been a military physician."

Gratillonius decided it would be politic to absent himself until Sunday. Besides, the idea of a man groveling among the crazy repelled him. He hired a boat and went fishing.

On the Lord's day, after sunrise prayers to his own Lord, he was early at the church. This would be far from the first Christian ceremony he had watched, but he wanted to observe everything he could. The energumens were gently but firmly guided out onto the porch, where a couple of priests with the rank of exorcist took them in charge. Trained by now, they gave no trouble. Meanwhile the interior was cleaned and made ready. The congregation arrived piecemeal. A comparative few went inside, most of them middle-aged or elderly, the baptized. Catechumens occupied the porch; of these, a majority were women. There was no objection to those excommunicated for sin or to unbelievers like Gratillonius, if they behaved themselves. Who knew but what the scales might fall from their eyes?

Solemnly, the bishop led his priests and deacons in. Martinus had changed little in a year and a half, save that he was freshly barbered, his sallow face smooth aside from the many furrows, his hair standing white —unkempt still—behind the ear-to-ear frontal tonsure which made his brow seem cliff-high. He wore the same slave-like garb, and went barefoot. His attendants were as humbly clad, and for the most part equally gaunt.

Folk knelt while the ordained led a prayer. There followed a reading from the Prophets. "—*Shall not the land tremble for this, and those who dwell in it mourn, while it rises up like a flood of Egypt and is cast back and drowned?*—" The people joined in singing a short response: "—*Glory unto God omnipotent—*" Standing, they heard the bishop read from an Epistle: "—*The natural man does not receive what the Spirit of God teaches; to him this is foolishness; he cannot know it, because it is only knowable by the spirit.*—" A choir sang a psalm. Martinus preached the Gospel. He was no orator. In terse soldierly words, he discoursed on the centurion whose servant Jesus had healed. *"—Lord, I am not worthy for You to come under my roof—"* Gratillonius wondered about that text. For all his devotions and meditations, yonder fellow kept uncommonly aware of what went on around him.

"Silence," enjoined a deacon. While bishop and priests prayed, the offerings of the faithful were brought forth in processional, goods and money. Some were earmarked—for the poor, the ill, a family member in need—and the deacon read aloud the names of those beneficiaries, and Martinus included them in his prayer.

It was the dismissal. Those in the porch left at its end. The doors behind them drew shut. What came next was the Communion service, for the baptized only. Well, Gratillonius thought, we bar our lower ranks from the highest Mysteries of Mithras.

He sought an exorcist, who was helping shepherd the energumens. "I have to see the bishop," he said, and gave his name. "Will you tell him? I'll be at the Imperial hostel."

"He receives supplicants—"

"No, this has to be a private talk. Tell him it's with the King of Ys."

The priest gaped and gulped. However, the man before him, big, healthy, well-clad, was not obviously a lunatic. To be sure, standing aside as a spectator, he had revealed himself a pagan. But Martinus dealt with many a heathen chieftain in the hinterland. "I can't approach him for some hours yet, sir, not till he's finished his Church business, and afterward his charities and austerities. Expect word about sunset."

Briefly, Gratillonius bristled; then he eased off and laughed. Maybe Martinus washed the feet of the poor, but be damned if he toadied to the mighty!

The message that evening, carried by an awestruck boy who had memorized it, was: "The bishop will return to the monastery immediately after worship tomorrow sunrise. He will be glad to meet you at the western city gate and have you accompany him. It will be afoot."

—On this side of the river, the road was unpaved. Rain had fallen during the night, and morning was cold and damp, though warming as the sun climbed. Mist smoked above the water. Dew glittered on grass and young leaves. The hills reached silvery with it. Birds twittered; high and high, a lark chanted its *"bi-bi-bi."* Few people were abroad. While Martinus needed a staff, he strode along without asking Gratillonius to slow down. A few monks who had come with him followed at a respectful distance.

For a time conversation went lively between the leaders. Martinus was ardent to learn everything Gratillonius had done, seen, heard, planned, since their last encounter. But when talk turned to the future, his mood darkened.

"—And so I've got to have a minister of your faith for Ys, soon," Gratillonius finished. "Please don't look on it as a political move. I am what I am. From your viewpoint, too, wouldn't it be best we get a reasonable man like old Eucherius?"

Martinus peered afar. Somehow his thin, snubnosed countenance came to resemble a Caesar's. "God rest Eucherius." His tone was steely. "From what I've heard, he did his pious best. He was weak, though. We require an evangelist there, who will take up arms against Satan."

"But not one who'll, well, antagonize the city. How would that help your cause? Give me somebody I can work with."

"Despite your own paganism." Martinus gentled. "Oh, I understand. Yours is a sore dilemma."

"Never mind me. I'm thinking of Ys. And Rome. What good will it do Rome if your man provokes the people into throwing him out? Maximus would—Well, remember what the Priscillianus business cost."

Martinus's knuckles whitened above his staff. "I can never forget," he said low.

Presently: "Let me confess to you." He wrenched the words out. "For we must indeed try to understand each other, you and I, for the sake of the souls in your worldly care, and—and Rome.

"Maximus did agree to call off his inquisitors, and to give the surviving Priscillianists in his dungeons light sentences. However, on this he put a price. As a sign of blessing, I must help celebrate the consecration of Felix as bishop of Treverorum.

"Now Felix was, is, a fine man." Martinus caught his breath. "But to share the Eucharist with Ithacius, the persecutor— Well, in the end, perforce, I did.

"On the way home, I walked through midnight of the soul. It seemed to me that whatever powers of well-doing had been granted me by God must be gone, because of this covenant with evil. Then an angel of the Lord appeared to me and said I had done what I must and was forgiven." He said that almost matter-of-factly, before he grew stark again: "Nevertheless, I have seen Satan at work within the Church itself. I will never attend another synod of bishops."

They trudged on in silence until Gratillonius had marshalled words: "So you realize how careful we need to be, choosing . . . a trustworthy servant of God for Ys."

Martinus had recovered calm. "I do. A man devout, learned, civilized, but also virile, familiar with the common folk yet wise enough to cooperate with you for the general welfare and . . . resistance to tyranny." He gusted a sigh. "Do you know any such paragon? I wish I did!"

Gratillonius's heart leaped. He had spent a great many hours thinking about this. "Maybe I do."

By then they had nearly reached their goal, about three miles downstream from Turonum. Sheer hillsides, honeycombed with caves and burrows, curved backward to wall in a broad, grassy flatland. Primitive huts covered the low area, wattle-fenced gardens among them. Although the community was said to number well over a thousand, most dwelling in the caves, few were in sight, nor did smoke rise from any but two or three shacks.

This was the Greater Monastery that Martinus had founded, to which men flocked who had despaired of the world and would seek salvation beyond it. Women came too, but were housed in the city; the bishop clove husband from wife as ruthlessly as he split away fleshliness from himself. Mostly the monks subsisted on donations, or on the proceeds of possessions they had turned entirely over to the Church when they enrolled. What food they grew, what fish they caught, were mere concessions to the body's need of some recreation. They shared a single meal a day, of the simplest kind. Nearly all their waking hours they passed in prayer, contemplation, mortification, reading of Scripture, attendance on the preaching of their master.

Gratillonius could not comprehend how any human being would seek such an existence. Yet as he beheld it, the power of it sent a chill through him.

"Whom have you in mind?" Martinus asked.

The centurion hauled his mind back to realities. "You know him. One Corentinus. We met last year, he and I, when I blundered onto his hermitage, and hit it off. On this trip, I stopped at Aquilo mainly so I could go back there and talk with him again. It went even better. I think he's right for Ys—since we must have somebody—and I hope you'll agree."

"Corentinus. . . . Hm-m." The bishop pondered, while his feet and staff ate the distance to sanctuary. "It may be. It may be. An old seaman, posted to a seafaring folk. . . . I must think. It's clear God has marked Corentinus for some high mission. You know about the miracle of the fish, don't you? Well, then—" More silence, apart from the scrunch of sandals, the song of birds. "I must think, and pray for guidance. But it does seem as though—He'll have to return here, get instructed, be consecrated chorepiscopus. That may take months. However, I could write to Maximus that it's in train."

"I'm afraid he won't be willing, Corentinus," Gratilonius warned. "What he wants to do is sit in the woods and beg forgiveness."

Also, those woods had been full of flowers, fragrances, peace.

Martinus laughed. "He'll take his marching orders if they're issued him. Stay a while, you. Let's talk this over at length. You're a soldier; you can survive our hospitality. If my decision is positive—and I suspect it will be—I'll give you a letter you'll convey to Corentinus on your way back."

Gratillonius bridled. "Sir, I *am* the perfect of Rome and the King of Ys."

Martinus laughed louder. "Why should you not also be God's messenger boy?"

2

Early summer brought a spell of calm, light, warmth. It had prevailed for days when Quinipilis's turn to have Dahut came, and she took the girl out on the water.

"I promised her this, the first chance we'd get," she snapped when her manservant expressed qualms. "Would you have a high priestess break her word? A promise to a little kid is the most sacred kind there is. And nay, we'll not want the royal yacht or any such cluttered-up thing. What you can do is carry my word to Scot's Landing. So get off your arse!"

As he left, the man grinned to himself. The old lady had a rasp for a tongue and a lump of butter for a heart.

Maeloch was quick to arrive from the fisher hamlet under Cape Rach. His *Osprey* was under repair after storm damage. Meanwhile he welcomed extra earnings, and this would be a pleasant job. When he entered the Queen's house he found woman and child on the floor playing with little animals that King Grallon had carved in wood. "Here he is, sweetling," Quinipilis said to her charge. "We can go now."

"Oh, go, go, go!" sang Dahut, and soared to her feet. She was taller than most three-year-olds, wand-slim, wind-swift. Beneath flaxen billows of hair, her eyes were huge, deep blue, in an exquisitely sculptured face. "We go sail!"

"The airs willing, princess," Maeloch said. "Else must I row." His coarsely clad, burly form, black mane and beard, rumbling voice, caused her no alarm. It did not seem that anything had ever frightened Dahut.

"Well, help me up, oaf," Quinipilis ordered with a nearly toothless smile. As he did, she caught a sharp breath.

"Does something hurt, my lady?" he asked.

"Of course something does. What d'you think 'twould do, in this wreck of a body? Like always having feet in a boiling kettle, if you must know. Let's begone."

"Uh, better if my lady stays home. I'll take good care of the princess, believe me. How I do remember her mother."

"Nonsense! Should I deny me a pleasure because of some verminous twinges? Fetch me my staff. 'Tis in yon corner; are you blind or only drunk? Give me your arm." Quinipilis leered. "I want all Ys to see I can yet snare a lusty young man for escort."

Dahut skipped with them down the winding street. Folk they met, mostly servants in livery, gave deferential salutation. Many recognized Maeloch as well as the Queen. He was not only a fisher captain, frequenter of taverns and sometimes joyhouses like most sailors; he was a Ferrier of the Dead.

"Why d'ye go in this wise?" he wondered.

"On Dahut's account," Quinipilis explained. "She's ever been wild about the sea. Can't get close to it, or out on it, enough."

A grimness crossed Maeloch's weathered countenance. He knew where and how the child had been born. Should that not have left a dread of the realm of Lir within her? Instead, it was as if He had touched her then, and was forever after calling her.

"Her dad takes her when he can," Quinipilis went on, "but he has scant free time, poor fellow. And then 'tis in his yacht. The notion came to me 'twould pleasure her to fare in a small boat."

Maeloch could not keep his forebodings while the bright small presence who already look so much like Dahilis skipped beside him. "We could land on a skerry I know and spend a while," he suggested. "Might get hungry, though."

"I'm not quite in my dotage! We'll have provisions aboard."

Thereafter Quinipilis must save her breath for walking. "Wan' a' hear a song?" Dahut asked the man. Her hand lay tiny in his. She pointed at the woman, who smiled as if receiving an honor. "Ol' Mama taught me." She lifted a voice clear and true:

"Starfish, starfish, what have you seen
Deep in the water, deep in the green?
'I saw the darkness, far from the day,
Where the seals go to hunt and play.' "

From the Forum, broad and busy Lir Way brought them through Lowtown to Skippers' Market and the triumphal arch. Beyond was the harbor. At early ebb, tide had drawn the sea gate open; but on this mild day, the basin curved almost waveless beneath the city wall. Shallops cruised back and forth, a merchant ship was standing out, more vessels lay docked, bustle went over the stone arc of the quay. Trade was reviving under the reign of Grallon.

A well-stocked boat waited at a slip as Quinipilis had ordered. They went aboard. Maeloch cast off, put oars in tholes, rowed powerfully. They passed between the awesome doors of the gate. He found sufficient breeze that he could step and stay the mast, set sail, pole it out for a broad reach, and merely steer.

It whispered, the breeze, cooling the brilliance that flooded from above and dusted diamond-sparkle across the sea. It stirred, the sea, in low waves that somehow moved as one, like a single huge being gently breathing in its sleep. Today whiteness did not shatter on the cliffs or the strewn reefs, only swirled and murmured. Otherwise Ocean was a million shifting shades of blue, save where a kelp bed rocked, or a swimming gull or cormorant. Such birds wheeled aloft in their multitudes, seldom crying. Dahut's gaze winged out among them, on past the dim streak that was Sena, to the line where vision met worldedge and lost itself in sky.

Her heed returned when a seal drew near. There were always many of the beasts around Ys, they being protected. Most were plunging through the water or basking on rocks. This one met the boat and swam alongside, a few feet away. Often it looked at Dahut, and she looked back, losing her earlier excitement, becoming mute and motionless though appearing very happy.

"That's strange," Maeloch said after a while. His voice, which could outshout storms, was hushed. "Dolphins'll play thus with a craft, but scarce ever a seal."

Quinipilis nodded. "I think I ken it," she answered as low. Clear sight remained to her. "Yon particularly beautiful coat, a kind of gold under the brown, and those big eyes. Could be the same as was there when the babe went overside. You've heard? I glimpsed it. And a few times since on the beach—"

"A seal saved me and my crew once. Guided us home through a fog, when else we'd sure have run aground."

Quinipilis nodded. "We're both wont to signs of the Otherworld, nay? As close as we are to it, in our different ways." She glanced at Dahut. "Sea child."

The girl returned to playfulness when Maeloch dropped sail and rowed to that skerry he had mentioned. It was large of its kind, an islet, bare rock but strewn with weed, shells, bleached and contorted sticks of driftwood. Tidepools gleamed on its lower ledges. She clapped her hands and caroled. Maeloch lay to, hung out rope bumpers, jumped ashore with the painter and made fast to an upright thumb of stone. "Come ye, sweetling," he called. "Nay, first put sandals back on. 'Twouldn't do having the barnacles cut those wee feet."

He assisted Quinipilis, then brought a chair and parasol carried along for her, then set out luncheon, while Dahut scampered round and round, shouting at each new marvel she discovered. After they had all refreshed themselves he led her by the hand, explaining things as best he could. Quinipilis watched, smiled, sometimes talked in an undertone to nobody he saw. At last he said, "Well, Princess, best we be starting home."

Dahut's face clouded. "Nay," she answered.

"We must. The tide's turning. That'll help your poor old Uncle Maeloch, for the wind's down and he'll have to row a lot. But if we wait too long, the tide'll close the gate, and we'll have to make for Scot's Landing, and your poor old Aunt Quinipilis can't get up the cliffs there."

The child stuck out her lower lip, clenched fists, stamped foot. "Nay. I *b'long* here."

"Not the way the sun's putting a flush in that white skin of yours, ye don't. No mutiny, now. Ye can play till I've stowed our gear."

Dahut whirled and sped from him.

When Maeloch returned to Quinipilis he found she had dozed off in her chair, as the aged do. He left her alone while he loaded the boat. Always he kept half an eye in Dahut's direction. She had gone down to the water and become quiet. The rock sloped in such wise that could see merely the fair top of her head.

Having finished his task, he gave Quinipilis a slight shake. She drew a rattling breath and blinked confusedly. "Dahilis—" she mumbled. Her senses steadied. "Oh, my, such eldritch dreams I was having." Painfully, she hobbled to the boat and got in with Maeloch's assistance.

The sailor went after Dahut. "Time to go," he said, and stopped and stared.

On the ledge beneath him, the girl was side by side with the seal. Maeloch saw that the animal was female. Her narrow, earless head (how much the head of a seal called to mind a human corpse) had brought muzzle against cheek, through a tumble of tresses. The fishy breath seemed to give no offense. Did a murmur, a hum or a tone, resound from the long throat?

"Dahut!" Maeloch bellowed. "What the thunder?"

The two started, rolled apart, exchanged a look. The seal slithered into the water and dived below. Dahut leaped up. The wet body had soaked her gown so that it clung to the curves of her, which were not yet a woman's curves but slender as if to cleave waves. Calming, she walked toward him without protest.

Maeloch squatted to inspect her. "Ye're not hurt?" he grated. "Damnation, whatever happened? Don't do that sort o' thing! A big beast like yon could tear ye in shreds. Saw ye nay its teeth?"

"She came and sang to me," Dahut answered like a sleepwalker.

"Sang? Huh? Seals don't sing. They bark."

"She did so." Sheer willfulness brought the girl back to herself. "She sang 'bout the sea 'cos I wan'ed she should." Turning, she called across the luminous, moving miles: "I'll come again! I'll al'ays come again!"

The mood flitted from her. She gave Maeloch an impudent grin, a wink, and her hand to hold. What could he do but lead the daughter of Dahilis to the boat and take her home to her father?

He knew he would never understand what he had seen; but he, who dealt with the dead as his forebears had done before him, need not be daunted by a mystery as tender as this. "She sang, did she?" he asked.

"She did, she did." Dahut nodded violently. "She tol' me 'bout my sea."

"What did she tell you?"

"I 'member. You wan' a' hear?" The treble that lifted toward the gulls was childish, but the words no longer were, and the melody ebbed and flowed. It was not a song that had ever been heard in Ys.

"Deep, deep, where the waters sleep
And the great fish come and go,
What do they dream in the twilight gleam?
The seals will always know.

"Far, far, from the evening star
Comes the storm when the wind runs free
And the cloud that lours with the rain that pours.
The seals will always see.

"High, high is the evening sky,
Deep is the Ocean swell.
Where foam is white in the changing light,
The seals will always dwell."

3

For the past three years, except when it was impossible, Gratillonius had given a day every month to open court. Anybody was free to enter the basilica during those hours, to watch the proceedings or to lay before him a trouble—dispute, complaint, need—that lower authorities had failed to resolve. Turn by turn, he heard them out, and rendered judgment with military briskness. He had neither time nor patience for subtleties, though he strove to be fair. In doubtful cases he generally found for the humble. They had less to fall back on than the well-off.

The setting was impressive. Tiered benches looked down toward a dais on which the King sat enthroned, the Wheel embroidered in gold on his crimson robe, the Key hanging out in view upon his breast, the Hammer across his knees. At a table to his left sat a recorder whose pen ran as fast as words were uttered, on his right a jurist with scrolls containing the laws of Ys before him. Behind the seats four legionaries in full battle gear stood at attention; and behind them loomed the eidolons of the Three, Taranis the Father, Belisama the Mother, kraken that represented inhuman Lir.

On that day, a rainstorm made dim the light from the glazed windows and laved the chamber with its susurrus. Candles in wall sconces and lamps on the desks cast their small glows, uneasy in the drafts. More people than usual had come to observe, for a notorious case was to be heard. The smell of wet wool garments gave sharpness to the air.

Gratillonius heard pleaders in order of arrival. Nagon Demari registered outrage, but Donnerch the wagoner guffawed, when they must wait for several of the lower classes. An elderly woman stated that she did not want the charity of the Gallicenae, for her son's widow could perfectly well pay her support as the son himself had done; having obtained the figures, Gratillonius so ordered. A man found guilty of theft brought friends, whom the magistrate had ruled unreliable, to declare he had been with them on the night of the crime; Gratillonius released him on grounds of reasonable doubt, but warned that this would be taken into account if there was another accusation. A sailor declared that his captain did wrong to make him suffer six lashes for a minor infraction, and ought to pay compensation for the injustice; after several of the crew had testified, Gratillonius said, "You were lucky. I'd have given you nine."

Thereupon it was time for Nagon Demari, Labor Councillor among the

Suffetes, and Donnerch, son of Arel, carter. Nagon spoke at length about his beneficence in organizing the longshoremen of Ys into a guild, now that trade was improving, thanks to wise King Grallon. He made a mouth as he said that: a stocky, cold-eyed man who despite aristocratic blood had been born poor and scrabbled his way up in the world till he sat in the Council. "Spare me this and get to the point," Gratillonius snapped.

Nagon looked indignant but explained that handling cargo obviously involved carrying it inland, wherefore carters should belong to the guild, pay its dues, require its fixed charges for their work, and perform such services for the guild as its leadership needed. Donnerch had not only refused these requests, made for his own good, and done so in unseemly language, he had brutally assailed two of the brotherhood who sought to persuade him.

Three newcomers entered the hall. Gratillonius drew a quick breath and raised his hand. "A moment," he interrupted. Louder: "Thrice welcome, honored sir!" with the same repeated in Latin.

Corentinus made salutation. A letter had declared he was coming, but Gratillonius had not looked for him quite this soon. He must have ridden hard, he and the two strong young men who must be deacons assigned him. The new chorepiscopus of Ys had shed much of the forest hermit. Nose, chin, cheekbones still jutted, deep-set eyes still smoldered under tangled brows, but hair and beard were neatly clipped and he had evidently bathed at hostels where he overnighted. His head was bare, the tonsured locks drenched and matted; but the paenula hanging from his shoulders to his knees, off which water dripped, was of good quality, and beneath it the long shanks displayed Gallic breeches tucked into boots.

"We shall hear you out tomorrow—" Gratillonius started to tell those who stood before him.

"Nay," said Corentinus. He used Osismian, but already he could throw in enough Ysan words that he was intelligible to every listener. How had he learned them?

"We have arrived early, and God forbid it be in pride. Let us abide your leisure." He folded his height down on a rear bench. Stiffly, the deacons joined him.

Donnerch answered the question in Gratillonius's mind. "Why, I know that fellow," he exclaimed. "Hoy-ah, Corentinus!" He waved. The clergyman smiled and made a responding gesture. "I got as far as Turonum, trek before last," the wagoner said, "and he heard about me being from Ys and paid me for a few days of language teaching. I earned it, lord.

How he worked me!" He was a big young man, yellow-haired, freckle-faced, ordinarily cheerful.

"*May* we get on with our business, O King?" Nagon demanded.

"If you'll be quick about it," Gratillonius replied.

Presently Donnerch said: "By Epona, but he lies, him! Hark'ee, lord. I'd no reason for paying into his mucky guild and doing his mucky will, did I? And so I told my fellow independent carters. Then this pair of toughs came to call on me. When they started talking about two broken arms, I snatched my mule whip off the wall. I have the cudgels they dropped on their way out, if the King wants to see 'em. Aye, they had me hauled up on charges of assault, but the magistrate didn't believe 'em, though he dared not call 'em perjurers either. So here we are."

"*Perjurers?*" shouted Nagon. "Lord, I've come on their behalf because their injuries are too cruel, too grievous, after that barbaric attack—"

"Silence!" Gratillonius commanded. "Think you the King is blind and deaf? I've stayed my hand erenow, Nagon Demari, for there's been much else for me to do, and it did seem you'd bettered the lot of your workers somewhat. But darker stories have grown too many of late. This is only the newest of them."

"Two honest men swear, against this known drunkard and brawler, that he fell on them with a dangerous weapon, unprovoked. Poor Jonan lost an eye. Cudgels? Donnerch could find two cudgels anywhere."

"Getting hurt is a hazard of building empires," Gratillonius said, "and I warn you to stop trying to build yours any bigger. Free carters are not longshoremen. Henceforth, leave them alone. And . . . Donnerch, mayhap you were needlessly rough. Tell your friends that next time something like this happens, there will be a full inquiry; and whoever has taken arms against a man without real need, he'll know the scourge or the ax. Dismissed."

Donnerch barely suppressed a whoop, Nagon did not conceal a glower. Gratillonius wondered whether he, the King, had won or lost today. He needed all the support he could call on, when he must protect not a mild Eucherius but a forceful Corentinus.

Luckily, just two more cases were left, and those minor. He adjourned before any further petitioners could arrive. In a rear chamber he exchanged his robe for everyday tunic, trousers, hooded cloak. The Key felt momentarily chill against his skin.

Returning, he ignored everybody else that lingered, to greet the chorepiscopus properly and have the deacons introduced to him. Those seemed like vigorous and dedicated men, but well under control of their leader. "It's good to see you again," Gratillonius said in Latin, quite sincerely in spite of awaiting difficulties. "I hope you'll like Ys."

"I do," the minister answered. "Too much. As I rode in, what memories came back." He squared his shoulders. "My friend, I don't know whether you've done me the greatest service or the scurviest trick; but Bishop Martinus said this is God's will, and that must suffice me. Will you show us to the church?"

"Why, you're here too soon. Nothing's properly ready. I'll quarter you in the palace till then."

Corentinus shook his head. "No, thanks. The fewer fleshly comforts and temptations, the better. To tell the truth, a reason I pushed hard on the road was fear that you, in mistaken kindness, would outfit our dwelling luxuriously."

"Well, come look, but I warn you, the place has lain neglected since Eucherius died."

"The more merit to us," Corentinus said almost merrily, "as we make it into a fortress of God."

Gratillonius thought of his Mithraeum, also an outpost lonely and beleaguered. Let Corentinus settle in, get some rest, begin to find out for himself what Ys was—not only a seaport with the usual gaiety, unruliness, swindlings, sorrows, vices, ghosts, dreams . . . though in Ys they were stronger and stranger than elsewhere—not only a city of wealth, power, beauty, industry, corruption, vanity, arrogance, like others . . . though in Ys these flourished as they had not done elsewhere since the high days of Rome—but a whole society with its own ways and Gods which were not akin to those of any other, ancient, pervasive, and enduring. He, Gratillonius, had not yet fully come to terms with Ys, and he was no Christian. He hoped Corentinus would not break his heart, battering against what the evangelist must needs perceive as wickedness.

They went out into the Forum and the rain. Wind sent the water at a slant, silver that glinted cold across the mosaics of dolphins and sea horses, and downward from basin to basin of the Fire Fountain at the center. The wind hooted and plucked at clothes. It bore a sound and a smell of Ocean. Hardly a soul was in sight. Gratillonius led the way across to the former temple of Mars.

"Sir—lord King—" He stopped and looked toward the voice. The speaker was young Budic, who as a legionary of his had today taken a turn in the honor guard at the palace. "Sir, an Imperial courier brought this. I thought I'd better get it to you right away, and you'd be hereabouts."

"Well done," said the centurion of the Second, and took a scroll wrapped in oiled cloth. He kept impassive, though his heart slugged and his throat tightened. Budic stood staring as he walked on.

In the portico of the church he said to Corentinus: "Let me read this at once. I suspect it's something you should know about too."

The chorepiscopus traced a cross in the wet air. "You're probably right," he replied.

The letter was clearly one sent in many copies through Gallia, Hispania, and perhaps beyond.

—Magnus Clemens Maximus, Augustus, to the Senate and the People of Rome, and to all others whom it may concern, charging them most solemnly and under the severest penalties to carry out those duties laid upon them by Almighty God and the state. . . .

—After four years of patient negotiation, it has become clear that accommodation with Flavius Valentinianus, styled Emperor, is unattainable. . . . Intransigence and repeated violations. . . . The abominable heresy of Arius. . . . The cleansing of the state, even as Our Saviour drove out money changers and demons. . . .

—Therefore we most strictly enjoin the people and those in whose care the people are, that they remain loyal and orderly, obedient to those whom God has set above them, while we lead our armies into Italy and wherever else may prove needful, to the end that the Western Empire, harmoniously with our brother Theodosius of the East, again have tranquility under a single and righteous ruler.

4

An autumn storm roared, whistled, flung rain and hail, throughout one night. It made doubly comforting the warmth of Bodilis's bed and body. By morning the weather was dry but the gale still ramped. Man and woman woke about the same time, smiled drowsily at each other through the dimness, shared a kiss. Desire came back. He laughed, low in his throat. "There's no call on me today," he said, drawing her closer.

That was not true. There was always something to clamor for the attention of the centurion, the prefect, the King. Only the day before, news had arrived from beyond the Alps, via the Duke of the Armorican Tract: Maximus was firmly in possession of Mediolanum and Valentinianus had fled eastward out of Italy. Gratillonius then made an excuse to visit the wisest of his Queens, out of turn, for her counsel and afterward her solace.

Nevertheless— "Just you and me," he said in the Latin she wanted to maintain for herself. "Later, let's breakfast with Una, hm?"

"M-m-m," she responded, and in other ways as well.

He often thought that if he could have his wish, she would be his sole wife. She had not the raw ardor of Forsquilis, good-natured sensuality of Maldunilis, dumb eagerness to please of Guilvilis; somehow, in her enough of each was alloyed. She was handsome rather than beautiful, and the years were putting gray into the wavy brown hair, crow's-feet around the blue near-sighted eyes, wrinkliness under the throat, sag in the breasts. But she was no crone, and good bones would endure. Though her monthly courses had not ended, it did not seem she would bear him more children, ever. Well, he had plenty now, and Una was a darling second only to Dahut. Before all else was the *wholeness* of her. She knew things, thought about them, gave him her judgments, submitted to nothing save the truth as she saw it. She was his friend, such as he had not had since Parnesius on the Wall; and she was his lover.

They met; together they went beyond themselves; presently they lay at peace with the universe. Outside, the wind hooted, rattled shutters, carried a noise of waves breaking mightily on the sea wall. Yesterday the King had barred the gate and locked it with the Key that he alone bore, lest the waters fling it open and rage into Ys. He did not expect to free those doors for a while; and few vessels would come thereafter. As winter neared, Ys drew into itself, even as he and his Queen did this day.

She chuckled. "What's funny?" he asked.

"Oh, you," she said. "Dutiful you, hiding away from work like a boy from the schoolmaster. It's good to see you taking your ease, dear, merely enjoying yourself. You should do it oftener."

Reminded, he sat up. "I forgot my morning prayer!"

She arched her brows. "For the very first time?"

"Uh, no."

"I'm sure your Mithras will understand, and overlook it. Belisama does." Bodilis's glance went to the figurine that occupied a niche in her otherwise plainly furnished bedroom. Carved of oak whose grain followed the folds of Her hooded cloak, it showed the Goddess as a woman of middle age, serene, an enigmatic smile on Her lips.

I could adore a deity like that, he thought, if this were Her only aspect. Putting solemnity aside, "We spoke of breakfast—" he began.

A knock on the door interrupted. "My lord, my lord!" called the voice of Bodilis's chief manservant. "Forgive me, but a soldier of yours is here. He says he must see you this instant."

"What?" Gratillonius swung feet to floor. His immediate feeling was of resentment. Could they never leave him alone? He took a robe off a peg and pulled it over himself. Bodilis rose too, with a rueful look for him.

His deputy Adminius waited in the atrium, wearing civil Ysan garb that he had donned with unmilitary hastiness. He saluted. "Begging your pardon, sir." The lean, snaggle-toothed countenance was full of distress. "I'm afraid I got bad news. 'Ard news, anyway, though I'm sure the centurion can 'andle the matter."

Gratillonius dismissed whatever happiness had still been aglow in him. "Speak."

"You got a challenger, sir. At the Wood. One o' the lodgekeepers came asking where you was, and I thought you should 'ear it from me."

It was as if the wind came in off the street and wrapped around Gratillonius. "Do you know more?"

"No, sir. Should I go look? I can tell 'em I couldn't find yer right away."

Gratillonius shook his head. "Never mind," he said dully. "Let me get shod."

He turned back toward the bedroom. Having covered her own nakedness, Bodilis had followed him and heard. She stood at the inner doorway, the color drained from her face. "Oh, no," she whispered. The hands that groped across his were cold. "Not already."

"The way of Ys," Gratillonius rasped. He brushed past her.

Returning with sandals and cloak, he found she had not stirred. Those widened eyes struck remorse into him. He stopped, clasped her by the shoulders, and said, "I'm sorry. I forgot how terrible this must be to you. A total stranger, who may be another Colconor or, or anything. Don't be afraid." It might be kindly of him to change from Latin to Ysan: "Nay, fear not, heart of mine. I'll smite the wretch ere he can slice a hair off my knuckle. For your sake."

"I dare not pray," she whispered. "This thing lies at the will of the Gods. But I'll hope, and—and weep for you, Grallon, who so loathes this need laid upon him."

He kissed her, quickly and roughly, and went forth with Adminius. The wind shrilled, sent dead leaves scrittling along the street, roused little breakers on rain puddles. It drove clouds before it, making light and shadow sickle over roofs, half veiling the towertops. Rooks winged dark on the blast. The garments of such folk as were out flapped as if they too were about to fly away.

"You'll take 'im, sir, same as you did the last 'un," Adminius avowed. " 'E'll've 'ad a scant night's rest in the wet. 'E can't be very smart, or 'e'd've waited till later ter arrive."

Gratillonius nodded absently. The rule that the King must respond at once to a challenge, unless absent from the city, was doubtless meant for more than the immediate gratification of Taranis; it gave him an advantage. Frequent changes were undesirable, even when the monarch was a political nullity.

"And if perchance you don't win, God forbid, w'y, 'e won't last out the day 'imself," Adminius went on. "Yer lads'll see ter that."

Shocked before he felt also touched, Gratillonius growled, "No. No legionary will raise a finger against him. That's an order."

"But, but yer the prefect o' Rome!"

"The more reason to maintain law. Including this damnable law of Ys. We *can't* have the city fall into disorder. Don't you see, it's the keystone of everything I've worked to build in Armorica." Gratillonius considered. His mind had become as bleakly bright as the sunbeams. "If I fall, report to Soren Cartagi. He'll be the effective governor for at least a while. Remind him of the need to continue my policies, for the good of Ys. Give him whatever help he requires. When he can spare you, bring the legionaries to the Duke and put them under his orders."

Anguish asked: "Wot about yerself, sir?"

"Let them burn me and scatter the bones and ashes at sea. That's what Ys does with her fallen Kings." And I shall go home to Dahilis. "My brothers in Mithras will hold their own rites for me."

Gratillonius stiffened his neck. "Enough," he said. "I do not plan on getting killed. Forward march! On the double, soldier."

At Dragon House he donned his centurion's armor. All twenty-four of his men formed ranks and followed him out High Gate, battle-arrayed. By then word had spread and the streets were aswarm, ababble. Where Processional Way started north out of Aquilonian Way, a squad of marines formed a line to hold back the crowd. Through the wind, Gratillonius heard shouted wishes for his victory.

That warmed him a trifle. He had much to live for, and live he proposed to do. This challenger would scarcely be another pitiable Hornach, but rather some sturdy rogue prepared to take his chances. Quite possibly he was a barbarian. It would be almost a pleasure to kill a Frank, say. In any case, a fair fight which Gratillonius had not provoked was no butchery. As always, he did not dwell on the possibility that he might lose. To do so would merely weaken him.

The road bent east, under sere hills, and the Wood of the King loomed ahead. The gale had torn off nearly all the leaves that earlier turned it bronze. Now trunks and boughs were winter-gray, though shadows still made a cave of the depths beneath them. Twigs clawed at the sky. Timber creaked. Wind eddied about, wailed and mumbled.

Half a dozen more marines had reached the courtyard of the Shield and Hammer. They saluted the King. Tethered nearby stood their horses, and leashed hounds whined impatient. If either contestant fled, he would be hunted down and brought back for the death stroke.

Red-robed, Soren emerged from the blood-colored house when an attendant called. He had been delayed by no need to equip himself; his was only to lead the ceremonies, before and after. "In the holy name of Taranis, greeting, King of Ys," he said.

For the sake of Dahut, Bodilis, Rome, Gratillonius bent his helmeted head to the God he abhorred. Mithras would understand.

"The challenger has chosen his weapons and is prepared," Soren said. Nothing in his heavy visage bespoke how he wished the combat would go. He was the instrument of Taranis. Turning, he cried: "Come forth, O you who would be King of Ys!"

A wiry, long-legged young man stepped from the gloom within, onto the porch and down the stairs. His movements were quick, suggestive of tension, but there was no hesitancy in them. A forked black beard, well trimmed, decorated clear features marred by poor teeth and a scar puckering the right cheek to pull that corner of his mouth into the hint of a sneer. From the oufits available he had chosen a nose-guarded helmet, knee-length chainmail coat, thick cross-garters over the breeches to protect calves, small round shield, long Gallic sword in a sheath, a javelin in his free hand. Plainly, he meant to make the best of agility against a larger opponent.

Plainly, too, he was not fatigued as Adminius had predicted. Springiness was in his gait and clarity in the green eyes. Browned skin gave a clue. This was an outdoorsman, skillful to contrive shelter and sleep soundly on the wildest of nights. He would be dangerous as a panther; and well he knew it.

He approached across the flagstones, peered, and halted. In Redonic-accented Latin he cried, "Are you the King? But you're the centurion!"

And Gratillonius knew him. "Rufinus!" Rufinus, leader of those Bacaudae whom the legionaries had driven from their prey on the road to Juliomagus—

The young man lifted spear and shield. Laughter whooped from him. "Why, you rascal, you never told me! I'd not've bucked you elsewise. Better to've asked for a place in your command, hey?" He sobered, apart from a savage grin. "Too late now, I suppose. Right? Pity."

"What's this?" Soren demanded. "Know you each other?"

"We've met," said Gratillonius. A knot formed in his guts. "He'll withdraw his challenge if I ask."

"Impossible, as well you remember," said the Speaker for Taranis. "Let us pray."

Rufinus glided close to Gratillonius. The smile kept flickering as he murmured, "I'm sorry, centurion, truly I am. You're a decent sort, I think. But you should've told me, that night in your tent."

They knelt at the royal oak. Soren signed them both with holy water and invoked the Father God. Wind boomed. A raven flew low overhead.

"We go off by ourselves," Gratillonius said bluntly.

Rufinus nodded. "They've explained."

Side by side, the two men pushed through snickering underbrush to the opening, out of sight from the house, where Gratillonius had killed Hornach and Colconor. Strange that underfoot were rain-sodden leaves and humus; this earth should be gory red.

His mood had not caused him to lose wariness. However, Rufinus attempted no sneak attack, simply leaned on his spear and sighed, "This is too bad. It really is."

"What made you come?" Gratillonius wondered.

Rufinus barked laughter. "I wish I could say a mischievous God, but it was just chance—and myself—though it did seem, one midnight, moonlight hour, that stag-horned Cernunnos danced His madman's dance before me, to egg me on. . . . Well," he proceeded in a level tone, "you roadpounders gave us brethren a nasty setback, you know. Not just our dead and wounded. You hit our spirits in the balls, and we skulked about for a long spell, living more off roots and voles than plunder and, hm, donations. My standing as duke was in danger, not that it meant much any more. Bit by bit, I rallied the boys, we got new recruits, till at last I had the makings of a fresh band. What it needed next—you'll know what I mean—what it needed was blooding, to prove itself to itself.

"Then the news ran this summer, civil war begun again and the Emperor marched off south with his army. I remembered Sicorus. Do you? My landmaster, who debased my sister till she died whelping his get." Fury went like lightning over the face and through the voice, and vanished as swiftly. "We all had things to avenge on Sicorus. The upshot was, one night we came and ringed Maedraeacum manor house in. We let women, children, harmless slaves go out, free; I told the boys that whoever touched them in anything but helpfulness would answer to my knife. Then we pushed Sicorus's overseers in to join him, and set fire to the building. That damaged the loot, of course, but next day we still picked a grand amount of gold and silver from the ashes."

Rufinus sighed once more, shrugged, and finished: "My mistake. I reckoned the Empire would be too busy with its own woes for doing much about this. That's how it was in past civil wars. But it turns out Emperor Maximus has driven his enemies before him right handily. The Roman—the Armorican Duke, is that what they call him? My fellow duke—I reckon he decided he could spare the troops to make an example of us. They scoured the woods for a month or more. Most of my Valiant are dead, the rest are fled. Me, I remembered a centurion who reminded me about wonderful Ys, and decided I'd scant to lose. So here we are, Gratillonius."

Wind brawled, swirled under armor, made the Wood groan. Gratillonius said slowly: "Too late, you thought of asking me for a berth in my service. How could I give you any, after what you did?"

"At Maedraeacum?" answered pride and reason. "Had I no right to bring Ita's ghost peace? Every ghost that Sicorus squeezed out of life? Hasn't Rome made friends of her foes, like you Britons or us Gauls? I could serve you well, King. I'm a good man of my hands. And . . . My own Bacaudae may be gone, but I know many more, up and down the valleys and off in the hills. Outlaws; but they could be useful scouts, messengers, irregular fighters, for a King who showed them a little kindness."

Gratillonius realized he must not listen. "Try that if you overcome me," he said. "But remember that Rome is the Mother of us all. And be gentle to the Nine Queens and—and their children."

For the first time, he saw complete calm on Rufinus. It was eerily like the peace he himself had felt this dawn after he and Bodilis made love. The wanderer traced a sign with his spear, in the wind. "I promise," he said low.

Thereupon he dropped into a feline crouch and asked, "Shall we have at it, friend?"

"We must," said Gratillonius.

They circled about the glade. Wind keened; the raven, settled on an unrestful bough, croaked hoarsely; fallen leaves squelped. Rufinus moved his buckler to and fro while his arm stayed cocked, ready to cast the javelin. Gratillonius kept his big Roman shield in place and squinted across its upper edge, the sword poised in his right hand.

Glances met and held fast. It was always a peculiar feeling to look into the eyes of a foeman, not unlike looking into those of a woman in bed, an ultimate intimacy.

They stalked, he and Rufinus, each in search of an opening. Now and then the Gaul made tentative movements of his spear. Gratillonius remained stolid. The wind blew.

Abruptly Rufinus cast. Immediately he snatched for the sword scabbarded across his back, and charged.

The Roman missile should have sunk its iron head into the Roman shield and hung there, its shaft dragging in the earth. Gratillonius was ready for it. His blade flipped it aside. It spent its malice in a rotten log. Rufinus was upon him. The Gallic sword crashed down. Gratillonius shifted his shield enough to catch the blow. His own weapon snaked forward. Rufinus sprang back. Blood from his left thigh darkened that trouser leg.

He's mine, Gratillonius knew. But let it be quick. Let it be merciful.

Rufinus gave him a wry grin and, again, circled, alert for a chance to pounce. Man for man, outlaw and centurion should be equal. It was not individual Romans but the Roman army that had broken the Gauls. Rufinus, though, had taken a wound not mortal but deep; and whatever carnivore skills he had picked up, he was untrained in the science of killing.

Gratillonius let him attack, over and over, wear himself down, retreat with more blood running out of him. Two or three times he got through the defense, but the injuries that the hare inflicted on the tortoise were minor slashes.

The end came all at once. Gratillonius maneuvered Rufinus up against a thicket, which blocked retreat. Rufinus hewed. By that time the long sword was weakly held. Through the wind, Gratillonius heard how Rufinus panted, while blood soaked his breeches and footsteps. Gratillonius's shield stopped another blow. His short, thick blade knocked the weapon from his opponent's grasp.

A moment Rufinus stared, until his laughter cried out. "Good work, soldier!" He spread his arms, while he swayed on his feet. "Come, what're you waiting for? Here I am."

Gratillonius found he could not move.

"Come, come," Rufinus raved. "I'm ready. I'd've done for you if I could."

"Pick up your sword," Gratillonius heard himself say.

Rufinus shook his head. "Oh, no, you don't," he crowed. "I bear you no ill will, buddy. You won, fair and square. But be damned if I'll let you pretend—*Roman*—you're still in a fight. Make your offering."

To Taranis, Who deigned to be Colconor. And Lir had slain Dahilis.

"Are you playing games with me?" Gratillonius brought forth.

"No," said Rufinus, feebly now as the loss of blood swept him further along. He staggered. "I only . . . want you . . . to stop playing games with yourself . . . and whatever Gods are yours, Roman,"

He lurched, sank to hands and knees, crouched gasping.

Mithras forbade human sacrifice.

It was as if Bodilis were suddenly there in the wind and the wet, Bodilis whom Gratillonius would seek back to as soon as he was able. Not losing time in cleaning it, he sheathed his sword. "I cannot kill you, helpless," he said, dimly amazed at his own steadiness. "Nor can I let you lie there. Not if you surrender to me, altogether. Do you understand? I think I can save you if you'll declare yourself my prisoner, Rufinus."

"I could have worse masters," muttered back around the reborn grin.

Gratillonius knelt and set about stanching the wounds of his man.

5

Throughout the years, Soren Cartagi and Lanarvilis the Queen had held many a private meeting. None was as grim as this.

The gale had died away, but seas still crashed against the wall and gate of Ys, spume flying higher than the battlements. Their sound went undergroundishly through the whole city, as if earth responded to that anger. Starless dark engulfed heaven, save for what towertop windows glimmered alone. Lights and luxury in the room where Lanarvilis received her visitor could not really stave off night.

Motionless in a high-backed chair, she watched him pace to and fro before her. Flamelight sheened on her russet gown and silver fillet. It flickered within her eyes, making them demonlike, though on her face was only compassion for him. He wore his red robe of office, the talisman of the Sun Wheel hung on his breast—so fateful did he think this occasion —but had removed his miter on entering the house. In the uneasy illumination, his hair and beard seemed largely gray.

"Aye, thus it was," he told her in his pain. "He came back upholding the bandit. Said he'd bed him down in the Lodge. Ere I could shake off stupefaction and protest, Gratillonius declared himself winner in the combat and that that sufficed; no good would come of slaying a captive. Instead, he would give Taranis a hecatomb of beasts, bought out of his own purse."

Lanarvilis nodded. "The Gallicenae have heard that much, of course," she said softly. "He sent a written account among us—written by Bodilis, with whom he stays closeted in the palace, his Roman soldiers standing by. They've brought the Gaul there too. That is all I know thus far. His words to us were few and hard, no matter that Bodilis tried to milden them."

"I'll give you the rest." Soren's feet thudded on the carpet, a drumbeat above the sea-noise. "I shouted my outrage. Ys lives by Her Gods, Who require Their ancient sacrifices. He replied that—he would fight future challengers, and those who did not yield must take their hazard of death; but he would not believe the honor of any God was served by—he called it murder!" Soren struggled for breath. " 'Stand aside,' he said, and began to help the scoundrel to the house.

"I called on the marines to kill the challenger, since this traitor King would not. 'Be still,' Gratillonius said—oh, how quietly. 'It is not meet that anybody die here.' His Romans trod closer, hands on hilts. Yet I— Elissa, Lanarvilis—I saw it was not they that stayed the marines. Our guards too were shaken, but 'twas the King they would obey, this king who scorns the Gods That raised him up."

Soren ground fist into palm. "I swallowed vomit, though it burned my throat," he related. "After the injured man was at rest and a Roman—not our standby physician for a wounded victor, but a soldier with rough surgical skill—was tending him . . . Gratillonius returned and I sought to reason with him. Whatever his beliefs, I said, surely he could see that this—blasphemy, violation of the Pact—this would make him hated and undermine all he has done for his Rome. He answered that he thought not."

"I fear he was right," Lanarvilis said.

"Aye," Soren groaned. "Have you heard? Late in the day, when that Rufinus was somewhat recovered, Gratillonius brought him to the city. Beforehand, he had sent for heralds and told them to proclaim his intent. Folk were packed along Lir Way. He entered High Gate at the head of his marching men and, and a squadron of our marines, he riding, with Rufinus tethered at his saddlebow—Do you understand? He gave himself a Roman triumph; and the people cheered!"

"I heard," Lanarvilis said. "I was not surprised."

"He has won them over. In spite of his alien God, in spite of his protecting that Christian priest, in spite of everything, he's their dear King Grallon, for whom they'll take arms against anybody. How long before the Gods take arms against them?"

"Have you thought, Soren," she asked low, "that we may in truth be at the end of the Age that Brennilis began? That mayhap Ys is once more offered the cup of youth, and if she will not taste of it must soon grow old and die?"

He halted. He stared. "You too?" he breathed at last.

She shook her head. "Nay, my darling. Never would I betray you. But my Sisters and I—other than Bodilis, though she laid certain words of wisdom in that letter—we had Maldunilis brought back from Sena and spoke together. I knew you would seek me out."

His bulk trembled. "What did you decide?"

"It may be that Gratillonius will satisfy Taranis with his hecatomb."

"I think not; for no sacrificial blood will flow in his heart."

Lanarvilis shivered likewise. "Wait and see. Taranis did not cast a thunderbolt this day. But if the Gods are indeed wrathful—Their revenge is often slow, but always cruel."

Soren traced a sign, braced himself, and said, "I'm concerned that all Ys not suffer because of a single man's wickedness. Might you Gallicenae curse him, as you did Colconor?"

Lanarvilis made a fending motion. "Nay! How could we? He may be mistaken, but evil he is not. A curse without passion behind it can no more fly to its target than an arrow from a stringless bow."

"And anyhow, several of you would refuse."

"The whole Nine would, Soren."

"So be it," the man said. "Well, Ys has been saddled in the past with Kings about whom something must be done. I mean not those who were . . . simply bestial, like Colconor, for to conspire against the Chosen of Taranis is an act of desperation—but some who posed a threat to the whole city. We'll send our agents out through Armorica, bearing gold and promises. Gratillonius will have challenger after challenger, month after month, till one of them cuts him down."

Calm had descended on Lanarvilis. "We guessed that idea would be broached, we Gallicenae," she said, "and we forbid it."

"What?"

"Some of us love him. But put that aside. We too can lay our hearts on the altar when it must be done. Think, though. You and I are the politic persons, the worldliest among those who serve the Gods. Is it not really Ys we serve, Mother Ys?

"Think what Gratillonius has done and is doing. He has strengthened us, within and without our wall. He has quickened our stagnant trade. He has reconciled the high and the low. He has kept us free. Who else has the least hope of holding Emperor Maximus at arm's length? Who else have the Scoti and the Saxons learned to fear? Why, his very Mithras is a counterbalance to that Christ Who would take from us our Gods.

"Dare you imagine that some filthy barbarian or runaway slave can replace him? I say to you, Soren Cartagi, and if you are honest you will concede it—ill shall Ys fare if she loses King Grallon."

Silence followed, apart from the subterranean thunder of Ocean.

Finally Soren dragged forth: "I am . . . aware of this. I awaited that response of yours. I have even begun talks with my colleagues. Hannon is bewildered with horror, but I should be able to talk him over, along with the rest. We will not rebel, not conspire, but bide our time. Let the Gods work as They will."

He stood quiet for a space before adding, "Yet we, Their worshippers, cannot sit passive. They make us what we are, our unique selves, *Ys*. How shall we make our amends for this harm that has been done Them?"

"The Nine have thought upon that," Lanarvilis replied gravely. "We, his wives, know what stubbornness is in Gratillonius. But patience, endurance, that is woman's weapon.

"Therefore we will lay the foundations of the future, that ineluctable morrow when he has fallen and we are done with mourning him. We will take triple care that our daughters grow up in the awe of the Gods. First and foremost will we instill devoutness in Dahut, child of Dahilis, whose nurturing we share. Forsquilis senses fate within that girl. Its form is unknown, but its power waxes year after year. We Nine will set upon her brow the sigil of the Three."

Again Soren signed himself.

"It is well," he said, took up the wine cups that stood on the table. handed Lanarvilis one and took a long draught from its mate.

Thereafter, soothed a little, he sat down opposite her, ventured a smile, and said, "You've lightened a huge burden for me. Thank you."

She smiled back. "Nay, you let it off yourself."

"Well, mayhap, but first you loosened the bonds holding it fast. Ever have you been kind to me."

"How could I be aught else . . . to you?" she whispered.

They withdrew from the edge of that. "Well," he suggested, "can we spend a while talking of small things? How have you fared since last I saw you? What will you share with me?"

"All I am permitted to," she said.

IX

1

Winter's early night had fallen when three Romans entered an alehouse in the Fishtail district. The first was well known there: Adminius, deputy commander of the legionaries. The second had come occasionally, young Budic; he, who carried a lantern, now blew it out and put it down on a remnant of mosaic. The third was a tall, craggy-boned, middle-aged man, clad in ordinary tunic and breeches, but with his hair shaven off the front half of his scalp.

This taproom had been the atrium of a fine house—long ago, before sea level began to rise, driving the wealthy to higher ground and eventually forcing construction of the great wall. Bits of relief sculpture and hints of frescos peered out of soot and grease. Tables and benches on what was mostly a clay floor were rough wood, though themselves time-worn, haggled by generations of idle knives. Tallow candles guttered and dripped on the boards, enough light to see by after a fashion. Shadows curtained every corner, flickered across peeled plaster and thin-scraped membrane stretched over windows, parodied each movement. The stench of burning fat mingled with odors of cooking from the kitchen, of sour wine and worse beer.

Withal, it was a rather cheery place. About a dozen fishers, merchant sailors, wherry oarsmen occupied two of the tables. They drank heartily, jested roughly, laughed loudly. A woman sat with one group, teasing them while she sipped what they bought her. As the newcomers entered, another man came in from the hallway beyond. He grinned in lazy wise and secured his belt. The rest gave him a ribald cheer. "Did your ram sink that hull for good this eventide?" shouted someone.

"Nay," he replied, "you know Keban better than that. She'll soon bob back to surface. Me, I'm thirsty. Mead, potboy, none of your horse piss but good, honest mead!" He was young, strong, ruddy of close-trimmed beard and queue-braided hair.

Adminius and Budic recognized him. "That's Herun, of the navy," said the younger soldier in his diffident way, and the deputy whooped, " 'Oy, there, 'Erun, come drink it with us!"

Their companion shook his head. "Poor, forlorn soul," he murmured in Latin. "Has he no wife, that he couples with a whore?"

Budic flushed. "W-w-we warned you, sir, what kind of place this is. Should we g-go away?"

"No." A smile. "It's not as if I didn't recognize the surroundings."

Herun trotted over. "We got a guest 'ere," Adminius said. "Corentinus."

The mariner halted, squinted through the murk, responded slowly: "Aye, now I know him. Every sennight he preaches at the Forum, from the steps of the old Mars temple. What would a Christian priest among us?"

Corentinus smiled again. "Naught to frighten anybody," he said in Ysan that had become fluent though heavily accented. "I hope to grow better acquainted with folk. These men kindly offered to show me where sailors hang out. After all, I'm a sailor myself."

"Indeed?"

"Or was. 'Tis another kind of sea I ply nowadays. If I pledge not to evangelize, will you let me drink with you?"

A staring, listening stillness had fallen. " 'E's a right sort," Adminius declared. " 'Oly man, but not sanctimonious, if you take my meaning. Nobody minds Budic or me or most of us soldiers being Christian, so why mind Corentinus?"

Herun recovered himself. "Welcome," he said, a bit grudgingly. "Shall we sit?" He joined the three at a separate table. "Only the mead here is fit for aught but swine and Saxons," he warned, becoming more genial, "but 'tis pretty fair stuff at the price."

The potboy brought a round. Corentinus watered his. "How like you our city?" Herun asked him.

"Oh, dazzling, a whirlpool of wonders," the chorepiscopus replied. "I've never seen aught to rival it, and I've been widely about in my time."

Adminius laughed. He waved a hand around. "This 'ere's 'ardly any palace," he said.

"Nay," Corentinus agreed. "But see you, I've had my fill of elegance. Thanks to the King, I've seen the inside of most wealthy homes in Ys and its hinterland. Beautiful, as I said; but my flock numbers few, and they poor and lowly."

"Get ye no Christians in summer?" growled a man at an adjacent table. "I've met 'em aplenty whilst faring to Roman harbors."

"Aye, aye. They attend services. But my true ministry is to Ys." Corentinus chuckled and shrugged. "Not that my sermons on the steps—my rantings, some call them—draw large audiences. So I thought I would go forth among ordinary folk and get to know them well enough that, God willing, I can find what words will appeal to them."

Herun frowned. "You'll find us a tough lot," he said. "For see you, 'tis by the favor and power of her Gods that Ys lives. Else would the sea overwhelm us."

"God, the true God, He has power to save Ys," blurted Budic.

Corentinus raised a hand. "Belay that, lad. You mean well, but I did promise no preaching this night. Can we not just spin yarns? Or continue whatever else your pleasure is."

"What is yours?" purred a female voice.

They glanced up. The harlot Keban had tidied herself after Herun and come back downstairs. She was pleasant to look upon, in her close-fitting gown over a buxom figure and her deliberately tousled hair. She drooped her eyelids and smiled. "Care for a bit of fun, you?" she went on in Corentinus's direction.

He shook his head. "Not for me, thank you."

She looked about, "Anybody? . . . Not yet, anyhow? . . . Well, who'll buy a girl a drink?"

"Allow me," said Corentinus, and gestured her to sit beside him on the bench.

"Huh?" muttered from another table. "Keban, don't you know that's the new Christian priest?"

"Mayhap I can seduce him," she said impudently, and settled down.

Corentinus laughed. "Or I you? We'll see. What'll you have?"

"Wine." She stuck out her tongue at Herun. "Despite what you say 'bout it." To the pastor: "I'm surprised. I truly am. I thought somebody like you would hate me."

Again he shook his head. "Nay," he told her solemnly. "I must hate what you do, but never you, poor child. Tell me, do you never weary of being a thing? Do you ever think what becomes of old whores?"

She defied him; forlornness lay underneath: "What else have I got, unless to be a scullion in some household where the master and, and all of them'll hump me anyway?"

Budic was appalled. "Why, Keban—" he began, and stopped.

"You've been sweet," she said to him. "Few are."

He withered under Corentinus's sardonic look. The pastor, though, merely declared to the woman: " 'Tis never too late for God's grace, while life remains. Did you choose to accept His mercy, I would for my part undertake to find you a decent situation. In due course, my church may found a home for those who were lost aforetime."

The outer door creaked. Boots thudded under the weight of a bear-solid man, roughly clad, who snuffed the link he had been carrying by scrubbing it against the clay and tossed it down. As he approached through the gloom, first Herun, then the soldiers and most of the mariners recognized his rocky visage. "Maeloch!" cried one. "What brings ye hither?"

The fisher captain spouted a laugh. "What d'ye think? A bumper of mead, and—Ah, two girls on hand, I see. Hoy, Keban, Silis, which of ye'd fain be first?"

The former caught at the table edge before her and sat unwontedly silent, but the second, merry, asked, "What, are you that well-heeled tonight, Maeloch?"

"Aye, and horny as a narwhal," he said, striding close to rumple her locks. "Been outside o' town this past month, helping Kadrach the cooper." No boats like his, and few ships, put far out to sea at this time of year. Maeloch sobered. "And now I'm done, well, looks to me like a spell o' calm weather ahead, after the blows and high seas we've been getting. Belike there'll soon be a summons for the Ferriers. I'll enjoy myself here, for I'd better be home tomorrow night."

Mirth had retreated as he spoke. Several men drew signs. "Lackwits!" Maeloch said amiably. "Why shrink ye when I bespeak yon duty? Would ye liefer the ghosts spooked about ashore, for aye?"

Since other benches were crowded, he sat down with Adminius and Herun. Opposite were Budic, Keban, and Corentinus. He peered past sputtering candles. "But ye be the Christian priest!" he exclaimed.

"Not precisely my title," the chorepiscopus replied. "No matter. I've heard talk of you, if I mistake me not." He offered his hand across the board, for a clasp in the manner of Ysans who were equals.

Maeloch ignored it, scowled, said harshly, "Why d'ye pester honest men at their hard-won ease?"

"My son, I came not to pester, only to make acquaintance. And ever since I heard of your strange task, I've wished to talk with one among those who do it. Somehow the chance has not come."

"Nor likely will." Maeloch grabbed his mead from the servant and swilled deep. "We be no puking preachers, we be plain working men, but this duty we have from our fathers, 'tis holy, and we'll not speak of it with any who share it not, let alone ye who'd mock it."

"Oh, but I would never mock," said Corentinus quietly. "You have right, 'tis far too sacred a matter. I wish to understand what happens on those nights."

"That ye may scuttle it?" fleered Maeloch. He drank more, snorted, grinned. "Enough. I seek no fight. Keban, honey, are ye ready to frig?"

The woman looked downward. "I don't—sudden-like, I don't feel so well," she mumbled. "I'm sorry, but could I just sit a while?"

Maeloch stiffened. "Next to the priest? What's he been feeding ye?"

"Let her be," Corentinus snapped. "Yonder's a wanton for you." His tone sharpened. "Or is it unthinkable you seek the wife that I suppose you have?"

Rage flared. "What business of yours, shavehead? I've heard ye deny the God's of Ys, the Pact of Brennilis, in the Forum; and I've heard the sea growl in answer at the gate. No more! Get out!"

"Now, wait a bit," Adminius urged.

Maeloch scrambled to his feet and around the table, to stand behind Corentinus and ask, "D'ye leave on your own shanks, or do I frog march ye forth? Quick!"

Corentinus rose, stepped over the bench, looked down an inch or two into the malachite eyes. "Are you that afraid of me?" he murmured.

Maeloch snarled and seized the right wrist of Corentinus. Instantly, the pastor jerked between thumb and forefinger and freed himself; and something happened with an ankle and a shove; and Maeloch sprawled on the floor.

Men swarmed up and around. "No brawl, hoy, let's ha' no brawl!"

"God forbid," said Corentinus mildly. As the fisher climbed back up: "Maeloch, friend, I know you're awearied, overwrought, and belike I provoked you. 'Twas not my intent. I humbly beg your forgiveness. May I stand you a drink?"

What could a sailor do but accept?

A fresh beaker, drained, had him asking where a priest had learned such a trick for a tussle. "Well, that's a bit of a story," Corentinus said. "Care to hear? Later I'll be happy to teach you the art, if you like."

Men crowded around. Corentinus leaned back, laid ankle over knee, and began: " 'Twas from a Sarmatian, on the south coast of the Suebian Sea, back when I was a deckhand. He was a wanderer himself, an outrunner of those Sclavonic and other tribes that're pushing in, now when the Goths and their kindred have pulled out. My ship was adventuring in hopes of getting amber at the source, 'stead of overland. First, you may know, we had to round the Cimbrian Chersonese and pass through the straits to the east. Those're wild and haughty folk there, Angli, Jutii,

Dani, not really German although they claim the royal houses of the German tribes stem from them; and they have some mightily curious customs—"

Keban, too, listened. Silis sat apart; she had no interest in geography. One hand cradled her cheek, the fingernails of the other drummed the table.

2

Merowech the Frank and his grown sons had been in Condate Redonum buying slaves. They did this four times a year—a healthy young male shortly before equinox and solstice. Everybody in the city knew why; nobody dared speak about it. A few times the Roman authorities had, in private talks, offered to supply condemned criminals free. The Frankish headmen spurned it. They would give their Gods nothing but the best.

Merowech always obtained the victim, using money collected from the laeti, because the sacred grove stood on his land. It was he who speared the naked body that sprattled strangling from a rope flung over a bough. (The corpse was left for the carrion fowl. Eventually the bones were taken away and stacked on that hill where the midsummer bonfire burned.) To other leading men of the neighborhood fell the honor of poleaxing and bleeding the animals that were also sacrificed, drinking some of the blood and sprinkling the worshippers with the rest. Afterward the carcasses went to Merowech's cookhouse, and everybody feasted in his hall. Thus nourished, Wotan and His sky-riding war band ought to grant victory in battle.

For the vernal equinox an additional purchase was required, a young woman. While the slain kine roasted, the men took her to a newly plowed field nearby. There Merowech swived her, followed by as many more as wished to call Fricca's blessing on their crops and their wives. She then went to work for the household whose turn it was, if she survived. Often she did not.

This day was glorious. Throughout the forest, buds had swelled and burst into leaf, blossom, a tumble of tender colors leading off toward reaches where sunlight speckled shadowiness, a whispering in breezes that were mild and laden with fragrances. The lesser birds jubilated. Overhead passed the great migrators, homeward bound.

Regardless, Merowech, Fredegond, Childeric, and Theuderich rode in helmets and ringmail, weapons at hand. Their dignity demanded it. They were not only the holders of acres broad and rich, they were garrison officers. It was on condition of the Franks providing the principal defense of the Redonian canton that the Romans had allowed them to settle there. Or so the official agreement read. Judging from what his father had told him, Merowech didn't think the Romans had had much choice, as weakened as the Empire was by its internal wars. Nowadays it seemed somewhat recovered, but the precedent had been set; and who could say how long till the next collapse?

A prudent man always went armed. If nothing else, the Franks had their own quarrels. Merowech, for instance, had a dispute over grazing rights under way with his neighbor Clothair, in which bickering half a dozen carls had gotten cut down. Clothair might take it into his head to waylay Merowech; success at that could be worth whatever weregild was negotiated afterward.

Wariness did not forbid mirth, as the warriors rode along the track that twisted toward their farm. They swapped tales of what they had done in town, brags of what they would do elsewhere. When their japes turned to the woman and her expectations, they used their German-laced Latin so she would understand. She gave small response. It was as if she had shed all the tears that were in her. Numbly, hands bound, she trudged along at the end of a cord around her neck, secured to a horse. The man still grimaced to hear, but kept his mouth shut. At first he had cursed the Franks, and when they bade him be still, gibed that he had nothing to lose. A couple of judicious kicks taught him that that was mistaken.

Talk veered to politics. Merowech kept his ears open and his mind well-stocked. "Yes," he said, "as nigh's I can guess, the latest news from Italy means Theodosius will indeed bring a host against Maximus. Which one'll outlive that day, the Gods will decide; but we'd best strengthen ourselves. At this coming feast, I mean to broach a thought—"

Abruptly men were on the road, ahead, behind. They numbered about ten, Gauls from the look of them, gaunt, ragged, unshorn, armed mostly with peasant's weapons, knife, wood ax, hook, sickle, sling, just a couple of spears and swords in grimy hands. The exception was a fork-bearded, scar-cheeked young fellow who must be their chief. He bore no marks of starvation or disease, but moved like a cat; though travel-worn, his garb of green had been cut from excellent stuff; a helmet covered his head, a metal-reinforced leather corselet his body; in his grasp were buckler and javelin, across his shoulders a scabbarded blade.

"Halt!" he cried cheerily. "Get down off those horses. Pay your toll and you can go unharmed."

"What's this?" Merowech bawled. "Who in Frost Hell are you?"

"The Bacaudae, the Valiant."

"No, none of them infest these parts."

"We do now. Dismount."

"Donar's whang, he blunders in that!" Merowech growled to his sons in their native language. He had heard about modern cataphracts, but those were afar in the South and East; his kind were fighters afoot. "Snatch your weapons while you jump down, and let fly. I get to cast at him. Then form a shield-burg with me, and we'll go reap them."

In the same motion that brought him to the ground, he released the francisca hung at his saddlebow and hurled it. The dreaded throwing-ax, which flew ahead of every Frankish charge, should have cloven the young Gaul at the throat. But he was alert for it, dodged, launched his spear—and Merowech's round shield had a dragging shaft in it that he could not dislodge.

From boughs and from behind boles on either side, arrows whistled. Childeric howled and sank to his knees, a shaft through his left calf. "Hold, hold!" shouted the Bacauda headman. "No more shooting yet!" He glided nearer to Merowech, his own sword free to meet the Frank's iron. "You're neatly ambushed, dad," he laughed. "Admit it, throw down your arms, and you needn't get hurt worse."

Merowech bristled. "Honor—"

"Oh, stop quacking. What use will you be anybody but the crows if you make us wipe you out? We can do it quite handily, you know. But we want you to carry a message for us."

"I fear he's right, father," Fredegond muttered. "I'm learning his face. We'll get revenge later."

Merowech nodded. "You do have us trapped," he forced from a throat that felt as if noosed. "What do you want?"

"To start with, drop your weapons," said the Gaul. "Then listen to me, and pass on what I tell you."

The Franks made themselves surrender. Horrible humiliations followed. The Bacaudae did them no injury. Rather, they removed the arrow from Childeric and bound up his wound. However, they took from them their arms, armor, horses, money, slaves, everything but undergarments—even shoes, because several of the brigands had only crude footgear.

The man and the woman who had been destined for sacrifice wept, she too, in the embraces of their rescuers. "There, now, there, now," said the leader, who called himself Rufinus, "you're safe, you're free, you'll come along with us to a wonderful city and I'm sure its King will make good places for you."

"What King is he?" asked Merowech.

"You've no need to hear that," Rufinus answered. "But listen to me. I went on a mission to such of my old comrades as I could find in our old haunts. They followed me back. I chose you to catch because of knowing what errand you'd be on. Your Gods gave you no help, though we were spoiling Their sacrifice. Think about that, Frank. Become a little more respectful of civilization."

"You say that, you, a highwayman?"

"We're none like that," Rufinus said sternly. "We're honest folk who want nothing more than to come back under law, a law that is just.

"Listen well. There are going to be more like us in the woods and on the heaths roundabout. In time they'll find wives and beget children. By then they won't be hungry ragamuffins, but well outfitted and dangerous to run afoul of.

"Their first equipment they'll get from . . . my master. Food? The woods have plenty of game, as shrunk as the population is. Whatever else they need, they'll trade for, or pay for out of some very reasonable tolls they'll levy. They'll harm nobody unless they're attacked, but if they are, they'll punish it hard. Do you hear me?"

"You mean outlaws intend to settle our lands?" Merowech choked on his indignation.

Rufinus laughed. "Not quite outlaws. They'll earn their keep. They'll keep down the real robbers. In case of invasion, they'll be scouts, and they'll harass the barbarians while the cities raise troops, which they'll guide. In a while, I think, they'll be ready to make you Franks settle for just giving animals to your Gods. That'll cost you a great deal less!

"Tell your people at their gatherings. I don't suppose they'll be overjoyed. However, my word may start some of them thinking. We don't really want to teach you the lesson with fire and steel. We've got better things to do."

Merowech stared a long while before he said, "This is no Roman thing. Who's behind it?"

"I can't name him yet," Rufinus replied. "But I will say he's the grandest lord any man could dream of having."

3

On the south side of Ys, between the city wall and the bluffs rising to Cape Rach, was a small crescent of beach. To the east the land mass butted against Aurochs Gate. Thus enclosed on three sides, the strand was often sunless and chilly. An incoming tide could make it dangerous, and the steeps were also a menace to the children whom they tempted to climb. Hence the place was not much used.

Occasionally, on sunny afternoons with ebbing water, Vindilis and Innilis took Dahut there. The girl loved it and was forever begging to go, no matter how raw the weather. She had discovered her chances were best when one of these two Mamas had her in charge. That woman would send for the other one, and the three would walk between those towers called the Brothers, and turn off Pharos Way onto the trail that went precariously down. Thereafter Dahut could do whatever she liked, within reason. Sometimes she wheedled her guardians into allowing what might seem unwise, but they had learned how sure-footed she was, and how strong a swimmer. Frequently, though, she would keep motionless for an hour or more, listening to a shell or the surf or the wind, staring out over the deeps where seals and dolphins played, gulls and cormorants winged, ships and great whales passed by.

On this day there was a slight haze, and enough breeze eddied past the headland to make the air nip. It smelled of salt, kelp, clean decay, things less readily knowable. Vindilis and Innilis settled themselves on a driftwood log. In front of them the sand reached coarse, tawny-dark, to a wet edge that was almost black. Beyond glimmered and surged the water, and the wall of Ys curved away, ruddy-hued, dizzyingly high up to the frieze of mythic figures and the battlements. On the other side the promontory bulked westward. Stones and boulders lay jumbled on its flanks, below scaurs where grass clustered silvery. Farther on, sight of land ended and the sea heaved gray-green, bursting white over the reefs. Birds skimmed about, creaking, or walked on the grit, to flap off when Dahut scampered their way.

The Queens had brought a large blanket as well as a basket of refreshments. No servant had carried these; they would not miss an opportunity to be by themselves. Vindilis's aquiline features softened as she brought the cover around them both. Once they sat wrapped in it, arms went about waists. Innilis sighed, almost happily, and laid her head against the taller woman's shoulder.

"How dear a moment this is," she murmured after a while.

Vindilis nodded. "All too uncommon."

"When . . . we go back up . . . and you take the child to your house . . . shall I come along? Spend the night?"

Pain replied: "Nay, that would be too risky."

"Why? Grallon won't be there, in spite of her. 'Tis Guilvilis's night, if he beds with any of us."

"I know. Yet—Dahut sleeps lightly at this stage of her life. Two days ago, with Forsquilis, she was wandering around thrice in the night. Maldunilis told me earlier, giggling, how when father and daughter were both with her, Dahut came in as they were making love."

Innilis flushed. "Really? What did G-Grallon do?"

"Oh, he scolded her mildly, shooed her out, and continued. She can do no wrong in his sight." Vindilis scowled. "You and I—She'd surely babble to him. Whether or not she saw, she has sharp ears and an uncannily quick little mind."

Innilis drooped. "I see. We must go back to stealing our times like chicken thieves."

"The Gallicenae require their secrets kept from the King, now more than ever." Vindilis glanced at the girl. She was piling sand together near the waves. Vindilis brushed lips across Innilis's cheek. Under the blanket, her free hand cupped a breast. "We will have our times," she promised, "and do not think of them as stolen. They are our right. Blame not yonder child. Through her, we may win a happier morrow for ourselves."

"What? How?"

"I know not. But clear it always was, Dahut has been born fateful; and the Gods have yet to claim Their due from Grallon."

"Nay, no harm to him, please," Innilis begged of the wind.

"I too hope 'twill be mere chastisement. We must wait and see. But, dearest, if They remain well pleased with us twain, and if Dahut is she who shall make a new Pact with the Gods—" Vindilis held Innilis close.

A seal splashed and slithered onto a rock not far off the beach. Dahut saw, sprang to her feet, strained peering into sunlight and sea-blink. The gown fluttered about her taut slenderness. She called, a wordless quaver. The seal rested quiet. Dahut's head drooped. She turned about and walked toward the women.

Vindilis released Innilis, who reached out from under the blanket and inquired, "Darling, what's wrong?"

"I thought 'twas *my* seal." Dahut stopped, stared downward, dug a toe in the sand, clenched fists. " 'Twasn't. Just an or'nary ol' bull."

Innilis smiled and, seeking to humor her, asked, "How can you be sure of that?"

Dahut looked up. Under the wild blond locks, her eyes were the hue of lapis lazuli, and as steady. "I know. She taught me."

"Indeed?" said Vindilis. "I've heard you make mention, and heard from others—But what is this seal you call yours?"

"She loves me," Dahut said. "Better'n anybody, 'cep' maybe father."

"Seals are sacred to both Lir and Belisama," Vindilis said mutedly. "I can well believe certain among them have . . . powers."

Dahut's mood brightened. "Can I get to be a seal? Like her?"

Innilis traced a sign against misfortune. Vindilis said, "Nobody knows. There are stories that—that sometimes good people come back as seals after they die, because the Goddess hears their plea at the Ferrying to Sena. That's so they can wait for those they loved and left behind. But nobody knows."

"I wouldn' be 'fraid to," Dahut declared.

"Peace," counselled Innilis. "Beware of overpridefulness. There are stories that bad people come back too, when the Gods are very angry with them—but as sharks, or things still worse."

Dahut suppressed a retort, flung her head high, and stood straight.

"I think," said Vindilis, "when we go home this evening, I should teach you a new prayer. *'Mother of Death, come softly, I beseech.'* You may, after all, not be too young for learning such things." She unbent. "Afterward I'll tell you about a vestal long ago, who by the favor of Belisama had wonderful adventures."

Likewise seeking to please the girl, Innilis said, "That's a splendid fort you're making there."

Dahut nodded. She was not shy about accepting praise. " 'Tis Ys," she answered. "I'm making Ys."

And she did, remarkably well, before she watched the tide come in and wash it away.

4

That year huge rainstorms arrived in succession, with lightning and hail. Harvests throughout western Armorica were meager, or failed altogether. There were those who muttered that Taranis was avenging the wrong He had suffered in the Wood. They were not many, though. King Grallon had long since established royal granaries and filled them with the surplus of good seasons, bought from the Osismii. Now the folk for whom his agents provided generally blessed his name. Rejoicing followed his proclamation that as soon as possible, he would commission ships to go fetch more from Britannia and Aquitania. As trade revived—in considerable part because of his measures against bandits and pirates—wealth had flowed into Ys until now the city could readily afford whatever it needed to see it through the next twelvemonth. Thus did disaster not undermine Grallon's authority, but rather strengthened it.

Corentinus therefore expressed surprise when Budic came to his church with word that the King had urgent want of his presence. He said nothing further, threw a hooded cloak over his coarse dark robe, and followed the soldier out. The midday was murky, rain driven thick and chill before a shrieking wind. It scourged faces, forced itself through garments, coursed down ribs and legs, swirled in the streets higher than shoesoles. Often heaven flared, and thunder followed like the wheels of a monstrous war chariot. The sea raged at the gate which the King had locked.

At the palace, the majordomo took the newcomer's cloak and offered him a towel and change of clothes. "I thank you, but nay," Corentinus replied. "Let my wet tracks be a sign to you that here also is no hiding from God. Lead me to your master."

Gratillonius sat in the upstairs room he favored for private conferences. Cups, jugs of wine and water, a lamp stood on the table before him. Next to them lay a papyrus roll. Neither the flame nor the greenish-glassed windows much relieved a dimness in which pastoral frescos became an irony, nor did a brazier give much warmth. Beneath his everyday outfit of tunic and trousers, Gratillonius huddled in a cape; and that was strange, for cold did not usually trouble him. He had left off any ornamentation. When he looked up at Corentinus's entry, the chorepiscopus saw the strong-boned countenance drawn into haggardness.

"Shut the door," Gratillonius rasped in Latin. "Be seated."

Corentinus obeyed. Gratillonius leaned over the table between them, stabbed a forefinger onto the document, and said in the same tone, "Magnus Maximus is dead."

"What?" Briefly, Corentinus registered shock. He crossed himself, bowed his head, whispered a prayer. When he again met the other man's gaze, his own was firm. "You've just had word?"

Gratillonius jerked a nod. "From the Duke. It happened well over a month ago, but couriers to bear the news were few."

"Theodosius overthrew Maximus, then? He died in battle?"

"No. Theodosius defeated him decisively near Aquileia. I think the Gothic cavalry made the difference. Maximus surrendered and renounced his claim to the throne. That should have been the end, hey? Exile somewhere, to an island, likeliest. Let the man who saved Britannia close his days in peace and honor. But no, soon afterward Maximus and his young son Victor were killed. This letter to me isn't clear as to whether it was beheading at the express order of Theodosius, or murder by stealth." A fist smote the table. The lampflame quivered. "Whichever, we know by whose will they died!"

"God rest their souls," Corentinus said. "And yet He is just, is He not? Maximus's rival Gratianus perished miserably too—and Priscillianus, and how many more?—because of that man's ambition."

"I'd grudges of my own against him. But he was my old commandant!" Gratillonius shouted. "He held the Wall for Rome! He should not have died like that!"

He seized the wine jug and sloshed full a cup. Without adding water, he swallowed. "Pour for yourself, Corentinus," he said. "Drink with me to the memory of Magnus Maximus."

"Is this why you sent for me?"

"N-no. Not really. Though I do want, need, to talk with you, and I expect I'll get drunk, and that's nothing a man should do alone."

Corentinus took a small measure of wine, diluted it well, and sipped. "May I offer a Mass for the repose of those souls?"

"Do. I meant to ask it of you. I thought of a funerary rite before Mithras, but—but Maximus wouldn't have liked that, would he? I'll pay what it costs to have you give my commandant a Christian farewell."

Wind keened, rain runneled down the glass.

"Am I the first you have told about this?" asked Corentinus.

Again Gratillonius nodded stiffly. "I've got to convene the Suffetes and break the news. But first I'd better have a plan to lay before them. Else they'll debate and squabble and bargain, while matters drift. That kind of delay could prove fatal."

"I am no politician or soldier, my son. I couldn't advise you."

"Oh, you can. You've been around in the Empire more than I have. You've got the ear of Bishop Martinus, who's more powerful than he pretends, even to himself. Theodosius has re-installed Valentinianus, his brother-in-law, as Augustus of the West; but Theodosius is staying on for a while in Italy, and you know very well who's really going to rule. From what I hear, he's a zealous Catholic. You can better guess than I how he'll use the Church, and it him."

Corentinus frowned. "Watch your tongue." He paused. "What do you fear, exactly? Won't everyone benefit from peace and a strong Imperium?"

"Once I'd have supposed so," Gratillonius answered starkly, "but I've learned otherwise. And . . . I belong here now, I belong to Ys. Rome is still my Mother, but Ys is my Wife."

Within the short beard, Corentinus's lips quirked the least bit. Sobering, he lingered over a fresh taste of his wine before he said: "I see. Maximus appointed you prefect. There will doubtless be a pretty deepgoing purge of his officials."

Gratillonius drained his cup and refilled it. "I'm not frightened for myself. I honestly think I'm not. But if I'm ordered back and—and obey, what then? Who'll succeed me? What'll he do?"

"Do you fear Roman occupation, the pagan temples destroyed and rites forbidden, Ys rising in revolt and Rome laying it waste as Rome long ago did to Jerusalem?"

Gratillonius shivered. "You've said it."

Corentinus regarded him closely. "Then I'll also say that this strikes me as being a terrible evil. They're not simple rustics in Ys, the kind whose sanctuaries I helped Martinus overthrow. There it was enough to show how the old Gods were powerless to stop us. They'd never been very large in the lives of the people. A spring, a hill, any sacred site meant more; and it can as well be under the tutelage of a Christian saint. The Gods of Ys will not fade away like that. Before yielding up Their worshippers, They would bring Ys itself down in ruin."

"You understand," Gratillonius breathed.

"My holy duty is to win your people to the true Faith. My single hope of doing so without bringing on catastrophe is by persuasion, patience, year after slow year. Not to attack the Gods, but to sap Them. If only you would unlock your heart—But at least, under you, Ys flourishes, open to newness as it has not been in centuries; and your protection is impartial. We need you as our King."

"If you'd write to Martinus—"

"I'll do that, and more. He, in his turn, can convince the bishops throughout Lugdunensis that Ys should be spared. The Imperium ought to heed them. Besides, in worldly terms, better a loyal foederate, a keystone of defense and a cauldron of trade, than wreckage."

Gratillonius eased somewhat, achieved a smile, said: "Thank you. The Duke is on my side already. I don't think they'll dismiss him; he goes back to before Maximus. If you can make the Church our ally as well—"
Impulsively: "Listen, Corentinus. You know the Ysan charities are mostly

run by the Gallicenae. I know your mission hasn't much to spend. Help me, and I'll endow your good works, generously."

"The thought does you credit," replied the pastor with care, "but the deed could endanger you. Your magnates would see it as yet another defiance of the Gods."

"What I lay out of my privy purse is no concern of theirs, or of Theirs."

"M-m, you realize that such of the poor and unfortunate as you enable us to aid—they will be grateful more to us than you, and this will incline them toward Christ."

Gratillonius laughed and drank. "Manly of you to warn me, but of course I knew it. No harm done. Why should I bar anybody from forsaking the Gods of Ys?"

Corentinus studied him. "Wouldn't you want them to come to your Mithras?"

Gratillonius shrugged. On the heels of his merriment trod pain: "Few ever would. His is no longer a conquering army. We hold the wall for Him while we can, but the foe has marched around it."

He upended his cup and filled it anew. "The Wall!" he shouted. "We stood on the Wall under Maximus. My buddies—How many went south with him? What's going to become of them? Those are men of *mine.* I barracked with them, and pounded the roads and dug the trenches and fought the raiders and diced and caroused with them, and after I'd made centurion I led them, punished them when they needed it, heard out their troubles when they needed that—my Second Augusta and—and there were others with us on the Wall that year, Corentinus. Like Drusus of the Sixth; we saved each other's lives, d'you hear? So they fought for our old Duke, and lost, and what's that Emperor who killed Maximus and Victor out of hand, what's he going to do about them?"

"You are getting drunk in a hurry," Corentinus observed in the sailor's lingo he used when he wanted to.

"I don't expect Theodosius can massacre them," Gratillonius went on. "Too many. But what, then? Think he'll send them back to their bases in Britannia, Gallia, wherever? I think not. He'll be afraid of them, and want to make an example, too. He'll discharge them, maybe. And what are they supposed to do then? They'll lose their veterans' benefits. Are they supposed to starve? Become serfs? Join the Bacaudae? What?"

"A knotty question, in truth," Corentinus agreed. "Christ bade us forgive our enemies, and I should hope Theodosius will, if only for his own soul's sake. But those men *were* mutineers, in a sense, and they'd too likely be an unsettling element in the army. You feel Maximus should simply have been exiled. But how can thousands be?"

Gratillonius straightened. Wine splashed from his cup as he crashed it to the table. "Here!" he exclaimed. "By the Bull, you've hit on it! Armorica's half empty. What we need most is more people, to make their homes and stand guard over them. And there we've got those fighting men, and here we've got a peninsula at the far end of the Empire where they couldn't possibly be any threat to our overlords."

Excitement seized Corentinus likewise. "Write to the Duke and the governor at once," he said. "Urge them to propose it to the Emperors. Offer the influence, experience, help of Ys in getting settlement started. God willing, you'll have a glad acceptance."

"I'll write tomorrow," Gratillonius roared, "and afterward tell the Council. Now let's drink and sing songs and remember Maximus and all old comrades."

Corentinus smiled—wistfully? "I may not do that myself. But I'll keep you company if you like."

They had been at it for a while, as the day darkened further, when a knock on the door brought Gratillonius there. He opened it and stood aside, still steady on his feet though the flush of wine was on his cheeks and the odor of it on his breath.

Bodilis entered. Her hair hung as wet as her garments. The hands with which she took his were cold.

"I thought you should hear this from me, beloved," she said, oblivious to anybody else. "Word reached me, I went to see, and, and I think Quinipilis is dying."

X

1

The agony that speared through breast and left arm, the stranglehold that closed on a heart flying wild, gave way to quietness. She slept a great deal, though lightly, often rousing from dreams. Her pulse fluttered weak, like a wounded bird, and she had no strength. Nonetheless she whispered her commands that she be helped out of bed for bathing and necessities. Such times left her exhausted for hours, but her head remained always clear. Besides the wedded couple who were her only servants, the other Gallicenae insisted on abiding in her house, each a day and night in turn. They allowed no more than very brief visits by the many who came, nor did they themselves tax her with much talk. Often, though, they read aloud to her from books she loved.

Rainstorms gave way to fog. As summer waned, Ys lay in a chill dankness and a white blindness that seemed to go on without end. Quinipilis could not get warm, even when the hypocaust had made the floor too hot for bare feet. The Sisters kept her tucked in fleece blankets and rubbed her hands and feet—carefully, as deformed and tender as those had become. They brought soup and upheld her maned skull while spooning it into her.

Innilis had musicans on call, for such times as harp, flute, song might briefly cheer. Bodilis translated some lyrics of Sappho into Ysan, because Quinipilis had admired those she already knew. Whenever she rallied a little, however, the dowager was apt to ask for something more vigorous, renditions from the Greek, original in Latin or Ysan: the clangor of Homer and Vergilius, sternness of Aeschylus and Euripides, comedy of Philemon and Plautus, or (wickedly grinning) the bawdiest bits from Aristophanes and Catullus, as well as Utican the Wanderer and Witch-

Hanai of this city. A couple of times she herself recited snatches of Gallic or Saxon.

That was near the beginning of her invalidity. Soon she slipped deeper down, and mostly lay with her thoughts and memories.

Then on the ninth morning she told Fennalis, who had the watch: "Bring my Sisters hither."

"Nay, you'd wear yourself out. I can scarce hear your voice, though you've had a night's rest. Take care so you can get well."

Wrinkles formed a hideous frown. Somehow the words loudened enough. "Stop that. I am not in my dotage, thank you. I *am* outworn, for which there is no healing." The scowl turned into laughter lines. "I've somewhat to convey to the lot of you—at once, ere the wheels altogether fall off the old oxcart. Prepare me your strongest strengthening draught."

"That could easily kill you."

"Another day or two would do that anyhow, with naught to show for it." Quinipilis must halt a while to breathe. Her fingers plucked at the covers. "Fennalis, I conjure you . . . I conjure all of you . . . by Our Lady of Passage."

The short gray woman wrestled with herself a moment before she nodded, bit her lip to hold it still, and scuttled out.

Presently there were seven crowded at the bedside. Guilvilis was absent, having the Vigil on Sena. Forsquilis, who was this day's presiding high priestess, had come directly from the Temple of Belisama in her blue gown and white headdress. Innilis clutched the hand of Vindilis, like a child her mother's. Maldunilis wept, striving to hold it quiet and not blubber. Lanarvilis kept stoic. Bodilis kissed the withered lips and stood aside. Fennalis plumped pillows, got Quinipilis half sitting up amidst them, fetched the decoction of foxglove, willow bark, and herbs more curious, held the cup while it went its way, took a post hard by.

Quinipilis's breath quickened and grew noisy. That was almost the single sound. Fog made windowpanes featureless. Within, candles kept shadows at bay, though they filled every corner. A few things were clear to see—a vase of aster and fern from the woods, shelved toys that had been her daughters' when they were small, the hanging sword of King Wulfgar who was her first man, in a niche with a taper at its feet a statuette of Belisama as a young matron holding Her infant. Air lay overheated and sullen.

A hint of blood mounted through the waxiness on Quinipilis. Her glance brightened and steadied. When she spoke, it was clearly: "Welcome. Thank you for coming."

"How could we not come, mother, mother to us all?" replied Vindilis.

"This is our goodbye, of course." Quinipilis's voice was matter-of-fact. She raised a palm against the protest she saw in some of their faces. "Nay, we've scant time left. Let's spill none in foolishness. For myself, I'm more than ready to go to my rest. But first I've a thing to deal with—or, rather, leave to you."

"Hush," Forsquilis bade the Sisters. "The Spirit is upon her."

Quinipilis shook her head and coughed out a chuckle. "I misbelieve that, my dear. 'Tis no more than the same vixen that ever made her den in me." She grew serious. "Yet lying here quietly, so quietly, feeling time slip away—that gives one to think, in between the visits of the living and the dead."

The high-crowned head nodded. "You've wondered whom the Gods will choose to reign after you, and why."

Quinipilis sighed. "Aye. I told you I am content to go. But I would have been earlier. Or I could have stayed longer, equally content to watch the seasons pass and the children grow. Is it chance that I must depart just now? I fear very much the Gods are not done with our King."

"Nay!" broke from Bodilis. She slammed control down on herself. "If They are still angry because of—that unfulfilled sacrifice and—other matters—why have They not struck him already?"

Quinipilis closed her eyes. The power of the medicine was flagging. "You can guess?"

"Mayhap I can," Lanarvilis said slowly. "This year agone has been the most dangerous for Ys since the year he came. The Empire has been in upheaval while the barbarians snuffed blood and grew hungry. Then the Imperial peace returned, but the victors would fain destroy everything that Ys has ever been. Who could cope save Gratillonius? Even his man Rufinus who should have died in the Wood, Rufinus has proven an instrument for him to begin shoring up our bulwarks. Therefore the Gods have stayed Their hands."

"Until now," whispered Forsquilis.

Quinipilis reopened her eyes. "So have I thought," she told them. "Also this have I thought, that They cannot yet spare him, but They will seek to humble him; and in that They will fail, but They can wound him terribly. He's a good man, under his iron—"

"He came to me yesterday, straight from having been with you," said Bodilis, "and that whole eventide he was swallowing tears."

"Stand by him, Sisters," Quinipilis pleaded. "Whatever happens, never forsake him."

"We can ill do that, like it or not," said Vindilis.

"W-w-we did bring him!" blurted Maldunilis. "We made him King. Could we have a better one? Nay!"

Fennalis began to reply but thought better of it.

"Help him," Quinipilis bade them. "Promise me. Give me your oaths."

"By the Three I swear," said Bodilis immediately.

Vindilis pinched lips together before she lifted her arms and exclaimed, "Hold! Hard is this to say, but bethink you, we cannot foreknow—"

Quinipilis gasped. She slumped into the pillows. Her eyes rolled back. Her breath raced in and out like riptides between reefs, then died away to nearly nothing, then raced, then died. Froth bubbled around her lips.

"Goddess, nay!" screamed Fennalis. She flung herself down on the bed. Her fingers sought to clear the foam away, let air get through. "Quinipilis, darling Quinipilis, are you there, can you hear me?" Only the rattling and whistling answered.

Soon they ended. Fennalis rose. Having signed herself, she beckoned to Vindilis, the blood daughter, who trod forward to fold the hands, bind up the jaw, close the eyes.

2

Lir's fog did not reach far inland. At the Nymphaeum, the end of the rains had brought a last upwelling of warmth and lightfulness. The forest that decked the heights glowed a molten green, a thousand hues which a breeze made ripple and weave. Likewise did the lawn in the hollow drink the sunshine that spilled on it from among a few swan's-wing clouds, and give it back to heaven. Blooms had mostly died, but leaves in flowerbeds and hedgerows lived yet. Brooklets glittered and chimed on their way to the glimmery pond. In the shadow of the linden above the sacred spring, the image of the Mother smiled mysterious.

Forth at noontide from the colonnade of the building came certain vestals, as was appointed for this phase of the moon nearest autumnal equinox. Their garments were as white as the walls and pillars. Their hair flowed loose and their feet danced nimble, for they were young girls, less than three years into their service—descendants of Queens in Ys unto the third generation, whereafter the Goddess released a lineage. More fully clad, a virgin near the end of her term led them, as did an aging woman who had returned to the Temple and become a minor priestess when she was widowed.

Blue sheened on peacocks; three spread their tails, like a salute of banners. The grown maiden put syrinx to lips and sounded the tune, while the girls joined hands and skipped the measure, on their way to do reverence before the eidolon. Their voices rose clear as the pipe-notes.

"Belisama, all-sustaining,
Lady of the golden year,
Now that summertime is waning,
Guard this world You hold so dear.
Soon the leaves must fall to cover
Earth grown weary of the sun.
Bring our lord, our King, our lover
Home to us when sleep is done!"
Suddenly one of them screamed.

The music stopped, the dance jarred to a halt. "What is it?" cried the maiden. "Come here, sweetling." She held out her arms.

The girl touched her bosom, "It, it burned," she half sobbed. "For a heartbeat, it burned." Her eyes widened. Her face went chalky. "I'm well again. I am."

The old woman approached her through the silent stares. "We must look at this." She took the small hand. "Fear naught. We love you."

The maiden mustered courage. "We have our rite to finish," she told the rest. "Follow me onward. Sing your song. Remember, we are children of the Goddess."

The procession resumed, raggedly. Meanwhile the priestess hastened toward the Nymphaeum. Semuramat, daughter of Queen Bodilis by King Hoel, stumbled at her side.

3

The fog lifted. After sunset, a nearly full moon dazzled away from itself the stars that otherwise crowded heaven. So wild was Gratillonius that at length Bodilis suggested they leave her house. "Space, air, a wholesome tiredness of the body, and then you may perhaps win to sleep for a while, my poor beloved." They dressed warmly and went forth.

Silence enwrapped them, save for their footfalls on frosty paving and for the sounds of the sea, rising as they drew nearer. He had ended the ravings and curses and desperate schemes he brought her after the word reached him. Their breaths smoked wan, like the utterances of ghosts. Walls shadowed streets from the moon but not from starshine. Man and woman found their way readily down the lanes that twisted from Elven

Gardens, and thence along broad Lir Way, over the deserted Forum, south on Taranis Way to Goose Fair plaza, across it and the pomoerium to a staircase and thus up onto the city wall. Guards at the Raven Tower challenged them; armor shimmered icy in the moonbeams from beyond eastern hills. Recognizing who came, the marines saluted and let them by. Under the high helmets, awe was on faces.

Gratillonius and his Queen walked onward along the battlements, past the war engines that slumbered in their housings, almost to the sea gate. There they stood looking outward.

The moon had cleared the towertops. Above the clustered roofs of Ys, they seemed spires of glass, ready to shatter at the least shaking from the sea, upraised out of a stonefield already sunken. Tonight there was no turbulence. The waters swelled and broke and swelled anew, fluid obsidian over which ran mercury. *Hush,* they murmured, *hush-hush-hush.* So clear was the air that Gratillonius saw a spark out yonder that must be light in the building on Sena, where Forsquilis of the Gallicenae held communion with the Gods.

Bodilis took his arm. "Let us take comfort from such great beauty," she said low.

"Beneath it lies terror," he answered.

"Great beauty is always terrible. Life is."

"Why? What have we done—no, not we, you and little Semuramat— that this has happened?" Gratillonius shook his head. "Oh, I know. You, as close as you were to me, must be hit when They struck. What worse loss than you could I suffer?"

"Dahut," she said.

He snapped after air.

"And you have not lost me," she went on. "Stop treading the same ground. You've pounded it barren. Let me tell you for the twentieth—or fiftieth or hundredth, but the last time—I remain your Queen Bodilis."

"Whom I may never again touch in love."

"That is your choice."

"My choice?" His gaze sought the Raven Tower, black against the sky. Beyond hulked Cape Rach, and at its end guttered the pharos candle. "My faith. Mother and daughter—Mithras forbids. If I denied Fennalis on that account, how can I do otherwise with you?"

"It would be . . . bad politics."

"No politics tonight, no damned politics! This is of the spirit, as well you should know."

She winced in the colorless light: she, both daughter and granddaughter of Wulfgar. It was not that her mother had sinned with her father.

There could be no incest when the Gods decreed the wedding. It was that he, who could not help himself once Their will was upon him, had afterward lost courage to live, and presently lay dead at the feet of Gaetulius.

Gratillonius saw the hurt he had given, caught Bodilis to his breast, and stammered, "I'm sorry, I didn't mean that, shouldn't have spoken so to you—you, half-sister of Dahilis—" through King Hoel: Dahilis, who perished in giving birth to Dahut.

Bodilis stroked his hair, stepped back, and smiled at him. "I understand. These are roads that double back and back on themselves, aren't they? Well, of course I'll long for you, but we'll always stay friends, allies; no God commands our hearts."

"Unless I refuse this marriage. The girl *is* too young. Oh, she's passed her Rite of Welcome; but so short a time ago, she so small yet and—and frightened."

"You will be kind to her. You've been like the father she never really knew."

Now he flinched. Casting weakness aside, he said, more calmly than he had said it before, "Best for her, too, if I balk."

"You would rip Ys apart. This is the holiest rite we were ever given, the renewal of the world."

"I meant, well, carry out the service, but not c-c-consummate the marriage."

Bodilis shook her head. "No, you can't escape that either."

"I did with Quinipilis and Fennalis."

"They were past childbearing age."

"Is Semuramat at it?"

"She will be. And . . . the bloodied sheet is given the Goddess next morning. No, Gratillonius, dear bewildered man. Unless you'd flee at once, abandon us forever, you must marry Tambilis tomorrow."

He battered a fist against a merlon. That was the name Semuramat had chosen, to honor her grandmother who died in the horrible reign of Colconor. Such was traditional. Yet the older Tambilis had been the mother of both Bodilis and Dahilis.

"At least this time you've said rationally the things you shouted in fragments at the house," added the Queen. She hesitated, glanced out across Ocean, added low, "We do have tonight left us, you and I."

A while he stood, hunched over. Moonlight caught a few tears. Finally he shook his head. "No. Your advice is right, hard but right. Then I dare not—"

"You are doubtless wise," she sighed.

He started back. "Go home, Bodilis," he said. "Rest yourself as well as you can. Your daughter will need you very much tomorrow."

She followed. "What of you?" she asked at his back.

He looked straight ahead. "I'll commandeer a lamp at the tower, and go down into the Mithraeum, and be with my own God."

4

There was the ceremony in the Temple of Belisama, where vestals sang and the Eight stood veiled together with her who would be the Ninth, flanking the altar behind which lifted images of Maiden, Mother, and Hag. The bride came to the groom, they knelt under the prayers and hymns, rose again when bidden; he lifted her veil while the Sisters raised theirs. "Gratillonius, King of Ys, in homage to the Goddess Who dwells in her, and in honor to the womanhood that is hers, receive your Queen Tambilis—" Fennalis, the senior, brought the consecrated wine for them to share.

Public coronation and festivity waited until Quinipilis should have had her sea burial. This day the Gallicenae merely accompanied the King to his palace, where a simple meal was set forth. They talked sparingly, Tambilis not at all. What conversation did take place was mostly reminiscence of the departed.

Afterward, one by one, each of the women kissed the girl and, in their differing ways and words, made her welcome, wished her well, promised her their help and love. By tacit agreement, Bodilis came last. The two clung together a short spell. Gratillonius stood aside, alone.

The guests and their attendants bade him goodnight and left. Dusk was blue beyond the doorway. The household staff were now free to come forth and, through the majordomo, request the benediction of the new Queen. "Blessing on you, blessing on you." Her voice was as thin as the hand with which she touched their heads where they knelt.

Thereafter they escorted the bridal pair to the royal bedchamber. They had cleaned everything that was in it, arrayed green boughs and, in lieu of flowers at this season, clusters of berries. Candles burned in abundance. The broad bedstead carried a richness of furs and embroideries. A table inlaid with nacre held wine, water, fruits, confections. Incense sweetened the air. Frescos on walls, paintings on shutters, mosaic on floor, gave images of woodland, meadow, lake, sea, cloudscape; beasts real and mythic pranced, swam, flew; youths and maidens were joyful together. Outside, in silence, the stars were coming forth.

The door closed.

Gratillonius turned from it, toward his wife. She stood with arms straight down, fists clenched, staring before her. It came to him that in the chaos of his heart he had not yet really looked at her. And earlier she had been only Semuramat, daughter of Bodilis, stepdaughter to him, a bright and blithe child with whom he enjoyed passing time whenever he was able. She had, indeed, been like a true older sister to Dahut, more and more so as she blossomed toward womanhood.

At thirteen years of age, she reached not quite to his throat, and much of that height was leg. The rest of her seemed to be mainly eyes, underneath formally dressed hair which had changed from the gold of childhood to a light brown. They were the deep blue of her mother's, those eyes, or of Dahilis's or Dahut's. Her features were delicate, lips always slightly parted over teeth. Because she was often outdoors, summer had tinged her skin and dusted freckles across the tip-tilted nose. Bridal gown and jeweled pectoral hung heavy from her shoulders.

Remembering his first night with Guilvilis, he willed resolution upon himself. There was that which must be done, and shilly-shallying about it would be no kindness. He went to her, smiled, and took her hands. They lay cold in his. "Well, dear," he said, "here we are."

She remained mute. Releasing her left hand, he brought his right under her chin and raised it until their gazes must meet. She blinked and breathed hard. "Be at ease," he said. "You know your old friend. He hasn't changed. I wanted this not myself." Louder than intended: "O Mithras, nay!" Softly again: "We've had a duty laid on us. We'll carry it out like good soldiers, you and I, eh?"

She nodded. It caused his hand, yielding, to slide down her neck. How frail it was, how silken the skin. A blue pulse throbbed.

"Come," he said, "let's be seated, let's drink to a happier morrow." Let her become warmed, at rest, wine-dazed.

She ran tongue over lips. "My lord is, is gracious," she whispered.

He guided her to a settee before the table and, with a faint pressure, caused her to sit down, before he himself did. "What nonsense," he chided, attempting laughter. "We'll have no 'my lord' any longer. You're a Queen of Ys, Tambilis. You'll be a guiding star to the people, a healer, a strong voice in council; you'll command wind and wave; you'll be—with the Goddess. Better I call you 'my lady.'"

He filled two silver goblets, diluting in neither, and urged one into her clasp. "Drink," he said. She obeyed. He saw her grimace and realized that the wine by itself, dry as most Ysans preferred, was harsh on a palate that had usually known water. "I'm sorry. Here, I'll pour some back and weaken the rest. I do think if you take a draught or so you'll feel calmer. And, uh, behold, wouldn't you like these raisins, these sweetmeats?"

Partaking did seem to help. After a few minutes Semuramat—Tambilis gave him a steady regard and said with childish seriousness: "Mother told me you would be kind."

"I promised her. I promise you. As far as lies in my power, I will." And may you never know how I miss her.

"Then do what you shall, Grallon."

His face heated. "Wait, wait, no haste, let's talk a bit, let me tell you something about what to await—"

He avoided grave matters but bespoke feasts, games, foreign visitors with wonderful stories. She drank faster, without noticing. A sparkle awoke. She leaned into the crook of his arm, snuggled against him, as she had done when she was a small girl and he yarning to her in the presence of her mother.

Desire flamed up.

No! he snarled to the Power. You'll have Your way with us, that's fated, but not yet.

"What's the matter?" she asked when his words stopped.

"Naught, naught." He went on with the tale. His loins raged.

—"That had better be all, darling," he said around the dryness in his mouth. Thunders went through his breast. "You need your sleep."

Her nod wobbled, her voice was slurred: "Aye. Thank you, kind Grallon. Now make me a woman."

She caught her wits back to her. "First I should pray to the Goddess, oughtn't I?"

He ordered his arm, that had been about to close tight, to let her go. He stood aside while she went to pray. He had long since had images of the Three removed from this room, but she found a nymph among the revelers who looked older and more modest than the rest. Her slight form took stance before the picture, she raised her hands, and Gratillonius stood fighting off the Bull. He heard:

"Belisama, to Your keeping
I entrust my soul this night.
Guard Your child while she is sleeping;
Wake me to the morning light."

Tambilis turned toward her husband, held out her arms. He went to her through the roaring. She did not know anything else than to let him undress her. Tortoise shell comb and ivory pins clinked to the floor. He had no skill in loosening hair, and she giggled a bit, while crying a bit, when he tugged a bit too hard. The pectoral and golden bracelets dropped with a clang. The girdle slithered aside like a snake. He shook as he undid the dress and pulled the undergarment off over her head.

Thereupon she stood with an uncertain smile on her lips. Hands flitted for a moment, seeking to conceal, but drew aside. As yet, he saw, her figure was almost a boy's. The crescent of the Sign burned red between tiny breasts. Hips and buttocks had, though, begun to fill out, and above her thighs was a shadowiness that caught glints of light.

Cast her down and have her!

Gratillonius stepped back. "I'll first blow out the candles," he said somehow.

Did the flush upon her cheeks pale? "Nay, please, can we keep them?" she asked. Thus could she see what happened, and maintain bravery.

"If, if you wish." As quickly as he could, he disrobed. When she saw him in his maleness, she gasped, quailed, rallied, stood fast. "Be not afraid. I'll be gentle."

He led her to the bed, drew blankets aside, guided her down, joined her, pulled the covers over them both. She shivered in his clasp. He stood on the wall against the Bull, while he murmured and stroked and kissed. Finally, of course, he must take her.

He *was* gentle. That much victory did he win over the Gods.

It hurt her nonetheless. She shed more blood than was common, and could not help sobbing afterward. He held her close. "There, there," he crooned into her ear, " 'tis done, you'll soon be well again, and we need do this no more until you are ready for it, years hence. I will not press you. Sleep, child."

That also was territory he could defend.

XI

1

"Maybe here at last we'll find peace," Drusus said low.

"I can't promise that," Gratillonius told him. "At best, you'll have to work for it, and most likely fight, too."

Drusus sighed. "It'd be worth it. If I could know my kids, anyhow, will have a chance to live their own lives."

Gratillonius regarded his comrade of the Wall with compassion. The centurion of the Sixth Victrix seemed grotesquely out of place in this frescoed, mosaic-floored room. The tunic upon his stocky form was patched and faded. A deep inward weariness bowed the shoulders and looked out of the weatherbeaten, ill-barbered face. There was even a listlessness in his grip around the wine cup that rested on his knee where he sat.

Through doors open to the summer's warmth drifted the sounds of Aquilo, voices, footfalls, hoofbeats, wheelcreak, hammer-clash, together with odors of smoke and of green growth beyond the town. Those too seemed remote from the visitor.

It was Apuleius Vero who found words: "Your life has been one endless march from battle to battle, homeless as the wind, over hill and heath and fields laid desolate, has it not?"

Publius Flavius Drusus cast a glance of startlement at the senator, the antiquated but immaculate toga that wrapped his slenderness and the handsome, still fairly youthful countenance above. "Feels that way, sir," he agreed.

Gratillonius harked back across the years. He had not been much together with this man, but those times were burned into him: combat against the barbarians, fellowship of miles and campfires and barracks, later a chance meeting in Augusta Treverorum and a drunken evening when hearts were unlocked. But Drusus had earlier fought the Saxons as they came reaving out of the eastern sea; he had crossed to Gallia to fight under his Duke Maximus and win for him the Imperium; he had stood guard on the German frontier and campaigned beyond it; he had tramped south over the mountains into Italy and done battle again with legionaries like himself; he had followed his Emperor eastward, and seen their cause go down before Theodosius's Gothic lancers; half a prisoner, he had done hard labor on lean rations through month upon month of autumn, winter, spring; then he had made the trek across Europe to Armorica and a fate still unknown. Gratillonius did not wonder at seeing him slumped.

I hope I can straighten that back of his, the King of Ys thought.

"You may indeed have come to haven," said Apuleius.

"Sirs, excuse me, but I don't understand," the centurion faltered. "I mean, well, all right, we veterans of Maximus have been sent north. We'll get our discharges, and places to stay, and—it's better than we hoped for, back there with the cataphracts on their tall horses herding us along—but what do you want of *me?* Why am I here?"

Gratillonius smiled. "That's a long story, old buddy," he replied. "Let me just give the gist of it now, because I think dinner time's close and we'd like to relax then.

"This resettlement was my idea, when I heard about the fall of Maximus last year. A priest—chorepiscopus, I mean, name of Corentinus, gave me a lot of help, and we got Bishop Martinus in Turonum and other big men interested, and—Never mind. The upshot is that here we have Armorica, half depopulated, screwed over by pirates and bandits and barbarians who've actually taken up residence. And yonder we had you soldiers, good men, but men that the Emperors could neither trust nor massacre. Let's bring them together.

"I thought of establishing a colony. If it was near Condate Redonum, it'd keep the Franks there in line. But that was refused. Not unreasonable, from Theodosius's viewpoint. He wants you dispersed as well as discharged, so you can't ever get up another revolt. So be it."

As he paused, Apuleius interposed gently: "None of you shall be left destitute. Each man shall receive his plot of land and the basic tools he requires. The tribesmen will surely help him, for they ought to welcome such a strong new neighbor. From among their daughters he can soon find a wife. Praise God for His mercies."

"We'd not every one of us make a farmer," Drusus objected. "Many of us wouldn't know one end of a cow from the other."

Gratillonius laughed. "True. Well, any legionary has skills that're in demand, what with trade reviving hereabouts. There'll be work for all. I can use a few engineers in Ys, as a matter of fact. And if nothing else, the granaries of Ys will keep you from starving before you can support yourselves."

Drusus shook his head dazedly. "My partner in the mud, a king," he marveled.

"Let's get to the point about why we've sent for you," Gratillonius went on. "You owe a heap—I think you'll agree—to my friend Apuleius. He kept up the correspondence and the political pressure and everything else I didn't have the time or the connections for. You see, I knew you'd be with your outfit if you were still alive, Drusus, and knew you could be depended on. So we managed to get a fair-sized number of men in your century assigned to this area."

"No gratitude is due me," said Apuleius. "I only wish to see the district well served, and therefore accepted Gratillonius's recommendation. Aquilo and its environs are poorly defended. We have nothing but a handful of native troops, ill-trained, and reservists with no training to speak of. Despite my repeated pleas, the Duke has never stationed any legionary regulars here.

"Well, of course you and your, ah, vexillation are going to be civilians. As such, you cannot, under Imperial law, form yourselves back into a military unit. You will be farmers, artisans, and so on. However, you will not have forgotten your martial trade, and equipment can be gradually obtained. I expect you to hold periodic drills and exercises which will include Osismiic men. Thus you will eventually provide us with a reserve force that is effective."

"Almighty God!" Drusus exclaimed. "You *mean* that?"

"I was never more serious," assured Gratillonius. "I'm hoping you'll take the lead, under Apuleius the tribune, in getting all this organized. Think you can handle it?"

Drusus put down his cup, sprang to his feet, squared his shoulders, and gave the Roman salute. "Sir, I do."

Gratillonius stood up too, refrained from hugging him, but said, "Splendid. We'll discuss details in the next couple of days. First let's enjoy ourselves. Isn't food about ready, Apuleius? My stomach believes it's been sent to hell for the sin of gluttony."

A trifle shocked by the irreverence, the senator nonetheless answered graciously, "Soon, I pray your patience. Would you two like to go to another room and talk? You see, we've developed a custom in my family. Before the main meal, I spend half an hour with my daughter."

"Verania?" asked Gratillonius.

Apuleius nodded. "I'm surprised you remember."

"Why shouldn't I? Charming child." Abruptly it came to Gratillonius: Rovinda, the wife in this house, was again pregnant; but there had been no sign or mention of another infant. Whichever she had borne since Verania must have died, as infants so often did, unless their mothers were Gallicenae who had medical arts and magics and the blessing of Belisama.

Impulsively, Gratillonius proposed, "We'll stay, if you don't mind. She might like meeting newcomers."

"Oh, that would be wonderful," Apuleius said. "You are too kind."

Gratillonius shrugged and laughed. "I'm a father myself, several times over." He regretted it when he saw the flicker of pain across Apuleius's lips, but dismissed remorse; he knew himself for a man not especially tactful nor the least bit subtle.

Drusus sat back down and reached for his cup, looking resigned.

Apuleius went to the inner door and called. A female slave led Verania in. She moved shyly toward him, her gaze big and hazel in the direction of the strangers. Gratillonius's heart lost a beat. O Mithras! Just about four years old, she was a trifle younger than Una, and her coloring was different, lighter; but how those delicate features and that graceful gait recalled the daughter that Bodilis had given him.

Daughter of Bodilis—A year had passed without much blunting his longing for Bodilis as more than a soft-spoken counselor, a carefully correct friend.

Gratillonius mastered himself. From Dahut he had learned how to court little girls. You didn't stare or beam or gush or grab. You were cheerful, casual, always respectful of the child's dignity; and before long she would listen to you, then come to you, with the dawn of adoration in her eyes.

2

"The centurion will be away," Adminius lamented. "Not the King, 'e don't matter now, but my officer Gratillonius, centurion o' the Second. Slice and gut me, wot a shame! The single thing wrong, that 'e can't be there ter stand me by and lead the celebration afterward. 'E would, you know. I've 'alf a mind ter put it all off till 'e gets back."

He knew that was impossible. The family into which he was marrying would have taken grievous offense. The Powers might too, since the astrological signs were propitious for the date set and for none other in the near future. Besides, nobody could say when Gratillonius would return from this latest journey of his.

Adminius found consolation in knowing that his whole Roman squadron would be on hand. This time the prefect had left them behind and traveled with an escort of Ysan marines. In part, he had explained, that was to allay a certain jealousy he had seen growing. To take them beyond the frontier not only gave them a pleasurable outing but acknowledged that he was *their* King. And in part, when he was to deal with former rebels, he had better avoid anything that might look suspicious to the Imperial authorities.

The wedding would be an event of some importance, joining the deputy commander of the legionary cadre to Avonis, sister of the naval officer Herun, who with her belonged to the Taniti clan of Suffetes. It would take place at the Nymphaeum, and a Queen would preside. Adminius proposed that his soldiers form an honor guard. They cheered, except for Budic. "What's the matter with you?" demanded Cynan.

The young Coritanean reddened like a maiden. He must gulp before he could mumble, "A pagan rite. The chorepiscopus was warning again, in his last sermon, about d-d-danger to the soul."

"Ha!" Cynan sneered. "Some faith, that won't let a fellow show friendship! When are you due to be gelded?"

"Lay off that," Adminius ordered. "Honesty's too flinking rare as is. . . . Budic, lad, I won't force yer. But well you know, I'm not the first among us ter settle down with an Ysan wife, and me a Christian too. It's an honorable estate, better than 'oremongering, 'specially when we'll likeliest leave our bones 'ere. You needn't bow down to 'eathen idols—I won't meself—just because you join our party."

Budic caught lip between teeth, shivered, and said, "I'm sorry. I'll come, and, and hope Corentinus will understand."

"Good." Mollified, Cynan slapped him on the back. "The centurion would be disappointed to learn you hadn't."

"I thought of that," Budic whispered.

—On the day, the legionaries departed in full and polished armor, up the valley to the hills. The groom rode ahead of them, finely clad, on a white horse, next to his intended father-in-law. Behind followed other kin and well-wishers, together with pack beasts carrying supplies for a feast. The weather was superb. Merriment caroled along the whole way. The bride had fared a day in advance, accompanied by attendants and Queen Forsquilis, that she might be purified and then well rested.

At noon the group reached the sacred site. A vestal guided them by a short woodland path to the barrack. They would sleep there—floor space and pallets were sufficient—before returning home in the morning. While they refreshed themselves and took their ease, the small garrison hospitably carried back the food and wine they had brought, for the women of the sanctuary to set forth on tables which had been placed on the lawn.

At mid-afternoon a procession of girls arrived, led by a full-grown virgin who was near the end of her term of service. Hair garlanded and flowing loose over white gowns, they sang and fluted hymeneals while they conducted the groom and his friends to the Nymphaeum. Beautiful among them danced Princess Dahut. Already she was often here, as well as in other places hallowed to Belisama. It was unusual for one so young, but she was being raised in piety.

Around the greenswarded hollow brooded forest, above it cloud mountains and blue depths, heavy with summer. The air was as sweet as the music. Peacocks walked on closely-trimmed grass, swans floated on the pond. That water came from several brooklets out of the hills and the spring at its edge; thence ran a stream which fed the slender canal that joined with rains to quench the thirst of Ys. The spring bubbled from a pile of boulders, atop which smiled a statue of the Mother, shaded by a huge old linden. Flowerbeds blazed with color, hedgerows and bowers drew the eye onward to the building. It was wooden and of no great size, but its white, colonnaded, large-windowed form was as of a jewel.

Adminius uttered a command. The soldiers formed a double rank below the stairs. Forth onto the portico came the aged chief priestess and her coadjutresses, in blue gowns and high headdresses. Gravely, they summoned the groom. He mounted the steps and followed them inside. After him went the rest of the wedding party, and then the choir. The legionaries stayed behind.

Through open doors came sounds of hymn, chant, prayer. Budic strove not to listen. He failed. Those word, those melodies were at once too joyous and too solemn.

They ended in a benediction uttered by a woman's purring voice. The bridal couple appeared, plump blond maiden on the arm of lean sandy man. They descended. As they passed between the soldiers, swords flew from sheaths and *"Ave!"* roared aloud.

The guests followed, the girls, the votaresses. Last was the Queen. Tall and stately walked Forsquilis, her face almost inhuman in its classic lineaments and pallor, save for the faint smile.

Dahut had been named to cry, "Rejoice! The blessing of the Goddess is ours! Rejoice!" Thereupon everything broke up in shouts and laughter. Folk mingled, embraced, made for the laden boards. Forsquilis went back inside. When she returned, her golden-brown hair was coiled around a silver coronet and cloth of gold clung to her litheness. She herself called for drinking to the health and happiness of the newly wed, and in the hours afterward chatted freely with any and all.

The gaiety, and perhaps the wine, soon overwhelmed Budic. Every nuptial feast in Ys, other than the King's, was mirthful, and apt to become erotically charged. Here there could be no stealing off with a newly met woman. However, nothing forbade the vestals to smile, joke, dance, exchange glances, murmur hints. When they attained their majority, most would want husbands, some would want lovers, and surely Belisama breathed higher the fire that She had kindled in young hearts. Budic blundered through a whirl of loveliness.

The sun went under western hills. Clouds burned golden. Forsquilis signalled to the virgins. They formed a line, their feet skipped, their epithalamium lifted, as they brought Adminius and Avonis back to the Nymphaeum. Dahut bore a candle before the two, lighting their way to the flowerful chamber that was theirs for the night.

Festivity outside continued a while. Twilight deepened, stars blinked into view, moon-glow silvered heaven above high eastern darknesses. First the oldest and the youngest yawned goodnight, then presently all revelers departed to their rest.

—Budic awoke. He could not have been long asleep. The barrack was pitchy black and steamy hot. He felt bodies pressed close to his, and for a moment a surging took him; but they were merely two roadpounders like himself, and snored. He rolled over, hoping to regain oblivion. The straw of his pallet rustled. He remembered youths in Britannia, when he was a boy, boasting of what they had done with girls in the hay. He remembered that he had not really been down in peaceful nothingness. Slim forms with voices like the chiming of brooks had undulated through his dreams.

Sweat prickled and reeked in his armpits. His member swelled and strained. Almost, he groaned. *Christ guard me from the demons in this haunt of heathendom!* Useless to lie here. He would only toss about till he roused his mates, who'd swear at him. Maybe some fresh air would soothe. He groped his way to the door, and out.

How solid, how soft the earth was beneath his feet. The night laved his nakedness; he felt every smallest cool ripple in it. The forest smelled of damp and musk. He heard rustlings, chirrings, a hoot, a wing-beat. They seemed to call him. Moonlight dappled leaves and ground. As his night vision strengthened, he saw the path winding off to the holy grounds. Yonder was water. Thirst smoldered in the thuttery thickness that held him by the gullet. He thought confusedly that he would not drink from the pond, for it was given over to the lustful she-devil; but the stream that ran from it, off to the canal and thus the city, ah, he could fling himself belly down, grip the moss in both hands, and bury his mouth in that chilly kiss.

He moved ahead. Twigs fingered him. A moonbeam touched a great fungus growing on a log. It stood forth like a phallus or the flame of a lamp in a bridal chamber. Was it a nightingale that trilled, or a girl's laugh?

The woods opened on the lawn. Budic slammed to a halt.

The full moon hid most stars behind a veil of brilliance. Trees, hedges, grass reached asheen. Above the spring, below the linden, the idol stood livid against shadow. Darknesses limned the rich curves of breasts and hips. Argency glimmered and sparkled over the pond. Around it, upon it, out from within it, the nymphs were dancing.

They were not vestals, innocently asleep, they were mist and moonlight made female, shapes that flitted, wove, flickered, soared, twined, caressed, parted to tremble on the edge of flight, came back together to embrace, one with one another and the night and the burgeoning summer. Not with his ears but with his soul, he heard them sing and cry and yowl desire. He knew not whether they were aware of him or cared; but he was about to plunge forth and lose himself in them.

Out of gloom that bulked against the northern sky trod a man. He was huge, naked, stallion-erected. Each fist held a writhing snake. It was as if stars glittered trapped in his unbound hair. From his temples sprang a mighty rack of antlers. Slowly he paced from the wood toward the nymphs, and their movements turned in his direction.

Budic huddled behind a tree. He could not help himself, he must peer around its trunk.

Moonlight flooded her who came down off the portico and across the lawn. White, white, blue-white was her skin, also nude except for the tresses streaming loose. She held out her arms to the man-shape. Distant though she was in this dimness, Budic knew that Athene countenance.

The male wheeled and strode to meet her. She ran. When she reached them, they halted and he took both her hands in his. The serpents wrapped around their wrists, moonlight icy along scales. For an endless while, male and woman stood unmoving. Then at last they went side by side into the forest. The nymphs took up their frolic anew.

Lightning through the thunder that filled Budic's skull: Everybody knew Forsquilis was deepest versed in sorcery of the Nine witches, and gossip muttered how she bore the air of a passionate woman and how hard it must be for her to share a single man. None, even Christians, ever

dared hint that any among the Gallicenae might betray the King. But
what about a God—a demon?

A nymph-shape left the dance and swayed across the dew toward
Budic.

He shrieked and fled. Yet he did not re-enter the guards' house when he
got there, but spent the rest of the night outside, shuddering, groveling,
weeping, and praying.

3

"Have you told anyone else?" asked Corentinus.

Astounded, Budic gaped at him. Dusk gathered around the minister of
Christ where he sat on his stool, in the room of his church that he had
designated private, like a black-feathered bird of prey on its perch.

"N-no, Father," the Coritanean stammered after a moment. "I
p-pretended I'd had nightmares, that was why I was so numb and weak
this morning."

"Good." The knaggy head nodded. "No sense in letting rumors get
started. They'll force people to take firm stances, which is the last thing
we want the pagans to do. Of course, you realize what you saw may well
have been just a dream."

"What? No, Father, that can't be. I mean, I beg your pardon, but I do
know the difference—"

Corentinus raised a palm to cut off the words. "Peace. Don't fret yourself. It matters little. The forces of Satan prowl always around us.
Whether they work as mirage or material, their purpose is the same, to
lure us from our salvation. If what you saw really happened, I'll feel sad
for that poor benighted woman. But you, my son, you may thank God
that He strengthened you to resist."

Budic wailed and covered his face. "No, Father. Th-th-that's why I
came—not even to warn you, but, but the vision won't leave me, the lust
is fiercer than fire, what shall I do, Father?"

"Ah. Hm." Corentinus rose, bent over the hunched figure, briefly
hugged the bright head to his bosom. "Don't be afraid. You have wisdom
beyond your years, that you seek help here instead of in a brothel."

"I have sinned that way before. But this, this *called* me."

"I know. I too have heard." Corentinus began pacing back and forth.
He made his voice dry:

"Listen, Budic. You've been a pretty good catechumen, and this isn't the first time I've given you some thought. Now, I can't compel you spirit. Only God can do that. But I can, in my left-handed mortal fashion, advise you. So listen, and think.

"Your trouble is that you're devout, but you haven't got the makings of a monk. No disgrace in that. The Lord bade Adam and Eve be fruitful and multiply. What're you waiting for?"

Budic gave him a dazed look. "Where'll I find a Christian wife? I knew I did wrong, going to that pagan wedding. Isn't this my punishment?"

Corentinus smiled. "I'm not sure you did do wrong. I've never reproached any of my flock who married unbelievers. It can't be helped, and grace may come on the spouses. I only require that they allow their children to hear the truth. You, though—you're not the sort who could live with an infidel woman. But you need a woman, in the worst way."

He took stance before he went on, almost sternly: "I have one, if you're Christian enough, man enough, to take her for your wife."

Budic stared up at him. The chorepiscopus seemed to tower as if he spoke from the peak of Sinai. "Who?" Budic whispered.

"You know her well. Keban, the harlot from the Fishtail."

Budic sat dumb-stricken.

"She has repented," Corentinus went on relentlessly, "she has washed herself clean with her tears, she acknowledges Christ her Lord and Saviour. But who among the haughty goodfolk of Ys will have her, even as a scullion? I give her shelter and employment here, but it's made work, as well we both know, and her days are empty, and Satan understands very well how to fill that emptiness with old carnal cravings. I've dreaded that she may fall by the wayside. But if not—what an example to shine before every wretch forsaken in this city of sin!

"Budic, she's still fairly young, healthy, a fit mother of sturdy sons, and reborn in Christ. What she was before is nothing in the sight of God. But is everything in the sight of man.

"Who will have courage to take her under his protection, for the salvation of both, and shield her, and turn his back on the sly, unspoken mockery, till at last it is outlived, forgotten, and an honorable old pair go hand in hand toward Heaven? Might you be, Budic?"

Silence lengthened, underneath harsh breath.

Corentinus eased. "Ah, well, I know better than to force things," he said. "Come, lad, let's share a stoup and talk a bit. I can always use barrack-room gossip. As for any sins of yours, consider them forgiven."

—But later that evening, summoned, Keban entered. In wimple and full, coarse gown, timidly smiling, by lamplight she seemed twice comely.

All she did was prepare and set forth a frugal meal, and answer a few inconsequential questions. Yet the glance of Budic followed her everywhere she went.

4

Often around the autumnal equinox, storms caused Ys to lock its sea gate, lest waves force an opening and rush through the harbor into the city. When calm was restored, the King freed the portal. It was his sacral duty. Only if he was absent or disabled did Lir Captain take it in his stead.

As usual, he performed the task at high tide, which this day happened to come in the afternoon. "You see," he explained to Dahut, "the doors are hung in such a way that they always want to be shut. As the water falls, the floats that hang from them do too, and draw the doors open. At low water, they would pull so hard that I couldn't get the bar out of its holder."

"But what if you *had* to close the gate then?" she asked.

Gratillonius smiled. "Sharp question!" There was quite a mind below those golden curls, behind those big eyes. "Well, we have machinery, so gangs of men can haul the doors shut against the weight of the balls. Just the same, it's hard work."

Lanarvilis had told him he should let Dahut witness the rite. All the Queens were touchingly concerned about the upbringing of Dahilis's daughter. Delighted, he had sent a messenger to temple school. She came from there in company with Guilvilis, whose turn it was to foster her. He was twice happy that that turn coincided with his night at Guilvilis's house.

Woman and child followed him from the palace. Guilvilis had donned finery, a silken gown that showed to disadvantage her tall, awkward, heavy-haunched figure. The thin dull-brown hair would not stay properly in its elaborate coiffure, but did call attention to small eyes, long nose, undershot chin. In a schoolgirl's brief white dress, Dahut went like wind and waterfall. Gratillonius wore a ceremonial robe of blue-gray wool embroidered in gold and silver thread with sea beasts. In full view on his breast hung the iron Key.

A squad of marines waited in their conical helmets and shoulder-flared loricae. Pike butts crashed a salute on the stones. They took formation behind the King. Traffic on Lir Way was thick and bustle was loud, but a path opened immediately before the procession. Many folk cheered, some signed themselves, a number of youngsters trailed after to watch from the wharf.

The Temple of Lir stood under the Gull Tower, just before the pomoerium. Ancient, it lacked the Grecian exquisiteness of Belisama's, the Roman stateliness of Taranis's. Despite small size, here was brutal strength, menhir-like pillars and rough stone walls upholding a roof of slate slabs. The interior was dark, revealing little more than an altar block within an arch formed of the jawbones of a whale.

Gratillonius entered. The man on watch today greeted him. Every ship's captain in Ys was ordained a priest of Lir; Hannon Baltisi simply presided over meetings of the guild and spoke for it and its cult in Council. Gratillonius knelt to receive on his tongue the ritual pinch of salt and voice the ritual plea that the God withhold His wrath. Emergence was like release from captivity.

It was a bright, bracing day. When he had climbed the stairs to the rampart heights, he looked out across utter openness. Waters shone blue, green, purple, white-capped, save where they burst on rocks and reefs, brawled against wall and cliffs; there fountains leaped. In this clarity he could see the house on Sena, miles away. Only wings beclouded the sky, hundreds of them soaring and circling on the breeze whose tang washed his face.

He looked inland, across the broad arc of the basin. How still it lay, nine or ten feet beneath the tide, lower yet whenever the combers climbed and broke. Ships and boats crowded the piers. Men were busy with cargo. Mariners of Ys would venture another voyage or two before winter closed in. The knowledge that he had put life back into that trade made a glow in Gratillonius.

And the city behind shone in roofs, towers, on its higher eastern half gardens, temples, mansions. Hinterland stretched beyond, valley and hills where homes nestled, the gaudiness of leaves muted by distance to a tapestry laid over the earth, a sign of ingathered bounty. God Mithras, said Gratillonius, watch over all this, stand guard upon its peace.

Dahut tugged at his hand. "Won't you start?" she piped.

Hauled from his reverie, he laughed and tousled her hair. "Ever are you the impatient one, eh, sweetling? Aye, let's. . . . Have a care! Lean not so far over the parapet. I know you love the sea, but remember, 'tis forever hungry."

He led her past the Gull Tower and the sheltered war engines to that fifty-foot gap in the wall which was the portal. Dahut, who had been here before, cried greeting to the block that jutted from the wall below the battlements. It had the time-blurred form of a cat's head. A chain ran from the inner top corner of the adjacent door, into the block, over the sheave within, and down out of its mouth. Most of the chain hung submerged, for the leather-clad bronze ball at its end floated not far beneath, idly swinging in the waves. Gratillonius heard the thuds when that great weight rolled against the wall. Those dry-laid blocks were well fitted indeed, to have withstood centuries of such battering. And even the doors, oaken though copper-sheathed and iron-bound, had only required replacement twice.

He let go of Dahut's hand. "Now 'tis single file," he said.

A flight of stone steps angled down the inside of the wall to a ledge beside the gate, halfway up. There stood a capstan, from which a chain ran through another cat's head to the inner top corner of the door. Opposite, fifty feet away, was a similar arrangement. "This is the machinery for closing at low tide," Gratillonius explained. "The doors are made so they never swing too widely for that. Follow me onward."

From the ledges, narrow, railed walkways ran across both doors, meeting in two platforms at the juncture. Dahut touched the riveted green plates and black iron reinforcing strips that she passed. "Why must you ever lock the gate?" she asked. "Less'n you want it shut up at low tide."

What a quick person she is! marvelled Gratillonius. "Well, think of a big storm with huge waves. They don't only have high crests, they have deep troughs. The floats drop down as well as bob up. Were it not for the bar, they'd jerk the doors wide. The sea would pour through and do terrible things to poor. Ys."

"Thank the Gods that They don't let that happen," admonished Guilvilis. Gratillonius thought, irritated, that man had somewhat more to do with it.

He reached the platform. There a titanic beam, pivoted on the southern door, fitted into an iron U on this northern one. A cable ran from its free end to a block and tackle above. The bar was secured by a chain through it and through a staple, closed by a ponderous lock whose hasp went between two links.

Looking down into the girl's eyes, Gratillonius wondered how he appeared in them. "This is my work," he said.

The marines had deployed along the walkway. Gratillonius unslung the Key from his neck and raised it aloft. "In the name of Ys," he called, "under the Pact of Brennilis that the Gods did grant unto us, I open the city to the sea."

He fitted Key into lock. It turned stiffly, with a clicking as of footsteps. He withdrew the Key and laid it back in his bosom. With both hands he removed the lock and hung it on a single link. Drawing the chain out, he fastened it in a loop by locking the loose end to the staple.

Crossing over to the opposite platform, he uncleated the cable and hauled on it. Cunningly counterweighted, the bar rose easily for all its massiveness. When it was almost vertical, he refastened the cable. Returning, he clasped his hands and bowed before the lock.

It was done. The party went back to the top of the wall. Soon, as tide ebbed, the doors would begin to draw apart. The sea would come hissing through, but gently, by that time not raising the level of the basin too much. Ys would again have the freedom of Ocean.

"I've other matters to attend to," Gratillonius said regretfully. "Guilvilis, there's scant sense in taking the child back to class today. Why not show her about this quarter? The Cornmarket, Epona Square, the Ishtar Shrine, whatever she'd like to see. She's grown enough for it. I'll seek your house this evening."

Dahut skipped for joy.

5

That ended an hour later.

Passing through the narrow, twisted streets near the waterfront, on the edge of the Fishtail slum, the girl halted. "What's in there?" she asked.

Guilvilis looked around. The cobblestones of Crescent Way lay nearly deserted, for dwellers in the tenements that hemmed it in were still off at work. On the right a building lifted four stories high, balconies cantilevered from the upper floor, the lower wall stuccoed and inset with shells which centuries had chipped and discolored. A couple of children had stopped their play to stare at the finely clad lady. A porter with a laden frame on his back had just come around a corner; Ys restricted draft and burden-bearing animals to a few principal thoroughfares. "Where?" the Queen replied vaguely.

"There," said Dahut with exasperation, and pointed.

Opposite stood a building unique to Lowtown. It was of black marble, broad and deep though not high. Pilasters flanked bronze doors on which were life-sized reliefs of a veiled woman and a man with bowed head. The entablature was granite, sculptured into a frieze: a row of skulls and at the center, floating above, an unborn babe.

"Oh," said Guilvilis. "Why, that, that's Wayfaring House."

"What's it?"

"You haven't heard? Well, 'tis, um, 'tis thus. You know dead people get taken out on the funeral barge and put in the sea."

Dahut nodded solemnly. "Father's told me. He says that's where my mother went."

"Well, the barge is supposed to go out each third day, but often the weather makes that too dangerous. Sometimes they have to wait a long while. They did this month, with those awful storms we got. Here, Wayfaring House, here is where they wait."

"Oh." Dahut's eyes widened.

" 'Tis all good and quiet for them," Guilvilis said hastily.

"Can we go see?"

"What? Nay, I think better not. Later, when you're older."

Dahut's face drew into an expression the Gallicenae well knew. "Why? You say 'tis good and quiet."

"Well, it is—"

Dahut stamped her foot. "Father said show me everything I wanted!"

Guilvilis searched her memory while the child fumed. "Aye, he . . . he did that, I think. But—"

Dahut darted from her, up the few broad stairs. The doors were unsecured. She pulled them apart and was inside before Guilvilis got there.

"What's this?" called the old man on duty. His voice made echoes in the twilight of a huge chamber. He shuffled forward. "My lady, you shouldn't bring a wee one here. Leave her with me. Which beloved would you bid goodbye to?—O-ah." He recognized the woman. "My *lady!*" Touching his brow in reverence: "How may I serve you?"

"I, well, 'tis thus—" faltered Guilvilis.

Dahut dashed past them.

Stone tubs, a few feet apart, covered the floor. She came to the first and looked over its edge.

Brine filled it. Within, full length, lay a dead woman. While a sheet wrapped her body, its soddenness revealed the bony contours. Cords bound wrists and ankles and held her to eyebolts. Hair floated loose. It had been an old woman, withered and toothless. The jaw had been tied up and the eyes closed, but lips and lids were shriveled back, while the waterlogged face bloated around the beak of a nose.

"You shouldn't'a done that, little girl," wailed the attendant.

Dahut made a mewing sound. Like a sleepwalker, she stumbled to the next vat. There was a man more newly dead. He had been young and healthy, though now his skin was ashen. Some mishap had shattered the right side of his head.

"Get her way from that, my lady," the attendant implored. "She's too young for the sight, she is."

"Aye, come, let us go, Dahut, dear, let's go see Cornmarket and I'll buy you a honeycake." Guilvilis lurched toward the princess. "Cry not, be not afraid."

"Nay," said the man, "these are but the harmless dead. We'll take them to their rest on the morrow, and the Ferriers will bring their souls to Sena and the Gods will make happy those who were good."

Stiff-legged, Dahut walked to the door. She stared before her, never a tear, never a blink. As daylight touched her, it showed a visage with no more color or movement than any in the brine.

Nor did she speak the whole way back to the house, and scarcely at all when Gratillonius arrived there. But when she had gone to bed, and man and wife were about to, they heard her scream.

—He stood holding her in his arms. She had hidden her face against his breast but did not give him back his embrace, only shivered and mewed. By the light of a single candle, he glared at Guilvilis.

"You dolt," he snarled. "You unspeakable clod, lackwit, bungler. What have you done to her? How could you do it, even you?"

She opened and shut her mouth several times, and he thought how very like a fish she looked, before she could stammer. "Y-y-you said take her where she wanted, and, and she got away from me. Oh, I'm sorry!" Tears coursed from her eyes. Her nose dribbled.

"A squid would have had better judgment, more command. And 'tis you who dwell in the home of Dahilis! Take you hence. Leave us ere you do worse harm."

She stared, and now he thought of a poleaxed cow.

"Get you to the nursery." To the Sasai, Antonia, Camilla she had borne him in such quick and glad succession. "Dahut and I will be together this night. . . . Not so, darling?" he murmured into the child-fragrance under her hair.

Guilvilis lifted her hands. "I love you, Grallon. I wanted to do what you said. I wanted to please you."

He brushed her aside as he carried his daughter out of the room.

They must cross the atrium to reach the main bedchamber. Every trace of Dahilis was gone. That had been at his insistence. Guilvilis would passively have left the dear things in place. He had ordered them brought to the palace. Guilvilis had acquired a few objects of her own. They were mostly garish. He didn't care.

He heard her weep on her way to the nursery. His anger sank a trifle. Thanks to her, Dahut had seen an unpleasant thing before she was ready for it, and it had given her a nightmare, but surely she could overcome any fears, as lively and self-willed as she was. Sometime soon he'd toss Guilvilis a friendly word or two.

He laid the ivory shape down on the bed. Though there was hardly any light here, she burrowed into a pillow. It was as well, since he must now undress and—better find himself a nightgown, which he generally did only in the coldest weather. Dahut was naked, but, Mithras, she was five years old. Yet, holding her, he had felt the first slight filling out of her slenderness.

"Be not afraid, sweetling," he said. "You saw no people yonder. You saw the husks they've no more use for. 'Tis like a—a dandelion, when the seeds blow away on the wind to become new dandelions."

Still she was mute. He got into bed and held her close. How moveless she lay, except for the faint trembling and catches of breath. Couldn't she cry, talk to him, have it out? Well, she'd always borne a strangeness about her. "I love you, Dahut," he whispered. His lips brushed her cheek. "I love you so much."

She did not answer. He got scant sleep that night.

6

Morning was bright and bleak. The funeral barge departed on the tide.

Dahut saw it from the heights. She had said at breakfast that she wanted simply a crust of bread and a cup of milk—which was true; she must force them down—and that she would make her own way to school —which of late she had been proudly doing. Father had left, and Mama Guilvilis was too crushed to respond. Freshly clad, Dahut set forth. Then she followed side streets to Northbridge Gate and went out on Point Vanis.

Few whom she passed paid her any heed. To them she was merely another lass bound somewhere, uncommonly pretty and curiously intent, but nobody to question. Women and girls walked about Ys as freely, safely as men. However, once on the headland, she left Redonian Way and went along the cliffs. A shepherd, carter, merchant, courier would have been too surprised by the sight of a child alone beyond the city wall. When she glimpsed anybody, she hid behind a bush or a boulder. Sometimes she stayed a while, staring out to sea or downward at earth and insects, before she wandered onward.

The promontory reared stark out of the water and stretched inland nearly bare save for grass turned sallow, gorse, thistle, scattered trees that the wind had dwarfed and gnarled, lichenous rocks. In a few places stood beehive-shaped stone shelters or menhirs raised by the Old Folk to Gods unknown. Wind boomed from the west, a torrent of chill. Clouds scudded before it, gulls, cormorants, a hawk on high. Shadows harried each other across the miles. In between them, sunlight made the waters flame.

Finally Dahut reached a low mound and a headstone, out near the northern end of the point. She sat down to rest. At school she was learning the Latin alphabet. She had not been here since that began. Now, slowly, with a tracing finger, she followed the letters chiseled into the stone.

Q IVN EPPILLO

OPT LEG II AVG

COMMIL FEC

Father had told her that a brave man lay beneath, who died fighting for Ys and Rome before she was born. He put off saying more, and when she asked two or three of the Mamas they put her off too. They seemed uneasy about it.

Abruptly Dahut sprang up. Her glance flung itself around. Against the dazzle on the sea she spied and knew the funeral barge, crawling out upon its oars. She choked down a scream and fled.

Nearby, where the cliffs turned east, a footpath led to them from the bend in the highway. Dahut sought it. Downward bound, it became a mere trail, steep and slippery. Father had held her in the past when they visited. Dahut picked her way alone, breathing raggedly but never losing balance.

A few blocks, canted and overgrown, showed that once a stair had led up. At the bottom were crumbling walls and the remnants of a jetty. Father had said this was a Roman marine station, smashed to pieces and fired long, long ago by the nasty Saxons. Dahut scrambled past the wreckage. Charred baulks and newer driftwood had jammed around the stump of the jetty to form a rough little ness. On this face of the headland the surf did not, today, assault it, though whitecaps smote and whooshed and sent spindrift flying.

Dahut stooped and took off her sandals. Barefoot, she could go out on the logs. Wind ripped at her. She cupped hands about mouth. "O-ho, o-hoo," she called. "Come to me, come to me!"

The wind flung her cry down into the waves.

"O-ho, o-hoo! Please come. I need you."

A shape appeared and swam rapidly toward her. It was golden-brown and huge-eyed. "Welcome, thank you, welcome," Dahut shouted; and tears started to run. She hunkered down into what shelter an uptilted slab offered. It was of planks, bleached and warped, still held by corroded nails to a pair of snapped-off crossbeams: a piece from the deck of a lost ship.

The seal came aground and slithered over the jumble. Dahut flung arms around her neck. The fish-breath was not foul, it was strong, like a soldier's trumpet. The wetness didn't matter, when such warmth and sleekness were there to lie against. A flipper enfolded Dahut. The seal nuzzled her. Whiskers prickled, then a tongue kissed, a voice hummed deep in the throat behind.

"O-o-oh, I saw the dead floating. They were all ugly an-an-and eels will eat them, *me too,* like my mother that father says was so beautiful, o-o-oh, they come after me in my dreams. I thought one of them was mother."

The seal held her close.

"Nay?" Dahut whispered after a while. "Not really? Never?"

Somehow the seal got her looking outward and opened her to what she saw.

"Papa told me 'bout dandelions—"

Radiance lit the wings of a hovering gull. Its voice was like laughter.

"Aye, shells on the beach, kelp, starfish, but they all go back, they all go back."

The waters no longer roared, they sang.

Dahut snuggled. Here, shielded from the weather, held in this comfort, she could let her weariness overwhelm her, she could sleep and be healed. "They all return. Ever'thing returns. . . ." The voice of the seal went lulling. " 'Tis mine."

Oh, darling, lie peaceful. The sea is before us,
The mothering, cleansing, all-powerful sea,
And borne on the wind and the foam is a chorus
Of surges and surf to your nest in the lee.
From depths that are darkling the billows lift sparkling,
As eager and salt as the beat of your blood.
No horror shall snare you, but life shall upbear you.
Dear sea-child, the tide of your hope is in flood.

XII

1

There was a man called Flavius Stilicho. His father had been a Vandal who entered the Imperial army and became an officer. Stilicho did likewise, rising high and fast until he was the mightiest general Rome had known for generations. This made him a power in the state. After military and diplomatic exploits in Persia and Thracia, he moved against the barbarians of the North. In Britannia his campaigns piled the bodies of Saxons, Picti, and Scoti in windrows and sent the survivors reeling back.

That spring, Uail maqq Carbri had led a seaborne raid up the channel to the mouth of the Sabrina and along the Silurian shore. Newly reinforced, the Romans fast marched from Isca Silurum, surprised the Scoti, and harvested a goodly number of them before the rest could escape. Uail's outsize currach did keep its load of booty from a town his reavers had sacked, including some captives. Among those was a lad of sixteen, a son of the curial, named Sucat.

Gallia had become an even worse hunting ground. Armorica guarded the approach, strengthened by the newly enlarged navy of Ys. No man of Ériu in his right mind would go there, unless it be as a peaceful trader.

Uail sought Niall maqq Echach, King at Temir, and gave his ill tidings. Unlike most of the chieftains who were on hand, Niall did not rage. Time had taught him patience. If the sun-brightness of his locks had begun, ever so faintly, to dim, the wits beneath were whetted as keen as his sword had always been. He accepted Uail's gifts out of the plunder, and made generous return. "It's kindly your mood is, lord," said the skipper.

Niall laughed. "It is not," he replied. "The Romans must simply wait their turn. I have built up my strength over the years. Now we will build it further still, beginning with an undertaking that men shall remember forever."

Toward that end, he had been seeking the good will of his Condachtach kinfolk. One of these, a tuathal king from the western shores, happened to be guesting him just then, a man named Mílchu. When this man went home, among the gifts he took along was the slave Sucat, whom Uail had presented to Niall.

Alliance was natural. Warfare between the Ulati of the north and the Firi Condachtae south and west of them was an ancient as when Cú Culanni stood off the cattle raiders of Queen Medb, if indeed the strife had not begun between the sons of Ír and Éber just after they conquered the Children of Danu. Being of Condachtach origin, the royal house that lorded it over the tuaths of Mide had inherited those feuds.

Equally haughty were the Ulatach kings who foregathered at Emain Macha. The chief among them claimed descent from Conchobar maqq Nessa, the lesser ones from the warriors of the Red Branch, as did the landowning nobles.

Tributary to them, between Qóiqet nUlat and Mide, were humbler folk. Ulati had established themselves in those parts as chieftains, but scorned the dwellers, calling them mere Cruthini or outright Firi Bolg, exacting heavy rents, being careless about rights. Often a poor man could only get justice by starving at the door of the rich. Sometimes this, too, failed to shame the defendant, whose well-nourished flesh could endure hunger far beyond the day when scrawniness must either give up or die.

Thus, when the chariots of Niall and his sons rumbled north at the head of a host, victory winged above them. They found few earthworks and strongpoints to overrun. The enemy leaders fought valiantly, but many of their followers, especially bond tenants, were half-hearted and quick to flee. Reinforcements from the King at Emain Macha arrived too late, too little. At the end of the second summer's warfare, Niall had prevailed as far as the headwaters of the River Sinand, almost to the Ulatach lands proper. The petty kings whom he had beaten plighted faith to him. He took hostages from them and went home.

There he would bide a while, waiting to see what happened in Ériu and overseas, before moving onward. Anything else would have been fool-hardly. What he had won promised wealth, power, glory, but also unfore-seeable trouble. It was more than plowlands, herds, salmon streams, for-ests for game and timber, gold, weapons, men. His now was mastery over Mag Slecht, the holiest place in all Ériu. He must be careful not to rouse the anger of its Gods or too many of Their worshippers.

2

The months wheeled onward, through winter and spring and again to summer.

Esmunin Sironai, chief astrologer in Ys, predicted a lunar eclipse some three sennights after solstice. His tables and formulae went back to the Chaldeans, with much added by the Greeks and no little by his own people over the centuries, hampered though they were by their climate. The Queen who would be in charge of the Temple of Belisama at the time prepared for a special service, and she who would have the Vigil on Sena rehearsed special prayers, for the moon was the Lady's. Forsquilis arranged to have neither duty; she would be casting spells and taking omens by herself. Bodilis planned to be at Star House.

The weather proved clear. The Symposium met early for dinner and discourse. King Gratillonius had attended such meetings when he was able, but now had Watch. The word went, very softly, that he intended a rite of Mithras.

At sunset the company entered the Water Tower and climbed a helical staircase to the observatory on top. Esmunin's students busied themselves with armillary spheres, goniometers, and other instruments. The old man sat in a corner wrapped in his cloak. He was nearly blind. "But we will tell you all as it happens, master," they said lovingly. "We will write it down with exactness, that you may draw forth meanings we would never find."

Bodilis went to the parapet. Ys made a basin of darkness, save where fire glowed from windows, but towers still caught light on their uppermost metal and glass. In the opposite direction, the canal drew a thread of silver through the dusk in the valley. Air was as yet warm, moist, full of scents and whispers. And yonder above the hills rose the full moon. Already a gap was out of its limb.

"A-a-ah," murmured voices, and "Goddess, be gentle us-ward," and "Quick, now, set the clock." Nearsighted, Bodilis squeezed forefinger against thumb to make a peephole through which she could more clearly see the marvel.

Blackness advanced until it became red. That veil gave way in turn to blackness again as it withdrew from ashen white. It has been an eclipse longer than some, shorter than some. It would go into Esmunin's book, another grain of truth laid down for a harvest he would never see. Bodilis wondered how many learned men in the Empire had troubled themselves to observe this, or watch at all.

A little talk followed, comparison, speculation; but most of the philosophers were ready for bed. Bodilis remained wide awake. As folk descended and said goodnight, she started home, thinking that she would read for a while, or perhaps attempt a little further translation of the *Oedipus,* or perhaps do a sketch for a painting she had in mind. Her place had grown lonesome since Gratillonius ceased sleeping there. Semuramat —Tambilis—was lonely too, but it behooved a Queen to maintain a household; and, to be sure, Tambilis was still studying those things a cultivated woman should know. Kerna and Talavair were good daughters who tried to see their mother often, but they had their families to attend first.

Bodilis had no need of a lantern, so brightly did the moon shine. The streets she took were empty, which made the glimpses she got through the windows of lighted homes seem doubly snug. Her rangy stride sent echoes rattling along the up-and-down twistiness.

It happened that her way led her by a house lately fire-gutted. That was rare in Ys, where only the upper stories of the tallest buildings were wooden. When conflagration did occur, the marines at Warriors' House were as quick to come put it out as they were to come stamp down violent crime. In this case, a high wind and a broken amphora of oil defeated them. The family moved elsewhere, pending repairs.

A man had climbed up to sit on the blackened front wall, whose roof had collapsed. Swinging long legs, he was dressed in forester's wise, coarse shirt, leather doublet, cross-gartered trews. The moonlight showed a silver headband, gold earrings, forked black beard. A scar puckered the face that he kept turned aloft.

The sound she made caught his attention. He came down in a rush via a windowsill and made a sweeping salute of deference. "My lady, Queen Bodilis!" His rather high voice spoke easy Ysan, though with a Redonic accent. "What a grand surprise. How may I serve you?"

She recognized Rufinus. They had met seldom and fleetingly, as much as he was off on errands of the King's about which neither man said much. "What were you doing?" she inquired.

"Watching the eclipse, of course," he laughed. "Such marvels are all too few, and then this wretched weather of ours most likely hides them." Immediately he grew serious. "Afterward I sat trying to think what makes such a thing happen. Surely the Queen knows, but I'm only a runaway serf."

"You've no ideas?" she found herself asking.

"Naught but folk tales. Not erenow have I had leisure to wonder about the world, thanks to King Grallon, best of lords."

Bodilis winced and replied in haste: "Well, 'tis simple enough. The sun and the moon move opposite each other when the angles are just right, and so the shadow of the earth falls on the moon. Have you not noticed how that shadow is curved?"

Rufinus stared. "Why—yea, my lady—but, but do I understand you to say the world, this earth, is *round?*"

"Indeed. That's well known. Think how a ship goes below the horizon on a clear day. First the hull disappears, then the mast. How could that be, save on a globe?"

Rufinus drew a long breath. His voice pulsed: "True, true! I said I'd never had a chance to think beyond the needs of staying alive, till lately, but—Yea, clear 'tis to see. But more riddles boil forth—" He fell to one knee in his extravagant fashion. "My lady Bodilis, wisest of the Gallicenae, may I beg a favor? May I accompany you to your doorstep, listening to whatever you care to share of your knowledge? If ever you'd make for yourself an adoring servant, here is how!"

Bodilis smiled. "Why, certainly, if you like." As devoted as he was to Gratillonius, this young man would be no menace to her; and he was charming and his appeal was touching. Besides, she recalled vaguely, gossip was that when in Ys Rufinus did not take advantage of the novelty that could attract many a well-born woman to him.

He capered for joy.

The questions he put as they went along showed ignorance, but also a mind amazingly quick to comprehend the truth. At her house she was tempted to invite him in. Few pleasures matched teaching a bright pupil. She thought better of it; but they agreed to meet again when opportunity allowed.

3

That had been a quiet year in Ys. Yet folk came to believe that mighty things were astir in the womb of time. One month the moon had darkened; then in the very month that followed, a comet appeared. For seven-and-twenty nights it followed the sun, drawing ever nearer as a wolf overtakes a stag. Even when clouds hid it, all knew that it prowled above, a maned star trailing tails of ghostly flame.

The Gallicenae met shortly after the apparition. "This fear is nonsense," Bodilis declared. "Whatever comets are—Aristoteles thought them mere vapors in the upper air—the chronicles tell us they've come and gone with less serious consequences than so many thunderstorms."

"The fear may be groundless," replied Lanarvilis, "but 'tis real just the same. 'Twould help were the King on hand, but—" She shrugged. Gratillonius was off to the Romans again, helping Maximus's veterans organize the training of reservists. "Unrest grows. Some mariners are afraid to put to sea. Nagon Demari stirs up the workers."

"And Christian Corentinus makes converts," Vindilis sneered.

"The trouble will die out, won't it?" ventured Innilis.

"One hopes so," Fennalis answered. "Still, 'twould be wise as well as kindly to quell these dreads now if we can."

"That's why I called you hither," Lanarvilis told them, and went on to explain her idea. After some discussion, the Queens reached consensus. Let heralds go forth, promising that at new moon, some nights hence, the whole Nine would be on Sena, there to divine the will of the Gods and set right any wrongs.

Toward the end of talk, Forsquilis proposed: "We should take Dahut with us."

"What?" exclaimed Maldunilis. "But we can't. She's no Queen. She may well never be."

"True, she may not go ashore with us," Forsquilis said. "But she can abide on the barge, which will wait overnight to take eight of us back." Her seeress's eyes searched them. "It should strengthen that awe of the Gods we want her to feel."

—Dahut was enraptured. The barge of state had always been so splendid, and here she got to ride on it, and to holy Sena! Tambilis, who was familiar with it because of the Vigils she took, led her about and showed her everything, from the swan's head at the prow, through the flagstaff and temple-like deckhouse at the waist, to the gilt fishtail at the stern. The sailors made much of the little princess; even those at the oars had a grin and a jest for her. It was a brisk day, wind whittering, the sea all gray-green and whitecapped.

The mainland cliffs sank into horizon haze. Low and flat, the island grew in view. Tambilis's pleasure dwindled. She had not told Dahut that she was often terrified yonder, alone after dark with the wind and the sea and Lir.

The barge docked. Guilvilis, who had been on duty, came down from the House of the Goddess to meet her Sisters. Its stonework bulked murky, foursquare, crowned by a turret of equally grim aspect. Beyond reached scrub, harsh grass, naked rock. Dahut tried and tried to see the two menhirs she had heard about, but they were at the heart of the island and she couldn't.

Tambilis bent down to hug her. "You shall stay with the men, dear," said the youngest of the Nine. "They'll want to amuse you, and that's fine, but remember we brought you along so you could think hard about the sacred mysteries."

Bodilis smiled a bit sadly down on the two. "You were ever a good girl, Semuramat who was," she murmured.

—While the high priestesses did not believe eclipse and comet were evil portents, neither had they come here as a political gesture. That would have been mockery of the Three. Their sundown rites were solemn. Thereafter they filed inland to the Stones. Wind hooted and bit, waves crashed. Low in the west, the invader star seemed to fly through ragged clouds.

Eight of the women formed a ring around the pillars. Fennalis, the senior, stood in front and called in the ancestral language, "Ishtar-Isis-Belisama, have mercy on us. Taranis, embolden us. Lir, harden us. All Gods else, we invoke You in the name of the Three, and cry unto You for the deliverance of Ys."

Tambilis had carried a firepot. She set alight the wood which a keeper of the Vigil always made sure was ready. The tasting of salt followed, and then the knife, to nick forth a drop of blood that each flung into the flames. Together the Gallicenae sang the prayer for guidance.

Meanwhile the clouds came in hordes out of Ocean, until blackness overwhelmed Sena. The wind loudened, the waves raged.

—By morning a full gale was under way. Noise, chill, and spindrift filled the air. Fury ran free on the waters. There could be no question of return.

The Queens were safe enough. Ascetical though it was, the House gave shelter and held supplies. In the unlikely event that combers washed over the island, the tower offered refuge. Yet this looked like keeping them weatherbound for days. Tasks ashore would go neglected while anxiety tightened its grip on the people, who would see this as another bad omen. Said Forsquilis bleakly: "Once the weather was at the command of the Gallicenae. We ourselves have summoned it. But more and more does the power slip from us. The world blunders blind into a new Age which holds terrors unknowable."

Tambilis and Bodilis went to the barge to reassure the crew and, especially, Dahut. They found the child wholly fearless, out on deck as much as the men dared allow, peering into the wind and chanting some wordless song of her own.

—Next morning the gale had dropped to a stiff breeze, while sunlight straggled down between rain-squalls. The seas remained heavy, and the captain of the barge told the Nine that he could not yet start forth. The reefs were too many, too treacherous. He guessed departure would be possible in another two or three days.

Dahut trilled laughter.

Toward noon, those on the island were astounded to see a vessel bearing in. On eight oars, it was a fishing smack, tarry, battered, but stout. *"Osprey!"* Dahut shouted, dancing in glee. *"Osprey!* Maeloch's come!"

Standing on the dock, Fennalis clutched her cloak to her. "What's this?" she asked. "Whom do you speak of?"

Dahut grew grave. "Maeloch's my friend," she said. "I called to the seal and got her to bring him for us."

"I don't understand," Maldunilis whimpered.

Innilis explained: "Maeloch, a fisher captain, also a Ferrier who knows this passage well. Sometimes he's been the boatman when Dahut's gone out on the water. I've taken her myself down to his home at Scot's Landing, where he fills her with goat's milk and stories."

"She's had me do the same," said Bodilis. "Child, what's this about a seal?"

Dahut paid no heed, and then the boat was close in, its crew looking lively under profane orders. They made fast. Maeloch sprang onto the dock. He drew the cowl of his leather jacket back from his shaggy-maned head, made a reverence like a bear's, and boomed: "Ladies, we'll take ye back. Fear nay. She be a cramped and smelly craft, but the crossing will be quick and safe."

The captain of the barge huffed. "Are you mad?"

Maeloch spread his huge hands. " 'Twasn't my thought, mate," he admitted. "A dream came to me last night, and when I stepped out at dawn I saw a seal that swam in a beckoning way. She led us. We might have been skerry-prey without her for a guide; but 'tisn't the first time we did well to follow a seal. She'll bring us to harbor again."

"She *will!*" Dahut cried.

Forsquilis came forward. "This is true," she said into the wind. "I too had dreams. I cannot read them, not quite, but— Come, Sisters, let us embark,"

Tambilis sighed almost happily. She must stay behind, today's Vigil being hers, but she would not be entirely by herself. The barge would convey her when the sea had calmed enough for that awkward vessel.

Maeloch beamed. "Aye, welcome aboard, ladies. We'll do our poor best to make the trip easy for ye. I did need to whack a couple of the crew ere they'd go, but they've come to see this be a right thing to do. We ask no reward but your blessing." His hand dropped over the head of Dahut. "For how could we leave the princess waiting here, the daughter of Queen Dahilis what everybody loved?"

4

The tower named Polaris was the westernmost of its kind, in Lowtown although on the mildly prosperous south side of Lir Way. Equidistant from the Forum and Skippers' Market, it contained something of both. Respectable folk occupied the lower stories, the poor and raffish dwelt higher up. When he was in Ys, Rufinus had an apartment on the topmost thirteenth floor.

Thither came Vindilis one winter afternoon. Fog had taken over the city, making its traffic a migration of phantoms, but a breeze from the south had now begun to rend and scatter the blindness. Clumps of it still grayed vision, and air remained raw. In plain black cloak and cowl, Vindilis strode unrecognized.

Approaching Polaris, she got a full view of it save where shreds of mist blurred vision. Less lavishly built and ornamented than some, it nonetheless lifted arrogantly. Marble lions with fish tails for hindquarters flanked the main entrance, whose entablature depicted a ship at sea and its lodestar. The first five stories were of the dry-laid stone the Gods had required, beneath tawny stucco inset with images of Ocean's creatures and plants. Construction above was timber, its paint shading from the same yellow to pearly white. Grotesques were carved into the vertical beams. The tower narrowed as it mounted to its roof. From that bronze cupola, green as the sea gate, curved four serpent heads. Each wall was agleam with window glass.

Vindilis mounted the low staircase, whose granite lay in concavities worn by centuries of feet. Entering, she found herself in a corridor onto which opened a number of shops and workplaces—a wineseller's, a spicer's, a draper's, a jeweler's, and more, including a small establishment selling food. Lamps lightened their dimness. Trade and craftsmanship happened softly. At the middle of the corridor was an alcove where a strong man sat by a wheel and crank. A rope went upward. By raising water and other needs, and bringing wastes and rubbish down for disposal, this hoist took some of the curse off living on the higher stories. Adjacent stairs went steeply aloft. Vindilis began the climb.

Doors on the first several residential floors stood mostly shut. Many bore the insignia of families that had lived for generations in the suites behind. Higher on, occupants were more transient. There was a measure of shabbiness, odors of cooking cabbage, loud voices, raucous laughter, children milling in and out of doors left ajar. Everybody goggled at the stranger lady.

Yet no one menaced her, nor did she see outright filth or poverty. Tower folk on the various levels formed their own self-policing communities, often with their own argots and customs. They were apt to scoff at groundlings. It added much to the intricate, many-colored tapestry that was life in Ys.

The thirteenth floor had space for just one apartment. The landing was a narrow strip lighted by a small window. Vindilis scowled at the door. Rufinus had replaced its former knocker with the penile bone of a walrus. Distastefully, she struck it against the wood.

He opened for her at once. Her messenger having told him she wanted to visit, he was neatly attired in a Roman-style tunic. "My lady!" he greeted. "Thrice welcome! Pray enter, let me take your cloak, rest yourself while I bring refreshment."

"Did you think I'd be winded?" she answered. "Nay, I keep myself fit, and forty years leave me somewhat short of senectitude."

Her coldness failed to dismay him. Smiling, he bowed her through, closed the door, relieved her of her outer garment. For a moment they regarded each other, his green eyes even with her black. She had drawn her hair straight back. The white streak through the middle of it seemed to recall the comet of summer. Whiteness had begun to fleck the raven locks throughout.

"Do be seated, my lady," Rufinus urged. "Would you care for wine or mead? I've laid in cheeses, nuts, dried fruits as well."

Vindilis shook her head. "Not now. I've business on hand that cannot wait."

"Aye, daylight wanes. Yonder door gives onto a balcony. Or would you liefer look through a window in this dank weather? The glass is fairly clear."

"Why do you live in an aerie?" she asked. "I know you could have quarters in the royal palace if you wished."

Startled, he said, "Why, well, I like my privacy. And the view is magnificent. The very fogs—I stand on that balcony under the moon and look down on a city become a lake of flowing alabaster. By day I am kin to the rooks and hawks around me."

"You certainly have changed your ways. Like your language."

"My lady?"

"You neither live like a Bacauda any longer nor talk like one. I'll step outside. What I see should tell me more about you."

Crossing the main chamber, she glanced everywhere around. The bedroom door stood shut. The kitchen was open, and ordinary: a cubicle minimally equipped, plastered and tiled against fire hazard. He kept the place clean. Rather, a hireling doubtless came in and did, for Rufinus had money these days. The atrium doubled as triclinium, with a table and chairs next to a sideboard. The ware on its shelves ran to the fanciful, sometimes the obscene, such as a ewer in the form of Priapus. Another table was of finely carved walnut inset with nacre. Likewise good were a pair of couches. A corner was taken up by his traveling gear, the weapons and tools and forester's outfit with which he fared on the King's missions. Two portrait busts on pedestals flanked it, one the beautiful ancient head of a boy, the second a modern likeness of Gratillonius. Elsewhere sprawled a jackdaw collection of objects, everything from a golden arm ring of Frankish workmanship to an earthen jug which must hold certain memories, whatever they might be.

Passing the central table, Vindilis spied a flute, a couple of books, writing materials, a shingle on which words had awkwardly been penned. "I see you practice your literacy," she remarked.

"I do, my lady, with more patience than is usually mine," he said. "You doubtless know Queen Bodilis was gracious enough to arrange instruction for me. She's promised me fascinating things to read when I'm able."

He hurried to fling wide the balcony door. Vindilis trod forth into a chill that braziers kept from the apartment. She breathed deep. "Fresh air cleanses," she said.

Rufinus smiled. "I pray pardon if my lodgings are stuffy. I get more fresh air than I care for, outside Ys."

The view embraced a semicircle, from the sea portal to High Gate and beyond. Rampart, turrets, triumphal arch, streets, plazas were hers, an interweaving made mysterious by the vapors that drifted through it. Towers like this lanced above, to catch long sunbeams and bedazzle heaven. Afar she saw Elven Gardens and the purity of Belisama's Temple like an island rising out of the mist-lake. The sounds were of wind, wings, bird calls, and, faintly, the pulsebeat of the city.

"Aye," Vindilis mused at length, "you've deeper reasons than you perchance know for roosting here. All this calls to you."

Rufinus blinked. "What?" He cleared his throat. "Hm, can I supply aught that my lady needs for her aeromancy? Shall I absent myself?"

Vindilis re-entered the room, closed the door, confronted him. "Not for that have I come," she said.

"But your message was—"

She smiled sardonically. "My message was to head off rumors. I have no gift for reading the future in patterns of cloud and breeze. If I did, I'd mount the pharos for it. Nay, my aim is to talk with you in private."

Unease passed through him. "Indeed? A surprise. I'm nobody."

"You are he whom the King defied the Gods to spare. That alone makes you fateful. Now you have also become his confidential agent, going to and fro on the earth. Surely you offer counsel as well. Sit down, Rufinus."

"As my lady commands. But first let me pour wine and—"

Vindilis pointed to a chair. "Sit down, I told you."

He folded his long legs and stared up at her. "Does my lady speak for the Nine?"

"Not altogether. Words concerning you have passed among us, but 'twas my decision to seek you out. What I tell anyone else will depend very much on what happens here."

He wet his lips. "I'll not betray my master's secrets."

Vindilis folded her arms and looked above him into the shadows that were gathering as daylight ended. "I need it not. I can guess, broadly, what goes on. The organizing of former Bacaudae into the King's forest rangers. Tasks they carry out at his behest. Linkage with the smallholders, the serfs, belike certain townspeople, the resettled veterans. He's gathering together a native Armorican strength, to protect the country better than Rome does. Yet the Imperial authorities would dislike learning that they are under surveillance and that so much they've mismanaged is quietly being done. *I* will bear no tales to them."

Rufinus had regained balance. "The Queen is shrewd. I beg leave to say no more."

Her gaze smoldered at him. "You may be required to. I think that from time to time you shall be recommending certain courses of action to Gratillonius, proposals that would not have occurred to him of their own accord."

Forgetting her orders, he jumped to his feet. Pallor made the scar on his cheek stand lurid. "Nay!" he cried. "Grallon's my lord?"

"Calm down," she snapped. "Think you his wives would wish him steered toward harm? I've his best interests at heart. And yours, Rufinus."

"Mine? My lady, I'll take no bribe—forgive me—no recompense."

Her smile was hard. "Not even silence?"

He stared. "What mean you?"

"Unwise you were, Rufinus, to take your pleasures freely in Ys."

He stiffened his back. "Why should I not carouse?"

"Wine, song, shows, gambling, aye. But you're never seen in Tomcat Alley, nor do you avail yourself of the girls so readily available in taverns near the waterfront. For that matter, given your status and, yea, your personal charm, I'm sure a number of elegant women would be glad of a little sport with you."

His hands lifted as if to fend her off. "I'm not impotent—"

"I never believed that."

"I've been with women—"

"Doubtless. After all, you came here intending to make yourself King."

"If I choose now to be chaste—"

"Curse me if you must," said Vindilis crisply, "but insult not my intelligence. I suspected early on what you are. The Nine have their means of finding things out when they care to. Shall I name the foreign sailors? Some you brought hither, the young and handsome. That was most foolish. 'Tis sheer luck that your fellow tenants have not paid much heed . . . thus far. They soon will, unless you grow careful."

The breath rasped in Rufinus's throat. "What concern is this of theirs? Of yours?"

The sharp features softened, and the voice. "It should be none. In olden Greece, I've heard, 'twould not have been, nor for a long time in Rome itself. But Ys is neither. Underneath all the sensuality, its heritage remains, of austere mariners from the South, ruthless charioteers from the East, and—who knows what of the Old Folk?" She laid a hand on his. "Would it were otherwise. But this must needs concern me, because the revelation would destroy your usefulness to the King. It would cast suspicions on him that would wound him in his soul and undermine him in his power. You'd not do that to Grallon, would you, Rufinus?"

He shuddered. Anguish answered: "O Gods, netherworld Gods, nay."

"Then, first, be more discreet," she said. "You can do as you like beyond our borders, though best would be if you use a false name. While in Ys, amuse yourself as you wish, save for this." Her tone thinned. "Engage whores, if your fingers will not suffice you."

He reddened. "I can. I have. 'Tis only—I think my nature is, is because I was a boy when I joined the Bacaudae, who seldom see women, and—Nay, I pledge caution in Ys, for Grallon's sake."

Warmth responded: "Then I will accept your wine. Come, light wicks ere dusk overtakes us. Set forth food also, though I eat sparingly. Let us sit down and become acquainted. For I do not abhor you. I understand you better than you imagine."

Heartened, he warned, "Gladly will I plan with you how we may both serve Grallon, my lady. But remember always, he is my lord, to whom my faith is plighted."

"Whom you love," she said softly.

Rufinus flinched. "He does not know."

"Nor shall he ever," Vindilis promised, "if you bear yourself toward me as I hope you will."

5

The Queens were all kind to Dahut, in their different ways, but she came to like Tambilis best and looked forward to her turns at staying in the house of the youngest. This was in spite of the fact that Papa never came there, with his romps and stories and tuneless but bouncing songs, as he did to the other Mamas whenever he was able (though he never spent the night with Fennalis or Bodilis). Dahut tried to find out why that was, but couldn't get any real answer from either one. They certainly smiled and spoke gently enough when they met.

No matter that eight years lay between their births, Tambilis and Dahut shared secrets, played little games together, went on trips, moaned about lessons, giggled at funny things. Tambilis had more learning, of course, which she could not readily explain to Dahut, only saying, "Wait till you get that far." However, she knew there was something mysterious and special about Dahut, which could still less be put into words. "I'm not afraid of you," she said. "You're my own dear cousin."

The Council of Suffetes met around the quarter days. Tambilis confessed to Dahut that she merely listened, sometimes interested, sometimes frightened, sometimes well-nigh falling asleep. On the days themselves, the meetings adjourned for various ceremonies. Tambilis looked on the vernal equinox that year as a liberation.

After services at the Temple of Belisama, she sought Dahut out from among the departing choir girls. She herself had been one of the high priestesses. "Would you like to come with me?" she asked, flushed and proud. "I have the Shrine of Ishtar this time. 'Tis just open two days a year, you know, at spring and autumn."

Dahut joyously agreed and got permission. She had heard that Ishtar was an ancient name of the Goddess and that the Founders had built Her a house when Ys was a new Phoenician colony. Nowadays Her first, simple dwelling stood unused, except when the wheel of the year bore back remembrance.

Hand in hand, the two made their way through crowds that respectfully parted, down into Lowtown. The blue gown and high white headdress of Tambilis only made her look as young as Dahut, who wore a flowing dress of silk, gilt sandals, and above her unbound blond hair a garland of primroses. The day was mild and sunny. Birds winged around flashing towers.

The Shrine was small, rammed earth and slate roof on a plot scarcely larger, which was marked off by four boundary stones. When Tambilis had unlocked the door, the interior proved equally plain, clay floor and rough altar block, though the Mirror was polished and the murals of Stars and Moon had lately been retouched.

After prayer, Tambilis seated herself on a bench together with Dahut and waited. In the hours that followed, a number of people came one by one or two by two through the open entrance. Mostly they were humble folk. Some simply wanted to make their devotions. Some approached the Queen and asked for blessing or help—a woman with child, a man who had lost his only son, a woman in search of her husband's forgiveness for adultery, a man soon to sail forth to distant lands, a girl who was deformed and lonely, a boy with soaring dreams. . . . Tambilis could give the benison. Aid and counsel she was seldom prepared to render, but she knew where they might be found. In this wise Dahut saw what power was the Goddess's.

At sunset, after a final orison, Tambilis closed the shrine. The weight of solemnity fell off her. "Now we are free," she caroled. "Come, let's go to the Forum. They'll be celebrating, you know, and the performers and musicians and, and everybody. There'll be stalls with food and drink and sweetmeats and, oh, all sorts of fine things. Innilis said I can bring you home as late as we want."

"Till dawn!" Dahut cried.

They danced off, Tambilis forgetting that in public a Queen should be stately.

Between the Roman-like buildings that surrounded the central plaza, a throng milled. Their feet hid the mosaics of dolphins and sea horses. Dusk had gone flickery-bright, for the Fire Fountain was playing, oil ablaze, pumped high to cascade in red, yellow, green, blue flames down its three basins. Voices surfed, laughter rang, melodies whistled, throbbed, twanged, drummed. Raiment made a rainbow, and few were the brows without a wreath.

Wandering about, little noticed in spite of Tambilis's garb, the girl passed near what had been the Roman temple of Mars and was now the Christian church. Words slashed through the merriment: "O people of Ys, hear the warning. Terrible is your danger."

Tambilis paid no heed, but Dahut stopped and stared. A tall, rawboned man stood on the top step of the temple portico. His beard was black but grizzling, his hair abristle behind a shaven slice of scalp that went from ear to ear. His robe was of cloth cheap and rough. At his back, drably clad, clustered a few men and slightly more women. "Amen," they chanted whenever he paused. His speech was quiet, but it carried.

"—yon cheerful ingle is in truth a will-o'-the-wisp leading you on to the burning that waits down in hell—"

The Ysans ignored him, talked, quaffed, japed, kissed.

"I beg you, listen. Ah, well do I understand, my plea tonight will win nobody over. But if you will hear it and think about it—"

Dahut's face paled so that the restless colors took possession of it. "Come," Tambilis said. "No matter that old moldy. Let's go on." Dahut seemed to hear only the preacher.

"I do not scoff at your faith. Your Gods have brought you to much that is wonderful. But Their time is past. Like those unfortunates whom senility has turned mad, They do naught but mislead; and the road They have you upon goes into the Abyss. I love you too much, God loves you too much, to wish that for you. Forswear those demons you call Gods. Christ waits and longs to save you."

"Nay!" Dahut yelled. She broke from Tambilis's clasp, dashed off and up the stairs.

An uneven sigh went over the revelry and damped it down. Many recognized the slim form with the beautiful face that ran to stand before Corentinus. They breathed her name to the rest. Eyes and eyes and eyes turned thither.

"Child," called the chorepiscopus shakenly, "beloved Princess Dahut, do *you* see the truth?"

She stamped her foot, clenched her fists, and shouted up his height: "You lie, old man, you're a liar! The Goddess is good, the Gods're strong!"

"Oh, poor darling," Corentinus said.

"You're horrible!" she screamed. Turning to the Forum, she raised her arms. The light from the Fountain picked out her bright garment and hair, while casting Corentinus into murk. "Don't you listen to him! The Goddess is good, the Gods're strong!"

"Child," Corentinus groaned, "you have but seven years in this world. How can you know?"

"I do know!" she flung at him. "The sea tells me, the seal comes to me, an' an' today—everywhere—" Again she faced the people. "Listen to me. We *belong* to the Gods. If we forsake Them, They will forsake us, and Ys will die. Please be true to the Gods!"

Weeping, she stumbled back down the stairs. Tambilis hurried to embrace her. The crowd swarmed around them. It roared. Corentinus and his Christians stood alone beneath the pagan frieze on their church.

XIII

1

At Lúgnassat, King Niall must by law preside over the great fair at
Tallten, its rites and sacrifices as well as its games and worldly dealings.
His older sons had fallen into the way of representing him at such other
gatherings of the kind as were important. They would be unwise to break
that practice, when no warfare had call upon them this year. Besides
keeping the glory of their house in view, it gave them a chance to gather
news and strike useful bargains. With their north-faring dreams, the lords
of Mide wanted no enemies at their backs. About the hostility of the
Lagini they could do little; however it seemed that Niall's punitive expedition, and the wealth he took back with him, had sapped the eastern
Fifth for a while.

Yet he was now master of Mag Slecht, where stood Cromb Cróche,
Who had power over earth and blood. If he wanted the help, the goodwill, of that God, he for his part must not fail to pay honor and make
offering. Having given the matter thought, he sent his son Domnuald on
his behalf, with a goodly train of warriors and servants, a druid for counsel and magic, a poet for solemnity and power, several bards for entertainment when the company had made camp at eventide. Though still rather
young, Domnuald had proven himself in battle against the Lagini and
afterward the Ulati. Among his own folk, his cheerfulness and common
sense boded well for the future.

As he approached his destination, he departed from the main road and
traveled about, collecting the tribute and rents due his father. These he
took in the form of kine. To landowners in whose houses he overnighted
when that was convenient, he explained his intention of giving the animals, in a huge slaughter, to the Bent One of the Mound. Thus should
there come no evil creatures upon Niall or the sons of Niall.

Certain men cast dark looks. After their guest was gone, they rode off with word. Having become a cattle drive, Domnuald's progress grew slow. Nevertheless he ended his journey ahead of time.

The past few days had been hot. Air stewed in the nostrils, clothes clung to skin, breath was heavy and sleep unrestful. Clouds brooded enormous, blue-black, with mutterings in their depths and sometimes a wan flicker of lightning; but the blessed rain did not fall and did not fall. The herd became skittish, hard to control. Men's patience wore thin, until tempers often flared into quarrels.

Mag Slecht was a plain out of which rose small hills. Here the menhirs, dolmens, and cromlechs were many. Such folk as lived thereabouts tended the cult sites and, in return, shared in the sacrificial feasts that outsiders held. Otherwise poor and lowly, they were still regarded as having something eldritch about them. Domnuald went by their homes without stopping, more hasty than haughty, until his band spied the halidom of Cromb Cróche from afar. Then he galloped his horse ahead of everybody else, up the track through the woods that decked the hillsides, reached the clearing, and reined in.

Awe smote him. He saw a huge circle of grass surrounded by forest. In this windlessness, leaves were utterly silent, as if cut out of green stone, and shadows made caves beneath the boughs. At the center blazed brightness almost too fierce to look at. It was the gold and silver that sheathed a giant standing stone which had somewhat the look of a hunchbacked man. Not much smaller were the menhirs that formed a ring around it, twelve altogether, themselves covered with brass kept bright by the rubbing of worshipful hands.

Domnuald's troop had remained below to set up camp, save for a couple of warriors who followed him more slowly. The trees hid them. Shouts, lowing and neighing of beasts, creak of cartwheels reached him faintly, as if the simmering stillness crushed every noise under its weight. He was alone beneath the thunderheads.

Of a sudden that ended. Three more roads led to this crest. Out from the eastern one trod armed men. Their spearheads flamed in the ruthless sunlight. Domnuald dropped hand to sword hilt where he sat. The leader strode toward him, a man as heavy as Domnuald was slender, dark as Domnuald was fair. "And who might you be?" called the Mide prince.

"I am Fland Dub maqq Ninnedo," growled the stranger, "king of the Tuath Ben Síde, who hold this land from of old. And you would be the upstart from Temir, would you not?"

"I am son to the Mide King, your high lord," Domnuald answered as steadily as might be. "What do you want? The rites are not till day after tomorrow."

"Hear me," Fland said. "You would take over our sacrifices, ours by right since the Children of Danu reigned here. You would glut yourselves on offerings we should have made—"

"The holy meat we will share with all who come!" Domnuald cried indignantly. "Do you think the sons of Niall are niggards?"

"Do you seek to buy the favor of our tenants away from us?" Fland retorted. "It shall not be. We, the landholders of three tuaths, say that." He tried to fight down his fury. The breath grated in his throat. "See here, boy. Let us be reasonable. We, my friends and I, we came early so we could catch you, talk with you, beforehand. Surely you and we between us can make a fair division of honor."

Domnuald reddened. "How can I parcel away my father's honor? If you bring livestock of your own to offer, I'll not be standing in your way."

"You have taken as much as the land can spare."

Youth and summer heat broke free like a lightning flash. "And so shall it always be, Fer Bolg!"

As if of itself, Fland's spear stabbed upward. Domnuald's escort, arriving just then, saw their leader topple off his horse, to thresh about with blood spouting and flowing.

Fland stared. "I did not mean—" he mumbled. Wit came back. As soon as the Mide men knew, they would attack. And they outnumbered his. Did he surrender, Niall would not likely take éricc payment for this young life, not though the honor price that a man of Fland's standing must add was high. Best flee north. The King at Emain Macha would have need of warriors before long.

Fland waved and whistled. His companions loped after him into the woods that they knew and the Mide men did not. Behind them, Domnuald maqq Néill's blood ebbed out, slower and slower, like the blood of an animal slain before Cromb Cróche.

2

Landing at Clón Tarui, Conual Corcc left a guard with his ships, his wife, and certain others. The rest of his followers, a large and well-armed band, hurried through Mide to Tallten. They had hoped to attend the fair, but a storm held them past Lúgnassat. Thus they arrived only on its last day, as it was breaking up.

Even so, what they saw was a mighty thing. Here Lúg of the Long Arm had buried His fostermother Talltiu and founded sacred games in Her honor, ages past. Here the Kings at Temir were buried, their grave mounds surrounding Hers like warriors asleep outside the house of a queen. Here the contests still took place, races of every kind, wrestling, hurling, games of skill. Here were music, poetry, dance, both solemn and light-hearted. Here was a market to which traders came from all over Ériu and no few countries overseas. Here too was another kind of dickering, for the fair was reckoned a lucky place to make marriages, so that families sought it to discuss arrangements and couples were united in the Glen of the Weddings. Laughter and song resounded through the river valley. Its grass disappeared under tents and booths, and must afterward grow back out of trampled mud. As they arrived and as they left, the lines of chariots and horsemen stretched for miles, not to speak of people afoot.

Above all, the fair was holy. The King himself conducted the great sacrifices; many lesser ones occurred as well. The laws were spoken aloud before the assembled chieftains and ollams. Serious matters were dealt with; an oath sworn or an agreement made here was doubly binding. For a crime committed at the fair, there could be no compounding by payment. Earth-walled fortresses frowned around Tallten, for it was among the royal seats of the realm, but at Lúgnassat season they stood empty; none dared break the peace, enmities were set aside, anyone could come from anywhere and his person be inviolate.

Conual Corcc made his way among the crowds, toward the hall of the King. It loomed on a rise of ground amidst its outbuildings, long and high, peeled studpoles gleaming from whitewashed cob walls, thatch woven in cunning patterns. Life brawled around it, warriors, attendants, artisans, visitors, men, women, children, horses, hounds, fowl—no swine, which it was gess for a King to possess though he could eat them; but prize cattle were there, sleek of red-white-black-brown coats, prideful of horns. Bright was the garb that swirled from shoulders and waists. Steel shone on weapons, bronze over shields, silver off brooches, gold about necks and arms. Talk surged like surf, along with clamor of children, beasts, smithwork, carting, footfalls, hoofbeats. Smoke from the cookhouse told noses that an ox was roasting.

This morning was brilliant. Conual stood taller than most. His hair burned above the hubbub. Folk stared, made way for him and his troop, but did not venture to address a lord unknown to them—until abruptly a voice cried his name. He stopped, looked, and knew Nemain maqq Aedo.

The druid had aged in the years since Conual went abroad. Stooped and skeletal, he leaned heavily on his staff and walked with the care of those who do not see well. Yet he made haste—a path opened immediately in the throng, and a hush fell—until he and Conual embraced.

"Welcome, welcome, a thousand welcomes, dear heart!" he cried. "How I have waited for this glad day!"

Conual stepped back. An eeriness cooled his spirit. "Did you, then, foreknow my coming?" he asked.

"Ah, there have been signs, not all of them good, but you strode into my dreams and . . . waking, I looked into the Well of the Dagdae." Nemain plucked at Conual's sleeve. "Come, let us go aside where we can talk."

"Forgive me, but I should not hang back from greeting the King. That would be an insult."

"It will not, if I enter with you, for I whispered in his ear that I must be off on mystic business. Himself is bidding farewell to his high-born guests who stayed here during the fair. It will take a while."

The sense of trouble grew colder within Conual Corcc. He gave the druid his arm and beckoned his men to keep their distance. A way downslope was a grove of rowan, with a bench for those who might wish to linger among the sacred trees and breathe of their magic. Overlooking the turmoil of leavetaking along the river, it was a haven of peace.

The two sat down. "Know that you have come at a time when grief is upon Niall maqq Echach," Nemain began. "The news has reached him that a son of his was slain at Mag Slecht by tuaths restive after he wrung their allegiance from them. Niall could barely keep showing the world a good face and carry on his duties. Now that the fair is ending, he is free to kill. Already he has sent for his hostages from those three tuaths. Tomorrow he will hang them. His vengeance will not stop at that."

"It's sorry I am to hear this," Conual said. "Who is he that fell?"

"Domnuald—Domnuald the Fair, we called him, child of Queen Aethbe."

Conual sighed. "Domnuald, indeed? Ochón! I remember him well. He was only a little lad then, but always bright and merry. May he reach Mag Mell and abide in joy."

"That is too strong a wish to utter at once," Nemain cautioned. "Well, Niall mourns the sorer because Domnuald, of all his sons, reminded him most of Breccan, his first-born, who died at Ys. You have heard about that?"

"Somewhat. I have been busy, you know, faring, warring, and . . . dealing . . . in Britannia."

"You return to claim a dream you have cherished, do you not?"

"I do. It is nothing that threatens Niall. Else why would I seek him first? Rather, he should help me, speed me on my way, for the sake of our common fosterage and the shield I can raise at his back." Conual frowned. "This redoubles the misfortune that has befallen him. As for myself—" He drew breath. "Nemain, dear, could I meet with those hostages?"

"I knew you would ask that," said the druid. "Come."

The prisoners were confined in a shed, tightly bound. Their guards durst not refuse admittance to Nemain, who led Conual in. The three men met his gaze proudly and spoke curtly. "You are ready to die, then?" Conual inquired.

"We are that," replied one, "thinking on what our deaths must cost Niall later."

"Hm, now," said Conual, "your three tuaths can scarcely stand against his might, nor can they look for much aid out of Ulati country. Would it not be better that he seek revenge on the killers instead of laying waste your homeland?"

He spoke with them a bit more. Thereupon he and Nemain went back out and talked at length.

The sun stood past noon when Niall's last guest had left. He slumped on his high seat, drinking horn after horn of ale. Uneasy stillness filled the hall. The rustle of movement and low voices seemed only to deepen it. Abruptly a shout broke through. The chief of the guard announced Conual maqq Lugthaci, who came in, resplendently clad, at the head of his warriors, at his right hand the druid Nemain maqq Aedo.

Niall roared. He bounded from his seat and plunged down the length of the hall to seize his fosterbrother to him. His folk howled, stamped the floor, beat fists against benches and shields, in their joy at seeing darkness lifted off the King.

Conual's followers carried gifts worthy of him, weapons, fine garments, Roman glassware of lovely shape and swirled colors, Roman silver which included a tray whereon were reliefs of heroes, maidens, and curious creatures. Niall made lavish return. Chief among the treasures he ordered fetched from his hoard and gave to Conual were a golden torc and a bronze trumpet whose workmanship drew cries of admiration from everybody who beheld.

Though the feast that day was hastily prepared, it was grand. After Laidchenn had hailed the newcomer in a poem and received a fibula in the form of a charging boar, he said, "Fine this is, but before I know what the deeds of our guest have been, I cannot properly praise them."

The building became still as heed turned toward Conual. He smiled.

"That story will take long," he answered. Scowling: "Much of it is sorrowful." Loftily: "But I shall go to wrest out a new fate for myself."

As he related or stopped to answer questions, he never conceded defeat. Yet clear it was that woe had betided the Scoti in Britannia. Under Stilicho's leadership, Romans and Cunedag's Britons had pressed in ever harder. This year, the last Scotic settlers in Ordovician and Silurian lands had perforce abandoned their homes and gone back across the water.

"But mine was not a sad leavetaking," Conual avowed. "I had gathered picked fighting men from among them. Others have I brought with me too. They wait in my ships, for they would be strangers and awkward in this company; but they shall soon be working wonders."

"What is your intent?" Niall demanded bluntly.

Conual laughed. "Why, what else but to claim my heritage in Mumu? I am of the Eóganachta; I will be as great a King as any of them, and afterward greater!"

Niall stroked his beard. "That would please me well, darling," he said. "I fear I cannot offer you help. There is too much on my hands. However, abide here until Nath Í returns from the fair he was attending. Do you remember him? He is my nephew, and now my tanist. He has traveled widely in those parts and should be able to give you sage counsel."

"You are very kind, darling," Conual replied. "So sweet are you that I make bold to ask a further boon."

"You need but ask."

Conual sat straight, looked the King in the eyes, and spoke weightily: "You will recall the command laid upon me, that I am to redeem any captives I meet whenever I can. This day I have met with those hostages whom you have condemned to die tomorrow. What I ask is that you let me ransom them."

A gasp went around the hall. Fists clenched, glances flickered between the two men and the hanging shields and the doorway.

Niall stiffened. The blood came and went in his face. At last he said, word by slow word: "Do I hear aright? My guest and fosterbrother would not mock me, I am sure. Perhaps you have misunderstood. Know, the tuaths for which they stand surety have murdered my son Domnuald. Shall his blood cry in vain for revenge?"

Nemain lifted a thin hand. "Not so," he agreed. "But they who slew Domnuald, Fland Dub and his fellows, have fled beyond the Walls of the Ulati. What honor lies in burning poor little shielings, driving off poor little herds, butchering innocent tenants? The Gods will raise the just man up, and They will cast the unjust down."

"I will pay, in gold, the éricc, and add thereto my own honor price,"

Conual declared. "Deny me not, if you love me. I may no more refuse to seek the freedom of men in bonds than you may traverse Mag Callani after sunset or let sunrise find you abed at Temir."

Niall hunched his shoulders. "Shall those men go home free, to boast that I dared not avenge my son?" he growled like a wolf at bay.

"They shall not," Conual answered quickly. "I will take them south to Mumu. I think they will serve me well. And we are allies, you and I."

"As for vengeance," Laidchenn reminded, "it awaits you at Emain Macha."

Said the druid: "The ransom that Conual pays will provide Domnuald a burial such as few kings have gotten, and endow honors for him for as long as Temir abides."

Niall gusted a sigh. "I yield you this, Conual. But it was not well done of you to trick me into making the promise."

With his pride thus bulwarked, he was presently at his ease, still somber but readier to talk than he had been of late. In the course of the time that followed, Conual remarked, "I was surprised to hear your nephew Nath Í is your tanist. Would you not liefer have a son of yours succeed you?"

"Nath Í is worthy of his father, my brother Féchra, whose ghost ought to be pleased," Niall explained. "Of course, I would have preferred a son of mine. But they all hope to win sword-land, kingdoms of their own." His gaze pierced the darkness gathering around firelight as the sun went down outside. It came to rest on one of the skulls fastened to the wall, a head he had taken in war upon the Ulati. "They shall have that," he said low.

3

Again the year swung toward equinox. Summer died in a last passionate outpouring of warmth, light, green, quick thunderstorms, high stars at night. Life pulsed strong in Ys, trade, shipping, foreigners from inland and overseas, readymaking for festival.

On such a day Dahut went from temple school to the home of Bodilis, whose turn it was to care for her. The time had been long, because first the Queen had had an illness that did not readily yield to medicine or even the Touch, then the princess had been a while at the Nymphaeum. That was customary with royal children, to get them used to the sacred site and its environs before they reached the age of full vestalhood. None had started these visits as young as Dahut, but the Nine had their reasons. Today the King had come back from business in Darioritum. He would not spend the night with Bodilis, he never did anymore, but he would call on her.

Thus Dahut burst into the atrium crying jubilantly, "Mother Bodilis, Mother Bodilis, is father here yet? He is coming, isn't he? He always wants to see me very soon."

She stopped, looked, and breathed, "Why are you sad?"

The woman smiled. It made crinkles around her lips and eyes, radiating into the cheeks as they had never done in Dahut's first memories of her. "Oh, I am not, dear," she answered softly. "I am happy, in a solemn way. Something wonderful is to bless us."

Dahut's eyes, the same blue as hers, widened. "What? I know father will bring me a present. What is it going to be?"

"I fear you must wait. You should have been told erenow, but—"

Footfalls sounded at Dahut's back. Turning, she saw Tambilis enter from the street. The daughter of Bodilis was finely dressed in a gown of white silk embroidered with doves, on her feet gold-inlaid shoes, on her head a garland of roses from which her light-brown hair flowed free past the delicate features. She looked quite different all at once. It was as if overnight she had grown taller, her body had filled out and her bosom swelled. Another strangeness was in her as well: she seemed frightened and resolute and lost in a dream.

Bodilis hastened to her. They embraced. "Darling, darling," the mother said. "Are you truly ready and willing?"

Tambilis nodded. "Aye."

"Be not afraid. You are now big enough, and this is Belisama's will, and, and be sure he will deal kindly with you. Be sure of that."

"I know."

Bodilis sobbed forth a laugh. "Come, then. Let me show you what I've had prepared, and tell you what I think will be best, and—" Hand in hand, they left the room and Dahut.

The girl stood where she was. Her face clouded, less with hurt than anger. A servant woman appeared from the inner part of the house. Bodilis must have told her to absent herself. She was an Osismian, blond, plump, one of many who sought to Ys and worked a few years to earn a dowry, unless they could catch a husband here. "Breifa," Dahut snapped, "what is happening?"

The maid was taken aback. "You know not, Princess? Why, tonight the King makes Tambilis really his Queen." She blushed, giggled, squirmed.

"Well, he knows not either, I hear. 'Tis to be an unawaited welcome-home gift for him. She is beautiful, the lady Tambilis, nay?"

"Oh," said Dahut tonelessly.

"I could not but overhear," chattered Breifa. " 'Twas Queen Bodilis who thought it should be done thus. Messages and such, arrangements, those would be too slow and stiff, they'd take the joy out of this. And Tambilis would be—passive, only a thing, is that what Queen Bodilis said? I remember not. Anyway, better Tambilis sweep him off his feet when he arrives, thinking he has just been invited for a cup of wine and a chat. Then he'll sweep her off hers soon enough, ha, ha!"

Dahut said nothing.

Breifa covered her mouth. "I talk too much, I do. What a bustle 'tis been, making everything right. Rejoice, lady Dahut. Someday you may be a Queen too."

"The Queen . . . of the man . . . who kills my father?"

"Oh, dear, I'm sorry. Well, such is the law of the Gods."

Dahut stalked off. She went into the street and stood arms folded, staring from this height out across the city to the sea.

Bodilis emerged, leading Una, her child by Gratillonius, a few months younger than Dahut but smaller and much more quiet. "There you are," the woman said. "I looked and looked for you." She paused. "What is wrong?"

"Naught," said Dahut, gaze held afar.

Bodilis laid a hand on her shoulder. " 'Tis disappointment for you, I know, not to see your father this eventide. Be brave. You will soon meet him, I pledge to you. You and Una and I shall stay in Tambilis's house tonight. Won't you like that? And I will tell you why, and you will be happy for him and your friend, I'm sure."

Dahut shrugged and trudged along.

4

At sixteen years of age, Tambilis had completed the education required of her. Each Queen served the Gods and Ys not only in set duties, but according to whatever special abilities she possessed. Tambilis had begun teaching elementary Latin in the temple school of Belisama, where Bodilis instructed advanced students of that language.

The young Queen was strolling about the flowerful intricacy of Elven Gardens during the noontide rest period. She smiled drowsily and crooned to herself. Rounding a hedge, she came upon Dahut. The child sat tracing pictures in the graveled path. What they were was hard to guess, because the stones rattled back together behind her finger.

"Why, why, good day," Tambilis said, astonished.

Dahut looked up like a blind person.

"But you're miserable!" Tambilis exclaimed. She hunkered down to hug her playmate. "What's wrong?"

"Naught," said the dry little voice.

"That's untrue," Tambilis chided. "Hark, you can tell me."

Dahut shook her head.

Tambilis considered. " 'Tis the King, nay?" she asked after a moment. "You feel your father slighted you. Well, he did not. 'Twas but that he—he and I—well, the will of the Goddess was upon us. Is. Have no fear. Soon he'll greet you, and he does have the prettiest cloak for you, that he found among the Veneti, and, oh, all sorts of adventures to tell about."

Still there was no response. "Indeed," Tambilis persisted, "you must visit us. We're staying at the palace now while we . . . get to know each other better. We shall for several days yet." Resignation laid a sudden burden on her voice. "After that, all will be much as it was before."

"I will see him somewhere else," Dahut said.

"But why? My dear, I've not turned my back on you. I love you always." Tambilis searched for words. " 'Tis only that times goes, things change. Later you'll understand." Impulsively: "This was not my wish at first. 'Twas Guilvilis who caused it, stupid, clumsy, loving Guilvilis. She mustered courage at last to tell me I did wrong, withholding myself when I could gladden him, lighten his cares, and—And, Dahut," glowed from her, "the Goddess gives me joy too, as She will you someday."

Dahut screamed. She scrambled to her feet and fled.

When she was not at her next class, the teacher sent an acolyte to inquire at the dwellings of the Gallicenae. Had she perchance been taken sick? It took hours to establish that she had disappeared, and then to organize search parties. They did not find her until sundown, after she had re-entered the city at Aurochs Gate and was stubbornly walking up Amber Street toward the home of Fennalis. Her clothes were wet, with smells of kelp and fish.

XIV

1

As autumn yellowed leaves, Conual Corcc bade Niall maqq Echach farewell. Since this must at first be a reconnoitering expedition, he left behind most of his men. Just thirty followed him south, among them the three hostages he had saved. His Cruthinach wife came too, for there is magic as well as comfort in women.

Shut off as Mumu was from the rest of Ériu, Niall heard nothing more until spring. When finally a messenger arrived to bid the remaining warriors now seek their lord, it was a strange story that he brought.

A day's travel northwest from the Mountain of Fair Women was the Plain of Femen, where Fedelmm the witch had troubled King Lugthach. It was fertile and well settled, save at one place where forest stood ancient. Few ventured in, for at the middle of the woods reared the Síd Drommen. This limestone outcrop, whose three hundred feet overtopped the trees around, was believed to be the haunt of elves, ghosts, every creature of the Other World. However, swineherds took their animals there in season for the rich mast. Though their trade be humble, it gave them ties to Those Beyond.

Once two of them were in that wood together. Each kept pigs for the king of a neighboring tuath: Dardriu for the king of Éle, Coriran for the king of Múscraige. To his master King Aed came Coriran and said: "We fell into a deep sleep, Dardriu and I. Adream, we beheld the Ridge of the Beings. Before it were a yew tree and a flagstone. Somehow we knew that that was the tree of the Eóganachta, and that he who stands upon the stone shall wax great."

The druid of Aed thought deeply, sought visions, and declared: "The Síd Drommen shall become the seat of the kings over all Mumu. From him who first lights a fire under that yew shall they descend."

"Let us go to light it!" cried Aed.

"Let us await the morning," counselled the druid: for it was late, and the sun hidden behind lowering clouds. Soon a snowstorm began, this early in the year.

It caused Conual, his wife, and their men to lose their way as they fared down from the north. They blundered into the wood and took shelter below the rock. A yew tree growing there, its leaves withered but as yet unfallen, gave a roof of sorts, letting them kindle a fire. A flat stone at its foot made a place to stand while shoes dried out.

So did Aed find them. Although downcast, the king did not venture to quarrel with the Gods. Conual had, indeed, a birthright claim. Moreover, he was a friend of the mighty Niall, of whom they had report. The upshot was that Aed acknowledged Conual king of the surrounding territory and gave him his own son as hostage.

Thus the story that Niall heard in spring. He smiled and let the men go whom Conual had brought from Britannia. Among them were several ollam craftsmen—engineers, stonemasons—who understood the Roman arts of fortification. With them Niall sent rich gifts.

A year passed.

For Niall it, like the twelvemonth before, was less warlike than many had been. Both years were nonetheless busy. His sons champed to be off conquering, but their father held them back. "Lay the keel, fasten the ribs, bind the strakes," he said. "When the ship is ready, we will sail." They did not fully understand, not being seamen like him.

Niall did complete the taking over of those nine tuaths which had been tributary to the Ulati. He raised new kings among them to replace those he had felled in battle, and a high King above these: all obedient to him. They were well content, because he returned to them that governance over the sacrifices at Mag Slecht which had been theirs from of old. Despite yielding this, which cost him little and won him much in the way of goodwill, he never let wane his resolve to have vengeance for Domnuald—and someday, somehow, for Breccan.

The hostages that the tuaths gave him he treated so generously that they vowed to fight at his side when he became ready for his onslaught against the Ulati. Likewise would their kinfolk. The kingdom he had founded for these became known as the Aregésla, They Who Give Hostages, a name borne proudly. People began calling him Niall of the Nine Hostages.

—King Fergus Fogae in Emain Macha was fully aware of the storm that brewed in the south. He thought of launching an attack himself, decided that that would be ruinous, and set about strengthening defenses throughout his realm. His poets reminded him of how Cú Culanni had brought Medb and her Condachtae low. Those songs echoed spookily in the hall.

—Next Imbolc came messengers from Conual to Temir. They bore gifts no less than those Niall had sent south, and fateful tidings.

Conual's power had grown like the antlers on a stag. While small, his force of exiles was schooled in ways of war unknown to Mumu. Each battle they won brought new allegiances, thus a larger host to call upon. Without fighting, even more chieftains swore faith to this newcomer whom the Gods had clearly blessed. Lately he had gotten for a second wife Ámend, daughter of Oengus Bolg, king of the powerful Corco Loígde. They holding land on the south coast, Conual thereby gained an opening to the outer world.

The magic that flamed around his name came not least from the seat he had chosen. It was the very Síd Drommen: an audacity that brought not disaster on him, but victory after victory. There he was building a stone stronghold of the Roman kind, impregnable to anything that Gaelic men could bring against it: Liss inna Lochraide, the Fort of the Heroes. Already, in the mouths of the folk, the name of the rock itself was changing to Latin Castellum, which soon got softened to Cassel.

The poet who related these things to Niall knew better than to say so, but unmistakably underlying his staves was glee, that his lord's rise was so swift that the deeds of the Temir King could not compare.

Niall sat silent a long time, staring into firelight darkness. Finally those who sat close saw his lips move. "The Síd Drommen," whispered forth. "He dared. He *dared.*"

2

Forty days after solstice, the diminishing gloom of winter was made bright in Ys. Queen Tambilis bore her first child. Mother and daughter were in the best of health. As he was wont on such occasions, the King decreed festival immediately after the hallowing of the new little Semuramat. Legionaries formed an honor guard when he led Tambilis from the Temple of Belisama to the palace. With them came the rest of the Nine— on as high a holiday as this, the Gods required none to stay alone on Sena —and the magnates of the city with their wives. Wine, mead, and rich food from the royal stores were distributed among the poor, that they too might celebrate. Entertainers of every kind, having anticipated the event, swarmed merrily about. After dark the Fire Fountain blossomed, though weather kept the Forum almost deserted.

In a house near Menhir Place there was no mirth. It was a small but decent house, such as a married soldier could afford to rent. The matron was having her own first childbirth. Her labor started about when the Queen's did. Still it went on. She was Keban, wedded to Budic.

Adminius had excused him from duty, never expecting he would be gone this long. He sat on a bench in the main room, elbows on knees, head bowed between shoulders. A lamp picked furnishings out of the shadows that filled every corner. His breath smoked in the chill. Outside, the night wind hooted, shook the door, flung handfuls of hail against shutters.

The midwife came in from the bedroom holding a candle. She shambled in her exhaustion. Budic raised his face. The youthfulness it had kept through the years was hollowed out. He had not shaved all this while; the whisker made a thin fuzz over jaws and cheeks. "How goes it?" he croaked.

"Best you look in," the woman said, flat-voiced. "You might not see her alive again. I'll keep doing what I can, sir, but my arts are spent."

Budic rose and stumbled into the other chamber. A brazier gave warmth that sharpened the reek of sweat, urine, vomit, burnt tallow. Enough light seeped through the doorway to show him the swollen form and sunken wet countenance. Her eyes were shut, except for a glimmer of white. Her mouth was half open, her breath shallow. Now and then a feeble convulsion shook her. Helplessly, he laid his palm on her forehead. "Can you hear me, beloved?" he asked. He got no answer.

A sound drew his attention—crash of wood against wall, suddenly loudened storm noises, the midwife's cry of amazement. He went back into the main room. A tall, grizzle-bearded man in a coarse robe and paenula had entered. One knotty hand gripped a staff. Beneath a half-shaven scalp his features jutted like the headlands.

"Corentinus!" Budic exclaimed in Latin. "What brings you, Father?"

"A sense within me that you have need, my son," replied the chorepiscopus.

The midwife traced a warding crescent. Tales had long gone about that this man of Christ sometimes had foreknowledge.

"Need of your prayers," Budic said. "Oh, Father, she's dying."

"I feared that. Let me see." Corentinus brushed past him. Budic sank down on the bench and wept.

Corentinus returned. "She is far gone, poor soul," he said. "This was just a little late in life, maybe, for her to start bearing. I thought she was barren, and beseeched God to gladden the two of you with a child, but—"

Budic lifted his gaze. "Can you pray her back to me?"

"I can only ask God's mercy. His will be done." Corentinus pondered. "Although—" Decision: "He helps us mortals, even unto an angelic summons, but we must do our share. My rough medical skills are of no use here. The Gallicenae command healing powers beyond any I've ever heard of elsewhere. I'll go fetch one."

Budic gaped. "What? But they're feasting at the palace. I know because Cynan looked in on us on his way to parade."

Corentinus rapped out a laugh. "The more merit in the charity, then. Who can tell but what this may start the pagan on a path to salvation? Hold fast, son. I'll be back as soon as may be." He went out into the night.

The midwife shuddered. "What did he want, sir?" she asked. Her Latin was rudimentary.

Budic shook his head, numbed beyond his numbness at the thought of such a raven breaking into the King's banquet and demanding the aid of the Nine.

Whoo-oo called the wind, and more hail rattled over the cobbles.

Budic returned to the bedside. Time crept.

The door thumped open. Corentinus loomed above a slight form in a cowled cloak hastily thrown over splendor. Emerging, Budic recognized Innilis. He pulled himself erect and saluted. Behind the two came a servant woman with a box in her arms, and then Adminius in armor that sheened wet.

"Stand aside," ordered the Queen. Budic had never before heard her anything but soft-spoken. She stepped into the bedroom. "Light." The midwife got the candle. "We'll want more than this. I've brought tapers." The servant, who had followed, began unpacking physician's things from the box. Innilis closed the door.

Adminius looked around. "Filthy weather," he said. "You got something ter warm a fellow's belly? The centurion 'ad us inside, of course. We'd get our share when the fancy part of the evening was done and 'e relieved us guards."

Mechanically, Budic set out wine and water jugs, cups, a loaf of bread and sections of sausage. "He let you go just like that?" he asked.

" 'E's our centurion, ain't 'e? Told me ter convey 'is sympathy and best wishes. 'E can't leave the feast, that'd insult some of their 'igh and mightinesses there, but 'e'll stop by in the morning. I came along on be'alf of the boys."

"The priestess Innilis—"

"She honors her calling," said Corentinus.

Toward dawn she trod forth. Her face was pallid, eyes dark-rimmed, hands atremble. "Keban should live," she told the men. "The child—it was a boy—I had to sacrifice the child for the mother, but I think he was doomed in any case. Nay, do not go in yet, not ere Mella has . . . wrapped him. Besides, Keban has swooned. But I think, by Belisama's grace, she will live. She may be in frail health hereafter, and I doubt she will conceive again. But your wife should live, Budic."

He went to his knees. "Christ b-b-be thanked," he stammered in Latin. And in Ysan, lifting eyes burnt-out but adoring: "How can I thank *you*, my lady? How can I repay you?"

Innilis smiled the least bit, laid a hand on his blond head, and murmured, "The Nine take no pay, unless it be in the coin of love."

"Ever shall I love the Gallicenae and, and stand ready to serve them, whatever their wish may be. By the body of Christ I swear it."

She declined his offer of refreshment and departed with her attendant, promising to visit later in the day. Adminius escorted them. Corentinus stayed behind. "Let us thank the Lord, my son," he said. His tone was harsh.

3

At Imbolc Niall Náegéslach gave out that after Beltene he would fare overseas. Unspoken was: "Let Conual Corcc down in Mumu have his fortress. The Romans threw him out of Britannia. I will carry my sword there."

Remembering what had happened under the wall of Ys, some men were daunted. Most, though, felt no forebodings. In the ten years since, the King at Temir had won back everything he lost, and far more. This foray could well begin laying the groundwork of his vengeance on the city of the hundred towers. Well-informed chieftains knew that the terrible Stilicho had not only himself quitted Britannia, he had taken with him many troops to use against the Germani who threatened Gallia. Complacent and thinly defended, the island east of Ériu offered wealth for the taking.

So it proved. Those who met with the King and followed him in galleys and currachs found easy pickings. From Alba to Dumnonia they ravaged. Men they killed, women they raped, slaves and booty they took. What legionaries there remained never got to a place the raiders struck before they were gone, leaving smoldering ruins, beheaded corpses, weeping survivors who had fled and then crept back home. The Britons themselves were ill prepared and fought poorly—save for Cunedag's tough hillmen, whose territories Niall steered clear of. Elsewhere he opened a way for Scoti to return, resettling along the western shores.

In blood he washed away his bitterness. As hay harvest and Lúgnassat neared he went home full of hope, he went home in glory.

He came back to wrath. In his absence, the Lagini had entered Mide and made havoc.

Eochaid, son of King Éndae Qennsalach, led that great inroad: Eochaid, whose first taste of battle seven years ago had become rank with defeat at the hands of Niall; Eochaid, whose handsomeness was forever marred by the scars of the blistering satire which Tigernach, son of Laidchenn, laid on him that same day. Since then he had known victory. He joined the Loígis clans when trouble broke loose with men of Condacht or Mumu, to repel the invaders and harry them past their own borders. He helped bring the allied kingdom of Ossraige to obedience, and collected tribute that subordinate tuaths in the mountains would have denied. Yet always the memory of the humbling festered.

They were, after all, as honor-proud in Qóiqet Lagini as men were anywhere. In Gallia their distant ancestors had been the Gáileóin, the Men of the Spears, which the Lagini claimed was also the meaning of their present name. Having entered Ériu, they formed their own confederation at the same time as the Goddess Macha of the Red Locks built Emain Macha to the north. Their seat of high Kings, Dún Alinni, was the work of Mess Delmon, who cast out the dark Fomóri, and pursued them into the very realms of the dead. The Lagini held Temir itself until the Condachtae who founded Mide drove them from it.

Long had Eochaid brooded upon this. When the news came that Niall was bound abroad with as large a following as could put to sea, he shouted that this was a chance given by the Gods Themselves. Éndae, his father, urged caution; but Éndae was weakened by age, while the country throbbed with fierce young men eager to hear the son.

Thus Eochaid gathered a host on the west bank of the Ruirthech, which near Dún Alinni flowed north before bending eastward to the sea. His charioteers led the warriors on into Mide, straight toward Temir.

They failed to take it. Those sons of Niall who had stayed behind held it too strongly. Yet bloody was the fighting ere the Lagini recoiled. Thereupon they went widely about, killing, plundering, burning. Countless were the treasures, cattle, slaves, and heads they took home.

Niall came back. When he saw the ruin that been wrought, he did not rage aloud as once he would have done. Men shivered to behold an anger as bleak as the winter during which he made his preparations.

It may be that at first King Fergus of the Ulati breathed easier, knowing that for another year he need not await attack out of Mide. If so, his happiness soon blew away, on the wind that bore the smoke out of Qóiqet Lagini. From end to end of that Fifth Niall and his sons went. They pierced and scattered the levies that sought to stay them, as a prow cleaves waves, flinging foam to starboard and larboard. His ship, though, plowed red waters, and the spray was flames and the whine in the rigging was from women who keened over their dead.

Éndae yielded before his land should be utterly waste. Now Niall exacted the Bóruma; and when he brought it back, chief among the hostages who stumbled bound at his chariot wheels was Eochaid.

Never did Niall show honor to this prince, as he did to those he had from the Aregésla and elesewhere. The Laginach hostages lived crowded into a wretched hut, miserably fed and clad. They were only allowed out once a day to exercise, and that only because otherwise they would have taken sick and died—which some did anyhow. When Niall fared in procession, most of the hostages in his train wore golden chains, the merest token of a captivity which was actually a life full and free in the royal household. The Lagini went in shackles of iron.

On his deathbed a few months later, the druid Nemain reproached the King for this. "You are ungenerous, darling, the which is not like you. Was it not enough to reclaim, in the Bóruma, threefold what that young man reaved us of?"

"I have my revenge to finish," Niall answered. "Let Eochaid meanwhile be my sign to the Gods that I do not forget wrongs done my kindred."

The old man struggled for breath. "What . . . do you mean . . . by that—you whom I love?"

"Eochaid shall go free," Niall promised, "when the head of Fland Dub is in my hand, and Emain Macha mine, and Ys under the sea."

XV

1

It had become clear to the Nine and many others that Dahut would embark upon womanhood in her twelfth year. Suddenly she was gaining height and shapeliness. There was never any misproportion, outbreak in the clear skin, or loss of self-possession. While always slender, she would be more tall and robust than her mother, though equally graceful and lightfooted. The buds of her breasts were swelling toward ripeness, the curves beneath becoming rich. Golden down appeared below her arms, and under her belly formed a triangle, the figure sacred to the Goddess as the wheel was to Taranis and the spiral to Lir. She strode more than she skipped. Her voice took on a huskiness.

Above, she eerily resembled Dahilis. Great lapis lazuli eyes looked from tawny arches of brow, out of a face where the high Suffete cheekbones joined a chin small but firm. Her nose was short, a little flared at the nostrils, her mouth full and a little wide. Her hair billowed halfway down her back when she loosened it, thick, amber-hued with a tinge of copper therein.

What she lacked was the sunny temper that had been Dahilis's. Despite her beauty and quick-wittedness, Dahut was a solitary child. The Gallicenae and their maidservants had tried to find her companions of her own age, but those grew inclined to avoid her. At home the boys complained that she was too imperious, the girls shivered and called her "odd." Dahut did not seem to care. She preferred adult company when she was not off by herself, which came to be more and more in her free time.

She learned fast, read widely, was earnest in her devotions. Athletic, she walked or ran across long stretches, ranged the woods when at the Nymphaeum, rode the horses her father gave her or drove a chariot he had lately added, was a crack target splitter with bow or light javelin, spent as many hours as she could arrange on the sea, sometimes even demanded privacy to strip and swim in its chill turbulence. Female skills she acquired, but without much interest. Occasionally she made use of Gratillonius's workshop behind the palace, and he laughed that an excellent artisan was lost in her as well as in him. She appreciated good food, drink, garb, together with art, music, theater; but it was as if she found her real pleasure in board games and other mental contests, or simply in listening to the King's conversations with visitors from afar.

His Roman soldiers doted on her. They called her their Luck, and practiced special drills when she was there to see. Likewise, the fisher captain Maeloch was her slave.

The Queens held her precious too, though in various ways and for various reasons. They agreed she must not be spoiled—if anything, more was required of her than of the rest of the princesses—nor should weight be laid on the fact that they perceived a destiny in her, without being able to see what it was. Nevertheless, inevitably, Dahut got intimations of this.

And so in her twelfth springtime she embarked upon womanhood.

It happened when she was staying with Tambilis. Gratillonius did not these days, because Tambilis was near term with her second child, whom she meant to name Estar. Dahut came into her room by dawnlight, shook her awake, and said somberly, "I have bled."

"What?" Tambilis sat up, rubbed her eyes, looked around. "Oh, my dear!" She surged from her bed and hugged the girl close to her. "Welcome! Be not afraid. Rejoice. Come, let me see."

In the guest chamber she examined the cloth that had been for some time laid atop Dahut's nether sheet. A spot marked it, brilliantly red against white, however dim the chamber still was. "Aye, this is your first coursing ever," Tambilis said. "May they be many and all easy. How feel you?"

"I am well." Grudgingly, Dahut pulled off her nightgown at Tambilis's behest and let the woman show her how to wash herself and attach a pad.

"Now you remember what you must do," Tambilis chattered. "And me, oh, the glad load of duties on me! What do you wish for breakfast, darling?"

Dahut shrugged. Well, girls were often upset on this day of their lives. Yet Dahut was calm enough, withdrawn into herself.

"We shall have *such* a festival! We begin with our prayers, of course. I'll help you dress."

Tambilis kept her image of Belisama in a room at the rear of the house. It was a miniature of the Goddess as Maiden, carved out of narwhal ivory and set in a niche painted deep blue with stars. Little of Quinipilis remained in this house; Tambilis favored things bright and dainty. She held up the spotted cloth as she and Dahut gave thanks.

Now the girl did not change lodgings but stayed where she was, avoiding company, saying her orisons and meditating upon the mysteries. When the flow had stopped, she bathed in water not from a cistern-well but piped from the Tower, to which it had flowed down the canal from the Nymphaeum. Then it was time for celebration.

Sumptuously arrayed, Dahut went forth from the house into a glorious morning full of songbirds. Ocean sparkled beyond spires washed by last night's rain. Flowers and blossoms dappled the valley and its guardian hills. Airs blew gentle. King Gratillonius waited outside in full regalia, love and pride radiating from him, together with all the Gallicenae in their blue-and-white attire of priestesses. The magnates of the city were there too, surrounded by their families. Light blazed off metal as legionaries drew swords and shouted, *"Ave!"* while Ysan marines crashed pike butts down on paving stones.

Musicians played fore and aft of the procession that went to the Temple of Belisama. Ordinary folk flocked to join it and follow it into the halidom. In that twilit chamber they stood quiet. From the aisles, vestals sang praise.

The Nine stationed themselves behind the altar, before the tall images of Maiden, Mother, and Hag. Dahut knelt and asked their blessing. She received wine, a drop of ox blood, and salt. When she had laid her garland on the block, Fennalis, senior priestess, placed on her brows a coronet of silver studded with emeralds and rubies. In lieu of her mother, her father bowed to the Triune and put a toy into her hands. It was one among many he had made, chosen by her because she was particularly fond of it, a gaily painted wooden horse with jointed legs. This too she laid on the altar and dedicated to the Goddess. That took but a single word: "Farewell."

Again outside after the service, she received the embraces and congratulations of her kin, the cheers of the crowd. She responded sparingly, though she did dimple up repeated smiles. Thereafter Gratillonius brought the party to the palace for a feast. At this she had a final tradition to observe, albeit an event regarded as merry rather than solemn. She gave away the rest of her playthings to her younger half-sisters.

Who should receive what had taken forethought. Bodilis's Una, Guilvilis's Sasai, Lanarvilis's Julia, Maldunilis's Zisa, Forsquilis's Nemeta, Vindilis's Augustina were close to Dahut in years. Guilvilis's Antonia and Camilla were not far behind either; but her Valeria was only five, while Tambilis's Semuramat was two—and that last mother claimed a rattle also, because it was lucky for an unborn child to receive a gift.

Thus went the Welcoming of Dahut. Commoners did likewise for their girls, though usually the blessing was by a minor priestess at a small sanctuary and the meal afterward modest. It was all the same in the sight of the Goddess.

For royal children, though, unto the third generation, more waited.

It happened quietly. In the morning Dahut rode to the Nymphaeum with an escort and a Queen. This one's task would be to stay there for a few days, consecrate the maiden a full vestal, and teach her certain secrets. Dahut would remain longer and receive training in her new duties. Thenceforward she would be at the Nymphaeum a sennight each lunar month, otherwise at the Temple in Ys, as housekeeper, gardener, participant in rites, and student. She would have ample leisure and a stipend which would enable her to live where and how she chose in the city, provided she remain pure. Her service was to end on her eighteenth birthday. Then she would be at liberty to marry, enroll as a subordinate priestess, pursue an independent career, do whatever she wished. Any daughters she might bear, and any daughters of these, must in their turn become vestals like her, enjoying the same advantages—unless, before the term of the vow closed, the Sign should come.

Bodilis had volunteered to be her sponsor at the hallowing. She had been half-sister to Dahut's mother.

The day of arrival went to settling in. Each virgin had a tiny room to herself. A newcomer was subject to japery and giggles in dining commons, but not too many questions. After all, she had been here before, Dahut bore it—neither cheerily nor ungraciously; aloofly—and retired early.

Her religious induction came the next morning, a brief ceremony. Later various instructresses interviewed her. They had already met the new votary, but hoped for closer acquaintance and some idea as to what kinds of education promised most for her. In the afternoon was a dinner more elegant than usual here, where everyday fare was simple. Later, until dark, pipe, drum, sistrum, and voice gave melody for dances on the greensward.

The morning after that, Bodilis drew Dahut aside. "Before I go home, I am to explain to you the secrets," she said. "They're not really close-veiled. That would be impossible." She smiled. "But tradition insists that certain knowledge may pass only between Queen and vestal, and otherwise not be spoken aloud. Let's avail ourselves of this beautiful weather while it holds. Go dress yourself for a ramble and meet me."

Dahut obeyed happily. When she and Bodilis had left the building, she could not forbear to prance about and bay the Wolf Chant. "Ah, you are young still, sweetling," the woman murmured. "Come along."

They took a trail uphill into the woods. A rivulet gurgled beside it. Birds trilled. Squirrels raced ruddy. Sunlight filled leaves with green fire and spattered on the shade beneath. Warmth and savor steamed from the earth.

"There is naught arcane about most of what I shall tell you," Bodilis said. "Special prayers. Cantrips to ward off certain misfortunes and certain creatures. Minor medical skills; we *are* healers, we royal women, though lay physicians practice too. At the least, dignity requires we be able to treat our own lesser ailments. It begins with knowing how to brew a tisane of willow against cramps, albeit many a goodwife can do the same. But let us commence with the greatest and holiest of all, the gift that the Goddess bestowed upon Brennilis and those who should come after."

They emerged where the hillside shouldered out to form a hollow. The spring that fed the stream was not much farther up, and here the water spread some three feet wide, ankle-deep, glittery beneath the sun. That light laid gold over the crowns of the beeches, hazels, and thorns walling in the grassy space. Masses of convolvulus clung to their innermost boles. Within their circle, blue stars sprang from plants with hairy stems and leaves, a cubit tall.

Bodilis signed herself. She knelt before a patch of them. "Here," she said, her tone now grave. "Look closely."

Dahut did perfunctory reverence and hunkered impatient. "Why, that's just borage," she said. "They use it for flavor and color in food. It helps against fever. What else?"

"It is the Herb," Bodilis told her.

Dahut reared back. "What? This?"

Bodilis nodded. "Aye. Our name for it is 'ladygift.' If a Queen of Ys eats a spoonful of these flowers, fresh or dried, a small spoonful, she does not conceive that day. When she wishes a child, she need simply leave off the use—" a fleeting, wistful smile— "and open herself to the King, if she be not too old. It is the bestowal of Belisama, so that the Nine may have sovereignty over their wombs and thus freedom to uphold the law of Ys against any of our random Kings who proves to be bad."

Dahut's fingers stole forward to touch the plant. "But this," she said, "only this? I thought belike 'twas magical vervain."

Bodilis chuckled. "Not that, of all plants! It works to cure barrenness."

"But the Herb should grow in a sacred place—the Wood of the King?"

Both now kneeling, Bodilis took the hands of Dahut in hers, caught and held the maiden's gaze, said slowly: "All the world is sacred, and perhaps the commonplace most.

"The knowledge of what ladygift actually is has gone about underground—that could never be stopped—but 'tis a thing folk do not bespeak. For the Herb, not mere borage but the Herb, is for the Nine alone. To every woman else, this plant is what you said, a simple, a seasoning, a decoration, naught else.

"Remember, Dahut, you must remain chaste until the end of your service. Else the wrath of the Gods would be upon you, and as for the law of man, you could be thrown off the sea cliffs or whipped from Ys into the wilderness. It has happened in the past.

"The ladygift will cease to ward you if you pass your vestalhood unchosen. After that, you must care for yourself, or endure, as has ever been the lot of women.

"But if ere then the Sign appears between your breasts and you become a Queen: then before each time the King comes to you, or you think he may, until you desire to bear his child—take a few of these little flowers, and kiss them, and swallow them. For the kisses of the Gallicenae raise the Power."

2

Very early in the shipping season, a large and well-laden merchant vessel stood out from Ys for Hivernia. The crew did not expect to have need for their fighting skills. Strengthened and vigorously used by King Grallon, the navy had scoured these waters clean. Beyond the Dumnonian end of Britannia there was a chance of pirates. However, Tommaltach had assured the captain it was most unlikely that they could bring anything more to bear than a few currachs; and such would not attack a ship with high freeboard, war engines, armored men. The peace of King Conual was spreading fast across Mumu, where folk preferred trade to war anyway. Two years ago, Niall, the King in Mide, had wasted Roman territories. Since then, though, his attention was aimed north; the question was not whether he would fall on the Ulati, but when.

No prudent man would have fared just on the word of a young barbarian. It was borne out by other reports that had come to Ys as traffic between his people and the city grew in erratic fashion. Besides, Tommaltach maqq Donngalii was no ordinary adventurer. His father was king of a tuath and a friend of Conual Corcc. Tommaltach, age about sixteen, was a blooded warrior when he joined a venture to Ys, less in hopes of profiting from gold, sheepskins, and salt pork than to see the marvels. He had taken the trouble beforehand to acquire some of the language, as well as basic Latin. Meeting him, Rufinus readily persuaded him to stay through the winter. During those months, the Gael living in Rufinus's aerie, the two of them had grown close; and Rufinus had gotten a working knowledge of Scotic speech.

After the stark headlands at Armorica, his goal seemed gentle, lushly fruitful, incredibly green. The Ysans anchored in a small bay, made camp ashore, gave presents to natives who approached. Tommaltach dickered for horses. The crew loaded three of these and put Roman saddles on the rest. It took a little while to get the animals used to that. Leaving most of their shipmates on guard, Rufinus and Tommaltach rode off at the head of ten. The journey to Castellum took a pair of easy days, broken at one of the free hostels which kings here endowed.

Rufinus observed carefully as he fared, and beswarmed his guide with questions. This was pastureland where it was not forest, sheep and cattle at graze, only a few small and scattered fields sown in rye, barley, oats. Some wattle-and-daub dwellings stood isolated, but most seemed to cluster inside earthen ringwalls with palisades on top. Towns did not exist. Armies were wild rabble, virtually without body protection, led by noblemen in chariots such as were four hundred years obsolete in Britannia and Gallia.

Withal, throughout Hivernia—Ériu, its people called it—arts and crafts excelled, while respect for learning was so high that the person of a druid or poet was inviolate. Women were almost as free as in Ys, infinitely better off than anywhere in the Roman world. Aside from slaves, who were mainly captives taken in raids, the relationship between master and follower, landholder and tenant, was contractual, either party able to abrogate it at will. Folkmoot and *brithem*—judge—gave out a rough justice; wrongdoing was generally compounded by payment, and a rich man must give more in redress than a poor man. When this failed, frequently the aggrieved person sat down at the door of the other and fasted until the latter, who was supposed to starve himself also, yielded. "Unless, I imagine, he outlasts the plaintiff," Rufinus drawled. "Still, you Scoti are not quite the two-legged wolves the Romans think you."

"Ah, it's grand to be home, that it is," Tommaltach exulted. "Not but what I don't mean to be often again in Ys, for the exploring of its wonders and to carouse with you, darling."

Rufinus sighed to himself. This race habitually talked in extravagances.

The youth had no idea what they implied to his listener. Tommaltach was beautiful: medium tall, wide-shouldered but supple, the snubnosed, blue-eyed countenance as fair-skinned as a girl's except for a breath of beard, under a tumble of black hair.

No doubt it was just as well. Vindilis had counseled wisely. Less for hospitality than for appearances' sake, Rufinus had from time to time brought a pretty harlot to the tower. He performed competently, thinking it could not be denied that women were better constructed for the purpose, then let Tommaltach have the rest of the sport.

The Scotian left the road, which was dirt but not badly laid out, to swing wide of a dolmen. In Ériu as in Armorica, works of the Old Folk brooded. "Christians chiseled a cross on that," he explained. "Ever since, the dwellers inside have been angry and spiteful." The religion had made considerable headway in Mumu.

Stepping from the hostel at sunrise, Rufinus peered aloft and conferred with Tommaltach and the inkeeper. He did not want to reach Castellum drenched. Opinion was that rain would hold off long enough. Rufinus ordered his men into full battle gear: peaked helmets, cuirasses with flaring shoulderpieces and spiral-ornamented loricae, greaves above leather breeks, studded shoes, leaf-shaped swords, long oval shields. He himself donned a silken shirt with flowing sleeves, jerkin of chased leather, woad-dyed linen trousers, calf-length gilt boots, belt and baldric set with carne-lians, over his shoulder a red cloak trimmed in ermine and secured by a cameo brooch. A show counted for well-nigh everything when you dealt with Celts. Besides, Rufinus enjoyed it.

The troop rode briskly on, beneath mountainous clouds through which the sun cast lances. The air was cool and damp. Soon the countryside turned into stands of woodland, meadows between them. Stumps showed that not long ago this had all been forest. "The King is having it logged off," Tommaltach said. "Settlers come, making strength and wealth around his seat." He pointed. "Look, my heart. On the horizon, the Rock!"

Nearing, the travelers saw the limestone mass lift ruggedly, an island in a green sea, its clifftops three hundred feet above. Buildings clustered at its base and strewed themselves out across the plain. Many were larger and better made than Rufinus had seen until now on his expedition. On the heights frowned a fortress. It was the Roman kind, foursquare, tur-reted, built of mortared stone, a thing that had never before been in Ériu.

Therefore it was twice important to impress the King. "Hoy-ah!" Rufinus cried. "Smartly, on the double!" The horses trotted forward.

Warriors hastened from the dwellings and along the trail up the Rock.

They were outfitted like other Scoti. Tommaltach galloped ahead to meet them. They cheered and formed a primitive honor guard.

—Inside the castle, barbarian ways remained strong. The feasting hall was long and lofty. Smoke from a pair of firepits did not escape out the high-set small windows as readily as through thatch. Benches lined the walls. Above them hung painted shields, while skulls grinned from the many niches. Yet there were also finely woven hangings, intricately carved panels on the seats, imaginatively wrought tableware of wood, bronze, silver, gold, a general rude magnificence in which Rufinus found more subleties the more he looked.

Conual Corcc, a tall man with flame-red hair, was gracious rather than boisterous as he received the Ysans. They distributed gifts from off their pack beasts, things as good as Ys could offer, and got thanks from the King's poet in intricate stanzas. Eventually, at their departure, he made them presents of value exceeding theirs. First they were his guests for over a month, and nothing was refused them.

During that time, Conual and his councillors made numerous occasions for private talk; and their queries were shrewd. "I am an envoy of my lord, the King of Ys," Rufinus said early on. "He has heard of your rise to mightiness. He hopes for friendship, oaths exchanged, benefits shared."

"He is afar," answered Conual. "True, I've no wish to make war on him or on the Romans like Niall of Temir. But what is to bind our two lands together?"

"Trade."

"You've come too soon for that, my dear. The great fairs do not open before Lúgnassat."

"I know. Granted your leave, we would like to take our ship's cargo round about and see what bargains folk wish to strike. But that is not why I am here, the voice of King Grallon. He in his wisdom looks beyond the gains that some Ysan merchants have made at your fairs. He hopes to arrange that many more will want to go, and many of your traders seek to us. We have much to give each other. Ys offers the harvest of the sea; amber from the Northeast, Roman wares transshipped from the South; the products of her own weaveries and workshops. Ériu has the yields of her fertile land, pearls, and also gold, which has long been draining out of the Empire. Surely, as traffic quickens, men will think of more than this."

"Hm. What might hinder?"

"War, pirates, the rapacity of overlords, ignorance and distrust. You, who I hear have spent years in Britannia, you will understand. Consider, King. Think of an alliance between yourself and King Grallon. Imagine

missions going to and fro, men becoming well acquainted, making agreements and planning joint ventures. Meanwhile, with help from Ys, your
people build stout ships like ours, to trade farther than ever erstwhile and
to patrol your home seas."

"It's like a Roman that you are speaking. I follow you, but there are
not many in Mumu who could. Just the same— Do let me think. Let us
talk more in days to come. Already I know that the message I will be
sending back with you will be a kindly one. May you come here again,
Rufinus."

3

Apuleius Vero and his wife Rovinda stared enraptured at the presents
Gratillonius had brought them. For her there was a woolen cloak from
the foremost webster in Ys, warm but light and soft as thistledown, its
dusk-blue worked with silvery figures of dolphins and terns. For him
there were the poems of Ausonius, done onto parchment by a calligrapher
who had access to Bodilis's collection, bound into a codex whose cover
was tooled leather with gilt trim.

"Oh," the woman breathed. "It's gorgeous. How can I thank you?"

Apuleius gave his friend a long look. "You *thought* about this, did you
not?" he said quietly. "You're less blunt than you let on."

Gratillonius smiled. "I've things for the children too, of course," he
told them. "How are they?"

"Very well." A cloud passed over Rovinda's face. She and her husband
had lost all but two. She dismissed memories in favor of pleasure.
"They'll be overjoyed to know their honorary uncle is back. Their tutor is
sick abed, so we've allowed them to stay on the farm. They love the
countryside so."

"And they deserve a reward," the father added. "You know Verania is
quite the little scholar, when she isn't outdoors. Well, now, Salomon has
begun taking a real interest in his owm studies. That doesn't come easily
to a headlong boy like him. Rovinda, dear, dispatch a slave to fetch them
before you turn the kitchen inside out preparing the feast I'm sure you
want to welcome our guest with."

"Hold on," Gratillonius suggested. "Why don't you and I walk there?
We can easily return with them before dinnertime."

"Aren't you tired after your journey?"

"No, it went smoothly. And from my arriving this early in the day, you know darkness caught us quite nearby. We camped on Drusus's property. He took me into the house and poured with a free hand. A walk will clear my head, if you care to come along."

Apuleius grew pensive. "Hm-m. . . . Very well. I'll let that replace my regular exercises for today. It will be much less tedious." His smile was a trifle forced. "Besides, I planned to take you there when we got an opportunity. I have something for you."

Gratillonius took the package he had not unwrapped. Donning outer garments, the men went forth. Aquilo was abustle. The approximately annual visits from Ys were always occasions in such a small city. The escort were already mingling with the people. He recognized a few former legionaries. Drusus had told him that after six years the resettlement was still working well. The veterans were gradually making the civilian reservists militarily effective—more than Imperial law envisioned. Most of them had married Osismiic women and become farmers, artisans, tradesmen. They had a stake in Armorica. No hostile barbarians would get close to Aquilo, unless as prisoners bound for the slave markets.

Apuleius conducted Gratillonius out the east gate and north on the river road. The day was clear, chill, a wan-bright sun above the heights whose steepness hemmed in this bank. Across the stream, the land rolled away, its northern horizon forested. Scattered farmsteads stood among dun plowfields, sallow meadows, orchards gone yellow and brown. Wind boomed from that direction. A buzzard rode watchful upon its torrent.

Apuleius must raise his voice against the noise. Indoors he would have spoken softly: "You've more than a walk in mind."

Gratillonius nodded. "Privacy."

"Nobody eavesdrops at the house."

"I know. But—your letter urging me to come said only that you've news for me. Now, I've learned your style. You have to be thinking of something unwelcome. I'd have trouble sitting still while we discussed it. This wind ought to flush the fret and anger out of me, so we can have a pleasant evening together."

"I see." Apuleius's Hellenic-like features showed the distress he had been holding back. "The truth is, I have little in the way of news. Mainly it's an accumulation of hints, overtones, mentions, incidents, the sort of word that the tribune at Aquilo, who sees higher authorities now and then and who maintains a rather extensive correspondence—the sort of word he gets, while the prefect in Ys, who is also the King of that nest of pagans, does not."

The wind slipped fingers under Gratillonius's cloak. "I have been notified that Lugdunensis Tertia has a new governor."

"You've probably not heard yet that the Duke of the Armorican Tract is also being replaced."

Gratillonius half stumbled. "What? But he's done well. He and I have kept the peninsula at peace."

"Precisely. He and you. Oh, I'm sure it will be an honorable retirement. No sense in provoking the many who feel grateful. But Honorius—Stilicho, rather—intends that his will, and none other, shall prevail everywhere in the West."

Gratillonius's gullet tightened. "If he means to recall me— Can you make them realize what insanity that would be?"

"My direct influence is slight. I do have communication with some men who are powerful. I will try. Just what I should write in my letters is one of the things we must discuss.

"Your policies were too successful, my friend. The Imperium has had unhappy experiences with such officers. Think back over the course of events since Maximus fell." Apuleius chuckled dryly. "If nothing else, those seven years were seldom dull."

Gratillonius grunted response and fell silent, trying to recall and order them for himself.

—Following his victory, Theodosius reinstated Valentinianus as Emperor of the West, but remained two years more in Italy, organizing its shaken government, destroying every relic of the usurper he could find, before he returned to Constantinople. As chief minister to Valentinianus, he left his general Arbogast.

This man had been the real director of the battle. A Frank and an avowed heathen, he favored barbarians over Romans for high office, pagans over Christians. On both counts, he was soon at odds with Valentinianus, and after a while he got the ineffectual Augustus murdered. Thereupon he proclaimed as Emperor a rhetorician named Eugenius. The real power was his. When Bishop Ambrosius appealed to him to desist from encouraging the cults of the old Gods, he threatened to stable his horses in the cathedral of Mediolanum and draft monks into his army.

After two years that army met the host of Theodosius, bound from the East to regain the West. For two days they fought, until Eugenius was killed and his cause lost. Arbogast fled, but committed suicide soon afterward.

Theodosius marched on to Rome. He was smitten with dropsy and knew he had not much time left on earth. The Empire he redivided, the East going to his son Arcadius, the West to his son Honorius. Thereupon he retired to Mediolanum, made his peace with God as best he could, and expired in the winter that was past, some nine months ago.

Arcadius was an indolent youth of seventeen, under the thumb of his praetorian prefect Rufinus. (Recalling that name, Gratillonius smiled wryly.) Honorius was a boy of eleven, said to be a weakling also. His father had made Flavius Stilicho and Stilicho's wife Serena joint guardians of him. They betrothed him to their daughter Maria.

Further strife was ineluctable. Stilicho had begun this season's warring on the Rhenus, where German tribes had gotten troublesome. But after quelling them, he marched to Thracia. There he still was.

—"It's given out that he aims to expel the Goths and Huns from that province," Apuleius said when Gratillonius inquired. "And no doubt he is working toward it. However, I've excellent reason to believe that his real objective is the destruction of the praetorian prefect Rufinus. If he can accomplish that, he will be the master of the whole Empire, both East and West."

"And then—?"

"The event is in the hands of God. But men can take measures."

Beyond the inflow of the Stegir they crossed a bridge over the Odita and followed a road that went north along the tributary stream. An oxcart lumbered far ahead, distance-dwindled; a tenant forked hay into a wooden trough for the cattle in a paddock; at the house behind, his wife strewed grain for free-running chickens: a peacefulness at which the wind gibed.

"I wouldn't look for immediate woe," Apuleius said after a time. "Stilicho will be busy. Even here in the Northwest, surely his first concern must be the Scoti. You know how they took advantage of his departure from Britannia to ravage it, two years ago, and have since been re-establishing their enclaves there."

Gratillonius scowled. His father's home had been spared, but barely. "That was the work of Niall. I hear he's now preoccupied inside Hivernia. Some good luck does drift our way sometimes."

"Who? . . . No matter. You're in touch with the Scoti as I am not, as I suppose no Roman—no other Roman is. That's one thing against you."

Gratillonius bridled. "See here, *I* broke the fleet that would have raided up the Liger a dozen years back. True, I'm cultivating relationships with Scoti, but friendly Scoti."

Apuleius sighed. "I don't doubt you. But they see it otherwise in Turonum, Treverorum, Lugdunum, Mediolanum—wherever it comes to mind that the man sent to be Rome's prefect in Ys has become its independent sovereign. For that you are, no matter if you continue piously calling yourself a centurion on special duty."

"How have I subverted any interest of Rome? By the Bull, I've strengthened us!"

"And strengthened Ys. The city that once lay veiled is today chiefest in Armorica, its brilliance and prosperity outshining any of the Western Empire. Nonetheless it remains as alien, as un-Christian, as the seat of the Sassanian King."

"Rome's made peace with the Persians."

"How long can that last? How long will Ys choose to be our ally? You will not reign forever, Gratillonius. You will not reach old age, unless you can end that barbarous law of succession. Ys would be a most dangerous enemy. Already the grievances are building up."

Gratillonius shook his head. "You're wrong. I know."

"You know what they think in Ys. I know what they think who govern Rome. When those men clamp down on the trade you have caused to flourish, how then will Ys feel?"

"Ha? But that's ridiculous! Why in the name of moonstruck Cernunnos should they do any such thing? We gave Armorica peace; we're drawing it out of poverty."

"By means that are . . . unsettling. The merchants and shippers of Ys, being free agents, undermine the authority of Roman officials, guilds, laws. Men disappear from the stations of life to which they were born. They reappear in traffic that goes unregulated, untaxed, yet scarcely troubles itself to be clandestine. This year Ysans began acquiring substantial amounts of Hivernian gold. It flows about, uncoined, driving the Emperor's money into total worthlessness, thereby making people mutter that perhaps they have no need of an Emperor at all. No, I tell you the authorities cannot indefinitely permit the life of the region to go on outside their control. They dare not."

Gratillonius decided to make no mention of his own irregularities. Some Roman officials must have some peripheral awareness of them; but to investigate would take those persons out of comfortable routine, into forests, heaths, slums, barbarian camps. Why force them to that? It could only make difficulties for all concerned—most of all for Rome, because the damned stupid government was not itself doing what was plainly necessary for survival.

"They certainly hold religion against us," he growled. "But we have a church and pastor. We persecute nobody."

"I hear that Honorius is devout," Apuleius said. "When he grows up, he may transform weakness into zeal."

"Maximus once threatened to invade Ys."

"He fell. Stilicho is more formidable."

Apuleius took his friend by the arm. "I don't mean to perturb you," he went on. "I only give you an early warning. You have time to prepare and take preventive steps. I've promised you to serve as your advocate with influential men. I believe we can forestall an order for your recall, because that would risk Armorica falling into chaos, a crisis which Stilicho surely regards as unnecessary at this juncture. But you must do your part. You must be more circumspect. You must forbid smuggling, and curb the most blatant of it. You—" Apuleius stopped.

"What?" asked Gratillonius.

"It would help mightily if you accepted the Faith and worked for the conversion of Ys."

"I'm sorry. That's impossible."

"I know. How often I've prayed to God that He lift the scales from your eyes. It's heretical of me, but I suspect that the knowledge you were burning in hell would diminish my joy in Heaven, should I be found worthy of going there."

Gratillonius reined in a reply. As he had told Corentinus in their generally amicable arguments, he didn't think an eternity of torment was the proper punishment for an incorrect opinion, and saw no righteousness in a God Who did. Corentinus retorted that mere mortals had no business passing judgment on the Almighty; what did they understand?

Apuleius brightened. "Enough," he said. "You have the gist of what I wanted to tell you. Think it over, sleep on it, and tomorrow we'll talk further. Let's simply be ourselves until then. Look, there's the villa ahead."

They walked on. Security from attack and revival of trade had drawn workers out of inland refuges. Maximus's veterans had additionally eased the labor shortage. Agriculture was again thriving around Aquilo, not in the form of latifundia but as sharecropping and even some freeholds. No longer neglected, the land surrounding the Apuleian manor house, which stood near the northwest corner of the cleared section with the forest at its back—this land showed neat fields, sleek livestock, buildings refurbished and permanently in use. At the house itself, whitewashed walls, glazed windows, red tile roof called back to Gratillonius his father's. But here the owner was no curial between the millstones, he was a senator, the closest thing to a free man that Roman law recognized.

The children saw who approached and burst from within, to dash down the garden path and be hugged. Only six, Salomon outpaced his sister regardless. Big for his age, he was coming to resemble his father, though Apuleius must have been a quieter boy. The parents had explained to Gratillonius that they named him after a king of the ancient

Jews in hopes that this would cause God to let him live. That had happened, but thereafter Rovinda continued to suffer stillbirths and infant deaths.

Verania followed. At ten she was well-made if rather small. She had her father's hazel eyes, her mother's light-brown hair, and a countenance blending the comelinesses in both. Near to Gratillonius, she abruptly blushed and became very polite, her greeting barely audible through the wind.

"Well, well!" he said. "How good to see you two again. I'll spare you any remarks about how you've grown since last. We're doing nicely in Ys. I've much to tell you about that. For a start, here're a couple of little things from there for you."

He squatted on the gravel and opened the package. Its contents were modest, because Apuleius frowned on ostentation. However, they drew a shout from Salomon, a soft cry from Verania. He got a Roman sword and sheath, scaled to his size. "A copy of my old military piece. Someday, I think, you'll lead men too." She received a portable harp, exquisitely carved. "From Hivernia. I know you're musical. Among the Scoti, some of their poets and bards are women."

Worship looked back at him, until Salomon sprang up. "I know what we've got for you!" he crowed.

"Hush," said Verania. "Wait till father's ready."

Apuleius laughed. "Why wait? Here we are. Before we step indoors and have a cup of something, let's go see." He linked his arm with Gratillonius's. "You've been so generous to us over the years, so helpful, that we'd like to make some slight return."

Salomon capered and hallooed. Verania walked on the other side of the prefect, not quite touching him, her glance bent downward.

The stable was dim, warm, smelling sweetly of hay and pungently of manure. Apuleius halted at one stall. From within, a stallion colt looked alertly out. Gratillonius would learn that he had overestimated the age, about six months, because it was so large—a splendid creature, sorrel with a white star, of the tall kind that bore cataphracts to battle.

"This is yours to take back with you," Apuleius said.

"By Hercules, but you're generous!" Gratillonius marveled.

"Well, as a matter of fact, my interest in breeding this sort began when you told me how your father's been trying the same in Britannia. I think we're having some success. Favonius is our best thus far. I suspect he'll prove the best possible. You're a horseman. We want you to have him."

"Thank you so much." Gratillonius reached over the bars, stroked mane and head, cupped his hand around the muzzle. How soft it was.

"I'll raise him right, and—and when I ride him here in future, help yourself to his stud services. Favonius, did you say?"

"Our name for him. You can change it if you like. It's a rather literary word, meaning the west wind that brings the springtime."

"Oh, it's fine. I'll keep it."

Apuleius smiled in the duskiness. "May he bear you to a springtime of your own."

XVI

1

Tiberius Metellus Carsa was of Cadurcic descent, but his family had long dwelt in Burdigala and mingled its blood with others that pulsed in the city. Its men took to the sea, and he himself inherited the rank of captain after he was trained and a position had opened up. For some years he carried freight between the ports of Aquitania and as far as northern Hispania. At last he encountered pirates. Many such had taken advantage of the strife between Theodosius and Arbogast, and not all were immediately suppressed after the Empire was pacified.

With Carsa in this battle was his oldest son Aulus, born to the trade and, at age fourteen, making his first real sea voyage. The boy acquitted himself well. He was expert with the sling. Though he had not grown into his full strength, from the cabin top he wrought havoc, certainly braining one man and disabling several. Meanwhile his father led a spirited defense at the rail. The upshot was that the reavers took heavy losses and fled before their vessel should be boarded.

That incident decided the owners to put Carsa on the Armorican run.

Those waters were tricky, but the human hazard had much diminished in the decade or so since Ys emerged from isolation. True, lately the barbarians had again been grieving Britannia. However, Ys kept them at arm's length; and now that he had disposed of his rival, the praetorian prefect of the East, Stilicho was dispatching an expeditionary force against them.

Therefore, when shipping season began next year, Carsa sailed the seven-hundred-ton *Livia* down the Garumna and north-northwest over the gulf. His cargo was mostly wine and olive oil, his destination Ys. With him went Aulus.

It was a rough passage, winds often foul, taking a full ten days because the captain was cautious. "I'd rather arrive late in Ys than early in hell," he said. "Although I've heard churchmen declare there is a great deal of hell already in that town."

Young Aulus scarcely heard. He was staring ahead. Wonder stood before him.

The day was chill and gusty, casting saltiness off the whitecaps onto his lips. Waves brawled green, here and there darkened by kelp, bursting white over rocks. Afar lay an island, its flatness broken by a single turreted building. Fowl rode the water and wheeled overhead, hundredfold, crying through wind and surf, gulls, terns, guillemots, puffins, cormorants. Seals frolicked about or basked on skerries. *Livia* rocked forward under shortened sail, the master peering now at the reefs and now at the periplus fluttering in his grasp, men at the sides ready to fend off if need be. This cape had a grim reputation. It did not seem to trouble the vessels, mostly fishermen, that were in sight; but Roman mariners supposed Ys had a pact with the demons its people worshipped.

The city lay ahead. Its wall bowed out into the sea whose queen it was, filling the space between two looming promontories, the hue of dark roses, up and up to a frieze of fabulous creatures and thereafter battlements and turrets. Farther back, higher still, spires pierced heaven, glass agleam, until the roofs flared into fantastical shapes. As tidal flow commenced the gate was slowly closing. The harbor beyond, docks, warehouses, ships, boats, life, seemed to Aulus a paradise about to be denied him.

Out of the basin hastened four longboats. Shouts went back and forth. Lines snaked downward, were caught and made fast. The Romans struck sail. The Ysans bent to their oars and towed the ship in. Aulus gasped as he passed the sheer, copper-green doors.

In a daze of delight, he watched the tugmen warp *Livia* into a slip and collect their pay; a robed official come up the gangplank, accompanied by two guards in armor unlike any elsewhere, and confer with his father; the crew snug things down for the stay in port and, impatiently, shoulder their bags; the captain at last, at last grant shore leave!

Among the longshoremen, hawkers, whores, strolling entertainers, curious spectators who thronged the dock, were runners from various inns, each trying to outsing the others in praise of his place. They all knew some Latin. Tiberius grinned. "Let's hope our poor devils don't get fleeced too badly," he said to his son. "We'll be here for several days. If we're to ply this route regularly, we need to familiarize ourselves with the port."

"Where'll we stay, you and I?" Aulus asked breathlessly.

"A respectable hostel. I have directions. Get our baggage and we'll go."

On their way, the Carsae found much—everything—to stare at. Nothing, not even those things the Romans had built, was quite like home; always the proportions and the artwork were subtly altered into something elongated and sleek, swirling and surging. The city throbbed and clamored with activity. Most Ysans appeared prosperous. It showed more in bright garments and jewelry than on bodies, except that folk were bathed and well-groomed. They tended to be lean, energetic, but basically dignified. Many resembled the aborigines and Celts who had been among their ancestors, but often the Phoenician heritage revealed itself in hawk face or dark complexion. Men usually had close-trimmed beards and hair drawn into a queue; some wore tunics, some jacket and trousers, a few robes. Women's tresses were set according to fancy, from high-piled coiffure to free flow beneath a headband. They generally wore long-sleeved, broad-belted gowns that gave ample freedom of movement, and they walked as boldly as men. The Carsae had heard their rights and liberties were essentially equal. Servants, too, were free agents working for pay, slavery being banned in Ys—an almost exact reversal of Roman practice.

Like the city it stood in, the hostel was clean and well-furnished. In the room that father and son got, a fresco depicted a ship at sea and, sky-tall and beautiful, a woman in a blue cloak whose hand upheld a star above the mast.

"Pagans," Tiberius muttered. "Damned souls. Licentious too, I hear. But they have a Christian church somewhere."

"We, we must deal with them . . . mustn't we?" asked Aulus. "They can't be *wicked*. Not if—" He waved an awkward hand at the view in the window. "Not if they made this."

"Oh, we'll mind our manners, you and I. The trade's too profitable. Also, we've got much to learn, and there'll be pleasures as well. Only be sure to keep your soul steady as she goes. I'm told the Armoricans have stories like ours, about sirens who lure seamen onto the rocks. Well, even inside wall and gate, the reefs of hell are underneath us."

Some of the food set before them in the common room was curious, all was delicious—marinated mussels, leeks cooked in chicken broth, plaice lightly fried with thyme and watercress, white bread wherein hazelnuts had been baked, sweet butter, blue-veined cheese, honeycake, and a dry, herbal-flavored mead that sang on the tongue. The serving wench, about Aulus's age, gave him glances and smiles that caused his father to frown.

However, Tiberius responded gladly when a messenger appeared, a boy whose red tunic had embroidered upon the breast a golden wheel. "Captain Carsa?" he asked. His Latin had a peculiar construction. "I am from

King Gratillonius. Ever is he desirous of making strangers welcome and hearing from them about the larger world. Therefore is word of them always borne to him. He will be glad to receive you this very eventide."

"Why, why, of course!" Tiberius exclaimed. "But I'm just a merchant skipper."

"One new to us, sir. Let me say as well that a ship of ours returned from Hivernia on the morning tide, and its chief passengers will likewise be at the palace."

Tiberius glanced at Aulus, saw strickenness, and cleared his throat. "Um, this is my son—"

"I understand, sir. He is invited too."

Joy kindled a beacon.

The two put on their best clothes and went with the messenger for a guide. Along the way he pointed out sights till Aulus's head whirled.

Four men flanked the entrance gate of the royal grounds, two in Ysan battle array, two in Roman. Beyond, labyrinthine paths among flower-beds, hedges, topiaries, bowers seemed to create more room than was possible. The palace was of modest size, but the pride was boundless. Its side walls bore scenes of wild beasts in the forest. A bronze boar and bear guarded the main staircase. Above a copper roof swelled a dome, whereon the image of an eagle spread wings whose gilt blazed against sundown.

Passing through an anteroom, the visitors came into a chamber great and marble-pillared, frescoed with pictures of the four seasons, floor mosaic of a chariot race. Clerestory windows were duskening, but oil lamps and wax candles gave lavish light. Servants glided about refilling winecups and offering titbits of food. Flute and harp trilled in a corner.

Only a few persons were on hand, none elaborately clad. Seated in chairs as if presiding over an occasion of state, they nonetheless appeared quite at ease. A big, auburn-haired man with rugged features lifted his arm as the new guests entered. "Greeting," he said. His Latin was plain-spoken, with a South Britannic overtone. "I'm Gaius Valerius Gratillonius, centurion in the Second, prefect of Rome, and—" he smiled— "King of Ys. I'd like to hear whatever you care to tell and try to answer your questions, but feel free to mingle with people. We'll have a lantern-bearer to take you back."

He introduced the others. Two were female, two of his notorious nine wives. They conveyed no sense of being more than handsome middle-aged ladies—until they joined the conversation as outspokenly and intelligently as any man. A couple of male Ysans were present, an old scholar and the head of a mercantile house. A fairly young Redonian—lean, tough-looking with his fork beard and scarred cheek—was one of those in from

Hivernia; Aulus caught his name at once, Rufinus, because it had been famous last year as somebody else's. With him was a fellow not much older than Aulus, defiantly attired in a Scotic kilt and a saffron-dyed shirt secured at the throat by a penannular brooch.

"Sit down," Gratillonius urged. "Drink. You aren't on stage. This isn't the Symposium, eh, Bodilis? Tell me, Captain Carsa, how was your voyage?"

He had a gift for putting company at ease: though Aulus suspected that when he administered a tongue-lashing, lightning sizzled blue. Before long, individuals were freely at converse with whomever they chose. Gratillonius drew Tiberius out about happenings in the South. Since Aulus already knew that, he shortly found himself off in a corner with Tommaltach.

That was the Scotian. His Latin was still somewhat broken, but had a musical lilt to it. Despite his having done battle in his home island, despite his being pagan and unlettered, his liveliness ranged so widely that Aulus felt like a child again. Yet Tommaltach did not patronize him.

—"Ah, you could do well among the girls of Ys, Carsa," he laughed. His glance probed. Aulus's frame was filling out into sturdiness; his countenance was broad, blunt-nosed, regular, beneath curly dark-brown hair. "Can you get away? The hunting's better with two. I'm not talking of some copper-a-tumble whore, you understand; not but what such aren't usually well worth it in Ys. I mean lusty servant women, hoping to marry someday but meanwhile ready for fun if they like you. They're apt to saunter the streets in pairs—"

The Roman wished his face would not heat.

"You could be staying over a while," Tommaltach said, "between two calls your ship makes. My friend Rufinus would take care of arrangements. Sure, and he's a good-hearted man. Your dad should be happy, if you ask him right." Seriously: "It's more than pleasure this would be. It's an e-du-cation. The learning, the folk from everywhere, the marvels, the magic—"

He broke off, turned, and stared. Silence fell upon the room. The girl who had entered, already more than half woman, was so beautiful.

In white raiment, garland of apple blossoms on the loose amber-colored hair, she flowed over the floor to Gratillonius. She murmured huskily in Ysan, then, observing the company, changed to excellent Latin: "Why, father, you didn't tell me you expected guests. I could have left my Temple duties earlier."

The King beamed. "I didn't know you meant to spend the night here, darling. Wasn't it to be with Maldunilis?"

"Oh, she only wants to lie about and eat sweetmeats. I *must* find a place of my own." The girl checked herself, lifted a hand, and said gravely: "Welcome, honored sirs. May the Gods look upon you with kindness."

"My daughter Dahut," Gratillonius announced. "Captain Metellus Carsa, newly from Burdigala. His son . . . Aulus. I don't believe you've met Tommaltach of Mumu, either. You should have, but it never chanced till now."

Dahut kindled a smile.

Gratillonius laughed. "Well, why do you wait, little flirt? Go brighten their lives for the young men."

Dahut lowered her eyes, raised them again, and demurely joined the elders. However, the time was not long before she was in their corner chatting with Tommaltach and the junior Carsa.

2

Summer lay heavy over the land. Westward, cloud masses loomed on the horizon, blue-shadowed white above a sea that shone as if burnished. Ys glittered like a jewel. Grass greened and softened the headlands, save where boulders of ancient stoneworks denied it. The heights leading east bore such wealth of leafage that most of the homes nestled in their folds were hidden. In between, the valley stretched lush and hushed. Warmth baked fragrance out of soil, plants, flowers. Bees droned through clover.

In the courtyard of the Sacred Precinct, two men fought. Wearing full Roman combat armor, they circled warily, probed, defended with shield or sword, sometimes rushed together for a moment's fury. Their hobnails struck sparks from the slate flags. Neither getting past the defense of the other, they broke apart and resumed their stalking. They breathed hard. Sweat runneled down their faces and stung their eyes. The sun turned the metal they wore into furnaces.

Maeloch the fisher arrived on Processional Way. His stride jarred to a halt. He gaped.

Menservants were watching too, from the porch of the great red house that filled the opposite side of the square. Right and left, its ancillary buildings formed two more boundaries of the courtyard. Black, all but featureless, they radiated that heat which the blood-colored lodge uttered to vision. The fourth side opened onto the paving of the road. High above roofs, the Wood of the King lifted its crowns, an oakenshaw whose rough circle spanned some seven hundred feet, silence and shadow.

The mightiest of the trees grew at the middle of the courtyard. From the lowest bough of the Challenge Oak hung a round brazen shield, too big and heavy for use. Sunlight dazzled away sight of the wild, bearded visage molded on it, or the many dents made by the sledge hammer that hung beside.

Blows thudded. They did not rattle or clash. Maeloch eased. Both blades were cased in horsehide.

The slender, more agile man saw himself about to be forced against the bole. He turned on his heel to slip aside. Suddenly swift, the large man moved at him, not in a leap but in a pivot on widespread, bent legs that kept his footing always firm. His swordpoint slammed at the other's knee and ran up the thigh below the chain mail. The struck man lurched and gasped a Britannic curse.

"Enough, Cynan!" called his opponent. "If this'd been real, you'd be bleeding to death now."

"Well done, sir," panted the other. "I'm glad you stopped short of my crotch."

"Ha, never fear. I need my roadpounders entire. Besides, your wife would have my head."

Cynan limped. "You did catch me a good one, sir. I'm afraid I can't give you any more worthwhile practice today."

"I've had plenty as is. Come, let's go inside, get this tin off us, wash up and have a drink."

Maeloch, whose Latin was scant, had gotten the drift. His rolling sailor's gait bore him forward. "My lord King," he said in Ysan, "I've sore need to talk with ye."

Gratillonius removed his helmet. He knew this man, as he did every Ferrier of the Dead. "I'll hold public court in a few days," he answered.

The shaggy head shook. "Can't wait, my lord. Aye, ye be standing your Watch. Never kept ye from handling any business you felt like. And—I also deal with the Gods."

Gratillonius met the unflinching gaze and smiled. "A stubborn lot, you fishers. Well, come along, then. Have a beaker while I get clean."

"I thank ye," said Maeloch, as he would have replied to an invitation from a fellow seaman.

The three mounted the stairs to the portico. Its columns were carved into images of Taranis and His attributes, wild boar, eagle, thunderbolt, oak tree. Beyond, the massive timbers and shake roof enclosed a feasting hall. Its pillars and wainscots were likewise carved, but hard to make out in the dimness. Age-eaten banners hung from the crossbeams like bats. The fire-trenches in the clay floor lay empty. Nostrils were glad to inhale cool air.

Gratillonius and Cynan stripped and went on into the modernized section for a bath and fresh clothes. Maeloch accepted a goblet of ale and sat down on a bench built into a side. Three men carried the military gear out for cleaning and stowage. A fourth took a feather duster and went about in search of cobwebs.

Maeloch beckoned to him. "What Queen is here today?" he asked.

The servant halted. "None, sir." Unlike his livery, his voice was subdued. A Ferrier of the Dead, in this house of the killers, raised too many ghosts.

"Why? He's no weakling, our King. Besides, 'tis plain justice to them, one man with nine wives."

"The Princess Dahut wanted to dwell here for the three days and nights of this month's Watch. She wanted no grown woman about."

"Dahut, ye say? What makes the child have such a wish?"

" 'Tis not for me to guess, sir. But her royal father agreed."

"Aye, he can deny her naught, I hear. And who'd blame him for that? Where be she now?"

"In the Wood, I believe, sir. She's hours on end in the Wood, both by daylight and moonlight."

Maeloch frowned. "That could be dangerous. What if a sacred boar turned ugly? Nay, Grallon yields her too much there."

"Pray pardon, sir, I must keep on with my work."

Maeloch nodded, leaned back against the smoke-darkened relief of a scene in an ancient tale—the hero Belcar combatting the demonic mermaid Quanis—and pondered.

Lightly clad, Gratillonius emerged with Cynan. He clapped his hands. "Cold mead for two," he called. "More ale for our guest if he wishes. Well, Maeloch, what would you of me?"

The seaman had not risen. "Best we speak under four eyes, my lord," he replied.

"Hm, you are in a surly mood, nay? Then wait your turn. Sit down, Cynan. I'd like to talk about a couple of things," Gratillonius said, pointedly, in Latin. "It was plain, stupid luck that you didn't nail me earlier today with that shield-hooking trick. I've got to overcome my slackness about it. Who can tell what the next challenger will know?"

A man brought the mead, which had been cooled by leaving its bottle in a porous jar full of water. Cynan drank and spoke hurriedly. Despite his centurion's protestations, he soon left.

Gratillonius dismissed the attendants and sat down on the bench beside Maeloch. "Well?" he asked.

The fisher drew breath. "This, my lord. We be angry at ye in Scot's Landing, for that ye had poor Usun and Intil flogged. I said I'd bring the grievance. Usun's my shipmate."

Gratillonius nodded. "I thought that was the trouble," he said slowly. " 'Flogging' is the wrong word. Three cuts of an unleaded thong, across those turtle backs, couldn't have hurt much. 'Twas meant for an example, a warning."

"A disgrace!"

"Nay, now. How often have you decked a man who was unruly or foolish, or triced him up for a few tastes of a rope's end, with no lasting grudges afterward?"

Maeloch's huge fists knotted on his knees. "What harm had they done? In this year of poor catches, they took a boat; they fared down the peninsula; they brought back Roman-made wares to sell. But your spies were watching."

"No spies were needed. Those two flouted the law with no special effort to hide what they were about."

"What law? We've aye been free traders in Ys, till ye made that bloody decree. Grallon, I be nay yet your foe. But I warn ye, ye're going astray. Ye whipped two men and took away their goods. Ye had no right."

Gratillonius sighed. "Hark, friend. Before Mithras, I wish I'd not had to do it. But they forced me. I'd made it clear as the pool at the Nymphaeum, henceforward our traders into Roman territory must go through the Roman customs. These men did not. Liefer than pay tax, they smuggled Ysan cloth to the Veneti, and took those wares in exchange. Let them count themselves lucky the Romans didn't catch them at it. I punished them for the sake of every lad in Ys who's tempted to try the same. If anyone gets arrested, I can do naught—naught, do you hear? —to save him."

Some of the bitterness drained out of Maeloch. Pain rose in its stead. "But why, Grallon?" he whispered harshly. "After all these years, why feed yon sharks?"

"I did not spell out the reasons as fully as mayhap I should have. My thought was that 'twould stir up too much wrath, too much pride. Some among us might go off and make trouble merely to ease their feelings. And we dare not have that. So I simply declared 'tis high time Ys honor her ancient treaties with Rome, and observe Roman law in Roman lands. The fact is—Think, Maeloch. Shiploads of soldiers are now in Britannia. When they've cleared it of barbarians, if they can, what shall they do next? The Emperor, or rather his guardian Stilicho, is already being urged to crush contumaciously pagan Ys. Naught but our usefulness to Rome keeps us free. We must not provoke Rome further. The Council of Suffetes agreed at equinox."

Gratillonius laid a hand on the shoulder at his side. "Bide a while, friend," he went on, softly. "I want you to understand, and make your comrades understand, that this is done for their sake."

He paused before adding: "Let me say at once, confidentially, I know those are poor men, those two, and confiscation of their cargo means hardship for their families. Well, I cannot let them profit by their misdeed, but . . . between us, surely you and I can work out some quiet way to see them through without undue suffering."

Maeloch choked. "What? Grallon, ye *be* a good man."

A slim form briefly darkened the open doorway. Dahut entered the hall. She seemed to light up its cavernous depths.

"Why, Maeloch," she cried, "dear old Maeloch!" and hurried forward to take both his hands. "Had I but known! You will stay and take supper here, will you not? Say you will!"

Helpless, he must answer, "Aye, Princess, since 'tis ye who ask."

Underneath his words rustled a quetion. What had she been doing in the Wood, why did she want to prowl it, the Wood where someday a stranger was to kill her father?

3

To the Greater Monastery in the Liger valley, near Caesarodunum Turonum, came a pilgrim. Autumn cooled and hazed the air but decked trees in brilliant vestments. The river glided darkling past the huts that clustered on a flat bank. Hemming this in, hills rose nearly sheer, riddled with caves where monks also dwelt. Many were in sight, coarsely clad, roughly tonsured, unwashed. The newcomer had to search before he found one who was not at prayer or meditation but spading a vegetable garden.

"In Christ's holy name, greeting," he ventured.

"His peace be with you," replied the monk. He saw a young man, fair-haired, rangy, in tunic, trousers, shoes of stout material though showing hard use. A bedroll and meager pack of rations were on his back, a wallet for minor objects at his waist, a staff in his hand. Nothing but a curious accent, not quite Britannic, marked him out from countless wanderers.

"Do you seek work?" asked the monk. "I hear they're short-handed on the Jovianus latifundium." And they did not inquire as to the antecedents of an able-bodied man. Imperial laws binding folk to the soil had succeeded in displacing thousands of them, as farm after farm went under.

The stranger smiled. "Not field work, at least not in any earthly fields. Of course, I'll gladly help if my labor is needed. Where may I find your bishop?"

"Holy Martinus? No, son, you've no call to interrupt him at his devotions. We'll put you up for the night, never fear."

"I beg you. This is necessary. He cannot have so entirely forsaken the world that he would refuse to see a kinsman returned from slavery among the heathen."

Astounded, the monk gave information. The founder and leader of the monastery occupied a single-roomed wattle-and-daub hut, as small and crude as the rest. Its door sagged ajar, to show him prostrate at his prayers. The traveler leaned on his staff and waited.

After about an hour, Martinus emerged. He blinked, for his blue eyes were dimming with age. Thin white hair made an aureole around a face shriveled and shrunken in on itself. Yet he still moved briskly and spoke vigorously. "What do you wish, my son?"

"Audience with you, if you will give me that charity," replied the young man. "I am Sucat, son of your niece Conchessa and her husband Calpurnius, curial in the Britannic town Banaventa."

Air soughed in between Martinus's gums. "Sucat? No, can't be. Sucat perished these . . . seven years ago, was it not, when the Scoti raided along the Sabrina?"

"I did not die, sir. I was borne away captive. Let me prove myself by relating family history. My father was a Silurian who joined the army and rose to centurion's rank. While stationed in Pannonia, he met and married your niece. Upon his discharge, he brought her to his homeland and settled there. He was a pious man, who despite becoming a curial became a deacon as well—"

Martinus cast himself against Sucat and hugged him with surprising force. Tears burst from his eyes. "God forgive me! Why should I have doubted you? Welcome back, beloved, welcome home!"

He took his visitor into the hut. Virtually its only furniture was a wooden chest and a pair of three-legged stools; but atop the box lay several books. The men sat down. "Tell me what has happened, I beg you, and how you escaped and, oh, everything." Martinus exclaimed.

Sucat sighed. "It's a long story, sir. I was carried away with unfortunates—ah, but how dare I call myself unfortunate when I remember the poor young women?— I came to Ériu, Hivernia. There I fell to the lot of a chieftain in Condacht—well, he took me to his estate in the far west of the island and put me to tending his flocks. For six years I did."

"You bore it bravely."

Sucat smiled. "It was no terrible fate. True, the mountainside was often wet or cold, but God gave me health to endure that. My owner was not cruel by nature, and some other people did me kindnesses from time to time, and often in good weather little children would seek me out in the pasture, to hear me play on a whistle I'd carved or tell stories I remembered from nursery and school—once I'd mastered the language, of course, which has many differences from ours at home. And then, alone under heaven, I found my way back to God. For I confess to having been a light-minded youth, who forgot Him and trod the paths of sin. Now I said a hundred prayers by day and almost as many by night."

"His mercy is unbounded."

"I might be there still, for escape across that wild land and the waters beyond looked impossible. But a dream came to me at last, and I knew it was from God and required my obedience. Pursuit never found me. I nearly starved, but always, somehow, there was something to eat in time to keep me from falling. They are so hospitable in Ériu. . . . When I could not ask directions, I guessed, and my guesses led me aright. In the end I reached that harbor on the Ulatach shore which my dream had named, and there was a ship loading for Britannia."

Martinus's military practicality struck through. "What? I've heard the army is cleaning the barbarians out of Britannia."

"It is, though I fear, from what I saw, that that's like weeding thistles. Anyhow, peaceful traders aren't forbidden. This cargo was a pack of the great wolfhounds they breed in Ériu. At first the captain spurned me, as ragged and coinless as I was. But I persisted, and God softened his heart."

"You have gifts of persuasion, it seems."

Sucat flushed. "Well, it was another hard journey on the Britannic side, as devastated as the Westlands are, but home I came in the end. My father had gone to his reward—did you know?—but my mother and various kinfolk remain, and made me welcome with hosannahs. They wanted me to stay forever."

"Why did you not?" Martinus asked.

"I am haunted, reverend father. I cannot forget the people of Ériu—the women who smiled and spoke softly and slipped me a bite of something sweet, the rough comradeliness of men, the innocent children who came to me—even the proud warriors, the majestic druids. It's as if they are all

weeping, beseeching, in the night that binds them, crying for the Light."
Sucat swallowed. "I believe I have a vocation. Because you are my kinsman, and have made this a famous holy place, a school for bishops and
missionaries—I beg you, in Christ's name, take me in, teach me, and if I
prove worthy, ordain me."

Martinus was silent a long while. Shadows crept across the floor and
lifted in the valley as the sun declined. Finally he murmured: "I think
you're right. I think you're in the hand of God. But we dare not presume
to know His will, not without much prayer and thought and austerity.
Abide here, dear son, and we'll see what we can do for you. I've a feeling
already that a great work awaits you, but you'll be long in preparing for
it." His voice strengthened, rang: "Yet if I am not mistaken, you'll reach
the forefront of ministry; you will be Christ's patrician."

4

Midwinter rites and festival, together with the Council meeting, went past
solstice. On the first midnight after they ended, Forsquilis took Dahut out
onto Point Vanis.

The air lay windless and cold. Stars crowded heaven; the River of
Tiamat foamed across it ghost-white, ghost-silent. By that light the sentries at Northbridge Gate knew the Athene face whose pallor a cowled
cloak framed. They presented arms. Mute, woman and girl passed by,
onto the short bridge to the headland.

Huge rocks jutted from the water beneath. An incoming tide roared
and snarled among them, dashing itself between wall and cliff, spurting
whiteness upward out of jet. Hoarfrost grayed the earth ahead. To the
west, Ocean bore a faint, uneasy shimmer on its raven immensity. A
gibbous moon was crawling from the eastern hills.

Where the road from the bridge met Redonian Way, Forsquilis left both
and led Dahut northeast across the foreland. The track she followed
wound almost too narrow to walk, between tussocks, gorse, dead thistles,
boulders. Dahut stumbled. "I can't see where my feet go," she complained.

Forsquilis, cat-sure of her own way, answered softly, "You shall become one with the darkness, I promise you."

"When? How?"

"Hush. There are those abroad who might hear." Each word blew
forth as a tiny white phantom, instantly lost.

The two went on. The moon crept higher. Stars coruscated. Frost brought leaves forth against shadow. Footfalls and the dry rustle of twigs being brushed were the solitary sounds, until sea-murmur deepened and loudened as the walkers drew near the northern edge.

The destination hove in sight. Centuries of weather had worn down earthen walls which once bulked threefold on the clifftop of a small ness. Grass and brambles had bestormed the fortress, covered it over, crumbled it away with their roots; timbers had rotted and rubble fill washed down into the surf; surely the very dead beneath had yielded their bones to the soil.

Forsquilis stopped before the ruin. Casting back her cloak, she raised arms and chanted, not in Ysan but in the sacred Punic of the Founders: *"Mighty ones, spirits asleep in the depths of time, be not wroth. Awake ye and remember. I, a high priestess of Ishtar, bring unto you Dahut, a virgin who bears fate in her womb. Bid us come into your dreams."*

It was as if the sea moaned.

The Queen turned to the princess. "Be not afraid," she said. "Where we go tonight, none but the fearless may enter unscathed."

Dahut straightened. Her hood had fallen off the braids into which her hair was coiled, held by a silver clasp in the form of a snake. Moonlight silvered the right half of her face; the left was in bluish darkness. "You know I am not afraid," she replied.

Forsquilis smiled bleakly. "Aye, well do I know. Of your own free will have you ranged along the borders of the Otherworld, all your brief life; or its creatures have sought you out, but then you never quailed. Ere ever your strange birth, the Gods made you Theirs for some purpose hidden from mortals—and, it may be, from Themselves. Every omen avows it, with never a sign we can clearly read. I have told you how the hope of the Nine has become this: that you, gaining skill in the Old Wisdom that men call witchcraft, may find your way forward to an understanding of your destiny, and make it not terrible but splendid."

Dahut nodded, wordless.

"It is a heavy load to lay on a young girl," Forsquilis said. "Once all the Gallicenae had the gift; but generation by generation, the Power has faded. We can still *sometimes* command the weather, cast a curse, lay a blessing, summon a wanderer, ward off illness or other misfortune, make a death gentle. But Innilis alone has the healer's Touch; I alone can make a Sending or call a demon or lure a God or hear the dead when they speak; and these are fugitive dowers, failing us oftener for each year that slips between our fingers. No longer do the Gallicenae teach a little of the ancient arts to each vestal, all to each new-made Queen. For most, that would be knowledge frightening, troublous, and useless. Give wings to a hare and they will but drag her down, make her easy prey for the wolf."

"The eagle's wings lift her!" cried Dahut. "They give her the sky and her quarry."

"Well spoken. I pray we have judged you aright, and you yourself. 'Twill be years until we can tell. This night is the barest beginning."

Forsquilis pointed to the earthworks. "Like most folk, you know this as Lost Castle," she said. "You have heard it was built by the earliest Gauls. It is shunned for no single reason—mutterings of bad luck, ghosts, mermaids who slither up from the depths—though I make no doubt you, Dahut, have explored it on your solitary rambles. Did you ever feel a presence here?"

"I am . . . not sure," the girl whispered.

"Hear what stands in the secret annals, and lock it away in your breast. This was Cargalwen, raised for Targorix, the first of the charioteer kings in our land. Because of a woman, the Old Folk whom he had conquered rose against him. Here on Point Vanis he met them, the sword-hubbed wheels made harvest of them, red rivers twisted down the cliffs to the sea. For a year and a day afterward, the slain lay where they had fallen, and their decay poisoned the air but enriched the soil. When flesh was gone, Targorix had the skeletons laid out on this tip of land, and said that would be the foundation of his stronghold. Human hands did not make it. His druid Vindomarix sang the dwarfs up from below the world and compelled them.

"Mighty for many years were Cargalwen and its lord. But the curse of the Old Folk hounded him. One by one, his sons died. The last and most promising did when he heard a song under the cliffs. He looked, saw a beautiful woman on a rock by the surf, climbed down to meet her, lost footing and fell to his death. Above in the fortress, they heard her laughter ere she vanished beneath the waves. They risked their necks to bring the body back. Crazed with grief, Targorix vowed he would bury the lad himself, in the heart of Cargalwen. Digging, he uncovered a skeleton. An adder nested in the rib cage. It bit him, and so he perished after hours of anguish, on a night of storm when folk thought they heard his soul shriek as it was ripped away.

"The Osismii took new leaders, who made their seat inland. When the Carthaginians arrived, the stronghold lay abandoned. But the earth, the stones, the waters remember.

"Come."

Forsquilis took Dahut by the hand and led her across the ditch, through gaps, over remnants, to the inmost circle. "This will be a long night," the woman said. "Dismiss haste from your spirit. We shall be seeking beyond time."

They sat down cross-legged on the withered grass. Forsquilis turned her face aloft. "Look on high," she said. "See, yonder strides Orion. The Dragon attends the Lodestar. The wheel of heaven is turning, turning, turning. Mount to the Wain, Dahut, enter, be borne down the centuries."

Vision and soul topple into endless deeps aloft.

The moon climbed higher. The witch crooned. Waves clashed and boomed, but as if very distant.

"—Oneness. All is one and one is all. Dream the dreams they dream who are dead."

Frost sends slow shudders through earth. Stones toil upward; on nights yet to come, the stars will shine upon them. Seeds asleep wait for springtime. There is a flicker of aurora in the north, a memory of burnings long ago. Surf rumbles like chariot wheels. A breeze rouses, sighs, seeks lips to kiss.

"What does the night says to you? Nay, tell me not, tell yourself. *Eya, eya, baalech ivoni.*"

Tide turned. The moon stood high and small.

Forsquilis rose. "May the Power be in us," she said. Dahut did likewise, stiff and dazed.

"Join me in the refrain," Forsquilis ordered. "I have taught you."

"I remember it," Dahut said. "Oh, I remember more than ever I knew erenow."

"Beware. Dwell not overmuch on that which comes from Beyond. But you shall feel the Power this night. Together we will summon the wind."

The song lifted. Out there on the headland, it was the loneliest sound in the world. But its undertone was the noise of the slowly retreating sea.

The stars turned, the moon mounted. That breeze which had drifted about began to whistle, ever so faintly. It could have been a melody played on a pipe made from a reed. Haziness blurred the western horizon.

Forsquilis danced while she sang beneath the moon. At first the movements of hands and feet and body undulated like low waves. The music loudened, now and then shrill, as if a gull cried. The swiftening breeze fluttered her cloak. Dahut stood aside near a briar bush, her whiteness limned against remnant walls and the sky. At the end of each strophe, she flung forth her lines: *"—Lords of the elements, Lady of evenstar, Your children evoke you by right of the Blood!—"*

Clouds lifted in the west. The moon dappled their shoulders. The wind could have been a melody played on a pipe made from a dead man's shinbone.

The dance grew violent. Clouds mounted, blotting out constellation after constellation. Moonlight found whitecaps. They burst on rocks with roar, whoosh, and hiss. Stars flickered in the wind.

Forsquilis grew still. "Enough," she said. Weariness flattened her tones. "The Gods are vengeful toward those who overreach themselves. We have learned that you are born to the Power. Let us go home."

Dahut's voice rang wild: "Nay, let me abide, watch, be here!"

Forsquilis regarded her for a long spell by the wan and waning light. Cloaks flapped and snapped. "As you will," Forsquilis said. "As you must, mayhap."

She set forth toward Ys. Dahut crouched down into what shelter was to be had. The storm strengthened.

—When it had overrun heaven, when rain and sleet slashed in on a keening gale while the sea tumbled and bellowed against the cliffs, Dahut stood naked, arms wide, face lifted to the blast, and shouted laughter.

—Dawn stole aloft in the wake of the storm, the late dawn of the Black Months, on the Birthday of Mithras. It was a light the hue of ice, above weather still roiling murky over the eastern hills. Elsewhere, streaks of cloud blew thin; the hunchbacked moon seemed to race among them. The waters raged like metal poured out of a cauldron, molten yet somehow winter-cold. Dahut stood on the highest cliff of Point Vanis and chanted:

"Green the sea and gray the air,
Flood come forth and wind arise:
Green flood, gray flood, windy cloud.
   All the sea is one.

"Blackling sea and silver air:
Clouds churn silver, silver tide,
Gales across the reefy cloud.
   All the sea is one.

"Wracking sea and rushing air,
Spindrift, skydrift, gale and blast,
Soar by spray and dive by cloud—
   All the sea is one.

"Sea is mine and mine is air,
Dark of star and wet of moon.
Wave I fling, I pile the cloud.
   All that's sea is mine."

XVII

1

Tommaltach maqq Donngalii returned to Ys with the springtime. Again he came as a partner in a trading venture, and again more for the sake of the visit than for any profit. It fulfilled his wildest dreams when he was received once more at the palace and, there, Princess Dahut offered to show him about the city on her first free day. His heart bounded. That night he lay sleepless.

She guided him to places he had never thought he would enter. A vestal of the first generation had admittance everywhere. Midafternoon found them atop the Water Tower, otherwise reserved for astronomers and philosophers.

Having looked with much respect at the fixed instruments, he let his gaze wander. To one side the city wall curved away beneath this parapet, behind it the blossoming valley. Nestled close was that red-tiled, colonnaded gem called Star House. Not far off, Elven Gardens lifted green and flowery, a chalice for the still more beautiful Temple of Belisama. Other fanes, together with mansions, graced this half of the city. Busy and stately, Lir Way swept down toward the Forum. Towers gleamed into a nearly cloudless heaven. Beyond sea gate and headlands, waters heaved blue and white, past holy Sena to the edge of vision. Sails were out there, and uncounted wings.

His glance went helplessly back to Dahut. She stood at his side, also looking afar. Air flowed cool, mingling odors of salt and flowers, to press her thin gown against a slenderness more full at bosom and hips than he had seen last year. It ruffled the hair that tumbled over her shoulders. The amber of those waves seemed to take into itself the light spilling from the sun.

He sighed. "Wonderful, wonderful. If only I could stay."

She blessed him with a smile. "You will come back, though," she said. "Often."

He shook his head. His Ysan blundered more than could be accounted for by lack of practice during his months at home. "The Gods alone know when I can. 'Twas all I could do to get leave for this trip."

How lightly her finger passed across his hand, where it gripped the edge of the wall. "You bespoke this not erenow."

"I did not, for I wouldn't be spoiling of the joy. But—my father, my tuath have need of me."

The deep-blue eyes widened. "Say on."

"The Romans advance in Britannia. We cannot be sure what they intend. At the very least, pirates who no longer find good pickings there will turn elsewhere. We must guard our shores. Moreover, King Conual, to whom my father is sworn, means to widen his sway. That will likely call for war. I cannot hang back and keep my honor."

"Oh, poor Tommaltach," she breathed.

He forced a laugh. "Why, glory waits for me, and booty, and many a tale to tell afterward. Will you care to hear my brags?"

"Of course. I will wait so eagerly."

"I too. Dahut," he blurted, "my kinfolk are after me to be marrying. But I'll shy from any such ties—I have hopes—"

Her lashes dipped. "What mean you?"

Hot-faced, he said in a rush, "I may find a way to settle in Ys. A fighting man or, or a merchant factor, or—something. Rufinus promised he'd help. Dahut, when you are free—"

She smiled anew and reached up to lay fingers over his lips. "Hush. I've five more years ahead of me."

"But then—why, Ys might even wish a queen of its own race in Ériu, or—"

Again she silenced him. Her mood darkened. "Speak not of morrows, I pray you."

"Why?"

"They're like yonder seas, when a ship comes in whose pilot knows them not. He must pass through, but he cannot tell what reefs wait beneath." Dahut turned and walked rapidly off. "Come, let's go down."

Gloom and echoes filled the circular stairwell inside the tower. Emerging at its base, youth and girl blinked, as if sunlight were an astonishment. Before them lay Star House. A tall man in a plain gown was about to mount its own stair.

Dahut stiffened, then strode forward. "What do you want, you raven?" she cried.

Corentinus halted. "Why, 'tis you, Princess," he said as mildly as his rough voice allowed. "What a pleasant surprise. And—aye, the skipper from Hivernia that I've heard about. Welcome, friend."

Dahut stopped before him. "Never call us your friends! This place is sacred. How dare you set foot here?"

"Did you not know? There is to be a meeting of the symposium. Your father has finally won for me an invitation to attend."

"Why would he do that?"

Corentinus shrugged. "Well, after ten years I've become somewhat of an institution. And my little flock has grown. The magnates of Ys must needs take us into their reckonings. The philosophers have wisely decided to exchange ideas with me, seeking mutual understanding, as civilized men ought. I seem to have come early. Wait, and the King will arrive. He's ever glad to see you."

Dahut's eyes misted. Her lip trembled. "I don't—want to see him—now," she gulped. "Come, Tommaltach."

She led the Scotian off. Corentinus stared sadly after them.

2

Wonder burst over Aulus Metellus Carsa.

Not only did his father agree, after much argument, that he could remain in Ys until the last voyage back to Burdigala in autumn: his term began shortly before midsummer, when festivities were fountaining. True, the captain gave his son into the care of the chorepiscopus, who was to see that the lad led a sober and godly life, pursuing proper studies and being introduced to just such aspects of the city as would be helpful to know about when developing commercial relations further. However, Corentinus knew what it was like to be young. Besides, one could not build goodwill for the firm if one refused invitations from Ysans who were interested in meeting this Roman—some of which invitations came from the very palace—could one?

And then Dahut asked him to be her steersman!

That happened in the course of the merrymaking which followed the solstice rites. It went on for days. After the Council adjourned, King Gratillonius was free to offer his distinguished guest, Apuleius Vero, his full attention.

Not that entertainment had been lacking. On this, his first visit to Ys, the tribune of Aquilo confessed himself bewildered by the endless marvels offered him. Some were of the Roman kind, banquets, games and races and athletic exhibitions in the amphitheater, performances of music and dance and drama in the odeion; but he exclaimed that everything was finer than he had encountered anywhere else, free of coarseness and brutality, yet tinged with a strangeness that freshened it like a sea wind. Other things he beheld were altogether alien. Certain of them he could admire artistically if not spiritually, such as the pagan temples and processions; certain he must deplore, such as men and women dancing together, or the general boldness of females, or the frequent hostility to Christ. But into much he could enter wholeheartedly—library, observatory, creativeness newly reawakened and breaking free of ancient canons, the Symposium, long private conversations with scholars or the learned Queen Bodilis, whipcrack wit, a sense of pridefulness and hope even among the lowliest, a feeling that the horizon was no longer a boundary.

When he told Gratillonius, the King replied, "Thanks. You don't see the underside of things. But never mind; you can guess what that's like. I'll tell you my troubles later, because maybe we can help each other. Now, though, let's enjoy ourselves. We've earned it."

"Have you something special in mind?" Apuleius inquired.

Gratillonius nodded. "I've decided to revive an old custom. It lay fallow a long time because of pirates and the like, but once it was a big event of the season and there's no reason it can't be again. I mean the yacht race."

Traditionally it had gone from the marine station to Garomagus and back, using boats of a single class. Today both terminals lay in ruins, and such pleasure craft as existed in Ys were wildly varied. Gratillonius had devised new rules. Participants would meet outside the sea gate, on the morning ebb. They would round Point Vanis and steer into Roman Bay. The murdered town would be too melancholy a rendezvous, but a short way past it, where the land bent abruptly north, was a fine broad bench. Small vessels could hug the shore; larger ones must stand farther out before turning east, a distance set by hull length and number of oars available; but those could only be used if it proved impossible to sail.

The balancing was crude. Gratillonius did not pretend that this would be a real contest in seamanship. To emphasize that it was simply sport, he sent people ahead to make a feast ready on the beach. The winning crew would receive their wreaths there and everyone would join in celebration before starting homeward.

"Will you be my steersman?" Dahut asked Carsa at the palace, in her fluent Latin.

"What?" he exclaimed, staggered. "Won't you go with your father?"

She tossed her head. "He won't compete, just preside. Anyhow, in that ship of his, with the high bulwarks, with crew babbling and bumbling, I never feel truly near the sea. He's given me my own boat; but he still forbids me to singlehand it." Candlelight glowed on her countenance, in her eyes. Harp and flute lilted around her voice. "He knows you for a skillful sailor. If I ask him in the right words, he'll agree."

That night Carsa lay sleepless.

3

The boat was a twenty-foot currach on the Scotic model, nimble and seaworthy, light enough for two men to row or one to scull. A small deck forward covered a stowage space and gave on a miniature figurehead, a gilt swan, wings outspread as if straining to be free. Otherwise the leather-clad hull was open, save for a pair of thwarts. The mast had been stepped but was still bare.

The day was lucent, the swells gentle beneath a northwest breeze. Vessels danced. Shouts and trumpet call mingled with the cries of the kittiwakes. Carsa accepted a tow from the royal yacht, which was rowed at the beginning, until safely out to sea. What he bore was immeasurably precious. Nevertheless, once he had cast loose and hoisted the azure-and-argent-striped sail, he had hard navigation. Often he must grip a sheet in either hand while his knees wedged against the tiller to control the steering oar. He gloried in it, for Dahut praised him.

After he turned the promontory, his task became much easier. Poled out, the sail bellied to the wind. The rudder felt like a live, responsive animal as he wielded it to maintain the proper heading. With shallow draft, a currach could scarcely point up, but on a reach such as this it surged along, lee rail low, parallel to a coast which grew gradually less rugged. Water hissed by, swirled in wake, murmured enormously all around. It was blue, blue-green, violet, snowy-foamed. Leather throbbed, frame and lashings creaked, rigging thrummed. A vast curve of land rimmed most of the world, distance-hazed. Boats and small ships filled its embrace. Afar in the west bobbed the dark hulls and drab sails of fishermen at their labor. Seafowl skimmed past. The air blew keen.

Dahut sat on the thwart immediately forward of Carsa. A rough gown and hooded cloak wrapped her. She looked out at him, radiant. "I'm still surprised your father permits this, my lady," he ventured. "It's not without danger."

"Usually I must have two men with me," she answered, "but today we've a whale-pod around us, and I persuaded him to let me . . . travel light, in hopes of winning." She grinned. "Fear not. We'll get another tow on the return trip."

"If we should capsize—"

Her glance ignored the floats kept against that chance. "I swim like a seal," she said haughtily. "I am of the sea." Concern flitted across her face. "You do swim? I never thought to ask."

He nodded. "These are chilly waters for learning how."

"I was born to them."

He sensed that this was no matter to pursue and fell silent, content to have her in his sight.

She said hardly anything more herself. Instead, she fell to staring outward, sometimes into the distances, sometimes into the deeps. Her vivacity had left her. Her could not tell what was rising in its place.

Time streamed past on the wind. The racers laid Ysan land abaft and entered Roman Bay.

Though Carsa used every trick of seamanship that was his, it became clear this craft would not arrive first at the goal. He nerved himself to say it. "I'm sorry, my lady. We should be among the earlier ones." Dahut shrugged. Her gaze stayed remote.

Now he made out the remnant of Garomagus. An islet guarded the mouth of a stream emptying into the bight. Behind it were roofless walls and gaping doorways. The view east, dead ahead, was more comforting, buildings strewn toylike. He could not be sure, though, which were inhabited, and certainly the signs of civilization were few; woods had overrun much of the land. It came to him that most of the clearing and plowing must be reclamation after King Gratillonius had given peace to these parts.

He pointed. "Look!" he cried. "The beach we want. The smoke of the cookfires."

Dahut threw back her cowl—light flared over braided hair—and cocked her head. Was she listening to the waves?

"The wind's fallen," Carsa went on after a while, in search of talk. "That northern headland blocks it. However, we'll have enough to make our goal." Several craft were already clustered there. The larger had dropped anchor and employed tenders to bring their people ashore, the smaller were aground.

Dahut shook herself. She regarded him where he stood in the stern, as if across miles or through sea depths. "Don't." Her voice was faint, but he heard her clearly.

Startled, he let his hand slip on the tiller. The boat yawed, the sail slatted. "What?"

Dahut turned from him to peer starboard. Her finger lifted. "Go yonder," she said.

"To Garomagus?" He was appalled. "No, that's ruins. I can't take you there."

She rose, felinely balanced. While she lacked her full growth, the cloak flapped about her shoulders as if she would take wing, and command flared forth cold as northern lights, in the language of Ys: "Obey! Lir speaks!"

He looked around. No help was in sight. The racers were veering away from him, ardent for landing. Laggards toiled too far aft. Nobody heeded this low little vessel. The King doubtless would have, but his yacht was at the destination.

"Christ help me," he pleaded, "I must not bring you into d-danger, Princess."

She scorned the Name. "I have heard Lir in the wind," she told him. "There is no danger. There is someone I must meet. Steer, or be forever my enemy."

He surrendered, inwardly cursing his weakness. "If you will have it thus," he said in her speech. "We cannot stay long. They'll wonder what's happened to you and come searching."

Her slight smile laved his spirit. "We'll join them in good time. And I'll remember your service, Carsa." Then he shuddered a bit, for she added, "The Gods will remember."

Lest he grow afraid, he devoted himself to sailing. The change of course astounded him, so easily it went; he could not account for it. And how peculiar also, he thought, that nobody whatsoever noticed the currach go astray.

To slip in past the isle looked too risky. Besides, he couldn't expect to find a useable wharf. He grounded on the beach just east. Its shoreline turned north, an outthrust of land hiding it from the Ysans beyond. Having struck the sail, he sprang forward, down onto the sand, and dragged the boat higher. Thereupon he gave Dahut his arm for her disembarkation. She had no real need of that.

Her visage was white, her eyes enormous, she shivered and spoke unevenly: "Wait here. I'll soon be back."

"No," he protested, falling unawares into Latin, "I can't let you go alone. I won't. What is it you're after?"

"I know not," she whispered. "I have been called." Her utterance rose to a yell. She stabbed two fingers at him. "Abide! Let me go by myself! I lay on you the gess that you not follow, by the power of Belisama, Taranis, and almighty Lir!"

Whirling about, she ran off, over the dunes, through the harsh grass that bordered them, past the snags of a defensive wall, in among the houses. She was gone. A cormorant flew black overhead.

Mechanically Carsa reached for the anchor rode and made the currach secure. What else could he do?

What else? It struck him in a hammerblow. She had forgotten that he was no pagan, to cower before the demons she called Gods or heed a word she had merely, childishly laid on him. He was a Roman. Anybody might skulk hereabouts. He *would* follow, and be ready to defend her. He wished he had brought his sling. However, a knife was at his belt, and he got the boathook.

Of course, chances were that this place was quite deserted, apart from ghosts and devils. Best would be that she never know of his disobedience. He'd stay cautious. . . . A haze had begun to dim the day. Wind had swung west and blew louder, colder. He summoned up courage to move forward.

Her trail was clear. Dust and sand had drifted into the streets to take footprints; plants grew to be bruised; her tread had splintered potsherds and displaced brickbats, as his did. He was vaguely glad that tracking kept his mind off what surrounded him. Weather had long since bleached the stains of fire and blood, but likewise colors, every human trace. Lichen was patiently gnawing walls which enclosed vacancy.

He found her at the mouth of the stream. It was an abrupt sight, as he came around a building. A few yards away, she knelt on a patch of silver-gray grass, limned athwart the islet beyond. He crammed himself back against the gritty wall and peered with a single eye. Sounds reached him above the shrilling of wind, mutter of brook and bay, half-heard rolling of Ocean.

She knelt before a seal that had crawled out of the water. Its coat shimmered golden-dark. Her arms were around its neck, her face pressed to its head, hidden from him. He heard her weep. He heard the seal hum, a deep plangency he had not known such a creature could make. A flipper reached to stroke Dahut's locks.

Christ have mercy, to this had the dream-voice called her, she who began the day so blithe. Carsa's knuckles whitened on the boathook shaft. Almost, he dashed to attack the soulless thing and save Dahut.

But she began to sing too. Her tone came thin and small; he was not sure how he made it out through wind and tide and the mewing of the kittiwakes. Somehow he knew that she was turning into Ysan words, for her own understanding, as well as she could in the middle of grief, the song that the seal sang.

"Harken, my darling. Hear me through.
Little I have to tell.
Now at the last I come to you,
To bid you for aye farewell.

"Hear what I say ere I depart,
That which I think you ween.
You were the child beneath my heart.
When I was your father's Queen.

"Torn from my side one winter night
Out in a wrathful sea,
You are the child whose fate takes flight
Beyond what is given me.

"Kiss me, my sea-child, ere we part
As it was long foreseen.
He that shall rip away my heart
Came down from the North yestre'en."

Carsa stole off. At the boat, he prayed to Christ. Presently Dahut returned. Beneath the cowl, her face was blank, a visor. As empty was the voice wherein she told him to launch her craft and bring them to the feast.

4

Osprey had fared under oars to the nets placed out the day before. Those having been tended, the smack sailed back, trawling. Her course brought her past Goat Foreland and across the mouth of Roman Bay. Heaven had drawn a veil across earlier brightness, the sun had gone wan and the air mordant. Then wind, stiffening, swung around until it blew almost straight out of the west.

Maeloch swore. Water chopped gray-green. Whitecaps began to star it. Land lay shadowy at the eastern horizon but rose and grew closer as it bent west; even across five or so leagues he made out the cliffs of Point Vanis, which he must round. Spraddle-legged against the rolling of his deck, he growled, "We'll nay be free of another haul at the sweeps, seems." A fisher captain took his turn on the benches.

A crewman laughed. "Well, nor will yon fine yachtsmen."

"Ah, they've hirelings to sweat for 'em," said another.

"Belay that," Maeloch ordered. "Be ye rabble for Nagon Demari to rant at? The Queens, the King, the Suffetes, they be as much Ys as ye and me. . . . We'll try how far we can beat upwind ere we run out of sea room."

The men moved toward the sheets to haul the sail around. He lifted a hand. "Nay, hold a moment." He went to the port rail and squinted. A swimmer had come in sight, outbound from the bay.

"Seal," declared a sailor. "I'll fetch my sling and give him a taste." The animals were sacred, but they had to be discouraged from raiding fishnets.

"Not that 'un," Maeloch answered. "I know her. D'ye see the golden sheen in her pelt? She be the pet of Princess Dahut." Recalling certain things he had witnessed, he drew the Hammer sign of protection with his forefinger, furtively, lest others notice and go uneasy. He himself did not feel threatened, but this was an uncanny beast.

The seal came alongside. She lifted her upper body out of the waves. Her gaze met Maeloch's and lingered for heartbeats. How soft those eyes were.

She swam onward, falling aft of the boat, heading into the boundlessness of Ocean.

"Fin ho!" bawled a man.

Maeloch ran to the starboard side and leaned out. Breath whistled in between his teeth. He knew that high black triangle, seldom though its bearers came this far south. "Orca," he muttered.

The killer whale veered. Maeloch realized where it was aimed. Did the seal? She swam on as if blind. Not that she could escape that rush—"To oars!" Maeloch shouted. "Bring us around! Ye, Donan, get my harpoon!"

Water foamed with speed. The black shape broke surface. Flukes drove it forward faster than Maeloch knew his craft could ever move. He glimpsed its belly, white as snow, white as death.

It struck. He seemed to feel the shock in his own guts. The mighty jaws sheered and closed. Hunter and prey plunged under.

"Belay," Maeloch said dully. "We'll nay see either of them again."

Blood colored the waves, so broad a stain that he could hope the seal had died instantly.

"Stand by to come about," Maeloch said. "We're going home."

It tore from him, a croak: "How shall I tell the little princess?"

5

"**F**ollow her," Bodilis urged.

Gratillonius hesitated. "She'd fain be alone. I've seen her thus erenow."

Forsquilis shook her head. "Something terrible happened this day. I know not what, but I heard ghosts wailing in the wind."

"Never mind that," said Fennalis. "I can tell when a girl needs her daddy. *Go*, you lout!"

Gratillonius reached decision, nodded, and hastened down the gangplank. Dahut had already passed between two warehouses and disappeared.

The Roman youth Carsa stood forlorn on the dock, staring in that direction. His throat worked. He had debarked at her heels, obviously offering—begging—to accompany her. She dismissed him with a chopping gesture and some or other word that crushed him. Earlier, she had quite neglected him, first at the beach when they joined the rest, afterward aboard the royal yacht when her currach was towed. But then, she had shunned everybody, giving the shortest of answers if directly spoken to, sitting at the trestle table with food untasted before her or wandering off by herself down the strand. The change from her cheeriness of the morning was like a fall into an abyss. It had spoiled the revel for Gratillonius; he must force himself to be jovial.

True, Dahut had always been a being as moody as Armorican weather. The small girl would flare into furies, the maiden would descend into gloom, suddenly, without any cause comprehensible by him. Her mirth and charm returned equally fast. Yet he had never hitherto watched anything like this. He thought that under a rawhide-tight self-control, anguish devoured her. Why?

Such of the Gallicenae as were in the party had withdrawn to the cabin on the way back and conferred. When the ship came to rest in the harbor basin, they had given him their counsel.

He brushed past Carsa—might have to interrogate that boy, but later, later—and those persons ashore who hailed him. Few tried. Ys had learned to let King Grallon be when he strode along iron-faced. Emerging on the street, he looked left and right. Which way? At eventide, folk off to their homes or their pleasures, the quarter was nearly vacant. He couldn't ask if anyone had seen a desolate lass in outdoor garb go by.

Wait. He did not really know his eldest daughter. No one did. She mingled easily when she chose, but always remained private to the point of secretiveness. However . . . she would not have headed left to Skippers' Market and Lir Way, nor struck off into the maze of old streets ahead. Wounded, she would seek solitude. Gratillonius turned right.

Dusk welled up inside the city wall. Foul wind and heavy seas had slowed the passage home. Hurrying along the Ropewalk, Gratillonius glimpsed vessels under construction in the now silent shipyard. Their unplanked ribs might have been the skeletons of whales. At the end he swung right again, to the stairs leading onto the top of the rampart, and mounted them.

His heart stumbled. He had guessed truly. Yonder she was.

She seemed tiny below the Raven Tower. Fragments of mist blew above, blurring sight of its battlements. The lower stones glowed with sunset light. Wind had dropped to a whisper, still sharply cold. Ocean ran strong, bursting and booming where it struck, purple-dark in its outer reaches. There fog banks roiled and moved landward. Sometimes they hid the sinking sun, sometimes its rays struck level through a rift. They turned the vapors gold, amber, sulfur, and cast long unrestful shadows over the waves.

Dahut leaned forth between two merlons, clutching them, to gaze down at furious surf and minute beach between the wall and the upthrust of Cape Rach. The noise rolled hollowly around her.

She heard Gratillonius approach and looked to see who did. Her eyes appeared to fill the countenance that was, O Mithras, like Dahilis's. He halted before her. Words were difficult to find. "I want to help you. Please let me try."

Her lips moved once or twice before she got out: "You can't. Nobody can." He could barely hear her through the sea-thunder.

"Oh, now, be not so sure of that." He smiled, put arms akimbo, rocked on his heels, anything that might make his talk more reassuring. "I'm your old Papa, remember? Your first friend, who—" his voice cracked— "who loves you."

Her glance drifted from him, back to the violence below.

Anger stirred. He knew it was at his own powerlessness, and allowed it only to put metal into his tone, as when he the centurion wanted to know about some trouble among the soldiers. "Dahut. Hear me. You must answer. What happened? Your companion missed his proper landing and the two of you came belated to the feast. They were teasing him about it, and he took it glumly. Did he do aught untoward while you were alone?"

When she made no response, Gratillonius added: "If I must brace him to get the truth, so be it. I'll do whatever proves necessary. For I am the King of Ys."

Then she whirled to confront him. He saw horror on her. "Nay, oh, nay, father! Carsa's been—courteous, helpful—He knows naught, I swear, naught!"

"I wonder about that. I wonder greatly. He's a sailor boy. He should not have made a stupid mistake in steering. He should not have been shaken to his roots merely because you fell into a bad mood. Aye, best that Carsa and I have a little talk."

"Father—" He saw her fight not to weep. "S-stay your hand. I swear to you—by my mother—nothing unlawful happened. I swear it."

He softened his words again: "I'll believe you, sweetling. Yet something has shattered you today. You cannot leave me in the dark. I *am* the King of Ys; and they say you bear our destiny; but 'tis enough that you are my child by Dahilis, Dahilis that I loved beyond all the world, and still love."

He held out his arms. Blindly, she came into them. He hugged her close. Her cheek lay against his breast. His hand stroked her slimness, over and over. He murmured, and slowly her shuddering eased.

"Come," he said at last, "let's go out where we can be by ourselves."

A few others had been astroll on the wall, and there were the marines at the tower. None had ventured nigh, and Gratillonius and Dahut had ignored them, but he knew what probing pierced the misty glow. He took her hand—it nestled in his like a weary bird—and led her by the guards, on past the war engines in their kennels, to the sea gate.

There they must stop, unless they would descend to the warder's walk. Fog smoked in, ever thicker, hooding them from view beyond a few paces. Its yellow grew furnace-hot to westward, where an unseen sun poured forth a final extravagance of light; but the breeze nipped keenly. Below them, at their backs, the harbor glimmered out of murk. At their feet, surf smashed in a smother of white. To the side, surges went to and fro between the doors, sucking and sobbing.

Dahut stared outward. "We can't see Sena," she said raggedly.

"Nay, of course not." He picked his way forward, word by word. "Would you fain?"

She nodded. "That . . . is where I was born, and—mother—"

"I've told you before, and I will again, never blame yourself, darling. She died blessing you. I'm sure she did, blessing you as ever I've since done myself."

"I know. I knew. Until today—"

He waited.

She looked up at him. "Where do the dead go after they must leave us?"

"What?" He was surprised. "Oh, folk have many different beliefs. You, a vestal, you must be more learned than I am about what the wisest in Ys think."

She shook her head. "They only say the Gods apportion our dooms. 'Tis not what I meant. Father, sometimes the dead come back. They are born anew so they can—watch over us— But what happens to them when they die again?"

He called to mind eerie rumors that had reached him over the years. Chill shot along his back and out to his fingertips. "That seal who comes to you—"

"She died. A beast killed her."

"How do you know?" he mumbled.

"*She* knew. She told me. I think the Gods saw that—if she stayed—she'd keep me from—from—I know not what, from something They may want of me— Oh, father, where is she now?"

Dahut cast herself back into the arms of Gratillonius. The tears broke loose. She clawed against him and screamed.

He gripped her and endured.

At length, still an animal hurt and terrified, gone to earth in his bosom, at length she could plead, "Help me, father. Leave me not. Be with me always."

"I will, . . . daughter of Dahilis." He dared inquire no further. Belike he never would, nor she say any more. Yet he felt within himself the strength he had reached for.

"Promise!"

"I do." Gratillonius looked above her tousled head. The sun must have gone under, for hues had drained from the fog and twilight was rapidly thickening. Wind cut through, though, and he spied the battlements of the Raven Tower clear against uneasy heaven, afire with the last radiance of the Unconquered. In a crypt beneath lay his holy of holies. The strength rose higher, defiant of the cruel Gods of Ys.

"I promise," he said. "I will never forsake you, Dahut, beloved, never deny you. By Mithras I swear."

They sought home together.

GALLICENAE

I

Chairs: In the ancient world these were usually reserved for persons of status. Ordinary folk sat on stools, benches, or the floor.

Augustus: At this time there was more than one Roman Emperor. The senior of two was titled "Augustus," his colleague and heir apparent "Caesar." Usually both the Western and Eastern parts of the Empire had such a double monarchy. (Occasionally a given Augustus had two or more Caesars, each responsible for a part of his domains.) Hence the name "Tetrarchy." Evidently Maximus's designation as Augustus amounted to recognition that the Empire had now split into three coequal realms, *de facto* if not quite *de jure.* St. Ambrose, bishop of Milan, had played a leading role in persuading him to settle for that, rather than trying to take over the entire West. In 387 he would break the agreement and invade Italy.

Augusta Treverorum: Trier (Trèves).

Early this year: Maximus made his terms with Valentinian and Theodosius late in 384 or early in 385; the date is uncertain, like the dates of many events in this era.

Africa: North Africa, exclusive of Egypt and Ethiopia.

Illyricum: A Roman diocese (major administrative division) occupying, approximately, most of the territory now comprising Yugoslavia and Greece.

Lugdunum: Lyons.

Burdigala: Bordeaux.

Sign of the Ram, etc: Precessing, the vernal equinox moved from Aries to Pisces about the time of Christ, and by the fourth century was well within the latter. To populations obsessed with astrology, this had an obscure but apocalyptic significance. It may in some degree have aided the initial spread of the Christian religion and (together with the ICHTHYS acronym) influenced the adoption of the fish as a symbol of Christ.

Pagans in high Roman office: Symmachus is best known from this time, but there were numerous others, despite Christianity being now the state religion and attempts made to proscribe all the rest.

Empire: The Roman state still called itself a republic, but had of course long ceased to be any such thing. Nobody took the fiction seriously. So, to avoid confusing modern readers, we have our characters speak the word which was actually in their minds.

Italian Mediolanum: Milan. Several cities bore that name.

Ambrosius: Today known as St. Ambrose.

(Gallia) Aquitania: A province of Gaul, bounded approximately by the Atlantic Ocean and the Garonne and Loire Rivers.

Ahriman: The supreme lord of evil in the Mithraic religion.

II

Tuba: In the Roman world, this was a long, straight trumpet, used especially by the military for commanding, signalling, setting cadence, etc.

Pontus: A Roman diocese, comprising Anatolia.

Hispania: A Roman diocese, comprising what are now Spain and Portugal.

Caledonia: A loose term, referring more or less to what is now Scotland. Cf. the notes to *Roma Mater*.

Juliomagus: Angers.

Namnetes: A tribe occupying the right bank of the Loire from the seashore to its confluence with the Mayenne.

Caesarodunum Turonum: Tours. At this time, those parts of city names that designated local tribes were increasingly displacing those parts the Romans had bestowed. Thus they often became the ancestors of the present-day names.

Laeti: Barbarians allowed to settle within the Empire on condition that they give it allegiance—a proviso observed only loosely, at best.

Jerkin: No such garment is attested until a much later date, but something of the kind must have been in use long before.

Redones: A tribe occupying the area around Rennes.

Maedraeacum: Médréac, a village near which we once spent a pleasant week in a *gîte*. The reconstruction of the ancient name is entirely conjectural, as is the history. However, many such communities did originate as latifundia.

Last Day: Chiliasm was rampant in this era. About 380, St. Martin of

Tours told a disciple that the Antichrist had been born. Countless people, high and low, educated and ignorant, were finding their own portents of the imminent end of the world. Like numerous other features of late West Roman society, this one looks rather familiar to an inhabitant of the late twentieth century.

Organization of the Bacaudae (also spelled *Bagaudae):* Little is recorded about this. A couple of chronicles mention an "emperor," though that word (Latin *imperator)* may there simply have its original meaning of "commander." Since the Bacaudae persisted for a long time and occasionally won pitched battles, they must have had more structure than, say, the medieval Jacquerie. But we can scarcely compare them to modern guerrillas; they lacked both a formalized ideology and the assistance of powerful foreign states. Our guess is that, as more and more individuals fled from an oppressive civilization and then perforce turned about to prey on it, they necessarily and almost blindly developed primitive institutions and a moralistic rationalization of their actions.

Hand to arm: The Roman equivalent of the later handshake.

Martinus: Today known as St. Martin of Tours.

The appearance of St. Martin: At this time there were not yet any particular vestments or other distinguishing marks for the clergy. Indeed, most still earned their livelihoods in ordinary ways and preached in their spare time; many were married; some of the married, when the husband had been ordained, vowed sexual abstention, but not all did by any means. Likewise, tonsures for cenobites were neither standardized nor universal. The kind adopted by St. Martin, which he may have originated, became that of the Celtic Church, eventually superseded by the Roman form with which we today are more familiar. Martin's looks and traits are described by his disciple and biographer Sulpicius Severus.

Martin's elevation to bishop: This story, given us by Sulpicius, is not as incredible as it looks. Ecclesiastical procedures were often *ad hoc,* especially in the provinces, and there are well-attested cases of laymen being called to the episcopate and only then receiving baptism. A full bishop had so much secular importance that ordinary people sometimes demanded a voice in the choosing of him.

Pannonia: A Roman province occupying an area now shared by parts of Hungary, Austria, and Czechoslovakia. Its inhabitants at the time were largely, if not exclusively, Celtic.

Avela (or *Abula):* Ávila.

Ossanuba: Faro, Portugal.

Manicheanism: A religion which was, like Mithraism, of Iranian origin, but if anything more of a threat to Christianity, since it incorporated important elements of the latter. Throughout the centuries, under one name or another, it has been a recurrent heresy. Among other deviations, it attributes creative powers to Satan.

Gates of Trier: In Roman Imperial times there were four of these, of which the Porta Nigra survives as a ruin. Its name is medieval; originally it was not blackened by centuries of smoke.

Mosella: The River Moselle (or Mosel).

Rhenus: The River Rhine.

Bonna: Bonn.

Juthungi: A Germanic tribe living near Raetia.

Raetia (or *Rhaetia):* A Roman province covering, approximately, what is now Bavaria.

Basilica: Originally this word meant an administrative center, civil or military.

The fate of the Priscillianists: Much is uncertain about events surrounding this trial, the historical importance of which includes the fact that it is the first recorded persecution of Christians by other Christians. The dates and the very year are debatable. We have chosen the 385 favored by most scholars and assumed that, because so much had been going on before, the trial took place rather late in that year. Some accounts say the heretics were burned, but it seems likelier that they were beheaded; the stake did not come into vogue until the Middle Ages.

IV

Fortifications: Legionaries on campaign had normally dug a trench and erected an earthwork around every camp, then levelled these upon leaving to keep an enemy from taking them over. By the late fourth century this cannot have been common practice, for the old-style legion was on the way out. We assume that it lasted later in Britain than elsewhere.

Lugdunum (or *Lugudunum):* Lyons. Several other cities bore this name.

Vienna: Vienne. (Wien in Austria, Vienna to speakers of English, was then Vindobona.) Remnants of a Mithraeum, such as are not found in Lyons, suggested that the cult persisted there, though by the time of Gratillonius's visit it had been driven into a private home.

Rhodanus: The River Rhône.

Circus: A space with tiers of seats on three sides, divided lengthwise by a barrier, for races, games, and shows.

Asiatic: By "Asia" the Romans meant what we now call "Asia Minor" or "the Near East."

The Mithraeum in Vienne: As the model for this hypothetical last survivor, we have chosen some that have been excavated in Ostia.

Tauroctony: A depiction of Mithras slaying the primordial Bull.

Rhetoric: Occasionally one sees Classical schools of rhetoric, such as the great one at Bordeaux, referred to as universities. This is anachronistic, but only mildly so. Rhetoric, the study of persuasive argument, embraced not just oratory, but languages, logic, history, literature, and much else. Thus a mastery of it amounted to a liberal education.

Garumna: The River Garonne.

Paulinus: Ausonius's grandson grew up into kind of life that the old man envisioned, but it was shattered by the arrival of the Visigoths and other calamities.

Duranius: The River Dordogne.

V

Mumu: Munster. The boundaries were probably less definite than in later times. Its association with women, musicians, and magic was ancient, and persisted into the Middle Ages.

Ériu: Ireland.

Children of Danu: Best known by a later name, the Tuatha Dé Danaan. According to legend, this race, the tuaths (only approximately equivalent to tribes; see the notes to *Roma Mater)* descended from the goddess Danu, held Ireland before the Milesians arrived from Spain. Overcome by the invaders, they retreated to the *síd,* mounds and hills whose interiors they made their dwellings. They themselves became the fairy folk. Most modern commentators think they are a Christian euhemerization of the pagan gods, and doubtless there is much truth in this view. However, the tradition of a war between them and the newcomers is so basic to Irish mythology that it must have some foundation in fact. Successive Celtic peoples did enter, taking land by force of arms. Our guess is that one or more of the earlier peoples, to whom their conquerors attributed magical powers, became conflated with the old gods, but that this had not yet happened at the time of our story.

Children of Ír and Éber: Later called the Milesians; tradition makes them the last invaders of Ireland before the Vikings.

The Mountain of Fair Women: Now Slievenamon, southwest of Cashel.

Síd (or *sídh): * Singular of *sídhe.* Both are pronounced, approximately, "shee."

Condacht: Connaught.

Qóiqet Lagini: Leinster.

The Ulati: The people of Ulster *(Qóiqet nUlat).* It should be remembered that the boundaries of all these territories were vague, and generally not identical with those of the modern provinces.

Trade between Munster and the Romans: This has been archeologically proven.

Christianity: The histories indicate that there was already an established and growing body of Christians in Munster, if not elsewhere in Ireland. For one thing, Palladius was sent to minister to them; and other bishops are mentioned, together with Irish clergymen serving on the Continent—all before the mission of St. Patrick.

Conual Corcc (today usually rendered as *Conall Corc):* His dates are still more uncertain than Niall's, and the stories about him that have come down to us are even more confused and contradictory. In both cases, we have tried to put together versions that make some logical sense.

Fostering: Children in ancient Ireland, at least among the upper classes, more often than not were raised in other homes than their parents'. The ties thus created between families were as sacred as those of blood kinship.

Alba: The early Irish name for what is now, more or less, Scotland. Sometimes "Alba" also included England and Wales. The name "Scotland" comes from its heavy colonization by Scoti, i.e. people from Ireland —just as Armorica was to become Brittany (Breizh, in its own language) after immigrants from Britain took it over. At the time of our story, the Scotic settlement amounted largely to an extension, into what is now Argyll, of the kingdom of Dál Riata, in what is now northern Antrim. (Some authorities put its founding as late as 500 A.D., but the event would have become possible soon after the Romans abandoned the Antonine Wall toward the end of the second century, and a date in the middle fourth century is consistent with other assumptions we have made for story purposes.) However, a king from Mide, adventuring in Alba, could well have defeated a Pictish leader and imposed an alliance in which the latter was a junior partner.

The ogamm (today *ogham) shield:* This is evidently a Celtic form of an ancient and widespread story. Quite possibly the vikings, in their day, brought it back to Denmark from Ireland. "Hamlet"—"Amleth (us)" in Saxo Grammaticus, Shakespeare's ultimate source—is not a name otherwise found; one scholar has suggested that it may be a Scandinavian reading of the Gaelic spelling of the Nordic "Olaf"! Ogham was a very primitive and limited form of writing, so to alter it would not have been difficult.

Ordovices and Silures: Tribes inhabiting what is now Wales.

VI

Éndae Qennsalach: Perhaps historical, perhaps not. The second half of his name refers to his ancestry.

Founding of Mide: This is the legendary version. See the notes to *Roma Mater.*

Origin of the Bóruma: This is also a legend, of course, but one which people of Niall's time may well have believed. The tribute itself and its evil consequences are historical fact.

Niall's warfare: The sources say nothing specific; but given our story assumptions, campaigns like these are plausible.

Ruirthech: The River Liffey. Then it seems to have marked the northern frontier of Leinster.

Chariots: Roman tactics had long since made the military chariot obsolete, but it persisted in Ireland, where it did not have to face well-drilled infantry and cavalry, until past our time. As for other equipment, see the notes to *Roma Mater.*

Niall's two queens: Not only concubinage but polygyny was accepted in ancient Ireland, even after the conversion to Christianity. (For a while canon law decreed that a *priest* could have only one wife!) The chronicles say that Niall had fourteen sons by two wives, whom we suppose to have been more or less contemporaneous. Surely he had daughters too, and children by other women.

Nobles and tenants: For a brief description of the classes *flaith, soer-céli,* and *does-céli,* see the notes to *Roma Mater.*

Combat tactics: Like the equipment, these too were little changed in Ireland from the old Celtic forms.

Lifting a knee: Stools and tables were very low. To rise when a visitor appeared was a token of full respect. Short of this, though still polite, was to raise a knee, as if about to get up.

Verse: Like Nordic skalds of a later date, early Irish poets used intricate forms, yet were expected to be able to compose within those forms on a moment's notice. Our rendition here is a much simplified version of one scheme. Each stanza, expressing a complete thought, consists of four seven-syllabled lines. Besides the alliteration and rhyme, it is required that end-words of the second and fourth lines have one more syllable than those of the first and third. Oral skill such as this is entirely possible and historically attested. The poet naturally had to have an innate gift together with long and arduous training.

Satire: The Celtic peoples were great believers in word magic. Well into Christian times, satirists were dreaded in Ireland. To a modern mind, it is not implausible that they could bring on psychosomatic disorders, even wasting illness. Our story supposes their powers went beyond that.

VII

Odita: The River Odet. (Our Latin name is conjectural.) The distances mentioned have been rounded off, as they would be in the mind of any ordinary traveler. It should be noted that this stream was deeper then than it is now, when impoundments in the watershed have diminished its sources.

Stegir: The River Steir. (This is also conjectural on our part.)

Aquilo: Locmaria, now a district at the south end of Quimper. While the existence of Roman Aquilo is attested, our history and description of it are still more conjecture.

Mons Ferruginus: Mont Frugy. More conjecture, this time based on the fact that there is iron ore in the area.

Durocotorum: Rheims.

Apuleius Vero: The ancient tripartite system of nomenclature had long since broken down. Some people still employed it, but others, in the upper classes, did not. "Vero" is a hypothetical Gallo-Roman name commemorating the family's most important connection of that kind. "Apuleius," the old *gens* name, now went from father to eldest son, much as the same given and middle names may pass through several generations in our own era. Upon succeeding to the paternal estate, this Apuleius dropped whatever other names he had borne, if any. In this as in several more significant respects, he typifies a man of his time, place, and station in life. More provincial and thus more conservative, the Gratillonii of Britain clung to traditional usages.

The Duke of the Armorican Tract: The Roman military official in charge of defense of the entire area. (This is a shortened version of the actual title, such as we suppose people employed in everyday speech.) Armorica was, in fact, considered a military district, not a political entity. Ravages along the coasts indicate that at this time the Duke's efforts were concentrated in the east and the interior of the peninsula. This was doubtless because resources were limited and, terrible though the depredations of pirates often were, they seemed less of a threat than a possible Germanic invasion overland. Gaul had already suffered the latter, again and again, and sometimes the Romans had managed only barely and slowly to drive the barbarians back. Under such circumstances, the Duke might be glad to delegate authority in the west to some competent leader. Our idea that this particular Duke was covertly opposed to Maximus is a guess—nothing is known for certain—but not unreasonable.

Troops: Increasingly, locally recruited soldiers were providing garrisons such as here described. Not being attached to any legion, they were known as *numeri* or *cunei* rather than auxiliaries. Civilian men, *limitanei,* were being made into reservists. These processes had gone much further in the Eastern half of the Empire than they had, as yet, in the West.

The Pulcher villa: Baths, such as would have belonged to a substantial estate, have been excavated at Poulker (near Benodet). The form of this place name is unusual in Brittany. However, we only venture a guess as to its possible origin.

The defenses of Aquilo: Our idea of what these may have amounted to is based on the lack of archeological evidence for anything else. Actually, the Gallic wall was a good, solid structure.

Corentinus: Known in France at the present day as St. Corentin. His historicity is uncertain, but there are many legends about him, including that of the miracle of the fish and his later career as the first bishop of Quimper. For reasons discussed in the Afterword to the last of these volumes, we have conflated him with the equally enigmatic figure of St. Guénolé.

Smoke: As we remarked in the notes to *Roma Mater,* primitive Celtic dwellings neither needed nor had vent holes for smoke. It filtered out through the thatch, killing vermin along the way.

Pictavum: Poitiers.

Pomoerium: The space kept clear just inside and outside a defensive wall.

Consecration of the Mithraeum: Our description of this draws in part on our imaginations, but largely on the ideas of such authorities as Cumont, Stewardson, and Saunders.

Pater and Heliodromos: Father and Runner (or Courier) of the Sun, the first and second degrees of a Mithraic congregation. Although knowledge of this religion is, today, fragmentary, what we do possess shows its many resemblances to Christianity, not only in belief but in liturgy, organization, and requirements laid upon the faithful.

VIII

Lugdunensis Tertia: The Roman province comprising northwestern France.

Church buildings: Most were quite small. The one here described we envision as being about the size of a fairly large present-day house. However, as will be seen later in the story, Gratillonius is mistaken in his impression that this is the cathedral.

Samarobriva: Amiens.

St. Martin as a military physician: This is not in the chronicles, but some modern biographers think it is probable.

Exorcists: In this era, such priests were not specifically charged with driving out demons, but simply with the supervision of the energumens and similar duties.

The service: Obviously this was very different from today's ritual. It varied from place to place; what we have sketched was the so-called Gallic Mass. Strictly speaking, though, the Mass was the Communion service, reserved for the baptized.

Biblical texts: Respectively Amos xviii, 8, I Corinthians ii, 4, and Matthew xviii, 8.

Martin and the bishops: His refusal to attend any synods after the Priscillian affair is attested.

Greater Monastery: Majus Monasterium, which probably is the origin of the place name "Marmoutier," although some scholars derive it from "Martin."

Chorepiscopus: The powers granted priests in the early Church were very limited. A chorepiscopus, "country bishop," ranked above them but below a full bishop. He had most of the powers later given a parish priest, but not all. See the notes to *Roma Mater.*

Paenula: A poncho-like outer garment. From everyday garb of this period and later derived the priestly vestments of the Church. The paenula became the chasuble.

Cernunnos: An ancient Gallic god.

IX

Sarmatian: What people the Classical geographers meant by this name is obscure, and evidently varied over the centuries. To Corentinus, we suppose, the word would designate one of those Slavic tribes that were drifting into what is now Poland and Prussia as the Germanic inhabitants moved elsewhere.

Suebian Sea: The Baltic *(Mare Suebicum)*.

Cimbrian Chersonese: Jutland. The Heruls, whom tradition says once inhabited the adjacent islands, had by now migrated south, and the Danes were moving in from what is now Sweden. Jutes and Angles were still at home, although soon many of them would be among the invaders of Britain.

Franks: This word *(Franci)* was a generic Roman term for Germanic tribes originating north of the River Main and along the North Sea, Moving into Gaul, they eventually gave that name to the entire country of France. Our account of their pagan religious practices draws on descriptions from other times and places; but it seems plausible to us. Whatever the details, we have scarcely exaggerated the brutality of the Franks. It was notorious. Even after they had become Christian, the history of the early Merovingians is a catalogue of horrors.

Cataphract: A heavy cavalryman.

Aquileia: Near present-day Trieste.

Death of Maximus and Victor: Authorities disagree on the precise date and manner of this, but it occurred in the summer of 388.

XI

The defeat of Maximus: According to one source, only two Romans died at Aquileia, Maximus and Victor. This implies that both armies were composed entirely of barbarian mercenaries, which seems to us unlikely in the extreme. Surely Maximus, at least, would have needed legionaries to drive Valentinian out of Italy, and then, lacking effective cavalry such as Theodosius possessed, would have brought them to meet the latter.

Maximus's veterans: There is a tradition that they were settled in Armorica, and some modern historians consider it plausible. If this did happen, then doubtless the involuntary colonists included certain of the troops Maximus had left behind in Gaul, though probably only those whose loyalty to the re-established Imperium of the West was very questionable.

The gravestone: Roman epitaphs, especially when military, were generally short and employed abbreviations. Expanded and translated, this one reads TO QUINTUS JUNIUS EPPILLUS / OPTIO (deputy) IN THE SECOND LEGION AUGUSTA / HIS FELLOW SOLDIERS MADE THIS.

XII

Thracia: Thrace, occupying approximately what is now the northeastern end of Greece, the northwestern end of Turkey, and southern Bulgaria.

Saxons in Britain: There is good evidence for some colonization, as well as piracy, by these barbarians as early as the later fourth century. Be that as it may, Stilicho had hard fights against them.

Silures: The British tribe inhabiting what is now, more or less, Glamorganshire and Monmouth.

Sucat (or *Succat):* Birth name of St. Patrick. As nearly as possible, we follow traditional accounts of him, including that interpretation of them which makes the year of his capture, rather than his birth, 389. It must be added that a number of modern scholars have called into question all the dates and other details of his story; some actually challenge his historicity. His appearance before Niall is our own idea. Even tradition does not make clear where he passed his time of servitude. Somewhat arbitrarily, we adopt the suggestion that it was in County Mayo.

Cú Culanni: Today better known as Cuchulainn, the greatest hero of the Ulster cycle. His king, Conchobar, was said by medieval writers to have died of fury at hearing that Christ had been crucified, though he himself was a pagan. This at least gives some hint at the time that tradition assigned to these sagas.

Emain Macha: The ancient seat of the supreme Ulster kings, near present-day Armagh. The Red Branch (more accurately, but hardly ever, rendered as Royal Branch) was the lodge where their chief warriors met.

Fifth: For the ancient division of Ireland into five parts, autonomous if not exactly nation-states, see the notes to *Roma Mater.*

Qóiqet nUlat: The Fifth of the Ulati people.

Cruthini and Firi Bolg: There were Picts (whom the Irish called Cruthini) in Ireland as well as in Scotland-to-be—and, for that matter, in northern Gaul. As we have noted earlier, they were not at all the dwarfs of modern folklore, nor backward with respect to the Gaels; however, they were a distinct people. The Firi Bolg were, in legend, the first colonists of Ireland, subjugated by the invading Children of Danu. Perhaps this tale embodies a dim folk memory of an aboriginal population whom the first wave or waves of incoming Celts overran and intermarried with. If so, pride of ancestry persisted well into historical times; and to this day, there do appear to be at least two racial types native to the country.

Conduct of the Ulati: Tradition does not say that the upper classes in Ulster were especially oppressive. However, the Uí Néill seem to have had little difficulty in keeping the Aregésla (or Airgialla), about whom more later, a puppet power. This has given some modern writers the idea that a malcontent population was present in the first place—a suggestion we have followed. Granted, at worst the yoke would have been far lighter than that upon the peoples of the Roman Empire or, for that matter, virtually everybody today. The Irish aristocrats were not saints or libertarians, but they lacked the apparatus available to organized governments.

Starving: Among the early Irish, a man who had a grievance against one more powerful, and could not otherwise get redress, often sat down at the door of the latter and fasted. If this did not shame the second party into making a settlement, then he too was expected to deny himself food, and it became an endurance contest.

Sinand: The River Shannon. The territory we have described Niall as taking includes present-day County Cavan and part of Monaghan. Of course, our depiction of events is purely conjectural, and some modern scholars deny that it could have happened this way at all.

Mag Slecht: The "Plain of Prostrations," in County Cavan, where stood the idols of Cromb Cróche (or Crom Cruach) and his twelve attendants. The chronicles say these were the most powerful and revered gods in Ireland until St. Patrick overthrew them.

The lunar eclipse: This took place on 13 July 390 (Gregorian calendar).

The comet of 390: It is recorded as having been visible from 22 August to 17 September (Gregorian dates). The magnitude is not known, but it was presumably conspicuous.

Polaris: Prior to the development of elevators, locations in a tall building were less desirable the farther up they were. Structures of this height were forbidden in Rome as being too hazardous, but we suppose the Ysans had more confidence in their architects, and knew how to make self-bracing frameworks.

Corentinus's sermon: Few if any Christians of this period denied the reality of pagan gods. Sometimes they were considered to be mere euhemerizations, but oftener demons or, at best, beings with certain powers and perhaps without evil intentions, to whom it was nevertheless wrong to pay divine honors.

XIII

Lúgnassat (later *Lugnasad):* A harvest festival taking its name from the god Lúg. In Christian times it occurred on 1 August. The English know it as Lammas, though that name has another derivation. Lacking the Roman calendar, the pagan Celts must have set the date some other way; we guess that the moon helped determine it.

Fairs: The ancient Irish held a number of such events, at various localities, each year. Religious as well as secular, they were open to all.

Cromb Cróche and the death of Domnuald: Our description of the sanctuary and the ceremonies that took place there is conjectural, though based on the chronicles, on local traditions in the area said to have held it, and on similar things in other milieus. Domnuald and his fate are imaginary, but the story does go that the slaying of a son of his made Niall ready to kill the hostages he had from the folk of the murderers.

Éricc (later *eraic):* Akin to the Teutonic weregild, a payment to an injured party or his heirs, the amount depending on the actual harm done and the possible provocation.

Honor price: Unlike the Germanic peoples, the Irish made some effort to equalize justice between rich and poor. A man of rank, who owed an éricc, must pay in addition an amount of goods which increased with his social standing.

Tallten: Now Teltown, on the River Blackwater in County Meath. Our description of the size and importance of the fair *(óenach)* there is not exaggerated; like its counterparts, it continued for centuries after Ireland became Christian, so reliable records exist. That an eponymous goddess should have been buried at the site is not unique. For example, though the Nordic god Baldr died in the early days of the world, he seems to have had a cult.

The Dagdae (later *Dagda):* A god especially wise. His well is our invention.

Mag Mell: The Plain of Honey, one of the paradises that Celtic myth located afar in the western ocean. Sometimes the name was applied to all of them together. The Celts do not appear to have had any clear or consistent ideas about an afterlife. There are mentions of favored persons whose souls were borne west to abide a while before returning and being reincarnated. Probably the most usual supposition was that the dead inhabited their graves, coming out to spook around on the eves of Beltene and Samain.

Irish arts and crafts: The glorious works that remain to us prove that, for all its violence and technological backwardness, this society had as keen a sense for beauty as ever the Greeks did.

Expulsion of the Irish from Wales: This is attested.

Eóganachta: The royal family, or rather set of families claiming a common ancestor, in Munster.

Tanist: The heir apparent of an Irish king, chosen well beforehand. It was doubtless done in the hope of an orderly succession. Any man with royal blood and no physical impairment, whether born in or out of wedlock, could become king if he had the power to enforce his claim. This could easily lead to war between rival pretenders. The laws and institutions of Rome had decayed so far that the Empire must needs invent something of the kind for itself, the Caesar associated with the Augustus.

Nath Í: Tradition says that this nephew of Niall succeeded him. The medieval account of his career creates so many chronological problems that several modern scholars have decided he must be purely fictional and that Niall—if he himself ever lived—should be dated a generation later than he is in the chronicles. It may be; or it may not. Given all the uncertainties, we have felt free to stay with the tradition, which better fits our story, and to put in modifications or new material of our own. The contradictions in the sources *could* mainly be due to their authors, drawing on oral history handed down for lifetimes, getting different persons and their acts confused with each other.

The Walls of the Ulati: Known as the Black Pig's Dyke, remnants of ancient fortifications—earthen walls and fosses—occur approximately along the southern boundary of Ulster. They may have been raised in imitation of Roman works, or they may be older than that. They were probably not a continuous line of defense, but rather a set of strongpoints for controlling movement along the main routes of travel. Elsewhere, forest, bog, and other natural obstacles would have sufficiently hindered invaders or retreating cattle rustlers.

Commandments and prohibitions laid on royal persons: Those mentioned here are in the annals. A taboo applying to an individual or a class of people was known as a *gess* (later *geas*), plural *gessa*.

The redemption of the hostages: This is in the tradition, though it does not state where they were from. We have put the incident just after Lúgnassat, partly so we could describe a little of the fair, partly because the chronicles say that the Rock of Cashel was revealed "when the leaves were yellow," which must have been in autumn.

Darioritum: Vannes.

Tambilis and Gratillonius: Most peoples, including our own until recent times, have considered a girl of sixteen to be nubile.

Veneti: A tribe in southern Brittany. Under the Empire, tribes had no independence and their identities gradually eroded, but they did constitute units of local government, not totally unlike American states.

XIV

The Síd Drommen (or *Sídhe-Druimm*): This is one of several names the great rock originally bore. They all suggest the supernatural.

The finding of Cashel: We have tried to synthesize the legends, omitting Christian elements that the chroniclers inserted. There are enough pagan ones. Swine were anciently associated with the dead, which may be why kings could not own them. The yew, one of the three trees the Irish held sacred (together with the hazel and the rowan), was a patron of the Eóganachta; the name of their ancestor, Eógan, means "yew." At his ceremony of accession, a new king always stood on a flagstone *(lecc)*.

The career of Conual: It is not known when or how Cashel and the kingdom that grew from it were actually founded. We have followed tradition as far as possible, including parts that some modern scholars hold to be purely mythical. For example, Byrne considers Conual's second wife, Ámend, a humanized sun goddess, daughter of the lightning (Bolg). That may be. Yet it seems quite plausible that Conual made a political marriage, and that his early successes were in large part due to the awe inspired by the seemingly supernatural circumstances of his advent—circumstances that may have been accidental or may have been engineered, but that he, who had been exposed to Roman civilization, was quick to take advantage of. Some authorities suggest that he was a Christian. We suppose not, if only because the chronicles declare that his grandson was the first king of Cashel to take the Faith, and the tale of that baptism by St. Patrick is too delightful to give up willingly. Hardly any historian disputes that a Roman-style fortress was erected on the outcrop sometime in the late fourth or early fifth century; that the name Cassel, later Caisel, now Cashel, derives from Latin *castellum,* meaning such a stronghold; and that from this nucleus developed the kingdom of Munster. Eventually deeded to the Church, the rock became an important ecclesiastical site.

Aregésla (later *Airgialla):* Occupying, approximately, what are now Counties Monaghan, Cavan, and Leitrim, this kingdom does appear to have been established as a puppet of Niall or his sons. Our account of the founding is conjectural. Giving local chieftains authority over the rites at Mag Slecht would not have debarred the kings of Tara from that ready access to Crom Cruach which the legend of St. Patrick says they had.

Niall of the Nine Hostages: By this name is the ancestor of the Uí Néill dynasties known to history. Just when or how he got the sobriquet is unknown. At any given time, any king of importance surely held more than nine individual hostages. Hence the reference must be to some who were especially significant. According to one chronicle, Niall had them from each of the Fifths of Ireland, and four from Britain; according to another, besides the five Irish, they were from Scotland (the Picts), the Britons, the Saxons, and the Franks. This makes little or no sense. For once we go along with modern commentators and suppose that the nine were of the Aregésla, whose establishment as subordinate allies marked a turning part in the destiny of the Uí Néill.

The hallowing of the newborn: There is no reason why a healthy woman who has given birth should not get up and walk about, at least for fairly short distances, a few hours later.

Niall Náegéslach (later *Noígiallach*): Niall of the Nine Hostages. It is our conjecture that he took advantage of Stilicho's departure to ravage Britain and so assert his power in the face of Conual Corcc's spectacular successes. It squares with the tradition. Certainly Scotic raids increased about this time.

The Loígis: Presumably this set of tribes gave their name to present-day County Laoighis; but the sources indicate that they held the western frontiers of Leinster as far down as the sea.

Ossraige: A kingdom occupying the western parts of what are now Counties Laoighis and Kilkenny. Apparently it had a subordinate relation to the Leinster high kings, somewhat like that of the Aregésla to the Uí Néill.

The origin of the Lagini: We repeat the legends.

Dún Alinni: Near present-day Kildare.

Fomóri: A legendary race who harassed the Firi Bolg in ancient times and whom the Children of Danu expelled.

Eochaid's raid: This, and its aftermath, are traditional tales, though of course we have filled in many details as best we could.

XV

Menstrual pad: Today's convenient sanitary napkins and tampons are quite a recent development, but people have always had the problem to cope with as best they could, and we may suppose the upper-class Ysan women had arrangements available to them that were better than most.

Vervain: Now more commonly known as verbena. Both the Romans and the Gauls credited it with numerous wonderful properties.

Irish gold: The country was rich in this metal, though in the course of centuries the sources would be exhausted.

Praetorian prefect: For some discussion of this high office, see the notes to *Roma Mater.*

Salomon: A form of the name closer to the original than "Solomon" and still common on the Continent. The early Church made little use of the Old Testament, except for a few lyrical and prophetic parts, so it is natural that Gratillonius would be ignorant of ancient Jewish history, while a scholarly sort like Apuleius could be well versed in it.

XVI

Carsa: Another conjectural family name. We fancy that it could relate to Carsac, a village in the Dordogne where we have spent pleasant days.

Cadurci: A Gallic tribe inhabiting the Dordogne.

The Armorican run: Archeological evidence shows that commerce was still going on between southern France and Brittany.

The shipping season: In the ancient world, this was generally from April through October. The virtual cessation of maritime traffic in the winter was less for fear of storms—most ships were quite seaworthy—than because weather made navigation difficult.

Tonnage: Mediterranean grain ships had burdens of up to 1200 tons. Ocean-going vessels were doubtless smaller, but not too much so. A typical merchantman is described in *Roma Mater.*

Speed: Merchantmen could do four or five knots under good conditions. They could point up to the wind to a limited extent and lie hove to, after a fashion, when that was the prudent thing to do.

Periplus: A set of sailing directions for a given route, describing landmarks, hazards, etc. Maps were so crude as to be virtually useless to navigators.

Clerestory: Not Roman; but we suppose there was some Egyptian influence on Ysan architecture.

Sucat and Martin: Again we are forced to select from among the often contradictory stories about St. Patrick; but we have invented essentially nothing. He may actually have been an Armorican rather than a Briton, and he may have been born as late as 389. However, this would probably rule out the kinship to St. Martin which tradition gives him, and certainly the story that he became a disciple of the latter. His career after escape from captivity is obscure in the extreme. The reconstruction that we employ has him come to Marmoutier in 396, seeking holy orders, and live there until the bishop's death, after which he went south to pursue his studies and devotions.

Banaventa (or *Bannauenta* or other variants): Mentioned in Patrick's *Confessions* (which some modern scholars consider spurious), this may have been Daventry, but may also have been one of three places in Glamorganshire called Banwent; we assume the latter. It is described as the home of his mother's parents, whom he was visiting when the raiders struck, but this does not seem to square with the claim that she was Martin's niece, so we follow the school of thought that makes Banaventa his father's and his own dwelling place.

Sucat's future: He spent many years on the Continent. Legend declares that Pope Celestine, in consecrating him for his mission, gave him the new name Patricius—now Patrick. There is reason to think he may have assumed it himself and, indeed, even consecrated himself a bishop. The traditional date for his return to Ireland is 432, for his death 461. Thus he, like Martin, had a long life, active until the very end.

XVII

Garomagus: Our conjectural name for a Roman town that, archeology has revealed, existed on the site of present-day Douarnenez. In fact, the entire littoral of the bay there was reasonably populous and prosperous in the heyday of the Empire. Local tradition makes the city Douarnenez the seat of legendary King Mark, and the islet bears the name of his nephew Tristan. This suggests that the area has ancient magical associations.

Roman Bay: Baie de Douarnenez. This is the Ysan name; what the Romans called it is not known.

Goat Foreland: Cap de la Chèvre. We are supposing that a name Gallic or even older has kept the same meaning though languages have changed—unless the identity is coincidental.

Geographical Glossary

These equivalents are for the most part only approximations. For further details, see the Notes.

Abona: Sea Mills.

Abonae: The River Avon in Somerset.

Africa: North Africa, exclusive of Egypt and Ethiopia.

Alba: Scotic name of what is now Scotland, sometimes including England and Wales.

Aquae Sulis: Bath.

Aquitania: See *Gallia Aquitania*.

Aregésla: Counties Monaghan, Cavan, and Leitrim in Ireland.

Arelate: Arles.

Armorica: Brittany.

Asia: Asia Minor.

Audiarna: Audierne (hypothetical).

Augusta Treverorum: Trier.

Avela: Ávila.

Banaventa: Banwent (?).

Bay of Aquitania (Sinus Aquitanicus): The Bay of Biscay.

Boand's River: The River Boyne.

Bonna: Bonn.

Borcovicium: Housesteads, at Hadrian's Wall.

Bridge of Sena: Pont de Sein.

Britannia: The Roman part of Britain, essentially England and Wales.

Britannic Sea (Oceanus Britannicus): The English Channel.

Burdigala: Bordeaux.

Caesarodunum Turonum: Tours.

Caledonia: Roman name of Scotland.

Campani: A district of Italy including modern Capua and Naples.

Cape Rach: Pointe du Raz (hypothetical).

Cassel: Cashel.

Castellum: Original form of "Cassel."

Cenabum: Orléans.

Cimbrian Chersonese: Jutland.

Clón Tarui: Clontarf, now a district of Dublin.

Condacht: Connaught.

Condate Redonum: Rennes.

Condevincum: A small city, now part of Nantes.

Confluentes: Quimper (hypothetical).

Corbilo: St. Nazaire.

Dalmatia: A province occupying, approximately, what is now much of Yugoslavia.

Dál Riata: A realm in Ulster, or its colony on the Argyll coast.

Danastris: The River Dniester.

Danuvius: The River Danube.

Darioritum Venetorum: Vannes.

Deva: Chester.

Dochaldun: An Osismiic village (imaginary).

Dubris: Dover.

Dún Alinni: Near present-day Kildare.

Duranius: The River Dordogne.

Durocotorum: Rheims.

Emain Macha: Seat of the principal Ulster Kings, near present-day Armagh.

Ériu: Ireland.

Etruria: Tuscany and northern Latium.

Euxinus: The Black Sea.

Falernia: An area in Campani, noted for wine.

Fanum Martis: Corseul.

Gallia: Gaul, including France and parts of Belgium, Germany, and Switzerland.

Gallia Aquitania: A province of Gaul, bounded approximately by the Atlantic Ocean and the Garonne and Loire Rivers.

Gallia Lugdunensis: A province of Gaul, comprising most of what is now northern and a fair portion of central France.

Gallia Narbonensis: A province comprising Narbonne and its hinterland.

Garomagus: A town at or near present-day Douarnenez (hypothetical).

Garumna: The River Garonne.

German Sea (Oceanus Germanicus):   The North Sea.

Gesocribate: Brest (?).

Gesoriacum: Boulogne.

Goana: The River Goyen (hypothetical).

Goat Foreland: Cap de la Chèvre (hypothetical).

Gobaean Promontory (Promontorium Gobaeum):   Cap Sizun.

Hispania: Spain and Portugal.

Hispania Tarraconensis: A province in northeastern and eastern Spain.

Histria: The area around what is now Trieste.

Hivernia: Roman name of Ireland.

Icenia: Norfolk and Suffolk.

Illyricum: A Roman diocese (major administrative division) occupying, approximately, most of what is now Yugoslavia and Greece.

Ingena: Avranches.

Isca Silurum: Caerleon.

Islands of Crows: The Channel Islands (hypothetical nickname).

Juliomagus: Angers.

Lemovicium: Limoges.

Liger: The River Loire.

Liguria: A region of Italy including Lombardy and present-day Liguria.

Londinium: London (in part).

Lugdunensis: See *Gallia Lugdunensis*.

Lugdunensis Tertia: The Roman province comprising northwestern France.

Lugdunum: Lyons.

Luguvallium: Carlisle.

Lutetia Parisiorum: Paris (in part).

Maedraeacum: Médréac (hypothetical).

Mag Slecht: A pagan cult site in present-day County Cavan, Ireland.

Maia: Bowness.

Massilia: Marseilles.

Mauretania: Northern Morocco.

Mediolanum: Milan.

Mide: A realm occupying present-day Counties Meath, Westmeath, and Longford, with parts of Kildare and Offaly, Ireland.

Mons Ferruginus: Mont Frugy (hypothetical).

Mosella: The River Moselle (or Mosel).

Mumu: Munster.

Namnetum: See *Portus Namnetum*.

Narbonensis: See *Gallia Narbonensis*.

Neapolis: Naples.

Nemetacum: Arras.

Odita: The River Odet (hypothetical).

Osismia: The country of the Osismii, in western Brittany.

Osismiis: Later name of Vorgium (q.v.).

Ossanuba: Faro, Portugal.

Ossraige: A realm occupying the western parts of Counties Laoighis and Kilkenny, Ireland.

Pannonia: A Roman province occupying parts of Hungary, Austria, Czechoslovakia, and Yugoslavia.

Pergamum: A former kingdom in western Anatolia, eventually assimilated by Rome.

Pictavum: Poitiers.

Point Vanis: Pointe du Van (hypothetical).

Pontus: A Roman diocese comprising Anatolia.

Portus Namnetum: Nantes (in part).

Pyrenaei Mountains: The Pyrenees.

Qóiqet Lagini: Leinster (in part).

Qóiqet nUlat: Ulster.

Race of Sena: Raz de Sein.

Raetia (or *Rhaetia)*:   A Roman province occupying, approximately, Bavaria.

Redonia: The country of the Redones, in eastern Brittany.

Redonum: See *Condate Redonum.*

Rhenus: The River Rhine.

Rhodanus: The River Rhône.

Roman Bay: Baie de Douarnenez (hypothetical).

Rotomagus: Rouen.

Ruirthech: The River Liffey.

Rutupiae: Richborough.

Sabrina: The River Severn.

Samarobriva: Amiens.

Savus: The River Drava.

Scandia: The southern part of the Scandinavian peninsula.

Scot's Landing: A fisher hamlet near Ys (imaginary).

Sena: Île de Sein.

Sequana: The River Seine.

Sinand: The River Shannon.

Stegir: The River Steir (hypothetical).

Suebian Sea (Mare Suebicum): The Baltic Sea.

Tallten: Teltown in County Meath, Ireland.

Tarraconensis: See *Hispania Tarraconensis*.

Temir: Tara.

Teutoburg Forest: Scene of a Roman military disaster at German hands in the reign of Augustus Caesar.

Thracia: Thrace, occupying approximately the northeastern end of Greece, the northwestern end of Turkey, and a part of Bulgaria.

Thule: Southern Norway (?).

Treverorum: See *Augusta Treverorum*.

Turnacum: Tournay.

Turonum: See *Caesarodunum Turonum*.

Venetorum: See *Darioritum Venetorum*.

Vienna: Vienne.

Vindolanda: Chesterholm, at Hadrian's Wall.

Vorgium: Carhaix.

Whalestrand: A fisher hamlet in western Brittany (imaginary).

Ys: City-state at the far western end of Brittany (legendary).

Dramatis Personae

Names of those who are undoubtedly historical (in the opinion of most authorities) are in upper case. When a full name has not appeared in the text, it is generally not here either, for it was of no great importance even to the bearer.

Adminius: A legionary from Londinium, later second in command (deputy) of Gratillonius's detachment in Ys.

Adruval Tyri: Suffete and Sea Lord of Ys, head of the navy and marines.

Aébell: A daughter of Cellach.

Aed: A tuathal king in Mumu.

AETHBE: A wife of Niall (name conjectural).

ALARIC: King of the Visigoths.

Allil: A half-brother of Niall.

Amair: Youngest daughter of Fennalis, by Hoel.

AMBROSIUS: Bishop of Mediolanum, known today as St. Ambrose.

Ámend: Second wife of Conual Corcc.

Antonia: (1) A sister of Gratillonius. (2) Second daughter of Guilvilis and Gratillonius.

Anmureg maqq Cerballi: A sea rover from Mide.

Apuleius Vero: A senator in Aquilo and tribune of the city.

Arator: A Gallo-Roman prelate.

Arban Cartagi: An Ysan Suffete, husband of Talavair and father of Korai.

ARBOGAST: A Frankish general in the Roman army.

ARCADIUS, FLAVIUS: Eldest son of Theodosius, his eventual successor as Augustus in the East.

Ardens, Septimius Cornelius: Praetorian prefect of Gallia, Hispania, and Britannia.

Arel: Father of Donnerch.

Artorius: The former steward of the Gratillonius estate in Britannia.

Aryagalatis maqq Irgalato: King of Dál Riata in Alba.

Audris: Daughter of Innilis by Hoel.

Augustina: Daughter of Vindilis and Gratillonius.

AUSONIUS, DECIMUS MAGNUS: Gallo-Roman poet, scholar, teacher, and sometime Imperial officer.

Avonis: Sister of Herun, eventually wife of Adminius.

Bacca, Quintus Domitius: Procurator of Lugdunensis Tertia.

Bannon: Headman of Dochaldun.

Belcar: A legendary Ysan hero.

Betha: Wife of Maeloch.

Blodvin: Osismiic maidservant of Fennalis.

Bodilis: A Queen of Ys, daughter of Tambilis by Wulfgar.

Boia: A daughter of Lanarvilis and Hoel.

Bolce Ben-bretnach: Mother of Conual Corcc.

Bomatin Kusuri: A Suffete of Ys, a sea captain and Mariner delegate to the Council.

Borsus: An Ysan.

Bran maqq Anmerech: A hostelkeeper in Mide.

Breccan maqq Nélli: First son of Niall.

Breifa: A female servant of Bodilis.

Brennilis: Leader of the Gallicenae at the time of Julius and Augustus Caesar, responsible for the building of the sea wall and gate.

Bresslan: A man of Carpre's.

BRICIUS: Successor of Martinus, known today as St. Brice.

Briga: Osismiic maidservant of Forsquilis.

Brión: A half-brother of Niall.

Budic: A Coritanic legionary in Gratillonius's detachment at Ys.

Cadoc Himilco: A young Ysan of Suffete family.

Cael maqq Eriai: An ollam poet at Niall's court.

Calloch: A Gaul, former King of Ys, father of Fennalis and Morvanalis.

CALPURNIUS: Father of Sucat.

CALVINUS: An agent of Maximus's secret police.

Camilla: Third daughter of Guilvilis and Gratillonius.

Carenn: Mother of Niall.

Carpre maqq Nélli: A son of Niall.

Carsa, Aulus Metellus: A young Gallo-Roman seaman from Burdigala, later settled in Ys.

Carsa, Tiberius Metellus: A Gallo-Roman sea captain, father of the above.

Cata: A female worker at the Apuleius manor house.

Catellan: An Ysan.

Cathual: Charioteer to Niall.

Catto: A fisherman from Whalestrand.

Catualorig: A former Bacauda.

Cellach maqq Blathmaic: The hostelkeeper at Clón Tarui.

Childerich: A son of Merowech.

Chramn: A Frankish warrior.

Cian: A name used by Dahut.

Claudia: A woman mentioned by Eucherius.

Clothair: A Frank settled in the Redonic canton.

Colconor: A Gaul, King of Ys at the time of Gratillonius's, arrival.

Commius: A Romano-Britannic senator.

CONCHESSA: Niece of Martinus and mother of Sucat.

CONSTANTINUS, CONSTANS: Elder son of Flavius Claudius Constantinus.

CONSTANTINUS, FLAVIUS CLAUDIUS: A Roman army officer in Britannia, later a usurper known as CONSTANTINUS III.

CONSTANTINUS, JULIANUS: Younger son of Flavius Claudius Constantinus.

CONUAL CORCC MAQQ LUGTHACI: Founder of the kingdom at Cassel.

Conual Gulban maqq Nélli: A son of Niall.

Corbmaqq (now known as *Cormac*):   An ancestor of Niall, remembered to this day as having reigned gloriously.

Corentinus: A holy man, known today as St. Corentin.

Coriran: A swineherd in Mumu.

Cothortin Rosmertai: An Ysan Suffete, Lord of Works, head of the civil service.

Cotta: A Mithraist in Vienna.

Craumthann maqq Fidaci: Brother of Mongfind, at one time King at Temir.

CUNEDAG: A prince of the Votadini

Cynan: (1) A Demetaic legionary in Gratillonius's detachment at Ys. (2) A centurion in Constantinus's army.

Dahilis: A Queen of Ys, daughter of Tambilis by Hoel.

Dahut: Daughter of Dahilis and Gratillonius.

DAMASUS: Pope, 366–384.

Dardriu: A swineherd in Mumu.

Dauvinach: An Ysan.

DELPHINUS: Late friend of Ausonius.

Dion: A youth from Neapolis.

Docca: A Dumnoniic woman, once nurse to Gratillonius.

Domnuald maqq Nélli: A son of Niall.

Donalis: A former Queen of Ys, mother of Quistilis by Wulfgar.

Donan: A member of Maeloch's crew.

Donnerch: A carter in Ys.

Doranius: A young man from Gesocribate.

Drach: Father of Vellano.

Drusus, Publius Flavius: A centurion of the Sixth and friend of Gratillonius, later a settler in Armorica.

Einiaunus, Valerius: A Britannic official in Constantinus's service.

Elissa: (1) Birthname of Lanarvilis. (2) Daughter of Lanarvilis by Lugaid.

Éndae maqq Nélli: A son of Niall.

Éndae Qennsalach: Supreme King among the Lagini.

Eochaid maqq Éndae: A son of Éndae Qennsalach.

Eochaid maqq Muredach: A former King at Temir, father of Niall.

Eógan maqq Nélli: A son of Niall.

Eppillus, Quintus Junius: A Dobunnic legionary, first deputy of Gratillonius.

Esmunin Sironai: Chief astrologer in Ys.

Estar: (1) Birth name of Dahilis. (2) Second daughter of Tambilis and Gratillonius.

Esun: A son of Catto.

Etain: A female druid at Niall's court.

Ethniu: A former concubine of Niall, mother of Breccan.

Eucherius: Christian minister (chorepiscopus) in Ys at the time of Gratillonius's arrival.

EUGENIUS: Briefly Augustus of the West, as a puppet of Arbogast.

Evana: Daughter of Vallilis and Wulfgar, mother of Joreth.

Evar: A maidservant of Innilis.

Evirion Baltisi: A young Ysan sea captain.

Ewein: A neighbor of the Gratillonii in Britannia.

Faustina: A sister of Gratillonius.

Favonius: Gratillonius's favorite horse.

Féchra: A half-brother of Niall.

Fedelmm: A witch, fostermother of Conual Corcc.

FELIX: A clergyman who became bishop of Treverorum.

Fennalis: A Queen of Ys, daughter of Ochtalis by Calloch.

Fergus: A half-brother of Niall.

Fergus Fogae: Supreme King among the Ulati.

Fland Dub maqq Ninnedo: Murderer of Domnuald.

Florus: A Gallo-Roman merchant.

Fogartach: A follower of Eochaid.

Forsquilis: A Queen of Ys, daughter of Karilis by Lugaid.

Fredegond: A son of Merowech.

Gaetulius: A former King of Ys, father of Maldunilis, Vindilis, and Innilis.

GAINAS: A Roman general of Gothic origin.

Galith: A name used by Dahut.

Glabrio, Titus Scribona: Governor of Lugdunensis Tertia.

Gladwy: Birthname of Quinipilis.

Gradlon: An Armorican version of "Gratillonius."

Grallon: An Ysan version of "Gratillonius."

GRATIANUS, FLAVIUS: Co-Emperor of the West with Valentinianus.

GRATIANUS: A legionary officer in Britannia, briefly claimant of the purple.

Gratillonius, Gaius Valerius: A Romano-Briton of the Belgic tribe, centurion in the seventh cohort of the Second Legion Augusta, later King of Ys.

Gratillonius, Lucius Valerius: Older brother of the above.

Gratillonius, Marcus Valerius: Father of the two above.

Guennellius: A Britannic curial.

Guentius: A Britannic legionary in Gratillonius's detachment.

Guilvilis: A Queen of Ys.

Gunnung Ivarsson: A Danic skipper and sea rover.

Gwynmael: Gamekeeper, later groom on the Gratillonius estate.

Hannon Baltisi: A Suffete of Ys, Lir Captain.

Herun Taniti: A Suffete of Ys, seaman and later officer in the navy.

Hilketh Eliuni: A Suffete of Ys, Transporter delegate to the Council.

Hoel: A former King of Ys, father of Dahilis.

HONORIUS, FLAVIUS: A son of Theodosius, by him made Augustus of the West.

Hornach: An Osismian who would be King.

Innilis: A Queen of Ys, daughter of Donalis by Gaetulius.

Innloch: Father of Maeloch.

Intil: An Ysan fisherman.

Iram Eliuni: A Suffete of Ys, Lord of Gold, head of the treasury.

Ita: Late sister of Rufinus.

ITHACIUS: Bishop of Ossanuba.

Janatha: An Ysan.

Johannes: Son of Julia and Cadoc.

Jonan: A laborer in Ys.

Joreth: A courtesan in Ys.

Julia: (1) Mother of Gratillonius. (2) Daughter of Lanarvilis and Gratillonius.

JULIANUS, FLAVIUS CLAUDIUS: Today known as Julian the Apostate, this Emperor (361–363) tried to revive paganism under auspices of the state.

Kadrach: A cooper in Ys.

Karilis: A former Queen of Ys, mother of Forsquilis by Lugaid.

Keban: A prostitute in Ys, later Budic's wife.

Kel Cartagi: A young man of Ys.

Kerna: Second daughter of Bodilis by Hoel.

Korai: A granddaughter of Bodilis.

LAÉGARE MAQQ NÉLLI: Youngest(?) son of Niall.

Laidchenn maqq Barchedo: An ollam poet who joined the court of Niall.

Lanarvilis: A Queen of Ys, daughter of Fennalis by Wulfgar.

Laurentius: A Britannic curial.

Lavinia: A lady in Mediolanum.

Lorccan maqq Flandi: A Scotic warrior.

Lugaid: A former King of Ys, father of Forsquilis.

Lugotorix, Sextus Titius: A Gallo-Roman tax collector.

Lugthach maqq Aillelo: A King in Mumu, father of Conual Corcc.

Lydris: Wife of Nagon Demari.

Lyria: Birthname of Karilis.

Maclavius: A Britannic legionary in Gratillonius's detachment and fellow Mithraist.

Maecius: Chorepiscopus at Aquilo, presently retired.

Maeloch: An Ysan fisher captain and Ferrier of the Dead.

Maldunilis: A Queen Of Ys, daughter of Quistilis by Gaetulius.

Malthi: A maidservant of Fennalis.

Marcus: Son of Verania and Gratillonius.

MARCUS: A legionary officer in Britannia, briefly claimant of the purple.

Maria: Daughter of Verania and Gratillonius.

MARIA: Daughter of Stilicho, who became wife of Honorius.

MARTINUS: Bishop of Turonum and founder of the Greater Monastery, known today as St. Martin of Tours.

MAXIMUS, MAGNUS CLEMENS: Commander of Roman forces in Britannia, who later forcibly took power as co-Emperor.

Mella: A servant and medical assistant of Innilis.

Merowech: A leader of the Frankish laeti around Redonum.

Mílchu: Owner of Sucat when the latter was a slave.

Miraine: A daughter of Lanarvilis by Hoel.

Mochta: A prostitute in Ys.

Moethaire of the Corco Óchae: Father of Fedelmm.

Mongfind: Late stepmother of Niall, said to have been a witch.

Morvanalis: A former Queen of Ys, mother of Guilvilis by Hoel.

Murena, Flaminius: A Duke of the Armorican Tract.

Muton Rosmertai: A Suffete of Ys and convert to Mithraism.

Nagon Demari: A Suffete, Labor Councillor in Ys, later expatriate.

Namma: Cook in the Apuleius household.

Nathach: A painter in Ys.

Nath Í: Nephew and tanist of Niall.

Nemain maqq Aedo: Chief druid to Niall.

Nemeta: Daughter of Forsquilis and Gratillonius.

*NIALL MAQQ ECHACH, later known as NIALL OF THE NINE HOS-
TAGES*: King at Temir, overlord of Mide.

Norom: A crewman of Maeloch's.

Ochtalis: A former Queen of Ys, mother of Morvanalis and Fennalis by
Calloch.

Óengus Bolg: A king in Mumu, father of Ámend.

Ogotorig: A hunter, formerly a Bacauda.

Olath Cartagi: An Ysan who became an ironmaker.

Osrach Taniti: A Suffete of Ys, Fisher Councillor.

Parnesius: A Romano-Britannic centurion, friend of Gratillonius in his
youth.

PATRICIUS: An advocate in the service of Maximus.

PAULINUS: A grandson of Ausonius.

Pertinax: A Romano-Britannic centurion, friend of Parnesius.

Philippus: An exorcist in Turonum.

PRISCILLIANUS: Heretical bishop of Avela.

Prudentius: A Redonian, deacon to Eucherius.

Quanis: A demonic mermaid in Ysan legend.

Quinipilis: A Queen of Ys, daughter of Redorix, mother not named.

Quintilus: A courtier in Mediolanum.

Quistilis: A former Queen of Ys, mother of Maldunilis by Wulfgar.

RADAGAISUS: A Gothic warlord.

Rael: A prostitute in Ys.

Ramas Tyri: A Suffete of Ys, Artisan delegate to the Council.

Redorix: A former King of Ys, father of Quinipilis.

Rivelin: Royal surgeon in Ys.

Riwal: A Durotrigian Briton who moved to Confluentes.

Ronach: An Osismiic Mithraist.

Rovinda: Wife of Apuleius Vero.

Rufinus: A Redonic Bacauda, later Gratillonius's henchman.

RUFINUS: Praetorian prefect of Arcadius, overthrown by Stilicho.

Rullus, Septimius: A curial in Gesocribate.

Runa: (1) Birthname of Vindilis. (2) Daughter of Vindilis by Hoel.

Sadb: Wife of Cernach.

Salaun: An Armorican version of "Salomon."

Salomon: Son of Rovinda and Apuleius.

Saphon: A former Ysan fisher captain.

Sasai: (1) Birthname of Guilvilis. (2) A daughter of Guilvilis and Gratillonius.

Semuramat: (1) Third daughter of Bodilis by Hoel, later known as Tambilis. (2) First daughter of her and Gratillonius.

SERENA: Wife of Stilicho.

Sicorus: The large landowner at Maedraeacum.

Sigo, Quintus Flavius: An Imperial courier.

Silis: A prostitute in Ys.

Soren Cartagi: A Suffete of Ys, Speaker for Taranis, Timbermen delegate to the Council.

Sosir: A painter in Ys.

STILICHO, FLAVIUS: A Roman general, half Vandal by birth, who became effectively the dictator of the West Roman Empire.

Subne maqq Dúnchado: A follower of Eochaid maqq Éndae.

SUCAT (or *SUCCAT*): Birthname of St. Patrick.

Surach: A son of Catto.

Syrus, Lucas Orgetuorig: Mithraic Father in Vienna.

Taenus Himilco: A Suffete of Ys.

Talavair: (1) Birthname of Bodilis. (2) First daughter of Bodilis by Hoel.

Taltha: A courtesan in Ys.

Tambilis: (1) A former Queen of Ys, mother of Bodilis by Wulfgar and Dahilis by Hoel. (2) A later Queen of Ys, daughter of Bodilis and Hoel.

Tardelbach: A man of Carpre's.

Targorix: A legendary Gallic king.

Tasciovanus: A Britannic curial.

Temesa: A maidservant of Quinipilis.

Tera: An Ysan countrywoman.

THEODOSIUS, FLAVIUS: Known today as the Great, Augustus of the East and eventually, briefly, sole Roman Emperor.

Theuderich: A son of Merowech.

Tigernach maqq Laidchinni: A son and pupil of Laidchenn.

Timbro: A follower of Ullus.

Tommaltach maqq Donngalii: A young man from Mumu.

Torna Éces: Great poet in Ériu, who fostered both Niall and Conual and taught Laidchenn.

Tothual the Desired: Founder of Mide.

Tronan Sironai: Husband of Runa.

Uail maqq Carbri: A henchman of Niall.

Udach: A servant of Gratillonius.

Ullus: A bully from Audiarna.

Una: (1) A Britannic girl, sweetheart of Gratillonius in his youth. (2) Daughter of Bodilis and Gratillonius.

Usun: An Ysan fisherman, Maeloch's mate on *Osprey*.

Utican the Wanderer: A classic Ysan poet.

VALENTINIANUS, FLAVIUS: Half-brother of Flavius Gratianus and co-Emperor of the West with him.

Valeria: Fourth daughter of Guilvilis and Gratillonius.

Vallilis: A former Queen of Ys, mother of Tambilis by Wulfgar.

Vellano: A Redonian who moved to Confluentes.

Verania: Daughter of Rovinda and Apuleius.

Verica: A Britannic legionary in Gratillonius's detachment and fellow Mithraist.

VICTOR: A son of Maximus.

Vindilis: A Queen of Ys, daughter of Quinipilis by Gaetulius.

Vindolenus: A former Bacauda.

Vindomarix: Druid to Targorix.

Vortivir, Flavius: Tribune at Venetorum.

Witch-Hanai: A classic Ysan poet.

Wulfgar: A former King of Ys, father of Tambilis, Quistilis, Karilis, Lanarvilis, and Bodilis.

Zeugit: An Ysan, landlord of the Green Whale.

Zisa: Daughter of Maldunilis and Gratillonius.